PETER TAUBER's

THE LAST BEST HOPE

The

LAST BEST
HOPE

Peter Tauber

BALLANTINE BOOKS • NEW YORK

Library of Congress Catalog Card Number: 76-0730

ISBN 0-345-27327-3

This edition published by arrangement with Harcourt Brace Jovanovich

Manufactured in the United States of America

First Ballantine Books Edition: September 1978

For my father,
Abraham Tauber,
1912–1977.

I am his son.

Fellow-citizens, we cannot escape history. We . . . will be remembered in spite of ourselves. No personal significance or
insignificance can spare one or another of us. The fiery trial
through which we pass will light us down, in honor or dishonor,
to the last generation. We . . . hold the power and bear the
responsibility, . . . honorable alike in what we give and what
we preserve. We shall nobly save or meanly lose the last best
hope of earth. . . . The way is plain, peaceful, generous, just—
a way which, if followed, the world will forever applaud, and
God must forever bless.

—Abraham Lincoln
Second Annual Message to Congress
December 12, 1862

Your generation was lucky. You already had a few years to
believe in something before it all fell apart. You know: God,
the United States, Good Guys Win in the End, Congress Can
Pass a Law, Here Comes the Cavalry, Take It to the Supreme
Court, Send the Marines, the Lone Ranger, Save, Work for a
Goal—you know, all that shit. With us I think, with my generation, all we ever knew was that they all lied—and not very well.
I mean, God was already dead; so was the government, right?
Everything's so—*existential*, you know? That's our reality. We
got born into free-fall. You want to know what I would ask for
if I had one wish? I wish there would be like God or Jesus
maybe or Bobby Kennedy—for real. Some guy who could get
on TV and be believed and say "Cut the crap, World! OK, life
is tough. End of Philosophy Lesson. Now let's get to work."

—Student in a suburban Boston high school
October 1971

I'm only sorry I missed the scene.

—Jack Downey, CIA operative
upon his return to the United States
after twenty years in a Chinese prison
March 1973

Part I

Heroes
and
Goats:
1969

THE MOON WAS IN THE NATION'S EYE EIGHT days that week; bright and big and beautiful. Empires of wealth and energy had come to this: the first men's footprints in the lunar dust. And so, the Capital proclaimed a holiday in celebration.

Soon, more men would come from Earth. And one would hit a golf ball.

An American flag was planted on the windless plain that first time, its stiff salute maintained by unseen wires within its fabric. Nearby sat the vehicle, nicknamed *Eagle,* that brought the two Americans. Overhead, their third brother circled, busy in his loneliness. On their lander's heel—they also called it "LEM"—a plaque declared:

WE CAME IN PEACE FOR ALL MANKIND.

Congress, though, thought otherwise, insisting that no flag or seal or emblem but America's be taken on this historic journey.

Half the globe observed their flight. And half those viewers thought the images on television demonstrated America's chief technological genius: they believed it was a fantasy, concocted on a Hollywood sound stage; and not as good as some.

No matter. It was real. It was more than real.

The holiday and flag revealed the mission's full conceit: that these first words—"(Contact light . . .) *Hello, Houston!*" and "Tranquility Base, here. The Eagle has landed!"—and those first steps, albeit backward, were the topping of a monument designed to stand forever. It was a pyramid, whose root was set on Earth and whose foundations lay back in time, before America

2

was ever conjured, somewhere in the dreams and long-tilled dust of Earth. It was pronounced a pyramid of hopes and history, with the future—America's, all nations', species *sapiens'*—hard beneath those fresh treads in the Moondirt. And we had got there first. The plaque was signed by the President of the United States, Richard Nixon.

The Moon was virgin, and she was not won, seduced, or even carried off in rape. Her time had come and she was surgically deflowered by two men in ghostly white, who danced in triumph at the easy virtues of her gravitation. They acted for ten thousand others also garbed in white: an army of technologists who saw this as the highway to the future. But of all of them, scientists and Presidents, only two had touched her. Only two were on the Moon that week.

One alone was First. One alone was Runner-up. And One alone hung waiting in that sky. These boyish men were the first, all alone, heroes in the dust and in the space besides. Certified.

A battery of computers and administrators had found them fit, all three, by every paradigm and parameter of need; every program yielded up their names. So they were chosen, elect, special: picked to stand for every family and genus. By nerves and skill and looks and names, they met the standards of a prescribed mold of heroes. They were protoheroes from the cradle, according to the press releases, cast resolutely toward a becoming greatness. Even their physical size was optimal: by genes and life's ingestion they contrived to fit machines that were born in time to bear them. By all means and measures they were suited, tailored, to act for the People who, by Merit and Resource, Genius and Grace—and Way of Life, it was insisted—were likewise meant to act for all humankind.

In all respects, the news which shone to Earth that week, flashed homeward by a blinkless camera's eye, was heroic, or rectified to seem so. For the event was asked to whisper something mighty—even before politicos and poets got their mitts on it—breathing in the silent marrow of its shout:

"Optimism!"

It was begged to say to doubters of the creed, "If you

3

can still believe, believe this: We're going to be *great!* We're going to be *terrific!*" For it is believed that by the actions of our heroes we are cursed or blessed, revealed as winners or losers, victors or goats for all time; known to ourselves by the fate of the best of us. So the monument they topped off on the Moon, the pyramid beneath the Nation's eye, proclaimed to all Eternity and ourselves American Faith's defiant optimism: "Let's let 'em know who we are and where we came from— America, on the planet Earth!" They'd hear our echo in the voids and black holes, where all the world's lost golf balls hide, a jolly lyric, "We're going to be great. We're going to be *terrific!*"

Garbage. They left it on the Moon. They fertilized the sterile plain with hope and garbage. They left an atmosphere of poison gases they expelled to start for home. But poison gases led to life on Earth. And historically, on Earth as well, the refuse of past hopes nourished roots of future ones.

In a darkened room that week one bright hope sat among a hundred men the Nation also prized but, unlike astronauts, hardly knew about. If their time would ever come they were now unseen, treasured by the Republic nonetheless, selected to act someday in its name.

While the Moon's light flooded Earth and filled the Nation's eyes, they were in the umbra. The youngest of them, and in many ways the most select, was Tyler Bowen. The very same computer systems which had combed the field for astronauts had also chosen him, though for a separate purpose by a slightly different program. Were he some years older and a pilot there is no doubt he might have one day walked the Moon.

In the brief biographical sketches compiled about the men in this room it was recorded that Tyler Bowen, twenty-four, middle name George, after graduating with honors in Biochemistry from Cornell University in 1967, had accumulated greater honor with each passing year: in 1967 he was awarded the Vera and Benjamin Trovato Society Fellowship to work at the Gila Compound National Laboratories in Arizona, returning to Cornell in 1968 as an Associate Fellow at the Advanced Studies Laboratory there, also serving as Assistant to the Dean of Students. His next year glowed even more brightly: his Cornell research team had been given National Institutes of Health grants, with White House sponsorship, to enlarge their project at Cleveland's Case Western Reserve University, where it was expected theirs might be a signal contribution to the understanding and treatment of cancer. That was the way to Nobel Prizes. He seemed a regular guy in spite of it, remarking of his résumé, "All it really says is I can't hold a job very long."

Bowen relaxed in the back of this room while the others, all in neat rows, listened to a lecturer who wore attire emblematic of a mixed and partly covert purpose. The man wore a white shirt and skinny knit tie. A bulging plastic pencil pouch swelled his breast pocket and fluttered when his heart beat quickly. The pouch had the name and logo of a pharmaceutical company printed on it, worn into illegibility. His tie was clipped by what appeared to be a circular Japanese slide rule of admirable tininess. The lecturer's left hand had no wedding band; instead, an MIT class ring the size of a walnut with an engraving of a beaver. On the man's collar were insignia of rank—not military, but nonetheless official. He looked, Tyler Bowen thought, like a cruise director.

Bowen's own clothing was casual. The first day there he'd worn jeans but it had made the others nervous. Those others sat in double-knits and seersucker; a few wore maroon pants with white belts and matching shoes. Some ballooned the uniforms of military and police organizations. Regulations did not require such official dress, but for some vanity did. There were high-ranking officers from every branch of service, men from the CIA, from the darker wayside corridors of other government agencies, several from the National Guard Bureau's Office of Inter-Agency Liaison, from strategic Reserve elements, from the FBI, the Office of Emergency Preparedness, various research and development facilities, a few from university defense analysis institutes—"we need more of that," an FBI man kidded Bowen, "a university defense analysis"—and from some semisecret installations known especially well to Tyler

Bowen. There was even a man from an office thought to be covered with ten years' cobwebs. And one from NASA: he looked infinitely crabby under his crew cut, especially when ribbed about being away from Houston during the long-awaited Moon Week.

For most of them this was an honored assignment. After three weeks of courses—lectures, films, and seminars—they'd go back to their jobs with special expertise and additional retirement points. For Bowen it was an honor he compared to wisdom teeth. He would have to stay for two more three-week cycles—this was the first of three—to lecture on "Principles and Applications of Biochemical Process," mostly through canned material and stupefying films. They could get along quite well without him. But the eternal vigilance which was the price of liberty meant specifically, by the lights of the sponsoring organization, the National Security Agency, that everyone, instructors or "students," had to attend every meeting and lecture, no matter how often they were repeated.

Bowen's tolerance for boredom was already saturated, for the banality of the proceedings was exceeded only by that of the participants. He wanted part of neither, but he had no choice. It would take a wheezing, sweaty effort, he knew, to make this time interesting. But that was what you got, he supposed, for letting yourself get stuck indoors in Washington while the better part of the world was playing tennis, and sailing, or taking a flying fuck at the Moon.

"I just want to give you people a few notes before the Kiddie Show," the skinny instructor told the assembly. "There's this goat, see. A kid, get it? Well, just you watch. And hold your breakfasts. Think on this, though: if'n you had half as much talent as this here goat's got—right?—you could be a movie star for your Uncle Samuel, too. With luck, maybe someday you'll get your chance."

The other men listened to the young instructor in that unventilated room. The stagnant air burned their eyes as he explained "the workings of the G- and V-series of nerve agents" which, of course, they all had clearance to know about.

"That's what the goat will be getting in this film," the

6

instructor said, without referring to his notes. "In the G-series, we have Tabun, which is Standard A, designated G-A. We have Sarin, Standard A, which is G-B. And we have Soman, which is G-D. We'll give the goat G-B: Sarin. Write that down."

"What about G-C?" a hoarse voice asked. Another volleyed back, "G-C is the clap, jerk. You don't give it to goats—you get it from sheep."

"He gives it to goats!"

"You get it from hippies—"

The instructor made a stab at regaining control. "Your government has not yet harnessed G-C for defense utiliza—" In the back, Bowen made a skeptical face, unseen by the others who continued to joke in the jargon they'd recently acquired. They volunteered to be "delivery vehicles" and "presamplers" until they were impoverished of silliness. Bowen shook his head at it all. The skinny lecturer's pink and beardless cheeks brought out the bully in these men, his Coke-bottle eyeglasses suggestive of timidity. Only Bowen was younger than this instructor, and though these men fondly ragged him, he took their locker room teasing well. Unlike the meek instructor, Bowen had presence and command of his audience, which was a large part of his value to the National Security Agency.

The day before, Bowen had to explain why the antidote of choice for cyanide poisoning, amyl nitrite, was not to be found in any poison detection and control kits developed with federal funds—"Because," he had said, "it has the correlative property of increasing sensation during sexual climax. Over the years the stockpiles have mysteriously disappeared." He sighed at the tragedy. "Some people have got no respect for priorities—and spoil it for the rest of us."

Now he spent most of his energies wrestling with a recalcitrant bar of Bonomo's Turkish Taffy in preference to the lecture, left with only that small device to put distance between himself and this program. He'd accepted the job, reluctantly, he told himself, to avoid direct participation in the greater evil of corporate slaughter. Prussian ancestors may have shot off toes to avoid the Kaiser's service, others further back torn off limbs to cheat the Crusades. He loosened a few teeth,

7

pulled the legs off laboratory frogs and winged a moral pinion by compromise, to avoid a mortal wound. His integrity might limp, but would survive. Still, he had to admit, it sure looked like they were getting from him what they wanted every time.

"About G-D," a voice two seats away from Bowen called out, in a distinct North Shore Boston twang, "in all due respect. It means the Good Lord to a lot of people, or God Damn, depending."

The instructor curled his lip and checked his notes. "Well, uh, yes. We don't see much of it anyway. Now then, in the V-series I can't give you the structurals—" he ignored a sarcastic noise from the class—"or much information, except that it's made from dimethyl polysulfide and ethyl 2-diisopropylaminoethyl—" They guffawed at the incomprehensibility of that intelligence, though Tyler Bowen began to doodle what the structurals might look like. "In fact, all I can tell you beyond that is catalog call letters for your TO&E entitlements." If any of them were representatives of some group whose TO&E—Table of Organization and Equipment —required them to have any of this stuff, they could at least order it. Similarly, the ordering of thermonuclear weapons was a rather simple matter, although shipment itself required proper authorization. "The V-series designation, gentlemen is . . . V-X." They made an impressed noise. "And I think I can tell you *this:* we do not choose our letters lightly. Same for G-D."

The logic of it all was exciting to the class, even Tyler Bowen, as if here they had the Supreme Stuff. No need to hold back the Big Letters. Nothing to save 'em for. A thimbleful will do for the world. Don't spill it. Call it V-X.

A rheostat dimmed the lights in the fetid classroom and all attention focused on a gelatin projected onto the hanging screen. The skinny instructor was out of the woods. In the semidarkness his technical guidance was the only light. "Look at these three structurals while I tell you how they work. The goat will get G-B."

"Do we need to know this for the finals?" someone called out.

The instructor chuckled into his microphone and said, "I just thought you might like to see them. You don't need to know them. Just the nomenclature." With the help of a declassified cleverness approaching Bowen's, the indicated compounds would enable anyone to rule a significant part of the world; a small but charming country perhaps, Philadelphia at the least.

The plate showed:

TABUN, STANDARD A (G-A)

(Dimethylaminoethoxy-cyanophosphine oxide)

$$\begin{array}{ccc} CH_3 & & CN \\ & \diagdown & | \\ & N-P-O-C_5H_2 \\ & \diagup & \| \\ CH_3 & & O \end{array}$$

$$(CH_3)_2 N(C_2H_5O)CNPO$$

SARIN, STANDARD A (G-B)

(Methylisopropoxyfluoro-phosphine oxide)

$$\begin{array}{ccccc} & & F & & CH_3 \\ & & | & & | \\ CH_3 & - & P & - O - & CH \\ & & \| & & | \\ & & O & & CH_3 \end{array}$$

$$CH_3(C_3H_7O)FPO$$

SOMAN (G-D)

(Methylpinacolyloxy-fluorophosphine oxide)

$$\begin{array}{ccccccc} & & F & & CH_3 & CH_3 \\ & & | & & | & | \\ CH_3 & - & P & - O - & C & - C & - CH_3 \\ & & \| & & | & | \\ & & O & & H & CH_3 \end{array}$$

$$CH_3(C_6H_{13}O)FPO$$

In the far back Tyler Bowen muttered, "Wonder how many guys died for typographical errors."

"All right, now," the instructor told them, "last slide." A few made approving grunts, but most sat glassy-eyed. "These three frames show the way G-B works."

Frame #1 showed a healthy body, resembling Dagwood Bumstead.

Frame #2 showed a primitive cage labeled "G-B Nerve Agent." This cage surrounded a molecule labeled "Cholinesterase."

Frame #3 showed the body lying down, quaking. Sinister molecules were all around it, labeled "Acetylcholine." A cloudlike thought balloon rose from the beleaguered head and the sufferer was thinking: "The culprit's my own acetylcholine! Wh-wh-where's my cholinesterase?" Frame #2 held the answer: it had been detained by the action of the G-B agent, that's where.

The instructor filled them in on the details of this message. "It's simplicity," he cooed. "Acetylcholine is what makes your muscles flex. Write that down. And cholinesterase—c-h-o—breaks it up. Write that down. Notice the '-ase'? It's an enzyme, as Mr. Bowen explained to you the other day. The G-series agents imprison that cholinesterase by being more chemically attractive than the acetylcholine. Isn't that nice? I suppose you could say it seduces rather than imprisons. It'd be hard to show you a slide of that, though!" The class offered a modest chuckle. "Without that cholinesterase to act as a check, the acetylcholine will keep flexing your muscles until you seize up. Same as if your carburetor was stuck—you'd rev until you threw a rod. In a sense, you kill yourself." An awed silence saluted the primitive grace of it all.

Then the lights went out completely, when the instructor signaled his projectionist to "bring on the goat." Over the film leader numbers he added hurriedly "the-antidote-is-atropine-and-hours-of-artificial-respiration." The curriculum used to call for an obligatory statement of the parallel between acetylcholine and freedom: too much of a good thing is anarchy. But that was preaching to the already convinced, and often hooted down by those who resented being so patronized. So it was dumped. The last few numbers were superimposed on a scratchy black Maltese cross. Then blankness, and then a white-suited man wearing rubber gloves dragged a bashful—indeed, sheepish—goat into the picture frame.

The man wore an M-10 Protective Mask, which made him look like a hooded executioner. The words "TF-3-3432: Nerve Agents and Their Effects" dissolved against the goat's mottled white hair as he filled the frame in a close tracking shot. The goat bleated, not unhappily, which made the class laugh. Then the picture went silent for a shift to voice-over, also shifting imperceptibly to a liquidy slower-motion for greater study of detail.

The white-suited man patted the goat's head and fed him a goat-yummy, then tied the animal fore and aft to stakes. His enhanced gracefulness and his white vestments made him resemble Neil Armstrong to some observers; floating slowly out of the picture frame, he was an enchanted Moonman on an earthly EVA. He soothed the goat as he went, rather like a parent leaving a child with a babysitter. The million eyes behind the camera would keep good watch, and the man's shadow hovered on the periphery, a short call away.

Another man, also in white garb and rubber gloves, but wearing the sportier M-9A1 Protective Mask, entered and patted the happy goat on the head. The goat upstaged him with a friendly toss of the head at the camera, vamping the audience. With an eyedropper, the man placed 0.4 milliliter of Standard A G-series nerve agent (Sarin, G-B: methylisopropoxyfluoro-phosphine oxide) on the goat's nose. Immediately, rhinitis set in: runny nose. A viscous droplet gleamed in the sunlight, as it fell; a stunning effect.

"Phase I of the standard reaction to nerve agents begins," the film's narrator recited in a bland, croaking baritone that sounded like a slow-running tape. It was obvious that the voice was postrecorded, light-years away from the strapped-down animal, soothing the audience like the hand that stroked the goat. "Phase I reveals these signs: running nose . . . pinpointing of the pupils . . . tightening of the chest . . . and sweating—*even if it's not hot out.*"

11

And the goat displayed the classic signs. The picture froze on each for a close-up moment.

At first, the goat showed minor confusion. But then he became passive, acceptant, evidencing a curious near-recognition, as though things had been this way for the goat before, though of course they had not; nor could the goat be said to have expected this.

"Now," the voice-over explained, "Phase I is ended with the onset of the J-T-S symptoms. They are . . ."—Tyler Bowen's mind raced the projector for the words, as the instructor was calling out "Write this down!" Tyler thought: Just Too Stupid? Jesus, This Shits? Johanna-Tyler—Someday? Jokes Tell Secrets? He doodled them on his scratch paper as the J-T-S symptoms appeared on the screen. The now-panicked goat searched in frenzied ballet for his unseen, odorless tormentor as each word captioned the symptom it stood for. The goat was powerless to avoid his role. "Here we see the goat exhibiting the J-T-S signs."

"JERKS—" The goat strained epileptically at his stays for escape.

"TWITCHES—" He fell to his knees, suddenly cut by an invisible scythe. Every muscle trembled. Tyler Bowen laughed to himself, thinking about someone he knew who was a jerk who twitched.

"STAGGERS—" It was too late for that one unless they went out and hired another goat. The goat was already on its side, eyes wide, imploring mercy from the class. The film left his screams unrecorded. The whirring sprocket cogs and the projector's fan were the only orchestration. The class's thumbs stayed down to the goat's petition. They were secure in the certainty that the plot was far from their hands, and so watched in a form of rapture. Some of them had never seen anything die before. None in such slow motion and lavish detail. They had never been the special beneficiaries of visual slaughter, felt such intimacy and experimental involvement. Many of them knew killing, but as either a sport or a job, as an operational, programmatic, impersonal thing. Now they could luxuriate in it awhile, enjoy its texture. A few felt liberated in the anonymous dark, heady and free from constraints of guilt, able for once to admire death, embrace it, peer into it as an equal, without fear of involvement or contagion. Their breathing grew heavy with the poisoned goat's.

Others, however, had grown fond of the goat, as they would any dumb animal who posed no threat. But they knew they could not help him, so they confined their pity to themselves. Tyler Bowen thought of the name Billy Goat, and the Kid, and thus of his brother Willie, sometimes called the Kid, captured in a way by the rubber-gloved draft, his neck and ass tied to splintery stakes, while antiseptic men in white suits did their worst and watched him jerk, twitch, and stagger.

"Phase II," the voice continued, "begins with paralysis and difficulty in breathing." The goat lay still. His chest heaved heroically, undulating against overwhelming mortal odds. The goat was clearly dying. Listlessly, he swished his tail to make sure no flies bothered his last moments, fussing over details, tidying up his room. He banged his head against the ground in a slow tattoo. And then he did a strange thing: the goat had an erection, a pink, vainglorious life-urge.

"Standard occurrence," explained the voice: Nothing to worry about. Dying for the camera was, in its way, like being victim of the biggest gang-rape in history. There was no limit to how many might watch. And there was certainly no more dignity to be lost when strangers watched you die in cold-eyed witness. So the goat's hips thrust forward and his pelvis shook, though death already had the rest of him, as if some primal force of Goatness commanded him to shoot his seed into the world, a message in a bottle for any surviving she-goat. The goat must nurse some hope that his race would yet survive. For his soma and germ cells must believe that they had not come all this way from the inert, conspiring to purpose, organizing against entropy's injunctions, willing themselves into community and sensibility, only to become extinct in a moment. So he readied his genetic legacy, as if no mere goat's mind, but the Great God of Goats alone, knew whether it was only this goat, or all goats everywhere, that were presently troubled.

Tyler Bowen thought, perversely in the face of this, of higher civilizations and lower media, of Superman comic books: Jor-El the Kryptonian scientist had launched his and Lara's baby, Kal-El, into unknown space when their native planet blew apart from internal stresses. One day Kal-El would land near Smallville U.S.A., be adopted by the Kents of Earth—who bore a remarkable likeness to the Harry Trumans—and become Superboy to the World, vulnerable only to the latent power of that original home's traumatic shards. So who knew, Tyler Bowen thought, what an ejaculation meant in the scheme of things?

Mighty sighs and heaves split the classroom air as the goat humped the air which had betrayed him and made love to living one last time. And in the process, as with love and radiation, the intensity hastened its passing. The goat's next thrust brought a mighty and fatal climax. Semen flew languidly about and settled on his coat and in the dust.

"Your Final Phase—Phase III," oozed the voice, an abrupt intrusion into the orgiastic symbiosis of audience and animal, "brings mental confusion, staggering, and convulsions." The goat was too dead for any of this, but he made a passing effort at convulsions. "Then coma." This was it. The goat's resistance broke under a siege of inevitability. His breathing became labored and shallow. Then at last: "The course of symptoms is concluded with C-N-S."

"Write this down!" the instructor yelled. C-N-S? Tyler puzzled: it usually meant Central Nervous System. What was it now? Cream Not Sugar? Comedy No Salvation? Christ, No Sex? Causation, Not Sense?—

"C-N-S," the unctuous voice explained, "is Cessation of Natural Signs: death." C-N-S would have the goat, a gift, brought all the way from A-OK, through the travails of J-T-S, by the NSA of the U.S.A. DOA.

And C-N-S crept in on the comatose animal. The goat had run down and out of time. His message was launched into an uncaring world. His erection died with his desire; all hope and will gone shortly after. Unconsciousness was embraced. There was nothing more for goats to do but snuff out their candles and return to a mineral state. The foe was too potent. Goats do not escape their destiny any more than mass defies inertia of its own volition. The universe had its laws. And death and destiny were matters of momentum and great controlling curves. C-N-S had come.

Suddenly, the white-suited men rushed into the picture. "These men are injecting the goat with atropine— a belladonna derivative," the voice said, and someone near Tyler Bowen yelled out, "*Heart*-Line! *Heart*-Line!"

Three times the normal dose of atropine was pumped into the stiff goat's veins. Wild cheers from the audience spurred the two men on, drowning out the explanation of the antidote's action: restoring the vital balance between the adrenergic and cholinergic nervous systems. The class was more interested in effects, not process; an American habit of mind. So when the goat edged back from death's ledge with a slight stirring, they gave a whoop and a howl. A heat of joy rippled up the aisle with applause for the timely arrival of the Cavalry.

Tyler Bowen nodded his head and grinned. Here was something to believe in. America was really something special. While flipping men up at the moon, it had time to order a lowly goat saved. Now no expense would be spared. They'd even find someone to give him mouth-to-mouth.

After a time lapse, the goat, once more dead than alive, rose haltingly and, by his expression a little bewildered, rejoined the bureaucracy. He seemed to bow. Shouting and table pounding, whistles and laughter rocked the sweaty classroom. The audience was as proud as so many new fathers. The lights came on and the skinny instructor let them smile themselves out. Uncle Sam had reached down and saved this kid. The Cavalry had come, as they deep down knew it would. And it pleased them, all of them, very much to be able to believe in this.

Tyler Bowen left for lunch in a good mood, amused at the happy voice which had called "*Heart*-Line! *Heart*-Line!" when the atropine relief came through in the clutch. Had it been live, on TV, Tyler thought, like the Moon Shot, that anguished seminal fluid would be placed in a gold bottle in the Smithsonian, and the Heart-Line would have rung right off the wall. Of course no one would ever see the goat's torment and rescue, for it was classified as fact and intent. But if they did,

15

he knew: America, with that Great Good Heart and Direct Distance Dialing, with its Native Generosity and Warmth as Big as All Outdoors, would be on the line, Station to Station from all over, Standing Up to Be Counted. Offers of help would pour in for the goat: money, food, atropine, nursing, scholarships, factory work, book contracts, bassinets, and golf clubs.

The goat would live by electronically interconnected Love, and no little Christian Shame, from the Great Good People.

During lunch, Tyler Bowen sought a moment's solitude in the Restricted Personnel washroom. One of the few unqualified liberties afforded to the much-valued toilers at the National Security Agency seminars was the right to visit the chaplain or john of one's choosing whenever one felt the call. Since he had reason to know that a cleric might have mixed loyalties, when Tyler wanted a moment's peace he chose the privy. He washed his face and scrutinized the rims of his eyes for redness. They still stung from the smoky classroom. "Hey, boy!" taunted a visitor, fondly patting Bowen on the rump. "How's it goin'? Moving in on the All-American pud-pulling record? Or ya just shitting your brains out from radiation fever?" Bowen laughed softly and splashed more water on his face. "Tell me," the man asked as he waddled up to a urinal, "how's a young punk like you qualify to be such a hotshot around here? Your daddy know somebody?"

Bowen shrugged. "Just lucky, I guess."

From the far stall, a voice surprised them. "That Bowen? Hell, from what I read you're quite the Golden Boy. Mister Cha-Risma hisself."

"Don't you believe it," Bowen answered, as the first man headed for the door. "Charisma? That's a death sentence in these parts. I'll plead to young punk." But he flashed a quick, flirty smile at his own face in the mirror, winking to it, "Hiya Ty. I know you're in there." It winked back, but how true were mirrors anyway? He'd be the first to suggest their fallibility. Perhaps he had never seen his face as it shone to the world, really. Nevertheless, there were many, too many to be lightly dismissed, who, like these washroom transients, insisted

16

they saw in Tyler Bowen's face some extraordinary thing.

Exactly what they saw would not appear in mirrors or snapshots, even holograms, for it was more precisely something sensed, as though beneath Tyler Bowen's skin was another face slowly rising to the light. In due time it would emerge, though for now, except in the dynamic of his features, it lay hidden, all potential.

To be sure, there were things Tyler Bowen had done to merit such regard. He was certainly a hero, even a minor legend, in his undergraduate days at Cornell. He'd been President of his class one year and for three years made a reputation as a great man in relief, leading the Ivy League in pinch hits and saves on the baseball diamond. By graduation in 1967 he'd acquired a solid faculty respect for his academic work, and his honors project was highly thought of in many quarters. He'd been a final-round candidate for a Rhodes Scholarship; now he was a candidate for a Fulbright. Most of all back then, he had the affection of his fellow students for the rumors of Bunyonesque pranks he'd precipitated; and the rigorous principle he displayed, hued with self-mocking humor. There were many at Cornell who expected him to act on a larger field some day, even to be a hero in some fashion, by native genius, simple fitness, or—a few hoped—moral rebellion.

Even rivals in his undergraduate years held him in respect, yielding like those Germans who raced toward American lines at the end of World War II: preferring, if they must lose, to lose to him. Elders encouraged him, friends gave him aid; people delighted in doing him favors. They wanted him to succeed and took joy in his triumphs.

Clear-sighted about his good fortune, Bowen attributed that local renown to the myth-making tendencies of others. One event in his senior year seemed to redefine all others preceding it. It was one defiant moment in the face of a losing cause which, he later joked, "somehow makes me uniquely fit for administrative duties." He had been a middling basketball player, and usually rode the bench until things were immutable. But in the last home game of his career, hopelessly

17

lost to Princeton by the start of the final period, Bowen and the other seniors were sent in for a last few minutes of play. He sparked a late rally which stunned the Tigers. He pumped in jump shots and stole the ball over and over, playing with the passionate, desperate abandon of a drunk on a high wire. The crowd sustained a deafening roar as this display continued. It grew louder and more frenzied, and then turned to eerie silence as they watched "the tragedy," according to the *Cornell Daily Sun*'s sports columnist, "of one man trying to undo what ten had determined and sealed." At the buzzer, Tyler Bowen took the final shot and made it, though the game belonged to Princeton, still. But the stands exploded anyway for they had witnessed "something vastly special," or so an editorial later that week insisted: "brewing legend, a near-rear-rangement of the pre-ordained, an electric moment of refusal," somehow finding more of an inspiration in the loss than a moral. And perhaps that is why they expected great things from him: his innovative talent was "resistance to quietus, a rare trait in the liberal arts community." Perhaps this is why, as well, those who knew him were sorely disappointed when after graduation Tyler Bowen took the first train to compromise and went for the tie with nature and the state.

That compromise, extracted as the price for other talents he could not hide and which the nation wanted a share of, landed him in this bathroom at the National Security Agency, where even momentary peace was likely to be ruptured in a twinkling. For complete safety he had to shrink into his thoughts. He smiled in the mirror, rolling his shoulders, thinking of heroes: basketball stars and the Men on the Moon, Inc.; Kennedys and the Babe, Jefferson and . . . Triumphant music and heavenly chords swelled in his ears, bleeding into other sounds. He squinted and he was a rock star, the Singer of the Age, in erotic agony on a blue-lit stage, inspiring energy by a distant glance and lyric. The screams and orchestration filled his head. Then he was the President: kind and wise, ironic, leveling with the people, calling them to faith in their own goodness. The music melted into the white noise of a deep lake: all sounds become one total sound, insulating like no sound. This roaring was the Earth's own sound or universal cheers, as pervasive as gravity and as unsensed. All of this occurred in the time of a few heartbeats.

Suddenly he crumpled a paper towel and wheeled. He stopped, faked a chest pass to one stall, a bounce pass to another. "Two seconds left," he muttered. "Bowen with the ball. Fakes once, shoo—No! Another fake! How does he *do* it? Double pump and UP for the shot!"

At the top of his jump, with a small head fake to confuse the guarding urinals, Tyler Bowen flicked his wrist to arc the wet paper wad over four booths. "One second left! Bowen *shoots!*" A perfect high floater it was, fluttering over the yearning fingers of the forwards and center and swarming guards; banked exquisitely off the far wall in the split second before he sounded the game-ending buzzer: *"Braaaaaaaaaaaamp!!"*

Two points to win the game in the last second over the feared and hard-playing foe, the bullying Urinals. Two heroic points against a stronger, obdurate team and great odds. A last-second game winner caroming neatly off the tile backboard and into the porcelain hoop with an efficient, wet "Hey! God *damn* you Bowen," squawked the occupant of that far booth as the paper hit his tender lap. "Cut-it-the-fuck-*out!*"

Tyler Bowen scampered out, yelling behind him as he went, "Goal-tending! Basket counts! Two points!"— laughing because he was at least glad to be inside his skin, if not inside this building.

"Charisma," he snorted in the hallway, *"Carumba!"* and jumped high to swipe at the soft acoustical tile on the ceiling. What people saw in Tyler Bowen was the hint that he would one day lie intimately with power. To which he would reply, "Yeah, if my wife runs for office." They saw him intersecting the path of public time with his special adrenaline, to leave it altered for the good. His usual response to such crystal gazings was a prudent, modest "Horseshit! Medium rare." For he also knew that malign things might be dormant in one's humors, like a canceroid melano-

19

blastoma. Yet, at another secret stratum, well below his skin, he would like to believe, and maybe did.

After lunch, they watched another film: *TF-3-9665 —Casualty Effects of G-B Nerve Agent.* The same goat starred. The same voice-over. Same film.

Only this time, they could see panic in the goat's eyes when the men tied him up. Or were they just looking more closely? Was it they or the goat who, knowing the plot, looked differently? The goat's ordeal had been etched too deeply in memory to be so easily forgotten. Yet it seemed to be the same film. And it surely was not the first time they'd been shown the same thing twice with the bald insistence that it was something else.

As a child, Tyler Bowen had a favorite cowboy record that claimed 1001 different stories, a new one for each time the needle was laid down. The first few times the trick worked well enough and too many stories to count were told by Range Rider Randy. But soon it was clear that Randy repeated himself a lot, dealing from a finite range of ridings. Each tale was tipped off to little-boy ears by the first few words or even the scratches preceding them. Over the months the ruts grew deeper and habits set in. Range Rider Randy told but three, then two, and then but one story, over and over and over, until he was discarded in favor of some magical creatures from a mythical dimension.

And so did this movie seem the same. Then the slight variations showed: the goat displayed symptoms of Phases I and II before they finished tying him up. Were there 1001 such variations? It might even be that this film had been shot before the other. Doubtful, though. For the goat seemed to know his part too well, offering, it seemed, a Stanislavsky dying act before the drops of nerve agent even came. If all they wanted was his dignity, he would offer it, and all his integrity, too, for a reprieve from further torture. He was telling them everything he knew. Inevitably, the nerve drops came. Again the goat fixed the silent camera eye with a silent screaming stare.

Once more his pupils pinpointed and his chest grew tight. He sweated in the cool air and then had sudden chills. He heaved his tormented chest. He jerked about as Phase I ended, straining at the dogging ropes. He twitched in anguished spasms. He staggered and he fell. By-the-book.

His head flopped about and he held it for a moment upside down, looking at the camera and audience like—God help us, Tyler Bowen thought: like Bobby Kennedy on the pantry floor. The look was acceptant, almost prescient, wise with resigned fatalism. He had sniffed the odorless air and thought: "Yes, of course—here." Having seen it before—you always see it once before—he knew his part and acquiesced, "God Bless the People and the Angels and the Angel of . . ." Tyler Bowen snapped his head to shake out the image.

Phase III brought the promised mental confusion, and the shadow of the atropine-bearing Cavalry. They stood just out of camera range, taunting hope. The goat began to whip his thighs in final embrace of life. He knew the Cavalry would cool its heels until he was really going. So he rushed headlong into the dying scene, mercifully denied the leisure of slow motion this time.

The convulsions set in, calmer this time. Then the coma. The goat slipped off from conscious pain, trusting his Uncle Sam to do his part. Quickly, again, the two men burst into the frame, and again cheers broke out in the classroom. But the cheers were mild and perfunctory. Bigger circuses would be needed to stir them one more time. This time it hadn't been a surprise. You could count on it. There was a net under the trapeze. It was a rerun.

The two men in white protective suits bent over the goat with stethoscopes and then stood up together. They put the stethoscopes in their pockets.

On the screen, white words subtitled the goat's body: "Cessation of Natural Signs." He was still. The Cavalry walked away. They never had atropine. It wasn't in the game plan. The camera froze at last in silent grainy close-up on the wide-eyed animal's head. And the credits rolled over his sightless eyes, as the goat lay in the dry brown dust. The Heart-Line never rings twice.

The whole world watched them when they walked the Moon that first time. And for a while the glow eclipsed the Earth, which was otherwise that summer ruled by mundane things: an auto accident on Martha's Vineyard, a war, some murders in Los Angeles, a music festival in New York State.

During Moonweek the men who spoke for Earth to the heroes in the sky withheld what news they wished and relayed ball scores and congratulations. Perhaps unhappy news might not survive annihilating airlessness. Or might, and thus despoil the Moon with Earth's infections, though it was the Moonmen who were quarantined upon return. Then, perhaps it was imagined what was censored might otherwise have drifted past the Moon, toward neighboring stars, to advertise us poorly in the later years when it arrived.

Whatever, the news of Earth was that week embargoed from the heavens. Events of epic scale were always edited for posterity. Even as we beamed the word back to ourselves we did not tell the least of our supposed best: the heroes on the Moon spent eight days in the nation's eye peeing in their billion-dollar trousers.

Reunited in the lunar sky all three astronauts sped for home, arriving with the same velocity required for escape.

When they were done with tests all three were strapped to white steeds for parades by PR men and lobbyists. Few people remembered their names.

One, the one who circled without landing, soon vanished in the vast untamed bureaucracy. One, the First Man on the Moon, dismounted his fame and retired, like Cincinnatus after victory, to the pastures of teaching, in Cincinnati. The third, the First Man Ever to Be Second on the Moon, found his nerves and marriage crumbling in the relative increased gravity of home. Someone should have told him: at speeds such as theirs time moves slowly, and those who travel are less old upon return than if they'd sat at home. His

22

equilibrium disintegrated like Moondust flaking off a foreign boot, in gold unfiltered luminescence.

The one who later came to hit a golf ball would be the first man to stand on lunar soil who was a millionaire.

The day they blasted out of selenic grasp all activities of the American Government were suspended in their honor except for two: these seminars at the National Security Agency, and the warring half a world away.

The day they landed, Tyler Bowen leaped higher than usual in a washroom and waited at the top of his jump for the perfect moment to make his shot. Leave him there for a while; it'll keep him out of trouble. Gravity is deadly.

Part II

Under the Sun: 1967

Two years earlier, between the summer and the winter solstices of 1967, Tyler Bowen was in a desert. He was on a graduate fellowship at the National Laboratories of Gila Compound, tucked in a fold of the Gila Mountain hills of southeastern Arizona. The hills are an offshoot of the Thunder Mountain flank of the Cochise Trail, a detumescent peninsula intruding in the hostile northern fringes of the Great Sonoran Desert. Chiricahua Apaches were once evicted from the area by settlers who now describe the place as a "lost pocket of a forgotten corner of nowhere"—by no evidence, save those deeds, a part of the United States.

Across the more fertile land surrounding that, a national debate raged over the length of children's hair, and over the psychotropic chemicals they swallowed, and over their music which was subversive of the old harmonies, and over their obligation to die for executive misjudgment. Vanities would collide and the battle turn vicious and bloody.

In the same general region as Gila Compound, an area defined chiefly by a grid of the firmament's most maintenance-and-police-free highways, and indicated by Tucson natives with a detached southerly sweep and a respectful "Out there," was another air-conditioned incongruity in the wastes, the Tombstone Center for the Applied Social Sciences. Such respect in their tone honored the land, not the traveler, for it was land the locals' forebears struggled for and then got the hell off of when they discovered it wasn't fit for anyone but asthmatics and the government and all that grew out there was blisters.

Tombstone Center was affiliated with Gila Com-

His Holiness, Pope Paul VI

GIOVANNI BATTISTA MONTINI

"Pope of Life"

Bishop of Rome and Vicar of Jesus Christ
Successor of St. Peter, Prince of Apostles
Supreme Pontiff of the Universal Church,
Patriarch of the West, Primate of Italy
Archbishop and Metropolitan of
Roman Province,
Sovereign of Vatican City
Born, September 26, 1897
Ordained Priest, May 29, 1920
Created Cardinal, December 15, 1958
Elected Pope, June 21, 1963
Coronation, June 30, 1963
Died, August 6, 1978

God, our Father, You willed that Your servant Paul be numbered among the Popes. We ask that he who served as the representative of Your Son in this life may be joined to the company of the Saints for ever. Amen.

———

Eternal rest grant to him, O Lord and let perpetual light shine upon him.

May he rest in peace.
Amen.

———

May his soul and the souls of all the faithful departed through the mercy of God rest in peace. Amen.

———

Nihil Obstat: James McGrath, J.C.D., Censor
Imprimatur: ✠ John Cardinal Krol, Archbishop of Philadelphia.

Jefferies and Manz, Inc., Phila., Pa. August 1978

pound and allied further by a shared style of architecture. When Warren Reigeluth, an associate fellow at Tombstone Center, first saw the place he described its school of design as "Reflecting the philosophy of competitive bidding." The main facilities were virtually camouflaged from altitude, consisting of sandstone blockhouses, a city-slicker's notion of environmental appropriateness and a source of endless amusement to area residents, whose idea of serving the desert well was to appreciate it from afar. Warren Reigeluth's wife, Johanna, had known the desert region all her life, loving its variety and textures, finding nuance where strangers found emptiness. She thought Tombstone's desert homage was not unlike "the passing eagle's— after he's eaten." But when she was asked by Warren to be diplomatic to his senior colleagues, she termed it "Just like the desert, only more so, and even better on the inside."

She in fact adored the cheerful and naive vulgarity of the place, and the way small units and wings were appended each year with a patchwork disregard of form or function: ersatz chalet, adobe, ranch-style, glass-walled. She admitted one day, with a studied seriousness that always told Warren she was being facetious, that she "finally understood the basic brilliance of the place. One can always know where one is by observing out the window all the places one is not."

One of the places Johanna and Warren Reigeluth were not during the first week of summer was Tombstone Center. They had gone to San Francisco for a week's working holiday. "Warren has to work and I need a holiday," she told her mother. A stagnant heat that would stay well past the summer's ebb was moving in then on the desert; so was Tyler Bowen, arriving at Gila Compound. And in San Francisco, too, that year, tidal pools of warmth would linger, an emotional tropicality reluctant to yield to fall.

A world away from this there was a jungle where the unluckier moiety of a generation bore pall. There, American power struck at will, invisible and irresistible, from clouds over Southeast Asia. Tyler Bowen's younger brother William would be there by late summer. Of the two, Tyler surely had the better of it.

27

All over, a dreary mood had settled in. No lever could be found to move the world. The war had become, for many at home, the source of fruitless contention; for others, a new idiom of entertainment: in the evenings they could turn a dial and "watch the war." To some it existed solely because it was on every channel. If not palpable, it was nonetheless undeniable. People had begun to chant that "things were in the saddle," and to feel that their lives were at the mercy of forces, great or infinitesimal, beyond their control: overwhelming vectors, insuperable momentum, genetic and historical.

But this was contrary to American Faith. To many it was hard to believe. And so it was not believed. It was not so much a heroic refusal as it was romantic. For belief itself was the greatest agony. What was held as true was disappointing; what was hoped for seemed impossible. Cherished values trembled. Dear faiths brought the most painful and paradoxical returns: the best intentions in the world murdered and maimed and ruined.

So the faithful, the hopeful, had few good choices then: acceptance, withdrawal, rejection, or revolt. They chose the romantic course.

To no use. The United States of America and the planet Earth would each go through a revolution that year, bound by inertia and gripped by the overwhelming Sun. After a year, both would be back where they'd begun in the summertime of 1967, with only the loss of energy and lives to say twelve months had passed. Nor was the Sun itself displaced. Only entropy increased.

In the early summer of 1967, Johanna Reigeluth lacked the energy of intention. If she was paralyzed by lack of will she was also swaddled by the force of home; she was an adverse witness to her own life, seeking only some way to survive another year.

Consider her eyes: green at the center, flickering hints of rainbows in the light; their impishness impossible to capture, only to be known from latent understanding in the penumbra of sight and memory. They had a lyric of light.

But her eyes these days held other things which

28

dominated all that: a nervous distraction that was at once fear and a faraway look; a disconnectedness and timidity; fragile affects strange in her. They told Warren Reigeluth more than she herself would say. Her eyes were for the moment silent, shut, and Johanna lay peacefully at dreams while Warren squinted in search of external clues to what was going wrong. He imagined himself a conscientious sleuth who worked while the suspects slept, a scientist of emotions, hoping the solution would reveal itself from the logical ordering of the evidence, even if the evidence wasn't logical. What he knew was that there were forces acting on his marriage from inside and without, tearing it apart; or, rather, eroding it. And he sought a measure to prevent that.

He watched Johanna sleep in the San Francisco morning light. She was serene there, her calmness interrupted only by an occasional spasm wrought by dreams. Like the great white buildings of the city, scrubbed bright by the daily fog, she seemed pink, glistening in those early rays. Warren cleaned up while she slept, determined that his wife should wake into an orderly world and a tidy room.

If only he could penetrate those dreams somehow, he thought, become part of her subconscious and crawl around inside her head. If only he could find out what she wanted, from life and from him. He hardly knew what might ever make her cry, and doubted now he knew what could make her laugh. Once, he had wanted nothing so much as her. And once, she said he was all she wanted. Now he wanted at best to make her happy, if that were in his power, and at least to make her want him still. She seemed to be resisting him these days, responding to affection with ambiguities, answering his touch with passivity, a detachment betrayed not so much by overt signs, but by subtleties of gesture, and vacancies, by slight or absent energy in her eyes and smile, and by indifference in her skin. Perhaps, he thought, he could sneak behind the lines, wake her by making love, and in that way catch her off guard: merge his reality with her semiconscious mind and take her, dreams and all, into mid-morning.

It seemed to Warren Reigeluth as though a mad

professor had scrambled up their lives with some deranged equation unresponsive to all known laws, just as weird chemicals interfered with the visions of reality among the kids in San Francisco's streets, warping everything, throwing time and space and all relations radically out of joint. The Reigeluths' union hung thus as a function of a magic, elusive variable beyond Warren's comprehension or control. If only he could touch her as she slept, where she dreamed. But that seemed impossible, owing to some new law of nature. It nullified all his best efforts. Doomed them. He tried. But things had changed. Johanna wouldn't say how, or what the key was, if she even knew herself. So he hardly knew where to begin. His hunches led him to her eyes.

Johanna's eyes were her father's gift at the iris; her mother's, the milky sea around it. In every feature and aspect Johanna was born her parents' child, the perfect mix of Carl and Maureen Poulson's blood, as though their two great beauties had crashed together at high speed to synthesize her. But her eyes were each, undiluted: her father at the live, blue-green center; her mother, the white broth, the fertile setting for the gem. The rest of Johanna was their sum and blend.

There was a spot that had no parent, though, Johanna's place alone. Just below the outer corner of her right biparented eye was a small scar; a tiny dot, pure white against her skin. It was a gouge cut by slipping forceps during her mother's delivery. Carl used to tease and say Johanna "came out all turned around." To Maureen it was more like "howling bloody murder." That dead tissue seemed a secret window, hinting of revelations. When afraid, Johanna was prone to rubbing it unconsciously, as though protecting the route to her last uncharted corner.

Some measure of Warren's inability to fathom her may have been that he saw this scar as nothing more than a slight imperfection, like an eccentric second belly button. She didn't like to talk about it. Not that it detracted from her facial beauty. But the truth was that Johanna's sense of herself proceeded from that dot. It had been born with her, the product of an artificial parthenogenesis she inspired. From a distance it appeared as an incongruous frozen tear, and gave the dynamic of her face added mystery and animation. Close up it betrayed Johanna and her eyes as part Carl Poulson's, part Maureen's, and all her own.

Carl Poulson had come to the western mesa in the War Year 1943, a young physicist recruited to work on a project at Los Alamos, New Mexico. Just what that meant he would not fully grasp until the end. The War was many things to those caught up in it, as for the nations themselves: a casting of their fortunes, a becoming or an end. By their actions and the War's effects they would be known for a generation after. But for many at Los Alamos and its satellite sites, the War was none of this. Many would leave as they came, itinerant technicians, hired for piecework, unemployable in peace. By the elaborate security labyrinths of atomic bomb making, most would work in ignorance of their labor's aim. For those who did know, any reservations they might have had were exiled from conscience for the duration. Necessity was infinite and the cause was absolute. All lived in analogue to their work in the desert: such was its velocity and momentum that time slowed down like motion through sand. The energy they released was greater than themselves.

Carl Poulson was luckier than most, having had a role of some importance. He left Los Alamos in 1947 with a citation for "Excellent and Meritorious Contributions to the War Effort." He moved his wife into a new house in Phoenix, Arizona, with what they called their "three prizes of war": two boys, Brian and Neal, and a baby girl, Johanna. Maureen used to say there might have been more if Carl had taken a fourth night off from work in those four years.

The marriage did not last many years of peace. Maureen Poulson, who had been an exquisite and fiery young woman with wit and ambition to match, had grown lonely in those years, bitter and scared. By the War's end she was drinking heavily. In Phoenix, Carl consulted for Hughes Aircraft and some electronics firms, and Maureen swelled and grew unreachably sullen. "The best thing Carl ever did for me," she later said, "was divorce me." Even before that divorce, though still under one roof, they lived apart. What War work had once required of him—reclusive abstraction from domestic life—he embraced as an escape from the war at home.

Brian and Neal were sturdy loners who were only seen for meals. They never noticed their father's withdrawn manner, more concerned were they with football and the call of vandalism. Johanna may not have noticed either, because she had a way to penetrate the wall. As Carl retreated more and more into his work, Johanna alone retained the power to tear him away and command his full attention.

He would lift her up and whirl her around, sing funny songs and tell her tales, make up rhymes and little poems. As an infant, Johanna would coo and gurgle when Carl poked her and sang, "Johanna-Banana/Elana-Mañana." As she grew up Carl's rhymes became his secret language with her; teaching games, instructing and sharing with her the special way her father saw the world. She learned to flirt before she walked, and as she grew it was clear—at least to Carl—that she loved the scent of her father's neck more than her mother's arms.

An ice cream truck used to come by in the evening, and Carl would race Johanna out the door to greet it. She'd hide behind him shyly and he'd say, "Well, there's no one here who wants this, so I'll just eat it all up myself." Then he'd poke his head between his legs and make a funny face upside down. She'd squeal and squeeze his nose, and like magic, Carl's clowning features would become her daddy's again. Her reward was the ice cream; his, watching Johanna-Banana's soft belly shake with happy laughter. Sometimes he'd glower with loving sternness, and then tickle her until she melted. He would pounce on her and pick her up on his broad shoulders, then swing her high. She would shriek in safe ecstasy as she fell forever into his strong arms. "Just don't be surprised," a friend of Carl's once joked, "if she runs off with a guy who runs a roller coaster when she's seventeen. You'll know why. My wife, she's got a thing, thank God, for baldness, on account of her old man. You can read all about it in *Agamemnon*."

"Which means," Carl laughed, "your daughter may run off with a camel driver, for all the time you spend in sand traps. Never can tell."

Johanna made Carl happy where his marriage, and even his work, did not. He and Maureen were divorced in 1952, but his work was indissolubly sanctified by a stricter church.

Patent royalties Carl had assigned to his family supported them comfortably in his absence, and his work was sufficiently respected that he was sought for teaching posts and industrial consultancies. He limited his government jobs to theoretical study groups on atomic energy matters, declining further weapons work, though the two were hardly separable. Even this brought a minor reward. His predictions and suggestions for instrument refinements earned him personal recognition when a team of theoreticians, experimentalists and warrior-scholars discovered a new element, number 99, synthesized in the debris of an atomic test. Other people were to win position and prizes for that same kind of work, including Nobel Prizes, but Carl Poulson's sole reward was a personal letter from the project research director acknowledging that Carl owned "a full share of credit for the fruits of our work." He treasured this piece of paper above all others. For there was in Carl Poulson a nagging sense of lack, an unfulfillable urge fanned by the Los Alamos years.

There had been a feeling among some of the workers there, in that aerie of urgency and brilliance they inhabited at Los Alamos, that their participation in the Manhattan Engineer District's weapons project made them scientific courtesans of the State, indecently recumbent; their theoreticians' virtue first compromised by cohabitation with engineers (an old intramural snobbery). For some of them the import would be so grave that they abandoned physics and turned to other fields. But for many the great lesson of their experience was oblique to matters of ethics and purpose: that by allying one's curiosities and talents to the public imagination (or manipulating opinion, as the newly arrived rocket scientists understood), one might forge a union of mutual benefit. "It is a vanity," they said, "to consider science as an art unalloyed by thoughts of commerce, or even to think of art that way. We live in a world where things are bought or sold, profit and advantage sought . . ." Thus, for contributions to the nation's material or emotional needs even a theoretical physicist could become wealthy and powerful and celebrated. And as much as he resisted domination by that urge, Carl Poulson felt another, more simple and more widely shared. He wanted most of all to do something very good indeed, something noble, well defined. Like any soldier or artist or philosopher, the scientist wants to advance the cause, the art, the state of understanding. So he toils countless hours in sweaty mines of played-out notions for every nugget of reward and piecemeal victory. Like a lover, knowing he may never fully consummate his most basic urge, still he strives. And human, too; there is in the heart of even an incandescent flame that carbon of incompletely burned ambition, the desire to make one's name and leave a mark. Carl Poulson shared all those human dreams.

He stayed in Phoenix for a year after the divorce and then, in 1953, took a chair in Theoretical Physics at the University of Utah in Salt Lake City. Maureen, retaining custody of all three children, received handsome support. The shock of their final separation helped her regain a measure of the self she had been before the War. She started off doing secretarial work at a local television station and within two years became assistant producer of a local show. By 1955 she was the first woman executive at the station, earning more than Carl's alimony and royalties brought in.

In February 1955, Carl, who had been unable to see the children during his holiday visitation period that Christmas, came down to Phoenix, and then took Johanna with him to a conference in Princeton, though Maureen initially objected to the idea of her missing school for three weeks. He always tried to make those increasingly rare times with Johanna special, and this was perhaps the most special of all.

It took a week by car and all the way Carl told his radiantly pretty daughter all she could handle about his work. Living with brothers and the sophisticated arrangements of interparent visitation had already equipped Johanna with a fine poise. She knew when and how to control her excitement, when to let go, when to hold back. And she had none of the saccharine cuteness in her manner that girls her age often affected. She was also attentive and bright, lapping up Carl's explanations with an understanding beyond her years. In fact, once that worked to her disadvantage: a poem Carl wrote for her about Albert Einstein and the Theory of Relativity cost her first place in a school poetry-reading contest. The teacher who judged the competition insisted Johanna could not possibly comprehend what she was reciting; the teacher didn't, at any rate, and instead awarded first place to a tedious rendition of *Curfew Shall Not Ring Tonight*.

During the trip to Princeton Carl wove long, spellbinding stories about enchanted, mischievous animals: Rickey the Cricket and his Sancho Panza friend and foil, Edgar the Worm. Each tale illustrated some law of physics. The gift for creating these stories was second nature to Carl, and Johanna's face shone especially when they made some mystery clear to her. At night while she slept he composed little ditties and longer poems about the great men of science and the character of natural law; even a song or two which he sprang as a surprise, set to some annoyingly repetitive radio jingles. So they sang over a toothpaste ad about the Laws of Thermodynamics, and resisted auto ads with ballads of Darwin and Copernicus. She memorized them rapidly, and where she hesitated, Carl patiently explained, until by her inflection he was sure she grasped it. Curiously, the one she understood least became her favorite:

> Quantum Mechanically
> Herr Werner Heisenberg
> Studied Uncertainty
> And in a wink—
> Said, "In all certainty
> (Probable-istic'ly)
> *Nothing* is certain!
> —I certainly *think*."

In every town along the way Carl introduced his daughter as a visiting princess from outer space who could not talk: on her world they communicated by giggle and blush. And she would invariably blush and giggle at her silly father.

At Princeton, the conference was to be held at the Institute for Advanced Study, and Carl promised to take Johanna to New York City as a treat when it was over. "Will Dr. Einstein be at the conference?" she asked. "I'd rather meet him than go to New York City." Carl laughed and said he didn't think so, as the man was geting rather old, but he promised to find out. He mentioned it to a colleague over lunch, just as a funny child story, and the friend shrugged, "I doubt he'll show. You know he hasn't been too well. Can't she just write him like the other kids—the ones who want help with their homework? Can't you buy her a doll?" Carl chuckled and told him to forget it. "Before you know it," the friend said, "she'll want to be a ballerina and you'll be trying to figure out ways to meet Adele Astaire. I guess that's the curse of being stuck with only visiting rights, huh?"

"She's been through ballerina," Carl said. "And cowgirl—and physicist. You may be right. I think she's coming back to ballerina."

"You sure you're not pushing for theoretician-just-like-poor-old-dad—not even a little?"

"Nope. She can even grow up to be her mother if she wants. In fact—you'll like this—she told me, very earnest, mind you, that she didn't want to do physics because she'd want to get out there and find out what the answers are for real."

"I don't blame her—what are you feeding her, Gödel Strudel?"

Carl beamed and said he had. "I told her not to worry about it. 'For all your days on Earth Isaac Newton's all you need.' But what can you do? She likes Einstein just the same. Her brothers met Bob Feller—"

"Some kid," the friend laughed. But the next day he grabbed Carl's elbow after the morning session, asking, "You still interested in seeing the Old Man?" Not if it was any trouble, Carl replied. "Well, this is crazy but, you know Tom Gressle? He's as nutty as you are—

he's got *four* daughters. He's *also* got a paper on Wave Mechanics and Quantum Field Theory he's supposed to drop off at Einstein's house. I told him, wait a minute, Tom, have I got a story to tell you. Anyway, I don't know if it's what you're looking for, but he said sure, you could run it over for him if you want. At least she could see the house." Carl thanked him and promised to come to dinner afterward, and then went off to collect Johanna.

When they rang the bell at the small white house at 112 Mercer Street, a middle-aged woman answered. "We've come to deliver a paper to Professor Einstein," Johanna chirped, as coached. Carl added, "From Tom Gressle at the Institute."

"Are you Dr. Gressle?"

"No. I'm Carl Poulson. I'm here for the symposium, and this is my daughter, Johanna."

"We've come from Salt Lake City, Utah," Johanna blurted, "to say hello to Dr. Einstein."

"Is he expecting you?"

"No. No," Carl explained. "He doesn't know, uh—" He straightened up from his embarrassment. He regretted having to employ this method, and winced to hear himself, but said, "He might know of my work slightly. I, uh, worked with Albert Ghiorso on 99— element number 99."

"Well I'll give him the paper and say you're here. But I don't know if he'll want to be disturbed. It's rather late in the day and he has not been well lately. Your name? Pultney?"

"Poulson," Carl corrected. "Johanna Poulson, age ten. And her father, Carl." The woman smiled and went up to the study. Carl shook his head while Johanna squeezed his hand eagerly. He felt like he was making Halloween rounds.

The woman returned and said, "Professor Einstein is unfortunately not feeling very well, so—"

"Oh, well," Carl exhaled with some relief, looking toward Johanna to cushion her disappointment, "then please give him our best wishes for—"

"But he says that a visit from a little girl might cheer him up," the woman said. Johanna squirmed in delight though she tried to control herself. "But please," the woman urged. "Be brief. He's really quite tired."

Johanna had never known her grandparents, yet the frail lion of science seemed, despite his moustache, to be an androgynous grandmother-father to her. She had heard her father speak of him so often and so reverently, and now he seemed as she'd expected. She curtsied, and color filled his cheeks. The room was neat and economically lit. The windows were closed to keep the breeze from piled stacks of papers. Only white lace curtains seemed a frill in the spare decorations. Beyond window shades half-drawn to mute the sharp winter sun, a small garden.

Dr. Einstein sat in a comfortable green chair, worn down at its arms, and asked Carl Poulson what role he had played in the work which produced element 99. Carl averred that it was minor.

"Then I really can't blame you," the old man said with a faint smile. "You know what Szilard said—" He sighed as if talking really to himself. " 'The first successful alchemist was God—and the second was doubtless the Devil himself.' Eh?"

"Some of us," Carl answered, "are just poor devils. At Los Alamos, we used to say that physics began with wonder, engineering with a crank." The old man rocked softly, adding that he'd rather have been spared the honor of donating his name to this new element, Einsteinium. Carl knew his embarrassment derived largely from the fact that the element was born of an atomic bomb. Surely that was the last thing Einstein sought connection with, though now it seemed inevitable.

The old man wore a gray flannel shirt and gray trousers, both of which must have fit better in hardier days. They gave him resonations of a laborer as well as a scholar. He wore brown slippers and a dark blue cardigan sweater. Carl thought he seemed to be defying his own most basic principle: in a universe insistently in motion, he seemed, in his easy chair, at perfect rest.

The famous white shock of hair was thinned, but it stood out against the dark colors and soft lighting of the room, as did the many-colored quilt on his lap, and the random tweed pattern of well-used haphazardly replaced books and records in the wall cases. In a near-whisper, the old man said, "They should name these new elements for pretty little girls. Again? . . ."

"*Johanna*," she said, with the proprietous stress she used to keep teachers from calling her Joanna.

"A pretty name," the old man said, "and honored too. *Johanna*. Fit for a Kepler or a Bach, eh?" He nodded to himself and then asked, *"Sind sie Deutsche?"* Carl understood it well enough to shake his head: no, they weren't German. Then the old man said something indistinct and added, "A pretty name for a pretty girl. An angel come to visit me." His laugh was gentle, soft. "If the other angels are so like you, I shall be very lucky, eh?" Johanna was puzzled by all this, but could tell from her father's hand petting her head that it was all well.

She took an extradeep breath and said, "My father has told me all about you."

"Has he now?" Dr. Einstein looked up. "And what has he said?"

"He says you are a great and good man."

Dr. Einstein looked away for a moment, then back. "And do good girls still believe what their papas tell them these days?"

She replied properly, and not without a little flirtation. "I do. Because my father is a very great man also." Carl winced, but the old man didn't see it, nodding at Johanna, saying, "Of that I'm sure."

"He's told me all about what you've done—" Carl pressed his hand on her shoulder to calm her down, afraid she was getting reckless. But she continued, "He wrote a poem for me about you," and Carl grimaced. "I have it in my notebook."

"I think it's time for us—" Carl interrupted.

"But I must hear this poem," the old man insisted.

Carl said, "It's very long and—it's for children."

"Say it for me, please."

Carl's chest sagged and he stood behind his daughter with his hand easily on her shoulder. She stood on the right of the easy chair and began to recite from the much-folded copy. Carl had taught her well. She hardly needed the cue sheet. Her delivery caught the flavor and meaning of the words, reading it to him almost as a bedtime story. She needed her father's help through only one rough spot, and otherwise her delivery was charming and strong. *"Ode for a Special Relative,"* she began, with great pride in her father's authorship, "by Carl Poulson."

> The Universe, to Newton's mind,
> Was like a clock in perfect time,
> With changeless fundamental rules,
> And Newton's Laws the perfect tools.
>
> But Albert Einstein found some flaws
> In Isaac Newton's cosmic laws.
> For Einstein said, "It seems to me
> That Mass is really Energy!
>
> "And photons act as if they wanta
> Show us that they're really quanta.
> Now space is curved, to Euclid's woe
> And Time speeds up as you go slow.
>
> "Time slows again, and Mass grows great,
> When Mass speeds near Light's Constant Rate.
> For all these things are just to say
> That Mass behaves a Special Way.
>
> "So too, Length, Time, and Energy.
> In Gen'ral: Relativity.
> For if through dark and lonely night
> There sped a beam of stellar Light
>
> "And near the Light there cruised a Mass
> Trying hard to go as fast
> (Like, say, a suitor pressing hard
> Against a maiden's constant guard),
>
> "Reports about the Mass's rate
> Would differ, causing hot debate.
> For all who look are moving, too,
> With different speeds and points of view.

Carl Poulson's embarrassment at having his professional credentials rendered to this man he admired above any other, as no loftier thing than a children's poem—one filled, as well, with minor license taken for the demands of poesy—gave way to larger feelings: glowing pride in his dazzling, fearless daughter. And Einstein's calm smile reminded Carl that the man's own priorities put the demands of beauty first. He was himself something of a poet, who felt that the laws of the heavens arranged themselves in designs of inherent grace, whose beauty was their basic simplicity—a truth which could be made sensible to children, perhaps more easily than to adults.

Her reading continued to hold the old man in her spell.

> "Now if we helped the Mass to chase
>   That Light beam through the pitch of Space,
>   We'd still fail by a little bit
>   For want of force near-infinite.
>
> "But Light's speed, on the other hand,
>   Won't change no matter where we stand.
>   Despite how fast its source may go—
>   —or you!—Light won't speed up or slow.
>
> "And only Gravitation's force
>   Can bend Light from its steadfast course.
>   While Mass, by neither work nor trick,
>   Can ever hope to go as quick.
>
> "The Speed of Light is Absolute.
>   So, you'd be vain, like King Canute
>   (Who ordered earthly seas to 'hold!'
>   But seas will not do what they're told),
>
> "If you desired starlight's rate:
>   You'd need push infinitely great.
>   By definition, then, your Mass
>   Would soon be infinitely vast!
>
> "Now back upon that speedy beam
>   The clocks go slowly, like a dream.
>   While on the laggard Mass, the clocks
>   Have quicker ticks, and quicker tocks.

"Though Time (and Tides) won't stop, it's true,
    All Time, and Speed, relate to you.
    Nor can you move as fast as Light.
    Thus one man's year's another's night.

"So King Canute could *slow* the tides
    By sending seas on spaceship rides!
    But try to *stop* them, and he'd get
    His royal slippers soaking wet!

With his eyes fixed on the top of Johanna's head, Carl didn't notice the momentary shift of the old man's gaze to him, carrying the same warmth. Carl interrupted to say that of course the attributions were not meant to be literal; and Einstein smiled graciously. Johanna waited for her father's cue to resume, then went on:

"Now here's a gem that I've prepared:
    E is really *mc*-squared.
    For Mass possesses Energy
    As times the second pow'r of '*c*.'

"And all you need are neutron beams
    To split an atom at the seams.
    But after you've achieved that fission
    Note the puzzled math'matician

"Counting up the Mass that's left.
    He's come up short! Was there a theft?
    The Mass that's gone's no mystery:
    It's now Atomic Energy!

"My great lament is that these rules
    Are seized upon by fighting fools
    Who'd rather than for Peace, employ
    The Laws of Nature to destroy.

"So take my theories, prosper, grow.
    But mind, you'll reap the crops you sow.
    The Knowledge Fruit is bittersweet:
    Both good and dangerous to eat.

"For long ago, 'twas said to Man:
'Get all the learning that you can.
But lest your Knowledge be your Fall,
Get Wisdom first, and most of all!'

Carl whispered softly that he thought she'd recited enough, but Johanna looked up at him confused, saying there was a little more to it. He assented when Einstein bade her continue.

"Our Father made the Heavens move
And Mother Nature added Love
In Peace these laws and gifts they give
To Man, their Special Relative."

Carl had been reluctant to attribute such simplistic faith to Einstein, who in no way seemed to mind. In fact, it was the coda, not meant to be Einstein's words, but the poet's tribute, that the old man found more uncomfortable.

So in the dark and starry night
At speeds approaching that of Light
As like a choir of angel-song
The mind of Einstein swept along

Universal in its scope
Racing at the speed of Hope
And only this was greater still:
Unending Love, Eternal Will.

She curtsied when she was done, and the old man clapped his hands together, laughing, "I wish I had said it so well myself." He nodded thanks to Carl Poulson and then turned to Johanna. "You are bright as well as beautiful." He blushed slightly and reached out to stroke her golden hair. Her head bowed in sudden shyness, and his hand fell to Carl Poulson's own, on Johanna's shoulder. Carl held the veined, age-spotted, delicate hand for an instant, squeezing it in his own gratitude. The old man's eye caught Johanna's most flirtatious smile and he said, "A bright . . . angel . . . I am pleased you came to see me. But now . . . I'm

43

afraid I must go back to work." He looked up at Carl for understanding, "I have very much left to do and it is so wearying." He smiled at Johanna, studying her eyes and soft cheeks. "But I am grateful . . . and I wonder? Might I have that fine poem to keep?—In case I should forget what I think?"

They happily surrendered it and he blessed them with "Thank you. You have made me happy today."

On the way out, Carl told her how proud he was. "You're a gift from heaven, sweetheart," and bit his lip to keep his vision from blurring.

Over dinner, Carl's friend was amazed. "I'm just glad it wasn't *my* kid who went along," he said. "Buddy-the-diplomat would've said, 'Oh, yeah! I know you. You're the guy that built the atom bomb!' As far as Buddy's concerned, you and me, well, we just held the screwdrivers. Let us be grateful."

Carl took his bright angel to New York City and squired her to puppet shows and ballets, on guided tours and through museums. And then he took his princess home again, back to her mother in Phoenix, spinning exotic tales of Rickey the Cricket and Edgar the Worm, while Johanna remained transfixed, in love with her daddy and his stories, her memories of the city and the feeling of being special. All the way back, the radio played "The Ballad of Davy Crockett," which was enjoying its last weeks of primacy, soon to be replaced by the carefree "Cherry Pink and Apple Blossom White," a mediating rhythm, easing the transition from the King of the Wild Frontier to his rude, upstart successor, the dark and dire "Rock Around the Clock," which boded of changing times. Indeed, though Carl Poulson found verses to fit "Davy Crockett" which could explain John Von Neumann's contributions to Games and Information Theory, and easily found words for "Cherry Pink" to detail the work of Gregor Mendel, "Rock Around the Clock" oddly resisted all efforts at domestication.

Later that spring, when Einstein succumbed to the grip of age and died, it seemed to many in the scientific community as though the center had fallen out of their solar system, the embodiment of its heart and conscience. In the lay world as well, the old man had personified the link between modern physics and its ancient roots in natural philosophy. Carl Poulson spoke a eulogy for him at the university chapel in Salt Lake City, which was as much a reaffirmation of his own belief as an address of appreciation. Excerpts were reprinted in several area newspapers and were among those selections from memorial remarks included in that summer's physics journals.

He said, in part, "The nonscientist often believes that Einstein added to the terrible uncertainty and faithlessness of our age, by giving us Relativity in place of Newton's comforting absolutism. What he did was free us from the authority of an invalid idea. And at bottom, not since, in the poet's words, Euclid 'gazed on beauty bare,' has there been a man of so devoutly simple faith and vision.

". . . His was an ancient faith, part Platonic, part Pythagorean, wholly poetic: that Nature is real, knowable, and based on the beauty of unities and simple patterns. In that way he was a Romantic, perhaps our last great one. He did not cause the great anxiety of our day. Rather, he was a holdout against the doctrines which dominate today's philosophy: existentialism, nihilism, dadaism—even Quantum Mechanics. He resisted Quantum Theory as repugnant to that faith, saying 'God does not play at dice with the world.'

"Before reason, it is beauty's truth, that he recognized as the universe's theme and mold. In a sense, his famous and noble formulation, $E = mc^2$, is an intellectual atom, a tiny bundle with enormous power. It conforms to that most cherished belief, for it hints, by its very grace and parsimony, of even more elegant wellsprings hidden deeper still. Inside this monad may yet be lodged some mighty and frightful understanding: unified field relations. They would link the atom's own heart—the interface of matter and energy—with the heavens' mind; the grace-filled fundament of all forces and being.

"Long ago physics was born, the child of awe and philosophy. It has come full circle, to full flower in

Einstein's work, to tell us the great reality of what he understood: his thought touched the soul of nature."

Other comment of the day spoke of the paradoxes in 'Einstein's life: his rejection of and contributions to Quantum Theory—which when wed to Relativity promised a closer approach to a unification of field relations; his seemingly hopeless quest for the Unified Field Theory, which most physicists regarded as an intuition which could never be borne out; his devotion to peace and his singular contributions to atomic theory—used as bombs. That, to Carl Poulson, seemed the most bittersweet paradox. News stories and obituaries summarizing his work invariably ignored the philosophical context, and often carried the subhead "FATHER OF THE A-BOMB." Carl cursed the clumsiness of headlines, and the dictions which sacrificed nuance for economy. A man's life was distilled in the retorts of journalism. What precipitated out was the essence; the printed residue was often the impurities and ironies which best fit newsprint's more pedestrian needs. Carl wondered if he, too, would be remembered as nothing more than a midwife to that beast, his penalty for four years' faithful service. He wished for some escape from such an immortality.

If it should come, Carl Poulson knew, it would only come by seeing something unbeheld by others. So he nurtured the hope that there was yet some clue beneath his sight, vagrant and alluring, some transforming inspiration which would enable him to transcend the limits of vision, and see further down the road the old man had set out on. It might require a stroke of imagination to leap the moat of logic's insufficiencies. Or perhaps instead, a stroke of luck. For understanding often rode on the kind of friendly breeze that blew mold spores onto agar. What was required was preparation, and belief in possibility. Such a moment, to one poised to see it, to one who did not limit what could be seen, would glow with awesome clarity. It would enable him, Carl Poulson felt, to give something blessed, understanding and hope, to the world.

He had seen the glow flicker before him at times, in sleep, or when near to some unraveling. He'd also felt in the heart of such a moment, without the words to define it, when he and Johanna and the old man had momentarily shared a common touch.

Twelve years later, in the summer of 1967, the memorial Carl Poulson wrote for Einstein had turned to yellowed pages among Johanna's childhood mementos. It had no apparent bearing on her life. She was informed enough to be aware that physicists had made some progress toward that long-sought unification, in terms too abstract for comprehension. They had halved the remaining distance in successive steps, though an ultimate solution, true unification, was afforded as much chance as Ecumenism; if it might be done, it might only be a physicist's conceit, of staggering complexity.

All of this had very little meaning for her, except as metaphors and images she might employ. For her primary avocation came from Carl Poulson's recessive traits. She had been an English major in college. And true to the prediction, the chief influence of physics in her life now was Newtonian: she and Warren were pushing off each other in opposite directions.

Their week in San Francisco was a search for an amnesty. Johanna had insisted she needed "time off from this day-to-day," the life they led in Tucson, though she suspected she needed time off mostly from the life she led.

When she married Warren in 1965, Johanna was still an undergraduate at Berkeley, and Warren was a first-year graduate student in Political Science at Stanford. The entire area was in an uproar in those years. This was not something new for the University of California at Berkeley, which had traditionally been on the cutting edge of political consciousness, nor for the city across the Bay, which smugly tolerated its Bohemian cultural enclaves.

But as never before, events in the dominant society served to link political and cultural nonconformity, creating hybrid and mutant strains which were as inevitable as they were unpredictable.

A Free Speech Movement begun in 1964 over local campus issues broadened with the commencement of large-scale American bombing of North Vietnam in

1965 to encompass the largest questions of injustice. In doing so it became necessarily radical, for the argument was no longer with specific policies, but with root causes which determined those policies. With that came changes in form, anger replacing the previous intensely academic, philosophical tone. Nor could the protest be limited to politics; it challenged all prevailing social values. So as with a revolution, there was room, in the beginning, under its accommodating rubric, for all who felt commonality by sharing alienation from a common enemy. Alternate forms of awareness beckoned, like side shows at a carnival. There was a tent for the Filthy Speech Movement, for the League for Sexual Freedom, for every kind of drug. And local art, from music to poetry to theater, was shaped by all this.

But for Warren Reigeluth these things held no attraction. While students rallied at Sproul Plaza and Sather Gate, he viewed their activity as counterproductive and inefficient. "If they're serious," he'd say to Johanna, "if they want to have a real effect upon the system, they should understand that they'll only be taken seriously if they take themselves seriously."

Access to the controls, he knew, came from acquiring the expertise needed by management. And, his friends liked to say, there was nothing Warren Reigeluth would do to impede his chances of someday becoming president—of anything.

To Johanna, this seemed mature and sure-handed. The confusing storm around her made Warren only the more attractive. Indeed, from that island of stability she could make forays, as a sightseer, into the exotica all around her, becoming fascinated by it all without the attendant risk of being swept off.

After they were married, Johanna transferred to Stanford and doubled up on courses. They set up modest housekeeping in Palo Alto that first year. And it was then that something began to happen to her. With the time and freedom to examine her goals she began to doubt them. Warren passed it off as symptomatic of both Junior Year Angst and First Year of Marriage Nerves. But to Johanna the prospect of attaining what she had previously sought became unsettling. In another two years, she suspected, they'd be a typical

48

faculty marriage, a likelihood more disturbing to her than to Warren.

For Warren, what he called "the demands of excellence" absorbed all his attention. He was preparing a thesis, taking graduate courses, acting as a teaching assistant, working at the Advanced Studies Center, so he hardly noticed Johanna's growing distress. Not that there was much to notice. Originally she had wanted nothing so much as marriage and a Ph.D. But things were changing: the world, to a great extent; Johanna, a little, though except for her doubts and her growing obsession with the musical metamorphosis around her, it was difficult to say how. She valued Warren for his dependability. And Warren was changing, dependably, not at all.

Then, in the spring of 1966, Warren was offered an ideal position. On the basis of an abstract of his doctoral thesis—an analysis of executive prerogative in modern government—he was chosen for the highly coveted position of Associate Fellow at Tombstone Center, not least of whose attractions was its freedom from the consumptive draft, by dint of government contracts. With this also came nominal faculty affiliation at the nearby University of Arizona at Tucson. His résumé, Johanna said, was getting longer than a Teuton noun. Warren felt that this move might also be just what Johanna needed.

She would be close to her family and on the edge of the desert she loved so much. Indeed, when they left Palo Alto she did lose some of her malaise. She finished her degree in the fall of 1966 and rolled over into graduate courses, busying herself otherwise with ballet classes and desert walks. By that spring, she had become intensely bored despite all this activity. Her view of her relationship with Warren became clearer in the distractionless desert. Perhaps, she thought, it was a mistake from the start. She'd married Warren for much the same reason her mother had married her father: stability and promise. In fact, she pressed him into it. They seemed to be in love back then, but now she thought those first months were largely make-believe, or the time of their greatest symmetry: Warren, the ambitious young scholar with all honor and opportunity his; Johanna, the pretty, brash, Phi-Bete-bound co-ed. Supplements and complements, they could stop the world like that, they thought then.

Now, she took little interest in his work, little glory in his achievements. She had typed an early draft of his thesis then; now she could hardly bear to read it. He was no part of her. When they made love, she felt distant, watching herself make love. She saw his skin as foreign and his touch as intrusion. At times, she thought it was something in herself that was wrong; at times, in him: he seemed a boy playing at manhood, doing checklisted things until by age and status he could claim a man's due respect. But she wasn't sure whether she wanted a man or a boy, or something in between; or of what she was.

When she walked around Tucson she identified less with those established citizens who owned the place and more with the scruffy kids who were continually routed from the city parks by the police. She became more than just a sightseer. She joined them, spent afternoons with them getting high in the desert, and then went home to Warren. She wondered if she wasn't getting a little schizzy. Indeed, Warren teased her before friends and family, calling her meanderings "Johanna's perilous adventures" and "her weekly nervous breakdown." But he reassured her that a small part of even the most stable individual was fascinated by disorder. She wasn't sure it was that simple.

Their attitudes toward many things took on a definition of determined disagreement. He accused her of being perverse, and she wasn't sure it might not be so. All they agreed on was they got in each other's way; often they couldn't agree on what it was they were arguing about. Even politics, a subject that had always seemed irrelevant to marriage, became a screen upon which every source of their discord could be projected and enlarged. Warren took a strict pragmatist's approach to issues, appropriating to himself the right of all authoritative comment. She conceded that her reactions were more emotive and intuitive than his, but he treated her as though she had the political acumen of a snail. Warren's study made the war in Asia continually germane. Johanna would say she thought it "a

50

mistake on the face of it. There's not much more to it. It's simply wrong, that's all."

"If you look at it simply. It's more complex than that. You have to deal with the *Realpolitik* in the light of competing interests on a world scale."

"You deal with it. I think it's terrible."

And Warren would laugh as though patting her on the head. Once he said, "You know, there are only two fields where the amateur is thought to be better than the professional—strategy and love. I guess I'll have to agree with you." She nearly bit him.

Tucson had seemed an ideal place for Warren and Johanna. There was work for him, some leisure for Johanna, and the desert out the back door as a room of her own. She had her studies, then a job, as further Band-Aids on the invisible wound. Yet all these things seemed to her mere conveniences to see her through a difficult time. She was not sure it was worth getting through this time. Admitting that to herself was even more taxing because she knew no other choices she'd admit to. Still, it seemed pointless, like her studies had, like the war she and Warren disagreed about, like many things. At first she drew further into her studies, into their fruitless interior landscapes. Then she abandoned that. Warren demanded reasons, did not respect mere feelings. She could almost grasp the reasons, but not quite. She grew absorbed in the fractious music Warren detested, combing its sounds and poetics for fragmentary insights, looking less and less to mend things.

Her mother suggested that she needed some consuming interest the equal of Warren's, that she was jealous of his work. Johanna wasn't sure.

Sometimes she thought the cause was just frustration, as they fell into a pattern of sexual incompletion. But that was not quite it. That was just another sign, an effect. Sometimes it seemed like lack of love, but not quite: she loved Warren, in a way, she was sure. She felt she'd grown up with him, that they shared many secrets. Unhappiness was a symptom, but she could not say flatly she was unhappy. There just seemed to be something missing, something that could make her feel intensely private with Warren, sealed off from the world and able to become herself in an ecstatic way. She remembered the feeling at its purest: losing herself in laughter when tickled as a little girl, falling endlessly, fearlessly. But now, not quite.

Waking up she felt herself bound by the limits of her own imagination and strength, with only the desert to escape to. She became as nervous and lonely as the other desert creatures, sleeping longer and longer into the day, burrowing into dreaming, devising strategies for survival. They were holding actions, really: talking to strangers wherever she was, stopping for hitchhikers or anyone who seemed to have the news of something new. Some of them thought her odd, or a doper, or a girl hungry for a pickup. Warren continually warned her that she was asking for trouble. Johanna marveled that he never asked what it was she was seeking. He said she seemed like a compulsive gambler looking for one lucky hit, and she agreed it might be so, but never admitted it to him.

Ultimately, she prevailed upon her mother for assistance, although the two women were on generally poor terms. Maureen had moved to Scottsdale, Phoenix's wealthiest suburb, and many of their mother-daughter differences were couched in terms of class: each believed the other could stand a little. Maureen accused Johanna at times of "exceeding bad grace. You don't attack your mother's manner of living from afloat in her pool." So it was with the sarcasm Johanna expected that, when she asked her mother for suggestions, Maureen replied, "Analysis." To that, Johanna said, "Warren claims it's an undeclared form of adultery."

So Maureen made another suggestion—"Adultery." It was only when Johanna made it clear that she was speaking of employment advice that her mother became less personal, saying, "The problem is you're educated to be either a Philosopher-King or unemployed. It's a real world, darling, calling for real skills. But I suppose that's why we need a welfare system."

"Mother, I'm not helpless."

"Not at all. We need one so young Liberal Artists can be social workers and minister to people who are happier than they are." She relented a bit by saying, "Many overeducated people without skills do rather

52

well in newspapers. Would you like me to call Arnie Logan?" He was editor of the *Tucson Intelligencer* and a man with whom Maureen had once had a notorious two-week affair. After Johanna offered the proper obsequy, Maureen made the call.

And for most of the spring of 1967 the *Intelligencer* absorbed Johanna's energies. She covered flower shows and shopping center openings, did cutesy animal features, publicity release obligatoriata, press handout effluvia, and one story on pruning the World's Largest Rose Tree in Tombstone—all of which was good training, if faintly demeaning, for a Philosopher-King.

Instead of being that hoped-for safety valve, her job seemed to add to the frictions of her marriage. When they wrangled about politics, Warren, waxing authoritative, would inveigh against "amateur, uninformed opinion."

"I only know what I read in the papers," she would reply.

"And you know how much that can be believed." He dismissed her field as "trivial," and she accused him in turn of revelling in the secretiveness his work at the Center obliged, too obviously enjoying the antidemocratic privileges of confidentiality. Then he turned it around, chiding her for her sometimes listless and unenthusiastic approach to her job. "I don't care if you want to be a butterfly collector or a Communist. Do it—but do it right." He was coming very close to touching an inadmissible truth. "You always do this, you know," he told her.

"Do what?"

"Set up little psychic paradises in your mind. Holy ideals of perfection and nothing can ever meet their standard."

"I don't know what you mean."

"You weren't happy in Palo Alto, so here we are, in your territory. You're not happy here, so you give up on grad school and take a job. Now you act like you're not happy with that. Or here, or me, or anything."

"We did not come here on my account, Warren. And the rest is really—it really isn't that way. I didn't

53

say I wasn't happy with the job. It has nothing to do with you."

"You can't tell me that. I see it spill over."

"How?"

"I don't know how, and I don't know why—but I can guess. All I know is sometimes I get the feeling I'm the embodiment of your second choice."

"Warren, that's not true."

"I'm telling you what I see, that's all."

"What else do you see?"

"I see you acting like a princess awaiting her coronation—who doesn't want to get her hands soiled with the here and now. But that's where we live, Johanna. It's the classic distinction between the 'is' and the 'ought'—"

"*Jesus!*"

"Make up your mind, Johanna. Shit or get off the pot, but don't leave us all dangling like this. I'm human, too."

Among Warren's virtues were a powerful insight and the cheerfully tactless way he shared it. Johanna promised that "things are different now." But she suspected that it might be impossible for them to maintain that independent third thing, a marriage. There was an irreversible drift, and an unmeasurable distance had come up between them in their sleep. Still, she'd try— "try to try," she said.

So they had gone to San Francisco for reasons individual and mutual, joining ten thousand weary-hopeful others there, all come like the cripples and indigestives at Lourdes and Baden, for the various miracles in the waters.

But there were no miracles. Only multicolored freaked-out kids in feathers and beads, journalists and tourists and sociological scavengers. It was a maze of troubadours and costumed children, princes and fairyladies looking for a crash pad, trying to score or sell some dope. Beggars, dealers, merchants, it was even more a freak show than they'd remembered, a bazaar. Things were given away free, and around the corner a brisk trade in scalped tickets to the music festival at Monterey flourished, side by side with street action in drugs. All values were inverted, it seemed to Warren: the material was worthless, while sensations commanded the highest price.

Johanna felt giddy in all this, and Warren tried to keep pace, as she shifted with the music and the wind. But it was hard for him, though he tried. For she had seemingly identified him with the things he defended, all things traditional. As Warren would make observations on the meaning of cultural rebellions, Johanna would withdraw into her own thoughts, that admixture of metaphors and intuitions. It seemed to her that musically, ontogeny recapitulated phylogeny: the sounds grew and evolved, summarizing in each incarnation the development of pop and hip itself, from its bluesy-beat roots to its new electric-grass-acid-madness-and-love forms; the generations and changes ever faster now. And its politics appealed to her. For it no longer mattered whether rock lyrics were explicitly political, it was implicit in the form: to appreciate was to defend was to espouse was to champion was to participate. Style itself became the banner of content; intolerance of doctrinal impurity the only common key. So music was no longer the mere shadow and agency of ideology, but the very stuff of it and whole of it, an inflated value that historically has one invariable result: assimilation and synthesis, after the war.

That first week the tide was at flood. The people all seemed beautiful. Johanna was enchanted. They called themselves flower children, moon children. The latter was an apt phrase, for there would also be a dark side rising later, and the tide would also run to neap. But for that moment there was something rare: every bright color and cheery hope, every naive intention in the land converged for a summer carnival, as though regarding the reality around as one they could ignore or alter by withdrawal. It spawned a breathless, celebratory style in all effects. Johanna brightened as she rushed into this, while Warren stood on shore asking about the water, regretting the trip entirely. He felt he was neglecting his work to let his wife become a child at an interminable circus.

But if it didn't work here, he knew, he stood little chance of wooing her back to a rational plane. Yet he feared that she would be hopelessly seduced by what he called "this self-indulgent muck of mindlessness." She called it "play," and he suspected she would set it up as some Elysium, holding all future ordinariness against him, unless somehow she could see its manifest flaws.

She did, at last, in ways Warren did not notice. For in the metaphor she used, there was in the hereditary information being passed from generation to generation of music the news of a mutant lethal gene which would doom it all. She'd watched at the Monterey Music Festival as something elusive of comprehension was enacted. She'd seen Janis Joplin stumble around onstage, tripping over a Southern Comfort bottle, consuming herself in her song. Other girl singers had riveted the men's attention as enticing fantasies. But here was something radical, riveting the women's. The woman devoured her band, it seemed, with still enough appetite for the cheap seats. She was every father's nightmare: rough and bawdy and insatiable. No man was good enough, none could move her down to here: but bring 'em on anyway, she's goddam hungry. The power of that naked revelation was overwhelming to the crowd. Johanna sat transfixed, idly rubbing the white dot by her eye. The roaring on stage gave off more energy than it took in; the singer might disappear, become her song entirely. She promised, it seemed, some release, but one that was infinitely distant. It was an exultant voice, being so close to truth, but one thus also perched precariously on the edge of heartbreak.

And so, in dreams in the San Francisco morning, Johanna understood, without the words to define it, how critical and hopeless was the distance between herself and Warren.

The images flashed in her mind, mixed with the sense of Warren as he loomed near her: the music, pounding and happy, revolutionary by its words and insistent upbeat, by its very demand to be heard, its rhythms coming through one's bones; the mixture of strangers and friends, theater and reality, Johanna and Warren. It was almost enough to lose one's definition in the wine and smoke and candlelight, to merge the flowing feelings with the morning's sleepy sunrise. Maybe they could make rainbows, feel more than is there, make something fragile last. Poor Warren, Johanna thought, awakening to his tender kisses. Poor Warren: he tried so hard, made love so arduously. He was desperate with passion, determination, and control.

Poor Warren. There were times he felt so futile making love with Johanna that his stomach knotted and will failed. He was like a man running marathons, afraid to give out short of the tape. And it receded before him. He was an earnest slice of matter hopelessly chasing a sunbeam, in different times at different rates, bound by relative limits, governed by the absolute, while the space between them swelled with night, left to drift, inertial and lonely, persevering with such fatal, mortal effort.

Poor Warren, Johanna thought. She would try. Poor Warren. Not yet, but almost. Poor Warren, slipping away, because he could never touch her dreams.

THE DESERT IMPOSES STRICT DEMANDS ON things that would survive it, and those that do are well and harshly schooled in simple purpose. The armadillo burrows deep to avoid the killing light; but the Sun evaporates the moisture in his tunnels' walls. He is patient and dauntless and perseveres. Some shade and trace water is found in the arroyos, and those minimal gifts are exploited into an unaccustomed local lushness. Bare yards away the competition for nutrients is fierce. The few creatures who brave the daylight, the antelope brown squirrel and the transient snakes, are lonely. Most do not stir until the night. Then, the animal life is, in every sense, frugal and cold-blooded. The zebra-tailed and leopard lizards and their venomous cousins manage, with tarantulas and Harris hawks, by preying on critters whom necessity exposes, and the cacti are cross-fertilized by vampire bats.

Strange lights play in the wastes, mirages, rippling waves of heat, lustrous glories, and ball lightning. At night, the pale beams of highway travelers who would not dare the day cast long shadows from the scattered Palo Verde nurse trees, and make the creosote bushes brilliant in oily phosphorescence.

On their way back from San Francisco to Tucson through the desert night, Johanna had watched the headlights devour space in silence. "Do you think they can do it?" she asked, idly.

"Do what?" It was the first exchange in an hour.

"Change the world."

"Who?"

"All those kids." Warren looked over at her in disbelief. "Wouldn't it be nice if—"

"No one can change the world who doesn't change his underwear," Warren said.

"Gandhi didn't wear underwear."

"They're dropouts, throwing themselves in the river. The current's too strong. It's a technocracy, Johanna."

"I thought you believed in sufficiency of numbers— turning ideas into policy."

"They hardly have the numbers. Or ideas."

"Maybe they can take it back to the cities and start an epidemic—"

"Of love? Or syphilis? A lot of acid-babies and mush-brains. A generation of cretins. Oatmeal heads."

"Not everything has to go bad, you know," Johanna said. She didn't really care for the point. She was just talking to make conversation.

"Great revolution!" Warren said. "The first thing a revolution does, Johanna, is sweep the drunks from the streets. Exactly what do they add or offer? You think the ditch that wards off typhus gets dug with a guitar?"

"Warren, I swear, you'd blame air pollution on outside agitators." She turned to watch the half-lit world outside her window, shaking her head to an imagined audience.

"Now what the hell's that supposed to mean?"

"Nothing. Forget it. I'm sorry," she muttered.

"No. It's not all right."

"Don't start. Please?"

"Johanna, it's all very romantic and sweet. But it's adolescent as hell. Aren't we beyond believing in fairy tales?"

"What do we believe in?"

There was no change in Tucson, no souvenir of San Francisco's Pope's Peace. Summer would stall that year through early winter, and the nights would be no relief from the days. In Tucson that can be murder. It is a desert within a desert.

There is evidence that Tucson is the coming American city. They named the big street in town the Speedway, and cut right to the core of things. The pace of Tucson's heart is set by an internal-combustion engine.

Speedway slices through the town, a free-access dragstrip with neon walls. Teenagers cruise past the blur of come-ons in their mothers' souped-up cars, a generation gap bridged by things and chrome, searching the streets for a promise of something. The lights lead them to the pit-stops: the sub shops, taco stands, pizza windows, and chicken joints wedged among the auto equipment stores, where drugs and casual sex are currency; means become an end.

Music blares from tire centers that also sell tape decks, but it cannot compete with the sounds of winding gears and screeching brakes. Nor can the fast-food smells and the aromas of adolescence overpower those of fuel oil and yesterday's burned rubber.

There are few homes on the Speedway. It is zoned for pinball lights and cashbox noises, the homes well back of the front-rank emporia. But the Speedway, calloused and sclerotic, is the center, leading from desert to desert, defining what lies around it.

To go back to Tucson, then, is to go back to heat laid upon the sand—pollution and concrete and exhausts, air-conditioner-vented hot air dumped back into the world beyond glass panes and steel doors—adding to the desert what a charge of light does to the crystal laser: a transforming surge, to make disarray into potent conformity. And there is this: a convergence of fear, sterility, and seasonless madness, a giant leap in crimes of frustration and boredom's desperation. Unreason reigns under a dome of superheated smog, a fit receiving blanket for the next assassin of the age.

That same June week, Tyler Bowen was peremptorily released from the Naval Officer Candidate School at Newport, Rhode Island, offered a civilian post at Gila Compound "in the national interest," in lieu of further military duty.

"I didn't even get my white suit back from the tailor," he wrote his brother in Army boot camp, "that's how fast it all was. I took the oath and then they said 'OK, bub, now you're in. How'd you like to get out?' Your mother didn't raise *only* idiots and, priding myself in recognizing a good thing when I see one, it occurred to me that the service was less than one. So I inked the pact. Which of us is Stalin and which is the other guy—you *have* heard about those two, haven't you? I'm sure there was a Classic Comic on the subject—I leave to your imagination. Regards to all in Tigerland."

His brother wrote back, "If they were federal, cut the cards."

Tyler Bowen became in that instant an Associate Fellow of the Vera and Benjamin Trovato Society for the Advancement of the Vital Sciences, on his way to the Gila Compound National Laboratories, with graduate credit in the deal.

The maps are ambiguous about Gila. They show its perimeters, and tell the public that within are National Laboratories. But not much more. They do not show, for instance, that those labs stand in the shadow of the World's Biggest Secret.

"Here's an odd thing," Tyler Bowen said to a man interviewing him on his first day at Gila. He pointed to a wall map of the Compound. Gila Mountain was not charted. The man said it had been that way for several years. To disappear from the sight of Rand McNally took an extraordinary act, comparable to becoming a bureaucratic black hole: a mass of grave matters so dense that no illumination might emerge. Tyler found this all amusing and reasoned that there was no accounting for the whims and mysteries of large organizations.

The Mountain rises sharply from the desert floor, without apparent reason, a monadnock, orphaned bastard of the Thunder Range, which also serves no earthly purpose save for meteorological mischief. From the Moon's vantage the Thunders might be seen as a deformed spine, meandering from Mexico halfway to Tucson, rickettsial, dividing southern Arizona into two halves: badlands and worselands. Only cactus and mesquite shrubs separate sand from sand.

But that stubborn, barren landscape of the Gadsden Purchase is misleading, for the open space is dense with secrets, paradoxes and creatures that thrive in different dimensions unawares. Flash floods rip across the baked washes, passing without penetrating. Hardy growths flower out of deadness with a will, cast short shadows and learn to coexist with desolation.

Some miles from Gila, across the here-painted, there-toneless desert, where the summer sun can last be seen each day from Gila Mountain's top, is a pioneers' outpost of the most modern sort, not unlike Gila Compound. Its back is to all civilization, looking for the future in the past. There, up in the Quinlan Mountains on the border of the Papago Indian Reservation, more than a mile above the bone-dry sand, atop Kitt Peak, the White Men tend the world's largest solar observatory, squinting at the unclouded Sun. Nearby, other telescopes plumb the nighttime sky for distant secrets and ancient news. A neighboring peak, Baboquivari, is considered by the local Indians to be the center of the universe. But it is behind and beneath the White Men's sight.

It is an unyielding land, most especially to constraints of category. Its parched reaches become, in winter, the home of more migratory birds than any place on Earth except the summer tundra.

Smugglers know the Gila area best, for they once wore paths through the hills and sandstone-spire monuments. Treasure hunters holiday among the bleached bones of those who never made it, searching for remnant silver swag. Older maps tell of long-dead zinc and copper mines up in the mountains. Nowadays, smuggling is chiefly in narcotics. But the stiffest penalties are reserved for those who trade in the more dangerous intoxicant, information.

Information, Bowen was repeatedly told his first day, "is shared at Gila Compound on a strict 'Need to Know' basis," because some of the work done at Gila required awareness of classified matters. The need of those who did not know was determined by those who did, an Access Committee whose main function was preserving others' notions of security.

It was tedious stuff such measures were arrayed against, confidential mostly by administrative habit: unless instructed otherwise, people who enjoy restricted access would deny the time on the wall clock.

That first day at Gila Compound, Bowen was told there had been a "slight change" in the program. He would not be, was never intended to be, a National Laboratories biochemist, but a technical liaison between the labs and the Compound's Public Information Office. "*Whaaat?* There must be some screw-up."

The man briefing him doubted it. Behind him was a bulletin board on which was an encouraging motto blazoned over a bull's-eye: "Zero Defect—That's the Target," fairly begging for a spit-ball barrage. The briefer smiled. "We like to say, 'We make mutations, but never mistakes.' "

"Yeah, but what I don't know about Public Information could fill volumes."

"You'll do fine."

"I think—" Tyler said.

"That's what you're paid for."

"I think I've made a mistake." The man looked over various forms and oaths Bowen had executed and didn't see any errors. "I signed," Tyler said, and the man laughed merrily.

The next office he was sent to—to be reimbursed for travel expenses—also had a motto on the wall: "Watch Your Hat and Coat at All Times." The bursar had him sign the pay logs and closed the book with a grin, saying, "One more for the Gila Monsters." It seemed to be the prevailing humor of the place.

Everyone he dealt with those first days treated him

with a similar country club informality. But underneath he sensed a queer reserve in them all.

Bowen had been chosen to fill this slot, or rather, this slot had been created, because of an accelerating series of problems at Gila Compound. At the Tombstone Center, where Warren Reigeluth toiled, the Department of Operations Research had been asked to devise a solution, and they hit upon a bold one. Tombstone resolutely and humorlessly called itself Gila's "thinking arm." And that usage, however strange, may be no less appropriate than the terms used to describe the astigmatic legislative committees supposed to keep good watch on such places: Congressional Oversight.

To understand what Bowen's job was meant to accomplish, Operations Research must first be understood. That can be done most easily by way of encountering the one and only intentional joke that the field of OR—a branch of applied mathematics whose uses are in management science, decision theory, and industrial engineering—has ever given rise to: An OR consultant was once called in to a consumer products rubber factory, where a downward sales trend had everyone unhappy. He learned that sales of its two main items—condoms and baby bottle nipples—were a "zero-sum" function. That is, he was told, "as condoms go up, nipples fall off. As condoms fall off, nipples go up." Moreover, total sales depended on product reliability. Consumers had to believe the perforations would be in the bottle end of things alone. But the engineering required to insure perfect safety for the condoms was prohibitively expensive. Indeed, as production increased, quality declined. And the conventional marketing wisdom held that quality was the key to sales. But the OR man saw through that fallacy. He knew that in a postindustrial economy, to break out of traditional cycles, one had to sell dangerous crud and open a repair stand. So he ordered those engineering funds which went into refining the production tolerances diverted into advertising, and recommended that production of both items be tripled. The unit cost plunged. As for quality, the public got the message when he had the price of both items raised. Sure enough, not only did condom sales boom, but after a short interval, so did nipple sales. The heavy profits enabled the company to expand, to service with new items (sports equipment and hospital supplies) the market they had, in a sense, spawned.

A more accessible OR story, though perhaps equally apocryphal, attaches to a nonprofessional, D. D. Eisenhower. During his brief tour as President of Columbia University, college construction plans called for ringing the campus with concrete walkways, because the students were killing the lawns as they trod from building to building. The first paths built were almost entirely neglected by the students, connecting as they did no place with no place else. "Where shall we build the paths, General?" the frustrated engineers asked.

Eisenhower knew what being a leader meant by instinct. He said, "Do you see where the grass is worn down? Build them there. That's where they walk!"

Conversely, he also knew what statistics did *not* mean. During World War II Supreme Headquarters analysts inspected the hulls of Allied planes returned from air combat and suggested plating be installed in those spots most frequently hit by Luftwaffe and ack-ack fire. An enormous savings could be made by that economy. But Eisenhower ordered, instead, they be armored everywhere *but* those spots: "These are the planes that *returned*," he said. Thus was the air war won, and perhaps thus was war averted during his subsequent tenure as President by the degree to which he declined to govern.

That's Operations Research. In a way. The most particular concern of that sober discipline is in the problem of allocations: resource allotment, scarcity, supply flow, budget participation, distribution of satisfactions. With similar bold logic, the OR Department at Tombstone addressed such questions for Gila's Administration:

"Projecting over five years, expected phase-out of manned space program and overseas military expenditures will create interagency competition for released funds and increased budget share.

"Most effective input on Executive Branch budgetary preplanning process derives from pressure of private sector and public wants.

"Present system of reflexive security tends to stimulate curiosity in unfriendly quarters, whereas *appropriate* interest should be encouraged to create a climate of enthusiasm, support and expectancy for Gila projects. Suggest PR focus on health, cancer, energy and food production research, downplaying other roles. . . ."

So Bowen was brought in because, in addition to having adequate credentials in the technical fields, he had attractive attributes that would sell. He looked good. He seemed discreet. He had the benign charm of a young astronaut, according to the worksheets. And he looked like a truth teller. His job would be to help make the public more aware of the important work carried on at Gila: heavily funded basic research, exotic experiments in the radiation labs, investigations into the nature and control of disease, treatment of debility. The benefits accruable from these things were exciting, and he would have to translate that to the laity, while steering them gently away from fruitless lines of inquiry not in their best interests. He would garner support for such vital work as much as did Space Agency people when they spoke joyously of national pride, the venturesome spirit, Teflon dinnerware and crystallized orange juice.

"What about the secret stuff?" he asked. "Is there any, really?"

"Oh, some. Not to worry. Ninety-eight percent of it's trivial and boring—and one percent entirely inane. Embarrassing, mostly. It's hard to make people realize that every step forward requires a few false steps, errors, and bad guesses. If you're going to be inventive, you've got to look foolish every now and then." That left one percent. "You don't want to know about it. Hardly a great moral burden with that split, what?"

As for the World's Biggest Secret, he was told, that was mainly a local joke, though one he should not refer to among the uninitiated. In any event, its protection was, to his main duties, a sidelight, though perhaps as much of one as football in the Big Ten.

Into the month of July his time was devoted almost completely to briefings, backgrounders, and study. As it would not be propitious to let him and the public at each other until his skills were honed and security clearance procedures completed, he was restricted to the Compound and confined to tedious tasks: preparing canned talks for the day when tour groups would be wheeled through, updating brochures and booklets about Gila's history. A colleague who'd worked for NASA offered him encouragement with, "Hell, until I was checked out in Houston I handled nothing more exalted than Coca-Cola invoices for two months. I couldn't get off the lot to buy a beer in all that time."

And soon, Bowen was trusted enough to be apprised of one highly confidential matter: within Gila was a whole class of personnel who shared his loneliness. Their work was so sensitive that they were recruited from the group of single men without dependents. They lived in splendid isolation at Gila, permitted only two leaves a year; feasted on incessant movies, recitals, and poetry readings; were encouraged to form badminton and chess leagues; were engaged in a continual round of wine-and-cheese-tasting parties. Gila was, in a sense, the pituitary and medulla of their operation, regulating maintenance, training, security, information control, and data processing. Tombstone Center handled the cerebral functions of operations planning, and Gila took care of everything else but the weather. A lab in Nevada was working on that.

But they were not happy. These highly prized men had nothing to look forward to. No incentive: No women.

Bowen was drinking alone one night in early July, in a place called the Crypto Club, whose sterile fittings rivaled what was available outdoors. The man behind the bar had seen him there two weeks in a row, every night, but they never had an extended exchange; Tyler thought he might be some kind of security operative. Now he didn't care. Bowen looked up at him in fatigue and said, "Tell me a secret, Mister Crypto."

"Pilkinton. All right, here's one: the rate of alcoholism here is off-the-fucking-charts."

Bowen nodded solemnly, mumbling "Ain't the only thing." Then he grinned. "But permit me," he said, raising his glass in toast, "to express my surprise."

"Trailed closely by self-administered laboratory drugs." Both men looked around edgily and Tyler brightened, relaxed.

"Buy you a round?"

"You're all right, Johnny. Waitin' on clearance?"

Tyler gave him a palms-open gesture, to say "Would I be here but as a prisoner?" Then he asked the man, "Suppose I got tired of working on my liver? Suppose I wanted to take the second route?"

But the man behind the bar was suddenly struck stupid. At length he suggested Tyler try his luck at "The Oh-Five thing tomorrow. Maybe you'll make some friends. I remember my first month—I never knew sleeping alone could be so *wearing.*"

"You think it's the thing to do, the Oh-Five?" Tyler asked.

"It's a tawdry little spectacle, but it's the best the bureaucracy can offer."

"Can't be much, can it?"

The so-called Oh-Five Event was, as with much of Gila, ultimately traceable to that very alcoholism rate. Tombstone had suggested several remedies. The primary level was, of course, a total blackout of information, Rule One in any Public Information Officer's handbook. Deny something often enough and it will slink away. The secondary level featured symptomatic treatment: a drying-out facility was added to Gila's Infirmary. The tertiary level saw an attempt to boost the morale of those travel-restricted personnel by artificial turf pitch-and-putt courses and outdoor swimming pools. The quaternary was a fizzled effort at outfitting the shadeless grounds with huge plastic conifer trees. But the sight and smell of them sizzling in the sun was more depressing than anything. Quintessentially, an effort was launched in the preceding year to remove the heart of the problem. Prohibition was rejected: the men's lives were dry enough.

The Gila Compound Chief of Operations, retired Major General Armistead ("Buzz") Sheaffer, joked that it was a problem with multiple horns. Security had to be maintained, but frustration was high. Then Tombstone suggested the Oh-Five Event as a form of profit sharing, community making, and Sheaffer saw it as a brilliant stroke of management, claiming full credit for the idea.

Whenever any project in the labs reached the .05 level of statistical certainty, that is, when its results seemed reliably significant, all would share in the rewards of success, even if they had no need to know what the success might be. It would serve as a bonus to all those who forfeited the right of transit. Output soared. Indeed, so successful were the first Oh-Fives that they became the full-time concern of one whole office, and so popular did they become that attendance was restricted to "the needy"—only those men who had nowhere else to go.

This particular Oh-Five, an Independence Day treat and Tyler's first, began modestly enough. The hot, heavy air of the Formica-ridden Crypto Club was broken only by the smell of sweat and the sound of hard breathing, and the slow, teasing circle carved in a jiggling dim spotlight by Patsy Ferraro's breasts.

Like a discus thrower set to loose the plate, she rocked back and forth, then let go. Her tassel-tipped breasts hove one way, then the other. Their angular momentum pulled the clockwise arc into a full circle. Round and round one hundred heads traced sympathetic orbits as the big breasts revolved. "I've seen this a dozen times in the last year," a man next to Bowen said. "Haven't got tired of it yet."

Tyler smiled, not to be rude. "Not much on spectation."

"Wait awhile."

She switched direction with a pert pirouette and a shake of her heavy fanny. Her breasts reversed course and unwound contrapuntally, to a snare beat from the back of the room, counterclockwise. A hundred heads drooled approval.

"A pro," the man next to Bowen said. "A true pro. Maybe the class operation of this whole place." The others gave her a pro's due in sighs.

Her right breast swung in one direction now, while the left spun in reverse; then a switch, then each in small circles, pinwheels, into the *pièce de résistance*. "Watch this. It's art," the man urged Bowen. Loop-de-loops. Overs and unders. Each breast moved independently, at different speeds. Figure eights! Each time they expected they'd seen the top-o'-the-line, she turned the screw a notch, until they were dry in the throat, limp. Hawaiian waves! Lazy jacks! Bongos and butterflies! The men watching did everything but bark.

"My God!" Bowen said, "They're gonna fall off."

Someone on his other side said, "They'll just subcontract for new ones—sealed bids and everything."

"Is she on the payroll?" Tyler asked.

"GS-12. Twenty years she pulls full retirement."

"And," the man on his other side added, "she's got that concession split."

"As it were," the other one winked.

She was carried on the payrolls as Entertainment Coordinator. So was Len Tobias, who managed Patsy and her shows. He was a tall, swarthy man, preternaturally dislikable, spade-bearded and smug. He worked for the Gila Special Services Administration, having been sacked from a research post for doctoring experimental results. He had no other responsibilities, and there were many in the room who would say there was no more important one. Patsy danced for these Oh-Fives, retirement parties, and other happy occasions. According to Tobias, her gross was, when concessions were added in, "equal to the Chief of Ops—if you don't count his kickbacks." She also picked up spare change from time to time with a little consulting work: "Sitting on some Tombstone panels," said the man next to Bowen. "And," the one on the other side added, "an occasional face. Twenty bucks the latter." She was forbidden, by regulation, to have "actual intercourse per se" with the personnel, a matter more honored in the breach, and at best interpreted with a perverse particularity.

Some people in Compound Central Security resented her, as she kept them from easily filling their quotas of security violators: whoremongers, sodomites, and the like. But they too learned to live with her, as a trust buster would a regulated monopoly. Her status was that of a utility.

How Len Tobias became her manager was sheer luck. But how he stayed that way was another matter. Others who offered a better cut made no headway. Because, Len Tobias liked to observe, "it boils down to the fact that I've got the biggest shlong in the state."

Now, as Patsy ducked into the Crypo Club Men's Room to prepare for Phase II of her show, Len Tobias mounted the stage and began his ritual patter. He rubbed his goatee and lit a cigar. He liked to say that he dined on Patsy every morning and sniffed the residue in his whiskers all day to keep calm. Rivals said he breakfasted on "juice and postnasal drip."

"Lady and gentlemen—" Tobias said, belching out a bluish cloud.

"Get the tits back here!"

Tobias loved it. On these rare nights he and these esteemed men were at last peers. "Marvelous. Marvelous. Really fine house tonight. Welcome back please, will you, the lovely and talented—"

"Cunt!"

"Dee-lightful," Tobias drawled. "Remind me how to spell your name, Doc, for my memoirs." He stopped, to agonize them, foxy in silence, barely containing a leering grin, stalling as Patsy sponged off in the wings. Then, *Gentlemen*—the lovely Patsy Ferraro! Let's give her a fine Gila Howdy—" He was drowned out by the explosion of approval, as she burst back on the stage to reclaim the light. She scooted him off with a signature wiggle up his back and he was followed to his seat by derisive, envious jeers.

Her second movement began slowly and the noise diminished in anticipation. Confident expertise masked her boredom. As any functionary, she tired of repetition, but as half-an-artist, she hid it well for the consumers. Heads bobbed appreciatively among the connoisseurs. "She's good," marveled Tyler Bowen.

"What's her booking?" someone asked Tobias.

"Two hours with a ten-minute break every forty-five."

"Can she deliver?"

"She'll deliver. In this business, your contract is your life."

But even Patsy needed to coast from time to time. Was she getting old at twenty-seven? Would the legs be the first to go, as with other brilliant athletes? The transition from largo to allegro never came. Her motor would not kick in, and Tobias looked worried. Her

70

muscles had lost elasticity from so much grinding work. Her bumps were down to pushes, her rotary action mere mashes. Yet a pro is not without resources. And so she tore a tassel artfully from her left nipple and flung it to the crowd, a scrap of meat. Another first-timer, near Bowen, speared it, holding it high for the fans, as a snared foul ball. Then he chewed on it. The other tassel went starboard and a small scuffle ensued. Then the G-string.

"Bush! Bush!" came a down-front whimper.

The man next to Tobias sighed, "Such a minor league place for a girl with her talent. Geez, I bet most night-club owners in New York'd grab her in a minute."

A massive gasp went up as the sequined G-string flew across the room. Bodies fell out of chairs and piled on the poor fellow who nailed the rhinestone liner. They forced it from his grasp. Fists and arms and legs tangled in a wild wrestling match over the prize. Gladiators, killing themselves for possession of the Robe, they one by one realized something truer: Patsy was heaving giant beavers while they fought for a sweaty piece of cloth. She sat on the table and waved her legs about, spreading her thighs. Pained moans floated up from the crowd. "I can't stand it! I can't stand it!" cried a fat enteropathologist who nearly had his nose in her crotch. Tobias leaned back and drew on his cigar in satisfaction.

Suddenly, Milt Armstrong—a/k/a Mad Milt—an enormous black man who was working at Gila in a laborer's capacity at the behest of the Arizona Department of Corrections, handling dangerous cargo in lieu of a jail term for the vehicular homicide of his high school guidance counselor, rehabilitating himself thus, who had twice been up on charges for precipitating brawls and for the threatened incineration of one of the people who bore true witness against him, *that* Mad Milt, who was retained in spite of his general undesirability largely because Chief of Operations Armistead Sheaffer thought he could be rehabilitated, and because at official functions he could sing "The Star Spangled Banner" like no one this side of Paul Robeson, which pleased Sheaffer greatly—and who, unlike Robeson, had never even *heard* of the Soviet Union—*that* Mad

Milt pushed his way through the groaning crowd and closed on Tobias with a cocked fist. Tobias flinched. Leaking through Milt's fingers were dollar bills. "Here, this!" he barked, shoving the money in Tobias's face. "You let me stick her. It's yours." Tobias eyed the waving green and agonized.

"Can't do it, Milt. I'd like to, but—she's here for the show. That's all."

"Take it. Take it," Milt hollered. "Just once."

"Milt, Milt. She's got a contract. If I let you, I'd have to let everyone. I'd have no control. I'm sorry. I really—"

"Motherfucker," Milt spat with murder in his eyes. But before he could strike, a line was pushing him from behind, all flashing money.

Patsy was oblivious to all this, her eyes half-hooded. She still waved her legs about, massaging the insides of her thighs, near to a dripping self-consummation.

"Look," Milt and some others croaked. "She's half-dead now—she'll never notice."

"Its the principle of the thing," Tobias stammered. "Patsy does not do that sort of—" Armstrong interrupted with a chesty laugh.

"Come on, man. Just once. Just a quickie. Hell with them. I was first." The others clamored irresistibly.

So Tobias went up to Patsy, and it was not clear whether she would explode, or kill him, or what. But she said, "Yes," and "yes, I will—as well one as another." She was opening for business.

"As you know," Tobias announced, "your government is a generous and compassionate employer. It stands ready to meet your deepest yearnings and most urgent felt needs. For some time it has offered this unique program of social care and is very encouraged by your response. The enthusiasm with which you men have risen to—"

"Cut the crap and get to it!" a physicist screamed agitatedly.

"Right. OK, here's the deal. You've got your entertainment scrip. Five bucks gets you thirty seconds touching one breast, personally. Ten bucks—a full minute, or both for a half."

"What about nookie?"

"Hands only. Three fingers max, deep as you can go: twenty. Or a combo ticket for twenty-five. Quite a buy. All names eligible for the big drawing for a butterball turkey—"

But the men had heard that before. It was the usual Phase III from holiday shows. They wanted more, now. They let him know it.

"And tonight," Tobias continued, as they drew breath, "we have something very special indeed." Ecstatic, wild orgasmic sobbing shouts and cries of delight. Quick loans arranged at killer rates. Anxious joy pouring out as tears. "One man—one man alone will be permitted to be private with Miss—excuse me, Mrs. Ferraro, for ten minutes. To bargain for whatever he can within the regulations." The *oooohs,* nearly indistinguishable from the *ahhs,* were no match for the *Me! Me! Me!*s.

Milt Armstrong waited until the noise subsided and then drawled in his best basso profundo, "The Biggest. The Longest."

Tobias arched his eyebrows and smiled brightly, "Suits me. I'll go with that."

But the others favored more democratic process, and so while two volunteers carried the Phase III buffet table onto the stage, and Patsy established her roost on it, Tobias weighed doing it by raffle. Estimating the house and the possible take, he decided on a simpler course, less luck-determined, more meritocratic: "The Highest Bidder."

"Yeah," complained a computer technician, "and who's got all the money?"

"That's the American Way, buddy," someone snapped. He added, "ten bucks!"

"Fifteen."

"Twenty."

"THIRTY!!"

On an off-night they could have had her for a mere sawbuck. But the night was crazed and the bidding soared to insane heights.

"Do I hear forty?" Tobias asked.

"You do."

"And five."

"Forty-eight sixty-five." They all laughed at the tension-breaker.

"Sixty." Heads turned to watch the high rollers.

"Seventy."

"Eighty-five," snarled Milt Armstrong.

Some yelled, "Higher, higher!" Others yelled, "Freeze, freeze!" But there was no further bidding.

Then Tobias eyed Milt Armstrong and said, laconically, "Ninety."

"Ninety-one," grinned Mad Milt.

"One century," said Tobias.

"One-and-twenty-five," growled Milt.

"One-fifty," Tobias spat.

With reflexes ever so slightly better than referee Ruby Goldstein, who let Benny ("Kid") Paret get slugged to death by Emile Griffith, Patsy herself interceded. Enough was enough. She knew that Tobias would bid Milt down, and then probably not pay her. So she suggested a way to accommodate both of them. "I'll take you both at one-seventy-five. Otherwise, this'll go on all night!" Loud whistles from the crowd approved her gesture. "Two winners, everyone's happy."

The lines formed right away. As usual, the physicists took one side, with the chemists and biologists, while the engineers and computer people took the other. But theirs was a common purpose, and one by one they paid their fives and tens. Milt and Tobias each went to the end of a line.

"This is the first time I've ever done this," confessed an agronomist, first on line, when Patsy said she hadn't seen him around before.

Tyler Bowen, fully caught up, dazzled by it all, was on the breast line.

They filed by solemnly, with no shoving, doing their individual duty. Gracious extra seconds were allotted those whose need was great. A few observed, "She's a saint." Each thanked her as they went by.

When the last man was through, everyone piled outside to wait while Milt took his winnings. Some wandered off, sated or disgusted. Milt approached her and slowly began to kiss her, tenderly. To Tobias, this was worse than her having been pawed by five-score others. His face twisted in torment as she greeted Milt's kisses

74

with sighs of apparent passion. Outside, hearing this, some wondered what it meant, this quickly contrived ardor, about what their own wives and sweethearts really felt when they were kissed. But, they reassured themselves, the lady did have an hour of foreplay.

Mad Milt took off his shirt and Patsy ran her hands across his muscular chest. It was sparkling ebony. But when he undid his belt she hugged him and said, "Uh-uh, that's as far as we go." Milt was boiling, but acquiesced, grinding unsatisfactorily for half his allotted time. Exasperated by these futile efforts, Patsy reversed her policy and loosed his trousers. His pants fell. Outside, Tobias paced around anguished, while some hung bug-eyed at the windows. "Not in me," she moaned as he lay her down on the table. She took his dark heavy organ in her hands, squeezing it and stroking it lightly, while Milt explored her foaming vestibule with his hands. She was impressed by the feel and heft of him, and when he swiveled around to kiss her where it would do the most good, she took the thick black hose into her mouth and sucked on it. Tobias, staggering back to the window for a progress check, fell away in horror, gagging.

She went through her entire repertoire until with one spurt that seemed endless, Mad Milt blew his charge. He gave a long, deep "Aaaaggh," and Patsy made noises of delight as she wiped her face and licked her hands.

Milt tossed his shirt over his shoulder and strode out with his chest expanded. The crowd cheered. "You're up, shit-eater," he said to Tobias.

"Uh, no, I'll take mine later."

"Now, little sucker," Milt commanded.

"Bigger than yours, buster," Tobias growled, stumbling up the steps, enraged. Patsy was standing on the buffet jumping up and down, fiddling with her crotch. Out fell a shiny silver quarter. "Goddam nigger tipped me!" Mad Milt was a solitary grin at the window.

"Jesus, Patsy," Tobias complained as he was about to kiss her, drawing back in distaste. "Wipe your stinkin' nose, will ya? Christ, you got snot all over—"

Patsy did as he urged, then beamed in reconciliation, leaning toward him for her reward, saying "It was just that black guy's, oh, you know, jizzum," and Tobias choked. He wiped his mouth in horror, then tore his pants open. They fell to his ankles. He pushed her down on the table. Patsy offered no objections. He needed no help. She was soaking, lathery from fifty hands and Milt's saliva. Tobias floated in as easily as a ferry in its slip, despite his size, charged with angered pride.

Mad Milt, at the window, boiled. "Fuck this shit!" he snarled. "Why my money's not good enough?"

Inside, Patsy ventured, "Milt's bigger," to which Tobias reacted by thrusting himself forward and deep until she thought he would come up her esophagus. Her ecstatic screams reverberated in the empty room and rattled the windowpanes. Outside, they rose to their feet at the sounds. Patsy tried to haul Tobias down from where he hovered at arm's length. He was remorseless. Her eyes were wide, head lolling, on the verge. Outside, Milt's sweat beaded at her shrieks, and he grew mad: Mad Milt! He shoved some others out of his way and stormed inside, the rest in close pursuit. In two steps and a dive he knocked the duo off the buffet table. Patsy's mouth hung unhinged in disappointment. Milt held Tobias around the head and socked away. Finally Tobias broke free and the two squared off: Mad Milt against Len Tobias.

"What? What?" Tobias croaked, backing up in shuffles, pants manacling his feet. "What?" He looked around to the others for an explanation. As he did, Mad Milt put a foot into his chest and knocked him sideways off the buffet to the floor.

Someone obtained a bucket of water and threw it at them. Others shouted, "Cut that out, you'll get us all wet."

Milt slopped around in that wetness, working the side of Tobias's head. A chemist picked up the quarter and said, "My mother always told me, never put coins in your mouth. You don't know where they've been."

Tobias was kneeling, already bleeding from several cuts, when Mad Milt stood up. The crowd parted to let him go. But he just wanted room to take a step backward, so as to go forward and drive his foot into the side of Tobias's head. The victim crashed backward, leaving a pinkish vapor of sweat and blood like a jet's exhaust to mark the spot his head vacated. Tobias hit the deck hard, still breathing.

Patsy rushed Milt as he was about to stomp Tobias, and pulled Milt sideways. His foot hit the floor at an angle, as though he were killing a cockroach. She hung on his shoulder but he groped back to bullwhip Tobias's head against the floor. Tobias's eyes began to shut and some of the observers were shouting, "Enough already! Stop!" But only Tyler Bowen stepped forward to wrestle Milt away. Armstrong struggled with him a moment, and for a moment Bowen had control.

Then Armstrong shoved him aside forcefully, and spat, "I got no fight with you."

Bowen looked glad for it, when a voice from the back boomed, "You do with me!"

"Oh, fuck," moaned one of those who had almost helped Bowen restrain Armstrong. "Gracie. We bought it now." It was Martin B. Gracie, Chief of Compound Security.

As this man Gracie surged to the front, an aisle parted for him like the Red Sea. Beside him strode two acolytic aides who bobbed their heads like men ducking for apples. "All right," one said officiously, "show's over. Ya got whatcha paid for. Sex and violence. Better'n a movie. Lessgo now."

"Now listen up!" Gracie bellowed. He squinted hard at one quivering member of the crowd and shook his head slowly, almost pityingly, saying with a calm power in his voice, an intimate half-whisper, as an aside to his aides, "Looks to be egghead for breakfast." Then he spread his glare upon the assembled multitude, hands on hips, eyes above the sway, fearsome in form and threat, promising dire consequences to those who withheld truth from him. Chemists, botanists, nosologists, etiologists and mathematicians began to re-assume their professional airs, grimacing nervously, spreading their ranks, eying each other with scorn, straightening their manners: worried more for the embarrassment of it all than any threat of Gracie's. He had no real power over them in such large numbers.

But Bowen was exposed. He stood vulnerable next to Armstrong. Those near to him shrunk back into the anonymous crowd. The man, Bowen thought as he stared at Gracie, looked like a killer. But also, like a large Walt Disney pig: the amusement park kind that hands out treats and makes little children squeal and wears a sailor hat but no pants. Gracie had puffy cheeks and tiny round nostrils which stared from his face as auxiliary eye sockets. His nose had been carved, it seemed, by a vertical slice of a knife. His belly swelled outward in a tight arch from chest to belt, muscular despite its shape, stretching his Banlon shirt into a glossy second skin.

"If you people for all your brains can't stick your pinkies in some twat without turning disorderly, then we'll just have to make some examples. Somebody thinks he can mouth his way out—your loved ones'll hear you died a hero." He gathered his witnesses, Bowen among them, and trotted them to his office for a midnight debriefing, dismissing the rest with this advice: "Any of you think you got a pair, you just try Martin B. Gracie. He'll show you something you'll never forget," tugging at his crotch for emphasis. "Fuckin' turkeys."

Bowen sat waiting in the outer office of Compound Central Security until two in the morning. It had an antiseptic cleanliness more pervasive than the labs, as prophylactic as a dentist's waiting room but without magazines. On the wall was a heraldic shield, a smaller replica of the one over the door to the Administration Building, the emblem of Gila. It depicted an ash tree whose roots, trunk, and branches were said, in myth, to unite the realms of Heaven, Earth, and Hell.

A plaque beneath the rendering said this was the Yggdrasil Tree of Norse mythology, and that one root led toward a malignant dragon, one toward a well of nourishment and renewal, and one toward the well of all wisdom. Up and down the trunk was said to run a squirrel representing strife. Deer fed upon the branches, and in the upper limbs perched an eagle and a hawk. The name *Yggdrasil* derived from the forms for Odin (*Ygg-*) and a horse (*-drasil*). It was all lost on Tyler Bowen, but they liked it very much at Gila, for it harkened to an old joke from Los Alamos, where men used to say of their clandestine enterprise that they were "building the front part of horses—to be shipped to Washington."

This emblem was designed, the legend behind the legend's legend held, by a young man in the Geodetic Survey's Cryptocartography, Cachet, and Insignia Section working late one Sunday. He was shown nothing more than some white spots on an aerial survey map and told to come up with something—"And for once let's not point to what-the-hell it is we're trying to keep a lid on." So he dug deep into his irrelevancy file, having studied mythology in college and having carried the information unemployed for years. It was an appealingly sympathetic gesture, this blind offer of symbol: a jest, a time capsule, a personal graffito on the map. It was the act, if the story is to be believed, of a man taping a dime to a water tower, hoping to find, years later, two nickels: a soul reaching out through lonely time and space to another who might understand.

When Bowen's turn finally came, he was light-headed from hunger and sleeplessness, less sure of his standing in this bureaucratic realm. Gracie's door flew open and Bowen could see Gracie leaning against his desk inside as the previous interview subject shuffled out. An imaginary line descended Gracie's length, from the trough between his golf cap's ventilation holes to the furrow of his frown, between those porthole nostrils to his chin cleft, down his breastbone to his polyester double-knit slacks, pulled tight in their egregious display of bifurcated pride. "Bowen. Get in here." Tyler stumbled forward, thinking that if one tapped the man lightly on the golf cap with an axe he would split in two.

Gracie pointed to a littered conference table where another man was looking through file folders, and Tyler took a seat across from him. "Zermatt," the other man said. "Baron—Baron Zermatt. With the Law Office." Tyler's face looked numb, until the man smiled. "Just a formality. Procedural. Some July Fourth, huh?"

"All right, let's get at it," Gracie snapped. "Bowen, I'm not too concerned about what you have to say. This matter is self-programming. I can tell you, though, I am deeply concerned about you."

"Why?"

"You don't even have full clearance yet. Don't you think it's a bit early in your career here to get into this kind of crap?"

"I—somebody was getting mashed and—"

"And you decided to be a hero. Right in the middle you were." Zermatt slid a paper from the file to Gracie; Bowen tried to read it upside down. It was apparently his personnel folder.

Their silence was unnerving. "If uh—the truth be known," Tyler tried again.

"Interesting phrase, that," Gracie grumbled. "We'll come to it." Zermatt looked up and winked. He was younger than Gracie and more consistently friendly in face and manner, resembling an overgrown hoppy-toad. He smiled and made a garroting gesture with the appropriate noise. Unamused, Gracie glared at him, saying, "You'll do that once too often, Zermatt, and we'll see what your head looks like on my watch fob."

Bowen broke this one up, too. "I was just saying that I think I'm here under false pretenses."

"That contract you signed?" Gracie said.

"Yes."

Zermatt answered, "You signed it."

"Your assignment here," Gracie droned mechanically, "reflects those facets of your abilities deemed most valuable to the national interest. You were in the Navy. Now you're not. We saw to that. You might also be aware that under standing provisions of the Emergency Powers Act, you didn't have to accept the offer—your special skills make you liable for compulsory service for the duration of the present emergency." Zermatt added that it had thus far lasted since World War II.

"So what's your end of it?" Gracie continued. "Three years of paperwork—and the lost opportunity to get your ass blown off in a swamp boat. In war some guys get shot at and some guys shovel shit. You're not getting shot at, are you? A little time, some mental effort. Everyone should have it so good."

"You said 'Special Skills'?"

"Of a technical nature," Zermatt answered.

"Come on. There were about ten better students than me in my department alone." The two men were resolutely smiling. Not friendly smiles. Confident ones.

"None of those better students volunteered for Naval Officer Candidate School," Gracie said.

"None of 'em were about to get drafted either. They split for Canada."

Gracie shuffled through the file folder while Bowen and Zermatt looked each other over with interest. Just out of Bowen's periphery of vision hung a wall placard, of such a color and mounted at such an angle to Tyler that it flashed in and out of his awareness with strobing annoyance. He turned to read it. It said, "Pay Attention." So did Martin B. Gracie when he sensed Bowen swivel around. Zermatt smirked merrily, "Gotcha!" as Gracie slid a document across the table to Bowen.

It was a photocopy of Tyler Bowen's senior thesis. Stapled to the top was a one-page abstract with four footnotes. With all the official stamps encrusting it, Bowen had to bite his lip to keep a straight face. "This is your work?" Gracie asked.

"Oh, yes. Every last word of it."

During his senior year, all of the students majoring in biology and chemistry had coordinated their theses and honors work at the behest of Cornell's Advanced Studies Laboratory, which was doing a special project for the Agriculture School. The idea was to search out pest controls which might deteriorate into growth stimulants, fertilizers, or vitamins. Since Bowen's special interest was cellular identity, he worked with a section which considered how well chemicals were absorbed or resisted by host plants.

Tyler had amused himself one day by analyzing his lunch, and stumbled upon an interesting thing lurking in the leaves of a head of romaine lettuce. What he found was an assortment of harmless inert compounds of no consequence to plant or animal. But, reasoning backward to the commercial insecticide which had spawned them, he conjectured, "It is fair to postulate a middle-generation parent molecule from the incomplete breakdown of the original, depending on photosynthetic and redox actions which may vary from case to case." He'd written it up and circulated the paper as an intramural lampoon of the study, and both his real thesis and this parody were well received by the participants. What was in front of him now was the parody.

He'd called it "Interference with Parasympathetic Systemology Related to Mid-phase Parameters of Short-term Catabolic Processes Specific to Residues of In-field Insecticide 'Y': Et Tu Caesar Salad."

A key line, generously footnoted, said "Various isomers are likely. Interestingly, one possibility is a close variant of phosgene oxime, which the Germans used to great advantage in World War I."

The footnotes read:

1. Assignment of olfactory signature, unnecessary. See note 2, Gross Indications.
2. Gross indications: Available (declassified) indices of phosgene oxime suggest following effects: (*a*) immediate whealing of impacted area, (*b*) scabbing, (*c*) dislocation. (Cf. "Blister Agents and Cauterizing Compounds.")
3. I.e., one whiff and your nose will fall into the salad.
4. While we do not know, therefore, what it smells like, we do know who has smelled it. And they are negatively reinforced from persistent smelling.

Gracie explained, "It is apparently assumed by those who matter that your gifts include one for expression. Given training—and a discretion not yet apparent—you will be useful."

"Now I know why my orals were held in the Chapel undercroft."

"The most secure place available. They were audited by FDA and other agency representatives."

"I thought it was the Dean's little joke. See, the year before up on the roof my friend St. Paul Hooper and this girl—"

"It's no joking matter," Gracie snapped. High authorities had determined that Tyler Bowen was, like Dr. Guillotin, too dangerous to leave at large. Who knew what political sympathies he had? So they had suggested he be "administratively acquired," but only got around to acting on that after he'd joined the Navy. Anyone who could speculate on the wonders in a leaf of romaine lettuce, they reasoned, might perform

82

miracles with a loaf of Wonder Bread. So he was commended to Gila Compound where he might be useful as a researcher or an instructor. A preliminary check, and his Naval Bureau of Personnel forms, showed him to be clean of political impurities, if not entirely immune to fits of juvenile exuberance. The latter was something they were used to among the scientifically gifted. What's more, he was, by all other measures, appealingly All-American. He was just what the doctor ordered for the Office of Public Information.

But Gracie had an eye for frauds and likely failures, and examined Bowen's folder closely. "What *is* this shit?" he demanded. Under "Aliases," Bowen had written "Red, Rusty, Skip, Skipper, Skippy, Spikes, Babe."

"Nicknames."

"Skippy?" Zermatt asked. "Like the spread?"

"Skipper. I was captain of my high school basketball team—I'm sure it's in there somewhere—the Madame Curie High Madmen. It stuck. Mostly it's—well, my dad would appreciate it if you called me Babe. But few people do. My sister calls me So Stupid. Like in 'You're so stupid.' Mostly it's Skipper, I guess." It was getting late.

Gracie made a prune face of impatience as Bowen volunteered that his father was buggy on baseball. "Named us all for diamond greats. Even my sister and the cat."

"We are more than aware of the contributions of baseball to your life, Mr. Bowen. That is not what you're here for," Gracie said.

Zermatt ran his finger down a sheet. "Led the Ivy League two—"

"Tough league," Gracie snorted. "The way I read it you rode the bench. A little luck—some hard-luck guys ahead of you—and some hits that dropped." Zermatt nodded at the description, and doodled the word *Luck* on his scratch pad, ringing it with concentric boxes. "And that's what makes you think you're a hero. I wouldn't try getting a job with this résumé."

"Haven't had the chance."

"Let me tell you something, give you a little advice, son. Don't get cute. You have that tendency, you know. Tobias was cute. People who get cute don't last long. We had a fellow a long time ago, thought he was kind of a card. He worked in OPI, too. And one day, he had to write an obituary, for our house organ, the *Ledger-Domain*. It should have been his own. Seems one of our people went home and found his wife with another man, and took remedial action. This joker wrote that she was 'survived by her husband, by his own arrangement.' "

"What happened to him?" Tyler asked.

"He thought it was funny. I didn't. That was a valuable man he was talking about. He's still here. Our joker spent the rest of his time loading chemicals on the shipping dock." Gracie pressed Bowen's folder shut. "Which is what jokers deserve. Keep your ass dry, Bowen. Martin B. Gracie is watching." He stood up, tugged at his crotch, and tossed his head toward the door.

Zermatt walked Bowen out, saying when they reached the safety of the predawn outdoors, "He's a stupid, mean, evil son-of-bitch. And when I find his soft white underbelly, I'm going to destroy him."

Tyler shrugged and laughed wearily. "A little generosity of spirit, now. He probably can't help himself."

Martin B. Gracie, as often as not, referred to himself by full name, title and GS rating, as though he were signing a letter, or still memorizing that information. He also liked to invoke his retired Army captaincy, often designating himself "Martin B. Gracie, Captain, USA, Retired." Those who respected him dubbed him, after this, Captain America; Zermatt and many others called him Captain Crazy. For Gracie also liked to refer to himself, whenever it was plausible without seeming like a fruitcake, in the third person, as though he were some version of a king, or alienated. He liked best of all to roar to faint-hearts, "If you don't got a pair, you come see Martin B. Gracie and he'll show you something you'll never forget!"

When Martin B. Gracie smiled he seemed almost human, appealingly Santa Clausian, though his face was ever porcine. But when he glared, as he did most often, ships at sea lashed their cargo to the decks. His hair was steel gray, tinged with blue, a crew cut gone to seed.

Zermatt's hair, in fact his whole head, incurred Gracie's disapproval. Zermatt's was a large globe-shaped skull, and his hair was a coarse black mesh of wires, as though several scrub brushes had been stapled to his scalp. Gracie was convinced that something was going on within it detrimental to his best interests.

Zermatt, for his part, liked Bowen's look. He thought it admirable. The boy seemed delightfully fearless in the face of the bureaucracy's primitive manner. Boys like Bowen were rare, and that was partly why he'd been chosen over even brighter young men. Boys like Bowen knew they belonged and became Navy officers with a certain reliability. The least of them remained such. Bowen, like Baron Zermatt, knew how to keep his options open. Tousle-haired and keen, here was a rising young star, a sure and natural winner. His was a look of confidence.

Baron Zermatt also radiated confidence, though of a somewhat different sort. He had a charm which he used in strict personal service. Once, after successively peeling the virtue off two stewardesses, a long-lines operator, a girl on the train to Washington, and one in an automobile, he observed, "Sometimes I think the entire Industrial Revolution was fought for my benefit."

He'd retired from such penny-ante combat into an opportune marriage which friends called "the shot wad heard round the world." After law school he was admitted to the New York and District of Columbia bars, and accepted a direct commission in the Marine Judge Advocate General Corps. He forthwith informed his fellow comrades in arms-at-law that he would be delighted to ease their burdens, for a nominal fee. "A smart man can make a buck out of all this misery. And I'm the smartest man I know." He acquired a quick reputation for enterprise when he began purveying green underwear to the junior officers. He also acquired the attention of his Commander, who called him on the deck at a Captain's mast.

The Commander shook his head. "I don't know whether to commend you or court-martial you. You'll either wind up in the Senate or in jail by the time you're thirty-five. Where the blazes did you ever come up with such a cockeyed idea?"

"Sir, it is as close to pure capitalism as man may ever get. I am simply filling a need. Plugging a hole in their sexual pride. Vaginal spray's the classic in the field. When they shed their Brooks Brothers habits and drop their briefcases their nerve fails them."

"Why do men down to their skivvies need your help?"

"Insurance. Green underwear is the best proof other than a wooden leg of being a returned combat vet. How's a nice girl from a nice family going to tell a man who's been there he's a lousy lay?"

"Why the hell didn't you just sell them a club?"

Zermatt huffed up. "The Baron," he said airily—a sometime affectation which annoyed many but pre-empted their making Is-that-a-name-or-a-rank jokes—"does not believe in fomenting disbarment as accessory to forcible rape."

The Commander arranged a transfer out of the Corps for Zermatt, to Gila, with highest recommendations. The economic lesson Zermatt drew from this was that power spoke volumes. "One must always have one's hand on the big lever," he told his wife. "Which or whose is key."

The transfer turned out to be a boon for Zermatt. He could minister to the needs of others at great profit to himself. His release, due before the year was out, would mark a translation of this to private life. His and his wife's professional stake was set in negligence and divorce work. And he was already no small force in New York clubhouse politics, with a reputation for good instincts and great fixings. His fortune would rise in every way, personally and professionally, *pari passu* with the misery of others.

And yet, if one could observe him as he slept, there would be seen his cool and detached waking self dissolving into a pageant of ferocious twitches, a rebellion of the body against the awful public self-control he exerted. They were the legacy of a distant, otherwise repressed, childhood torment.

But in waking, he was capable of glib surety. "Someday," he liked to say, "I'm going to be so wealthy I can afford to hire a man to come in and take care of the foreplay and the three hours of talk afterward."

86

"Cup-a-coffee?" Zermatt asked Bowen.

"It's four o'clock in the fucking morning!"

"You got something special to-fucking-do?"

Over coffee in the Gila canteen, Zermatt marveled, "Boy, why Gracie didn't bounce on you with both feet for all that shit about baseball names. That's perjury, pal. You don't get to pull his chain twice."

"The tragedy is it's all true. See, my dad's convinced the right name's a passport to glory or some shit. I'm not so sure."

"It was, for the people who had them first."

"Yeah, I guess. I'm part Ty Cobb and Babe Ruth—on paper."

Zermatt sucked his cheek, still dubious. "I thought Cobb was Tyrus."

"Sounded too foreign for my mom or something. And there was some Scottish rebel named Tyler—maybe a cousin, so they compromised. It's kind of presidential, too, I guess. And my middle name is for—da-dum!—George Herman Ruth."

"Least it wasn't Herman—or Ruth."

"Lemme tell you, it's a little staggering, all that baggage. I'm dragging my life and my dad's hopes in one load."

"So're we all. Just be glad you didn't get Jesus Lincoln. What's Bowen, anyway? English?"

"These days," Tyler said. "Think it used to be Bowenzork or something. Goes back through thirty generations of great Romanian fruit-and-veggie men who couldn't hit left-handed pitching. Neither can I."

"No wonder they picked you up for OPI. You making this up?"

"Hell no! My brother Willie? Ted Williams."

"You're full of shit," Zermatt laughed. "Why not Theodore?"

Tyler leaned across the table and confided, "It has to do with a Romanian King in the middle ages, named Theodore, who slept with his sister—and may have thus founded Poland, according to reports."

"And I take it your sister's named Casey."

"That's the cat. She's Connie. Willie's never laid a glove on her, though someone should. It'd do wonders for her complexion. Her animal husband's out of town a lot, mostly when he's home."

Zermatt's head was swimming. "Connie like in Connie Mack, I suppose."

"The one and only. Cornelius McGillicuddy. Owned and managed the fuckin' Philly A's for half a century, wore a suit in the dugout and everybody called him Mr. Mack, which is what I call her to piss her off." As big sisters go, she started it. "When she was fourteen she realized that I was born an uncanny nine months after V-J Day, on account of which she began referring to me as a 'victory party wine stain in the rug that took,' which wasn't far wrong."

Tyler didn't elaborate on Willie who, in his opinion, was gangling proof that (a) what you don't know can't hurt you but might kill you, and that (b) there are probably more vitamins and minerals in marijuana than in half a pound of calf's liver, saying only, "He's sixty-two already, three years younger than me, and a congenital jerk. But lovable—especially if you ask cheerleaders. Lately he's taken to telling people he was named for Willie Mays, but you could look it up: Little Willie B. was wetting his pants a full season before Mr. Willie Mays ever swung a major league Louisville Slugger."

"If he gets mileage out of it," Zermatt conceded.

"Maybe. When we were kids, though, Teddy Ballgame was in the papers every day, spitting at fans, conking ladies with his bat. My guys—Spikes and the Babe—were clipping coupons or in that Big Clubhouse in the Sky. You got any?"

"What, sibs? Nah," Zermatt said, as though he'd participated in the decision. "They hysterectified my mother after me. Tied her tubes and put a stop to this nonsense once and for all. All my relatives are a wife, pleasantly distant. May get her fixed, too."

"Typical. I'm aboard, haul up the gangplank. No offense. Think of all those Zermatts who never got to be."

"Fuck 'em if they can't take a joke. What're you anyway, some kind of Catholic?"

Bowen smirked. and flipped his empty coffee cup into a plastic wastebasket. "Unitarian. Recessive Presbyterian on my mother's side." Zermatt laughed unaccountably, and Tyler got up, dramatically tugging his own crotch to mimic Gracie. "See ya round the yard."

Zermatt followed him out and grabbed his elbow. "Listen. I want to show you something. What's a good word for you?"

Tyler's eyes stung from fatigue and the first rays of light made him squint painfully. "Me. *Tired.*"

"Another."

"Lucky, I guess." At which Zermatt unfolded the piece of paper he had doodled on earlier. "Hey, that's great. Looks like a bar of soap on a TV. You do card tricks, too?"

"It's true, Tyler. You're lucky. And with the right management, you could be even luckier. Lemme tell you something about luck. My uncle was a guy who was temporarily rich several times. Between rolls of the dice. You know what I mean? So one time he borrowed some money from my father, about seven grand. Swore it was an emergency. Bingo: off to Vegas. And I mean he was busted within the hour. A new indoor record, maybe. Called my father and begged for more, to win it all back. Well, my old man went ape-shit. This fool'd just pissed away the Baron's college money. So my uncle was very remorseful, you understand. Which helped."

"I bet."

"Really. At the airport he sticks a quarter in a slot machine, and what do you know? Three lemons. So does he buy me a toy to apologize? Hardly. But he's got this bag of quarters."

"Life's a gamble," Tyler said helpfully.

"Precisely. He pumps 'em into an Insurance Vendo-mat on the Big Bet. Of course, he lost."

"Landed safely, eh?"

"No. No. *He* lost. *We* won. Accepted his apology completely when his plane smacked into another one going the other way over Brooklyn. You might have read about it. Came up double-zero. Christ, it practically delivered him to our door with the stub in his hands. It was touch and go for a while."

"I'm waiting to hear about luck."

"Well, if he'd have lived we wouldn't have collected

a centavo. And figure the odds on his not being incinerated with the claim stubs. As it was, they were bastards about paying off because of the hospital expenses. Anyway, he expired soon enough—"

"And glee reigned in the Zermatt household."

Baron laughed, "Well, funerals are sad enough, you know, without a lot of unnecessary crying. I mean, the main matter is already resolved." After that, Baron was set: Princeton, Columbia Law, believing in the Grail of the Perfect and Essential Angle, the Platonic Profit. Like a wealthy doctor, Baron would prosper ever by rampant misfortune, and was not at all unhappy about the frailties flesh was heir to.

"What does that have to do with my being lucky?"

"Just, sometimes luck needs a little push. And you've got to make sure you take the right risks. Like breaking up that fight. That was the wrong risk. You listen to the Baron. It could make all the difference."

Lucky he was, all right. But if there was anything that worried Tyler Bowen at night, counting the mental rosary of his gifts in his circumstantial loneliness, it was precisely his unconscionable luckiness. He was alive, having beaten a billion sperm in a grand chase for the One Main Chance, tall, good-looking, bright, and perpetually amused. He was no genius plagued by erratic fires of invention. His instincts and values were sharp: he'd rather be Bill Russell than Bertrand, DiMaggio than da Vinci. Yet, other than his worry for the safety of his dumb kid brother, it was his very luckiness that bothered him most.

He was afraid he would never be super, because he would never dare. Leaping to play collegiate basketball was one thing; flight itself required trusting a hunch on a window ledge. Risk and Gamble were the keys. Yet the lures of safety were compelling.

Something within him was afraid he would never: lead a great slave revolt, conquer the stage and screen, pitch a perfect game, love a World Class Woman, write a perfect sonnet, visit Mars, leap tall buildings or conduct at the Met, solve an impossible riddle, create a new vaccine, or make a Golden Record. He was afraid

he would never be scared and hungry enough to concentrate and risk everything for real.

His father and mother had rendered to their children
many gifts and curses in their chromosomes. His
mother was Scottish and she insisted there was deposed
royalty in her Ainsley line. "Maybe the Used Car King
of Glasgow," Tyler's sister liked to say, "but sure as
hell no Thanes of Cawdor. From mother we have inherited a lasting and inspiring tendency to sunburn and
not a lot else."

His father, who was so keen on the destiny of names,
liked people to call him Victor, or Big Vic, which they
didn't, instead of Vlad, which they did because it was
his name. He thought that name a curse, for there was
an early Romanian Prince named Vlad who may or
may not have been the Original Vampire, Dracula. Expert opinion is divided. Vlad Bowen's children called
him Vladad, Big Vlad, or Vampops. "But always," he
would say, "collect." And they would reply, "For a
Vamp his bark's worse than his bite."

But among the many endowments Vlad Bowen gave
his children was the cursed gift of his own desire that
each be something special. He scoffed at modern
heroes: they did not go through recognizable hells any
more. No one spent long evenings swinging weighted
bats from both sides of the plate, or running aching
miles through cornfields of gloom. Today's heroes
sprang fully formed from Golden Wombs in Santa
Clara, dined on Coke and Fortified Twinkies, and
popped steroids with fluoridated water.

It was precisely that which made computers believe
Tyler Bowen was select and thus to be trusted with
great secrets, including the World's Biggest Secret. But
that was a large class of people nonetheless. Vlad
Bowen knew better. He told his children that the sword
would remain in the stone until someone took the
American Dare, and no one in forty years had. A hero
who could turn his times around and wind his people
up when all faith flagged would be someone who, say,
could get up in a small plane, alone, over the Atlantic.
Someone who with a single act could grab diverse
imaginations, galvanize two hundred million meanings
by the single myth of himself.

It would not be a selfish thing, for personal glory. For by such a thing, such a person could epitomize the Nation's best impulses, make his visions theirs, and theirs his acts. That hero could return something fine to the world, an American promise.

The Bowen children thought this largely nonsense.

Vlad Bowen often said, "Life means nothing if it does not mean leaving the world better for having been here." To which his daughter Connie once replied, "Then it means nothing."

Except that they had invested so much time in being wed and that custom required greater energy to dissolve a marriage than to make one, and that Warren still held out hope of Johanna reverting to what he had fallen in love with—not realizing that she was precisely that ungovernable girl still—Warren would have given up and cut his losses. And she persisted because she could not identify the source or cure of her discontent. So they tried, employing pretend games to break the stalemate. Warren tried everything he knew. He suggested they have a baby, assuming that women wanted children the way children wanted puppies, with a species instinct. He was stunned, insulted, when she rejected it out of hand. He'd hoped it might be just the marital glue. But Johanna could not explain that a child would be even further crippling to the more pregnant sense inside her.

Still hoping to convince her of the joys of parenthood, and searching for an experience they could share, Warren suggested they take one or another of her nephews for a weekend. The most tolerable of the lot was six-year-old Michael Poulson, who had just completed a year believing he was a fire truck, peeing on neighbors' flower gardens. The others were less inventive. They were rigorously trying to earn their bones as renegade Apaches, one having blown the belly off a cat with a cherry bomb, the eldest having no conscious thoughts he could not modify with "motherfucking."

They took the nephews to every tourist attraction between Mexico and Phoenix, to amusement parks and rodeos, to ghost towns, county fairs, and cowboy movie sets, to caverns and museums. Warren played doting father while Johanna wiped their noses. He hoped the children would be a new catalyst in their lives, while she stared at strangers' faces.

She would try, even as Carl and Maureen Poulson had not. Yet in the deepest corner of her scar-touched eyes, where she had worn a wavering gold star at Monterey, high while Warren wouldn't touch the grass, in the white dot that was herself to herself, she already knew it was just not Warren. It was missing with him. And in Tucson. She felt like a prisoner of her own life. But too many people accused her of running away from things for her to act. So she would wait for some climatic change, some cool breeze to sail her out of town, some bright hope to make her a Princess in the City again; some someone else, some somewhere else. But all that came were siroccos, date winds from the south, hot air from the desert and what Tombstone Center and Gila Compound generated.

During August, Johanna's editor asked over lunch if she enjoyed the assignments she was receiving. He took an avuncular interest in her, partly because of his friendship with her mother, but partly because he liked her unaffected spunkiness. She didn't claim to be a reporter, but she had a disarming way. "Well, let's see," she said. "In the last two weeks I've done a go-cart jamboree, an elementary school pageant, and the Betty Crocker Bake-off Regionals. I can't say I'm not getting experience. Only, it's also what I do on my days off."

"It beats reviewing books," he said.

"Oh, yes, and that nursing home transfer! That was a nice piece, I liked that one. I just wish I'd been there when that poor panther broke out of his cage at that dreadful restaurant during their little party."

"That," he told her, "and white space and stock tables is what sells newsprint. Every night I say a prayer of thanks for parakeets and pussycats."

Johanna broke into a broad grin. She liked him for the relaxed way he traded teasing. "I just love hearing you rhapsodize about Freedom of the Press, Arnie. It's so inspiring."

"Don't kid yourself," he replied. "When I got my start in newspapering, my editor came up to me and said, 'Logan, lemme tell you the facts of life. You are not a journalist. You are a newspaperman. And the primary function of a paper is sale of space to advertisers.' My salary came from the number of ads I sold between stories. Which brings me to my question. How would you like to do a piece for the Arizona State of the Art series?" This was a weekly feature celebrating Arizona's contributions to the Moon Race and other technological gymnastic events. In previous weeks they'd described the work done at the NASA Geological Research unit at Flagstaff, the Deep Space Communications Center, the Optical Research facility at the University of Arizona, asthma research and the Heart Institute in Phoenix. "Would you?"

"Sure," she brightened. "What?"

"Well, you do have an in at Tombstone Center."

Johanna looked at him askance. "Where they took a desert and made a Los Angeles. Ah, progress! Aren't you the man who says that sleeping with a news source is screwing the readers?"

"Depends on the source," he said. "I'm not anticipating an investigation. It's a feature."

She dipped a finger in her water glass and sucked on it thoughtfully. "I'd really like to, Arnie. Really. But talk about busman's holidays. And, uh, I honestly don't think I could trust my utter objectivity."

"OK, lady. I know some people who'll be very disappointed."

"Would most of them be my mother? Sounds like something she'd suggest."

"I am entirely free of outside influence, Johanna."

94

He stirred his drink and grinned. "Except when I'm not."

"Is that really fair to me, Arnie?"

He nodded apologetically. "I am chastised. How about something on Gila Compound?"

"I thought they didn't talk to people."

"Times change. After years of being sons-of-bitches whenever we wanted some friendly answers, suddenly there's a big PR push on. They're running tours, yet. They want us to know all about their sinks and computing machines and why the monkey wants the banana at 50 Gs a throw."

"Why now?"

"Even as you and I, they must hustle for a buck. You've got to read their press releases to fully appreciate it. Every other line invokes the Big C."

"Communism?"

"Only at elections. Cancer. How our support in this critical hour is—"

"Kind of gets you right here," she said, holding her tummy.

"It's going to get you right there," he said, slapping his rump, "if I know them. I once sat on a committee with the Director of Public Information there, Mrs. Carver."

"My mother knows her, I think."

"Yup," Logan said. "Same committee. She could be your godmother here—she introduced your mother and me. The lady once said to me, in an expansive mood, that she's an Absolutist on the First Amendment, thinks it's an absolute outrage. Quite a gal."

"Why do her any favors?"

"I ask myself that. And then I think, the hell with her. The story is the story. And if it's a favor for anyone, sweetheart, it's you. Unless you like cutting your teeth on kindergarten plays."

As well funded as Gila Compound and Tombstone Center were, they pimped for more by salvos of self-congratulations. Their work was counter to the fatalistic view, for they were asked to conjure ways to manage and exploit the forces that burdened good hopes, and they had the best minds available for the task.

At Gila, press releases claimed, one of the more fruitful approaches to research problems now in general use had come through a conceptual breakthrough of the first magnitude: the application of characteristics seemingly anthropomorphic to the mysteries of natural process. Gaps in scientific understanding could be bridged by simple terms which, taken literally, implied intention and personality for events of ignorant atoms and blind energy. Physical entities were described as having "strangeness" and "charm" and peculiar affinities; various biochemical units were deemed to have "sociability" and "identity" problems they never dreamed of, perhaps even dreams and fears. Things had urges—aspirations and anxieties—that were experimentally valid. They were true only as matters of pragmatism, but useful nonetheless. For they explained sufficiently well properties and behavior otherwise difficult to describe. From that came fruit in diverse places, as means of prediction and control. For once the proper metaphor was determined, a bold analogy system could be erected to reveal new truths about the matter under study.

This took on proportions of paradox when Tombstone Center was considered. Work there sought to depict social process—historical, psychological, political—in terms of reliable natural law. The rules of the universe were taken as Holy Writ, deemed unexceptionable, in ways no Gila scientist would dare. One of those laws declared, "An inertial course cannot be altered from within an inertial space." Of necessity to their work's purpose, they chose selectively to ignore that.

Johanna and two other area reporters took a tour of Gila in early September, along with twenty Tucson civic leaders. Their smiling tour guide was Tyler Bowen, who told them, "Although unschooled, the Mexican Indians who named our mountains Thunder have much to teach us regarding meteorology. But they could not have known how apt would be the name they gave. They could not have dreamed of the lightning-fast computers housed here in Arizona's largest computer complex—"

He walked them through what had been, until that

week, a classified area. They were taken into confidence, given this information as small, inconsequential morsels for the sake of public relations, the reporters told exactly what they could and could not write about as a condition of their visit.

"These computers serve as the spinal cord for the Global Electronic Message System, which rings the world." Tyler beamed, and once again apologized to the man from the Phoenix paper for not permitting photos. "They could not have dreamed, sending smoke signals, that—"

No, indeed. Neither could the Indians nor these guests have dreamed that at Gila Compound the loco gringos would play with lightning. For not only were mechanisms perfected there which conveyed the secrets of a great nation, but also were great advances made in hard- and software to jam the receptors of the nosy. This place was chosen for these functions because it was perfect by isolation and climate. "The air is—hot —and still, free from factory grindings and radio waves. I understand that transistor radios die regularly of broken hearts," Tyler said. And here was further evidence of that isolation: news came in by invitation and went out by sufferance. A.P. was just the name of a Mexican border town, Agua Prieta. Only on the highest hill and in a few privileged, wired quarters was Walter Cronkite known. To the rest he was mere memory, and legend, his name whispered at delicious peril, like Napoleon's during the exile. "So the desert"—and security and secrecy—"creates a *cordon sanitaire* around Gila Compound."

"What are you walling in and what are you walling out?" Johanna Reigeluth asked.

Bowen nodded to her. "Interference. Static. You might say 'the meaner influences of the world.'"

"Sounds dreadful."

"To be honest," he answered, "it drives some people, the isolation, half-crazy." He smiled at the rest of them. "And if you wonder how I've gotten the rest of the way"—they all tittered at this little joke—"you may know that the temperature here in the summer is a reliable 109. It's nice and cool now at 98. Which is why we also lead the state in use of air-conditioning facilities."

As the group went through a tunnel between two buildings, on their way to the biology labs, an older woman, sweating like a glazed ham, asked Tyler Bowen whether he had been in residence during a fall season.

"No ma'am. I still have that to look forward to. Though I'm kind of used to cooler weather and foliage, back East."

"People from back East don't realize how much the desert changes. There are wonderful seasons. Such colorful bloomings, if you look closely."

"Yes, Ma'am."

Walking behind them, Johanna Reigeluth said to the man next to her, "That explains about the Indians."

"What do you mean?" Tyler asked, turning around.

"Unschooled they may have been. Stupid they were not. When they said Thunder, that's what they meant."

It was true. While there is no deciduous foliage to speak of, there is excitement. And it all but wrecks the serenity so vital to those GEMS computers. The intrusive presence of the mountains in the broiling flatland creates a drafty corridor in the upper atmosphere. Every drop of moisture over Sonora and the Gulf of California gets sucked north in the fall and the air explodes with cloudless rain for a savage ten minutes each day. It is more reliable than the temperature. It comes down hot and fast and is no relief. At ground level it has been gauged at between 98 and 100 degrees. Wags call it "cumulo-urine." In late September it falls around noon and by December has precessed to dusk. In five minutes the moisture is gone as though it never came.

Tyler saw them to their bus, smiling at each, thanking them for coming, offering any further help they needed, apologizing again about the cameras, and specifically requesting that no mention be made of Gila Mountain. "And if there are no further questions—have a good, safe trip home and come back soon. If you do have any questions you'd like answered, please don't hesitate to call. The number is in your press kits." He showed them all the teeth in his mouth.

"Nice young man," Johanna's seat-mate said as the bus pulled out. "Don't you think?"

"Which?"

"Mr. Bowman."

"Um," Johanna nodded, opening a book to read for the ride back, saying idly, "I wonder what he's doing in a place like this."

"Why, nice things, what do you think?"

The stories which came of this tour uniformly reflected that impression. Gila and Tombstone were pleased with themselves. At higher levels publishers and editors and broadcast executives were invited to sit on joint policy committees, made to feel part of "the team," encouraged to take the lead in their own seduction. As journalists, all liked to preen that they were not for sale. And they were not. They were for rent. The stories spoke of great possibilities in the understanding and control of the biochemical process, and plumbing the secrets of the atom.

But it wasn't all cancer research and it wasn't all message transmission. Hints were all around, secrecy the greatest hint of all. Yet the axe of silence fell to slice every intriguing thread. Even Bowen did not know all that was going on behind the curtain, though with each passing week it became more obvious.

There was sufficient study of socially beneficial things going on there to justify the elaborate claims he made in Gila's behalf; and his wasn't the only hand on the mimeograph machine. But it might also be said that at Gila Compound they dealt with the World's Smallest Secrets, peering through a glass in one direction, encouraging the public to join their gaze in wonderment, while, much like their brothers atop Kitt Peak who scour the skies, the Biggest Secret loomed behind their sight in another.

There was nobody in the *Tucson Intelligencer* office one Friday night in late September except Johanna Reigeluth. She rubbed her eyes and played with a short lock of her hair as she read the material in front of her for perhaps the fifth time, not knowing what to do with it. She did not have enough experience to feel confident at this. Indeed, she wanted nothing more than to stretch languorously in that solitude, but felt she owed the material and the process greater dignity. She felt like an outsider, still, tiptoeing in a room where she was alone.

Arnie Logan had asked her to generate another story from her Gila Compound notes, something on the specific good deeds of the place.

She had a marked-up copy of the original Charter of Gila Compound that had been given to all the people on the tour. With it was other material from the press kit. Every page was stamped: "Confidential: Use of this material conditional on prior release from Gila Compound Office of Public Information. Unauthorized use prohibited by Law." Each copy was numbered.

Logan had suggested she call Gila's OPI and arrange for another visit. But all they did was send her more handouts. When she told him this, he said, "Keep on it. Maybe you've got enough already. See what you've got."

The Charter said that Gila was commissioned in the early 1950s under the joint auspices of the National Institutes of Health and the National Science Foundation. Because of difficulty in gaining access to classified material held elsewhere, Gila was transferred in the early 1960s to AEC-NASA cosponsorship. According to the press kit, the Executive Order which gave Gila life set it on an inspiring mission: "To develop American treatments for the infirmities of the world." It seemed a magnificent, noble purpose, grand in scope and gallant. "A little tinged by jingo," Logan had remarked when she'd shown him that. "But forgivable, when you're talking about assuaging the suffering of the globe, I guess."

"I have friends," Johanna told him, "who call themselves radical historians, who say all that secrecy's very suspicious."

"Your friends are very suspicious," Logan replied. "This stuff's really weapons?"

Johanna opened her notebook and flipped a few pages, locating a quote. "Or national treasure—inexhaustible, more precious than gold. Its impact on political economy would be immense."

Logan leaned back and sighed. "Your friends are better radicals than historians. At the time, it was not in America's nature to horde such things. They'd be shared."

"That's what Gila says, too."

His jaw dropped. "You asked them? Wonderful. I wouldn't've had the nerve. Give me a novice any day. Let me tell you something, though—you can tell it to your revisionist friends. In those days—I don't think your friends were even born yet—the very name America was filled with explosive, benign connotations. All the forms of goodness lay in the word. No country ever had so much, was so unladen by discredited dogmas, or broken histories, was so willing to use its resources and give its best away in help—"

"You could write for Gila," Johanna teased.

"As for secrecy, well," Logan shrugged, untroubled by it, "that's just the way the world works. Hell, even Santa Claus doesn't tip off his shots. You know, they nearly blew the Marshall Plan like that, sweetie. Should've waited 'til they had Congress in line and the crops on the boats. Now I don't know the Easter Bunny's policy, but I bet he keeps his eggs to himself too, keeps those good little girls and boys guessing— and good. Look, it was pretty humane stuff any way you slice it. I forget, how many famines and plagues've your revisionist friends cured?"

"It's just, you should see the way Gila describes itself. Here: 'The finest voyage of discovery since . . .' I mean, *honestly,* Arnie. The Easter Bunny doesn't pimp for himself either."

"Compromise is always the entry fee; just pick the good guys."

So Johanna sat trying to make sense of her notes, trying to find a story and a peg for one, and a band in the spectrum of conscience to tell it in. She stared at the page for another fifteen minutes, blankly. Then she wrote:

Dear Arnie:
    During the Civil War, Gila Compound was known as Fort Compliance. It was the farthest-west outpost captured by the Confederates. They abandoned it a week later after a little-talked-about affair with the Indians that included some perfectly grim activities

with one of the horses. This is why southerners, although they may savage other minorities, have nothing but the highest regard for the Indians of the Southwest, and rarely, if ever, speak ill of horses.

As for Gila, from drawing board to scaffolding must be a perilous journey. Hard to trace just where it happened, but I estimate that somewhere in the first fifteen minutes it got off the track.

They have yet to cure a foreign wart.

Our files are filled with funny stories relating to Gila that don't add up and seem kind of batty. That silly mountain, for one. I don't get it. There's a weird story about *aardvarks,* for Chrissakes, that is simply implausible. I think something's under our noses and we don't know it. I made a small check on their latest medical triumph and found this:

In fiscal year 1966, the National Laboratories at Gila Compound did little more than perfect cures for three harmless but annoying skin rashes indigenous to five southern states exclusively, among whose sufferers, I'd bet, were numbered several members of important congressional watchdog committees, their wives and/or girlfriends. Am I in over my head?

She stared at it for a few minutes then slowly pulled it out of the typewriter. She folded it carefully, pressed the creases flat, and then dropped it in the wastebasket on her way out.

At Gila, the labs were working overtime and the Public Information Office triple-time, pouring out more and more elaborate tales of loping strides toward cancer treatments, new energy sources, enlightenment. Mobile trucks were being saddled with displays to take to school science fairs, story boards and dioramas mounted for exhibits at trade fairs and conventions. It all told of happy, peaceful profits from the national investment, rather like prospectuses for a new series of bonds to pay for old ones come due.

But this was just a small share of the work at Gila.

Inside of fifteen years, from the bright goodwill of its conception, Gila Compound's major energies were

102

focused on an entirely scholastic question: How many demons could ride the head of a pin?

What had happened was that the construction of Gila required the cooperation of many agencies. To appease them, a few dollars were at first set aside for "incidental identification of affliction factors resisting ameliorative measures." That is, finding pestilences that had no cure. These might be used not at all; or to protect Americans from the similar concoctions of others; or in paramilitary and political exigencies, should those prior offers of succor be unpersuasive.

Accordingly, in early 1960 the most highly developed insect vectors, for efficient delivery of disease, were produced at Gila. The Tombstone R&D team in charge of this project wrote in its report, "Let's get the bugs in. Insects should work. People should think." At Gila, men first harnessed melioidosis, which, despite its pleasant name, has no cure and militates toward universal mortality. Trypanosomiasis, African sleeping sickness, was refined, crossbred, and mutated into a tactically ready state. Varieties of spirilla and Q fever tumbled into the stockpiles. Soon the versatility and depth of American disease was second to none.

As one of his last acts, shortly before giving the go-ahead to the Bay of Pigs invasion planners, President Eisenhower ordered all such work halted and Gila confined to its original purpose. This was backed up with extra appropriations to recatalog stock, close files, and paint new signs on the lab doors. More money was siphoned in to find cures for what was in hand; those that had no cures were serendipity.

Special steps were taken to tighten security. One was to populate the place with people on fellowships sponsored by bountiful organizations with no corporeality except as budget-line items somewhere, figments of the perfervid imagination of the National Security Agency. The other step was that Gila and Tombstone reported directly to the NSA, which stopped telling the President what he couldn't handle.

The Oh-Five Event before the July Fourth rumble celebrated the development of a mutant herpes simplex. And the next one in the wings would commemorate the isolation and perfection of a new, vaccine-resistant strain of polio.

Gila wanted to go civic in the worst way. Toward which end Tyler Bowen was assigned to sit in a booth for a morning at the Cochise County Fair in front of a story board of Gila Compound's contributions to Agronomy, surrounded by gigantic blowups of hydroponic tomatoes, immense turnips, and mammoth cabbages, while a creepy-voiced narrator on a tape loop recited a litany of achievements. The Fair was an adjunct to the annual Tombstone Helldorado Days, a yearly Wild West show, stampede, and carnival commemorating Hollywood's version of the past. In previous years the Fair had been held at Bisbee, but few people could be found to drive that far from Tucson just to look at livestock, so it was merged with the Tombstone rodeo.

"You gotta hand it to Ma Nature," Baron Zermatt said as he drove with Tyler toward the Fair. The early October air above the desert was crystalline, a still and shiny blue made brighter by the gold refracted from pyrites in the ground.

"Delighted to hand her the whole place."

"No aesthetic, Tyler. That's your problem."

"Tell you what. You sit in the booth and I'll go play. You can tell everyone about your love of nature."

"Yeah, but what I love is her style. She's kind of puckish. Gives you a leg, then takes it away. Puts the tits on the right sex, but wraps her own best stuff tighter than an otter's twat in February. I mean, here's this glorious day, all these people out in the ozone— and she's gonna piss all over 'em for ten minutes even so."

"You're really in the wrong line, you know? You should be working for OPI."

"I respect her too much. Shit, I'm the guy you have to thank for keeping her best jewels from getting raped."

"Truly now," Tyler said.

"Bet your ass. Up in the plateaus of Gila Mountain are fields of lush grass and mountain brooks that start off green and cold. Granted they're flowing kind of brown down below. But it's beautiful up there. How'd you like that overrun with tourists? I'm the guy that permanently chased 'em out."

"How?"

"Well, the forestry people were running it, because there was a stand of trees up there that predated humans on the continent. The damned canyon wasn't even discovered until this century. And the Interior people wanted to make it into a monument. You know what that means? Campers, litter, destruction. I did the paper work that sent 'em packing for good. Can't have the Interior Department running a sideshow on a mountain that doesn't exist, can you? So now it's happily getting along without us."

"You're a saint, Bar."

"Better. I'm a good lawyer."

"Then why don't you help me figure out how to get out of here with a minimum of damage to my conscience?"

Zermatt stared at him blankly. "A small parable, Skippy. From lawyers and saints you don't get miracles. You just get mediation."

"That's not a parable."

"Sue me. Play the game."

All morning Tyler sat at his booth, hoping the proverbial farmer's daughter would come by. But only Baron Zermatt did, trying to bring him cheer. He kept reporting on the "gorgeous girls hanging around the livestock show—if you can handle that kind of competition."

When Tyler's relief came after lunch, and he was free for the day, he realized it was his first unregulated fresh air in months. He and Zermatt watched some of the cowboy shows and went on rides, and Tyler won a raggedy Kewpie doll for meritorious foul-shooting in the midway. It restored his self-confidence a bit. "Listen, Bar," he said, "I think we ought to break up this act for a while. The lies told in the name of lust are better told alone. You go ply your trade for a while and let me ply mine, OK?"

Zermatt put a fatherly arm on Bowen. "I've talked to these women. They all want a down payment on a house first."

"I've got a hunch."

"Me too. You bring that stupid doll back and Gracie'll run you out for buggery."

Tyler looked at it fondly. "Considering my choices?" Then he swatted Zermatt away and disappeared into the crowd, happily liberated, totally lost, his face crossed with the delirious release of a child leaving detention on the last day of school before summer recess, paralyzed by the candy shop of opportunity around him. He wandered around like a ghost at a party, effectively lacking substance, knowing no one, ignored by all as if by prior concord or maybe, he began to think, ostracism. They were natives, families, and he was a stranger. They lived in a different reality. There were a few college students, but they were in groups, at peace among themselves, apparently stoned, and they paid him no attention.

Johanna Reigeluth was standing by the Ferris wheel in the Funland section, idly picking at some cotton candy. Warren and their nephew Michael handed two tickets to the ride attendant as they boarded. If Tyler Bowen saw them, it didn't register. The sense of freedom was enrapturing, and no part of it begged for personal involvement. Johanna saw him first and watched him look around like a lost child. He seemed different in this environment, friendly in a downcast way; resembling a fuzzy red cinnamon bear with a pine needle in its paw, bewildered and harmless. Quite different, just by movement, from the glib and opaque tour guide at Gila Compound. She smiled, recalling that cinnamon bears were cute but dangerous. Tyler noticed her then, looking his way. He brightened at this first familiar face, but she only nodded, as one might wordlessly acknowledge a stranger in a familiar plight before walking on.

She was turned away, picking at the cotton candy, looking at strangers, and he stared at her still, hoping he didn't seem threatening, bathing in the isolated thoughts of one pretty girl's presence while the rest of the Fair faded for a moment into its noises and smells and grease. He walked around the Ferris wheel closer, feeling as though he were sneaking up on a lovely sun-speckled damselfly. There would only be a few more

106

seconds of study, he knew, before she detected him and exploded in nervous flight.

"Hey, Babe," Zermatt pounded his back from behind. "Any luck?"

"Oh, hiya, Bar." By the time Tyler ducked away, she was gone.

She had noticed him watching her, even enjoyed the objectification for a while. For by the strange economics of her life just then, a mild, wordless minuet was worth the price for its relief from tedium, but then she thought better of it. She was still standing by the Ferris wheel, but once again directly opposite him. He saw her again through the workings and noticed her humming to herself as if on a moment's secret cues.

This time, as he approached, she stayed put, waving cheerfully to Warren and Michael on the ride. He saw a flash of wedding band and thought there was no point, except to talk to a human. But when he reached her, all he could manage was an embarrassed gargle. He looked quickly to the ground, laughing at himself, clearing his throat and reddening. When he looked up, she was smiling warmly. Her smile had every trait he imagined his own, nonprofessional one did: a friendly center, flirting corners, hinting, by a mixture of modesty and delight, that its owner was conscious to the toes.

"How's the weather?" Johanna asked him.

"Huh?"

"You're the weatherman, aren't you?"

"Oh. Fine. Terrific. *Hot.* I, uh—actually, that's not what I really do, you know."

She pursed her lips, trying to be kind. "It was hard to guess."

"Yeah, well—my name's Tyler, uh—*yours* is—"

"Johanna. You're at the Gila Public Information Office, aren't you?"

"Sort of. That's not what I do really either."

She tilted her head, bemused. "Why don't you do what you do?"

"That's a good question. Actually, I'm a grad student, sort of—Biochemistry, sort of. I'm hiding here on a fellowship."

"Sort of?" she asked. "What are you hiding from?"

"The war."

"Good place to hide. Do you work at the labs when you're not running tours?"

"No, uh, I guess I'm kind of hiding from that, too."

"Which is why you don't do what you do? If you did do what you do—what would you—?" And both started laughing.

Tyler shrugged, "I don't know. I was—I hope I'm not bothering you."

"Would you like to tell me why nobody's supposed to know about a whole mountain?"

"What're my alternatives? It's a secret, that's all. It's a dumb secret, so don't let it bother you."

"Just curious. You're the one who wanted to talk. Why do I get the feeling that the job of a Public Information Officer is to make sure no information gets to the public?"

He began to laugh, then assumed a dour expression. "That laugh was off the record. Mostly, you're right—it's PR and hooey. But it's our hooey, and a lot of people seem to love it."

She said, "Your turn to ask a question."

"Uh, you live around here?" And they both started to laugh again.

Warren took passing notice of their conversation as the ticket attendant collected another stub for a repeat ride. He couldn't remember the last time he'd seen her laugh. Then he watched them intently as the buckets lurched him upward and out of earshot again.

"What are you doing here?" Johanna asked.

"Playing hookey."

"Hookey," she repeated softly, more to herself. "When I was in high school I used to play hookey by going to the desert. Singing Beach Boy songs. I still do."

"Big beach," he said. "I guess it's a matter of taste. I used to go to the zoo."

"Really? Tell me, what do you know about aardvarks?"

He recoiled in surprise. "Aardvarks? Are we working our way to zebras?"

"Just aardvarks."

"Not a whole—" He gestured vaguely and lost his train of thought. Her eyes were dazzling, and the uncombed pile of hair drooped over her sunburnt ears. "Not, uh—not—" His fingertips went up to brush some strands from her face, and he blushed at his own rashness. "Excuse me." He wished he could drop his hand to touch her cheek, when something caught his attention beyond her. The quick snap of his head was startling, and he took a tentative step forward, confusing her. "Excuse—" he mumbled, brusquely shoving the Kewpie doll into her breast, brushing her aside as he burst past, breathing, "Oh, God," thinking he was the only person in the world with eyes.

A small boy in a blue-bibbed pair of jeans had reached out of his car on the Ferris wheel to swipe the ground as the gondola passed its perigee, and tumbled out. He hit the ground and the next car knocked him flat as it passed. The operator didn't notice: he was hustling up new customers. In that first moment, only Tyler Bowen and Warren Reigeluth knew something was wrong, and Warren was stuck in the gondola headed for the top, yelling for help.

Tyler ran the few yards to the spot and vaulted a low fence. The bystanders who saw the accident remained stunned, refusing to believe it, trying to rearrange the information signals until it all made sense with a different message. Ferris wheels do not hurt children any more than Santa Claus would beat a baby with a lollipop.

As the first clap of shouts and screams enveloped the area, and Warren's gondola reached the zenith, Tyler lay his body in a belly-flop dive on Michael Poulson's. A car passed over them and then Tyler scooped the boy up as the next one approached. It hit Tyler in the side and pitched him forward into the grassy gear area, onto his knees, still holding the boy. He fell on Michael, unhurt, and cushioned the boy as they hit the ground. Michael was bleeding profusely along the scalp and seemed unconscious. When the operator pulled the emergency stop cord, Warren was halfway down.

The screams attracted a Trooper in the Midway who broke into a fast trot when he saw other people flowing in the direction of the Ferris wheel. He signaled his partner to bring the ambulance which lay in wait for just such an emergency, and its siren attracted Baron Zermatt who followed closely after.

Tyler looked up and saw no help on anyone's face. Not knowing what to do, or even if the boy was alive, he decided to try mouth-to-mouth. Blood slipped down the boy's face and ran into his mouth, and Tyler had to suck it out and spit it free. He pinched the wound to staunch the bleeding, reassured as Michael screamed in pain and instinctively tried to push Tyler away. He's alive, screaming and fighting, Tyler thought, raising up to order someone to "get some *help,* will you!"

Two men soon arrived and placed the boy onto a stretcher, nearly covering his face with an oxygen mask. They wheeled the stretcher to an ambulance and lifted it in, shoving Tyler in as well. Then the ambulance began to roll slowly through the crowd, its siren a low animal moan. Suddenly it stopped and the back door was pulled open. Warren Reigeluth got in and someone in a white jacket told Tyler to get out. As he did, the State Troopers elbowed him back into the crowd.

As the ambulance pulled out of the melting hemisphere of people, Warren yelled out of its window to Johanna to follow in the car. "His sweater's in the Ferris wheel thing!" Warren shouted. But she didn't hear it, for she was already running to the parking lot.

Tyler ran back to the Ferris wheel and grabbed the sweater, then raced toward the parking lot. He saw her running, hugging her arms to her chest, squeezing the Kewpie doll. She hopped into a tan Volkswagen and pulled out. Tyler ran toward the exit to head her off, and just caught her as she came to the gate. "His sweater," Tyler said, breathless from the run.

Johanna looked at him quizzically for a moment. Tyler's face was dirty with the dust and Michael's saliva and blood, and she hardly recognized him. "Thank you," she said. "I'm sorry." She shook her head quickly and stepped on the gas.

"No, that's all—" Tyler said as she pulled into the street and raced away. "That's all," he repeated to himself. He stepped into the street and watched her rear window, partially obscured by decals, one of which said "Tombstone Center/Staff Parking." He wondered if she saw him in her rear-view mirror, diminishing, ever smaller. Strictly speaking, he supposed, he would never disappear, unless she turned a corner. She turned a corner and headed after the speeding emergency vehicle.

It was shortly before sundown when Baron Zermatt finally found Tyler at the Funland section. "Jesus, Babe," Zermatt whistled. "You are a mess. You want to get us all killed?"

"What are you raving about?"

"There are cops looking for you with accident reports. Operators want to buy you off or rub you out. Christ, if you get involved in a lawsuit and have to go under oath—boy, Gracie'll eat you alive."

"Where's the car?"

"It's a damned good thing we're not hitchhiking. Who'd ever pick you up looking like that?"

"Hey! I don't need this abuse. I nearly get my bean bopped off and I get shit for change."

"You want a medal? Fine. Keep it up. But do it when it counts: when the money's on the line and the whole world's wired in. Don't get busted up in some sideshow. You get the slammer for premature heroism, pal. And all the medals in the world won't get you in the Oval Office then."

"I don't want to be in the Oval Office, jerk."

"Everyone does! You don't? OK: you sit in the hall and I'll sit at the big desk and take your calls."

"You're out of your fucking mind."

"Babe, I'm going to make you a star. Get used to it. But don't make my job any harder—"

"You are out of your—you should have seen her, Bar. She's lovely."

"And married, from what I saw, with a kid in stitches. And you are now part of a very bad memory. Listen to the Baron; he knows women."

"You're crazy. You are just plain stark, staring—"

"Am I? You watch. In the meantime, just don't fondle the wrong people and blow the whole waxworks—"

"How about if I screw the experimental sheep?"

"Careful, pal. The Coke machines have ears. Never

say anything you don't want coming back at you in twenty years from a Senate Committee."

The Monday *Intelligencer* had a small story; and it said the injured child, "Michael Poulson of Mesa, was attending the Fair with his uncle, Warren Reigeluth, a Research Associate at the Tombstone Center for the Applied Social Sciences, and the boy's aunt, Mrs. Reigeluth, a reporter for this newspaper." Tyler was described as "an unidentified carnival worker" who "gave first aid on the scene until medical help arrived." Tyler wondered why his name and affiliation had been dropped. It was because Johanna had forgotten. No action was taken against the Ferris wheel.

Tyler called the hospital in Tucson to inquire about Michael, but they wouldn't give out information except to say the child had been released to his parents.

Baron Zermatt understood the hospital's procedure completely. "It's like they never tell you your own damned IQ or let you see your chart, either," he said. "And it's your own damned body. I'll tell you something. When I was a prefreshman on my way to Princeton, the Admissions types sent out requests to parents, asking them to list the strengths and weaknesses sonny would be bringing with him. Mine must've been the only ones who did, I swear."

"A short postcard, your strengths."

"You laugh. Boiled down to 'Kid comes from terrific home.' But the weaknesses!"

"Three pages, single-spaced—"

"Just about," Zermatt grumbled. "Hell, I didn't think my old man laid his paper down long enough to notice. Must've asked my mother. This, to an All-Ivy halfback in the Freshman Office who couldn't stay sober enough to get a real job! For two years the Dean used to pop that shit back at me, too. You know: 'Baron, we know you come from a fine home, and we are not unaware of your various problems—' "

"May I ask what prompted this outburst?" Tyler laughed, Baron having distracted him from thoughts about the child.

"Hospitals. It's the same—deans, parents—an interlocking directorate, a big horizontal monopoly. Now,

112

you can either join the cartel by growing older and moving in—or you take direct action, which has traditionally not been fruitful. Although in my case, I did manage to leaven the Dean's files before I left. But that's only because they trusted me to work in the Dean's Office by then."

Tyler's attention lapsed again. "You know what she said to me, what she asked, just before it happened?"

"My place or yours," Zermatt leered.

"If I knew anything about aardvarks," Tyler said.

Zermatt watched him blankly. "What'd you tell her?"

"What do I know about aardvarks? Strange girl."

In the next day's mail, Tyler received a short note:

Dear Mr. Bowen,
   It's a very small way of saying thank you for your help today, but if you are ever in Tucson and need someone to talk to still, my husband and I would be most happy if you'd come to dinner. It's a pleasure to be able to tell you that Michael only had a broken arm. In our family, the best place to drop us is on the head. I make no promises about the food, but I can promise not to ask you about aardvarks.
                              Very truly yours,
                              Johanna Reigeluth.
P.S. What *am* I to do with that rag doll?

It was hard to say where fact left off and legend began about Martin B. Gracie. It was known that he had been at Gila for some years, and prior to that had served at other installations which coveted privacy. It was also known that from this post there was nowhere to go but Washington. But Gracie's dream of dreams, a staff post on the National Security Council, seemed closed to him. Such positions went mainly to academic and political types, and some career military people, but rarely career security persons, men who, as Gracie often said, "gave their lives and the best part of themselves to their country."

Perhaps it was such remarks—midst the otherwise unalloyed loyalty of the man—which stimulated the irrepressible wits at Gila to mold Gracie Lore. It was known, for example, that as an enlistee in Korea the man had pulled down every medal for reckless valor in the catalogues. It was there he was first heard to bark as he swaggered around, replete with a newly won battlefield commission, "Here's Martin B. Gracie, Lieutenant, Infantry, Commanding!" No one ever had a chance to forget. "If you don't got a pair, you come see Martin B. Gracie, and he'll show you a pair you'll never forget." In his belt he was said to keep a cyanide spansule in case of capture. They said he still carried it in case he ran into reporters from the *New York Times*. Back then he also wore a pearl-handled revolver, which added to his maniacal, terrifying leadership aspect, and made him a cinch for Major someday.

Legend, or fact, there was no way to tell, held that one day, somehow, fortunately in private, the pistol misfired. Which is to say, fired. And only by the sheerest luck did it not blow off either of his legs.

What it did blow off all but wrecked Martin B. Gracie's sense of humor. Word was that it taxed the imagination of a team of surgeons, working in relays, and the resources of the Special Products Division of du Pont merely to replace what was lost with a prosthetic appurtenance.

As it was told around Crypto Club tables, and as Baron Zermatt told Tyler Bowen one evening over drinks, Gracie took the characteristically heroic route, telling his wife to divorce him. In a voice cracking with unaccustomed emotion, Gracie reputedly said, "It's all off. Over. Dead. Finished."

But she, not willing to yield him and the house, said, according to Zermatt, "Oh, we could have had such a damned good time together."

"Yes," he said. "Isn't it pretty to think so?"

And she said, "Eat me, you son-of-a-bitch," in Baron Zermatt's telling. "That really saved the game for her. She's quite happy. He's prick enough."

"How much of that is true?" Tyler asked.

"They're unnaturally happy. Fact. He's a *putz*. Fact."

"And they never adopted?"

"Gracie likes to say the men of Gila are his children. His days and nights are filled with the joys of drum-

114

ming them out as incompetents or risks. Keep yourself off both lists."

For those who didn't, the consequences could be similar to those that befell Len Tobias. He had been released from Gila Hospital after the Oh-Five brawl, but had gone back a few days later with a mysterious complaint. The symptoms indicated *N. gonococcus,* which made Martin B. Gracie equal parts angry and jealous. In short order Tobias found himself being interviewed by a colleague of Baron Zermatt's in the Law Office.

The young lawyer explained that if Tobias would plead nolo to the charge of "unauthorized association," things would go easy for him. As an example, he pointed to Milt Armstrong, who had suffered no loss of status for his part in the fight.

"Yeah, because he said I started it."

"He cooperated. You didn't."

"I was unconscious!"

"Now is your chance to cooperate. Save everyone a lot of paperwork."

"But I didn't do anything."

"The dispensary says you have a venereal infection."

"Yeah, but—isn't that confidential?"

"No but. It might have been confidential. It isn't anymore. It is now fact."

"What about my rights?" Tobias insisted.

"In an administrative matter? I wouldn't categorize it by saying you have a wild excess of them. And most of all, you have this infection."

"Is that a crime?"

"Yes and no. Having it isn't, per se. Conspiring to acquire it from person or persons unknown—and you can't get a toilet seat admitted into evidence."

"Aw, come on, this is silly."

"You don't seem to understand the gravity of the charge against you. You have Victor Dog. Now, if you would like to plead sodomy—find two others and we can talk. Do you have medication?"

"Yes."

"May I see it?" the legal staffer asked. Tobias handed over a vial of tetracycline pills, and the man dropped them into a manila envelope. "I'm afraid we'll have to put this under seal until this matter is disposed of. You'd be destroying evidence." Tobias slumped in his seat and the legal staffer told him to "sit up straight. Where do you think you are?"

So Len Tobias, acknowledging that they had him by the short hairs, took his medicine. That is, he did not contest the allegations against him, and received his medicine back. He was transferred to duty as a laborer loading chemicals on the docks for the laboratories. It was a Tombstone OR theory that punishment for the white-collar people when they needed straightening out could best be accomplished by the simple expedient of changing their station in life, and the color of their collar, for a brief period.

Tyler Bowen walked past Tobias on his way to a biology and chemistry lecture, not recognizing him for his shambling look and workman's overalls. Nor did Tobias know Bowen, having been insensate when Tyler intervened in the fight.

Bowen stopped to lean against a wall and finish reading his mail. His friend Saint Paul Hooper had sent him a letter which he'd shared with Baron Zermatt over coffee that morning.

Tyler had been a sophomore dorm counselor at Cornell when he first came across Paul Hooper, a bite-sized freshman from Minnesota temporarily known as Small Paul. One night during Fall exam week, Small Paul Hooper came into Bowen's room glassy-eyed, stoned, and dripping wet. He had been out in a thunderstorm talking with his "Friend." It was six-to-five-pick-'em in the dorm whether Paul's Friend would speak in tongues of lightning and assume Paul straightaways to Heaven. On his way to an oxygen tent, he stopped in to see Tyler Bowen, who complained that Paul was making a mess on the floor.

"I'm just doing the Lord's bidding," Paul said.

"You sure He's got so much free time He—sorry, *He*—could bother to send some half-pint freshman to drip on my shag rug?"

Paul conferred skyward—to an electric light on the ceiling, strictly speaking—for a moment, and replied, "Yes." He insisted that Tyler was being baptised through him.

"You're baptising my shag rug, chowderhead—and I've already been. I need this like another Comparative Anatomy final, Hooper." Yet Paul's studied perverseness appealed to Tyler, and they soon became best friends, though the only religious act he could get Tyler to try was his first baptism of marijuana. While others saw Paul as a confirmed lunatic, Tyler valued him as a very sane order of maniac, a peculiarly motivated guy, who had anointed himself Tyler Bowen's conscience. And as consciences went, he had his compensations: Paul was a devoted Promiscuite, suffering from what Tyler called the "Heartbreak of Satyriasis."

When a fight caused Tyler to write a letter to the Dean in the name of his own roommate, saying that he, the roommate, could not stand living with Tyler Bowen and wanted out, which caused the roommate to be suddenly removed, Tyler invited Saint Paul, though only a freshman, to move in.

It was his religious fanaticism which led people to dub him Saint even though Paul often confined his passion to pragmatic forms: he used his tolerance for nearly any crackpot belief to score his way through both the Eastern freaks and the higher echelons of the Campus Crusade for Christ. "I can believe sixteen impossible things before lunch," he often said, "if necessary." At other times he restricted his activities to very reasonable expressions of faith: during the flu season he only screwed Christian Scientists.

Because of his size and his home town, Minneapolis, and his studied Swedish accent, largely derived from an overdose of Ingmar Bergman movies ("English should have melody as well as lyrics," he insisted), people began to call him Saint Paul Mini-Hooper. It seemed to fit.

He could quote scripture for his purposes and was fond of statements which seemed biblical, though no one could find their source: "Verily, I have lain with over five score women and if their mean age be one score I have scored with two millennia of womanhood in sum—two thousand belly-annums, four thousand nipple-years! A bridge of thighs from Jesus to me! And lo, I still know not wherefor and what they do want." As a Classics major he was fiercely gifted, and a difficult match for anyone who caught him in a debate on matters of morals and ethics. Saint Paul spewed forth aphorisms and ancient wisdom to support his causes, in the unanswerable original. He gave the Dean a case of ileitus. Once, in a debate, Saint Paul had whipped the students into a froth with a succession of Latin slogans, leaving the Dean lathered, whimpering French proverbs and homilies until a chaplain led him off. It was obvious, the *Cornell Daily Sun* wrote, they didn't speak the same language.

Saint Paul wrote: "Bad gnus for moderate man, Babe." Tyler scanned the rest of Saint Paul's letter for that bad news but still only found tracks of Saint Paul's imagination. "Ty, M'Guy," the letter said, "you know we have always maintained that there is a small but convincing likelihood that you are the Big Guy's Nephew. I know, you claim dumb luck. But it won't wash. And what do you think—I'm having a talk with Him last week and I think you've got the Big Fella sore. He wouldn't be mad if He didn't *care*. I think He wants you to Cut the Crap, whatever it is. The way He put it, and I quote, was 'A fucking abomination in the sight of Me is what it is.' Mumbled something about 'fixing that boy's wagon for good.' There were floods in the lowlands, Ty. I'll see what I can do to patch it up. (He used to speak so highly of you.) But if it starts raining, stay indoors, Skip. OK?"

When Tyler had shown the note to Zermatt, Baron said, "If that's supposed to be a direct quote, He's written better stuff."

"Don't look at me. Paul gets these notes, not me. He just passes 'em on. The consensus is—well, nobody knows where he gets 'em from. The consensus is he's in great need of psychiatric help. I for one can attest that he hasn't spent a lucid day since 1965. But sometimes he's pretty canny. Predicts some things right on the nose; you've got to hedge your bets just a little."

The profound belief of most of Saint Paul's fellow students was that his frequent cryptic messages were less than Divine in origin. Even Cornell's Catholic Chaplain, who was on the lam much of the time, had some doubts. Most agreed that Saint Paul was "brilliant, but flawed." Once, he'd gotten into an argument with the goalie of the lacrosse team. Observers commented, after Saint Paul had been decked by a straight left hand, that he was "brilliant, but floored."

The letter was dispiriting to Tyler Bowen, as his best friend and supporter seemed to despair of his redemption. And hadn't they always been a team? Hadn't they used hypodermic syringes to inject the football squad oranges with vodka? Hadn't they, together, pulled many beards of several deans? Hadn't they contrived to found a Great Tradition at Cornell by getting an acid-freak girl from Elmira College to ball with Paul on the Sage Chapel roof facing the Engineering Quadrangle? Hadn't Paul's neglected girl friend guessed who it was when she heard, and called the Ithaca Fire Department, sending the entire event deep into the annals of Ithaca History? They had conspired on many an adventure. Had Tyler grown older, apart, made too sudden and thorough a compromise? Paul was now treating him like a lost sheep, as though he really knew what Tyler was doing.

Tyler slipped into the amphitheater, late, through the back door. He was nearly reconciled to taking license with truth; it was no more, ultimately, than rearranging Christmas ornaments on the tree. And the alternatives the world outside presented were equivalently unacceptable: service in or resistance to the war. He was not predisposed to radical action, for most of all he was marked as an inheritor of society's best benefits. He knew that he had a spot, however far down the line, on the list of Presidential succession. There was no reason to overthrow that. The small dissemblances and perversions required of him in the national interest were in his interest, too. The previous week he'd shepherded a flock of "opinion leaders" from favored industries and institutions through the labs, and suffered through a series of staggeringly dull dinner-seminars. A few had left him their cards, suggesting he call when he was out in the job market.

But with each step in his growing grasp of his job, as he impressed the Director of Public Information with his capacities, he also became more familiar with

119

things he wished to remain ignorant of. Here, in this classroom, was something personally subversive.

Tyler was there to pick up the cudgels of a colleague who'd gone on home leave. He had to prepare reports for a new group of visitors to take home and deliver as their own. This group came mostly from government quarters: agency liaisons, military representatives, select staff from trustworthy congressional supporters, administrators from friendly research installations; carnivores from police and security organizations, obligors from strategic reserve elements; and perhaps a few herbivores, like Bowen, who bought in to avoid impersonal mayhem. As he eased into his seat in the back row he wondered if he hadn't bought in to a more subtle and thorough kind of murder. For these guests were being briefed on what the best minds of the nation were up to. Some honed malign skills indeed, laboring to find ways to cause earthquakes in the service of country, unraveling the world with their wits. Some pursued equally deadly trades, and some pursued those who worked at those trades. Some, like Tyler Bowen, wrote alibis for them all. Most he saw one day and never again, in a community square dance of training and work: do-si-do and off again. Zermatt he saw frequently, for the Law Office's job was, with Security's, close to his own: keeping the lid on. Zermatt's attitude was completely adaptive: "It's a living," he shrugged.

Down front, the biology instructor lectured with fine flourishes, peddling Dark Angel wares to the entranced. A team of social scientists at Tombstone had deduced the best way to sell this stuff was to make it fun, and to some it was. Behind the instructor and on the flanking walls was an exquisitely mapped-out chart of the cornucopia of pathogens ready to be employed as the nation saw fit, a brightly colored medieval nosology splayed on the pastel-green chalkboards. There were zootoxins for the fauna, phytotoxins from the flora; partially obscured by the instructor himself were the most domesticated arthropod vectors.

"Maybe you'd like a fungus," the man offered. "Not your common household variety, no sir. More like something to go to a masquerade dressed as a cancerous tree. Or maybe you want to cover somebody with

120

toadstools?—" He tapped his finger against the board on the spot where he had written *"Phytophthora infestans*—late blight of potato" and waved softly over *"Piricularia oryzae*—rice blast," *"Erysiphe graminis*—powdery cereal mildew," and *"Erwinia carotovara*—bacterial soft rot." "Grass greener on your neighbor's lawn?" the man asked. "Make it browner with herbicidal foams. Warring with an agrarian nation?" He flicked his head jauntily toward the anti-plant-and-cattle bacteria.

Tyler was impressed by the orderliness of the man's blackboard work, although his classroom manner was a bit flamboyant.

By determined daydreaming, Tyler managed to finesse the more depraved parts of the biology lecture, and just as well. What he did hear was enough. His study and love of biochemistry formed the cornerstone of his faith. He believed in sense, and beyond that, in the synthetic integrity of natural processes, that against all odds and discouragements nature worked to build and organize, to reach sentience and well-being. There was a benign conspiracy of elements which railed against oblivion, an optimism in the energy of life. But here was dismal contrary news. Flipping through the *Review Manual* for some small show of grace or mercy he found a choice paragraph which made him wonder what colleague had been set to the task of composing it; and what up-tempo revision of it would be required of him soon:

4. FEASIBILITY AND MISCONCEPTIONS OF BIOLOGICAL AGENT EMPLOYMENT

   a. Biological agents have not been employed as major weapons in modern warfare. However, there is much evidence to convince the most hypercritical skeptic that, under certain circumstances, the intentional use of pathogens to cause casualties in a target population is feasible. Understandably, new and untried methods of warfare lend themselves to a sensationalism and exaggeration. History, through the ages, has a tendency of emphasizing mankind's suffering as a result of disease from such killers as bubonic plague, typhus, yellow fever, cholera, diphtheria, and

121

smallpox. "Black Death," or plague, caused a pandemic in Europe from 1347 to 1352 during which it was estimated to have killed approximately one-fourth (25,000,000) of Europe's population. Unfortunately, some writers, either through incomplete knowledge or as a means of drawing attention, adopt extreme positions. On the one hand, the "Black Death" example is one which illustrates that pathogens as military agents have their place in a military arsenal. On the other hand, it also illustrates that disease if unleashed on a populated area will not completely exterminate the inhabitants as some would have you believe. Some writers attach a science-fiction connotation of savagery, horror, and complete decimation of a population to the intentional use of biological agents. And still, for reasons difficult to understand, individuals are ready and willing to accept the use of conventional weapons such as flame-throwers, or even the employment of nuclear weapons, but are unable to accept the use of "germs" as a means of gaining a military advantage.

Indeed, he realized, the penalties of doing his job poorly were only exceeded by those for doing it well. If he washed out as an information officer, they'd probably put him to this sort of human tape-looping; eminent success might win him a research assistantship. And the only way to top those, he imagined, was to swallow pointed objects.

"So don't give the flu back to the Asians," the instructor exhorted the class in his spirited conclusion. "You've got so many colorful choices!" His arms swung out at both sides as though he were about to flap off in a cape, while behind him strobed foot-and-mouth and rinderpest, Rift Valley fever; simple vesicular stomatitis, encephalomyelitis; hog cholera, African swine fever, fowl plague. "You can send Newcastle disease to Coaltown, and cold sores *(Herpes simplex)* to Newcastle!" Even Bowen's attention was seduced by all this travelogue nomenclature; it was arresting for its exotic promise of relief: Bombay dung beetle infestation, Trobriand Island elephantiasis, Dipleptic Mensis. There were available kidney diseases which, the joke went, could start a regatta at Henle's loop. It was jolly stuff to sprinkle on parched imaginations. Then the biology lecturer attempted a grand segue, fulfilling a promise he'd made to his chemical counterpart who'd complained that, compared to biology, chemistry left the classes cold. "Now then," he yelled, hastily trotting over to a red-chalked section of his elaborate display, "if you really want to understand Brucellosis and botulinum toxins," rapping his knuckles against them on the slate, "as well as they understand *you,* the only way is to ask 'How do they work?' Thought you'd never ask. And if you're going to travel in high defoliation circles—" his other arm flung backwards to pass over diagrams of 2,4,5-T and IPC—"then you must pay attention to the next lecture. It's very sexy. I say this as a biologist: Germs are cute; but molecules, in the final analysis, are where it's at."

Still, the chemistry lecturer was a surpassing disappointment, and quickly lost the class of esteemed visitors to pre-lunch restlessness and reflexive resistance to anything scientific that could not be made to have personality; it took a stretch of the imagination, but disease names were proper nouns of the sort one might give to children. Not so, chemical compounds. There was a charm to *Escherichia* that was lacking in sulphur. "If you will check the chart in the back of your books," the lecturer nearly begged, as they opened a gate-fold compendium of poisons, "you will see why we can say that not all the fruits of victory from the last war are employed in the space race. How can I justify that statement?" He looked down at his notes and read with care. "What are the shared traits of all these compounds?" He was proving them geniuses at Tombstone, for a replacement chemistry lecture was already being readied. "One: no matter what else they do, they make you throw up. Even if your teeth are falling out, you are flashing lunch. That is a classic German signature. And two: they all tend—militate—toward 'maximum pain and suffering.' " He smiled. Well begun was half done.

Someone came in late and the momentary distraction made the whole class swivel, while the man up front pimped for the splendors of phosgene, which "causes so much lung secretion its victims die standing up, drowned." Tyler shook his head and sighed. "Remember Caryl Chessman?" the shrill instructor asked. "How many of you know what they gave him? It was—*right* —hydrogen cyanide, though in some places they prefer cyanogen chloride." The man erased part of the biology tree—salmonella, Bullis, masculatum, trench—to put the structural formulas for HCN and CNCl on the board. As he erased, Tyler Bowen thought to himself that it was the most humane act yet committed in that room.

The man waved contemptuously at the remaining biological menaces and tapped the HCN for emphasis. "That," he pronounced, "is a heap of trouble for the body. Even its cure, amyl nitrite or sodium thiosulfate, can kill you in the wrong dosage, without symptoms." Now the class was riveted. No more valence charts and resonance concepts. This was the straight stuff.

"What happens is this. There is an enzyme—" he wrote it on the blackboard in expert backhand strokes —"Cytochrome oxidase. Say it." They pronounced it like children. "Now pay attention to this. This enzyme hangs around the body helping most of us utilize oxygen . . ." Tyler stared resolutely out the window into the desert sunshine; he could have been thinking of the biological elegance which arrayed itself for the purpose of oxygen processing, how oxygen, a most notorious and corrosive poison to much of life, became the very stuff of higher life; how similar were the mutable proteins hemoglobin and chlorophyll, and how radically opposite in effect; how simple, yet complex, the uses of porophyrins, sugar and the phosphates in the energy storage and release cycles, and all of it dependent on oxygen for kindling; the eons it took the atmosphere to fill with sufficient oxygen and how its early noxious gases came to become oxygen producers and consumers, all in balance, with a cap of triatomic oxygen, ozone, to shield them all from necrotic rays. How fragile was that balance, how intimate the helix-weave of nourishment and poison: the small window in a killing range that let organic things emerge; the whole cosmology of body chemistry, so delicately contrived and yet so hardy, weathering so many rude shocks, but

124

then succumbing to the barest tipping of the scales. He floated in this rapture, conscious of the miracle circus in his veins and its kinship to all things around him, as the instructor bore on. "Now I say this enzyme, cytochrome oxidase, helps us utilize oxygen. The majority of us, that is. A small minority are getting no help at all, because here come all those—" he pointed to the structural diagram—"Hs and Cs and Ns and Os. And maybe a little Cl, too. Now if it's an old darkroom where this is happening, you're in luck. Reach for the fixer. Sodium thiosulfate. If not: *you're* fixed."

Tyler's thoughts coincided with the instructor's just then, as the man explained how the ironies were just beginning. "If you took all these atoms and rearranged them—" He drew lines from the appropriate positions to a new configuration, nearly an anagram of the first —"you could work up a nice batch of amino acids, and maybe some proteins." The audience muttered, impressed with the magic. "But not today. First, there's this smell, and the olfactory indicator is—look it up— peach kernels. Sweet and lovely. Then, breathing speeds up, and male subjects develop erections. It's Hydrogen Cyanide! On the other hand, cyanogen chloride makes your breathing slow down. Which is swell, because the less you get the healthier you stay— for a while anyway."

"What does it smell like?" someone called.

"Well now, if the first was peaches, would you bet that this is plums?" He smiled impishly. "Check your manuals and you'll see. It says 'causes such choking and tearing that its rather disagreeable odor usually goes unnoticed.' Furthermore it penetrates gas masks and in sufficient doses can cause sudden death without symptoms."

Suddenly he fixed them with a grim look. "None of this, regardless of what you may have read, is much fun to watch. It's disgusting. And all the victim does is object a little and die a lot. Often he doesn't object. It's not very dramatic and makes you unmindful of just what kind of transformation is occurring. To really get a handle on that you'd have to look at Insidious Blister Agents. They are uniformly cruel and unusual. And

125

slow enough to enjoy. Slower than slow. Like arsine—arsenic trihydride: it gives you anemia."

"What does that smell like?" someone asked, part of the Socratic ritual.

"Garlic."

"Jesus."

"It isn't used much any more," the man explained, "because it has this unfortunate tendency of exploding in its storage canisters—and has therefore acquired a very bad rep. But it smells like garlic, so if you're in the neighborhood, and you smell garlic—well, if you're lucky, it's just a Mafia luncheon in the back room. But if you don't smell that real good mozzarella soon, and it gets chilly but it's August, and if you start vomiting a great deal, you'd better start eating well and not stop for about three years."

More of this Tyler could not take that morning, so he shuffled through his briefcase and pulled out a letter pad in which he had placed, as a reminder, the first letter he'd received from his brother since Willie'd left Fort Ord. The return address did not say "Republic of Vietnam" or anything so "controversial." Just Willie's name, rank, serial number and "APO/SFO." Something about its efficient address troubled Tyler, that very incompleteness: what if the world caught fire? How would he ever locate his brother and drag him out? Yet that very "APO/SFO" notation meant he'd not been able to stop his brother from walking into an already flaming world.

Saint Paul had another approach: he and a caravan of students, Paul had written, were going on a trip to levitate the Pentagon. Tyler harbored no doubt they were going on a trip. But he wondered whether they would discover what he already felt: that they lived in a glass bottle with a pentagonal stopper, little genii, possessed.

Both Bowens were beyond the comforting logic of civilization. Both had taken the best offers bad circumstances made, convinced their inherent luck would see them through—but both offers stank.

No thunderbolt loomed in the wings, despite Saint Paul's earlier warnings, to change Tyler's fortune. No special letter or superoffer, to convert this straw to gold. Indeed, the only women he had touched in three months turned to dross in the touching. And if there was anything Tyler Bowen held as a supernatural belief, it was that his life would not find its adult shape until some magic, golden woman came along to give it compulsive meaning. Then he'd see himself become himself, fulfilling every destiny and promise. So, like his younger brother, he felt indefinitely postponed from his life's fruition. Some deal this was; though, unlike Willie's, his was easier to outlive.

. . . and I'll tell you one thing, I'm not gonna let nobody send me home in a bag, that's for sure. Not to save this stinking half of the world. And sure as hell not to save my buddies. Not to save some poor asshole's dreams of a ranch house and a Mustang from melting with his bones. None of that shit for me, thanks. If I am to get my name in the papers, it'll be for a string of selectively discriminating rapes. Fuck of a lot better than diedofhiswounds.

Apparently, other than picking up the pieces, my special military skill is waiting. That's what they have me doing all the time: all-the-fucking-time waiting. In between waiting is nothing. Which is OK with me. It's like you say, reading the big fortune cookie to find out what's on tap for the next 24. You just wait for some mad-assed general to unzip his plans for tomorrow, and hope he didn't write you down in the wrong book. If he feels like getting out of bed.

. . . If I ever see a medal, I sure hope it's not like this guy I know who stepped on a mine and traded his ass for a Purple Heart. Blew his melons clear across the highlands and now he's got this pretty ivory cameo of George Washington to wear instead. The man who cannot tell a lie goes to the guy who cannot get a lay. (Keep your tin shit, Lyndon, give me back mah cheeks!) Most likely I'll haul some guy in on my back and get my head lopped off by a sentry. It'll turn out the guy was aced—and I'll get the PH badge for meritorious pallbearing, above duty and beneath stupidity, eh? Well, don't you fret, big bro, because there isn't any of that shit going down. The only VC I ever saw close up was dead on Huntley-Brinkley, and the biggest noise around here is my friend's battery tape deck with its music to get offed by (he inherited it). One big noise was this punk Lieutenant, but a few of us straightened him out with simply stated death threats. He's OK now. Haven't heard from Gooktown Charlie-san—or even Mom and Dad. (Or you! Come on, Babe, write me, please!) Did Mack let Animal screw her again? Any more grandbrats? Tell her to write, too. Tell that pigdog Animal husband of hers to fuck himself and come on over and fight. Tell Mom to wish the old Vampire happy birthday for me and buy him a present and I'll pay her back as soon as I can find a guy to bury with change in his pockets.

Jungle rot starts in your head. So I'm going to do some dope now. Adios, you yellow-bellied lucky sort-of-civilian.

The chemistry instructor was having his own difficulties staying with his material. He'd cited many colorful examples to maintain class interest, but it was hopeless. He even tried pretending a perverse fondness for the fiendish armamentarium, but it was much too arch to maintain. And, like Bowen, his enthusiasm was restricted to the chemical process itself. So he found it hard, ultimately, to mask his disapproval of the sadistic twists which changed altogether happy energy bondings to deadly arrangements.

"In my Johnny-come-lately opinion, ever-popular classic distilled mustard gas may be the all-time champ," the instructor said. "Basically, it sears and blisters the lungs and makes your skin crawl. Your flesh tries to make a fast getaway from your body."

"Why?" one of the attendees asked, amid snickers as though he'd broached a theological matter.

"Because inside you've got a breakdown of cell mitosis and other functions and you've got hemorrhagic diarrhea, and your skin has, to all intents, been set on fire. You are a hero to bacteria. A moveable feast." They shuddered at the images but turning away from the lecturer was equally painful, for along the side blackboards was the whole biology curriculum: Characteristics of micro-organisms, growth, reproduction, survival, inhibition; their forms: bacteria, rickettsiae, viruses, fungi and protozoa; the toxins; vectors; infection and immunity, suppression of immunity; herbicides, defoliants; dissemination methods (aerosol, vector cutaneous, sabotage); targeting and detection—and a bushy chart of the specific biological agents that would have made Darwin and Linnaeus proud:

Bacillus anthracis (anthrax), *Shigella* (bacillary dysentery), *Brucella, Vibrio comma* (cholera), *Corynebacterium diphtheriae, Pasteurella tularensis* (tularemia), and *P. pestis* (plague); *Actinobacillus mallei* (glanders), *Pseudomonas pseudomallei* (melioidosis), the *Salmonellae: S. typhosa, S. paratyphi, S. schottmuelleri* and *S. typhimurium, Mycobacterium tuberculosis; Rickettsia prowazeki* (epidemic typhus), *R. mooseri* (endemic typhus), *R. tsutsugamushi* (scrub typhus), *R. rickettsii* (Rocky Mountain spotted fever); *Coxiella burneti* (Q. fever); *Psittacosis* (parrot fever), *Encephalitis* and *Encephalomyelitis; Influenza* (la grippe), *Variola virus* (smallpox), yellow fever, dengue fever, hepatitis. And the fungi he had earlier been cavalierly bandying: *Coccidioides immitis, Histoplasma capsulatum,* and *Nocardia asteroides.*

"It's a funny thing," the chemistry lecturer said quietly, almost sadly, as though in regret at using snake-oil techniques to sell not balm but snakes, "but nature works overtime to tip us off to what's good and bad, arranging things so we don't get hurt. You know, our sweet tooth carries us to sugary foods. Sex gets us reproducing. It all works so well. Even when things are unhealthy—and that, too, is part of the plan—there's a clue. Most natural poisons taste bitter or sour, or sting in some way. If it's odorless and defenseless generally, it's a patent process. Even a rattler gives a warning. . . ."

It was the lowering of the lecturer's voice that drew Bowen's attention back from writing his letter. "It used to be SOP," the lecturer confided, "for everyone involved with these compounds, and everyone in the military, to experience it by having a drop of mustard gas placed ever so gently on his wrist, to see what it's

129

like. But, you know the times. An angry horde of mothers and Congressmen made them cut it out. The claim was it was a budget nuisance, but I myself think too many people remembered some Polish cities with ghastly names and . . . So, it's just another small but incredibly painful experience denied us by the bleeding hearts." A thankful pair of eyes in the front row rolled heavenward, and the lecturer winked at him paternally, as though to say it was just a scary campfire story between middle-aged men. But its truth was indisputable.

On the blackboard were the formulas of the mustard varieties: nitrogen mustard, with its fishy smell and its cousin that tended to cause bronchopneumonia within a day; mustard-lewisite, combining all mustard's meanness with the viler attributes of lewisite; and one that, as though seeking a symptomatic metaphor, "could knock your eyes out, or at least the corneas," he'd said. Blood agents, incapacitating agents, tear agents. It all swam in chalk before them. And all those "olfactory parameters," the characteristic odors, so redoubtably whimsical: fruity, geraniumlike, apple blossom, pepper, soured milk, soapy, camphor, new-mown hay, bitter almond, flypaper. "These are generally aliphatic acid groups," the instructor had explained. "Pheromones, they're called in animals, sex-attractants. We're working on some stuff that comes off the line smelling like a woman. You wouldn't know it consciously, but your body would. Your nose would send the message, and after all it's your body chemistry we're talking to, not you. You'd modify your behavior in that regard and you'd go happily, ever after, whether you thought so or not. Against this, the only defense is an army entirely made of queers. Which somehow brings us to the two boys that've come into great repute in overseas quarters among our armed forces: adamsite and lewisite. They are an unnatural act. Very simple really. Adamsite, puke for a week. Lewisite, on the other hand is, as many of you know, less kind. Lewisite gives you cold symptoms." There was some muttering in confusion by the listeners, which only signaled to the lecturer that they had paid close attention. "Yes, it causes cold symptoms and is less humane. Because

130

it also causes, I feel obliged to point out in footnote, systemic poisoning, pulmonary edema, permanent blindness, deep burns, cell poisoning, nausea and death."

"Is that all?" someone laughed as the buzzer went off.

"I should think that would be enough. It also causes depression. Understandably. Oh, by the way, I think you should know our adversaries are every bit as advanced as we are. Their Gretcha-44 series is quite comparable to lewisite and distilled mustard. As for its smell: . . . think of, well, think of a Big Mac, Coke, and a side of french."

They filed out, shaking their heads like sophomores who had just been led through a tour of the dirty parts of Chaucer, nodding "Good lecture," one by one.

Tyler sat in the back until the class emptied, trying to collect his thoughts. There was some truth to the notion that only man-made poisons were odorless or seductively perfumed. But looking for morality lessons in natural events was a tricky business: after all, carbon monoxide, whether belched from immoral engines or naturally occurring, bonded with hemoglobin more readily than oxygen, and killed without warning. Strontium-90 was more chemically active than calcium, replacing bones with radioactive, carcinogenic, flaky talc. Where was the morality in that losing footrace, except to say that these were largely products of man's manipulations?

Now he was not even sure that his own gifts did not have their ultimate effect in deadly ends.

WARREN WAS FURIOUS. JOHANNA HAD spent the evening stalking around the house in sullen silence after a quarrel they'd had. Now she was engaged in a puttering around he called "sarcastic cleaning." He'd gone into the kitchen to get something to drink and found, taped to the refrigerator door, a paragraph in Johanna's hand:

It's among the intelligentsia and especially among those who like to play with thought and concepts without really taking part in the cultural endeavors of their epoch that we find the glib compulsion to explain everything and understand nothing.

—Joost A. M. Meerloo, *The Rape of the Mind*

He stormed back into the living room, demanding, "Where'd you get that? You pulled that from one of the books on my desk!"

"I was straightening up and it was open—"

"Johanna, I'm going to try and reason with you, but it's getting harder."

"Try."

"You are putting me in an impossible position. Do you want me to have to say it?"

"No."

"You want me to quit? Will that make it better? I will. Where do you want me to go? What would you have me do? Will you be happier if I get drafted?"

"No."

"Then what?"

"It's—nothing. Oh, I don't know. I'm sorry."

"No you're not."

"I said I was."

"But you're not. Tomorrow it'll be something else. Dammit! Sit still a minute. You're doing an absolutely classic thing."

"I'm not a case study, Warren."

"You're blaming me for a situation you asked me to be agent for. One you created."

"I created!"

"Dammit, yes. You want security. You want to be held and taken care of and appreciated. I accept—"

"I have never heard such swill in all my life!"

"Deny it, but it's true. I give you an island of stability. Go swim off, splash around. But you know there's dry land behind you. OK, quit your job. Become a hippie or something. Whatever makes you happy—but do it quick—"

"Oh, Warren, it's just—forget about it. I don't want to talk about it any more."

"I do. You never want to talk about it."

"I started it and I'm sorry."

"You can end an argument, Johanna. It doesn't mean you've won. You really don't see what you're doing. You're adopting strategies that don't come close to getting you what you should want."

"What I *should!* You can bully someone all day, Warren. It doesn't mean you're right."

"I'd be angry if I thought you were serious."

"I *am* serious. I'm so serious I might just leave."

"To what? To the next thing you won't be satisfied with? Last year you complained because we were 'defined by course catalogues.' This year it's something else. What'll it be next year?"

"Nothing. I'm sorry."

It was already too late.

When he first got to know Johanna, Warren Reigeluth had been in a position odd for one so full of drive as he—flat on his back. She was then a junior in high school and he a whiz-kid sophomore at Stanford, wowing the Political Science Department, whizzing himself into mononucleosis. He spent the spring semester of 1962 recuperating at home in Salt Lake City, wishing he had someone to tell how furious he was at what Kennedy had done to Big Steel.

Carl Poulson lived down the street and was friendly with the Reigeluths. Although Carl was an Episcopalian, they, Mormons, put him up for membership in their country club—three times, until he was accepted. During Warren's illness, as a good neighbor, Carl dropped by from time to time for a visit. Warren's parents had determined that even illness should be gainfully employed, so Warren was taking some courses at home to keep his class standing. Carl would talk to him about one of them, Science for Humanists, a requirement of all liberal arts students, easing him over some conceptual humps; Carl found the name of the course mildly insulting.

The Reigeluths, whose eyes Warren was the apple of, were Salt Lake City's apotheosis. They were devout, hard-working, no-nonsense citizens. They believed in the Church of Jesus Christ of Latter-Day Saints and 10 percent tax-free municipals. They respected all credentialed professionals and all duly constituted authority. And they were sublimely intolerant of anyone ignorant of the truth as revealed to Joseph Smith by the Angel Moroni on Hill Commorah in Palmyra, New York. Mr. Reigeluth once thought he saw a flying saucer, but kept it to himself. Warren, they despaired in modest amounts, was a jack-Mormon, whose soul was endangered by a reluctance to attend any but Christmas services at the Temple, by a collegiate taste for grain alcohol, and a flat refusal to do missionary work. Other than that, his mother said, he was the perfect son.

Carl Poulson was considered by the Reigeluths to be a perfect gentleman, although strictly speaking a heathen barbarian infidel. He was just the thing for Mrs. Reigeluth's single friends when they needed a fourth for bridge. He rarely mentioned how much he detested bridge. Nor did he ever mention his reactions to the Temple Square displays for the propagation of the faith, to which he was repeatedly taken after concerts at the Tabernacle: they all depicted blue-eyed Jesuses with altogether Ashkenazic Patriarchs; it seemed wholly and naively American, unabashedly the insurance policy of religions.

During Easter that year, 1962, Johanna Poulson was visiting her father. Her brothers had made brief refueling stops during their semester breaks the week before, negotiating never-to-be-repaid loans and then departing. Johanna was Carl's real Easter present, and she proceeded to take over the running of his household for two weeks. She also filled in ably for Carl as a tutor, to Warren's delight and embarrassment.

Though only a high school student, she knew this material well, teasing Warren that it was "kid stuff." To demonstrate, she used some of her father's old stories and jingles. Warren's recovery and the learning process were both speeded considerably by his entrancement with her. He had seen her in passing over the years since 1954, and each year she looked prettier. But in the last year a quantum leap had occurred. His feelings toward her, always those of a neighborly surrogate older brother, also changed radically. Her skin shone and stretched tightly over long and graceful swimmer's muscles. Her quick smile and dancing eyes made her seem the embodiment of everything his temporary anemia denied him. Behind those eyes there seemed to be small fires of demonic light, and at times Warren thought she must know what effect she had on him, was toying with him.

Each night he anguished over lost opportunities to say bright things the day before, worried that she would not show up the next day, prepared clever remarks he never found a chance to use when she did show up. He assumed himself ballast, to be left behind when impatience spun her toward new, more rewarding adventures. Yet every day, for two weeks, she returned, and every day Warren was overwhelmed by some new marvel in her character. By turns she was lively, as though her thoughts were ruled by quixotic dervishes, then considerate and calming, alternating moods when he least expected it, but always when he most needed it. She was funny and friendly and intelligent. She was young, but had a serene sense of herself. And he was flat on his rump, under her spell. He wished he could lock her in the cellar like a wine bottle, or a savings certificate, to be drawn on when she reached acceptable maturity. He ached. By every measure and index she was everything he valued in a woman: smart (maybe smarter than he was, he shuddered), poised, and, without being self-conscious or vain, she was one good-looking girl. She gave no second thought to the unfairness of so many gifts when half the planet hungered for a single one. She was just herself and wore it well.

Every part of her touched his imagination and turned him weak: her peach-colored skin and graceful limbs, her way of walking. It was, curiously, her teeth that appealed to him especially: tiny, baby teeth, with a modest, almost imperceptible space between the front two, and a slight chip on one which made her smile all the more dynamic. Johanna's ears were small

135

and the part of her most prone to blushing. They seemed to Warren public versions of her breasts, fine and round and economical in design. He wanted to know more about each.

As for Johanna's face, there was where his chief problem rested. When he looked at her he could not stop looking. She would be telling him about Lagrange's formulations and sense his attention wandering, and his gaze focusing. "What are you doing?" she'd ask, and he would snap back, "Um, uh, nothing. Nothing. Oh, yeah, right——" Her face moved like a body, expressing too many things with every angle. It spoke to itself while it spoke to him, losing him in its many messages. When she smiled her face flared up, her mouth quivering to expose her lower teeth, as if she'd encountered something delicious and forbidden. White strands of hair announced the birth of amber from her scalp, seducing his attention from her eyes, which were hypnotic even when they looked away from him—he wished he knew what tunes those eyes danced to, and why they were so delighted with themselves. She took few pains arranging her hair, and generally piled it casually on her head to cool her neck. Ringlets fell out, curling down her neck and over her ears. It was no color he ever knew—gold as tea or peanut butter. Were it not so clean, that loose fall might have seemed almost bohemian, compared to the lacquered ladies of Salt Lake.

At Easter's end she was gone and Warren moped like a miserable dog, angry that he had made no overt gesture.

With a prompting Warren had no inkling of, and studied offhandedness, Carl Poulson asked him that summer if he would like to join Johanna and himself on a Labor Day weekend camping trip to the Grand Canyon. "If you feel physically up to it, that is." Warren looked around frantically for a piano to lift as testimony to his recovery. Carl said, "If you feel that good, Neal and Brian and I will be taking the Snake River in July. That might be more——" But he didn't pursue the jest. So elated was Warren at this prospect that he nearly suffered a relapse. Here was his chance to spend solid time with this girl who captured his thoughts. His own attractive competence would be manifest. And Warren was, by all accounts, as fine a catch as a girl could want: tall, well mannered, deep-voiced, and handsome, with jet-black hair and excellently balanced features. At Stanford, when his health was better, he was something of a fraternity row legend for the way he parlayed his high class standing and good looks into a charm the most sought-after girls found affecting. Most of all, in a short year-and-a-half, he had made his scholarship so beloved by the Political Science faculty that his future was no color if not rosy.

The last few weeks of summer are rainy in northern Arizona and southern Utah. But that year, the rains stayed themselves for the tourists. For two days, Johanna and Carl Poulson and Warren Reigeluth camped on a small promontory on the Grand Canyon's North Rim. For two days, every shift in the sun's angle gave the canyon a new look. The thousand ages of its evolution were reenacted in a smaller cycle with each day's maturation and with each stratum of the canyon's depth, the way a growing fetus tells the story of the ascent of its kind.

The place was peaceful, still, as though a hole in time. The only evidence of strain was a giant tree—Warren said it was a sequoia—on its side, as though the Earth had opened or let go its grasp. Carl said it probably had to do with soil depletion: the tree had grown too big and its roots could no longer anchor it in the dry ground.

The encampment gave Carl Poulson a chance to point out evidence of the things he often talked about. They felt more keenly what he meant about how the limitations of senses determine the reality they saw, even in such lavish surroundings. There might be alternate or concurrent universes, Carl suggested, even more beautiful to some sight, made of antimatter or other things in other dimensions. When Warren sounded skeptical of that, Carl pointed to a bat who had no trouble seeing at night, with sonar and infrared detection—but couldn't see through a windowpane in broad daylight. "I think you'll only convince Warren," Johanna said, "if you put it in terms of Rickey and Edgar." Warren accepted the good-natured teasing and joined with Johanna in coaxing Carl to make up a Worm and Cricket tale. But Carl demurred. She pressed, saying, "He's such a good storyteller, Warren. Not to mention a wonderful teacher—"

Carl looked at his sixteen-year-old adoringly, and said, "Johanna is a perfect example of why a computer will never replace a woman. Spoil a computer and you get an electricity-gobbling mess. Spoil a daughter and you get compliments and flirtation." Johanna frowned at being caught at it. "Women know how to maximize their input better than any machine we could invent. And what drab packages machines come in! Why the legs alone—" She made a cross-eyed face which broke them both up.

"I think you're stalling," she said.

"Suppose there's nothing new under the sun to tell about— All right. Let's go over the difficult concepts first—"

Johanna raised her hand like an eager student, preening, "Rickey is a rogue cricket and Edgar is a not-too-bright worm who is always getting into trouble because he doesn't do his homework and therefore doesn't understand what's happening to him." Carl nodded at her recitation. "And it always mysteriously explains some law of physics—not to mention having a perfectly silly moral."

Carl raised his eyebrows. "If you make up the story, you can make up the moral. Invent one where it's good to watch TV and eat chocolates all day if you like. In my stories, the morals are mine. Now then: In this one, Rickey owes Edgar ten dollars. And in return, Rickey says, because he can't get the money just yet, he'll teach Edgar how crickets sing. Besides, he tells Edgar, it's so much fun to rub yourself all day. Of course, worms can't chirp—at least not to our ears. So Edgar rubbed and rubbed: Nothing."

"Is that it?" asked a surprised Warren Reigeluth.

"Well, he grew so fond of himself he fell in love with his tail and tried to swallow it." Carl winked to tip them off. "He became smaller and smaller until— he merged his outsides with his in, his start with his

138

finish, his today and yesterday and—Poof! All gone! All that was left was a worm-sized pair of glasses. And a little noise—*chirrip*—when he disappeared."

"What's the moral?" Warren asked.

Johanna blurted out, "Don't lend a worm ten dollars if you want to see either one again."

Carl had another in mind. "This story has a negative moral. It couldn't happen because of my Second Law of Wormodynamics which, as you know, says 'Critters can neither be created nor destroyed.' So maybe that chirp was Edgar turning into pure energy. But the rub there"—he laughed as they groaned—"is that there are practical limits to possibility. There's a limit to how much a worm—even a dopey worm—can swallow. That is, before he reduces his power to swallow the rest. So for Edgar to vanish, or for Rickey to chirp so fast he becomes invisible, they'd have to be perfect. And nothing is perfect—except maybe God, and fools."

Warren was right on top of it. "I always thought that most scientists were atheists—"

Carl started to respond, but instead answered, "Tomorrow." He got up, yawning dramatically. "Enjoy the fire. And don't forget: I may be old and decrepit, but I'm a dead-eye with a shotgun." Johanna shooed him off with a patronizing kiss, embarrassed at his suggestion.

They sat by the fire and a cricket chirped when Warren tried to put his arm around Johanna. She just raised her eyebrow in the same manner her father would, whispering, "Daddy's spies," and lay her head against Warren's shoulder.

He kissed her and they lay on the soft ground, Johanna permitting Warren to caress her stomach and small breasts. She felt happy and warm against the heavy weight of him, and hugged him tightly, until Warren nervously sat up, saying, "I like you very much, Jo—"

She kissed him on the cheek in answer, then looked off in the dark woods. Searching for conversation, Warren said, "I bet I know what the other Law is—that the rules are more important than the story."

She shook her head kindly. "It's really the other way

around. If the story makes sense, and the rules don't, look for new ones."

"What if they contradict other rules, or make paradoxes?"

"Paradoxes count double, like four-leaf clovers." She kissed him on the ear and Warren wondered if she was as relaxed and happy to be with him as he was happy and nervous to be with her. She was comfortable, even though she said, "I think we'd better go to sleep now."

The weekend was one of tranquility for Carl Poulson. The tapeworm of ambition lay dormant in his belly. He was pleased that Johanna was with him, and genuinely fond of Warren. He seemed a good boy, although Carl wished he weren't so annoyingly devout a social scientist. The boy insisted on talking politics much of the time, and Carl was just as pleased to be infinitely far from news of segregation, Laos, and nuclear testing. Johanna apparently liked Warren, too, and that made Carl glad.

Their last afternoon on the rim, Carl called Johanna over to him while Warren gathered firewood. "Come here, love. Look. I was wrong. There's *always* something new under the sun." He gestured to the canyon before them: its buttes and arroyos and rainbow-striated ridges had an amber glow in the afternoon light. The red clay's phosphors sparkled in the dusk and bled to shades of purple and gold. Greens swam with blues. "Look. Nothing electronic within a hundred miles. No TV. No phones. No airplanes or computers. Just the three of us."

"It's like the Garden of Eden," Johanna said.

"Oh, now hold on! I'm too modest to be God, and I am not about to be cast as the Snake, thank you. No: Just a primitive family. What a lovely, peaceful day. I'd like to hold it forever, except that tomorrow might be just as lovely. And different. It's a perfect day. See, I was wrong again! *Here's* something perfect."

"It's like swarming rainbows, all around," Johanna said, hugging his side.

Carl looked down at her "—and in your eyes, too. God, I'm a lucky man, sweetheart. All these rainbows." He inclined his head for a moment, something recalled. "Isn't that funny? Do you remember when we went to

New York and—what Dr. Einstein called you? He called you a 'bright angel.' "

Johanna reddened with embarrassment.

"Do you know what we're looking across? Here—toward there—that is Bright Angel Point. Or Vista. Isn't that odd?" He squeezed her waist very tight. "I'm a very happy Daddy, you know. But I think I might rather be Warren."

"Warren? That's the silliest—"

Carl held up a hand and whispered, "He gets to kiss you." She clucked her tongue and then hugged his big chest with all her might until she squeezed her muscles dry and felt rapturously light inside.

The firewood Warren brought back to camp was dry from the rainless summer, and the pine needles on the ground were brittle, so they built a small cooking fire and dug a moat around it.

"What do you think, Warren?" Carl asked as they cleaned their skillets. "You think we could have passed muster as pioneers?"

"I think if we were with the Donners or Brigham Young we'd never have made it past St. Louis," Johanna laughed.

"I apologize for my beans," Warren said. "I didn't know it was possible to ruin them."

"Ah, but they had nothing on my steaks," Carl said. Johanna rolled her eyes. "Well, I think it took skill—talent to destroy all the flavor. And as for your punch, my darlin' daughter, you'd better marry a man who can afford to hire a cook."

"The Donners had better food," Warren suggested. "Fillet of Reed."

"They got their just deserts," Johanna said, and both frowned at her.

"Now here you see a modern problem," Carl told Warren. "How could you ever describe a day such as this and make it sensible to a computer? You'd only get a shadow, and miss the fullness. Even what we see has to be described through a veil of perhapses." He engaged Warren in a little game. "Give me an operational definition of Happiness—so that some political authority might dispense it more evenhandedly." Warren tried, offering an elaborate chain of words about

141

"maximizing the life-sustaining capacities of an organism—within the framework of the social system's own collateral interests—and minimizing the, uh . . ."

"Unhappiness. Friction maybe. Sounds grim."

"That's politics," Warren said.

"Grim," Johanna seconded.

"It's engineering," added Carl. "I wouldn't dare to try what you did just then. We theoretical folk are really humble about such matters. That's why we like to say that engineers and social scientists make lousy lovers. Women and God's intentions are beyond man's comprehension."

"You said that last night," Warren pressed. "I don't understand. I always thought God didn't fit into equations. Women I'll grant you. But I don't really understand the other."

"Oh ye of little faith and ye of no imagination," Carl laughed. "That's just what I'm talking about. It's a tough racket, the seeking-truth biz. When you try to plumb reality you get into awful problems. Suppose, for example, we could somehow know the truth about something. Everything there is to know. Really know it, the simple, graceful truth. Could we express it? There's an inefficiency between our urge—what we feel and know—and what we can state. Expression is a frictive process. Watch a poet try to hold emotion motionless, watch a mathematician have to resort to 'imaginary' numbers to describe the square root of a negative number. The problem is built right in—"

"I'm not sure I follow," Warren said, looking to Johanna for translation. But she gave a shrug of equal confusion, and said, "Humor him. He gets these fits often. It'll all be over soon, poor man."

"All right, you two wise guys," Carl said, preparing to deliver a long explanation. But, instead, he sighed. "Children—and parents. It's not fair for me to rattle on like this, I guess, with a captive audience. After all, I've got the car keys. Now, someone's going to have to carry you two back to civilization tomorrow. So I, for one, am retiring. Good night, honey. Warren. Oh, Warren. That thing about social scientists making lousy, uh—I just made it up. Nobody told me."

"Daddy, get *out* of here!"

142

Johanna and Warren sat up by that last dying fire of summer half the night, talking and kissing. She let him get bolder this time, wanted him to touch her. She was relaxed, comfortable, curious. Warren was no threat, really, and he was going back to Stanford in a few weeks. Sandwiched between the pine needles on the soft black dirt and Warren, Johanna let herself float under his touch. But her fondness had limits, and though she warmed to the sensations of his tentative explorations, she felt bound by an ambivalence. For his part, Warren was bound by other constraints. He liked this girl very much, so much that he felt compelled to show he "respected" her.

She was so lovely and bright that he felt shyly deferential, mustering all the propriety and maturity he could. No one had said as much to him, but he firmly believed girls thought boys to be monsters whom they must reconcile themselves to living with; girls themselves were something more complex—outwardly confection and purity, which clothed a sleeping beast in some. When awakened it made the animal of maleness seem a hairless thing. He felt like a blind man in a foreign country: wherever he got with uneasy steps, he was grateful for it. Kissing her was a thing of wonder for him. It flattered him and made him feel privileged, slightly defensive, slightly resentful of his imagined need to court. In the middle of his reverie he heard a sound and sat up startled. "There are no bears around here," Johanna teased, tugging him back. Warren silenced her.

"Your father made a noise. I think he's coming out." They quickly arranged themselves.

"I don't hear——" Then she heard the noise: a low rumbling sound, as though Carl was having trouble sleeping, or perhaps clearing his throat, warning them he was about to come out. "Daddy?" Still the noise, in a broken pattern. "Daddy? Are you all right?"

Warren was on his feet, moving closer to Carl Poulson's tent, Johanna quickly after. "Dr. Poulson?" The noise.

"Daddy?"

Carl moaned inside the tent and then his broad shoulders and head pushed through the door flap. "I'm all right——" But his face was sweaty and florid. "Just a little heartburn. Damned steaks, I think." Warren watched him carefully and then looked at Johanna. "I'll be OK. Get some sleep—beat you both to civili—" He winced again. "—in the morning."

"Warren, go get help," she said, kneeling down to support Carl's shoulders in her lap. "Hurry."

"It's nothing, Angel. Just gas. It'll clear—"

Warren got his jacket and flashlight and brought over the remaining water. "Here. I'll be back as fast as I can. The Rangers should have medical supplies."

Carl looked up and said, "I just need some sleep and some aspirin. In the morning—OK." He relaxed in Johanna's arms to show he was ready to sleep, while Warren soaked socks and towels in water and poured a cup for Johanna to use.

"I'll be back as fast as I can. Before light, maybe."

Carl looked up and grimaced from a pain in his chest, making no effort to hide it now. "Off you go, Diogenes —don't fall off the rim. Thank you, Warren." The boy nodded and took off down the trail they had come up.

"You know, Sweet—"

"Daddy, lie still, *please?*"

"Was I in time to save your virtue?" He smiled at the thought.

"Never in doubt. Now be still—or I'll drown you in a towel." He closed his eyes while Johanna mopped his face.

Warren ran as fast as he could over the unfamiliar rocky trail and through the dark woods. Several times he fell over roots and bloodied himself. But he got up and ran all the faster until he reached the Ranger Station after nearly two hours.

At one point during the fitful night, Carl clenched in sudden pain, and pushed Johanna away from him. "Go away!" he cried, frightened. "Go away!" he said, not wanting her to see him as he was. But she held him in her arms and soothed him, kissed his brow and cleaned his face, until he calmed; and he felt comforted and loved, and proud of her.

The Rangers had to return on foot, for a jeep would not make it over some of the rocks and through certain chutes. The Rangers were still a mile away when the first light came and gave Bright Angel Vista a bath of Coronado's chimerical gold.

Carl lay outside the tent, Johanna still swabbing his face in vain war against the beads of sweat which gushed from him in pulses. The full moon was sinking in the west, still up, and with the rising sun, it made Carl viscerally aware of their being on a rotating planet in a sea of other bodies. His eyes shut and opened, wanting to rest but afraid to. His pain made him fear that in sleep he might lose the will to hold his parts together. He was afraid to lose the pain which kept him conscious. Over Johanna's shoulder the light danced on the air's moisture, making rainbow parhelions in the sky.

Warren and the Rangers climbed over dewy rocks, Warren near exhaustion. Carl rested his head in Johanna's lap, a giant, huge-chested man supported only by his daughter's will. "Life of my life," he sighed, pain ebbing.

"I'm right here, Daddy," Johanna soothed. "Just lie still. They'll be here soon." Carl smiled at her and thought of light, blindly looking at her eyes. He squeezed her hand and it pumped a tear from her which momentarily broke his delirium.

"Oh, not for your old Dad, honey. Don't cry, Angel . . . bright." He sighed long while looking at the rainbows in her eyes, and fell into a spectral dream.

"I'm here, Daddy. I'm right here," she was saying, hugging his empty husk for dear life, enfolding Carl's shell, rocking in denial, crushing him to her chest so hard the Rangers had to pry her arms loose when they arrived with their first aid and medical emergency supplies—digitoxin, glyceryl trinitrate, practolol, ephedrine, and amyl nitrite—too late.

They drove Johanna and Warren to Jacob Lake, Arizona, where transportation to Cedar City was available. Carl's car and body would be held until some adult relative made arrangements. In Cedar City, Johanna called her mother, and Warren called his parents, and they waited for the evening bus from Las Vegas to Salt Lake. Sleepless and dirty they took a room to get some rest and wash and wait.

Johanna showered and lay down on the bed, and when Warren was clean he came in and sat on its edge to hold her hand. She pulled him toward her and he hugged her, stroking her back, but would not kiss her when she turned her face toward his. It confused him, afraid to appear cruel and disrespectful. He knew his mission: to be compassionate and kind. So he rubbed her shoulders and caressed her gently, and kissed her on the forehead. She wanted him to make love to her, but to Warren it seemed like preying on a wounded girl and he was brought up too well for that.

So Warren, nervously, but giving off all the signs of clear-eyed command and control he knew he should, calmed Johanna and supported her. He smoothed a sheet over her up to her neck, despite the humid closeness of the room. Then he kissed her on the cheek and held her hand tightly.

Warren went back to school that fall and Johanna returned to Phoenix. But she and her mother did not get along and with both brothers away at college, Johanna and Maureen Poulson fell into a constant battle of will. Johanna spent more and more time in the desert, thinking, often of nothing, just soaking up its infinity and letting it absorb her feelings.

Something about her eyes changed that year, temporarily, in the synapse which translates emotion at the junction of mind and body. It replaced her accustomed luster with a wary aspect.

After New Year's Day, 1963, during her senior year semester break, Johanna defied her mother and ran away to see Warren in Salt Lake City. The Reigeluths were livid, said they were *"most* displeased," when they learned that Johanna had not told them the truth, though when an attack of appendicitis laid her low they cared for her as though she were their own daughter. But to Warren they made plain "what kind of girl" they thought she was. "It's a good thing," Johanna told him, unaware of their harsh judgment, "your mother's not a Jehovah's Witness."

Her brother Neal was dispatched to bring her home after she recovered, and to Warren's mind Johanna looked, as she left, like a felon being returned to the pen. That's exactly how she felt, failed and just shy of desperate.

When she enrolled at Berkeley the next fall, distance from home restored her. Her new surroundings replaced the illimitable range for imagination she had found in the desert. Though she dated many boys, it was Warren most of all.

That was four years gone.

Now, she found it hard to remember why. Nor could Warren. "You know what it is?" he told her after yet another quarrel.

"You're just going to have to ask one of us, sweetheart, Daddy or me, to step out of bed."

"My father! Do you ever have a case!"

"Three's a crowd, Johanna. There isn't room for—"

"Why don't you deal with me and not some half-baked hypothesis!"

"I'm telling you about you. Someone has to. I see it —maybe better than you do."

"I don't have to put up with this."

"I swear it. It's always somewhere else. I just despair of ever reclaiming your Daddy's spoiled darling for the love of the living—"

"That's precious, Warren. I saw my father three weeks a year. Do you think fathers spoil their only daughters for the sole purpose of driving future sons-in-law up the wall? He knew you, remember? He wouldn't bother. Oh, hell, Warren. He's been dead for five years."

"Then bury him."

"I did."

"I wish you'd remember that."

"I remember it," she said.

"I mean remember you can't find the past in the future." Warren stopped and looked away for a moment. "Look, I'm sorry. I don't like to be this cruel—"

"You're not hurting me."

"Maybe someone should, then. For your sake. Because the only way you're going to start acting like a human is when you decide it's worth it. Maybe you need somebody who'll *inspire* you to behave yourself. But I can't do it. And I'm tired of congratulating myself on my patience, Johanna. I'm tired of living with— with a . . . social imperialist. You just spread into every

147

corner. Well, that's not the way I want to do it. It's a very simple problem. *We* don't have a problem. You do. And it's called self-discipline, self-control. I've been listening to you mewl about leading a postponed life for a little too long now. You're absolutely right, except it's not because of me. It's because you've got some crazy notion that it's some kind of house you build, a life, and you don't move into it until you like the way it looks. Until then you camp in the yard or something. I just wish I had the capacity to look at life so dispassionately, Johanna. It's my life that's getting postponed, because you're my wife and you don't seem quite adjusted to it."

"Is that all?"

"That's all. And there's not a God-damned thing I can do to help you except leave you alone. So if that's what you want, you've got it."

"It's not," she said, with a meek kind of wonder in her voice, that her own inaction and irresolution could precipitate such consequential occasions. "Really."

"You've got it anyway."

The road from Gila Compound to Tombstone Center is a long, circuitous path, as tortuous for autos as for memos. Gila Compound's orientation is idiopathic, its back turned on the American world, while Tombstone's arms reach toward the city of Tucson to embrace the academic and political communities there. But with Gila making its own bid for public favor, that once-kind topography was less the boon than it had been.

There is a shortcut from Gila to Tombstone that skirts Gila Mountain and winds down an ill-tended dirt road beside a desert rillet. It is open only to those with the proper clearance, for it has a vantage on the World's Biggest Secret. Down this road jounced an interagency motorpool sedan, windows sealed tight, its air-conditioner working madly to hold the out-of-season hot evening at bay. The desert night in late October should be chilly, for there is no cloistering vegetation nor retentive features to stand for the absent sun. But the evenings remained hot by the upper atmosphere's refusal to haul off or chase the months-old, over-

148

breathed air below. The nights were only remarkable this year in that they were barely less hot than the days.

The car descended from a high grassy canyon bounded by hills that glowed yellow in the Indian summer dusk. It looked like a good night for an assault, Tyler Bowen thought, peering up from a file of notes in the sedan's back seat, a personal guerilla attack. Out the side window he watched the World's Biggest Secret disappear as the car sunk down onto the desert floor. It was emblematic of his disloyalty to his best interests, the schizoid nature of the life he led just then, that his urge was antithetical to his mission. He dreamed of defiant gestures and arrived, chauffeured, by armored car.

He persuaded himself, after his first exposure to Gila's least savory corners, that his own sin was mere literary mischief, telling tall tales after a fashion and, he persuaded himself anew each morning after, that it was not much mischief at all. Indeed there was, from within, at least the possibility of having a creative effect, spreading ameliorative notions, pushing, however slightly, against the general drift. As a logical exercise it was, to his daily chores of lying, as brushing his teeth was to smiling. And as Baroque as his rationalizations became, they were less satisfying.

"Roll with the punches," he'd been advised the previous morning as he reported for his mandatory daily audience with Susan Carver, the Director of Public Information. "She's on the rag today," Carver's assistant warned him before he went in. Halfway into her office Tyler heard the assistant close the door from the outside, as though he anticipated noise.

"Sit, Bowen," Susan Carver said, and as he did, this forbidding woman tossed a folded proof sheet of the Gila house organ, the *Ledger-Domain,* in his lap. Circled in black Magic Marker was a guest column written by one of the National Labs biologists; Tyler had arranged for it, hoping to sneak some merry wit into those slick pages. The man had written a light personal essay describing "the application of the scientific method to a local problem." The piece parodied the quandaries of conscience raised by those who question "all technical progress," in this case the exorcism of a parasite, concluding, "And thus, in one fleeting act of

149

biocide, were my interior subtleties reduced by one degree, another world destroyed, and a being that was a better guest than I a host. . . ."

"Less than funny, Mr. Bowen," Susan Carver growled. "Toilet jokes in the *Ledger-Domain!*"

"Oh, I don't know," Bowen said. "It's—"

"Stupid and inexcusable. Don't apologize for him! I expect this sort of garbage from those people, but I expect you to be a backstop."

"I never saw it until now."

"Damned scientists. Oughta cut off their tongues and feed 'em to the animals. It's dumb casual attitudes like this that start those damned rumors." She pushed around on her desk and gathered up a handful of telephone message slips. "This week alone—wild stories, wild queries. Somebody thinks we're running a torture factory here: lasers, ultrasonic crap, alpha wave. Where do they come *up* with these ideas?"

"You can't blame people for being curious," he said, glancing at the question slips, all of which seemed to originate from some radical newspaper in Phoenix.

"You'd think they'd mind their own business. I think next week or the week after I'm going to send you up there and let you sweet-mouth them. Maybe they'll recognize one of their own." He began to grin broadly at the prospect of being sent to a campus, despite the attendant risks.

"Save it for the public, Bowen. As far as I'm concerned, you should be taking a larger role around here."

"Thank you, ma'am." She shook her head to silence him and rose half out of her seat, as though about to transfer the helm right then, but settled back down again, content to swivel her great bulk instead of carry it. She did so with a girlish wiggling of her feet, perhaps the only unbusinesslike habit she had.

He watched in fascinated horror as she talked of his perceived virtues, for a lip-locked Camel nonfilter's ash grew precipitously, hypnotically. She wheeled around to gesture at two wall-mottos, which hung behind her desk: *"Let us begin then, by laying facts aside, as they do not affect the question"*—J. J. Rousseau, Second Discourse on Political Economy; and *"Truly, to tell lies is not honorable, but when the truth entails tremendous*

150

ruin, to speak dishonorably is pardonable"—Sopho-
cles. The ash hung on.

"We had some bad luck before you came. Had a
problem with some thieves. People committing crimes,
right here at Gila." The ash twitched at each nod of
her head, for she agreed with herself vigorously as she
spoke. "Local press had a field day—and they just love
it when they can make fools of us."

"Did you find the people responsible?"

"Oh, yes," she beamed. The cigarette hung by will to
her lower lip, the ash by less than that. "I personally
had the leaker transferred to a less sensitive position.
It's happened before. It'll happen again." She rose
abruptly, but the ash held firm. "We've tried," she said,
gazing out her window to the desert's comfort, "so
many ways to keep security, from geography to penalties, from necessary deception to—" without warning a
nod of her head bullwhipped the ash high into the air
and it crashed down on her mammoth bosom in chunks,
a powdery boulder-slide, skidding to the edge of that
bluff. She strode away from the window and a heaving
bounce of her bosom flipped them high again. "—to
establishing a corporation." It seemed she might do this
trick forever. "That way it's our business if we want to
keep it off the market. *Comprende?*" The ashes crashed,
obliterated on the floor as lonely dust, ten feet from
where she stood by the time they hit. Tyler watched
them, his head bobbing at her words, as they blew into
anonymity. "But finally it all boils down to the willingness of good men and women such as us. And, as they
say, honesty turns out to be the best policy. That's why
your job is so vital. You have to tell the truth."

"All the truth?"

"You do and I'll have you shot," she winked. "Just
the believable truth. My truth. Here," she gestured
around her office, "is where truth lies, in a manner of
speaking." She smiled faintly to herself, calmed in ru-
mination of something; perhaps it was that plans hidden
deep in the National Security Agency headquarters
nominated her for a top-level job in any post-holocaust
caretaker regime. "You see, Mr. Bowen, I'm not all
bluster. I like to pass on compliments when I have
cause. A lot of people have commented on the quality

151

of your work. You've been showing me great potential. You give us a fine public face. Keep it up."

Tyler bowed his head, blushing in blotches, then looked up. "Would this be the time to raise the question of maybe a weekend off?"

"No. What I wanted to see you about, is this." She picked up a file folder from her desk and flipped it to him. It was heavy with material he had prepared for her to use at a symposium at Tombstone. "Very good stuff. I think you can pull eight hundred words to fill that hole in the *Ledger-Domain*. We're dumping that column. *Now* my only problem is how to be in two places at once."

"If you had a tapeworm . . ."

She ignored it, and then erupted in her own fearsome dark-toothed grin, revealing a cavernous mouth whose gentian recesses were forbidding, apparently pleased with some turn on the phrase she'd discovered. "Well, you're going to be my other half, young man. They've let this little Tombstone tea party get out of hand, and set up a chat-o-rama at the University, too. A panel on Saturday. We'll need more material."

"If I get on it right away I can have it done by tonight."

"Tomorrow morning's soon enough. I want those excerpts first. You can have the final draft copied to me on the TeleNet."

"In Tombstone?"

"No, no, I'm going to some think tank in Monterey. So you'll have to handle both ends of this nonsense here. You'll get some time off soon, I promise. I have no intention of working you to death. And you'll have all day Saturday to rest in Tombstone. They have fine facilities for relaxation there, just like we do here."

"Yes, ma'am. Thank you." He wished he could raise the idea of switching assignments. He had family near Monterey. But doubtless Susan Carver had her own reasons. Probably, he thought smugly, has a girl friend there.

"I'm counting on you, so don't let me down. It's a credit to your work, you know, that these invitations are doubling. Funny that it should wind up increasing

152

your work. And don't bother making me separate material. We can use the same notes. Who'll know?"

As he backed out of her office he faintly bowed, then blinked humbly to show glad acceptance. He was learning a whole repertoire of obsequious mannerisms. Outside he sagged wearily at the weight of masks he carried, recalling something Baron Zermatt had said about the power of smiles when it came to exerting bureaucratic leverage: "Cash is handier."

"Give you the treatment?" Carver's assistant asked.

Tyler cocked his head, saying, "I've been screwed worse, and I've been screwed better. But I've never been screwed without knowing it before."

The assistant agreed. "Ladies are no gentlemen."

Neither the panel at Tombstone nor the one at Monterey was as well attended as the sponsors had hoped. Few people without a vested interest could be moved to travel far from their televisions to hear such a sexless discussion as one on Public Policy and Technology. So the panelists in each place addressed each other in auditoriums whose population density rivaled that of outer space. At Tombstone, Tyler Bowen felt the formality of his prepared remarks embarrassing in this intimate gathering. He delivered them in an efficient manner, but in a soft monotone. Nonetheless, there was considerable glee among the Operations Research people attending. He'd justified their every expectation, and they told him what excellent reports they'd be filing.

Susan Carver, in similar circumstances in Monterey, felt no such compunctions of shyness. She delivered her identical remarks with a gusto suited better for a medicine tent.

"Small wonder that Nature is called Mother," she bellowed to the two dozen others in the tympanic hall. "It is a truism, acknowledging that we exist by grace of her umbilicus. We are burst from the womb of her utilitarianism. We acquire her laws, as immunities, frailties, and possibilities, the genetic legacy of all past trials and failures.

"We children sometimes view her as intransigent. Our needs do not always coincide with her offerings. So we push against her tolerance. And sometimes we fail. We at the National Laboratories at Gila Compound know failure and disappointment—and know it as the price of success."

At both places an informal cocktail party followed the discussions. Unsure of protocol, Tyler Bowen stayed at his until a majority of panelists had left. Susan Carver headed straight from her panel to San Francisco, for the weekend.

"There'll probably be more of a turnout tomorrow," the Tombstone panel's organizer reassured Tyler Bowen. "Tomorrow's topic's more of a grabber." He showed Tyler to his room at the Tombstone Center guest house and told him he could get a ride to Tucson any time he wanted on Saturday just by calling for it. "You need anything to help you sleep?" he asked.

"Nah. I'll just reread my remarks."

In the meantime, his host told him, he was free to enjoy the hospitality of Tombstone Center, such as it was. The man handed him a visitor's booklet listing the diversions available at Tombstone, and as Tyler settled into his lace-filled room late Friday night he flipped through it, laughing to himself softly that it must be somebody's idea of a joke.

It was all somebody's idea of a joke, he continued thinking: the alternate forms of cushioned imprisonment, the tradeoffs between various subversions of conscience.

He dreamed about a girl he'd known from his Intro Psych class three years before. She'd become an Ithaca legend for her own dreams. Their professor was a funny little fellow who looked like a gingerbread man. He would sit on a stool in the lecture hall before five hundred students, checking his progress against an alarm clock he placed on the experiment table next to him, lecturing in a diffident near-whisper. With two minutes left after a lecture on dreams he asked for questions. The girl rose to ask what he made of a recurring dream. Tyler always imagined her backside to be halved tennis balls, small and white and fuzzy; a friend who admired her efficient design said, "She should be cast in bronze and put in the park—on a low pedestal so little children can climb on her." Her apple cheeks flushed in full virginal flower as she de-

154

scribed her dream: "I'm in the kitchen making pudding, stirring the batter very hard when the spoon jumps up and chases me around the room until I grab it and lick it clean—" The professor crashed to the floor groping for his alarm clock.

Tyler was dreaming he was the spoon. And he woke, flushed and tense, wondering what it meant that he was now dreaming about other people's dreams. How much of himself was left if even his dreams were forfeit?

WILLIE BOWEN COUNTED THE BODIES. Sometimes there wasn't enough of one to count, so he reverted to a standing rule of thumb: a thumb counted as a hand; a hand counted as an arm; spare arms and legs were totaled and counted three-fifths: any five being scored as three whole people. Someone suggested the Constitution itself was the source of this convention.

Willie moved cautiously out from his position at the end of the fire fight and counted the bodies, like a center in a touch football game ticking off the delayed-rush seconds: "One Red Tomato, Two Red Tomato— Hey, Pilsner! Score me a leg, left one. Marked down one foot! McCready's got a spare one? It's a bonus, what d'ya say?" Arms and legs hung from corpses at grotesque angles and the tabulators often felt a sympathetic pain for the contorted positions the bodies seemed to be enduring. Dead faces peered up with wide eyes. An occasional scent of petroleum blew in on the breeze, a welcome smell. Without it there was nothing but the stench of the older bodies with their putrefying blood and decomposing skin. Pilsner, the squad leader, who would live to be fragged in his tent, whistled while he wrote down the figures for each quadrant. "WETSU!" he yelled, when the numbers came shouted across the field. "WETSU!": a shout he had learned in Basic Training: "We Eat This Shit Up! WETSU!" "With a spoon," he laughed, "WETSU, m'boys, WETSU!"

"Cram it," someone yelled back, gagging on the smells.

On a mission in the Delta once, Willie had cleaned up after a fight and his unit of cadremen had fished bloated gray bodies from the green water. No one knew how long they had been dead. Some were rotted and half-chewed by something, some partly saponified.

But the bodies he counted today were fresh and mostly brown from flame and dirt. Ugly, too, Willie thought, from mud and festering wounds. Uglier still in the way they seemed to look back at him. He turned a boyish Vietnamese face away with the toe of his boot and moved on to the next charred body.

On that Delta mission there was also a sweet smell, from the dense countryside, and a cocky-assed Navy j.g. who ran their river sweep boat and somehow managed to smell like a flower when everyone else smelled of fear. This place now also smelled of fear, and the overwhelming odors of decay.

When Willie first smelled his own fear, he reflexively reached down and felt the seat of his pants, then sniffed his fingers. Nothing. It puzzled him, for he sensed an aroma of loose bowels. He mentioned it to a buddy, who laughed. "First time you ever smelled it? Christ, my first time was on the motherfuckin' plane over. Bet you picked your asshole for a whiff, right?" Willie was amazed. "Shit-and-spinach," his buddy gloated. "Smells like shit-and-spinach. If Charlie had any kind of technology, he'd put shit-and-spinach in a can and toss it over on us. You and me and half the rest'd figure it was us and run so-fuckin'-fast—" Common lore had it that shit-and-spinach was the smell of fear, an effect with a known cause. Yet the same lore held that it often preceded another smell: the smell of blood in your nose, from taking a punch full in the face or missing a step on a staircase. Everyone said you smelled it just before you stepped on your personalized mine, or your monogramed round came calling.

There was shit-and-spinach all around, nearly half the time, Willie knew. But he hadn't smelled the other one yet. Not all legends worked all the time. In fact, there was another smell he kept with him and recalled, like a lucky rabbit's foot: the odor of sweat and alcohol and vinyl and conditioned air on the Pan Am charter plane. When he smelled that again, the bad dream would be over. He could open his eyes for he'd be on his way the hell out of there.

The land around the bodies he counted was bare, wider than he had imagined from pictures at home, broader, more open and forbidding. Giant holes pocked the hillsides, like acne scars, Willie thought, on a giant's face. Cattle lay about in comic twisted heaps. Willie wondered whose side they were on. But he knew: one member of his squad counted cows and added them to the total VC bagged. Willie looked over the scarred, steaming hillside. Except for the Moonmen bodies, he realized, you'd never think men had been here; we might be the first American visitors to a barren planet, the first Earth rocket to land on the giant's face.

Small fires burned in scattered areas. Some were the still-smouldering, ferocious-smelling bodies he had yet to count, sizzling embers, slowly dying coals from the happy campfire, percolating still from the rush of napalm which had gripped them.

Willie's platoon had seen the attack called in from their hiding place on a distant hill. Some mad Captain had called in a napalm assault on his own position. "At least we'll take 'em with us," was his last radioed message. A Colonel at Operations broke in to say, in an emotion-charged, gravelly voice, "Dave, I promise you this: there are going to be two planes coming over you. That second one is going to drop every God-damned medal we can find! We're proud of you!" The strike had wiped out his entire unit. He had simultaneously been nominated for the Medal of Honor. If he left children behind, they would be automatically admitted to West Point. His platoon would also get medals, though not the Big One, for he alone had died by choice. They would get Bronze Stars, and individual plaques and/or urns, depending on their next-of-kin's request for disposition of remains. In either case, a grisly package would be ceremoniously presented to their stateside survivors by a Community Relations Officer team, who would preen unctuously about the noble sacrifice the zapped had made. (In the case of the Medal of Honor nominee, the blow would be softened by the knowledge that he had actually been put up for it twice: once earlier in the month for an equally suicidal gesture, which he outlived; and now this. Red tape had prevented him from learning of his first nomination with meaningful timeliness.)

Willie's body counters had moved out from their position while the fire fight was still raging, before the napalm was called in. When they saw the plane, Willie's unit sought cover behind the crest of a hill. The explosion sent a wave of heat rolling up the hillside and Willie ground his face in the mud afraid for his eyebrows. The roar of the canister and the accompanying fifty-pound bomblets sent a cannonade boom through the bowl beneath them, and it resounded in Willie's chest, making him feel hollow.

"You through there?" an eighteen-year-old Sergeant called out to the body counters in Willie's quadrant. "Add ten to y'all's count and let's move!" They slowly regrouped and began the walk back to base camp.

It was Willie Bowen's third day in the field this week. In spite of his lassitude, he welcomed field missions. Without them there was nothing but interminable boredom. Boredom he had never known in his life. Boredom that he and his buddies decided in one stoned late-night's reverie was a Pentagon plot: the Brass knew that the troops didn't give a crap. They knew the troops would just as soon surrender as fight. They knew the best of the troops were stoned half of the time, and the worst of the troops all of the time and maybe vice versa really. So the Brass invented Boredom: put them in the boonies until they were itching for something, anything to break the monotony: bring on Charlie and his 800 million ChiCom cousins and all the Red Indians in the World. Anything but another day of nothing. But day after day there was nothing. *Nothing* was the war's byword:

"Watcha doon?"

"Nuthin'."

"Watcha think?"

"Nuthin'."

"Out in the field?"

"Yeah."

"Watcha see?"

"Nuthin'."

And when something would come they would be jubilant, happy to fight, uncaring about the outcome. It was that, or "What's up?"

"Beaucoup nuthin'. Mox nix. Nada."

"Nada?"

"Nada."

"Nada what?"

"Nada fuckin' thing."

Willie Bowen was three years younger than his brother Tyler, and received his high school diploma by mail simultaneous with his certificate of graduation from Fort Polk's Basic Training School in a place they called Tigerland. He followed that with "marching orders," as they used to be known: orders to attend school at Fort Ord, California, for Military Occupational Specialty 11-Bravo; Craps-Bush it was also called, Advanced Infantry Training. In the barracks they called it MOS 13-69, which was no known military designation, but merely a way of acknowledging that 11-Bravo effectively meant "Hard-luck Cocksucker": 13-69. At least, Willie thought, Ord would put him close enough to visit his sister Connie—the sister Tyler called Mr. Mack—and her family in Carmel. By August he had visited her only once, and then they got the word: "Leaves canceled and prepare your wills." Westmoreland wanted fifty thousand more of them. So Willie and his crop of war babies flew west to find the East.

At this point in his life, Willie thought, the word *Nothing* could easily be etched on his tombstone. It had somehow been his calling card since even before he was born. Tyler used to tell him the story of how Mr. Mack had lobbied long and hard for another brother to torment until Willie came. To pacify her,

159

their parents bought her a ventriloquist's dummy. When Willie was born, she decided she'd stick with the dummy and the hell with a baby brother. But Vlad Bowen piled the two kids in the car and they drove down to pick up their mother and her new baby, William Charles, from the hospital. On the way down the car caught fire and nearly blew up. Vlad and Tyler and Mr. Mack piled out and the firemen soon arrived on the scene to hose down the car. While they were dousing it, Vlad called his wife, and Mr. Mack, who took her dummy everywhere she went, suddenly started to scream, "My brother's in there! My brother's in there!" jumping up and down, screaming, pulling her hair. In retelling it, Tyler would say, "The firemen risked their lives and everything, pulling all the doors open and tossing everything out."

Nothing! Mr. Mack cried, "He's in the trunk! He's in the trunk!" So they busted open the trunk: Empty! The trunk was empty. The firemen were horrified. They went back and pulled out the seats. Maybe the kid had slipped behind a crack. Nothing.

When Vlad got back from the phone, the firemen were visibly upset. "We're sorry, sir. We did everything we could . . . but, we're afraid it's too late. The Chief would like you to know how truly sorry we are. We—"

The burly firemen were near tears, so Vlad Bowen reassured them: "Don't worry about it. We're insured," and hailed a cab.

"But the little girl's *brother*—" the firemen said. Vlad looked at Tyler and Mr. Mack, and then understood.

"Oh, the Dummy! No loss." He laughed, "We're going to get her a new one right now." But when they got home, Laura made him call the Fire Department to tell them what they had found: "Don't worry. We found the little girl's 'brother' right where we left him —at home—yes—in the living room in a suitcase."

Mr. Mack split her time between tormenting Tyler and telling Willie, "If we kept you in a suitcase, maybe you'd stay out of trouble." Perhaps so, Willie now thought. At least he wouldn't be creeping around the jungle and the swamps, pretending that he was a great team player.

Another time, when Tyler and Willie were just boys,

Tyler had to take his younger brother to a Cub Scout meeting at a new pack. It was the dead of winter and Willie insisted on going in a loincloth and war paint, for they were having an Indian Pageant that night. Most of the others wore snowpants and maybe a feather. Willie was wrapped in seven blankets to keep warm. He had left his old pack because a punk of a snot-nosed bully whom Willie had given a black eye and a broken tooth to on behalf of the rest of the pack, had had his father ascend to the Chieftainship, become the Big Bear.

At the new pack Willie sauntered in, cool, half-naked, and immediately started making friends. At his old pack they had a custom: if someone did something terrific and spiffy, you gave him the old wolf howl—"Ooowooooo!" The kids would scream and it made you feel just grand, according to Willie. Just before he was to be sworn in with some other newcomers, one desperately trying to master holding two fingers up together, the pack awarded silver arrowheads to this Big Bear's son for doing something patently impossible, like building a canoe in his apartment. The boy took his bow and Willie Bowen let go with the World-Famous Wolf Call: "Ooooowoooo!" The church basement reverberated as Willie really let it roll: "Ooooooooo-woooooooooo!" Then the Big Bear grabbed Willie by the neck and dragged him to the center of the floor, Willie going "Ooooooowooooo!" all the way.

"What are you doing?" the Big Bear demanded.

"Nothing," Willie said, innocently.

"You're booing my son!"

"No, I'm not. I'm just giving the Wolf Call."

"I never heard of any Wolf Call! You were booing Barry. I want you to apologize to Barry in front of the other boys." The children were laughing and screaming. Howling. Just loving it, like precious little cannibals. Willie stood there in his loincloth, shivering, about to cry. "Well, what do you say, young man?" the Big Bear demanded.

Willie muttered, "Nothing."

"What? Now you tell everybody you're sorry. Acquit yourself like a little man." The boys were stamping and cheering, and Willie took a sullen deep breath.

161

He yelled, "Fuck You!" and bolted out of the room, straight into the snow, with Tyler in hot pursuit carrying the blankets.

"That same attitude," as he was too often told, had landed him here in the bog. Willie and Tyler had visited Mr. Mack and her husband, whom they called Animal, in Carmel, the summer before he was drafted. Animal had served in the peacetime Marines and imagined himself a war hero, though, as Willie took delight in reminding him, he "only left his little boat to get drunk and the clap in port."

Mr. Mack had been acting as a superego for Tyler, doing a lecture tour through his entire personality on "the destructiveness of your behavior." She found it "unbelievable" that Tyler and a girl were living together in Ithaca. Mr. Mack used her otherwise unemployed M.A. in Philosophy to remind Tyler continually that "you're so stupid." What his family didn't realize was that Willie had spent much of his adolescence popping elaborate chemicals down his gullet. When they did, it nearly caused a small riot.

"The body is like a set of pipes, William," said Animal, who was in hardware and should therefore know. "You're letting down not only yourself, but your family—and your country."

Willie pushed his potatoes around his dinner plate and said, without looking up, "You know who you are, Animal? You're the kind of guy who, if your daughter came home fifteen years from now and said, 'Pop, I'm a nympho,' you'd find it hard as hell not to try and slip her the old wazoo." Mr. Mack ran one way, while Animal came growling at Willie across the table, right through the vegetable tray. Tyler grabbed Willie and ran the other way. When they were safe outside, Willie stopped and said, "I would. Wouldn't you?" and nearly threw up laughing. Tyler told him, "If the American Civilization and Empire should last a thousand years, men will still say, 'Willie Bowen was an idiot.'"

As much as Tyler Bowen was charmed with luck and grace and many gifts, Willie had the knack of doing things wrong which turned out right. He won a high school football game—and later the alleged virtue of the prettiest cheerleader—by falling on his head in the end zone, and won a baseball game once by being beaned, thus producing the winning RBI. The wave always broke in front of Willie, as for Tyler, sweeping him to an even better shore. This time, though, for the very mortality of the tsunami, and the Red Tide on the current, one might be inclined to doubt it.

Still, surviving was a talent he had in abundance, and if he survived this strait, his grip-tight pass-catching hands and reckless regard for his own safety guaranteed him a safe seat in any major football borough. For the only thing which stood between Willie and the free ride his gridiron skills insured was his ungovernable arrogance. His senior year in high school, Willie trotted off the field after practice one afternoon with the stride of one who liked himself immensely. As he jogged past the coach's table, the coach flipped a suggestion to him like a short flea-flicker pass. "Bowen," he called as Willie loped by, "cut your hair."

"No, coach," Willie said, and kept on trotting.

"What did you say, Bowen?" the coach hollered.

"I said, 'No, coach!'"

Across a twenty-yard space the coach called, "You don't cut your hair, bub, you don't play. Your choice." Willie flipped his hair all over as he jogged back to the beer-swollen little coach.

"You tell me to run and I'll run. Just say where. Say catch and you got it—"

"Cut your hair."

"Say jump and how far. Move and how fast—"

"Just cut your hair."

"Tell me about my hair and I'll tell you to fuck yourself."

"Cut your hair, Bowen."

"Fuck yourself."

"You're off the team, Bowen!" the coach sputtered like an apoplectic umpire calling the last strike.

"Sure thing, coach," Willie shrugged and flipped his helmet into that paunchy belly.

"You're not so good as you think you are, Bowen. We can win without you."

"I'm sure you can," Willie said. And they did. He and the coach insisted all season that they didn't miss each other. But in the spring, Willie got himself into terminal trouble and it was that very coach who bailed him out. Sort of.

A near-riot on the high school grounds had caused the Principal, protected by the Varsity Club, to berate the students over an outdoor microphone. Willie mounted the platform and the Principal warned him to step down, as Willie tried politely to take the mike away. "I think you ought to go now, sir."

"I really don't think that's for you to decide."

"I think you've done enough." The Principal demanded Willie relinquish his grip on the mike, and Willie said, "No." So the Principal told him he'd be suspended on the count of three if he didn't leave. Everyone stopped what they were doing to watch the show. With only two months to go until graduation and four years at Stanford (Amherst having withdrawn its scholarship offer after the hair incident) in the balance, Willie relented. "Oh, hell. Don't let me stand between you and your ambitions."

"And just what be they, Mr. Bowen?" the man demanded, principals not enjoying being accused of ambition.

"To make yourself a public asshole—" Willie mumbled, thoughtlessly, loud enough to be picked up on the microphone. He hopped off the platform while the crowd roared as not since his gridiron heroics. Their delight nearly drowned out the Principal's blasting rejoinder, delivered like a preacher exiling an unrepentant sinner or a referee calling a technical:

"You're out Bowen! You'll never go to college. You're through." The riot rekindled itself in Willie's behalf, but he was off the team again, until the football coach interceded. Punishment was just what Willie wanted, he insisted, in his secondary capacity as head of the school Guidance Office. A scheme was evolved whereby Willie would receive his diploma if he quietly withdrew. Stanford was irrevocably queered. All right, he resolved, so it's Trial by Fire. With college temporarily out of the picture, no one wanted him anyway, except the Big Picture.

The draft board was having the devil's own time finding bodies, because wild rumors abounded that "they're shooting people dead over there," and round-trip tickets were not always issued. Not many young men in Westchester County were enlisting, and the vulnerable busied themselves writing philosophical essays justifying their allergies to homicide. Many were safely tucked in colleges, or on drugs, or so Christlike in physique if not philosophy that they appeared better suited to washing socks in the Ganges than wading through Mekong Country on the A-Team. When Willie Bowen ambled in, the dottering clerks at the draft board drooled in the manner of starved alley cats seeing a giant white albacore float by in black garters and spike heels. Sorry Charlie, hell: they'd take anything they could get. For months all they saw were boys in pink pedal pushers.

At Willie's physical, one fellow peed on the eye chart, and another came in with a microfiche library of needle tracks on his arms. A brisk market thrived in the bathroom: oxblood for dropping in urine samples; similarly, sugar bottles kept disappearing from the coffee shop next door. One had a tampon protruding from his anal passage and he told the doctor, "It's a surprise: pull the string and read the message!" In all, the quality of upper-middle-class medical care suffered undue slander by the number of poor specimens parading by. Few, at least not the AMA, connected it to a foreign policy's more severe health risks.

Willie Bowen seemed, thus, Tarzan among the Fairy People. Tyler's friend, Saint Paul Hooper, had urged Willie to resist when Willie visited Tyler in Ithaca the weekend before. "Physicals are very anti-Darwinian," Hooper said. "If you can't pee in the paper cup, you go home and prosper. If you can pee in the cup, they have you shot."

"So how come Tyler's not going to grad school? He's joining the Navy." Tyler insisted he was a lousy example to follow and "grad school is like not being able to pee in the paper cup. You're safe, but after a while your shoes smell funny." They tried to argue him into throwing a show, but Willie was ambivalent. "Look at my alternatives," Willie said. "Shit all around. I might as well let them make me a war hero. I could become Jack Kennedy."

"Dead," Tyler answered. "Look, jerk, a lot of guys

165

are getting cut to pieces trying to become Jack Kennedy—it helps if your old man owns Boston instead of a lot of junk yards."

"If I'm lucky," Willie shrugged, "you'll get sent first and they'll have to send me to Europe." They blew it, Tyler and Hooper agreed. In compensation, they fixed Willie up with the most resolutely willing girl they knew, to ease their consciences. But Tyler was furious with himself at his failure. It reminded him of when Yogi Berra's manager told the Yog, a notorious first-ball and bad-pitch swinger, to "go up there and think, Yogi. Think." Yogi thought through three called strikes and never took the bat off his shoulder. "I told you to think!" the manager moaned.

"Ah, how d'ya expect a guy to think and hit at the same time?" Yogi grumbled.

Tyler wondered, in the face of his ineffective suasions, if maybe his wasn't the wrong approach: you don't make Cooperstown, or Canton, Ohio, by thinking. The Kid's got natural reflexes, good talent, nerve. Tyler wished he himself could stop thinking, because once he got released from the military, and Willie was subsequently shipped overseas, he mostly thought that Willie was going to get killed.

The first day in the field that week, Willie Bowen volunteered to walk point, virtual ambush bait. But instead of being ambushed, his patrol got the jump on whatever was in the rattling bushes. They emptied their M-16s until the bushes were completely blown away, replaced by a hanging blue cloud. Nothing.

Later they saw a figure move, and the word passed silently but excitedly, as a crow's nest lookout might tell his doldrums-locked shipmates of a distant flatness below a breeze. Two men moved right and two— Willie and another—deployed left, creeping off the trail into the high grass. Willie was the one who found him, catching a glimpse of the back of a head moving into bayonet range. Fire would attract other VC or draw it from his own nervous patrol: he would not like to bet his life on their coolness. So he lifted his M-16 high and took a deep breath. He plunged the bayonet down toward his prey, with a grunting thrust-cry,

166

"Hruuh!" Blood pounded in his ears and his eyes were obscured by panic as he lunged, his face twisted in fright. His victim was cringing, arms raised in helpless defense, jaw quivering, old blood and infected skin matted on his swarthy cheeks. He whimpered for mercy as Willie plunged toward him, a noise that was half-gargle, half-English. Willie could not slow himself and could not miss his feeble quarry. He extended himself more fully with a desperate stretch and crashed bodily into the man. The bayonet flashed past the man's head, but the muzzle smashed him in the ear and both men tumbled to the ground, the bayonet in up to the hilt in the soft soil. Willie's partner piled on to help subdue the prisoner. It was an American airman, shaking and sniffling beneath the two terrified soldiers. "Jesus Fucking Christ," Willie muttered to the spongy black dirt.

The airman lay there whimpering, and Willie got up and whistled for the others.

On the way back in, Willie sat down with the flier and offered him a smoke.

"Haven't had one in three weeks," the grateful flier said.

"Maybe you shouldn't have it. You're halfway to quitting," Willie said. "Want some canteen water instead?" But the man wanted a cigarette, as tangible proof to his body that he was safely on his way home, and told Willie his story.

Weeks before, the flier had been shot down near the DMZ.

"DMZ?" Willie whistled. "Do you know where we are? About a hundred kliks south is all."

The flier had been captured by some noncombatants, who handed him over to the VC.

"Were they VC?" Willie asked. The flier shook his head no. "Then why'd they give you over?"

"Week before," the flier said, "some of our boys came through—interrogated the locals and they didn't take to it too well, is how I heard it." Willie asked what was done. The airman sweated and looked nervous. "I'll tell you what was done, fella—'cause they done it to me. Got one of their women down. Real pretty little poontang. Boy friend or what-have-

167

you's a local VC organizer. Course they say they weren't. They say they was neutral. Bull*shit!* Got her down and interrogated her out back. With a snake. Pulled her dress up and goddam let that snake go to work. I don't think it was poisonous on account one took a nip outa me. But that snake goddam ate her out. Snuck its way right up her pussy while four guys held her down." The flier trailed off in a mutter: "Goddam fucked her with a snake—bitch probably loved it. Don't know if she talked, though."

Willie looked pale, but the flier continued. "Well, they evened the score. Scumbags. I just fell on the wrong town. Put that motherfuckin' snake right down on me and let it—well, it wasn't poisonous." Then the flier laughed and said, "Only thing's been keepin' me going these last few days: I wanna watch some Colonel pin that fuckin' purple heart on my wound. Nurses'll have to dress it—put salve on."

Willie said if it had been poisonous, maybe he could have gotten someone to volunteer to leech out the venom.

"That's right. That's right. I never thought of that. Course, I'd be dead." The VC had walked him all over the area after that. Several times he heard the sound of American motor traffic moving by. Once, in a ditch, he saw an endless line of U.S. and ARVN vehicles and TV camera crews, But his mouth was taped and he might as well have been watching it on television.

"They got us later in a rocket assault," the airman said. "I thought that time I'd bought the farm."

"Who's us?" Willie asked, confused.

"Me," the airman said. "I'm's us. Me and Charlie. Them was *you.* I was rootin' harder than *shit* for us. Hoped we'd clobber you."

"What happened?"

"Rockets blew the whole place apart. We all took off. Them one way. Me th'other."

"Who's them?"

"Them: Charlie. I'm us. What's the matter with you, boy?" He was free, but lost. For two weeks he wandered in the jungle eating leaves and roots, not knowing if he would run into more VC around the bend or simply starve. "In all that time I was movin' I musta seed a dozen VC movements. Not one single friggin' U.S. troop. I don't understand it."

Willie said, "Fuckin' Charlie's never where he's supposed to be. But we're always there looking for him."

"God-damned if that ain't the truth. I figure you boys is VC too, when I hear you."

"Same difference if I'd put it to you."

The airman raised his eyebrows in surprise, and Willie thought he looked like Howdy Doody. "Bullshit, same diffience! I'd rather you than some Slope any day. You want to be buried in Hanoi?"

"Same difference," Willie said.

That night, Willie sat up and passed on an opportunity to get stoned on stuff that was certified as "dynamite," in order to write a letter to his brother, Tyler.

He wrote that becoming a hero was too dangerous. "I'll settle for malaria and a ticket home, thanks." It was flip, with blithe contempt for the threats around him, though he was increasingly aware of them.

There were recompenses for all this. Despite the danger, his service was "something like letting a junkie loose in a heroin factory." That was not a simile, but a direct appraisal. So, he went over to his buddy's tent and joined the bunch. He lifted up the M-14 barrel and smiled at the joint peering north from its operating rod assembly.

"Damned fine weapon," his buddy grinned. "Shouldn't never have switched to fuckin' 16s. Mothers jam too much anyway." He coughed out a lungful of smoke as he laughed.

"Yeah, but," Willie said, inhaling between phrases, "they knew we were doing evil things with these suckers. Gotta keep the boys clean enough to kill, ya know."

"Shut up and smoke it, Bowen. You're way behind. You're Bogartin' the best shit in I-Corps." Willie took a deep drag from the barrel's end, the little roach glowing orange at the other end of the rifle. He passed the glowing source under his nose. His eyes widened as the smoke poured into his lungs. Then he held the rifle stock against his shoulder while the next man took a drag. He fiddled with the trigger as he aimed

169

the barrel down the man's throat. It was his turn again, and his head swam as the smoke, purplish from hash and supergrass from Laos and who-knew-how-much opium and kif and heroin and whatever, curled from the corners of his mouth. This was some fancy shit: two tokes and you'd be on the wall looking like a fucking Martian, if there were walls around, not giving a good goddam what they did with your body for a week. No one was sure whether the source, seemingly a VC sympathizer, didn't really work for the brass. No one cared. Willie's buddy called the stuff Primordial Goo. It was indigo, a tacky hash resin, like the sticky plastic little girls used to blow into bubbles. And it was incredible. "You subversive son-of-a-bitch," Willie coughed, as his buddy leered. Willie wondered what the devil he was doing on the wrong side of an M-14.

"I'm not subversive. I'm a pay-tree-ot."

"You're a pay-*toilet!*" another laughed.

"No joke. Cap'n wanted me to do him some D.A. notes to tell the replacements Why We Are Here—"

"Why *are* we here?" Willie laughed.

"Dope's cheap."

"*I* know why we're here!" said another, struggling upright, singing: "We're here because we're here because we're here because we're here!"

They fell back giggling and rolling, gone on two tokes.

"Hey shut up, man. You'll wake the fuckin' dead!" one whispered hoarsely. All were on their sides in the smoky hooch, laughing until the juice dried in their throats. "Come on, you'll wake the fuckin' dead."

"Yeah, and they'll take our places for a tour."

Willie's buddy poured a little wine in the muzzle and shook it around, then poured it out. They put another joint in and drew it in with wine vapors. "Man," Willie said with awe. "Guy who owns this thing's gonna be a long time cleaning."

"He's been wasted a week," Willie's buddy said, giggling, as he aimed the rifle at a third who took a drag.

In the morning, Willie was sent out on a mission, stumbling along without complaint. It was his second field mission in two days. One more and he'd be rotated back to base guard, and get some rest. At his lunch break, he looked over a letter he'd written Tyler but never mailed. If he made it home alive, there'd be no sense sending it. If he didn't, well, the Army was pretty good about those details. So it remained in his hip pocket, getting damp with sweat. Near evening, they were ambushed. Willie's buddy and the patrol leader were killed immediately. Another was busted up in the leg. While they poured cover fire in the direction of the ambush, they called in a Med-Evac chopper on the patrol leader's phone.

When the chopper arrived, the ambushers opened up again, and Willie and his patrol hustled the wounded onto the chopper, while four others dragged the dead as fast as they could. They heaved Willie's dead buddy aboard and the dead patrol leader with him, and then they all scrambled on, firing back at the bushes.

"Get this thing the fuck out of here!" Willie yelled to the frantic crewmen. The engine roared and mixed with the pock-pock of weapons fire. A Spec/6 told Willie in the din that they'd better have a solid story why they rode the chopper if they weren't wounded.

"Preventive medicine!" Willie shouted back. "Protective offensive retreat!" The chopper took off and brought them all back to base camp. It dropped them off and flew away again.

Willie went to see the Operations Officer with his after-action report, since he was the senior survivor. He justified his patrol's evacuation with a story about "enemy saturation of the area."

"Hundreds of 'em, sir. They only got two of us and one hurt bad."

The Operations Officer picked up his phone and radioed Willie's story to Intelligence, who relayed it to Brigade Operations, who relayed it to a strike force. Air strikes were pounding the area in an hour. Mortar and heavy artillery poured in from every angle, blocking every route of escape. Napalm canisters cracked open and the bushes and trees sizzled like a beef fondue. From the attack group to the strike force, to Brigade Operations to Intelligence, to Battalion Operations to Willie's commander came the news: the half-hour barrage was a complete success. Pilots had spotted hundreds of running VC, trapped in the flame's embrace like ants in a bonfire.

Willie and his patrol were sent out the following morning to count the bodies. Sure enough, there were some. Maybe twenty. Who knew who they were? It took all a man could squeeze from his intellect just to determine that they were once humans.

It was from there that Willie's group was sent to the moonscape to count the bodies and cattle in a fresh napalming. When he returned to base, he reported that the earlier mission had been a huge success: dozens of dead, by the count; dozens of dozens. The wounded had been dragged away, natch. Operations was happy. Brigade was happy. I-Corps was happy. Far away, where all the bodies were boiled down to final statistics, somebody was happy, and chalked in some fresh numbers on a running count of "WHAM!" successes, to determine how many Hearts and Minds were Won that week.

Willie was rested for three days as a base guard. The fourth day he would be off duty.

On his second day of respite, Willie found some time to be alone, and curled up in his sleeping bag holding onto himself. Persistent in his mind was a girl friend of Tyler's, now, according to Tyler, a free agent. She had carrot-red hair which Tyler said was nature's way of attracting male humanoids in the jungle. Nature sure knew her stuff, Willie thought. He had begged Tyler to fix him up, but Tyler always said, "You're too young to fully appreciate her, Kid." When he visited Tyler in April of the past year, Tyler and his friend Saint Paul Hooper arranged a date with Mary Marshall. She was at the School of Hotel Administration, majoring, Tyler said, "in one-night-stand studies." Saint Paul thought she should transfer to Indiana: "She could split time between the Dental School and the Kinsey Institute; do great work in oral prophylaxis." He refused to elaborate. But Willie got the general idea, and looked forward to the date with great anticipation, hoping, as he put it, to "find out about this blow-job business that everybody talks about so much."

On the third day of his rest, the squad in the field

was decimated. No one survived. And that night at the base camp, sappers and infiltrators switched the direction of the trip-wire-triggered, spring-loaded, Claymore mines. A noise was heard near the camp perimeter and the auxiliary string was pulled. A cordon of rounds would cut down anyone moving near the barbed wire. But the rounds came zinging in on the base. "Fire in the hole!" they screamed as white phosphorus lit up the night. Magnesium flares and tracer rounds came in like clotheslines across the barbed wire toward the center of the camp. The sounds of whining rounds zigzagged across the base, glancing off aluminum sidings, mingling with the soft thud and thump of slugs hitting sandbags, the howl of mortar and its sudden detonation. Then something hit the ammo dump, which went up like the Fourth of July. The enlisted men's barracks in one area was turned to dusty splinters. The senior officers' latrine collapsed in on itself and disappeared in a self-suturing wound.

When the base camp stopped exploding, everything grew silent. No charge. No attack. No descent from the hills. Nothing. Willie spent his day off helping clear the wreckage and setting up new defenses.

"Not too good, now," a fellow working with him on new booby traps said. "You make it too good and it'll kill us. Make it lousy. I want to go home. Fuck it up and maybe we'll have a chance." Willie was convinced the VC knew it was his day off.

Willie was still alive, and so the letter in his pocket remained unmailed. It would soon be nearly unreadable from sweat and mildew, itself smelling like shit-and-spinach. So for safekeeping, Willie placed it in the hollow stock of his rifle with his cleaning kit. The letter read, in part:

. . . a vast emptiness out here. No front. No time. No sides. If I was hit in the mouth and on the floor —at least I'd know which way was up. It's spooky. There's nothing here. Nothing.

They say there's no fear in a fire fight. Bullshit. We were in one. They say your hands don't shake. Whoever *they* are. Only because you can't *see* them. You're so blind with fear you can't see past your

173

fucking nose. But believe it, Babe: your hands are shaking all the goddamned time. I'm so scared sometimes, so crazy fucking scared it's silly. I may run away at any time. And I'm afraid it might be too late.

I only have one heroic thing in me, and it's not very much: I'm having them send you this letter if I get killed. Don't believe it if they tell you I was a hero. I probably got it running away. Let some other guy wear the ribbons and medals I win, some guy who can use 'em to get laid. Tell anyone you want what a coward I was. Tell your kids and Mr. Mack's especially, so that they don't come over after me. It's a little late for me to worry about pretending to be a hero.

So if you're reading this, I ask you to do me one favor, Babe. Go out and get laid once for me, 'cause I'm dead. That's the only thing I want done in my honor. And maybe once a year in my name. But let the lie stop with you. It wasn't because I was a hero that I got offed. At least not by choice. And oh yeah—Hey, Babe: you were a fucking good brother.

D ECLINING TO SPEND ANOTHER NIGHT trying to sleep in a place designed for thinking, Tyler Bowen checked into a motel in Tucson. It was as close as he could bring himself to finding a whore; paying a price for liberty.

He had wandered in the morning from Jacome's Department Store—disappointed that there was no branch of Goldwater's—to the Pioneer Hotel in silence. "You have any out-of-town papers?" he asked the smoke shop clerk.

"Last week's Sundays."

"They'll do," he said, buying the New York, Washington, and Boston papers out of a homesickness for real news. "Know a good motel?"

The man, in a sea-isle nylon shirt, sweatless and straw-hatted, said, "Tucson's full of motels, son."

He wandered in silence up First Street to Stone and over to Speedway, where a passer-by gave him directions to the University; it occurred to him that if congeniality was to be found, it would be there. Perhaps some fresh-faced girl awaited him, whom he might invite to the evening's session and show off for.

But after an hour of watching students play keep-away with some campus dogs, and floating in and out of a Frisbee toss, he grew melancholy with reminders of undergraduate afternoons, and retreated to the Student Union for a Coke. It closed at noon and everyone was headed for a football game, so he returned to his motel and papers and slept away the afternoon by the pool, his sweat running news ink onto his skin.

An editorial in one of those old papers said, "November coming in the country is cold. In New England and the Northwest, damp air freezes the ground hard at night; the shortened days are brown and brittle. In the South and Midwest it is a season of mists and sudden chills. All over, early gloamings." Indeed, time and seasons' moods make landfall in the East, from whose great cities is sent the news of new sensations to the country. "November is a time of gloom," the paper said. "Color has fled the world and only memory shelters hope through growing desolation."

But in Tucson, the time before November's arrival was uncommonly warm. A dome of hot air clung to the southwestern tier. And the jolt of reverting to Standard Time was also muted in Arizona, for it "Remains outside," as the *Intelligencer*'s editorialist put it, "the national delusion of easy sunlight and Daylight Savings."

Yet even Tucson shivered to the approaching November spirit with its country this year, despite its singular warmth. It too had no hope. This November was an "off year," with no great election to supply at least the fantasy of effect against the flow.

What would stand for the spirit of November 1967
175

as October buckled? The cheap sunlight bargains that become bad debts? The papers had suggestions in their coverage: "The vain charge of the young and self-proclaimed humane," said one, "wielding frail arms of incantation, wish, and witness," referring to a rally at the nerveless, unscarred Pentagon in October's barren maw. A Washington paper told of how the ground of reality trembled and buckled under lotus eaters of every station; hallucinations were not exclusive to the dispossessed. It described "orgies of speculation in the front rooms, drug traffic in the back rooms, chaos in the paper work" of great financial houses. In Boston, American biochemists were honored for their research into the nature and principles of true sight's chemistry. News of this was, of course, well known at Gila. But the Boston papers made more fuss about another honor, of greater interest to Tyler Bowen, one that he'd missed at Gila: Boston's Carl Yastrzemski had walked off with the Most Valuable Player award, after leading the Red Sox to the pennant and winning the Triple Crown. Tyler dozed off, wondering if the press would now feel kindlier toward Ted Williams; after all, he had taught this kid to hit.

As he dressed for the evening panel, and its distinguished collection of experts, Tyler recalled something Cornell's dean once told him: "Sometimes, Bowen, I think you know two facts about everything, and you're just clever enough to use them as if you knew more, and to get the hell out before someone sticks you for a third." The sting of which was first undone by Saint Paul Hooper's assessment, "When they make the Great Cornell Movie, the entire administration and Board of Trustees will be played by Jim Backus."

The admonition weighed on Tyler further when he arrived at the auditorium and considered his fellow panelists' credentials. Some had academic degrees and titles cantilevered upon each other, some had exquisite affectations which bespoke critical intellect, all making him feel a dilettante. He was no longer shooting hoops in an empty gym; this was a full-court press by a major conference team in front of spectators. And it was the spectators he had figured to be the greater problem.

Experience at Cornell had led him to expect outbursts of moral wrath from the University audience, justly angered Christians with the lions finally in the dock, a Jacobin tribunal holding them to answer for various technocratic sins. It was not a role he looked forward to: he imagined his placard might read, "Tyler Bowen, Co-opted." Nor were any pretty girls likely to be at a dumb panel on a Saturday night. In any event, at Cornell the classiest women would be the molls of the most articulate syndicalists.

Memory of Cornell also suggested that visiting poets had the best time of it, primarily with faculty wives who'd run off with them, at least as far as the next lecture stop, on the slim promise of evacuation—yet another reason why he came suddenly to regret his major. But neither were they in attendance. The faces in the audience were scrubbed clean, eager if a little dull, and apparently innocent of worldly crimes. They appeared, for the most part, comatose. "Around here," a junior faculty member had told Tyler over pre-panel coffee, "S.D.S. is quite well thought of—as a football power, San Diego State. The most pervasive political influence on campus is Moral Re-Armament. You know them? Christian Anti-Communist Crusade."

"I've heard of them," Tyler had said.

"Well, we're kind of winter quarters for their circus, the Up With People show. As for the war, mostly it's a viewing habit. *Gunsmoke* starring your neighbors."

"Might help shut it down," Tyler had ventured. "Ratings fall—" But his own innocence of faculty—even junior faculty—upmanship was showing. The game was to score points, off which team didn't matter. He'd been trapped, gone for the ball on a fake only to watch a young faculty hot-dog drive through with a favored thesis:

"Perhaps, but to me it's inconceivable that it could have lasted this long *without* TV. What that tells me is it's entertainment, or fiat, and that people now accept their foreign policy as dictated by *TV Guide.*"

All Tyler could muster was, "Didn't help Ed Sullivan," and the resolve to avoid this buck further. As his thoughts wandered during the initial statements and early exchanges, he pictured his esteemed co-panelists

177

as a basketball team: some were intimidated by elbows and hustle, one had no outside shot, while another made his point by driving hard just to draw the foul and take an easy bucket. And like many a basketball game, the referee distracted from the show. This one, a moderator who was a Professor of Political Science at the University, did so by percolating tiny puffs of smoke from his pipe, apparently indicating cogitation. Each exhaust, Tyler imagined, matched a morpheme of thought, the smoke's density no doubt revealing levels of meaning, all perhaps sublime but which, when translated, made dirty words to any Indians attending. He wanted to flip a wad of paper down the length of the table and see if he could pop it into the pipe's bowl unnoticed.

To the extent that the audience made their concerns felt they distracted the panelists from the announced theme, Public Policy and the Academy, shaping a desultory discussion on the consequences of increased governmental influence and whether that boded of creeping socialism, certainly a Bad Thing locally.

"I think there is a pernicious myth we must dispel," one panelist said. "I call it the D-Day Myth, the rotten harvest of success: that by throwing enough public money at things we can overwhelm all problems. Whether we like it or not we are not immune to the harsh economics of reality, or the harsh realities of economics."

Another enjoyed repeating himself with citations of the "irony" of liberal governments inhibiting personal choice, during which revelations Bowen stifled a yawn and thought to himself "All right, it's ironic. So what?" No one in the hall was willing to take a stab at the announced topic. Prepared only for the original theme, neither was Tyler armed for an ad lib debate with anything more pointed than good intentions. Still, he felt the burden of his silence oppressive. Credentialed or not, he at least had the privileges of a panelist, if not the art or good sense of one. So when the next speaker looked down the panel table and invoked Tyler's opening statement, he was all-too eager to respond. "If I understand what you said in your earlier comments," the speaker remarked, "I might add that

178

I agree: we do live in a world of alcoholics with but one bottle of booze. Shall we draw lots? Give everyone an unsatisfying little? Cut it with water, set up a political process, a hierarchy of subordinated needs established under a social contract whose price is—well, anyway, shall we do all this to foil nature's cruder means of dictating survival or—"

"That ain't what I said," Tyler interrupted. "And if I may say so," he added, deferentially suppressing undue glee, "there's a fallacy you're attributing to Darwin, about survival being identical with fitness."

"By definition, with all due respect to our young guest, it is. *De rerum natura.*"

"I think you'd agree," Tyler tried, "that certain valued members of the human tribe need assistance surviving. I mean, we may not be what nature has in mind either. We may just be a false step, too. There may be some species who'll make monkeys out of us."

"They'll just have to make it on their own though, won't they?"

"Yes, but," Tyler tried, twice turned around, "the field on which we contend for survival may not be appropriate for us, either in terms of our advantage or our standards. I mean, I assume that at some level what distinguishes us from things that do our own tricks better, computers and robot systems and insects, is our capacity to generate values that exceed our experience, and supersede the struggle. Things not in 'our best interests.' I mean, principles for which we would abandon all advantage, things we would die for, and ought to live for."

The older man said, "I confess I find this a peculiar tack coming from the National Laboratories. I do get this from some students, who would abandon 'linear' thought for some sandbox of emotionalism, replacing reason with sincerity, reason being, to my mind, beyond them, or unavailing in their attempts to remake the world as a teenager would dream it. So I'm a little chary about where you're trying to lead me. Do you know where? Not back to the jungle, I trust."

Another panelist stepped in to help Bowen off the hook and the conversation drifted even further from the program in a Brownian movement of conceits. At the

179

end, each panelist was asked to summarize and Tyler began with a ritual rubbing of his chin and a disclaimer. "I'm afraid I feel a little out of place here, and have all night. We've been listening to a lot of expert spokesmen, and I'm hardly an expert, just a spokesman. I am what you see in the papers referred to as 'an official spokesman.' And of course, no one believes what *they* say anymore. In fact, I'm only an assistant official spokesman. But when I look toward you in the audience, and I look at all this high-priced talent, I think 'well, we've got 'em outnumbered, anyway.' " The other panelists made sounds of tolerant amusement, a patronizing noise, but the audience was silent.

He looked up and smiled wanly. "I seem to have made a little problem for myself. I can't remember why I wrote what I'm supposed to say, and the only other thing I brought with me is a story about a tapeworm which—well, let me go at this another way, try to work what I want to say and what I'm supposed to say together. Uhmm—when this area was a good deal wetter than it is now, millions of years ago, it was the happy home of dinosaurs. Now, they were fierce, but not the brightest reptiles, and they roamed these parts mostly trying to remember where they'd been. Where they were and where they were going escaped them entirely. Not to do further violence to Darwin, we can adduce the dinosaur's passing to a dud time-bomb, its brain.

"Well, we too will leave our dinosaur bones: monuments, spires, trackbeds and bomb craters. But . . ." He began to range over some evidence of Nature being a fickle judge of survival, diseases whose point in the grand scheme was both elusive and short-lived. "So it seems to me that our ability to remain free from the tyranny of microbes or bad ideas, to throw our imaginations over the wall and follow . . . uh, well, anyway, here's the pitch: our work at Gila is hardly more valuable than a poem. It is not guns. It is not even butter. But it is inspired by Nature's own dynamism and ingenuity, by Biology's passion for temporary survival amidst hostile and amoral forces, not every one of which is becoming for a species wise enough to think on such things."

A note was passed hand to hand down the line of

panelists as Tyler Bowen finished speaking. He was so bored, or perhaps nervous, that he paid it little heed, scanning it without comprehension. He assumed it was a cutoff note, and stuffed it in his pocket without a hitch in delivery.

"Defending the past and present is brontosaur's folly. There is adventure enough for us, just stumbling into the future. And it will not be the lawyers who will mend a fractured world or lift it from malaise; they will just litigate the remains."

The largely catatonic audience applauded politely, cued by poetic closure, though generally numbed by the preceding statements.

"I hope Mr. Bowen will take it in good spirits," the moderator said when he commended and thanked them all in turn, "if I say how warming I found it to hear an 'official spokesman' come out so strongly for freedom from the Party Line." Tyler reddened slightly. "I only say that because, speaking of good spirits, all this listening makes one thirsty—and the party line is forming at the Faculty Club buffet."

Small clusters of audience members formed around each panelist, eager students with questions and arguments to try. Over his shoulder, Tyler heard one assaying, "But from David Hume to Kenneth Arrow, the impossibility of perfect satis—" Bowen sought quick escape and grabbed the moderator's sleeve as he passed, asking, "That bad, huh?"

"You did fine," the moderator said as they pushed toward the door. "Sorry about the joke. Come, you can meet the rest of the department. Help us drink up our meager budget."

"I think I'll just go soak my wounds in a nice warm therapy pool at—"

"Bah," the man scoffed. "False modesty. When you get back and they see the Monday papers, why, I bet you'll get a five-dollar raise. You made all the good quotes."

"Only about half of which were in my prepared text. When they see how far I deviated from Scripture . . ."

The moderator insisted Tyler was unnecessarily concerned. Then, spotting a familiar face, he said, "Here's half your problem, now. Warren?" he called, reaching out to snare Warren Reigeluth's arm. "Our guest here wants to amend his remarks. He wants to deny everything."

"Good idea," Warren said amiably, as he and Tyler shook hands. "Listen, I never really got a chance to thank you."

"You two have met?" the moderator asked.

"In passing," Tyler said. "How is he?"

"Fine. Just fine," Warren said, and explained what they were talking about, overly praising Tyler's effort.

"He's a tough little bruiser, huh?" Tyler asked.

"Yeah. No permanent damage," Warren said.

"You heard Bowen's presentation," to which Warren nodded efficiently. "What did you think?"

Warren deadpanned, "No permanent damage. But it's not me you have to worry about."

"Ah, yes," the moderator beamed. "Now, Bowen, if only you can convince our favorite newsgal that you didn't mean anything you said—or better, weren't here —I don't envy your problem."

"She covering this?" Tyler asked Warren, as the moderator ducked off to catch someone else.

Warren half-smirked, "She'd just love to make us all look silly."

"And I've given her the chance."

"I would think so."

"What's her beef?"

"She's on some sort of tear, who knows. She's got a favorite quote from Bertrand Russell she's sprung on me a few times. You may be the next beneficiary of her wit. 'There is no nonsense so arrant it cannot be made the creed of the vast majority through adequate governmental action.' "

"I didn't think I was that bad."

"You were—adequate," Warren said. "I mean that sincerely."

"Either way," Tyler groaned, "I'm wiped." For most of their walk to the Faculty Club gathering Warren talked about his work and explained the methodology of his thesis project, while Tyler pretended to listen. Finally, Tyler said, "I don't suppose she'd do me a favor on account—"

Warren shook his head solemnly. "If I knew where she was, I'd ask. I doubt she'll come back for this. She gets bored easily. And if I asked, I doubt she'd listen."

"If I asked?"

"She'd just start hollering about the First Amendment—which I doubt she has either read or understands. You're better off taking your lumps, believe me."

At the party, Warren quickly disappeared into a cluster of his colleagues. Tyler was left nursing a drink, wandering from conversational node to node. Then he had another drink and continued his aimless circulation, smoking too much, drinking more than was prudent.

A room full of chatty strangers is an uncomfortable thing and the internal dynamics of parties always made Tyler lonely despite their crowding. One could either join a group and stay with them, thereby missing the party's whole, or wander freely, an eternal newcomer in each group. The feeling was disorienting, promiscuous at best, distancing at worst, rather like trying to partake entirely of a big city, or toying with every mood and scene of one's age. He felt part of none.

Then he saw a familiar back of a head. He'd seen it so often in his imagination that he forgot they were barely introduced to each other, and nudged her as she passed, as though old friends. "I was told you weren't coming."

"Who told you that?" Johanna asked.

"Your husband."

She arched an eyebrow. "He lies, as you can see."

"He said you'd be bored here."

"Oh," she said, stopped in her tracks. "I'm sorry. He does tell the truth."

Cocking his head to the crowd around them, as though to say except for her he was at their mercy, Tyler said, "I had no idea these things were a worldwide bore. I used to think it was just Cayuga's waters in the drinks."

"Don't be silly. Why, people come from seven states to be bored here. We're very famous for it. Is that why you came?"

"I came to ask you something."

"But you didn't think I'd be here."

"Well, your husband kind of dragged me here and—well, why are you here?"

"I'm supposed to ask the questions," she said. "You answer them."

"Only during working hours. I need a favor from you. I want to kind of unsay some things I said tonight, for the record."

"Not your rhapsody on freedom for dinosaurs!" she gasped.

"Did I say something about that?"

"Mr. Bowen, you said something, at one time or other, about nearly everything. And I for one agree with most of what you said, even when you were on both sides. Anyway, in this state extremism in the defense of liberty—*especially* for reptiles—isn't supposed to be a vice."

"It's also not supposed to be my job," he said, worn out, half-resignedly, half-cavalierly tossing back his drink, seeing her friendliness as a journalistic ploy that would simply further heat his soup. "You finished asking me questions?"

"No. Did Warren tell you about Michael?"

"Said he's okay. *Actually*, he compared being dropped on the head to listening to me."

"More or less," she agreed, a kind smirk emerging from the corners of her mouth. Then she grew serious, or appeared so. "I just wish I knew how to thank you properly."

"Well, I asked you a favor but—in fact, as I recall I have a dinner invitation from you guys."

"That's right! And you see how smart you were not to cash it in right away? You may be able to get two dinners soon." She craned her neck to see if she could spot her husband. "I wouldn't let what Warren said worry you," she winked, almost to no one in particular, then said in a mutter, "but I wouldn't lend him my wife or my car."

"Actually, he said to watch out for you. Especially if you told me my stuff was 'adequate'."

"But it was! I assure you," she said.

184

"Some Bertrand Russell quote about governmental nonsense or—"

"Oh," she giggled, delightedly. "Why, I never suspected he was such a sensitive boy! And you! If he bothers you again you just tell him that Bertie also said 'Politics is largely governed by sententious platitudes which are devoid of truth'." It did not seem to cheer him up much. "How are you on truth?"

"Adequate," he mumbled.

"Want to start with the A's? Let's try aardvarks."

"What is that anyway with you, the litmus of the universe? 'Cuz I don't know a God-damned thing about it! Except every time I see you, you either ask me about anteaters or tell me you're not going to."

"Would you tell me if you knew?"

"I don't know. Maybe not. But I also don't know what you're talking about, besides which I happen to have a very sweet note from you promising not to pester me about it. Why not escapes me. But then, so does why, so I'd be just as happy to move on—" and he started away.

"Not to tapeworms," she said, tugging at his sleeve to keep him.

"Baboons, I was thinking, actually." Neither said anything for a moment, and then Johanna dropped her grip on his sleeve. He asked, in the softest voice he owned, "Have we run out of conversation so fast?" Despite her persistence with a question, and her partiality to annoying ones, there was something almost wantonly intimate about her manner, as though she shared private places with strangers, or used glimpses of herself, the self usually hidden by social formalities, as a coping tool. She was flirting, he decided, but probably for a reason. Her studied frankness, almost rudeness, was ingratiating in its way. It was as though she was without that faculty which mediates between impulse and expression. It was charming and rather breathtaking, yet it surrounded her with a furious cloud of diffuse energy that was ultimately obscuring. For example, at that moment she was mugging at him quizzically, as though he'd overthrown some merry game they'd been playing. It was the expression of a bewildered puppy, a lopsided head-hanging and a half-pout. Out of its conversational context it would have served but to scramble her motile beauty and make it foolish-faced. To him just then, it made her seem the most unique and mesmerizing woman he'd ever met. "Uh—how's, uh, my Kewpie doll?" he asked.

She threw a hand up to her mouth, abashed. "Still on the floor of the car. Sorry. I can get it if—"

"Just fishing for things to say so's you don't leave me to the sharks."

"I have no intentions of. You are all that stands between me and a lot of embarrassing looks from Warren's colleagues."

"Huh?"

"You talk so well, but you don't hear so good, do you?" she laughed. "My dear, patient husband has determined that I am less fit to live with than I used to be, so he's camping at some friends while I enjoy what he calls a 'cooling off period.' The longer I stand here talking with you, I hope you don't mind, the more shady I seem. In slander, the best defense is increased offense."

"Excuse me if I don't look entirely thrilled about being used as a prop. Why are you bothering to stay?"

"I get the car as long as I pick him up and drop him off." Tyler was watching her carefully, an easy expectant look on his face, having decided that this latest tack of hers was simply mere perversity and, in fact, was perversity to conceal herself again. By silence and distance he was flirting as much as she, more aware of it perhaps than she. "Tell me," she asked in the next breath. "Do they pay you to look and act like this all the time?" He shook his head very slowly, as though he could walk in on her without hurry and ward off the fastest things she could send up. She felt she was in slow motion. "What *do* they pay you to do?"

"Get you a drink?" They walked by a professor who nodded at them politely while he continued lecturing two middle-aged women: "You can see the trends in art as well. Manipulation all around. Gimmickry with the medium itself. Narcissism. They drop their pants in public and celebrate it as now and hep."

"Of all the arts," Tyler whispered to Johanna as

186

they filled their glasses, "politics alone still rest on illusion."

"Tell him!" she dared Tyler.

"Oh, no. Gotta show some residual politeness. I, my lady, am a guest who's learned his lesson. I got bounced from one of these shindigs once at school— for telling a visiting State Department honcho that a Ph.D. didn't give him the preemptive right to bomb the shit out of dropouts."

"Now Warren would call that anti-intellectual."

"He's already let me know. Basically, he said I was full of it."

She gave a giggling noise and said, "Whether that's true or not, Warren has usurped the Reasonableness Square. If you disagree with him you're an extremist, and if he does with you, you're an idiot. He has the singular capacity to be logically indisputable but completely wrong."

"Sounds like you've made this quite a study. Is it an art or a science?"

She brightened faintly. "A craft. Now I know why they don't let Popes get married. Infallibility's a bitch. You're a very strange person, you know that?"

"It's the company I keep."

"You do the most contradictory things. You play with whatever it is you're so furtive about down there, and then this talk tonight, and that thing you did at your school."

"I got carried away a little. I've generally held my peace."

"And that's why they trust you?"

Rolling his eyes he sighed, "Check me Tuesday. Isn't there something more pleasant we can talk about?"

"How's the weather? How's your war?"

"Listen, I don't know why you're so convinced there's terrible stuff going on at Gila."

"Aren't you?"

"No."

"Off the record?" she said, and he nodded confidently. "Bullshit."

"Oh, yeah, lots of *that*. Hey, you should know: most

bureaucrats'd deny cause and effect. Doesn't mean they're tampering with it."

She examined him again carefully. "Know why they call the space people NASA?"

"Sure. National Aero—"

"Never A Straight Answer."

"Oh, c'mon! You've got conspiracies on the brain. OK, look, you want a quote? 'Kid says the war, she bites. Badly.' On the record. 'Comes out strongly for children and flowers.' But it won't sell many papers."

"I'm not taking notes," she said, offended. "I was talking to a friend, I thought." Out of the corner of her eye she saw Warren and said to Tyler, "Maybe the Holy Father'll grant you absolution." She smiled broadly for Warren, kissing him with antiseptic daintiness on the lips.

"I see you two found each other," Warren said.

"Your wife has just saved me the pain of circulating and having to talk about what I don't know."

"I thought you did rather well at that," Warren said. Tyler and Johanna stole sideways glances at each other as though to distinguish their own rough teasing from this. Johanna made a move in the direction of the drink table, but Warren held her forearm firmly, not letting her go. So she added, "But it was quite *eloquently* nothing."

"I get that kind of compliment all the time," he said, bowing to Johanna. "Once when I was in school, the Dean called me in and said 'Bowen? You know a thing or two about physics, don't you?' "

"What does this have to do with anything?" Warren asked.

"Well, I thought he was going to question me about coaxing a friend of mine to commit an indecent act in the Advance Studies Lab's particle accelerator. My friend thought he could achieve weightlessness and—well, I admitted I knew exactly two things. I was in biochemistry, actually."

"You've lost me," Johanna said.

"I'm not sure this story has a real point, but—" he was getting nervously glib, afraid for his credibility to Johanna and no longer concerned about Warren's opinion. "So he said, 'What about action at a dis-

188

tance? How particles signal their existence to each other through time and space?' He'd just blasted right past my store of physics goodies, and I told him he'd have to stick to concrete matters, like baseball."

"What does that have to do with anything?" Warren repeated.

"Nothing, I thought. I figured it'd hold him. But never underestimate the nonsequiturial capacities of a Dean. So he said, 'Very well, consider baseball and American literature.' 'I'll try, sir,' I said, and thought that was it."

"It wasn't?" Johanna asked.

"Nope. He went into a long thing about baseball and myth and how it was the field on which we expected the American Messiah to arrive."

Johanna enjoyed this more than Warren, who excused himself to get a refill. In fact, it was at Warren's expense, a kind of secret chatter to chase him off. "I wonder," she said. "There's Paul Bunyan and his Blue Ox and Babe Ruth—I bet there is a funny connection—"

"Well, the real guy might've been Ted Williams, but they drafted him. Then they pulled him out of the showers and made him suit up for Korea. It was a twinighter."

Warren returned, amazed that they were still talking such nonsense. "But see, here's the point," Tyler said, trying to draw Warren in. "The guy was right."

"About what?" Warren asked.

"That we're really waiting for some divine hero to reveal our central theme, to symbolize our best meaning and galvanize the whole stew—before some microscopic neoplasm erupts to undo the whole thing."

"Too late," Warren said, comfortable now in this realm. "You can blame the Kennedys for that."

"I don't know," Tyler said. "My father thinks Lincoln might be the guy—"

"Lincoln is a myth—and dead," Warren said.

"Well, see, that fits right in. If you follow the whole line, there's got to be a—a cleansing act of blood—to presage a Parousia—a Second Coming."

"Who said that? Your Dean or you?" Johanna asked, half-laughing.

"Oh, he said, 'I know who you are, Bowen—you're the one who put—who put—'"

She giggled, "The ram in the rama-lama-ding-dong?"

"Close. The methylene blue in the Faculty Club coffee. It made the whole Poli Sci Department pee purple for a week."

"Did you do that?" she asked admiringly.

"No comment. The man was a crackpot anyway. No doubt about it. Not the first in the Ivy League and not the last."

"Is that it?" Warren asked. "End of story?" He was looking for an opening to get Johanna to drive him home.

"Well, except that, uh—well, I was reminded of it by thinking what a goof it would be to do it here—everyone's so *serious*—and also by the point about heroes and myths. Everyone seems so passive, as if they're expecting someone to pull the whole thing together for them—as if it's tied by some magic threads."

"Not only not necessary," Warren said, suddenly engaged, "but dangerous—and in fact really what you're arguing *for,* I think. Meanwhile, Johanna, your friends grab for Kennedy artifacts like pieces of the cross. His name's spoken like Buddha. It means a thousand different things. Talk about your demagogues! And then you tell me 'wait till Bobby has his turn'—he's the biggest bully of them all! Some liberal champion. You like him because he's cute."

"I like him because he cares," Johanna said, reddening in exasperation. Warren turned away as she stuck out her tongue.

Tyler cleared his throat and tried to pacify, saying that "the myth is pretty compelling. I've got a kid brother who thinks he can pick up a medal and run for Congress. Everyone wants to be Jack Kennedy."

And Warren modulated his attack by admitting that his first impulse to study Political Science came because Kennedy had made it "well, sexy. And I was entranced with the argument in his Harvard thesis, that democracy has to adapt itself to compete with totalitarian systems. There's a real point there. And an opportunity—as you know, the Constitution's grant of legislative power is restrictive, while the executive power is self-defining and expansive. But, after watching him work, I think his canonization should be postponed for a seemly period. There's an unrequited-love thing that's got the liberals possessed. A pout. They all think history was derailed—the nightmare land entered, when he died. To them it's one bracket of a historical period —they're waiting for the other shoe to drop. Hence, Bobby."

"I either don't understand you or you're speaking contradictions," Tyler said. "On the one hand you're against executive power and on the other you're for it. Just depending on who wields it?"

"Like the liberals, one can be foolishly consistent on this. What I am saying is simply that the fulcrum of history may, in fact, be an individual, yes. In this particular case, I think the individual died about six months before we would have learned what a monster he was. The way he changed the nature of electoral politics—that's the key: he made it out to be closer to the Tong-wars. And what he did to the office itself, him and his brother—I think it'll be a long time before we have the kind of pre-Kennedian stability we once knew. They marketed him like a face cream. Sex appeal! Threw out all the rules. Try to put *that* Humpty Dumpty together again—the sky's the limit and the rules are out the window. If Bobby has the nerve to run someday, he'll probably win. Most people would vote for Tab Hunter over Lincoln. Any pretty show-bizzy tough guy with the bread's a good bet now."

"From the description," Johanna smirked, "it sounds like you expect an announcement any day now from Lassie."

"I think it's time we were going," Warren said.

"Where would you like me to drop you?"

"Home."

"Whose?" she asked. "I want the car."

"I'd rather not talk about this in front of strangers."

She turned to Tyler, "Can we drop you somewhere, stranger?"

"Uh, thanks—no. If you'd like, you're both welcome to come use the therapy pool back at the Royal Inn—"

"Some other time," Warren said. "Nice talking to you. See you again, I'm sure."

"Sure," Tyler said. He looked at Johanna for a second and bit his lower lip, feeling the same pressures he had as an athlete, with two seconds left and one chance to do it all—an artist with one fragment of a lifetime to use all his powers and finesse in one statement. This was his second good chance, and you did not get three. He felt an urgent message he had to convey—that he was inside his skin and knew who she was—before she slipped away again. An extra beat of silence was all he had to offer, and a slight wavering smile. "Good-bye."

"Do you know why they have therapy pools?" she asked. "Because Tucson is the elephant burial ground. Republicans come here to die. And the Mafia. Bye." A moment later, she came back. "Say, I want to apologize."

"For what?"

"For what Warren said. It makes my question look pretty silly."

"What?"

"Didn't you get it? I sent it up while you were finishing. Owello, mox nix."

As she left, he reached in his pocket and pulled out the scrap of paper, which he had totally forgotten about. He'd thought it had come from a fellow panelist. He read it and swallowed the rest of his drink before leaving. The note said, "When are you announcing your candidacy?"

Around midnight, Tyler was lying on the Vibramatic Magic Fingers bed in his room at the Royal Inn, depressed at his prospects. Who knew what would await him when he went back to Gila? On the television, postponed because of a night rebroadcast of a football game, was the local news. A man was being awarded the "coveted Green Jacket as Carter and Hauler of the Year." It made Tyler think his own father would be happy there. Vlad Bowen was in junk, scrap actually, and now mostly in real estate. He'd started before World War II, made a pretty bundle during the war, converted most of that to landholdings—Tyler and

Mr. Mack used to joke that he had an option on World War III—and made a recent killing in the '50s, when his last remaining scrap yards were bought for the site of an abortive amusement park called Freedomland, Inc. It was meant to be an eastern Disneyland, but its fantasies were just unsatisfying. Vlad kept à token scrap yard in Port Chester, New York, just so he could tell people "I'm in junk." That Tucson gave honors to its jetsam archeologists made Tyler think his dad would be most happy there. He loved honors, awards, and decorations. Anything official hung proudly from the den wall, regardless of how lowly the origin. Mostly, Tyler thought, that was his mother's influence, as though she needed certified, tangible proof of her excellence-by-association. At any rate, Tyler was sure he'd love to wear that Green Jacket. Instead, he was saddled with directionless children. The world thought the Bowen children were glory-prone, but Tyler knew better.

He was exhausted and uncertain. Whatever filtered back to Gila about his performance was likely to buy him trouble. He'd displayed precisely the opposite of that cocktail party skill his Dean had once chided him about: he'd lost control of himself and very likely exposed how little he knew; nor was it his inexpertise that was at issue, but his imprudence. That's what Susan Carver would go full-tilt berserk about.

He still held Johanna's note tight in his hand, fingering it, squeezing it like a piece of flotsam after a shipwreck, wondering to what use she would put the things he said. Whether she merely reported them, or pointed up their conflict with the Tombstone Center's spokesmen, his sin was the same: he'd been hired to speak for others, not think for himself. Susan Carver would doubtless find him unfit for further public consumption, perhaps even be forced to renounce what he'd said. Still, he treasured the note for its very intimacy of taunt. Of all the people attending, and of all the things he might have done, Tyler was at least glad to have engaged this one woman's interest on such a level. She was, he imagined, more intriguing to him than he was to her. She was probably doing her job, and better at it than he was. Nonetheless, he sensed a common pitch. He liked her odd asides. Her remark about Tucson matched his own feelings: even the toilet came wrapped in Sani-Check, as though the slightest infection might tip the scales and send an aging codger to his reward with an unpaid bill for room and raisin bran. He wished he'd said it.

The television was buzzing incoherently, and he was nearly out, ready to fall asleep in his clothes, when he sat up with a start. He reached for the phone book and found Warren's home number. He reconsidered: probably too late to call. Maybe in the morning. Have lunch, talk about the story, explain his problem at Gila. Maybe she'd bend. But maybe he'd seem too obvious in the morning. Maybe—he dialed impulsively, ready to hang up. No answer. Maybe neither lived there any more, or —who knows what it meant. He hung up to dial Information, when someone knocked at his door. Probably complaining about the television, he thought, and opened the door, hoping it wasn't the Police, to see Johanna Reigeluth. "Is this where the therapy pool is?" she asked, poking her head inside. She clapped her hand to her mouth in a favored look of mischievous forgetfulness. "Forgot my suit. But I brought back your Kewpie doll. Are you going to invite me in?"

"Yes! No! Please! Wait! Uh, just a min—no, here." He shoved the telephone book to her in trade for the rag doll. She grunted at the blow and leaned against the door jamb, enjoying his antics. "No, keep it, the doll. Let's get some food, OK? I'm starved. You know I was just about to call you?"

"Uh-huh. That's what they all say."

"What else do you think I'd be doing with a telephone book?"

"Did I ask what you were doing with a rag doll?"

"That was a long time ago, wasn't it?" he said, and she said nothing.

They settled on an International House of Pancakes on a street Tucson, for unknown reasons, called the Miracle Mile. As they ordered, he realized something odd. With any other girl he might have made a joke about having breakfast on the first date, but with this one he felt cautious, club-footed, sensing both worth and fragility too great for the risk of crass jokes. The restaurant was harshly lit and they sat squinting in the Formica glare. "Tucson," she whispered across the table, "is the world's largest natural deposit of fiberglass and stainless steel." He decided there was no point trying to parry everything she said, so he just nodded.

"I'm glad you came over," he said.

"Impulse," she shrugged. "Action-at-a-distance."

"You didn't really come for the therapy pool."

"Absolutely. My mother's been suggesting therapy for years."

"Sure took your time."

"I had to drop Warren off, and then there were these two hitchhikers going to Sabino Canyon."

"Boy, if I ever got in your car, I wouldn't get out."

"I'm not a boy. You were in my car. And you did get out. As for your room," she said, "you wouldn't let me in!"

"Oh, yeah, well. It's rented. You are exhausting. Do the jokes ever stop? Do I make you nervous? You still haven't told me why you came over."

"Should I leave?" she asked.

"No. No. It's just that I wanted to talk to you so damned much without all that cocktail party junk and all those questions, but each time I tried I either said something dumb or something happened. At least I didn't spill a drink."

"Why?"

He looked in one of her eyes then the other, putting fast-chatter aside. "It's been a long time," he said. "Between friends."

"That's why I came. Syrup?"

"Look, I have a confession to make. I've got a conflict of interests about three ways here."

"It sounds like you have a terrible problem," she said.

"Make you a deal. Let's both forget all about how we earn our livings for a while. I'm not very happy with mine."

"I can't ask you any irritating questions? You look so sweet when you're lying."

"That's the deal," he said.

She thought a moment, making rubbery faces, then agreed. Over multiple coffees they tumbled out words to reveal themselves, telling about their pasts, and families and friends, as though in a rush to begin or a desperation not to end.

"My friend Saint Paul," Tyler said, "talks to God daily sometimes. Claims He calls collect, 'cause He can't be bothered with a lot of change. I asked him once, since miracles are no big deal—after all, He isn't the prisoner of logic, He just does what He wants, right?—how come He couldn't whip up a dime now and then?"

"Did he have an answer?"

"He said God doesn't trust money, or the phone company. So I asked why He even had to bother with it, why He didn't just speak person-to-person, without the wires. He said the Lord works in mysterious ways."

"You don't believe?"

"Oh, sort of. In the implacable optimism of the universe. It's supposed to run down but there's an awful lot of us running up."

"Maybe that's just probability."

"Maybe. It just depends on which straw you get, what you believe, I guess. Until some clown in a super-chrome Pontiac hands me the short one and walks away unhurt I'll just keep believing I'm cosmically lucky."

In turn, she told him about an old childhood superstition of hers: that there were two beasts loosed in the world at one's birth; each roamed the globe in different directions, taking random paths on any given day. Of the two, one would get there first, the race simply to see which: the bogeyman of childhood fears, or some best hope and champion to restore one's faith.

"Who's in the lead?" Tyler asked.

"Let's just say I await my fortune with interest." She had been idly touching the white dot near her eye as she talked, and Tyler reached up to touch her hand. He held it there, alongside her face, and reached a finger tentatively toward that spot, but she began to tell about her father's stories and rhymes with animated movements of her head, avoiding that touch.

"The thing about scar tissue," he said, "is it's hardier than skin, in a way." She seemed not to be listening.

"Less elastic. It's neutral to pain and immune to dis-
app—"

"I think the only thing my father ever told me that
wasn't entirely optimistic," she said, disregarding him,
"was once, I was about fifteen I think—"

"What was it?" Tyler asked, distracted by her cheeks,
examining her at leisure, cruising her face. "God!
You've got the pinkest gums!"

"He was talking about Einstein, I think, about an unfinished theory he'd been working on, and one that
Fermat, the mathematician, had proved, or said he did
—but he died before he could write it down. And my
father said, 'Everything that is fine and elegant and fitting isn't always what Nature or History had in mind.' "

"Don't you believe it," he winked conspiratorially.
"C'mon, let's get out of here. I'll sing you flat songs
and tell you sad stories—"

"I don't want to hear sad stories."

"Too bad. Only know one. The tale of my cat, who
was a son to me—"

"What happened to him?"

"Died of a hairball on a Tuesday. Now all you have
left is flat songs."

"Sing me flat songs. It's the best offer I've had in
weeks. Months. Maybe years." Her eyes flared, then
clouded over with a mist that might have been fatigue,
shy hope, or some sudden interior rue.

"What else can I offer?" he asked.

"It's enough."

He decided he would stay with her as long as she
would let him. They drove aimlessly about, Johanna
offering a suggestion for a turn here and there, saying
little. He turned to her and smiled, then turned back to
the road, shaking his head. "What?" she asked.

"I'm just afraid you'll suddenly get tired." She
reached over, and placed her hand lightly on his forearm.

It was nearly three in the morning and they had
driven past the roads to Sabino Canyon and Redington,
bumping over the Tanque Verde Wash. "Where are we
going?" he asked, hoping it was someplace infinitely
distant.

"Out of Tucson." With every turn they rose, up toward a pass in the Santa Catalina Mountains, to an overlook that commanded all the places they chose not to be.

Below them, the city blinked in dots and blips of light, answering the faraway stars above the black desert, with no more intelligence in its information; but harmless now, like the stars' ultraviolet rays, when seen through the right filters. Tyler stopped the car near the top of the pass. Both felt apprehensive, excitement tingling in their tailbones, embolisms of anxiety bubling in their blood. Johanna got out and stood in front of the car. She spread her arms and waved at the hemisphere's horizon, pointing out where Spud Rock and the Little Dragoons lay, "and Fort Defiance, from all those old cowboy movies. Way, way over there's Kitt Peak, looking for messages."

"I wonder what Tucson's blinking?"

"You're supposed to be the expert," she said.

"I'm trying to forget."

"Probably GIGO: Garbage In, Garbage Out."

"Well, computers are only human."

"No they're not. They're very stupid. They can't weigh anything important. More power to the people who pull the plugs!"

"Don't be so hasty, now. All those little ones and zeroes—every nanosecond and they're doing some mighty philosophizing: on/off, yes/no, existence/absence. Every junction's a great to be or not to be. And they keep on going."

They walked around aimlessly, talking of nothing at all. A small fog settled in on Tucson, a second filter, on the shroud of warmth in which it lay buried. Up on Redington Pass they imagined they were two survivors, the last two, of a planet that had warred itself into extinction: together by accident and need before desire. Johanna fell silent and then looked at him. "Say something," she asked. He grinned and squeezed her around the shoulders.

"We're going to be great," he said, "we're going to be terrific." And her eyes tossed prodigal green flecks of night in return. "You know what? In the light, your eyes are—you're going to think this is dumb—but they're the exact blue-green color of a xenon oxide laser beam."

"Is that good?" she laughed.

"It's wonderful. That particular laser may be the key to harnessing fusion. See they aim them——" She put a hand over his lips. "OK. They're also the color of blue-green algae."

"That's terrible!" she said.

"It's beautiful. Blue-green algae just about invented the whole concept of sexuality."

"It's just a pigment of your imagination. I think you're a little crazy, Tyler Bowen."

"I'll have you know I've got a note from my doctor. It's notarized. Says no loose diodes. No aliens controlling my body. Except my blood is four-fifths Vampire and one-fifth Scotch."

"Which makes you what? A Macaroon?"

The circles they walked in grew smaller as they approached a caution point. She was a little scared, having learned to distrust her instincts over the years. He was also, afraid that if he told her how lonely and trapped he'd felt, she would not believe his gladness at meeting her, once and again, was genuine. With sudden intensity, she asked him, "Are you honest?"

"Where I come from, honesty is another gambit."

"So is that. I meant you."

"And I still mean that where I come from it's a gambit. In New York people trade off small pieces of themselves. They hedge their bets by playing different games. They've got six locks on their doors and ten on their lives—and half are in the Civil Service. Never look you in the eye. Just like Gila."

"And you?"

"I'm trying. I want to believe I will gamble everything vital for something I might cherish—"

"What would that be?"

"Ah, if I knew that, Miss, I'd understand what my old thymus and Marshall glands are talking about."

"I hesitate to ask where that is."

"It's *why* we hesitate. Somewhere up by the heart is a kind of soft tissue that's just along for the ride. It doesn't want to do any work at all. So it looks like the whole show is organized to walk it around and find food for it. You know where it is." She nodded her head: it was a place she would shrink to. "Well, it turns out it's more than a metaphor. There's a hormone made there, called thymosin, and it looks like a big key to immunology. It helps the body establish its identity. So it really does tell you who you are."

"But you can't hear it."

"You can see it, reflected in people's eyes. That's why it's good to look. And sometimes you see the most wonderful eyes looking back, and you forget who you are, long enough."

"You said no one does that where you come from."

"I've learned a little, lately. Most people are afraid to have their secret hiding places defiled by uncaring strangers. So they show the Fool's Gold and touch each other's skin but never go very deep."

She said nothing, indeed seemed sad by her quiet, and he felt as though he had been misunderstood or seen as trying to steer the discussion to sex. But the truth was all things in their lives were its next-door neighbor, all were related radially from that hub. She was thinking something similar: that every person had a private note, a personal tone as atoms have their individual spectral bands. It was an interior thing, and not something in one's control, too intimate to share with passing strangers. It came, songlike, as a violin string caressed by a tender concertmaster, when spoken to, held, loved, by someone who cared enough to understand. Then was one's sex flowered fully: one's swoon was perfect sympathy with every tissue's pitch and timbre.

A layer of their protection was now shed; their commitments and ambitions fell away, replaced by a paramnesia of the moment. Garbed in that forgetfulness, of anything but each other, something held them back despite their attraction. "I want to be your friend more than anything right now," he said. She leaned toward him to kiss him on the cheek and pressed against him lightly, both vulnerable and expectant, then leaned back to examine his face for honesty.

"You know," she said, tracing his mouth with her fingertips, "you have what they call an archaic smile. It's a very fine thing to have if you're a Greek statue."

"Do you want me to take you home now?"

"We've come this far. It seems a pity not to see the show."

The sun was not yet up, but the stars were the better part of memory, erased by advancing light, when he first held her close to him. "I want to be your friend. I want you to believe that," he whispered, touching her chin. "I can only promise you I'll try. I'll take you home now, if that's how to show it." She silenced him with a timid thrust up to meet him closer.

"Friends can kiss," she said, and he answered that with a strong hug to hold her as she wavered on her tiptoes. Then she pulled away slightly, asking oddly, if he was really descended from vampires.

"A little," he said.

"Do you disappear in the daylight?" He said nothing, just looked at her unwaveringly. The shift from night to day created a convection current that cooled the air even as sunlight came. "Let's watch it come up," she said, "like Indians." So she fetched a blanket from the storage well and they wrapped it around themselves for woolly warmth. He hugged her with one arm and stroked the curve of her jaw to her ear, playing with the ringlets of her hair, and she rolled her face into his big palm and kissed it. Slowly, deliberately, still masquerading their intent as imitating Indians they pulled each other's clothes off, then sat haunch to haunch, afraid to proceed without some final lie; naked, asexually joined at the hip, happily Siamesed, pressing at their junction, dissembling by their inattention, as if to claim they had disrobed to show mere friendly honesty. And odder still, they were content, hugging gingerly, prepared to remain that way, deriving warmth and protection from this.

As Spud Rock and Eagle Peak gleamed of copper, and the Little Dragoons woke, the dying moon settled over the western range. Both Tyler and Johanna were unconsciously informed by this, as Carl Poulson had been at the Grand Canyon years before, of being small creatures on a large planet which spun ever into sunlight and out again, moving bodies in a universe of change. They pulled backward from each other briefly, self-conscious of the moment and their own small fibs.

It was a fraction of their time, but convoluted with interior times, a weighty instant that held the future's clue, a future already written by the sum of moments prior and the additive fibs that contrived to be truth. As a drop of water totters on the Great Divide, precipitous history would be charted from an angle, an attitude, a bare inclination. It embraced them with the moment's whole point, ripeness, and the question of what they might become. "We're going to be great," he said. "We're going to be terrific," and winked in glad conspiracy.

"Sunrise," she answered, "is a thing unappreciated by better vampires and lesser lovers."

They were safe, beyond mistrust and fear in mutual vulnerability. They were not so beautiful as they had seemed the night before, now pale and stiff-limbed. Still, they reached up from that and kissed again. Her breath fluttered and he calmed her. Like two rising birds shot with a single arrow their paths crested where they met. They glided easily to Earth through the window of chance, their boundaries melting, seducing each other no more than themselves. Wearily and shakily they made love.

Their hinge was moist and not without a droplet of fear. For such moisture was both the last step and the first in a chain begun before the blue-green algae swam. Ignorant atoms engaged to make molecules, molecules wed to form amines, changing partners, dancing, mating, divorcing, recombining to form amino acids united by a peptide bond that was where poisons linked, recombining once again to make some wholly new, wonderfully proteinaceous thing, with the power to re-create itself and feel the pleasure of its act, to aspire, to articulate its needs and then achieve some temporary fulfillment, within which was more hope and dread, desire and risk and information than in all the things they might say or do or feel again. That sensate power brought news of pleasure, and with it, the ability to be afraid. But even that added energy to their bonding. Union itself was paramount. So neither worried that the other might be more concerned with the act's mechanics. For by the promises of novels and movies and what dreams suggested, theirs would fail. It was not the gymnastics people searched for in their poverties, believing in. It was trembling and clumsy, gently shy. Its energy was all potential, well intentioned, and so received. "I was better at this when I was younger," he whispered, and she hushed him, accepting that clumsiness, too. She floated under the desperate feelings entrance had brought, the irreversible commitment to a brand new path, the shattered virginity of discarded ways. This was dangerous new ground, but she had plunged ahead heeding only the murmurings of her own thymus. It would not do to regret the step and doubt one's instincts now. And she held him with a tenacity whose meaning he could hardly guess.

All they could manage in their warming morning fatigue was a gentle lullaby rocking in each other's arms, coital in afterthought, a mixture of fluids at their tangency and on their sleepy cheeks. Johanna felt full inside, as if she had found, despite the artlessness of the dance, a partner who offered a rhythm she could move to, by the way he responded to hers; after ages of one who watched his feet with every step and led by simple force. Tyler felt the blood in his ears cease pounding; then the veil of urgency lifted from his eyes. But nothing changed. He wanted to be nowhere else but where he was, within her, beside her. Drowsing in embrace they lay together while the striated sun, with parhelion changelings on its wings, scattered the Tucson mist.

"What would you do with me?" she asked on the way back to his motel.

"Run away to a neutral country and write the Great American Joke."

"What's black and white and red all over? Give up? A campus riot."

"I'll go alone."

They slept away Sunday like kittens in a box and in the late afternoon drove down to Tombstone. When he pulled his belongings out of her car, he shook out her blanket and refolded it. Stuck to its nap was a burr acquired while they had shivered in its shawl. "Exhibit A," he said, and pocketed it for a memento. Someday, he thought, he could have it gold-plated and give it to

203

her as a charm, unafraid to let such thoughts get the better of him.

Johanna was more modest in her thoughts, wondering if it was wise to draw the temper of a fine encounter by stretching it through time. Perhaps good memories should be enough. Certainly they had lost some energy in their exchange, for both were now overcome by centripetal forces, drawing them back to their obligations. Who could know what grim presents might await them and what new pressures such a conflicted association might create in those already turbulent vortices?

When she dropped him off at the Tombstone Center, from which he would arrange a ride to Gila and she return to her office to write her story, they divided up the fresh Sunday papers between them. On the front page was a picture of young people and troops facing each other at the Pentagon. "My friend Saint Paul's in that mob somewhere," he said. "Said something about trying to levitate the place. Looks like it weighs a ton."

Johanna was looking at another picture, one that would cause a recession in even the most ardent revolutionist's heart. It announced the death of Dr. Ernesto Guevara, called Che, in the Bolivian hills. The CIA-trained posse displayed their prize catch as an object lesson. "It looks like *The Anatomy Lesson*," Tyler said of the man holding the body for the cameras.

Johanna shook her head. "John the Baptist in the hands of Salome, by Artemisia Gentileschi. Or Judith cutting off the head of Holofernes."

"Maybe. Smartass."

And the cusp of times is also time of paradox, so there was news of resurrection, a return of the Undead: Richard Nixon, slain a thousand times by popular rebuke and serial rejections, was stirring once again from Southern California's precincts, where self-belief coalesced to self-creation. He was speaking wherever they would have him; he was in Phoenix the day before, according to the papers, salivating over an election still a year away, one yet unseen by keener eyes.

But those things were still only October's epitome, the haunted surreal images, hobgoblins and headless horsemen as well as befits a Witching Time. November and the fall itself would not see its metaphor delivered, despite the Sunday editorialists, until the days after Thanksgiving. Then would something new and desperate flicker into being.

"I wonder," Johanna said, thinking of the Washington marchers, "what they really thought. Did they think they could—do anything?"

"Probably not. But I wonder if they really know they can't—that's the thing. A friend of mine says, 'Without the proper lever, you'll only get a hernia trying. But *with* one you can move worlds—' "

She kissed him on the cheek. "Mountains, certainly."

"Please? You promised. Now, don't spoil it."

"Am I too, too terrible?" She pouted like a kitten that, however independent, wanted just then to be petted, or rather demanded to be.

"Too terrible?" he said. "No: adequate. More than adequate. Superbly terrible. Monstrous. If you weren't, little poison, I wouldn't risk getting shot by an angry husband."

"Warren? He wouldn't dream I would—I mean, not that that's why, or that you wouldn't worry him. It's just outside of his imaginative frame, I assure you."

"Actually, I was thinking of the angry husband who is chief of Gila Security. Never met his wife. But he'd just love to fire a few warning shots through my back before he got serious. I'd almost rather face your husband."

"You sure you'll be all right in that horrible place? We don't want to arouse suspicions, do we?" she smirked, pleased with herself.

"I knew I could count on you. I await the reading of my fortune with"—he sighed forlornly—"interest."

Let me put it to you this way," Susan Carver bellowed, waving a copy of the *Tucson Intelligencer* in Bowen's face. "I am the judge, the sole arbiter of what is pertinent, what is news and what—when it comes down to it—is *fact*. You leave Truth to philosophers from now on. It's not your department. When I open the paper—and I don't care if it's the *Ledger-Domain* or the Tucson rag. I don't want to see what *you* think. I want to see what *I* think!"

"I'm sorry I—"

"Don't be sorry. Be smart. Didn't you have enough to say that you had to go think of more? If they don't have enough copy, maybe they'll run a press release, or lead it out—white space, that's what sells. You want philosophy? I'll give you a little: newsprint is a body without a soul. You must be very careful what gases you breathe into it.

"Now the problem you've created is very interesting. In a sense, you've cushioned your fall. I've got to keep you on view now, don't I? And it's not even that I disagree with what you said. I just disagree with your right to say it. At the moment, Mr. Gracie and everyone in Security is wondering who let the mad bomber loose, and why. I have to explain it to them."

"I'll take full responsibility—" Tyler tried.

"You can't. You have none. You just have a job. Do it."

"Yes, ma'am."

"I still think you'll work out, Bowen. You're a promising lad. Stop promising and start delivering. Because another gag like this and I'll throw you to the wolves at Security. And your body and soul will go in different directions. Have a good day."

The business of keeping secrets, bureaucrats and philosophers agreed, had deadly consequences, as did the business of spilling them, dating back to Eden. But the pragmatic admitted certain lies one lived with, and by, and for. And it would be naive to say they did not become then true. Still, philosophers and bureaucrats shared a hunch of faith: that somewhere, something is so, worthy and right, something so basic and true that all things derive their value and veracity as ratios of its unity. It must also say something about what gods reign, if any at all; for with none, "all things become permissible."

"What do you figure, Bar?" Bowen asked Zermatt with an earnest look one morning. "Which way is it? On the one side you've got people going, 'Someone is dying for every lie,' so when the last secret is known men will no longer die——"

"Are you sick or something? Who the hell knows? Who cares?"

"Think about it. The other side's pretty strong too. If we knew everything, and had no reason to fear death we'd be as good as gods. Somebody there would be pointless, and——"

"I don't know anything about any of this. All I know is there's the World's Biggest Secret and if that breaks I know just the guy who's gonna be terminal. You figure it——"

"You do your job, you get your check, you get drunk——"

"There's not a whole lot more, Babe. Listen, check out any of your historical heavies, they'll all say the same thing: 'I did it for the money.' "

"Jesus, Bar, they're not baking cookies at Gila."

"Well, I wouldn't let it give you bad dreams," Zermatt said, pouring his cold Sanka out. "For all you need to know the place is creepy with cancer work."

"What'll they do with the stuff when they——?"

"Calm down, will ya? You got years of this ahead. Get used to it."

"How?"

"You hang around, you learn—you learn to live with it."

"Maybe you're wrong."

"Sue me. Just don't go do something stupid."

"Hey," Tyler looked up, offended. "You know I wouldn't do anything to get you in trouble."

"I'm not talking about me, babycakes, I'm talking about you. You got reflexes—but use 'em in the right place. Swing for the fences, but hit the pitch.

"Look," Zermatt said, clapping his hand onto Tyler's shoulder, "in case of National Emergency, you're a valuable asset. You guys are a nucleus of talent. Some'll be called on to piss in reservoirs. Some'll give college kids mono—I want priority on that levy. Some'll *teach* people stiff. And you? My boy, when the balloon goes up someday you'll be mobilized to say nothing's happened. You'll be attached to the Office of Denials. You could make your mother proud by dying early so she doesn't have to worry. But come the revolution and you'll make your papa proud: it may be necessary to lie for your country."

Tyler rolled his eyes skyward. "Just glad I'm not a Catholic."

"Me, too, Babe," Zermatt said. "Me, too. Never confess. Always take the Fifth!"

At the Tombstone Center for the Applied Social Sciences, Tyler Bowen's petty excesses at the Tucson symposium had caused little concern. And this diminished to the vanishing point as more of his work was observed. It was apparent that he had made a slight "human error" but had been brought under quick control. Things were working as they had planned. Tombstone considered that its work for Gila was now largely completed. The systems and patterns they had devised for Gila proved adequate to every task and contingency. Tombstone still believed themselves the farsighted peers of the Constitution's framers, equal to anything history might throw at them. At Tombstone the image they preferred was "proud parents": Gila was their ward, and theirs had been a careful, thoughtful home, full of good example and moral guidance. They had seen the child through blemishes and growing pains,

208

brokered it into a fine marriage to its purpose. Now it was time to let go. Gila was trustworthy, self-programming, and Tombstone had new, more enticing challenges.

In a sense, the work at Tombstone, of which Warren Reigeluth was a valued asset, was also an exercise in constitution making, of systems invention, of ideograph conjuring. Its scope dwarfed the work they had done before, paled Gila Compound's activities, and taxed the imagination of all participants. No more were they concerned with refining the instruments of a political system and creating effective agencies for its will; nor with finding ways to cope with what history offered, but to anticipate, and predict, by finding new ways to envision and describe history itself, withal to master it. For at the end of that rainbow lay El Dorado, the true gold of perpetual power.

They sat around polished oak tables, in tinted-window rooms, toiling over these conceptual things. They were uniformly addicted to pipe smoking, and toying with ashtrays that were built into the tables. And they never soiled their hands with anything more dangerous than hot coffee.

There was a certain urgency to their work, for the future seemed to approach with increased speed every day. New elements had entered human affairs in recent centuries, more frequently in recent years: new techniques, new insights, new understandings and exigencies. Systems of thought and behavior based on obsolete views would not be suitable for this new world's coming age; cracks in the architecture of the old were already evident. As Houston brought brains to bear on winning the Moon, and Gila struggled to control Biology, Tombstone tried to outrace the impending vestigiality of thought styles. In doing so, they hoped to "get there first" and thus maintain order and conserve the world's distribution of authority.

So they pondered whether the appropriate models for human interaction were to be found in poker or Poetics, in Dialectics or in Physics. A given model would suggest new forms and possibilities, new devices to be reckoned with. They considered the forces acting on human affairs and wondered how to equate them:

209

there were drives intrinsic to the species, it seemed—greed, lust, vanity, territoriality, dreams of immortality; and extrinsic ones such as Meteorology, Agronomy, and other controlling cycles. And there were internalized patterns derived from crude interpretations of surrounding systems: Astrology, Socialization, Ethics, Comity.

In early November, one of their first working papers was circulated. It said, in part, "In approaching the question of historicity and historiography, care must be taken not to impose two-dimensional constructs on a four-dimensional system." What this meant was that history's *fleuve* was not necessarily linear, pocked with "important dates" of discrete action. "The direction of social time is traditionally defined as a changing state of information and organization. We are now seeing an inverse relation between these two."

It was largely unarguable that history was not spotted with sudden happenstances and rupturous events whose causes were entirely local and immediate. Nor were there ideas whose time arrived on a given morning. Such asumptions, as comforting as seeing the past as a purposeful march toward some inevitable culminating present with obliged tomorrows, were a function of vantage; and inept. Unless one was concerned with when Columbus discovered America out from under its inhabitants, it had to be conceded that linear views were rooted in circular reasoning.

Still, Warren Reigeluth's study group found it an important tool to analyze the clustering of events at certain historical moments. They were concerned with questions of stability, crisis management, incipient revolution, and they were troubled by the increasing frequency and intensity of modern social tremors; but most of all their very suddenness.

So they pored over what looked like maps of the sky, computer printouts of historical constellations. The major clumpings and first-magnitude events coincided with those years when the balance of forces was disturbed and "everything happened": 1492, 1609, 1776, 1789, 1814, 1848, 1859, 1872, 1905, 1932, 1956, and so on. Of course, those dates only told of great eruptions. Causes were subterranean, their ultimate effects like so many pumpkins. So the analysts drew tracks on their charts and inferred from these paths insights about process.

What was missing was an explanation of the independent variables which created these causes. There was apparent self-generation of transformation, arising from within continuing systems. Was this an iron rule, something about the limits of perfectibility, the relationship between liberty and order? Or were there various fulcrum points of opportunity for increased purchase? It seemed in the more recent years as though the tools of mediation magnified the rifts in the vessel, enabling tiny menaces to lay low Goliaths, in a twinkling, as the smallest rays might cause the most maladaptive mutations.

Warren struggled with this for days. There was something missing in it all. A larger framework, a more accommodating equation with no loss of grace or parsimony, was required, or a different kind of computer projection. There were other confluences that made social eddies, phenomena that built to tides. Much that was threatening in the modern world, upon the evidence, could be attributed to technics in the grip of passions. New indices were important now: gross tonnage of newsprint consumed—if that didn't simply reflect a net gain in domestic pet population—and number of journal articles printed, amount of time sharing at computer terminals, net draw of electronic information media, gross garbage produced. Hell, he thought, the sunspot cycle was a good economic indicator, better than the rise and fall of hemlines; though the economy was a perfectly good indicator of hemlines in turn.

His disagreement with the methodology flashed into the open at one session, when he suggested that their procedure lent "false importance to precisely that notion we're trying to avoid. Big years. Are there 'off years'? Look around you. This year's a perfect example. Intense what? Cultural cage rattling. It all hinges on what you call a happening."

His study group's leader admired Warren's spark, but reminded him, "We're really best off sticking to the well-trod middle of the road."

"The trouble with the middle of the road," Warren said uncharacteristically, "is that's where all the horses shit."

"What I suggest you do," the study group leader told him, "is prepare a monograph on it. Why don't you take a representative year and trace both what *you* call happenings and what we do. See what you get."

"It's been done, Sid," Warren replied.

"Do it again."

With impatient vigor, Warren attacked the idea. At least it kept his mind off Johanna. But then he had a second thought. Why not debunk the thing he disagreed with by underscoring how naive and simple-minded those notions of what constituted popular history were. It was then he thought of Tyler Bowen's prattling about baseball. There was certainly a subject of inordinate public attention and no lasting effect. So he called Tyler at Gila. "I was thinking of you," Warren said pleasantly and Bowen nearly had an occlusion.

"Oh."

"I asked a computer for some raw data on events in 1957 and it started to tell me about Ted Williams. Can you imagine that? It must have been programmed by a friend of yours."

"Is that why you called?" Tyler asked skeptically.

"Not . . . exactly. I was intrigued by our discussion the other night, and I thought we might extend it. I was a little testy about some things, you might have gathered. Can you come up to Tombstone for a drink?"

"What did the computer tell you?" Tyler asked.

"Ted Williams nearly hit .400 but Mickey Mantle won the Most Valuable Player award."

"It's true. Mantle was well liked by the voting scribes. Kept his real personality under wraps." He agreed to come up as it gave him an official excuse to take a car to Tucson.

The year that Warren was considering was fruitful for his purposes. In 1957, as every schoolchild once knew, the Soviet Union helped ring in the International Geophysical Year by launching their first Sputnik. (The computer bank was overstuffed with data on this.) They followed it with another, carrying the little doggie, Laika. That much could be traced to that was

212

a commonplace. It gave America the national heebie-jeebies: every ranch house and convertible was suddenly vulnerable to an attack of dogshit from outer space. Vast sums were appropriated for science and education, and for military hardware. Engineers became ascendant. The United States decided it was in a race, though later it would be partial to football similes.

More important, Warren thought, was the year's failures, what didn't happen. Project Vanguard was rushed in order for America to launch at least one baby moon before the year was out and share the line in future history textbooks. Such haste, Warren knew, came from being prisoner to one's own propaganda. Fathers who've convinced admiring sons they can lick the Heavyweight Champ know its dismal consequences, and Project Vanguard was thus ripped untimely from its launching pad, haplessly premature. It proved the greatest public embarrassment to American technology since . . . the data bank said it was contemporary with the Edsel.

So 1957 passed into the printers as a Russian Year and the U.S. resolved not to see that happen again. Harnessing the talents of its brightest captured German scientists, America got on the scoreboard with *Explorer I,* the satellite, in early 1958 and never looked back.

When Warren sketched out for Bowen what he was doing, he added, "Now, 1957 was just about when John Kennedy was gearing up for the 1960 run—"

"Fascinating." Tyler peered at him hard, trying to figure out what was up. "Exactly what the hell does all this have to do with baseball, if anything?"

Warren bit the inside of his lip and said, "I was hoping you could tell me."

"I don't know what you're getting at."

"See: we know, for example, that the Vanguard failure ushered in that national inferiority complex Kennedy exploited, with his inflated rhetoric."

"From which we can adduce the Space Race and the Vietnam War. So what?"

"Well, I'm interested in his psyche, and that of his

whole Boston crowd. Now, let's say he was frustrated by missing the vice-presidential spot in '56—"

"The best thing that ever happened to him," Tyler said.

"Well, failure being a spur, what about the general Boston anger over the national humiliation of Ted Williams, home-town hero?"

"Either you're playing games with me or you've got a little bit of crackpot in you."

"We're talking about mood, about gestalt. You're the one who gave me the idea. I think you're right. All the attention those things get—"

Tyler had no idea where he was coming from now. "Look, 1957 was also the year after elections weren't held in Vietnam. One of many. *That's* a contribution."

Warren answered, "It was also the year of Khrushchev's 'Secret Speech' and his announcing support for wars of national liberation. What I'm after is what, on a popular level, structured self-regard, particularly at the prime focus, which I think you'll admit was Boston, for Kennedy."

Tyler leaned back and studied Warren carefully. "I think I'm the wrong guy for you. I've never given it that much thought."

"Enough to give me some background. For instance, what was it about Williams that made him unpopular? He delivered, didn't he?"

Tyler said, "So did Muhammad Ali. He was too aloof, and they jumped all over him for it. Look, um, if you're really serious about this, I think you should forget baseball. From what you tell me you're after, it's more a question of, well, morphology."

"What?"

"Structural—you guys 'n' your billiard ball models are missing the point. And from what I hear about what you're into at Tombstone you may just prove the world is flat as a billiard table."

Warren smiled vaguely. "You do a *lot* of talking about things you don't know about."

"Maybe. That's because I get paid *not* to talk about the things I do know about."

"Such as?"

"Oh, lots of things. Take, for example, your study.

214

Now you guys are so enthralled with the calculus as a social science tool that you miss the fact that there's a central inadequacy in it."

"Elaborate," Warren said expressionlessly.

"Not all change occurs in continuous, deterministic ways. Now it happens that while you guys are trying to boil society down to physics, the people who *do* know what they're talking about are trying to get up from the bottom. Maybe you'll all meet somewhere in the middle, around the level of microbiology. One of the mathematicians at Gila has been working on some stuff advanced by a French guy, René Thom. It's fascinating stuff with all sorts of implications about time and motion. See, he started looking at biological events and—in fact, social change—and he's busted through to a whole new approach to calculus, by getting a new angle on topology: shapes."

Warren tried to follow as Tyler explained how for hundreds of years, the calculus of Newton and Leibniz —whose simultaneous discovery of that very concept also spoke of historical ripeness—brought mathematics to bear on questions of flow and change. At Tombstone, in their attempts to regard social movement as imitative of physics's principles, this was a way a system's movements through time, space, and alteration of condition could be precisely symbolized. Great and complex matters could be thus analyzed and perhaps manipulated. It all had to do with infinitesimals and differentials, as a way of making curved paths straight, making flowing things stand still. "But some stuff," Tyler said, "doesn't work that way. Panics, mitosis, fertilization, densities of breeding populations or saturation of poisons—"

Tyler was making his point now, with Warren tagging behind. He enjoyed having Warren dangling. "Now the only disconcerting thing about this whole business is its name: Catastrophe Theory. See, as I understand it, the likelihood of a catastrophic event increases as a function of the variables. At about six, it's a sure bet. I find that a little discouraging when you think this is exactly the kind of system they'll use to set up nuclear strategies."

"I suppose that's what they pay you for," Warren

215

said, shaking his head like a swimmer clearing water from his ears. "But I ask a question and you give a speech."

"You want explanations or you just want to be a snot-nose?"

"Go on. Examples of social applications."

"Well, I don't know. It's time-stress-motion stuff. It makes sense in biology and—see, it's about limiting forces and stuff. I think. The sudden change is called a 'catastrophe,' and it happens in just about no time. In biology I'd think of mutations, after mitosis. For example, first there's the event of a cosmic ray changing a gene to make a rogue cell. But then the thing remains dormant. And then it starts to work. Why does it suddenly go berserk? And then there's the question of its setting up a vascular system to support itself. And then there's the question of its metastasizing. It's a series of plateaus and catastrophes."

"How about a physical model," Warren asked. "Something I can visualize."

"The universe. The farther out you go, the nearer you are to returning."

"On a smaller scale," Warren said.

Tyler thought a moment. "The dead letter office." Warren remained impassive, and Tyler thought that he either knew, and was incredibly slick, or didn't know and was incredibly stupid. And Tyler began to sweat a little from the question, his own internal interrogation. So he thought to test Warren by surfacing it a little. "On a social plane," he said, "you'd have to consider falling in love—and out."

"Catastrophe's the right word," Warren muttered. "Say, I was just going to ask if you survived my wife's story all right. That was a pretty nasty trick."

"What?"

"Well, I didn't agree with very much of what you said but I heard that part she quoted quite differently. The thing about specific adaptions being temporary local phenomena and not necessarily universally purposeful. I was struck by your point about sickle-cell trait being a defense against malaria—"

"Useful when we didn't have quinine and no one lived past thirty-five, yeah. A burden now. I don't see

216

how she could have gotten it so screwed up. Well, that was the least of it. It only hurts when I laugh."

Not unlike the shapes they'd been discussing, their discussion had worked its way back to a point of origin turned inside out, for now they shared an attitude, admissible in polite society, decorous in both locker room and drawing room, a despair of Warren's wife. From this common plane Tyler was allowed to speak of her. "I take it you two aren't on the best of terms."

"Breathing space," Warren answered. "Do us both good."

"I don't doubt it."

"Tell you what," Warren said, in his hale best, "you got a girl?"

"Yeah."

"Maybe we can all four have dinner."

"Who?" Tyler asked incredulously.

"You and your girl, me and my wife. I'll tell her it's all off the record. I owe you a favor. A little charm and she can be had. She won't bother you again."

Warren made his point with the study group's leader, by his debunking pseudomonograph on "Calamities of 1957." But the leader was intrigued by the notion of "Catastrophe Theory," saying "it's a perfect Finagler's Variable for post hoc analysis." Warren was content with this resolution, as it had afforded him the chance to make an individual and unique presentation. That it was a fanciful one hardly mattered. He had been brought to the attention of those who counted at Tombstone, and they liked the way his mind worked. A position of prominence in drafting the study's final report might come of it, and that would be a major career break. For those who knew said great store was put in this study.

Tombstone was often given such hardtack to chew, and usually succeeded in turning it quickly to jargonized bubble gum wrapped in Latinate nonsense. Sometimes they ruminated over the bright idea of some bureaucrat who, when they were through, would shine like the genius his family and friends never imagined he was. Often, their work proceeded from the request of a high but unnamed source; and just as often, that source had picked up the idea from another wing of Tombstone. At times like that they wondered if perpetual motion machines weren't so impossible after all.

Now they labored to render human action sensible to computers, a matter that would not startle anyone but the most devout believers in pre-Beardian myth.

With paradigms based on physics and mathematics, their first working papers enjoyed the felicity of the multiple meanings of "The Democratic Model." They had derived elegant postulates: "Conservative are the great principles in nature, in realms of Physics and Politics. . . . The inertial propensities in mass actions prevent sudden revolutionary change in the absence of substantial pressure external to the system." That this ignored the evidence of history seemed a trifle, for they argued, "The Theory of Large Numbers does not discriminate as between objects and people. Probability always obtains." This was their most favored premise, and it was not incompatible with new refinements and understandings, even Thom's Catastrophe theory.

The degree to which Johanna had resisted seeing him again surprised Tyler and confused him. He was certain that as much as he and other men found sexual acceptance by women validating, and rejection devastating, women were most frightened of not being called the next day. Johanna was frightened by her own forwardness. "I practically seduced you," she said.

"Only because you didn't give me a chance to try. And I was afraid to. I thought I'd outrage you. Anyway, it wasn't practical. So it wasn't seduction. So stop being crazy."

"You have an awfully swell opinion of yourself. Besides, you work for the platitude machine."

"Sweetheart, it's a relative world. And I've seen your husband more times this week than you. Believe me, he owns the machine. I just read the printout—not willingly, but pretty well. And even *he* says we should have dinner, you and me. Sort of."

So they did, and so did she go through the same catechism the third time round. In fact, a courtly formalism reigned at the beginning of each of their meetings, until that, too, became a kind of play between them.

And every few days when he had to go to Tucson or Phoenix to boost the work of Gila, or to deny it, he devised some way to see her for a few hours. Between times she would drive down to Gila and meet him at the public gate, no matter the hour. On those nights the desert became a play house for them, far away from authority and bogeymen. "That's the only good thing about this whole region," Tyler said one night. "You can trust the fact there's not a damned thing for miles."

"Your specialty, again? Biology? There's more going on in the desert right under your nose, Mr. Bowen—"

He confessed, "Sense has a very dampening effect on my conversation, Miss."

"So I hear." And he worried, at odd moments, that she would compare him unfavorably to Warren; at other moments, that she would compare them at all. And he also worried that his value to her was the simple virtue of not being Warren, and that his other virtues were too subtle.

"He likes his work," Tyler would say. "Christ, he loves it."

"What's to say you don't?"

"Me."

"To me." So he also worried that one day she would turn serious in her game and tell him lying was no longer charming, was no way to make a living, none that she cared to lie next to, and would cut him loose for her own needs; or make him choose between safe duty and her. Or remind him of the things he'd said he'd stand for. Then she would suddenly cease her game and he would revert to the more comfortable state of a moon-calf.

For his part, Warren told Johanna he thought divorce was "not necessary at this point," and he made awkward reconciliation gestures she resisted. He remained ignorant of her liaison because informing Warren, Johanna told Tyler, was "not necessary at this point." Then she grinned and kissed him on the nose.

"You kiss me on the horn one more time, sweetheart," Tyler said, "it means we're married in six states. That'll make your old husband suspicious." She then kissed him on the mouth with a great feigned swoon, so he tickled her into submission. "I'm going to tell Warren," he insisted.

"What?"

"I'm going to tell Warren."

"What are you going to tell him?"

"What a knucklehead he is. The next time I see him. Just for the hell of it. Not about us—just what a knucklehead he is. I've got to tell the truth about something to someone."

"Just be careful how much truth you tell to whom."

"I swear, I must be the only man in captivity who is continually urged by women to lie—but of course, never to them."

"You poor, used boy."

"As my friend Baron likes to say, 'When it comes to sex, there is nothing I won't resort to—including pity.' C'm'ere." And it was kind love they made.

Later that same week Tyler and Zermatt sat in an open area, drinking beer from paper cups, on the bench of what used to be a softball field. It was overgrown and choppy from disuse. No one was playing there, or walking, for it was late and hot. Zermatt said, "In a way, it's a privilege to be here."

"It escapes me."

"This is where some of man's most useful inventions were thought up, some of the biggest things since the utensile thumb."

"Prehensile."

"Whatever. Sue me."

"I'd like to sue the guy who sold me this bill of goods."

"Nobody said you had to buy it. But you did. Mostly you sold yourself. Caveat emptor. And you gotta take the little itty-bitty pieces of the program, too. Like the honor system. It's very simple. The honorable people get screwed. Look at Tobias—well, he doesn't count. The whole place works on popular gullibility."

"That wasn't invented here," Tyler said between sips.

"No. You, for example, came fully equipped. Factory installed. See, people believe what they want, what's easiest, what's most comforting. What upsets them least. Then they act surprised when it bites 'em on the ass."

"You were telling me about the great inventions. Name one."

"Well, let's see," Zermatt said. "Tombstone came up with 'Human Folly.' "

"It's going to come as a shock to Erasmus."

"I know," Zermatt brightened. "Not folly. *Error.* Human Error. That's what."

"They pay people for that?"

"You kidding? They pay 'em *mostly* for that. But Tombstone's thing was conceptual. You ever notice when a plane falls out of the sky, the investigators write it off to Human Error? Or when a reactor melts a town? Hummin' Human Error! It's brilliant."

"You're sick."

"Ah, you got no sense of humor," Zermatt grumbled. "I'll tell you though, I think they're making a mistake with that line, scaring the customers away."

"Can't admit the plane was at fault."

"Why not? There's gonna be new models out next year. But where the hell they gonna come up with improved humans, tell me? Maybe they should blame it on swamp gas and ball lightning."

"Have you ever read the press releases we put out? You know how many times they use—we use words like *cleave* and *sanction* and *render*—we sound like Wuthering Fucking Heights!—and all those words mean exactly two opposite things."

Zermatt said, "It's an enormous breakthrough."

"It means half the time I'm lying."

"And half the time you're telling the truth. And half of the time you're just repeating what you've been told. If it's a fib it may not be yours."

"It's still lying."

"You keep saying that. Let me tell you something: All lies are not false, you know. And all truth isn't necessarily real."

"Where'd you read that?"

"On TV, I think. It's really very harmless, Tyler. Look, first principle: in our day power confuses. And absolute power confuses absolutely. It's just a job. It's

221

creative. You're making truth commercially safer, more interesting, too. Realigning the little scraps of fact."

"Molesting is more like it. Marauding."

"Look around you. What do you see? Antimatter? Reality? Hell—not just this wretched place—there's a whole civilization out there built on a dense fabric of deception. And it's the public reality. That's just what we *know* about. Whole careers are fashioned out of whole cloth. Willful mistruths! Love 'em. Embrace them. Make them the bottom for logic and they'll be next year's elected truth. You watch."

"What ever happened to issues?" Tyler laughed.

"Issues? Issues, son, are the muleshit of politics. Running on it's tricky. And you only throw it if you can make it stick on someone else. You don't run on issues. You run *against* issues."

Bowen shook his head in wonder. Zermatt could salvage from whatever baleful mischance some spoor of gluttony and cheer, by a logic so warped it was irresistible, and contagious.

Keeping a cover on the World's Biggest Secret was no mean task, for the World's Biggest Clue covered an entire mountainside. In the main, it was a political act, requiring the cooperation of an ever-widening circle of those who knew. Someday that circle might spread to encompass everyone, but the trading of information about it would still be a violation of the National Security Code, itself a classified document. Curiously, it was only a code, and violation, for those enfranchised to know. One dyspeptic and suicidal privy soul could blow the whole waxworks. Upon that fragile spirit of community hung Tyler Bowen's career, for it was his task to tend the secret, and co-opt the curious.

The mountain itself had been judiciously excised from Geodetic Survey maps, but the heaviest security was intended for the mountainside. The higher up one went in security circles, the less was known. In the E-ring of the Pentagon, the information was shared on a strict "Eyes Only/Need to Know" basis. Memos were destroyed when read. NATO hadn't an inkling. Such information necessary to store was kept at the National Security Agency, in a room so infiltration-proof it was not marked on the floor plans, and was therefore neither wired for electricity nor ventilated. In case of a break in the silent circle, the NSA maintained priority lists of those persons who were to be evacuated to non-English-speaking climes. Among the Joint Chiefs of Staff three were entirely ignorant, and no one knew for sure how much the President had ever known.

Information about many things going on at Gila could be had for a price, a woman, or a few bottles in most cases. But so jealously was this one secret held that it exceeded the cryptolevels for missile launch-and-destruct codes and SAC wing attack-and-recall plans.

On the mountainside was this: a sign, so huge it was measured in football fields, three wide and seven high; twenty-one acres of painted rocks and logs. The sign was a large, flaming globe split by a giant white lightning bolt. Below it, a mammoth white rubric, spelling out: GLOBAL ELECTRONIC MESSAGE SYSTEM. Captioning the whole was a logo: GILA NATIONAL LABORATORIES—YGGDRASIL RESEARCH INSTITUTE—In Sickness and Health!

All of that frantic secrecy, including the excision of the mountain from the maps, was not because of the less exalted doings in the shadow of the mountain at the Labs, but because of the very fact of the sign.

In 1962, the Chief of Operations at Gila National Laboratories had retired abruptly, opting for more lucrative work: doing subcontract research in the private sector. He'd discovered that presenting the government the bill was far more profitable than taking its salary. With the expertise he'd gained he quickly became Gila's major supplier.

Upon his departure, higher levels of the National Security establishment designed to put a military man at the top at Gila. Certain exciting new projects were being inaugurated then, requiring the utmost discretion. This could be best achieved, all agreed, by employing a man whose pension was dependent upon his efficiency reports. And they had just the man.

Brigadier General Daniel ("Shorty") Nibelung, who was a pain in the Joint Chiefs' side. To begin with, he was an albino, which they considered somewhat flamboyant, and he was something of a darling to the press.

He'd graduated tops in his class at the War College and was always sought out when newsmagazines needed a colorful quote. *Time* had dubbed him the "Brilliant White Dwarf Star." As well, during a lull in the action in the Aleutian Islands during World War II, he had not been satisfied with acquiring a simple, tasteful tattoo on his arm: he went ape and had an outstanding example of scrimshaw carved of his upper left canine. When he smiled, or growled, *Old Ironsides* rode the waves. Rivals sneered that it was probably the *Potemkin,* and that, in any event, fighting ships belonged in *Jane's,* not on one's chompers. Finally they had their chance: on a Washington, D.C., television show in 1962 he advocated the mounting of personal machine guns on family fallout shelters. With appropriations hearings coming up, it seemed wise to get him out of sight. So he was tucked away as the new head of Gila Compound.

Once there, he surveyed his domain, and though considering its new projects wasteful, "science fiction boondoggles," assumed proud command. He quickly determined that what America truly needed to keep 200 million Russians and God-knows-how-many Chinese at bay was a sign on the side of Gila Mountain that would glow in the dark.

Employing all the skill he had acquired in years of command—indeed, his thesis at the War College had been on the very subject—he embarked on a breathtaking display of budget chicanery. He managed to camouflage two million dollars in expenditures, including forty-three burned-out trucks. His diversion of funds was so great that it nearly stopped all research on ticks, kala azar, parrot fever, glanders, and brucellosis. But a study group found that slight increases in the thermal input of microorganism cultures, and a suspension of the prevailing segregation of arthropod sexes, would result in increased species production at minimal cost. Nonetheless, for several months the Labs had to limp along on dangerously tight rations of boutonneuse, anthrax I and II, and plague. The spotted fevers were nearly all exhausted; and as for basic research in the public interest, that all but disappeared for a while, as the need for more typhus and mumps had priority.

Nor was this great construction project easily accomplished. In his first month, Nibelung learned that the canyon in the Gila highlands was a historical forest entrusted to the Department of the Interior, many specimens predating Christianity. His response was to the point: he ordered the Forestry Service off his mountain within twenty-four hours; if not, every Ranger would be shot and every tree turned into a picnic table. In half that time white flags were hanging from every Ranger tower, makeshift banners in all cases, underwear and pillowcases mostly. Individual security oaths were required, and also what the Undersecretary of the Interior testily called an Instrument of Surrender; a document Baron Zermatt three years later drafted into formal legislation.

When the work on the mountainside was at last completed, General Nibelung held a massive unveiling. He invited Cabinet members, military brass, Arizona's Senators, key members of Congress and the National Security Council, Intelligence chiefs, and others of national stature. The big day was timed to coincide with his twentieth anniversary in the service. After a banquet all assembled for the ceremony. A chaplain implored them to "lift your eyes into the hills," as General Nibelung threw on the arc lamps. The brass applauded, and the Senators, security people, and Cabinet members went "Oh, my" together. The circuit was cut by the then-Chief of Security, Armistead ("Buzz") Sheaffer, who explained, in the darkness, that he was acting under regulations to usurp General Nibelung's prerogatives: Nibelung had demonstrated prima facie evidence of an inability to exercise compos mentis authority. Sheaffer was decorated for this act and took over as Chief of Operations when General Nibelung was retired with full rank, honor, and pension a short two weeks later.

A few efforts at camouflage saw planes from Tucson's Davis-Monthan Air Force Base and from Fort Huachuca in Sierra Vista brought in to blast it and recurring attempts to paint over the whole in dark green. But the original paint job had made the rocks nonporous and the green washed off with the daily rains, leaving the sign proudly luminescent. The attacking planes had little effect, so it still stood, a Mount Rushmore of embarrassment, a monument to man's ability to work his vulgar will on nature. Fortunately, it faced toward a canyon closed to the public, and the air space over it was likewise restricted. Various ideas were considered for dealing with the problem, from painting the whole with radioactive tailings to whitewashing it.

Forty thousand gallons of AG-44 drab-green paint were used to cover the sign, but it slid off with the rains. The painting, like that of the Golden Gate Bridge, became perpetual. And every year the cost rose. A mathematician in the Office of Statistical Analysis at the NSA plotted the cost-growth graph of the paint job, which resembled a tangent curve, and compared it with that of the GNP corrected for inflation. It was such a depressing exercise that the results were destroyed.

Reality, Johanna decided, was entirely manipulative. In the scheme of things, this coincidence with Gila and Tombstone's philosophy was no less surprising than Newton and Leibnitz's simultaneous discovery. The time was right and all evidence commended the conclusion, as ancient Greeks and Indians peering at the night sky's mystic speckling deduced strikingly parallel shapes and meanings.

After all, Tyler seemed reconciled to doing things not in his nature, even detestable things, when they proved inescapable. "Just another form of taxes," he shrugged. "What can ya do? I don't love it, but I don't have to let it make me all bent out over it." She rationalized similar concessions to her greater interest.

So she could continue working at the *Intelligencer* and not trouble herself over its insignificance. Once, it had seemed important, contrasted to what it took her from. But she had dropped her graduate courses without remorse and let her marriage dissolve into a de facto nullity, without worry over law or custom or others' expectations. So she could continue to build a reality around what was most nourishing, defining truth by what was most organically rewarding, same as Tyler Bowen. Reality was in their hands, entirely.

Nights and weekends they spent wrapped in each

226

other, isolated from the world, sometimes adding the extra remove of shared marijuana or hashish. Whatever state they chose, their freedom was in mutuality, equivalence, a commutative understanding. They had a similar language and truth. If it was an escape, each thrived by it, and even their work reflected an increased energy.

Sometimes, though, Tyler Brown worried, alone, over inchoate matters. Sometimes he worried over how quickly they had become dependent on each other, and wondered how wise it was.

This time, cause supported his worry.

Johanna was always late, and he considered it one of her endearing traits. She would pop out of her car, explanations tumbling over one another, often contradictory; self-conscious, vulnerable, giddy. It was hard to stay mad. The later she was the more delightful would be the melange of reasons, the greater the cockeyed patter. His anger gave way to delicious anticipation well before she arrived.

This time, his neck muscles were weary from turning his head to peer into every teen-packed car tumbling down the dirt road in front of Gila's gate. He envied the insouciant innocence of those kids who plunged into the desert night toward road-stand bars. This time Johanna's lateness was inexplicable, his worry grown intense. Maybe she was in trouble, he thought, preferring that idea to his fear of simple abandonment. He imagined her car in a ditch, its wheels spinning frictionlessly while he was too far away to help. Perhaps she and Warren had had it out, though Warren seemed blithely ignorant or smugly unconcerned. Was Tyler's name ripping through the air in a vacuum gouged by bullets' paths? Or had she simply floated out of his life as she had floated in, without good-bye as without hello, tired of his twists and gyres and her alliance with the liberties he took with truth, leaving him adrift again. For every pair of headlights he fashioned an expectant smile. He would forgive her lateness, for the hour had long since passed when a man waiting for a mere date or lover would slink away defeated. "Six more cars," he told himself. "Three more sedans." Then, "two more with one headlight."

227

Finally, he trudged back into the Compound and called her at home. There was no answer. It made no sense. They had such plans.

He dragged himself over to the Crypto Club and found Zermatt holding court in a corner, regaling friends with triumphant tales. Convinced this was his lot, Tyler took a seat behind Zermatt like a deputy delegate to a ministerial conference.

Zermatt was encouraged by one to retell of his proudest coup from JAG days. "OK. So I promised these guys I'd get 'em plums, you see. It was simplicity itself. So the guy in charge of assignments was this little runty guy with rosy cheeks—you know what I mean? And he's got all sorts of medals with—what are they?—*pecan* clusters—right!—oak-leafs, you got it—oak-leafs on 'em, all this crap hanging from his tit. Heroic paper shuffling in the Battle of the Coral Sea. And he says to me, 'Wal, wutzya law school, boy?' Am I gonna tell the man Co-*lum*-byah? Or even In-Wah-*Yoo?*" Some bleary-eyed heads shook loosely, children at a puppet show, warning of an overforeshadowed danger. "Betcha sweet bazookies I'm not! Looked 'm right in his lovable puss and I went, 'Duke, sir.' 'Duke?' he cries. 'Duke, you say?' 'Yup,' I go. 'Duke,' he goes. 'Lova God, boy! That's mah school. Wah dinja—So ya say Duke, do ya? That put's a diff'nt laht on thangs. Duke, do ya?' 'Yessiree Bob,' I say. 'Dooooooooook, sir.' "

"Sombitch, sombitch," another lawyer mumbled, pounding his fist on the table in admiration. "You gotta speak to where the jury lives." There were seven of them around the table, all lawyers save Bowen, and Tyler wondered if they could ever agree on anything again, except the Baron's excellent deceits. He imagined the simple matter of their seating must have taken delicate negotiations, and come the bill and they'd look like circus elephants, each one's trunk up the other's tail, all eyes straight ahead.

"One by one they fell," Zermatt concluded proudly. "Down the line. Four outa six—'cept two guys from Fordham, which I wouldn't touch with an injunction. I mean, you had to see it to really appreciate it. My costs? Some calls, some index cards, a magic marker. Months of research and all of it culminating in a blitzkrieg: One guy's from BU. Sure thing, I tell him: Ray Hanratty. One guy's keen to get in at Kimble and Garmezy, right? Tell Barney Esterhazy I sent you—and do me a little favor here on these forms. Mal Farber at Scrooge and Marley's a pal of mine, I say to one. Sure thing. Use my name. Interviewing at Baubles, Bangles, Beads, and Berkowitz when you get out? Funny thing there: Betty and Philly Battenberg—old, old friends of mine. Knew 'em when we were kids. Ollie Cromwell, too. And one by one—like ducks. Like fuckin' ducks. Four outa six. *Eeeeeasy* aces."

Zermatt sat back to soak himself in their admiration, sipping his beer smugly. "You're a fuckin' noble, greedy, evil genius," Tyler whispered in his ear.

"Yes, I—Hey, boy. Have a drink with a genius, why don't you? You know these guys?" Various heads nodded in welcome. "Take a good look, Babe. Anybody here you trust to be your executor?"

"It looks like the Last Supper."

"Damned straight. On any given day, any guy here can help pull your fat out of the fire—and any one of us can put it back in again. Comforting, isn't it?"

"Listen, Bar. I gotta talk to you," Tyler said, and both went over to another table for privacy.

"What's up?"

"It's just this girl—"

Zermatt grabbed at his elbow and leaned into him. "Tyler, my man. This is the Baron. Listen to me—she's just a twat. There's lots more floating around—get it? So you get laid. So what. She's not preg—she didn't give you something, did she? Holy shit! She gave you—"

"Shut up, will ya? She just stood me up."

"Of course she stood you up! You both got what you wanted, maybe a little extra. Christ, you're acting like a juvenile romantic. This is war! You're not supposed to take those things seriously—whores de combat and all—"

"Do me a favor, Bar? Drop it. I like her. She likes me. She's stood me up and I can't reach her. Maybe something's wrong."

"Listen to the Baron. He knows women. They're like gems. There's rubies and pearls—and *swines,* by God!

—and emeralds and zircons out there. There's sapphires and moonstones and just too many precious and wonderful varieties to give up for just one little diamond—"

"Who said anything about—Jesus, Bar. I just want to see her, that's all."

"Well, let's go call her or some damned thing. You want me to drive you to Tucson?"

"I don't know what I want."

"Come on, we'll go look up a few numbers and—who is this honey you're so bent over about?" Tyler had told him about Johanna, but not her name, or the salient facts about her husband and her job.

"You remember that girl at the County Fair?"

"Holy shit, Babe—are you out of your fucking mind? Have you any idea what would happen to you? Good riddance! Leave her alone, man! Do you have a clue what Señor Crazy would do if he found out—you're supposed to be screwing the press, not the reporters!"

"Lay off, will ya?"

"As far away as I can. Whatever you've got, it may be catching. You're self-destructing. You're incredible. All the right instincts and all the wrong moves. I'm telling you, as a friend—"

"Or a lawyer?"

"A lawyer—not *your* lawyer. And I won't always be here to advance for you or clean up your mess, Babe. I'm short. Christmas and I'm home. New Year's and you're on your fucking own, pal. I just hope you don't have some incubating bug—"

"Come on, let's go to Tucson," Tyler sighed. "I'll sport you to gas."

When they reached the gate, there was Johanna, arguing with the guards in vain to let her in. Zermatt grabbed his shirttail as Tyler tried to leave the car—
"Break it to her easy."

"What?"

"Break it off, idiot."

"I haven't broken any laws—"

"It's the appearance, Babe—do the smart thing, guy."

"I am."

"When your brain goes soft and your meat falls off
230

don't say I didn't warn you. When you get the screws on your thumbs—"

"I will specifically exonerate you, Bar. Follow us to town. I'll buy you dinner." Zermatt begged off politely, shivering.

Johanna's apologies splashed all over themselves and she talked a mile a minute. He relaxed, happy to be sealed in that hermetic carriage with her. "Oh, Tyler, I'm sorry. They wouldn't let me in and there was this accident on the highway. A car broke down and there was a whole carload of Mexicans and this drunk had run them off—"

"If I wasn't his alibi I'd say it was my friend Baron driving."

"Just ran them off the road like dirt. And there was nobody to help but me."

"You're better than the Highway Patrol—you're Saint Jude—you're the Lone Ranger!"

"And the guards wouldn't let me in or call and I had to go back the other way for a phone. You have to understand. It's not like the city. You have to stop for people in the desert. They could die."

"If I was stuck in the desert, I'd hope you got there before the vultures, Gunga Din."

"You were," she said, leaning over to kiss him.

"I still am—that's why I worry when I slip down the list. I have to go batty over Florence Nightingale! How did I ever get so lucky?"

As they neared Tucson, Johanna dropped the other anvil. "Warren's coming by in the morning for the car."

"Maybe I should be scarce."

"I might need your protection."

"I might take a rain check. Warren knows me, sweetheart. This isn't the most proprietous arrangement, you know."

"Always there when I need you. My hero."

"If he doesn't wonder what I'm doing in his pajamas he ought to be written up in journals—"

"It's what you're doing in mine that counts—and he doesn't care."

"Not to be unflattering, but it's *me* bopping around in a bathrobe that's the problem. Maybe we should at least make a stab at looking businesslike. But if he

231

can't figure it out by my face, he's ready for Johns Hopkins."

"You're supposed to be such a good liar—I'm sure you can look the part."

"Some things I just can't hide," he said.

"Such a romantic. That's why I like you."

"You'd toss me over in a moment for Bobby Kennedy," he said.

"He hasn't made an offer."

"Wait till he gets to the state. He will."

"I might choose you still."

In the morning, Tyler remembered a similar time, when he had visited his girl friend's parents as a junior at Cornell. Earlier that year, she had thought she was pregnant, and out of compulsive honesty told her father. "Don't tell your mother," he commanded, "it'd kill her."

Her mother had said, "Don't tell your father. It'd kill him." A false alarm anyway, but when Tyler showed up for dinner with the family they gazed at him like he was a 170-lb penis.

"What do you plan to do after school, young man?" her father asked.

"It looks like I'll be drafted," Tyler acknowledged.

"Do you think that's very responsible?" her mother wondered.

Tyler admitted that he'd "almost rather go to grad school."

"Well, what are your ambitions, son—if you don't mind my asking?" queried her father.

"To survive."

"And otherwise?" her mother demanded.

"There is no otherwise," Tyler shrugged. "That's all I know."

Her mother found a bright spot even there. "You could become an officer, at least. That's honorable. Do you have any ambitions in that direction? A war can be a wonderful opportunity—what are your goals?"

"To outlive it."

"And otherwise?" her father picked up.

"Haven't really thought about it, actually," Tyler admitted.

232

"No, you haven't," he grumbled, "have you."

When Warren came by, the same feeling was about. They talked of Michael at first, as they did each time they met. The boy was having trouble in school. It was an odd bond: two expectant fathers in the same waiting room, claiming the same woman and child. Warren shrugged off the worry. "According to current thinking —hell, he's ahead of his class, an early dropout. What a head start."

Johanna broke in to say that was the most "awful, terrible thing. It's just like you, Warren. I swear, you don't have a feeling bone—" Both turned to Tyler for moderation.

"My brother Willie used to have this dog," Tyler began, inspiring Warren's respect for the sheer irrelevance of the utterance. "His name was Grover. Grover Cleveland Alexander John Stuart Mill Bowen, actually."

"That's a pretty weird name for a dog," Johanna laughed. "Did he answer to that?"

"Well, yes and no. My dad named him Grover etc. And my brother, who was crazy about him, swore he'd teach him to talk Greek by the time he was four. So my sister put the Mill around his neck, see?"

"Does this have any bearing whatsoever on anything?" Warren asked.

"I'm coming to it. Had to tell you his name, though. See, it didn't matter what you called him. He couldn't hear a thing. Deaf as a post. Willie got him out of the pound just before the gasman got there or whatever they do. All he would do is wag his tail and ask to be loved, and give off the world's weirdest bark. This little pup making the wildest noise. My father called him a hyena. Willie slept with him because he said dogs cry just like people when you tie them up in the yard, only we don't recognize dog language."

"Soon enough we'll be letting them vote, with that thinking," Warren said.

"Just like women and Negroes," Johanna added.

"Well, Willie was very keen on this, because my mother used to drag him around shopping when he was too young to protest, while she got girdles fitted and such. Or tell him to sit in the chair like a good little man—for three hours. Willie's been very sensitive to those things ever since—"

"I trust this story has an end, or is it a shaggy dog—?"

"All right: One day, we're out tossing a ball around and old Grover ran into traffic. Couldn't hear the horn a-tall. We used to have a sign that said, 'Watch Out for Deaf Dog,' but kids were always stealing it. The driver was really upset. But we couldn't blame him. Now, a lot of dogs that can hear get hit. But Grover—well, maybe he'd be able to stay out of the way of that Pontiac, you know?"

"And your brother," Warren said, "with all his senses, is running for Congress in Vietnam."

"From his letters I gather he's running mostly from danger—he's got all his senses back."

"Well, for his sake," Warren said, tossing the car keys up and down in his palm, "I hope the President doesn't cave in to all those demonstrators." He looked at Johanna as if she were now flanked.

"I'm missing your point," Tyler said.

"His safety depends on our keeping up the pressure. You know that."

"I don't," Johanna said. "I know the sooner we clear out the sooner he'll be out of danger—and not before. If he gets hurt, you can blame nobody but good old LBJ—killing all the Orientals in the world won't make a little bitty damn."

"The United States is not shooting at his brother."

Tyler smiled wanly, "The Viet Cong didn't draft him."

"Or fly him over there," Johanna added. "Or set him loose in someone else's country where there were people shooting—"

"Who don't belong there," Warren interrupted. "Who use Soviet and Czech weapons." He turned to Tyler for confirmation.

"I have a hard time pretending it's a noble Crusade. Especially when I see rubber patriots posturing on Johnny Carson."

"Fine," said Warren. "Super. At the next Nuremberg we'll hang the comedians."

Johanna exploded, "And the consultants! And the

social scientists, and the lying poli—bureaucrats and— the people who stayed home while other people got shot at—"

"Bravo!" called Warren. "Don't forget the draft-dodging women. Politics, Johanna, is not a parlor game—"

"Let me tell you something," she fumed, "both of you. Someday they'll run out of little boys to dump down the hole. Someday, they'll run out of no-deposit, no-return kids to junk for imperialism on the cheap. And they'll come get you both out of your hiding places. And they'll start picking on the middle class—"

"It's that same damned moral arrogance," Warren snapped, "that ethical superiority. Why don't you quote a rock 'n' roll song, too?—"

"—and all those mommies, even Mrs. Reigeluth in Salt Lake City who never even thought about it, and the women when they draft us—are going to hit the ceiling. And they'll raise a noise that will curl the braids on Westmoreland's cap and open Lyndon's bladder scar!"

Both men applauded and Johanna's eyes flashed angrily. She stormed out of the room and slammed the bedroom door behind her. Warren shook his head and sighed, "Thus, the objective press. I wish you luck with your interview. I think if I were you right now, I'd rather be your brother. She's going to be merciless. What's the story?"

"Oh, uh—you know, Thanksgiving, cancerberries, crop-spray stuff. What are we doing about it and all that. There was that lettuce crop a couple of months back, and people are wondering."

"Good luck, bub. Don't say I didn't warn you."

When Tyler went in to see her, she spun away from him and stalked around the room. "What was I supposed to do?" he yelled, "take your side? Tell him not only do I think he's full of shit but I'm sleeping with his wife?"

"You don't understand any more than Warren does. Go away. Leave me alone. I'm so tired of—"

"Johanna, I'm sorry. I really—"

"Why should I believe you? You use words—they come too easily and they lie too well."

"I've never lied to you and I wouldn't. So don't go holding me for moral ransom."

"You don't even know what I'm saying. You just don't listen."

"I'm trying, dammit. Now look, you get one apology per incident. That's all. I think I show enough faith in you with my neck sticking out. How about a little faith in me? Just a little."

"I like your neck. It's good for necking. Can't I get mad at the rest of you?"

"It comes with the territory, sweetheart. It's all connected."

"Life would be a lot easier."

"I'm sure if you put your mind to it, you can find some good reasons. But make 'em good."

She stuck her lower lip out in a poutish way. "Am I that awful?"

"Not usually. Maybe Warren fouls the air. Come on. Let's get out of here and go for a walk or something."

In a small civic park off Speedway, Johanna asked, "What did you and Warren talk about?"

"Nothing."

"Man talk."

"Not that kind. He asked me what you were interviewing me about, and I made up something."

"What?"

"I can't tell you."

"Why?"

"Because it's dumb—"

"You didn't make it up. It's something you can tell Warren but not me."

"It's just a dumb story. It's over and dead, but he'd never know."

"Well you'd better tell me what it is, smart guy. In case Warren asks me."

"I don't think I like this game."

"I'll tell him you gave me science's longest no-comment, but you'd better tell me what I was curious about. I promise your silly secret's safe with me."

"Well, see, a couple of months ago—before I got here—there was this crop thing. I came across it the other day, doing some research on our wonderful contributions to Agribiz. There was this farmer who had a crop of romaine lettuce that got hit by a blight. It just happens that I did my senior thesis—sort of—on the crop spray he used. If he didn't spray, he'd lose the crop, and the government wouldn't reimburse. Only for not planting. But the thing about the spray is it breaks down to a pretty nasty chemical. It's against the law to use it within two weeks of harvest. Big fine, though it's probably classified or something."

"So what did he do?" she asked.

"Well, you gotta have values to be a farmer. You have to choose between letting your crop die and losing a bundle, or risking a fine—and maybe killing a couple of thousand people. So he sprayed. It might have come out all right. They might not have caught him. Except the guy who sold him the spray informed. The beauty of free enterprise. By the time the FDA closed in, though, the stuff was on its way to market. They grabbed it off the boxcars and took it to the FDA station in San Luis Obispo where they tested it. The stuff was practically ticking. So they burned most of it in their furnace at Ojai—they've got an operation there with the Theosophy Society for a front."

"That's terrible."

"It's a lot less terrible than standard practice—which is to give the stuff away to hungry nations. Anyway, a funny thing happened. When they burned it, all the chickens within a ten-mile radius dropped dead."

"You're making this up," she laughed.

"And if you print a word of it, no one will believe you. So anyway, they towed the chickens out to sea—and there was this mysterious tide of dead fish that stretched from San Clemente to Rosarito in Baja."

"Why is this such a secret?"

"Well, first of all, you don't want to tip off half the loonies about how to make their own toxins. And you don't want to cause a panic in the truck farmer world. They'd have the FDA budget sliced to ribbons. So they want to be discreet."

"That's wonderful. The FDA lives to fight another day—declaring toothpastes fit for use—"

"And keeping crops off the market, toots."

"What would you do if you had to cover it up?"

"My best. So don't ask me if I'd be a hero. Until the crunch comes, I don't know."

She smiled. "I have faith in you."

"Sometimes I wish you didn't."

Waking into possibility was what made them rise up gladly on their weekend mornings together. "Have you been watching me sleep?" Tyler asked, one eye still shut, Sunday morning.

"A little. I've come to a conclusion. You're not as interesting as you think when you're unconscious. Except for that Kouros smile when you sleep."

"I never looked." He reached over to kiss her good morning. "Maybe it's because I like where I'm sleeping." She kissed him back. "I think we're getting better at this," he said.

She folded her arms in a pseudofunk. "I thought it was pretty nice from the start."

"Except I nearly froze to death."

"No one said you had to."

"You inspire me. You have to understand men. We're very delicate things. It's only when we get charged up with energy and desire that we can do all that stuff—build the Taj Mahal, climb Mount Everest, sit up all night and talk about classical music, go to foreign movies."

"You didn't do any of those things."

"Or sit on a cold cactus. Same thing."

"Why do you bother?"

"Well, the old hormones get rolling and—did I forget to mention it was love at first sight?"

"You did. Maybe you'd better stick to hormones."

"Well, the real test is when they go splashing back the other way. You feel like you're going to die. Or maybe have, just a little. It's sort of like being a pitcher with a sore arm. You feel like there's just no point. Mostly you feel like having a roast beef sandwich."

"It sounds so absolutely sad."

"Yes, we're more to be pitied than scorned. Such a gloomy hopelessness at the end. A quick mortality lesson. You grow weak and just give out. It's a losing cause, a vain chase for—it's the same in just about anything: work, sports—"

"That's not what it's like for me."

"Only women and roosters crow afterward."

"How do you know?"

"Oh, I've officiated at a few, uh, presided—attended the ceremonies—there's a difference, if you haven't noticed."

"Oh, good, I want to watch this carefully. Tell me about women now so I can pick out the highlights."

"Forget it."

"Really!"

"Johanna, you're toying with me."

"I want to know."

"All right, wise guy. Now, I'm not talking about what it's like when you really like someone—I'm just talking about biology."

"Don't apologize for your chemistry—"

"OK. With men—unless it's love or something—it's like being fired from a cannon. Up. Explosion. Mess."

"You're such a romantic."

"Are you going to make fun?" She sat up powwow style with her chin in her hands and teased him by rapt attention. "Now, the way I see it, with women, it's more like reaching an escape velocity. You get parked in orbit for a while and it's fine. You can just stay weightless forever. You might not even care to go any further. But if that engine gets fired again, and with a little luck, you just go, and go, and go and go!"

"Lyric poetry," she sighed dreamily. "No wonder they have you writing releases! Tyler, I think you've got what everyone's been looking for: the great sexual metaphor."

"You're more of a pain in the neck than you realize. I'm hungry."

"Already? I didn't notice that we—"

He grinned. "We will."

"No, wait. Let's see. I know. How's this: there are three times when time stops—at absolute zero temperature, which we can't achieve; at the speed of light, which we can't achieve; and orgasms, which we now have the technology to accomplish. What a slogan! 'If we can put men in orbit, we can put women out of orbit!' Industries springing up to—"

"I should have stayed asleep—or gone to church."

"I just feel so sorry for you. The way you describe it, it must be hell for you, poor dear. And such a bother. Is it a bother when we——?"

"No. You inspire me. It's the best way I have of telling you everything I can, with every single cell and corpuscle. It's a whole lot better than a lot of words."

"I think," she said, curling up beside him, "that if I am to survive with someone, I'd need a little bed off somewhere that I could go be in by myself now and then." He kissed the top of her head. "But not just now." She turned up to kiss his face and ears. He kissed her where he could, her face moving in eccentric patterns. She seemed a bit apart, controlled, until he nuzzled a part of her shoulder near the nape of her neck. She shuddered anxiously, as though this were a special place, endowed by past occasions with great meaning; how else did such odd loci become so magical, transcending nature's bare design, except as the site of buried treasure from long ago forgotten?

Barely brushing, hovering beside each other, they both blinked good-byes. It was, in joining, a leaving, for they were in the way of becoming different people by their act. Their minds slid down the long tubes of their bodies, lodging at their tangencies. All he could sense was a gracious entranceway, enveloping him entirely. His whole consciousness had shrunk to one engorged place for one tumescent purpose.

She too slipped southerly, leaving the realm of her head for a larger empire, diffused through her whole body, a democracy of tissues embracing his slim monarchy. His body wagged like a vestigial tail outside her, mindless, unconnected.

Every time he explored this space it seemed new and limitless, infinite with messages. He stirred his own poor thoughts within her; wrote hieroglyphics, painted a cross, an infinity, a Christmas tree on which to hang a world of ornaments. Only seraphs speak as much so silently.

Johanna could not sense the world around her, only her inner world as it changed with every pulse, polymorphic as a shoreline.

He bit his lip and she smiled from the lower corners of her mouth, a smile of mischief bearing fruit, as she felt the pressure of his awful, mortal fate build up to bursting.

There was a delicious pain in all this pleasure, he understood despite his earlier jabbering: a man who can feel his heart as it beats can only be cured by a death, however small, and seeks release instinctually from the paradox of pleasure. The heartbeats intensified until Johanna also knew the height he'd reached was Icarian. Her ground rushed up to meet him, as he feathered down to Earth. It was a well, and he fell far past the Earth into a dark circle that closed behind him, squeezing, unlit. He left nothing but a remnant shell outside, having discarded his self to mingle and swarm with hers.

Proprioceptive distractions came to him then: a tingling in his head, a brief stinging all about him. A chill in his freshly sensed arms and legs, a newborn first discovering himself. Then he discovered something finer.

The soft shower within her as he flew apart, his endless breath let out, made him want no more than to be wrapped by her completely, urgently and helplessly. And she was also trying to ingest him whole. She held him and blew soothings in his ear, taking energy from his, recharging his with her own. His first shrink and ebb stirred her drastically. She was gasping, squeezing, seemingly afraid to let some deadly secret loose, as though asking to be pushed at knifepoint to divulgence. He held on for dear life as she was transformed by herself, breaking in a wondrous detonation, by her own suggestion, one that tore and overwhelmed her. She was far more a fountain than he, spilling back on her source, splashing wider and wider patterns as she also rose.

Then they were both still and quiet, letting breath and wetness blend. His face was buried in the golden nest on her shoulders. Looking sideways he could see her cheeks, flushed and damp, as though embarrassed. She brushed the matted hair from his still-sleepy eyes.

For nearly fifteen minutes they lay glued by sweat and happy gravity, with syncopated breathing, until his stomach rumbled. It made her laugh and her inner muscles flexed, clamping tight on Tyler. He moaned and rolled his eyes. "I'm sorry," she whispered, laughing again at the grimace on his face.

"It only hurts when you laugh," he said.

"A sweet paradox."

"Just like us."

"Tyler," she gasped, biting her lip. "The bed moved."

It was a good day for sermonizing in the church they did not attend that morning; a better day for not attending, as among the benefits of the Sunday slugabed estate were: not bumping into Susan Carver, who was also in town for the weekend, and who was worshipping, however perfunctorily, with Tucson's most Episcopal opinion leaders; and not being observed by Warren Reigeluth who, in his self-imposed continence, had contrived a renewed lust for the spiritual. From the steps of his local Mormon congregation, the University First Branch, he watched Susan Carver and her band of civic luminaries entering the church across the street. One of the deacons approached him as he stood there and said how glad he was to see Warren after such a long absence. "And how's your lovely wife?" the deacon asked, one hand on Warren's shoulder.

"She's fine," Warren said. "Just fine."

"Will she be here with us this morning?" Warren shook his head efficiently, his eye still across the street. "I'm sorry for that," the deacon said.

"It's a lovely day, yes."

Members of the Mormon congregation rose that morning to speak to their fellow worshippers, offering homilies, scriptural guideposts and lessons drawn from their own lives, all as Christian testimony and shared participation in their religious life. One lay minister told a near-endless story and capped it with a selection he'd memorized from the minor prophet Micah, preaching to the confused but the more or less confirmed, "Wherewith shall I come before the Lord? . . . Shall I come before Him with burnt offerings? . . . Shall I give my first-born for my transgressions, the fruit of my body for the sin of my soul? He hath shown thee, O man, what is good: and what doth the Lord require of thee, but to do justly, and to love mercy and to walk humbly with thy God?" Most felt it was a light sentence; they could do it standing on their heads.

After the service was over, Warren stood and watched the group across the street pile into waiting cars. Some had chauffeurs, private or municipal, all were expensive and more highly-shined than the teeth of the day itself. Even from twenty yards away he felt part of this display of civic station. His own church was no less larded with clout. The inspiration he'd drawn from the meeting was the joy and comfort to be found in regularity. He decided to walk the two blocks to his house—his wife's house; maybe she would be as pleasant as he felt.

Over lunch at the Devil's Hills Country Club, Susan Carver's group listened to more sermons from their own ranks, hers beginning, "Luncheon speeches are rather like wars: they can never be too short, and no one can remember what they were about when they are done. Because, unlike wars, no one takes them seriously. I pledge to be brief if you promise . . ."

When Warren arrived home, there was no trace of Johanna, who'd gone to cover Susan Carver's luncheon speech; nor Tyler Bowen who, in a separate car, had gone to listen.

V IRGINITY," SAINT PAUL HOOPER WROTE, "like football, is a game of inches." Tyler dropped Saint Paul's latest missive beside his coffee, thinking that if anyone was an authority on such matters it would surely be Saint Paul Hooper: he had fondled his way to new indoor records in the venery series. This letter recounted some recent campus escapade which must have been chaotic because the telling of it was beyond comprehension. All that filtered through were

Saint Paul's quasi-theological prattlings. "There's going to be a Hell of a line in Purgatory for all the folks who bought the New Morality, pleading Guilty With an Explanation. The thing is, circumstances are *always* extenuating." With his usual scattershot approach, Saint Paul had hit a plexus. Tyler knew he'd remain alive, healthy and thriving as a result of a judiciously ablative innocence, and that his work's dubious virtues would not fool any but the most inattentive, myopic, deaf or naive Deity.

In a sense, Bowen was more Saint Paul than Saint Paul: his subconscious believed in a kind of moral accountability, holding his mind to answer for his body's crimes in daydreams that were like the cranky noises of a hungry child.

This distracted Tyler Bowen from his work, which that morning consisted of writing pre-Thanksgiving releases for the local press on what Gila Compound should be thanked for. His torpid pecking was interrupted suddenly by a grim Susan Carver. "We have a problem," she said, blanched. In ten minutes Bowen was on his way to the town of Tubac with Baron Zermatt.

"Nice day for a drive," Zermatt said. "Pity to ruin it with a gig like this." A body had turned up in a giant Lawn 'n' Leaf Bag in the middle of town. "Middle, outskirts, they're all the same," Zermatt laughed. "Town's so small the local Mafia chief's a Filipino." The bag and the body in it were ripped in several places, the abrasions caused when it rolled across the macadam. That had happened when it bounced off a truck passing through on its way to Gila. "The game seems to be Keep the Lid On—you with your magic gift for euphemism, me with a writ for the local deputies."

"Any idea what happened?" Tyler asked.

"Apparently some kind of accident. They were on their way back in. Must have hit Tubac's only pothole. We won't know the whole thing until they get the sucker back for an autopsy."

"What's the big rush all about?"

"It may not be in the interests of all concerned to let the locals do the postmortem. Probably your best bet is that same line you put out on the suicide last month."

"Wait a sec. It's one thing to take a boy who's just chugged a bottle of pills with a Red Mountain chaser, to use a little poetic license—"

"Hunting license's more like it."

"I just gave out the acute causes—pleuritic condition leading to pulmonary blockage and cardiovascular depression."

"Pneumonia is what you said. In Arizona. In a closet. So say this guy drowned or something."

"Fine. Now tell me what he's doing in a Glad Bag in Tubac."

"Civic neatness. Make it up as you go along. Answers are the farthest thing from anyone's mind. You just put that catnip in front of them and they'll love it. Beg you for more."

To divert attention further, Susan Carver had assigned Tyler Bowen to this task precisely because he was of the second rank. At that same time she was calling a high-level press conference starring herself, attracting the more important editors and reporters, so as to announce "significant new achievements" wrought by Gila, every one of which was premature in its release and destined, indeed selected, to make like mist in the sunlight.

Several Troopers were milling in the corridor of the Tubac mortuary when they arrived. Zermatt and Bowen went over to one and showed their IDs. To gauge the drift of things, Bowen asked, "What does it have the earmarks of, Officer?"

"Ears is about the only place that ain't marked. You got a sorry-lookin' bird in there. Biggest cockeyed smile on his face, though. Whatever he was doin' inside that bag, musta been the time of his life. Beats sugar-lickin' hell outa me."

"Has the press been told anything?"

"You kidding?" the Trooper snorted. "I got a look at that stiff. Damned details'd scare 'em out of their minds. I think we'll leave that to you fellas. Wish you luck."

"Thanks," Bowen said.

Zermatt told Tyler that he was going in to see the

245

coroner. "I'll get you details as soon as I can. Stall 'em—and for God's sake stay out of trouble."

"You too, Bar."

"Huh?"

"I'm under the impression you'll fuck anything—"

"That moves, Tyler. That moves."

In a small room used as an interfaith chapel were the waiting members of the press: three middle-aged housewives from nearby towns who were stringers for area papers, two semiretired men from the Tubac area, one of whom also compiled sports statistics for the University of Arizona Athletic Department's News Bureau, and Johanna Reigeluth. She sat in the back with a pair of sunglasses perched up in her hair, and Tyler's first instinct was to pirouette out of the room and hunt up Baron Zermatt. "We'll, uh, have full details for you shortly," Tyler told them, "as soon as the examination is completed."

"Take your time, honey," cooed one of the women.

"What we know at the moment is that there seems to have been a traffic accident. There are, as you may know, some irregularities and, between the autopsy and further investigation, we hope to have it all sorted out, uh—I would, however, imagine that there may be a legal question as to the rights of the people involved, which none of us would want to jeopardize. We have a legal representative here, and I will find out from him what it is appropriate to release at this time—"

Johanna followed him out into the hallway and caught up with him as he neared the autopsy room. "Not very original," she said.

"I'm a public information officer, not a novelist."

"Could have fooled me. How come you can be so charming—but not to me?"

"Because I have a problem—"

"And I'm it?"

"I don't know—and if I did, I couldn't tell you. Now, you go do your job and I'll do mine and if we're both lucky there'll be no problem."

"But I won't know if you're lying to me or not," she said.

"You want me to wear white feet or something so you can tell?"

246

"I want you to keep your word. But I don't want to get you in trouble."

"I don't know what to tell you. You can believe me if you want or not if you want—" He shrugged his shoulders and turned down the hallway.

"Grouch!" Johanna called after him.

In the autopsy room, the coroner closed the stomach incision he had made to weigh the internal organs, telling Baron Zermatt, "All his parts're back. Aren't attached. But they're back."

Zermatt was perched on a table in the corner and he said, "I don't think he'll mind. What's your tentative diagnosis?"

"Hard to say. Lungs filled with fluid, I'd say he drowned, except he's dry as a bone—and the other stuff."

"I think we can all agree on drowning, don't you?" Zermatt smiled. He lifted the sheet gingerly from the body to admire the coroner's suture, when he noticed an oddity. "There's something missing, Doc."

"That so?" the coroner asked with a professional's disdain.

"Where's his *balls,* Doc?" The doctor looked sheepishly at the floor. "They inside him? Doc—if you're holding out . . . If they're not inside this boy when we open him up—"

"I, uh—"

"Doc—if we gotta come looking for a pair of balls— we're gonna start at your house."

"They're over here," the doctor admitted. "In the jar." Zermatt looked at a shelf of organs floating in various aqueous solutions: saline, formaldehyde, and pickling compounds.

"They're government property, Doctor. Sorry to break up your collection. But they may figure in evidence."

The coroner took the jar from its shelf where it sat amid similarly admirable specimens, each floating merrily in preservative. He removed the organ from its amnion with a pair of tongs, dipped it in acetone, and dried it on a gauze pad as if it were a piece of Canadian bacon. "You got something to carry this in?"

Zermatt's face twitched momentarily at the sight of

247

the thing. It looked grotesque in its eviscerated state. Gagging, he said, "Put it back in the jar, will ya?" waving it away. They wrapped the jar in aluminum foil and put it in a brown paper bag, depositing the whole thing in the doctor's lunch pail, which Zermatt had claimed through eminent domain.

"Doc?" Zermatt asked the coroner numbly, "would you see if the Troopers won't get us some kind of body bag for this thing?" As the doctor left, Tyler Bowen came in, to ask what he could plausibly tell the reporters.

Zermatt was too wound up for such concerns and testily suggested Bowen make up anything he wanted.

"I can't. My friend's out there. She'll know it's a crock."

"Tell her to mind her own fucking business!"

"What's eating you?"

"Look, just do what you have to."

"How about doing it straight?"

"Jesus Christ. I like you, Bowen. You're a little sentimental, but I like you. So let me tell you a few secrets of the deep. You go out of here two ways—over Gracie or under him. But lying either way. Now nobody told you the rules when you were born. But there *are rules*—"

"What the hell are you raving about?" Tyler asked. Zermatt gripped him by the arm and dragged him over to the body. Then he grabbed him by the scruff of the neck and thrust him toward the destroyed face, pulling back the sheet. "Look at him! Look at him, dammit. It's real life, pal. Wise up."

"Oh, my God—" Bowen jerked away from the table, groping, retching. Len Tobias lay in pieces on a slab.

"It's not a fucking *game,* Tyler. There's rules. So play the game."

"I've never seen—" His head was still reeling. He gagged, heaving convulsively.

"Sue me. Cry! This guy got caught being cute. That's all. Nobody killed him. It was an accident. Accidents happen. He was in a place where accidents happen—"

"How?"

"I'll tell you later. A dumb, stupid accident, that's all. But ten weeks ago this guy was 180 pounds of

248

living asshole who thought he could be cute. So play the fucking game, babycakes. Play the fucking game."

From the Troopers, Tyler pieced together what little was known and, though ashen-faced and shaken, his breakfast caught half-way up his throat, he went back to brief the reporters, able to construct a plausible story for public consumption. "It looks like drowning," he said. "From what we know now it appears the man was with some friends and had some sort of seizure. We'd like to withhold his name until notification of next of kin, but we have positively identified him, yes." Tyler's eyes betrayed a kind of crazed nervousness, straining to stay wide as though fighting a cold wind. "Concerning his arrival here in Tubac, it seems his friends were panicked and all of them were drunk, and well, the details are pretty easy to imagine. They put the body on the back of their truck and perhaps they were a little hysterical as they drove back. Certainly upset. The problem, frankly, is that some sensitivity is called for about the details. I don't think any of us would want the misfortunes that befell the body to be plastered across the newspapers. It's just—it's painful to the bereaved. So perhaps we can be fair to them and just leave it at drowning, with a mortuary as the appropriate place to deliver a body, and pass over the unfortunate manner. As to the others, whether there was negligence will be looked into. But it would be unfair to bandy their names about. They too have suffered enough. I think that about covers it. I would like to call your attention to some material we have prepared at Gila of a more pleasant nature, regarding the Thanksgiving season. If you would all call me this afternoon, I'll see that it is directed to each of you, rather than—well, I'm asking you to give up one story, in a sense, so it's only fair—"

"Mr. Bowen?" Johanna called out.

"Yes?"

"What is the truth here?"

He smiled wanly at the assembled six. "Well now, the truth is that a man went swimming with some friends. They drank too much. One drowned and his friends panicked. Now, I've told you what I know and I've also admitted that it is a matter of some delicacy, calling for a certain *maturity* in its presentation. That is simply a suggestion. I can't write your stories for you. You're free to say what you want."

"What is your assessment of the cause?" she asked.

"Human error."

"Mr. Bowen?" Johanna asked then, "what do you know about aardvarks?"

His smile dropped, but quickly rehabilitated. "About as much as you do." The others tittered at the odd colloquy. "If there are no fur—"

"And that is?" she asked again.

"I don't know what you know," he said patiently. "But I would describe them as creatures who keep their nose to the ground and wind up swallowing the damnedest things."

Everyone in the room chuckled, and Tyler took the opportunity to detail some of the more exciting work going on at Gila concerning cancer and other afflictions. Johanna's ears still burned at the derisive laughter, and while he lectured the rest she folded her notebook and left.

On the way back to Gila, Tyler cursed the air about Johanna's flight, but Zermatt said, "There are some things that should not be known in our lifetimes, Babe."

"What do you know about this?"

"That they shouldn't have an open casket."

They dropped the body off at the Security Officer's loading dock and Zermatt took Tyler for a walk. When they reached the abandoned softball field, Zermatt finally looked up at Bowen and asked, "What are the effects of that nerve gas you told me you studied?"

"Your nose falls off."

"Don't crap around. What did they teach you about it?"

"Tachycardia, dry-land drowning—is that it?"

"Well, if he was working at a test site loading dock, he'd have a mask on. That stuff doesn't penetrate, does it? And what about that freaky smile?"

"Maybe a couple of things combined. We've got stuff that penetrates masks with similar effects. We wouldn't be testing phosgene anyway."

"That's what I think. Suppose, just suppose, you're getting hit by something and it's shaking you up. The

250

stuff's coming in and you don't really know it. What's that stuff smell like?"

"Green corn. New-mown hay, according to the book."

"OK. You're a farmboy and, by God, it's like you're going home. Away from Gracie. Straight to new-mown hay and green corn. All those memories and you start to smile—"

"And you drop dead."

"Uh-huh."

"What do we do now?"

"We do our best to avoid repeat performances. We get out the forms and send it to whom it may concern. That's what we do. We tell them that we're sorry your son/husband/brother/debtor drowned."

"What am I going to tell Johanna when she asks?"

Zermatt eyed him sternly. "Not a God-damned thing, you hear me? I mean it, Babe. If this leaks, I won't cover for you. That's a promise." Then Zermatt went back to type out a draft of the letter, cribbing off precedent forms, simultaneously putting Tobias in for a citation, SOP. He thought how he would make Martin B. Gracie pay for his part in this. He'd show Gracie a pair, all right. If the man had any conscience at all, it'd haunt him the rest of his life.

"I'll tell you something, Babe," Zermatt said later. "You'd better be damned sure your little chiquita's in line."

"Well, she doesn't know any more than anyone."

"That's exactly the point. If she decides to really stick it to you, she doesn't know what's under the sheet."

"I trust her."

"With your life? The point is she doesn't know the consequences."

At the OPI and *Ledger-Domain,* Susan Carver congratulated Tyler Bowen on what the state wire service indicated had been a very skillful handling of the matter. "You keep this up, Bowen," she said, "and pay attention, and you'll be a first-class Public Information Officer by-the-by. Wonderful work today." He hardly heard the praise. His mind was everywhere but there.

Johanna answered none of his calls and wasn't in

when he called to volunteer "late details" on the Tubac story. Her editor, Arnie Logan, was grateful, as Johanna had claimed a flat tire prevented her from getting there. "Yes, that's why I'm calling," Tyler replied. "She left a message to that effect yesterday. This is my first chance to get back."

"I'll have her buzz you when she comes in," Logan said. "She's doing a piece she'll have to check out with you people anyway."

"Glad to be of help, anytime." But when Tyler finally reached her, she hung up. He called her later at home and tried to reason with her, but she said, "I don't want any part of you. I don't want to fall in love with you and be stuck here with you and your cheesy—" She slammed the receiver down without finishing.

Alone, saddled with more criminal intelligence than he desired, cut off from all sources of love and afraid of everything, Tyler went out and shot basketballs all evening by himself. He couldn't even go home for Thanksgiving.

"Mr. Bowen, come in here," Susan Carver's voice called through the intercom Thanksgiving morning, a soft, modulated tone in her request. When he went in, she asked him, "You know Arnie Logan at the *Intelligencer?*"

"Yeah."

"Look at this. He sent this down for a courtesy fact check." She handed him a story under Johanna's byline. "Pretty damned funny, don't you think?" Tyler read the lead and scanned the rest, his mouth agape.

"Where'd she come up with this?" Tyler asked, dumbfounded.

"Damned if I know. I've asked Compound Security to get on it."

"It's true?"

"That, for the moment, is irrelevant. I've already told Logan it's absolutely without substance. Obviously, his reporter or her source has more imagination than good sense."

"Will he buy it?"

"I doubt it. But I also doubt he wants to go to the mat with us, so we'll just deny it up front as absurd.

What I want from you is something we can give him in trade."

"Well, we've got that thing at the Radiation Labs. We could break the release date and give him a nice national beat."

"What is it?"

"As I understand it, they're trying to synthesize some new elements—superheavy ones—about twice as massive as the transuranic series. They expect them to be extraordinarily stable."

"Sounds dandy. Get on it."

"There may be a problem. Talking to one of the physicists I get the impression it's chancy. It may either be an enormous new source of energy, or collapse in on itself from its surface mass, kind of like a black hole." He shook his head, bemused. "You know the proverbial acid that eats through anything? Well, the problem might be that this'd gravitationally swallow its neighbors. It'd be like giving the Earth a fungus."

She rolled her eyes at his imagination. "Downplay that, do."

"What about this?" Tyler asked, shaking Johanna's story. "Other than her sentences being too long."

"I'll handle it, don't worry," Susan Carver said. "And don't worry about her. Neither that story nor the reporter are going anywhere. As far as this office is concerned, she is cut off. We're going to dry her up. Not a phone call. Not a query. Arnie Logan understands the way the world works. Now you get that other thing for me by this afternoon."

It proved to be no problem getting Logan to kill Johanna's story. All it took was a call from Armistead Sheaffer to the *Intelligencer*'s publisher.

The story that Johanna had put together made some earlier Gila statements look ridiculous. He had no idea how she developed the story, but if her using it was out of anger at him, to hurt him, it was as close as he wished to having his head taken off. So he was only relieved that she had not somehow worked in his name.

That the story made Gila look ridiculous did not mean it wasn't true; it sounded like the typical kind of boondoggle for which Gila had acquired fame within covert circles. Johanna's story proceeded from two stray bits of information, one provided by an *Intelligencer* copy editor who delighted in recounting the most bizzare Police Desk stories he'd handled, the other a product of Johanna's persistent curiosity in the face of Gila's, and Tyler's, repeated denials of already-public information. Too many "No comments" greeted her inquiries about aardvarks, when in fact Gila's published budget supplement for 1966 led off with: "Aardvarks, 15." But it was not until she'd heard about how some guests at a Nogales motel in 1965, arrested for possession of hallucinogens, had tearfully welcomed their own capture, insisting that they had been terrorized "by a pack of berserk animals" the previous night, that she imagined there might be a connection, and began to scratch around for the other pieces. The story was something of a classic, and it was precisely the stupid way things like this experimental accident were handled that had sent the Tombstone Center Operations Research Department to the drawing boards to invent Tyler Bowen's job.

An entire year at Gila had been devoted to training army ants to attack on command. They were crossbred for viciousness and mobility, and starved into a state of high agitation. Previously, Gila had helped develop the kamikaze porpoise for the Navy, with discouraging results. The porpoises had proved whimsically uncooperative, stubborn even. But the ants were something else.

All looked well for the first major demonstration of their land-engagement capacities. Tombstone, Gila, and RAND executives, Defense brass, and Congressional guests assembled to witness the event at Gila's Astroturf proving ground, when something went wrong.

The regiment of ants marched in well enough, "Like Lee's Legions," Susan Carver had said, "perfect ranks and iron discipline," straight toward their quarry: a tied-up old cavalry horse. But they got sidetracked by an ineradicable instinct, and made a right-column maneuver to the refreshment stand picnic tables. Colonels and Generals and research directors, executives from consulting firms, and agency chiefs dropped their beer and punch, jumping aside in an unseemly stampede, while the swarming ant brigade thundered down on the canapés. Millions of ants, schooled in warfare at huge expense, descended on the buffet and overran it. By sheer force of numbers they toppled a beer keg, whose pressurized contents burst out in a shower. What was left of the ants' discipline crumbled. They waded through the lager in a frantic *sauve qui peut* confusion, drawing up new ranks as best they could on the opposite shore. And then, they marched again: a hundred thousand sullen, drunken ants, tearing through the Compound like tiny Cossacks on a rampage. They swept across the plains, swarmed through offices, and stormed beneath the finest security devices ever assembled, into the labs, without a hitch in stride.

All permission to enter or leave the Compound was revoked that week as the wild and stupored ants laid siege. Several ant battalions found their way into the labs which housed the advanced BZ experiments. Crazed with hunger from their trek across the sterile lab floors, they waded into the BZ vats like Marines in a whorehouse.

BZ is rated one hundred times more potent than its psychotropic relative d-lysergic acid diethylamide-25 ($C_{20}H_{25}N_3O$), known as LSD. BZ's symptoms range from the preliminary vomiting which is the cachet of all U.S. chemical weapons, to various psychological manifestations, most dependably "persistent maniacal behavior."

Many of the ants died from the merest vapor, but a huge majority were affected by-the-textbook, and the entire installation was evacuated until the plague of hallucinating ants was ended.

A guerrilla war settled uneasily on the Compound, for, though most of the ants died out soon enough, some survived and bore mutations, which surfaced in belligerent bands for some months thereafter. The most offensive species was a bellicose flying ant with latent schizophrenia and a tendency to vertigo. Imagining themselves whatever a crazed ant's mind does, they attacked in queasy squadrons. "Damn good thing we didn't use bears," commented Susan Carver when it was all over, after the imported aardvark mercenaries had carried the day.

The chief result of this near-calamity was increased

appropriations for ethological research. It was also rumored that four entomologists were transferred to Antarctic weather ships. Susan Carver had successfully kept the lid on, and she wasn't about to let it slip off now because of some silly girl.

To Tyler Bowen, Johanna's attempted story was a shovelful of dirt on their relationship. She'd not only made it very hot for him, but for all practical purposes made it impossible for him to see her again. If that was the way she wanted it, he thought, so be it.

It was a rueful time for a boy so clearly golden by everyone's insistence. His parents were subdued Thanksgiving night when he talked to them, no doubt feeling the emptiness of having a house without children for the first time in thirty years.

Gila supplied creamed turkey and canned cranberries and Zermatt supplied bad company. "I for one," Zermatt said, "am grateful to be here on this of all days. The whole thing is a pain. I used to go home when I was in college, and my mother'd come blasting into the living room like a lanced blister, snapping pictures of the boy to show at canasta parties. Conspicuous Conception, that's what kids are. Snaps've entirely replaced her ego."

"You're nuts," Bowen said as he pushed his food around aimlessly.

"It's true. They're all alike. They're Everymother and we're Anyson. After you leave they file reports to the World Assembly of Moms: 'I have seen the progeny and he is ours.' They learn it when they're little girls. And when they're our age—it's the same thing only different. It's not fair. They get to sit on it all day long, not using it at all. And we have to take 'em out to dinner and listen to them talk for hours just to borrow it for a while."

"You're a sick dog, you know that, Bar?"

"No more than anyone. We're all trying to get back to the womb—anyone's we can. It's a limited resource and they charge monopoly prices."

Loneliness filled Tyler Bowen, replacing the keen sense of his own sinew he knew when happy. It was a sorry weekend's business to cling to nothing, as though his heart were hollowed out. Leading into his heart was worry, not only for himself, but for those he loved; even for Johanna, if she would permit it.

Maureen Poulson was neither wholly cynical, manipulative, nor blind, though she was all of these in some measure. Nor would she regard the first two as character flaws. Rather, she was a determinedly complex and intelligent woman with mixed feelings toward her life and family, feelings she had nurtured too long in the glow of television, as a producer and then a station executive, to resolve. So she was at pains to persevere in the most banal forms of family togetherness, while nonetheless respecting more those individual urges that worked against it. She required her family for the maintenance of her private self-image, but treated the most docile and domestic of them with condescension. She viewed herself with few illusions except as a parent, and saw her children and their mates with acute perception. She had a keen understanding of their individual worth, if not their values.

Her daughters-in-law were fat and fertile and devoted to acquisition. So she treated them with a mild contempt. Neither had any personality she could discern, clearly none to threaten her. Both feared her more than she feared anything, suffering her invasions in their lives—the forays she made heavily armed with gratuitous advice. Brian and Neal, conversely, were her chief sources of public pride. They had been with her all along, had never been in trouble, brought honor upon themselves in college, entered good professions, and looked to be pillars of their communities, bulwarks of consumption. Both boys had been athletic stars in college and enjoyed the kinds of knee scars and back problems that entitled them to draft exemptions. Neal was a Tucson dentist, and Brian was rising in a Phoenix mail-order firm. Both were prosperous and able to discuss golf until dinner companions were past the far shore of slumber.

Johanna and Warren were another matter entirely. Maureen knew things were not good with their marriage, and took it as a sign of fealty that they came to her Thanksgiving dinner together. Whatever Maureen's relations with Johanna, Warren was always in clear focus. At first she considered him "Johanna's teddy bear," believing he was a means for Johanna to cling to Salt Lake City after Carl's death. Maureen predicted the marriage would be a mistake, saying, "You don't see it, but in many ways Warren is like your father, only not as warm."

"I don't know what you're talking about."

"He is a stuffed shirt who thinks he knows it all. There isn't a drop of humor in his blood. At least your father had that, whatever else he was."

"It's not your business."

"You are my business—especially when I see you making my mistakes all over. I used to know a man who was like *my* father."

"What did you do?"

"I married him and had three children."

"I'm not you, mother."

Lately Maureen found Warren's manner all the more offensive. As the marriage foundered, he became more solicitous of Johanna's family. Once, Maureen sarcastically said that she thought he was "jockeying for position in my will." Now she had a different view. He was trying to outflank Johanna. Just when it appeared that he had all but given up dealing with Johanna by reason or affection—unreturned—and treated her flings at chasing childish fancies with salutary neglect and a grinding jaw, he turned. His patience was evaporated. All entreaties had failed. Johanna was steadfast in her rejection. So he geared for diplomacy, family combat by other means. He was concluding secret alliances with Johanna's family. She'd be isolated, her access to family approval blockaded until she met his demands. Warren was a bright son-of-a-bitch, Maureen conceded. But blood, even the runny Poulson blood, was always thicker than guile.

Johanna was Maureen's special heartache. There were days Maureen was sure she had two different daughters, and other days she wondered how she could be two such different mothers. Their relationship was often tense and bitter, yet there was more to it. Maureen knew that, but it dwelt in such a tender and rarely used part of her she almost could not bear to touch it, let alone act upon it.

Things between Maureen and Johanna were never quite oriented right for Maureen to expose her true feelings. In truth, her fearless style aside, Maureen was timid, afraid to reveal even a mother's love, afraid to risk being scorned. She adored Johanna intensely, loved her all the more for her obstinence and willful independence. She saw herself in her daughter and ached when Johanna headed for the same mistakes. She cried when facing the thought she led Johanna to them, bled for the absent and seemingly impossible chance of having a daughter she could talk to as a woman. She walked out on two psychiatrists who suggested she might have destroyed those opportunities herself. They said her ability to deal with Johanna was "poisoned by resentment over Johanna's relationship with Carl." That wasn't it either, Maureen felt. But it was so confused. No psychiatric sword could slice the knot. And more painful by far was that in spite of all, through separation and every pain Johanna endured, she had grown to respect and love Johanna more. And now she had no vocabulary to reach her with.

There was no real conversation at Thanksgiving dinner. Each family member lived in and spoke of their own world, going through the form of reunion but hardly touching. Throughout dinner, Johanna talked and played with Michael. She saw him as a memento of Tyler, their secret child by an impromptu marriage, proof of better days. She wanted Tyler but not what came along with him. And Michael's hardly chastened spirit, reckless despite having been dropped from Ferris wheels, was an encouragement to her. By her third glass of wine she was convinced that had Warren fallen out instead, there might yet be hope for their marriage.

By dinner's end, she wanted nothing more than to call Tyler and put their argument behind her. She could hardly remember what it was about. All dinner long, only Michael could coax her smile, and afterward, they played conspiratorial games while the others watched two separate televisions. Johanna was a little tipsy, and found herself slightly shocked at the sexual character of her flirtation with this six-year-old.

When she got back to Tucson, late Thursday night, she called Tyler. This time it was he who was enraged.

She had hurt him and been recklessly cruel to him. His own pride had limits, too, he said, and she was the last person he needed badgering him and making life difficult. "So maybe it's just better off this way," he said, and hung up.

Well, she thought, angry and headachy, the hell with him, and went to sleep.

By Sunday night her resistance broke. He hadn't called back to apologize, and she wasn't about to apologize, and she couldn't decide who really owed whom, so she gave in to her feelings and called him again. But his line was busy. She tried two more times and it was still busy, so she gave up, deciding it was just as well, best to leave it alone.

Though Johanna's story didn't run, the papers were that weekend filled with other oddities that were the season's truest knell. The brass band of America's manifest destiny was being challenged by a former contemplative novitiate, part-time poet, and philosopher manqué turned U.S. Senator, lightly fingering a political harpsichord. It made as much sense as anything else.

The Senator, Eugene McCarthy of Minnesota, had announced a modest assault against one rampart of despair, challenging his own party's President, Lyndon Johnson, for the nomination.

It had long been conjured in meeting rooms in Los Angeles and cloakrooms of the Capitol, and in the pages of the chicer urban journals. Now it acquired reality by the checkbooks of the elite in the drawing rooms of Boston and New York.

It would fill the dead time between Thanksgiving and Christmas for the journalists, at least. Its ironies were appealing. For the likelier man to make so rude and ambitious a move was New York's junior Senator, Robert Kennedy. But he scuffed his toe in the dirt and demurred. So the writers had great sport with the fancy, pointing out how rare were regicides among the ranks of philosophers; and that not since David had a poet worn a crown; nor since Disraeli or Paderewski had any man of artistic bent been seen to rule.

Cynics conceded, though, that theologues and mystics were quite common in high councils. And at this time of year particularly, American politicians spoke of God as a colleague, if not a constituent.

Small jokes break like November twigs in the air so sharp with disconnection's fear. So McCarthy's announcement was met with sighs, derision, and as much respect as ever granted romantics at a rumble.

For here was a sane man, eminently sane, charmingly sane, doing a queer thing, embarking on a delusion's course while all illusions crumbled. With Nixon, all agreed, it was different: he had a sickness, a ballota psychosis, needing validation by election. He was like the ersatz culture of his region, a gangrene march on the map. This man McCarthy, though, should know better. For, where he came from sensible people were indoors, banking logs on their fires. Only fools and lovers, madmen too, gamboled nude as Henry at Canossa in the cold.

That was November's spirit. The pioneers who'd plunged against all risks into a hostile wild, the immigrants and pilgrims who had planted a nation with the tender seeds of optimistic faith and work were stale and full of doubt, grown weary from the feasts of success. Uncertainty roosted in their fibers, complacent satiation in their bellies. Energy was lavished on televised football games, to surrogate adventure, spectation and smart-cracking.

So McCarthy's effort was christened with rhythmic nods of understanding: just another November breakdown.

In Pelham, New York, the turkey was cold. It had not been touched. Giblet gravy congealed and fat globules agglutinated on the sauce. By Sunday afternoon most people were stuffed from a surfeit of turkey sandwiches and football games. This Sunday, in Pelham, a color television rang tinny with announcers' voices, while Vlad Bowen dialed the telephone to speak to his children. The voices were saying, "There can't be many viewers who don't know about Rodnie Elkant, Dale, the great running back for the Wolverines."

"Right you are, Merle Glean. He's been suspended for the season, as you know, for signing that letter of intent with the Winnipeg ballclub up in the Canadian

Football League. I spoke to him earlier and he assured me it was definitely not because of his draft status."

"Right, Dale. So you people at home can be reassured. And I have a sneaking hunch, Dale Bartok, that he'll work it out and we'll see him real high up in the NFL draft rounds this winter."

No one was listening. The television was just noise to fill the emptiness. Vlad Bowen, who liked to be called Victor but seldom was, talked softly with his daughter Connie, who liked not to be called Mack or Mr. Mack, but often was. He called her Constance now. He said he had something to tell her. He didn't say it had been waiting since Thursday. His wife had urged him not to call the children until after Thanksgiving. And neither Tyler nor his sister had sensed any portent in Vlad's voice when they checked in earlier with obligated calls, though Tyler did wonder why his father, having all but retired "Babe" as a sobriquet, squeezed it till it bled this time. Both children concluded it was typical parental fog, long-distance. Then Sunday Vlad called each of them back.

All weekend, in the middle of their beautiful mahogany family dinner table, where the turkey putrefied from inattention, lay a Telex message, hand-delivered with fine efficiency Thursday afternoon despite the holiday that night. They'd stared at it hard all that first evening, hoping by merged concentration to rearrange its message:

23 November 1967
Washington, D.C.
   The Secretary of the Army has asked me to express his deepest regrets that your son, PFC William C. Bowen, SSN 233-47-8187, US21021657, has been reported missing in action in the Republic of Vietnam. He was on a combat operations mission when a hostile force was encountered. This confirms notification made by a representative of the Secretary of the Army.

The space for the signature was inexplicably blank. But the equally blank messenger added what the telegram would not: there was only one survivor from

Willie's unit, who confirmed the worst suspicions. All of the men were lost at the hands of the enemy, the messenger said, but not all the bodies had been recovered or identified, nor was it likely they would be.

Such bare and slim uncertainty was part of the corpus delicti of a war that consumed sons and eliminated them as doubt. A neighbor's boy had been listed missing once, but then turned up, dead. Yet those neighbors had clung for all those months, and two months more after the final word came, to the thorned stem of a clerical error. Then they accepted that it was no reprieve. Others with missing sons wrote letters to their boys each week to reinforce their resistance to the inevitable. They waited for the other shoe to drop. But always, whether by official word or by the pressure of reason, they acquiesced to the truth, and understood that death's courier was a one-legged man.

"Don't bunch up!" Willie Bowen's Lieutenant had hissed to his men. "How many times do I have to say it? *Don't bunch up!* Come on now: Spread 'em out. Spread 'em out!"

The unit had snaked through the winding trail, each man turning every-which-way as they walked. They were warned not to crowd, for if they did, an antipersonnel mine or boobytrap might enjoy undeserved efficiency. A sniper shot missing one might hit another by mistake. Make Charlie earn his scores. But in their turning and nervous flank-watching, the gaps would close, and they would pile up on each other's heels, bunching up. The men at the rear were constantly hustling to catch up with the file's middle as it closed ranks with the head, jangling under the burden of sweaty jungle fatigues and fully weighted utility belts. The file moved like a Slinky Toy. The boys at the rear were in a constant state of panic, more so than the head. For when the middle met the head, the rear guard was exposed alone.

They had entered the village area unchallenged, except for some small-arms fire from a flanking hill a mile or so back. A fusillade of M-16s tore open the brush on the hillock, silencing the threat. Each of them watched the dust kick up on the hillside as the ringing of their weapons and the smell of spent cartridges enveloped them. They wondered about the hill. It was the end of a ridge which guarded the village in gentle embrace, the tip of fingers loosely holding something precious. But the hand was more likely a fist. For over the ridge was a plain, more vital to the enemy than the village. Control of the plain would be simple from the hillcrest. So if there were any VC in the area— and none had been reported in over a week—they would be on the other side, waiting to harass large troop movements. As much as the hills protected the village, it would protect them, too.

The sniper was most likely a lone man—but still, his fire had put them on guard.

So great care would be needed entering the village: it might yield unexpected surprises. They were reconnoitering it, for it was the stepladder to the near side of the hill. From there, the hill could be controlled, and safety on the plain ensured. As they approached the village there was no further fire.

They circled around behind it and climbed halfway up the slope to get an overview.

The Lieutenant indicated where they would enter. And where, if trouble developed, they would leave. He pointed out an alternate escape route if the first was blocked. "Here," he said, "let's not have any fuckups. OK. We enter here at twelve o'clock—"

"What's that in azimuths?" someone asked, and the Lieutenant glared at him.

"—and if we have to scramble out—here: four o'clock. Back up's here, at eight."

"A.M. or P.M.?" the same joker asked.

"Even for you, moron," the Lieutenant said, "this should be a piece of twat—in and out. Any questions?"

The jokester took his bayonet and connected the points on the circle's perimeter where the Lieutenant had indicated entry and exit. He drew radii from them and made the map into a peace symbol, nodding to a black buddy, "On this play—NGL—Niggers Go Long."

"You're brilliant, asshole," the Lieutenant sneered. Most of the unit had little patience for this clown also. "You think you've got a monopoly of wanting to go home? You just do your job—or *I'll* waste you."

The rear of the column made sure no one followed them as they descended into the village. They paused behind each large bush to deliberate their way to the next. At the last bush before the entrance, the Lieutenant whispered into his field phone, "No movement. No reception committee," and reconfirmed his coordinates. "OK. We'll wake 'em up and take a look." He turned to his NCO-in-charge: "Get 'em outa bed."

The Sergeant fired two shots in rapid succession, and the unit waited. There was no return of fire, but much action in the village. On field maps, this area was designated pink, and leaflets had let the villagers know how to act when they heard two rapid shots. Previous patrols had trained them well. They lived in a free-fire zone, so after those shots, anyone who wasn't standing in the center of the village, testifying to his "friendliness" by all but reciting the Pledge of Allegiance, would be considered hostile.

Clutching children, furnishings, and food, the villagers crowded in a mass. They never knew if they would have to relocate, run, or watch their houses burn. Only the skinny, scabby dogs moved with impunity, jumping up one bare leg after another for the scents of sweat and meat. The dogs did not bark, or at least they could not be heard over the nervous, high-pitched chatter of the villagers.

The patrol spread out in a tight hemisphere at the village edge, and the Lieutenant indicated a small woman to his ARVN aide, who yelled for her to come to them. She began to put her child down, and the ARVN man snapped off a stream of angry noises, telling her to bring the child. The other troops looked nervously about. The woman's walk was slow and purposeful and the ARVN man made her walk back and forth on different paths from the people to the perimeter several times. Then the Lieutenant was satisfied there were no booby traps in the path.

The unit counted heads in the middle of the village, and the ARVN man asked one old man and his wife where their children were. The old man replied that all of them were dead in the war.

"Ask him which side," the Lieutenant said, looking off obliquely toward the animal pens. The ARVN man asked and the old man replied with a flurry of Vietnamese and a shrug.

Several troops searched the homes but came back with nothing to report. The Lieutenant still looked about nervously, then settled what was bothering him. He snapped his fingers and ordered Willie Bowen and two others to the empty animal pen to look around. He turned to the ARVN man with ill-contained pride at his detective work, saying, "That damned dog over there bothers me." The ARVN man nodded in appreciation.

Shortly, one of the soldiers called out, "Hey Bowen! Look what we found!" In the feed box, cowering under a layer of grain and a canvas cover, was a teenaged boy. They dragged him over to the others by his neck, and Willie's buddy said, "Sort of remind you of yourself when you were younger?"

"I was better-looking. More hair and all—"

The ARVN man seized the boy by that hair, and kicked him in the butt. The boy fell to his knees with his head arched all the way back.

The ARVN man put a pistol to the boy's ear and cocked it. He demanded softly in Vietnamese to know where "the others were." The boy shook his head though it hurt his scalp, and spilled a torrent of Vietnamese words, half-crying.

"He says he's just a draft dodger," the ARVN man told the Lieutenant.

"You believe him?"

The ARVN man looked at the boy, who trembled, scared. "No."

The Lieutenant looked around at the huddled villagers and then said, "Question him again—without the gun."

The ARVN man put his sidearm away and tossed his automatic to one of the troops, who pondered where to point it. Then the ARVN man pulled the boy's ear, almost fondly, and walked him back toward the grain box, with another man as guard. He grabbed the boy's hair again and yanked it hard, while booting him in the small of the back. The boy fell face down in the dirt. The ARVN man dug his heel into the boy's back, then yelled in his ear demanding information. But the boy didn't cry out, or beg, which only convinced the ARVN man the boy was indeed VC.

The Lieutenant was talking to his senior noncom when Willie Bowen came over and muttered something. The Lieutenant said, "Make it quick," and Willie wandered over to the bushes near where they had entered. He took one step into the brush and began to urinate. Over his shoulder he could hear the ARVN man yelling strenuously, and the villagers had begun to yell as well —apparently, Willie guessed, pleading for him to stop. The ARVN man began to dig his heel in harder, with short chops. Still the boy wouldn't talk, and looked, if anything, more defiant.

Willie shook out the last few drops, and then lowered his pants to relieve himself further.

The ARVN man asked the Lieutenant what to do. The Lieutenant still respected the ARVN man's judgment, and said, "Talk to him in plain English—get him to talk. And do it quick. If he won't, he's still a draft dodger." As the ARVN man began to trot over, the Lieutenant called him back. "Tell these people to stand up straight. Tell them if they think Green Berets are sons-of-bitches they haven't seen anything. Tell them I can be meaner than any VC they ever saw, and if I don't get some useful answers starting soon I'm going to shoot them one by one." The ARVN man looked at him, and the Lieutenant shook his head to say he of course wouldn't do anything of the sort. But threats were useful when precedent made them credible.

It was no big deal to the ARVN man, and he relayed the message. Then he returned to the boy. A flurry of Vietnamese was traded and the boy put his hands behind his head. Stepping hard on the boy's rump made him moan, the first sound of pain he had uttered. The ARVN man pulled the boy's pants down, and placed a foot on his coccyx. He pulled a long silvery needle, thick as copper wire and as long as his forearm, from his utility belt. It was gnarled and twisted, and he unbent it to moderate straightness. He held the boy's neck down with his foot and pressed the wire against the boy's skin into a soft tuft of hair by the tailbone. No sound. He pushed it in, pressing firmly. No sound. Blood from capillaries trickled out, and the boy began to sweat profusely. His muscles tightened. No sound. His eyes twisted in advance of pain. Then the ARVN man cursed, pulled the wire free, and kicked him in the side. The guard let go his breath at the same time the boy did.

The Lieutenant looked around, bored, edgy, impatient to finish this detail. If boredoom was to be the price of service, he thought, why hadn't he had the good sense to join the AirCav, and ride to work? Or the Navy. He'd heard from men on R&R that the height of action on the carriers was found in front of flashing electronic screens. Success was measured by how quickly the ship's complement of planes could be launched, how close to twenty-four seconds the interval between each plane. It was, to them, a war of time-and-motion studies, theoretical systems tested in a vacuum, for the enemy, and danger, were well over the horizon. It would be just a short walk to work, with all the amenities in easy reach. They said the continental shelf off North Vietnam now gave off false sonar readings from all the crates of beer and Pepsi cans dumped off the picket line of carriers and destroyers. Those lucky bastards, he daydreamed, if they wanted some information, they just punched it up on their machines, or sent machines out after it or, finally, suckers like us.

There was probably no useful information to be gotten here, he knew, but he needed something for the reports. He checked out his troops and looked over to the ARVN man's interrogation. "Stop jacking off over there," he hollered, shaking his head in wonder.

The ARVN man spat something angrily at his captive and began again with the needle, this time in the boy's ear. Tears flowed down his silent face. He grunted in short, stabbing breaths and the ARVN man stopped again, afraid he might kill the boy. He cuffed him in the back of the head in his own frustration, and began again with the needle.

This time he pushed the wire up the anus, and sweat slid off the boy like a sheet of rain. He whimpered, and the ARVN man barked questions at him, twisting the wire further, deeper up the bowel, and the boy let out a scream that frightened the ARVN man. The scream stiffened the boy's body and increased his own pain.

The scream grew louder, into a wailing cry, and blood slid between his quivering buttocks. The guard looked away and swallowed air to keep from retching.

The ARVN man pulled the boy's hair and bellowed in his ear, but the boy only took that moment of relaxation to yell of his pain. The ARVN man saw a noncom running over from the Lieutenant to tell him to desist, and in his own anger, he took the needle and rammed it in as far as it would go. The boy howled and the ARVN man stood up tall to threaten the boy with a heel stomp to the face. The boy rolled on his side and whined frantically, and the noncom was yelling for the men's attention. The guard took a step over to stop the ARVN man. But the ARVN man drove his heel down at the boy's face as hard as he could.

He missed the boy's head entirely: a short, sudden flurry of fire rang from the hillside and blew off his leg, knocking him backward into the guard. A torrent swept the spot where they were, killing the boy, the dog, the guard, and the ARVN man; the noncom hit the ground and tried to low-crawl out of his exposed position. More fire poured into the center of the village from all directions. Villagers and patrol members hit the dirt and scrambled beneath the huts for safety in the shadows, while Willie Bowen, in the bushes, didn't bother to pull his pants back up. He just pressed himself against the ground and waited.

"Elvis! Elvis! Elvis Two!" the Lieutenant croaked into his radio "This is Delilah! Hello, dammit! Where the—Hell-vis! All right, man! This is Delilah, Elvis Two! Pinkville 6. Fire from all-the-fuck-over. Gimme cover, will you? Yeah! Take out hills clockwise SSW through SSE. Yes, God damn you! No—I don't *remember* the coordinates. I gave 'em before. Come on, man! We're in trouble. Figure out the fucking azimuths yourself! We need help!"

The fire poured from all angles. Willie Bowen lay flat in the bushes. He couldn't move. The open area was awash with bullets and mortar rounds. The hills on all sides and behind him were alive with the sound of machine guns. Willie thought of sneaking up the hillside to outflank them, but then thought better of it. He lay with his head on his wrists, wondering who'd win. There wasn't anything else he could do.

In minutes, the big jets streaked overhead, raking the hills with cannon fire and small bombs. "Goddam jets," Willie thought. "Five minutes and they're here. Ten minutes and they're back having coffee" Artillery looped in under the jets, and shook the hills without warning.

It did little to slow up the barrage of small-arms fire, and so the big flame ships came. They split like a blossoming lily, each in a half-roll, to attack the hillside from different angles. They spat foo-gas and the gelatinous orange-black fire swept the hill, curving around the bowl.

The Lieutenant screamed in his phone, "Give me a *pounding,* God damn it! Lay it all in. Every-fuckin'-where! That's what I said. Everywhere. Up the hill and down. Leave me one slot at SSW to pull out. Thirty seconds. Diggit!"

The Lieutenant motioned for the men to prepare to move out at his command, and they low-crawled through the reverberating dust to a position closer to their escape path.

"Here she comes!" the Lieutenant hollered. "On the money! All right! On my signal: Move out—Ready—"

Three planes split in three wing attacks. One peeled off right and took the hills counterclockwise. Napalm surged over the already-blackened hills in a wave. One took the hill clockwise, and the two waves splashed together and frothed in a wild confluence. The third jet hung, seemingly motionless for an instant, as if in aesthetic contemplation of the soufflé-mix peaks, the eddies and swirls made below it. Then it made up its mind with a slight hitch of its stride, and plunged down in a dive, aiming straight for the gap the patrol would be heading for.

"Now . . . GO!" the Lieutenant bawled, and they all raced toward the opening in the bush. A trail of machine-gun fire chased them, hitting half. Willie Bowen broke from his hiding place and dashed ten steps toward the fleeing unit. Dead and wounded were strewn across his path. The third jet, in its dive, was aiming at his nose. "Hurry up, fucker!" one of his buddies called, then a mortar round blew pieces of another man across Willie's friend. Blood washed him and a flying arm sent him sprawling into the bush, unconscious. Willie stopped in his tracks. Explosions blocked the path in all directions, and his fear was mixed with embarrassment—"You're gonna buy it for taking a leak!" he thought, and he almost laughed. The plane turned upward and opened its hatch. The drum tumbled out as Willie ran back as hard as he could. The blood-drenched friend at four o'clock lifted his head in spinning pain, and saw Willie Bowen let go of his rifle and dive horizontally into the bush he had been watching from a few minutes before, seeking safety in his own fecal pile. That was the last thing the man saw.

Everything in the village was sucked into a brilliant cauterizing fountain, everything within its boundaries incinerated in a fire that could be seen for fifty miles. Nearby treetops were blazing from the heat of the fire. Then the heat set off explosives under the huts. Had anyone been able to observe this they would have understood why the little village was so fiercely defended. Detonations sent rocket and mortar casings hurling through the fireball's orange skin, crates of explosives made new eruptions. Then the flame turned black and rolled inward, having consumed what could be consumed, sated, leaving the bowl from ridgetop to village edge a scar of ashes, with only the scent of oil and burned flesh to say it had once been inhabited.

Those who escaped ran like hares for a hundred yards, bunched together in panicky flight. They ran into a trap of preset American claymore mines and all were killed at once.

Late that night, a search patrol found the bodies and took back one dogtag per man. Near the village rim they found Willie's blood-caked friend, under his dead buddy's severed arm. He was not expected to live. His hair and eyebrows were burned off, and his skin smelled foul. His face and hands had deep oozing burns nearly beyond repair. The medics thought he would be luckier if he did not live: his face was virtually gone. But their emergency work was excellent and he was stabilized, then rushed to the Long Binh burn ward where he made some progress. He was able to fill in the gaps for the

271

after-action report. Later, a little stronger, he was able to elaborate. Through a mask of gauze which stuck to the pus on his face, he said the "last thing I saw was old Willie Bowen looking for a place to hide. In his shit. Never made it." And he said, judging it worth the pain it cost to move his remnant lips, his voice so hoarse and low they had to bend close to hear, only aware that he was still speaking by the bare trembling of the gauze, that it was "the biggest—goddamn waste I ever saw— Nada—Shit—Noth—" But they didn't put it in the report.

Laura Bowen had to be sedated most of the weekend, but by Sunday was reconciled to waking into a world turned on its head, strong enough to stand by her husband Sunday evening while he made his calls. He'd suggested she take a nap when he called Mack and Tyler, but she insisted on being near at hand for their support. "How's Mom holding up?" both children asked, grimly, and Vlad said, "Fine. Just fine. Your mother's a pretty strong gal. Here, you can talk to her." And it helped both Tyler and Mack in those first moments to feel they had to comfort and support her.

Vlad told them what details he knew, calmly, and it set the tone for them. The control and determination in his voice said all that could be done would be done, and that he felt things would work out all right, no matter how they seemed. It was as though he were telling them he had experience with these things, that he understood their nature, and that by the strength of his resolve it could be undone.

Then he walked around his spacious house to find some place to be strong. No corner of it served, not his den and not the living room, not his bedroom or the kitchen. They were too stuffed with comforts, too jammed with things that seemed no part of him. He felt naked and oppressed by clutter. The playroom in the basement was too teeming with the tinkle of glad echoes, a chilly wind of distant sounds, hollow and indistinct. He remembered walking barefoot there and finding cherry pits on the floor. Up in Willie's room he kneeled down by the bed and put his head upon the spread, clutching that cloth with all the strength in both hands. Then he rose and went into the bathroom Willie shared with Tyler. His little boy's electric razor was standing on the sink, lined up like a toy soldier by his electric toothbrush. His hands gripped the sink's sides to steady himself but he slid down to the cold tiles of the floor, bumping his head on the porcelain bowl, squeezing his eyes shut to fight tears. He rested his bruise against the cool hard surface that had hurt him and then sank further.

He stared blankly at the underside of the sink, the sweating pipes and streaks of solder. This would do for a chapel and he prayed, as prostrate and as supplicant as a mendicant can, asking mercy for his boy Willie: *"Please."* His rough bearded jaw quivered as he begged the pipes and tiles and porcelain to hear him.

He sobbed tormented whispers to a God he did not believe in as the only thing left to do. "Give him *back*. I beg you, please, give him back!" And then he squeezed harder still, in prayer to one he did believe in, addressing God but holding an image of the President in his eyes. Lyndon Johnson was a man, he knew, but something more than that. He had the stench of potency about him, resting in Vlad Bowen's mind like something animated from a leaden New Deal post office mural, a social realism steed, all rump and bile and stomach juices, with the hearty odor of ball sweat and manure. He'd always thought of Eisenhower as tiny clean white feet and Truman as a man with bleached eyes whose ears had fine silk angel hair spinning out. Kennedy was something else. He never trusted Kennedy: he was an ad for a classy car; some kind of ballet dancer who didn't perspire, or Whitey Ford's arm when they took out the sweat glands. There was no show of labor. He had a gorgeous body and was poison magic to millions seeking union with his beauty, but he wasn't real, not a man. Johnson was a man. He was, to Vlad Bowen, a man inside of whom was super-human power, enough to burst through every mortal limit, all logic and constraints. He had power in his guts and belly, he was a dark and fearsome star. He was America, and could hit one out for an orphan or a cripple any time. "Please," Vlad Bowen whispered hoarsely. *"Please.* O God Almighty give him back to his mother, *please!"*

Baron Zermatt was good, walking Tyler down in the first feverish days after this news came in. He distracted Tyler with an endless store of small talk and cockeyed homilies. "The institutions of the world are very strange," he said at one point over nothing in particular. "Take the Church. What a value system! The highest good is that teenaged boys and girls mustn't get laid. Doesn't matter to them they're putting a lot of overcharged teenies on the streets who go beat the snot out of everyone and turn into alkies——"

"I could've kept him out of this——"

"There's no point, Babe. Just wait. Don't chew yourself up."

Tyler said softly, "I guess hand holding is a large part of the practice of law, huh?"

"Maybe. Friendship isn't."

"I'm sorry. I appreciate it, really."

Zermatt punched his shoulder. "My pleasure entirely. It has a certain *exotic* feel."

For his parents, Tyler manifested as much self-control and hopefulness as he could. They'd taught him well at Gila, and he could lie convincingly, reassuringly, with a comforting authority. He said from what he knew mistakes were often made, statistical propensities did not govern individual cases, there was certainly hope, though he knew better. But to Mr. Mack he confided his helpless feelings, his sense of impotent responsibility. He wanted to take evil—the draft board, football coaches, principals, and Lyndon himself—and wring its neck until it loosed its grip on Willie. He imagined them all in some vile blood-ceremony, a coven of Babbitts chewing on his brother's flesh for their belly's greed in some black-spirited banquet. The worst part was, of course, that he just didn't and might never know a resolution. They were left with insubstantial things from which to conclude it was beyond repair. There was no recourse, and no revenge available. Both Tyler and Mr. Mack said they worried most about their parents, and didn't say they also worried about each other. In talking they searched the spectrum of responses for an appropriate case or tone. All failed to meet the needs of feeling. There was none fitting the event or their reactions, for they only knew a message, a shadow of the event, a well of illusion and bureaucratic expression, with no solid thing to hold or rail against. It was a desperate, nauseating, weightless sense, and so they avoided it as best they could and coaxed each other from it.

December entered with a sense of time warp. The electronic speed of dire messages had outpaced the mails. Postal miscarriages ushered in the pre-Christmas season. A letter, not the one Willie had placed in the stock of his weapon, but one mailed earlier that month, arrived. It was vintage Willie, sublimely nonchalant, tossing about mortal possibilities with the confident bravado of a man who had read the last page of his story and knew it said "happily ever after," that he could not be jinxed. Or perhaps Willie was scaring off bad spirits by speaking their name in the daylight. The letter might be true Willie, announcing his emergence from whatever Phantom Zone he had been mired in, by the same insensitive arrogance with which he packed off to war. Tyler wondered whether some hypersensitive computer at Gila might be subtle enough to discern which hand the letter had been written with, and whether its diction bore any clues to its date. But he knew, in the heart of that wish, that the letter was cold and Willie was gone, not to be resurrected by the hamhanded U.S. Post Office. It may have been his last souvenir of his brother. It read:

Hey, boy!
. . . besides the usual fighting and dying—getting good at one, pretty much a voyeur of the other—I have taken what time I have off in the pursuit of pussy, here, there, and everywhere. I'm sure you are thrilled to learn this. Do they censor your mail?
. . . I got three days off in Sydney and everything is a little hazy but I woke up next to this super-boobed piece, halfdrunk. She said I offered to drive her to Japan (by the way, in three days I never saw a *single* kangaroo)—which I agreed was a little rash (luckily, I didn't get a little rash a week later!)—

275

and she did the driving. I may be crazy but I'm not stupid. Once we were in a small fire fight and I was stoned, but I straightened out quick enough. Anyway, I looked over at her and I Wanted Those Breasts. So I said, "Did we . . . ?" She said we did, boy, hot damn, and it was just fine. So I grabbed her ass for the next 48 and went back to the war with the biggest hard-on in Combat Engineer History.

. . . gotta go on patrol and WHAM some village. Guy I knew got creamed the other day, by a mine. Couldn't tell he was a person when they checked him out. Interesting thing here about this stuff. Imagine the most outrageous thing that could possibly happen in any war or anywhere. It probably happened here already. It's like the action's in a big comp with your imagination. And it's *winning,* Babe. Gotta go kill—time—now. . . .

Very interesting thing about fire fights. You never know what hit you or who or from where most of the time. It's just like getting tagged out of some game you don't understand. That's all. Bingo. Short straw. Check out time. Adios.

On the whole, I think letting them draft me may have been something of a mistake. I don't know.

Willie/The Kid
XXXX
(His mark.)

The Bowens used all the tears and pressure desperate constituents can mobilize in Washington. But nothing came of it. The antiwar emissaries who periodically emerged from Hanoi's catacombs with grotesque holiday baskets for America—lists of dead and captured— brought no relief from the suspension. Willie's fate was spoken of in short sentences in each call to Pelham and Carmel. "Any news?" And then not again. The information was exhausted in the first few calls, but they declined to remove Willie to the past tense idiom which now best became him. Tyler told his sister about the letter and sent it off to her, both agreeing it was not suitable for their parents' eyes. Both agreed as well that it certainly predated his last fire fight. They did not want to upset their parents' process of adjustment, and send settling hopes into an unwarranted renascence.

And yet, each of them, as programmatic as they felt they were being, entered into a process of denial. For children believe in immortality, measured as their imaginations' ability to conceive more tomorrows than it can remember yesterdays, and a kind of omnipotence, measured by the inability of great grave forces to hold them down for long. So they chose not to believe what they could not believe. Not until Willie's agonized body was dumped in their laps would they accept the final seal. Not until the war was over and the last man out accounted for, until all searches ceased, would they take second-hand word that Willie had been swallowed whole by Asian Earth and American Flame, no longer to be found, assumed whole into some new existence. Maybe not even then, though by that time they would learn the art of resignation, and truth of gravities and gravities greater than will and hope, the reality of impotent mortality.

The wire services buzzed in early December with stories of new fighting in that faraway place, "potentially as bad as Hill 875 or Dak To," as though there were magnitudes to be considered. To Tyler it all seemed a struggle for possession over his brother's fallen shell.

He sweated out his frustrations beating Baron Zermatt at one-on-one basketball in the Gila gym at night.

In the locker room, Zermatt was cheerful despite the whipping. "I ever tell you about this girl I knew? She was a stewardess and they called her Andrea Doria, 'cause one night in a fog she went down with the crew."

"Some other time, huh?"

"True enough. Got pregnant, and her mother, who was very devoutly Irish, thought it was a miracle. Liked to do it in the same room as her twin sister when she could. This psychologist wrote 'em up for a journal. Maybe you read about it. Claimed it was an instinct to reassemble that original, uh—"

"Monozygote," Tyler volunteered lazily.

"Yeah, that's the one." Zermatt slapped Tyler's naked knee and pushed himself up. "I knew I could get you interested if I talked trash."

"You know something? That's as close as I've ever come to doing what I signed up to do."

"Tough job. All you gotta do is smile at people. Gums, that's what they want to see. They'll eat whatever treacle you slop down in front of 'em. You got it easy! My work's gotta pass under the nose of people who know what they're looking at."

They drifted out to the pitch-and-putt course and mechanically went about the business of playing, though it was really a social convention to have something to do while talking. "I think," Tyler said, holing out a short chip, "I should have been a Catholic. I make a great celibate. I could've made Pope."

"I can't see it," Zermatt said. "Other than the tax advantages."

"It'd be refreshing, all that straight-up right and wrong. Makes life easy. And that elaborate mojo and that sturdy sense of continuity. They know what they're gonna be doing next year, the Church. I used to worry, really worry, that the Unitarian church we went to wouldn't be there in the morning. Just an empty lot and no forwarding address."

"Now there's a perfect example," Zermatt said, kicking his ball away to concede himself a putt, "of a major piece of philosophy. It's what I mean when I say there's always some good come out of bad. Take me."

"Do I have a choice?" Tyler said, kicking Zermatt's ball back to where it had been. Then he walked over to it and picked it up. "Let's get out of here. I'm bored with this."

They dumped the balls and clubs back on the equipment rack and just walked around.

"I mean it," Zermatt said. "Good out of bad. Now, I hate the Catholics. Really hate 'em. But if it wasn't for them, I'd have about six months more of Gracie than I do."

"Divine Intervention?"

"In a way," Zermatt said. "See, I'm an Ethical Culture Person."

"Could've fooled me. Let's go get beer."

"Lapsed. But I was trained, you see, as a Mobile Roman Catholic." Tyler made a joke about Mass Transit, but Zermatt pressed on. "I was raised in this Nazi ghetto in Brooklyn—the parish line between two churches, Saint T'resa's and Mount Saint Ursula. Which I always thought was a command. A very Irish part of the burg, you might say. They used to have jurisdictional gang wars over who had primary rights to beat me up. Christ, they held Crusades right through our junior high school cafeteria. Only without the horses."

"Why were they after you?"

"Because I, uh, went to the public schools and was fair game. I thought they should have been off chasing the kids who were still Jewish, myself. Anyway, one time they got me up against a fence and one sticks a knife under my chin. Neighborhood ladies walking by, going, 'Hello, Tommy,' 'Hello, Chris,' 'Hello, Kevin'— all afternoon, like they weren't doing anything strange —just the Lord's work."

"They wanted your money?" Tyler asked. "Little Kevin and—"

"The hell they did! They wanted me to recite Catechism, the damn Saracens—Trial by Liturgy."

"What did you do?" Tyler asked, trying to keep from laughing.

"What do you mean, what did I do? I recited Catechism, is what I did. What do I look like, a schmuck? I picked it up from another gang the week before. Christ, I knew it cold. I bet I still know it better than any of those little heathens." He laughed, proud of his ability to incorporate it in a funny memory, confirmed that he probably did know it better. "That's what your poet types call GUP—Grace Under Pressure, buddy. I spent the next two years running down the street with a dozen RC's in pursuit, yelling portions of the Mass over my shoulder. I looked like a fucking processional—"

"I see you've survived it well enough," Tyler said.

Zermatt smiled a checkmate smile. "That's half the point. Tyler, you can survive anything as long as you're not too proud. Go with it. Renounce your faith if you have to. Lie, if they make you. But don't get your ego confused with your ass. Survival's the whole game. Get it?" Tyler nodded numbly. "And it pays dividends."

"What does?"

"It pays sometimes, to seduce your rapist. Now, I've

never told anyone this, but that little disgrace turned out to be a great opportunity in later life."

"How?"

"You swear on a stack of whatever shit you believe in? OK. I got wind once they needed someone for a special NSA assignment, which is a rare treat. You get to travel on a per diem, a bonus incentive, and it's early release if you do well. I earned six months off my three years like that. Plus it was a thing back in New York, and my wife had just decided she'd had enough sand in her shoes. She'd decided to go home and wait for me there—for three years. Anyway, what it was, was they used to have this real stand-up priest on the payroll. He did nothing but shuttle between various churches for them, and he'd do reports on Luci Baines and Jackie Kennedy—what they were confessing. He got sick—"

"Maybe an attack of conscience?"

"You may not like the rest of this story, then. Maybe it was gout. All I know is they needed a sub in a flash."

"The archangel Baron."

"This whole program came from someone in Very High Authority. Well, Luci Baines didn't confess to anything worth listening to. But Jackie . . ."

"She didn't know? She didn't guess?"

"Would you? I mean I was in a God-damned confessional in Saint Tom More in New York, for Christ's sake! Hell, she didn't bat an eyelash. And they were lovely." Tyler asked how they knew where to find her. "It was her regular place, I figure. Up on the wall on my side of the booth were three Holy Name Society pictures: Jesus, Pope John, and Jack himself. It was really something. My act was so good, when she was through, she gave me a little, I don't know, a tip, a little souvenir. This tiny glassine envelope. Inside it was a beautiful silver-plated PT-109 tie clip. Don't know where I was supposed to hang it—but I still have it at home."

"What'd she tell you?" Tyler asked, but Zermatt shook his head slowly, saying, "Some things are sacred, you know."

"You lousy—" Tyler said, shoving him.

"You—*layman*. I'll tell you this, though. She had this

real teenyweeny voice like Jayne Mansfield's. I think she had an endangered species on her feet, too, but I'm not sure. And when she stepped out, into the nave, the place lit up with this blue—almost holy—glow. Turns out there was a guy from *Women's Wear Daily* in the choir loft with a Sun Gun. Could've sold the snaps on the Continent for a fortune, said it was—well, the Secret Service nabbed him bad." Zermatt smirked merrily at Tyler's frown.

"You're disgusting, Bar."

"Maybe. But, see, I blessed her. Though I don't think I had to. I think there's some kind of heaven where all those High Church types go—Popes and thieves and babies and big winners like Kennedys and Notre Dame halfbacks and quiz show emcees and the merely famous and the well-born and the thoroughly rotten."

"Your place is assured."

"And they all fight it out over the three parking spots and dream up next week's history over cocktails."

"That's the funny thing?" Tyler asked.

"Oh, yeah. Just before I let her go, I asked her to return it, the blessing. And she did. Didn't miss a beat, like it was the most natural thing in the world for her to bless the Church. And here I am, Baron Duncan Zermatt, with Jackie Kennedy's blessing and most of her best secrets. Let those guys from Saint T'resa's put that on their wafers. So it pays, see? There's always gonna be some good come out of the bad. I'm living proof."

"I suppose it follows that out of good—"

"Sure. Take that high school you went to, the one with the Catholic name—"

"Madame Curie? That's not Catholic, jerk. Maybe *she* was, but it was public. Jesus, it was practically federal. They rebuilt it when the Russians put up *Sputnik* and the dog. We were supposed to be the next generation of scientists."

"Right. Now follow this. Bad out of good. America looks vulnerable, and lucky you gets picked to be a genius. So what happens?"

"I wind up here."

"You're getting smarter."

"Listen, man. We were very proud of that place. The Defense Department assured us that we were individually targeted by the Kremlin. Right after Niagara Falls and Disneyland. Sure made for a lot of shelter drills— sitting next to the prettiest girl you could find who didn't want to die a virgin. Boy, I'd hate to see what the clean-up crew after the bomb'd find."

"That's some distinction: last in the league in football, first on the Kremlin Target List, high school division."

"Well, we were the Cape Canaveral Farm Club—"

"That's Cape Kennedy," Zermatt corrected.

"Sue me," Tyler laughed.

"Yeah, but, you see? There's another one. If you'd got shot instead of him, circumstances would be different. You wouldn't be here. Maybe none of us would. You blew it, pal. You should've taken that plane to Dallas when you had the chance."

Tyler sniffed something strange then, but couldn't trace it. Just a funny scent of gasoline, or cleaning fluid. He checked his beer. Nothing. "All that time," he said wagging his head, "we kept waiting for it to come in through the roof. It came in through the TV, didn't it? *Jesus—*" He rose, stretching to full height, "I gotta get out of here before I go crackers like you."

"I have my dreams of Jackie to keep me warm," Zermatt said, as Tyler left him to the stars.

Stumbling back to his quarters, Tyler felt like he had during his freshman fall at Madame Curie, when the girl next to him was called on the first day of classes. She opened her mouth and, in her utter nervousness, vomited all over his desk. He escaped, charmed by inches. Freshman falls did not begin well. His first autumn at Cornell was a long, dry season of successive disillusionments. "You *think* this is Ivy League," his upper-class advisor had sneered. "There's one piece of ivy and we keep it in a glass cage to roll out at football games. It's a mascot. Other than that—and not without good reason—ivy steadfastly refuses to grow here." Throughout that freshman fall, Tyler plotted mightily to shed his virginity, which had become an embarrassing and troublesome bore.

The prospect consumed most of his waking thought.

Then one day, a girl he had known in high school, and had lusted after to no avail for years, came toward him on the strip of pavement which led from Olin Library to the Student Union at Willard Straight Hall. Her name was Robin D'Aimont and she had taken up with a succession of pre-Engineering Hockey Jocks in her two short months there. It was certain she was no virgin, but Tyler Bowen had yet to lay a waking finger on her. Every time he saw her it was "hello" and "see ya."

But that day she came straight at him. Earlier in the day he had found fifty cents in a phone booth, and by all omens it was shaping up as his lucky day all around. Robin came right-the-hell at him, and with a murmured "Oh—" (he couldn't remember now whether she called him Skip or Ty or even Babe, but he recalled it as the most intimate sound he had ever heard, his own name breathed with such urgent, vulnerable passion that he was aroused to the point of lost control), Robin threw her arms around him and buried her head in his neck.

He pulled back, smiling with unrestrained joy until he saw her face closely: her eyes were flooded and red-rimmed and her nose was stuffed, running; the form which held her together in thrilling alliances of features had been suddenly violated. Her lavender eyes had no focus, and the midnight hair he so long wanted to bury his own face in was a wild mess. He wondered if some Quad dogs had not pulled her roommate into a gorge, or a truck had hit a child. Somehow that image stayed: a wild and brakeless truck bearing down on a wide-eyed child.

Robin stood against him, crying, holding onto his coat, and then he noticed other couples in the same pose on the chilly sidewalk. Surely war had broken out, he thought. Cornell would not be far behind Madame Curie on the target list. The Russians probably wouldn't want America to keep the Finger Lakes, either. That or—had the Singing Nun run off with Elvis? Some of the others ran toward The Straight and Tyler had an urge to get the hell off the streets before the bombs hit. Grab Robin and steal some cafeteria food for the siege. He shook her and demanded at arm's length, "What? What's happened?"

283

"Don't you know?" she asked, surprised at his innocent ignorance, giving no thought to sparing him.

"I've been in the Libe till just now—" Her eyes
pulsed out new tears, and she shook her head violently.
She told him, "They've shot the President in Texas."

As he walked across the Gila Compound grounds,
he remembered the phrase and detail, and the linkage
particularly, as though it stood for a common fate:
Texas and Death sounded so well mated. Someday
everyone would be shot in Texas. An image burned in
his mind like a brand. Texas: a shadeless suburb from
end to end. A giant Lone Star, filled with the street of
a movie western town. The hostile lynch mob nearing
the jailhouse door, dust from the street kicking up. A
levee of tension breaking and then: the President down
in the street somehow, the mob swirling about him, de-
vouring his body like vultures in an unholy Eucharist,
seeking transubstantiation; trampling him, not content
with merely shooting him down, satisfied only with a
bloody dismembering; a ripping storm over the fallen
body. The mob closed in to prevent all rescue. They
would not give back the body, turned him bone and
brain to stringy carrion. Not shot in the head. Shot in
Texas.

He wondered about the images and why they flooded
back now, just as he had wondered about the odd odor
in his beer before. What were the antecedents, and the
subsurface runners linking causes with such effects, and
creating those causes in the first place? It was strange,
he thought, walking away from the spot of his wondering, that his mind's impression of Dallas should be so
surreal, when he'd actually been there twice. Once, in
June, on the way to Gila from the World, for a twenty-
minute stop. And before that, once when their parents
took Tyler and Willie on a western trip. They'd stopped
in Dallas so the boys could have the supreme uplift of
bowling at Mickey Mantle's lanes. The only demise of
note that day was in the papers: Marilyn Monroe, in
California. But in both cases, in memory, though the
name was the same, Dallas seemed like someplace else.

Whatever hopes had gone into however small a rebirth quickly died when the next letter came. It was

runny and half-charred from having been through sweat and fire and repose in a weapon's oily stock. It arrived with its injunction to "get laid once a year in my name," and Tyler cried in private all night on Gila's old softball field. He looked up at the constellations in the rapturous night sky. Willie's voice was in his hands, but like the light of long-dead stars, it was just evidence of what once was and is no longer. He could hear Willie in the music of the words, the melodies of every syllable, feel him in the intimate relations between thought and sound and idea and action. Intentions turned into a thumping, grinding, scraping symphony of noises built toward meaning, each sentence the sum of the universe's most complex process, all of them a universe in small, now flung by the energy which once bound it into infinite disorder's shards.

Zermatt felt an equivalent helplessness and was moved to take a risk for friendship. He called Johanna Reigeluth, but he didn't get a chance to explain before she cut him off, demanding, "How many people know about us, anyway?"

"I'm a close—friend. Listen, he's got problems and—" She was bristling. This Miles Standish business put her in a position she found strangling: categorized, classified in people's minds, pigeonholed as half of a fixed pairing.

"I don't care about his problems. You tell him to do his own dirty work," she snapped, and hung up.

Zermatt slammed his own receiver down and took a long, deep breath. He dialed her back and before she could hang up again he barked, "Now listen to me, you little self-righteous monster! I'm trying to talk to you —about somebody who needs you—"

"He's a big boy."

"Just shut up for a minute, will you? Look, I don't know why and I don't think he's particularly smart about it but he never stops talking about you. Maybe he likes you, I don't know. I do know he needs you. Now you don't have to believe this, but he's had his ass in a sling from the first day he started seeing you— and now he's in trouble."

"Because of me?"

"No. But if you care, you can help." He told her about what had happened and Johanna was overwhelmed with contrition.

"Oh, I feel so stupid—I . . ."

"Don't tell me," Zermatt said. "Tell him. Just don't tell him I spoke to you. I think he's crazy, but he thinks your act is cute. And *be careful.*"

"You're a good person," she said. "I'm glad you're Tyler's friend."

"It's a nice feeling."

She called Tyler immediately, giving no hint in her voice that the call was anything but self-generated. Nor did he suspect. She said cheerily, "I surrender. My Lysistrata streak is too thin. I can't take it."

"I don't believe you," he said fondly.

"Then we'll have a perfectly balanced relationship, tra-la. Besides, if you multiply minus one times minus one you come up with plus one. Look at it that way."

"It's a convenience."

"Owello, it's still true, funny as it is."

When they finally met for dinner, Tyler was alternately animated and quiet, as though filled with a fluid that would either burst from him or drown him if he kept containing it. "Johanna," he said. "I've never said this to any girl—woman."

"Girl," she admitted.

"—before. Christ, I don't know. Maybe you're better off without me."

"Why don't you let me be the judge of that?"

"I—don't know what more to say. You don't need me, really. But—I need you, Johanna. I need you so much that—I need you to want me. Does that make any sense?" She reached for his hand and took it to her face.

All across the country, girl friends were attempting to inspire their men to acts of moral outrage and resistance, but she, now, by an instinct that was greater than politics or reason, offered unconditional comfort, feeling once again a wife.

Later, Tyler told her about Willie in his own way, and said, "It's just so damned stupid. So God-damned stupid. They drag him away and don't tell you a God-damned thing. Just phase him out like last year's model." He told her how he and Willie were always "doing a 'Slide Kelly, slide!' " She looked puzzled, and Tyler explained that Kelly was a ballplayer who stole home plate from second base, sliding between the legs of a man who was tagged out stealing home from third. "The fans were screaming, 'Slide, Kelly, slide!'—and he did. Scored the winning run while the guy in front blocked for him. Since I was older we always used to do that sort of thing. I'd block for him, and clear the path, or he'd—oh, Christ. He just got tagged out on his feet, I guess."

"Tyler, don't."

"My friend Saint Paul likes to say that the potential for miracles is a ratio of God's force over the Universe's resistance—infinity over nothing. It's nice, but the fucking VC never heard of Campus Crusade for Christ. It's like that freaky cloudless rain. Nada. Human error. Ah, *shit!*"

While looking for a funny picture she had of herself, one in which she was braided and bunny-toothed with other serious-looking first graders, to make into a present for Tyler, she came across other old mementoes, brittle and crumbling, and brought some along one night to show Tyler for what mid-December cheer they might be.

One was from Carl Poulson's eulogy for Einstein. ". . . His final great work was evidence of that most potent and pervasive faith. Let me tell you of it. He sought to unlock one final riddle, as he had so many times before. He sought to divine a workable Unified Field Theory—to synthesize those great forces of nature he had done so much to explain, gravity and electromagnetism. To weld them into a basic theme, suggested by their similar actions, might reveal one last great secret truth: their common root. It is presently unpopular in sophisticated Physics circles to believe this.

"But this unfinished work of his is more than just a theory to be proved or disproved. It is his gift to us. For it says something remarkable—that the Universe may be traced to a basic set of relations, suggestive of an Original Event—from which all variety is but an arithmetic function. Without this, I believe he meant to say, we are left with several streams, all flowing into the sea of time, with multiple, warring truths and manifold creations, untrustworthy laws. Nor is it far from this to inferences of good and evil.

"You see, men of science are men nonetheless, sharing this small sphere with all other men. We are entitled from time to time to think of the essence of things, of meaning as well as fact. On one level that is what separates us from computing machines. One another, it marks the boundaries of theory from engineering. Einstein, as a great spokesman for humanity and humanism, was first among us in this. It permeated his work.

". . . To Einstein the secret was plain. Only the symbols were lacking. He believed in its truth. But how do you translate into language and symbol anyway the essential beauty which binds all things?

". . . For the leap from nothing to something, from inert to organic, from happenstance to chance to propensity to purpose to consciousness is more than Math and Chemistry can account for. The universe is more than mere information scattered in random clusters. It is just. Whim does not have total reign yet over reason. . . ."

"Oh, Christ," Tyler said, kissing her on the cheek. "Maybe we'll wake up and this'll all be a dream. Wouldn't that be nice?"

"I don't want to be banished with your dreams."

"At the moment," he said, "you're all the dreams I allow." She was a life preserver in his dry sea, whose support made him the more aware of the nature of that sea. The contrast was too plain, and it stoked his fears of being without her.

The next day after lunch he could not face going back to his desk, nor Zermatt, nor even the empty commissary. So he went to the Crypto Club and had a midday series of drinks, wishing he could get stoned instead. He called Johanna from there, calmer, but spinning with desperate ideas. "How'd you like to fly to New York?" he asked her.

"Don't you think it would be seemly if I got a divorce before I met your parents?" she replied.

"Why? They're always saying it'd be swell if I

brought home a wife. Look, I got some days coming at the end of the week and it'd be a goof if you could swing it. I gotta go away from here for a few days, and I don't want to go anywhere without you. So there you are and what do you say? I'll even pay your fare!"

"Why don't we just drive up to the Grand Canyon? That would be nice, wouldn't it?"

"What? Drive eight hours just to freeze in some Kaibib—"

"Yavapi," she said.

"Yeah, whatever— With a half-day's drive on either end? Well, that's in no way superior to flying two hours to San Francisco."

"I thought you said New York."

"Either one. Paris. Doesn't matter," Tyler said.

"Transporting a woman across state lines for immoral purposes, Mr. Bowen? A fine kettle of flounder!"

"Well, that way, Warren could have the car—"

"Let him eat roller skates!" There was no use trying to resist her. The only thing he could think to do was squeeze her. Tyler was completely her prisoner. When she was playful, he was helpless; when she was serious, he was breathless to keep up.

"Listen, Cassandra, pack a bag and come get me Wednesday, OK? We can figure out where on our way."

"Is that an invitation?"

"Details, details. Please?"

"It's a date."

He'd made a decision. Over the weekend, he'd ask Johanna's help in choosing. If she said, "Go," he'd find some way out of Gila. If that meant back to the Navy, he'd do it. As sole surviving son they'd never send him overseas. Besides, they couldn't risk it, considering what he knew. If she said so, he'd go out the gate and just keep going until they reached that neutral country to the north. He'd come a long way since he took the oath at Newport as a fledgling Naval officer.

JOHANNA LEFT TUCSON EARLY THAT WEDnesday afternoon, eager to show Tyler she could be punctual. More than anything she wanted their holiday to be perfect from beginning to end: she was going to reseduce him. She wore a leather miniskirt with a linen shirt and sandals. The first time he'd seen the skirt, Tyler had said his blood pressure had spiked.

Johanna had come to terms with the one problem gnawing at her. Her job was just a job, not a career; quite by accident, she had met Tyler Bowen, and that seemed a more fruitful and providential thing than a stopgap job, and far more important a thing to cling to. He was required by impossible circumstances to compromise; so, she recognized, could she. She would cease badgering him about philosophical questions, go anywhere he wanted, help if she could, share if he'd let her. She carried his presence even when he wasn't there. He seemed to be in the car with her, laughing with her, teasing her, smiling when she was happy, singing to the radio's songs in blithe ignorance of his own dreadful voice. She wanted to help bridge the gap in his life, be an antidote to the poisons afflicting him. If he had been forced to lie to her, it had not been by choice, but by forces larger than either of them which imposed special burdens, impossible choices, on those who had no choice but to be men. She wanted to see him through that time, not make it worse. She would tell him that. And they would celebrate a rebirth at Christmas, start a new year of their own devising.

At the point where the last road stands proclaimed the terminus of Tucson's mid-desert hegemony Johanna saw a hitchhiker standing by a dusty backpack and thumbing for a ride. He stepped onto the pavement as she approached, and all thoughts of passing him were exiled when she considered her manifest good fortunes. Having decided that good living was the main thing, this was no time to be stingy and hard-hearted. Hitch-hiking on a public highway was illegal, and giving a ride was both a favor and a small act of sheltering sub-version. It made her feel good. Here she was between Thanksgiving and Christmas, in her own Epiphany. She had to share her cup, at least. So she stopped, pulling onto the gravel shoulder. She had to back up fifty yards. It was only four o'clock. She could even give him a lift into a nearby town and still be early. Tyler would be so happy she was early, and she could tease him all weekend about the small cost of a desert favor. He looked so funny when he was proven wrong.

"Give me a lift to Benson?" the hiker asked.

"Easy enough," Johanna said. "Hop in." She pulled back on the highway and studied him through the side of her eye, then looked back at the road, fully in command of her world.

"Tell you," he said. "I really appreciate this." His voice was low and halting. Attractive in a rustic way.

"You took an awful chance, you know," Johanna said, "hitching in the desert."

"You're right there. You're right. Hot. Real hot. It can be like forever out there, when you're tired. Desert can be sore and mean."

"That's why I stopped."

"Well, I'm surely glad." He smiled and shook his head. "But if I was your daddy, I'd tan you good for pickin' up strangers. Girl shouldn't do that."

"Oh, I don't know——" Johanna laughed, a little patronizingly.

She looked over at him briefly in a friendly way, indicating her self-confidence. His weather-seamed face was open and broad, like a mellowed old prospector, a desert neuter full of nothing but sand and advice. Ruddy, sunburned cheeks, shiny with sweat and road grease, gave him a Kris Kringle aspect. She noticed him cocking his head to one side, watching her long, tanned legs work the pedals. He smiled at the pleasure of being in her aura. She winked at him and said merrily, "I guess I do lots of things I shouldn't do."

"Name's Richie," he said. "Live up around Flagstaff." Perfect, she thought: he had a child's name to match his childlike artlessness.

"I live in Tucson," Johanna replied.

"I guess I've lived on the edge of one desert or another all my life," he told her, somewhere between proud of that fact and resigned to it, "but—she always looks like you're lookin' at her for the first time. You ever feel that?"

"Yes," she smiled, turning toward him to agree. "I love the desert. It's beautiful a thousand different ways." Her luck held: she picked up hitchhikers and they turned out to be gentle souls who validated her view of the world. Tyler would shake his head in bemusement. "Is your family in Benson?" she asked.

"Only people I got left. Couldn't get out of Flagstaff at Thanksgiving, so here I am."

"I missed my people at Thanksgiving, too," Johanna said, thinking of the dreadful dinner she had passed at Maureen's with Warren.

"Man says to me, 'People go places at Thanksgiving, to relatives and such, just to remember why they don't go see them all year.' I expect it takes a whole year to forget." Johanna laughed at that, but he said, "Anyways, I don't hold much with that. They're all I got, like I say. So here I go—better late than never. You got people down this way?"

"I'm going to get my—husband, for the weekend. We're going on holiday."

Richie nodded warmly, mulling it over, "I bet you're a real handsome couple." He leaned back to enjoy the afternoon scenery, breathing shallowly with an audible wheeze, while Johanna traced some melodies on the radio with *la-la-la*s as they bounced down the highway. Soon he rummaged in his rucksack and pulled out a calico-hide canteen. "Want some?" he asked, holding it near her chest. He held the wheel while she took a swig.

"Thank you," she said. "Won't be long now." Richie swiveled slightly in his seat and rested on his left hip.

"Yup. Just down the road a piece."

"Well, fifteen minutes, maybe." She caught a glimpse of him looking at her intently and thought that Tyler would really laugh now to know he made her a little nervous with his watching.

"Here we go," Richie said. "Slow down just up ahead and pull onto the shoulder."

"I thought you wanted to go to Benson," she said, turning to him. His face was inches away and he was staring straight at her. She looked down suddenly at the feeling of something hard at her side. Richie was pressing a hunting knife against her just above the belt-line of her skirt, in the unprotected soft flesh of her waist. "What do you want?" she asked timidly, a different girl in that moment's change. Still, she tried to appear controlled and retain some purchase on the situation.

"Just slow down and pull over. Take it easy." His voice was soothing, calm. They were near the Mescal exit. She pulled to a stop and squirmed toward the corner of her seat. But he followed with the hunting knife.

"What do you want? What?"

"Just be nice. I'm not going to hurt you."

"There's money in my bag. It's not much, but it's all I have." He stuffed the money in his knapsack and commanded her to pull off the road into the desert. She obeyed him in silence, hoping to find some way out, as she drove deeper into the desert.

"Now stop." There was nothing in any direction but mesquite, cactus and clumps of earth, but enough of those to hide them from the Interstate, two miles away. To the south were the Thunder Mountains, their flat-topped ridge stretching from one arbitrary point to another in the middle of nowhere, and Gila a somewhere in that nowhere. Richie took the keys from the ignition and got out of the car. As he did, Johanna fumbled in her bag for her spare set. He was going through his own bag looking for something. He approached her door just as she was nervously jabbing the spare key into the ignition. "Don't do that," he snapped angrily, and reached through the open window to grab her hand. He took the spare set of keys and pocketed them. "Now get out."

"What do you want? What?" He had a rope in his hand, and he moved toward her with it. A bloody hurt filled the inside of her face, as if she had been punched in the nose or missed a stair and fallen into space.

"Don't make this hard," he said, still in a calm, reassuring voice.

"We can be friends. I'll come to Flagstaff. You don't have to do this. I'll see you in Tucson—I like you, Richie. We—"

He ignored it. "I'm sorry, miss. You're a nice girl. I'm sorry it has to be you."

"I like you, Richie. We can be nice together. We can be friends. I don't just see my husband. I—" He slapped her across the face and it shocked her by its suddenness. Tears rose, but did not fall.

"Take off your shirt." Johanna unbuttoned the linen shirt and let it fall off her arms to the desert floor. Her breasts stared at him like two children roused from bed to greet an intimidating stranger, wide-eyed and quivering. She hugged herself as if to protect them like a mother. "Put your hands out," he said, his voice never changing its singsong quality. He tied her wrists together and attached the rope to the car's bumper, holding her on a six-foot tether.

He held the dirty hunting knife in front of him and pointed it at her belly. Johanna's face leaked fear, but she said nothing. He pressed the knife at her neck then, and tugged at her skirt belt. A strong tug snapped the skirt zipper open and ripped it apart, hurting her in the small of her back. The skirt slid stiffly down her legs and lay around her ankles like the apron and pedestal of a statue. Again he pointed the knife at her belly and pulled her blue bikini panties down her long, smooth legs. She stepped out of them and stood before him naked, somewhat more composed now, for she had gauged the perimeters and was less anxious, more resigned. "It doesn't have to be like this. Really. It doesn't. We can—" He cracked her across the face and she brought her head back, in pain, as if it were on a spring, her eyes twitching with a desire to cry, though nothing came.

Richie pushed her down to the sand and threw the knife out of her tether's range. He grabbed her by the hair and kissed her mouth. His breath seemed beery, not drunken, but hot and wet. He kissed her on the neck and it sent a shudder down her spine. Her head fell backward. He grabbed her jaw and kissed her so hard it hurt. His nail cut the skin by her left nipple and she had to muffle her cry of pain in his scratchy cheek. Then he pulled back from her and pulled his fly open, to let his half-erect penis flop out. With all his weight on Johanna he tried to penetrate her, but she was cramped up with fear.

He sat up quickly and slapped her across the face three times. Blood trickled out of her nose and into the corner of her mouth. She swallowed what blood she could, and gritted her teeth to keep from gagging. Then Richie rolled her sideways to clot the rest with sand.

He took a rough hand and brushed her pubic hair free of sand. He slid down her and licked at her vagina for a few seconds. Her face twisted in anguish from the pawing, and when he couldn't see her she loosed her urge to grimace. He too wore a look of disgust, in some way hating exactly what he was driven to tear from her. Pulling himself up her front he tried to enter her again. He pushed and she spread her legs to let him. He twisted her ear as he did. Slowly and with some pain, he slid inside her. Her throat dried up and her stomach went weak. The sense of entrance made her head reel, dizzy in some new dimension of divested virginities, this one ripped from her.

He thrust inside her a few times, and then came with a short burst of air and a collapse of strength. Her mind played tricks, mean ones, leaving her no place to hide. She was terrified of what turn he might take. He was sweating profusely and Johanna's body was damp from him. Her mouth tasted of sand and blood and saliva and his breath. He lay on top of her for another moment then pulled himself up, opening his eyes slowly, as though waking from a dream that merged well with the subtle sounds of morning. He grew angry at what he saw, more scared than she was. He struck her in the mouth and cheek until the left side of her face was numb. "Please," she begged, "please," pinned beneath him. "I'll be good to you. I'll—"

"Stinking, filthy—" he hit her again, and she rolled sideways against his leg, whimpering. Her fright at his brutality was increased by the insensate look on his face and the threat in his voice. A dark cloud had come over him. His eyes were turned back where no reason could approach him. "Lousy— C'm'ere, you!" he yelled. Johanna edged away on her knees, but he grabbed the tether to reel her in. "Cunt! Lousy whore slit!" He wrapped the rope around her ankles until she was casually lashed like a calf in a rodeo event, shivering fetally. She began to lose clarity and strength, and was mortally afraid now. He hit her again and the blow fell on her shoulder and bounced off her face as she hunched over. She tried to crawl backward, but tripped over and nearly hit her head on the bumper, whimpering in the sand. He pulled her back and fell on top of her, trying to enter her again. He pulled her hair until her head flopped back and her mouth fell open in pain. She made no sound, not wanting to frighten him. She twisted about as he tried to enter, as though to give him the pleasure of a fight, and it excited him. He tried to rub himself into an erection, but it was no good. Sweat stood out all over his face and his features grew hard and black. He heaved himself up and down on her with force. But the erection would not come.

"Bitch!" he whined. "Filthy *rag!*" he cried. He spat in her face, and put all his weight on one arm pressing on her stomach. She moaned beneath it as he tried again to enter her. But he was still not hard enough. "I'm sorry," he said softly, as if a detached narrator of a story he could not control. "I don't want to have to do this. You're a nice girl, but—" He retrieved the knife and stood over her with it. She lay crumpled on the ground, bruised outside and in, semiconscious, a sleepy girl who did not want to be awakened for a difficult day.

He pressed the knife against her throat, kneeling by her head, saying, "I'm sorry, girlie, I'm sorry," tearful at his actions. He pressed it against her soft and sticky skin until she could feel its heat slice the first stratum of skin, and blackness in her mind began to tear like a drop of dark water on a razor's edge, pulling unnaturally in two directions, yet oddly graceful, a delicate mitosis, parting painlessly, like a dying dream. But her eyes jumped open and she pulled backward quickly by sheer instinct, staring at him with resistance for the first time. Her own killer sense had been awakened. No longer was her head throbbing with fear, nor even pain. Something deeper than sensation had resolved that fear and pain were incidental and neither would avail. Balanced on the blade were survival and death and she was not prepared to lay down and die, not yet: she was possessed with the belief that there was some purpose she must still strive for. So she scrambled backward in the sand, gaining moments to think, naked except for a sandal on her left foot.

She thought of many things: her father, Warren, Tyler, and no larger thought than "Johanna, you're an idiot. And now you're going to pay an unbelievable price for being foolish."

Now she murmured, "Please. No. Please," in short hysterical sobs. She backed up on her knees, half-standing. What art could she summon? she wondered frantically. "We can still be friends. I won't turn you in—"

"Yes you will."

"No. I won't. We'll meet. It's true. Anywhere you want. I swear. I'll be your girl. You can have me any time. Anything you want. I'll be good to—I stopped for you. I'm nice to you."

He moved toward her and she minced backward again, guerrilla-fashion, stalling for advantage and time. Richie's eyes were bloody now and her words had no effect, bouncing off his ears unheard.

He grabbed her by the throat and stood shaking in front of her naked body, trembling as much as she. He hit her across the side of her head with the handle of his knife and she sank to her haunches. A surge of relief filled her momentarily: she had thought that slash was the blade itself, that she'd be dead now, without a last effort in her own defense. It lulled her into false safety for a second. Then Richie yanked her hair and put the knife at the nape of her neck. Her eyes rolled backward, preparing to see blackness. Blood slid down her face from the scalp wound, stinging her eyes, falling to her shoulders and breasts. Her mind spun furiously.

"I'm sorry, girlie—" She saw him take a deep breath and her own stuttered. Her hands mediated on the knife blade, trembling. She knelt before him, unready for slaughter, her eyes darting about, unwilling to focus.

"I'm sorry, girlie," he repeated. Something stirred, and she leaned forward, into the knife, reaching past it, groping toward life, barely touching his still-limp penis. Richie's knife hand grew slack for a moment: Scheherazade was being given a short stay to finish a tale. She reached out and took his twitching organ in her fingertips, gently, frightened but determined in spite of her pain. She closed her eyes and caressed it, kissed it softly, stroked it with her lips and tongue, lapping it as a cat tastes milk. She drew it fully into her mouth. Her throat parched by the desert and by fear, she nonetheless suckled his penis until it grew hard as the knife at her throat had been, and tried to ingest it entirely. Her hands reached up past his waist, begging him to come down to her. She was breathing hysterically.

Richie dropped to his knees. His erect penis fluttered and nodded between them, a child they had conceived, the object of their mutual adoration. She slid her hands around his buttocks and pulled him down over her. He was stiff and dumb and tumbled on her with a crash. But she writhed beneath him like an adolescent enjoying back-seat fooling, until by sheer force and the aid of her hand, he entered her. She circled her hips to permit him deeper still, almost proud, in her pain, that she had done it: seduced him even in his unreason.

Each pull and thrust tore her skin inside from her dryness. His fingernails dug at her shoulders. Blood still trickled down her face. He stiffened even more and jabbed her in the side. As if understanding this prod, she brought her ankles up to permit him as deep as she could, trying to read his moods, like a performer working a hostile audience. She kissed him with faked heat, panted as he drove deeper. He felt like emery and she could hardly remember any existence but this. Only her left eye, staring out for help and mercy into the empty desert space, betrayed her unwillingness. A casual stranger might even mistake them for ardent lovers. But that eye fixed unyieldingly on the distant plateau, while Richie poured his energy into her.

Then, in a seizure, he gasped and flexed all of his muscles, smacking her shoulders and back. She cried, "Yes! Come! Fuck me! Yes! Oh, yes! Oh, God, oh, yes, oh yes, damn, yes, damn, *yes!*—" arching her back to take still more of him and felt the surge of moisture within her as he squeezed and tore at her shoulders, slowing her hips to a rhythmic round carousel.

His face lay against her blood-splotched hair and he breathed hard and heavy in her ear. He lay on her for a few minutes, still half-erect, and she began to arouse him once more. And again, though each movement seared her, she brought him to a dark release. He pulled her hair so that the roots ached, and came in her with a great rumbling moan and a sudden fall, as though shot by a distant rifle. Then he rolled off and lay beside her in the sand, the knife on the far side of her head. She thought about picking it up. But even if she had the strength to use it, he could surely overpower her. Instead she put her head against his chest.

"Richie?" she begged. "Let's be friends. I like you. Here's your knife—see?" He reached over her and picked it up, standing astride her, a Colossus with his pants down. "See? I could have taken it." Her mouth was numb and the words were hard to make out. "But I didn't. I want to be your girl—" The blood was caked on her face, and she looked ugly, but she smiled as sweetly as she could. "Your friend—all right?"

His mind was fuzzy and he told her to stand up. He untied her hands and told her to walk away from the car. She was still naked, but she walked, a sandal on one foot, into the desert further, toward the butte. She limped from the pain of her assault, but began to run when she heard the car's engine start. He would run her down, she thought. She stumbled, sprawling to the sand, whimpering and crawling madly like a desert lizard. Richie puttered off in the direction of the Interstate, leaving her lying naked in the sand.

Johanna stumbled back to the spot where it had happened and found her other sandal with her skirt and blouse. She smoothed a place in the sand and sat, numb, gathering her strength and wits, preparing a small nest to lie in for a while. The afternoon rains came and, in fifteen violent minutes, left. She stood up and undressed in the rain to let the water wash the bloody evidence from her body, then lay back like a sunbather to let the downpour splash and run over her skin. The rain slipped in rivulets amid clotted blood and dirt congealed with sweat. Only the taste and feel of the event remained. The rain could not go inside her.

She felt like an odd and special child, one now with rare gifts: more senses than she had been born with. The native five might outlive pain but two more now ached, and these two could not forget or be repaired. They had been born of a tearing: her sense of personal space, and her integrity. And to save herself she had assisted in their ripping. They were matters of apprehension, not perception; the damage might not be undone.

Heat followed the rains to dry her body and clothes. She pulled her sandy panties on, draped her blouse around her shoulders, and pulled her leather skirt up to her chest for a wrap. Then she pulled her matted dirty hair in front of her eyes and lay down in the sand to wait for dark.

Johanna watched the sun set over Kitt Peak and wondered whether the insistent gaze of the astronomers remained fixed in the heavens yet. What more was there to learn about the sun with their poor tools? Their back was to her now, while below the sun and their sight she lay beaten. Behind her, as she rose in the waning light, lay the Cavalry trail in the shadow of Apache Peak. Ten thousand horses thundered by in movies every year. Westerns made the landscape known around the world. The Cavalry always rode that way on the trail from Fort Defiance to Tombstone. Beyond that, just out of sight, Johanna knew, but maybe less than twenty miles away, toward the bluff, was the abandoned back door of Gila Compound, the winding trail to the Gila Canyon.

Darkness comes fast in the desert, when the sun slips over flat-topped peaks on the western edge. And darkness in the desert is like nowhere else. The desert life awakens. The stars are so bright and plentiful that, though blessings to navigators, they can create a disorienting rapture. Only the smog of Tucson, sitting as a cap on that city over the horizon, like emanations from a golden pot, gave Johanna any clue. The lights of cars and street lamps shimmered and created a Tyndall effect, fluorescing the suspended particles of poison in the city air, lighting the north rim of the world for her..

Behind her, Gila Compound shone like a world of neon.

Johanna walked at an angle oblique to these two glowings, guided by the southwest-leaning barrel cactus, following her own tires' tracks on a path to intercept the Interstate.

She was tired and thirsty when she reached the highway, as weak as before. But she stood gamely on the shoulder and hailed down a diesel tractor-trailer, gratefully accepting a ride.

When she sat down, something stuck her leg and she jumped slightly. "You all right?" the trucker asked her. She nodded. "Hiking through the desert, huh? There's advantages being a girl—when it comes to thumbing down a ride, good thing for you." She paid no attention, reaching behind her leg to the hemline of her skirt for the annoyance.

"Yes." She spoke slowly. "Could you drop me at a gas station or a lighted house? I'm not feeling very well."

"Sure thing, miss," the trucker said, looking at her sideways. He thought if he helped out, maybe she'd let him grab a little ass. It was one way of making up for being on the road at night. Maybe she was lonely and wanted a little friendly cornholing. But she looked like trouble, as he considered her, all scraggly and torn up. Probably on drugs. Maybe there'd be a freebie in it yet —but maybe she was diseased. He'd wait and see what he'd have to do for it.

She pulled the sticking object from her skirt, a burr, and held it in her palm, wondering whether she should keep it as a sarcastic memento. But she closed her eyes, leaned back, and lightly dropped it out the window.

They pulled in at the first service station near the road, a family store with a home attached and two pumps in front. She knocked and a gigantic man in an undershirt answered. "Weellll! What have we here?" he smirked, pleased to see the bedraggled girl at his door. Johanna began to howl. Not a cry, not a tearful bawl. Just the howl of a frightened animal, an animal who had been unable to cry out earlier for fear of betraying its hiding place to a predator, dry-eyed and desperate. It scared the man in the doorway and brought the trucker in a hurry. "Carol!" the man in the T-shirt hollered. "You'd better come out here. Hurry!"

The man's wife pushed him aside and took Johanna by the arm. "Come in, dearie. Come in." She sat Johanna down and brought her water, offering some leftovers "if you're hungry."

"A man stole my car," Johanna said, and the trucker, weighing his odds, left quietly. Johanna said she wasn't hungry, but asked to make a phone call. She reached her brother in Tucson. He called Warren and the police and Maureen Poulson in Phoenix.

While they waited for Johanna's people, the woman sat staring at her, smiling solicitously, but scrutinizing her as though she were a visitor from Mars. "Arthur, go get a basin of warm water," the woman said. He left to fetch it and the woman leaned forward with earnest interest. "What happened, child? You've been hurt—did he—did he rape you?" Johanna just shook her head and said a man had stolen her car and left her in the desert. "You can tell me—you're sure he didn't—?" Johanna said nothing.

The woman's husband returned with the basin and Johanna opened her eyes to ask meekly for some water to drink. "Don't be silly," the woman said, urging the basin on her. "You've got dirt up in your scalp and blood—you really should wash off. You'll be more comfortable." The man strutted to show how cool one could be. But Johanna stayed sunk in the chair until they brought a glass of ice water. She held it in both hands and rested her head against the chair back, periodically pressing the glass against her forehead.

When Warren and Neal arrived, Johanna had fallen into a light sleep. They took her to the University Medical Center in Tucson, where her nephew Michael had been. She was dosed with antibiotics and given a dilatation and curettage, after which she was sponged with witch hazel and alcohol, sedated, and allowed to return to fitful sleep.

After a few hours, she woke and found two policemen sitting by her bed. They asked her a few brief questions, which nevertheless made her relive the entire afternoon.

At eleven she woke up again, and found Warren,

her mother, her brothers, and her sisters-in-law sitting in a circle around her bed like a witches' coven. Each time she opened her mouth to thank them for coming, one would move forward, touching her sheet, reaching out to interrupt her with a word of care, pressing her arm with a hand.

At midnight, just before she fell asleep for the night, she took some juice and a light meal and another sedative.

Warren and her mother remained and asked her at that time whether she didn't think picking up strangers on a highway was "foolish and dangerous." They demanded the confession as though, it seemed to her weary and sedated mind, there was some urgency in wringing that admission from her before dawn. Johanna said nothing. Then she asked for some more juice, and rubbed the white dot by her eye distractedly for its familiar touch, as though to check that it was still there, while they clucked their cheeks in despair of her.

When she didn't arrive Wednesday afternoon, Tyler called her house every half-hour until ten at night. Frustrated and worried, he located a beery Baron Zermatt at the Crypto Club. "Hell, she's probably stopped to help some peon fix his ailerons or—I bet she's off organizing the braceros. Why, her goodness knows no bounds! When her Band-Aids run out, she'll show up, just in the nicotine, to get you in more hot chili."

"I bet there's a simple explanation," Tyler said.

"You know what? I bet she's run off with her husband!"

After two more hours of no answer, he gave up. Zermatt dragged him outside into the stagnant air of the Compound, and they wandered over to the outdoor pool. There, Zermatt took a piece of tin foil out of his wallet and opened it carefully. "Here. It says, 'Eat me.'"

"What is it?" Tyler asked, eying the pink speckled pill. "Cyanide?"

"Mescaline from Mescalo. Part of some evidence in a very quiet little security hearing."

"How'd you get it?"

"Oh, some guys were making a little extra swapping

303

this stuff for some better stuff out of the labs. A regular operation right through the hills into Sunny Meh-he-ko. Didn't need the whole stash for evidence, so some of it got into circulation. You want?"

"What for?"

"Make you feel good, dope," Zermatt laughed. "Tell you what, just to show my bona fides, I'll take half. OK? I'm trying to help."

Tyler lay on his back by the pool and counted the stars, waiting for the pill to take effect. "Are we dead yet?"

"Depends how you mean."

"I'm feeling no pain, that's for certs—"

"That's the idea." Under the moon and the warm shawl of night, the two men were alone. In the sand by the fence they built a sand castle, happy and playful as two little boys with no cares. An aqueduct curled from its turret to moat, and before they abandoned it for other toys they stood over it and urinated into a single stream. It reminded Tyler of the time he and Willie were taken by their parents on a western trip, the same month they had bowled at Mickey Mantle's. Then, Vlad Bowen had taken his boys to a point high in the Rockies, along the Great Continental Divide. In a small clearing in the bushes, all three Bowen men passed their water. Bowen family essence would seek the oceans and seas throughout the American continent, some east, some west, by random movement and happenstance. They'd be in the soil and water and flesh of all citizens. Then, they were peeing on the fulcrum of fate. Now, they fertilized the American desert and the floor of a distant jungle.

Zermatt was smiling like a foggy jack-o'-lantern at his good medicine. They slipped into the pool and watched the stars walk around until the effects of the drug made each feel he was dissolving. All Tyler could sense was an anesthetic overloading of his skin. The water and his body joined to shed their separate identities. He wished Johanna, angry as he was at her, was there to play with him instead of Zermatt. What a time they'd have with this candy and playground. He tilted his head back and lost himself among distant galaxies, dulled by unbearable awareness and a sense

304

of participation in all around him, as if his matter and energy were in constant flux, as though he had been part of that golden fluid in all his countrymen's veins; as if his very self was a temporary station for entities and energy in transit. His mind spun dizzily. There was no reason to consider oneself apart from the cosmos, no real boundaries of self and the void.

"Hey!" Zermatt shrieked, jumping out of the pool, shaking Tyler from his reverie. "This is weird, boy. That stuff's dangerous. I didn't know where I began and where the rest of the place ended."

"So much for private property."

"I'm serious. I had no idea what was inside me and what was out—and it just kind of ooozed . . ."

"What did?"

"I'm trying to tell you I peed in that pool, Babe. But I didn't know it."

"You peed in the pool. In this one? The one I'm in? Wasn't the sand castle enough for you?"

"Uh-uh," Zermatt said, nodding and shaking his head at the same time, calm, reposed, twitchless.

"You peed in this very pool? What's left for you but to commit a lewd act on the Sign?"

"You're floating in my whizz, fella."

"This pool? This very pool? This very night? My God!" He jumped out, examining himself. "I'm unclean!"

"Jump back in," Zermatt laughed, following his own advice.

"Are you crazy?"

"It's my pee, ain't it? Won't kill me. It was in, now it's out. Big deal. Sue me!"

"Sweet fuckin' paradox it is." They dressed and tripped back to their quarters, crashing wildly.

It was three in the morning, and Tyler asked Zermatt to call Johanna for him. "Why do I feel like Friar Tuck?" Zermatt asked.

"You've got the wrong play, Bar."

"Saw the movie. Maybe she's asleep. She's probably got a rational explanation, for her. Or will in the morning."

"Thanks, buddy, I'll do it myself."

"That's the spirit that made America great—and kept lawyers from going to jail with their clients."

There was an answer. "Hello?" Tyler asked timidly.

"Who the hell is this?" Warren bellowed.

"This—" Tyler hung up quickly. "I think it was Warren," he said to Zermatt. "What's he doing there?"

"He lives there," Zermatt said. "Maybe they've reconciled. What'd I tell you. Everything works out for the best—a rational explan—"

"That's not rational!"

"Neither are women. And neither, my friend, are we."

"Unreal," Tyler muttered. "I mean, *really* unreal." Then he grabbed at Zermatt's sleeve, wild-eyed, saying, "When they make a movie out of our lives, Bar, they'll make this scene significant. They'll make it stand for something—"

"I don't see how."

"They'll do it. They lie about these things. You've got to stop 'em!"

"Babe, I got bad news for you. They can't make a movie out of our lives. It's all classified, and pointless."

"It'll be a point about pointlessness," Tyler insisted.

"I just hope it goes down better than it lived."

"They'll make it a musical, Bar!"

They retired to phantasmagoric drugged-sleep visions, as real as any other.

In the morning, Thursday, Tyler Bowen lay in bed in self-pitying hibernation, a protective fetal curl to conserve his warmth against the winter's threat.

He was alone, without friend or lover, in a place he hated and a time he could not deal with. There was nothing in his world to be a lever, and no place of purchase to stand.

He lay there, thinking, "One more time, Johanna," and then dragged himself out of bed to call her. Maybe she had a good explanation. Maybe Warren had popped over unexpectedly and she had stayed at home to keep him from suspecting.

On his way out, Susan Carver's assistant hailed him. "Hey! She's looking for you."

"Who?"

"Who do you think? She is positively cumulo-nimbic today!"

"How can you tell the difference?" Tyler asked. "Any idea what's up?"

"I wouldn't be surprised if she runs your ass up the flagpole just to see who shoots."

"How come?" Tyler asked, resignedly, unable to be anxious.

"Just that kind of morning."

When Tyler arrived at her office, Susan Carver said nothing, and pointed to a seat. She flipped expressionlessly through a pile of phone messages while Tyler squirmed in the hard chair on the side of her desk. "A good thing you were still here, Mr. Bowen. It pains me to think about Central Security scouring the countryside for you."

"I don't understand. What's the problem?"

"Maybe you can tell me. Quite a little holiday you had planned for yourself."

"That? You agreed to that two weeks ago. It's on the sched—" She waved him silent with her left hand while her right lit a cigarette. He was still fumbling with matches when she exhaled a blue gray cloud.

"There was a phone call for you this morning," she said, pulling one message out of the pile. "A very important member of the media. So—" Smoke bubbled out of her mouth as she spoke—"they put it through to me when they couldn't find you."

"Well, I told you. I had comp time coming. I'm sorry but—"

"I told you once: don't be sorry; be smart. We had a very nice chat. You know, Mrs. Poulson's an old friend of mine."

"Mrs. Poulson?"

"From KPTV in Phoenix."

"Oh, *that*. She's probably calling about the—that special you wanted me to see if—you know, that idea you had about a one-hour—" Susan Carver stopped him.

"I advise you to think very carefully. She was calling at the request of her daughter, our friend Mrs. Reigeluth. Suggestive, don't you think?"

"Not at all. You know how she's been trying to bust

307

our chops. I was going to stop in today and have a chat with her—on my own time."

Susan Carver stubbed out her cigarette with a disgusted twist, and said, "Not only are you a liar. You're a bad liar. These are her calls to you this last month." She waved a stack of message slips almost laconically. "She certainly is persistent. You must be doing a better job than I dreamed. Except this"—she held up a one-page typed sheet—"is the log of *your* calls. Do I have to tell you which numbers stand out?"

"Hey, wait a minute! If you think I gave her that damned—"

"It's not a matter of what I think. As far as you're concerned, it's what Central Security thinks."

"This is all a mistake," he protested.

"The mistake, Mr. Bowen, was entirely yours. Mine, too, perhaps. I believed in you when I should have known better. *Consorting* with—I can tell you, I am extremely disappointed." He slumped in his chair, and she looked up from her desk. Her face was no longer angry, more drawn and fatigued, as though truly pained. "You know, I really thought you would work out. I really—but you're just not our man. You're a child. We should have put a bell around your neck or some damned thing."

"This is all a horrendous—"

"I'm not interested in what you have to say."

"We're just friends. I was doing my job!"

"You know, Bowen, I'm a mother, too. Yes. You didn't know that, did you?"

"No. But—"

"It hurt me very much, talking to Mrs. Poulson. Not only for what it means for you, but I feel for what she's going through. Now how do I tell her that her daughter's mixed up in something like this? I don't want to add to her pain any more than it is—"

Tyler sat up abruptly. "What?" Susan Carver's eyes were hooded, her face choleric. She shifted her gaze from Bowen to her desk several times. "What—?" he asked, no longer sure of her meaning, and she handed him a piece of copy from the State Police ticker.

"Mr. Bowen?" she said, as he shuffled to the door, reading the news. "This time, you do what you're told."

"I'd like to call—"

"No contact. None. Don't dig yourself in any deeper. You are confined to the Compound until this matter is disposed of. Your name is at the gate. No travel."

He nodded absently. The words on the pink page stood out and seemed to turn into scrambling animals, darting off into a thick, throbbing blackness. First Willie, now Johanna was troubled and in need of him, and despite the depth of his concern he was neutralized, impotent, imprisoned by his own contractual compromises, by latent chemical stupor, self-concern, and second-hand telegraphed news.

Frantic and scared, he sought out his only friend. "I've got to talk to her, Bar."

"Leave her alone, man. She's bad news."

"I've got to."

"Drop it. You've got more than enough to worry about."

"I have to."

"For *her* sake. Look, I told you. This place runs on a modified honor system. The honorable people get the shaft."

"What if I honorably take off?"

"They will honorably chase you until they honorably find you and honorably throw away the fucking key when they catch you."

"What if I threaten to tell what I know?"

Zermatt sighed and looked heavenward. "What? Are you kidding? You'd never hear Gracie count ten. You'd get the Len Tobias Scholarship. A small parable: when you're fighting a big heavy-arm type, don't stand outside calling him names."

"That's not a parable."

"And you're not gonna be around to keep telling me if you don't wise up. You threaten with what you can't deliver and you can just forget it. Get inside and clinch. Guerrilla warfare. Jab, jab, jab. You can beat this, maybe. But don't make it harder."

"I've got to see her, Bar."

"That's the other part. Go with the percentages. Don't fight two fronts at the same time. It's a sucker's bet. Play the fucking game and know the rules. Between the two of us we can figure out some way to

309

walk out of this winners. But, Jesus Christ, Babe, don't go threaten them with blackmail. This is the Majors, pal. You're talking about things federal now, not some candy-ass college rumpus."

It was not until Friday noon that Johanna was released from the hospital. Police in Benson had taken Richie into custody on Thursday. They had found her car sitting unmolested in front of a house belonging to Richie's aunt. He made no attempt to avoid capture, and in fact was quite willing to tell everything. However, the local police were too shrewd to permit that without first getting him a lawyer. The attorney, Gary Stanton, imposed silence on his client and Richie was booked Thursday afternoon on grand theft, automobile (the Desk Sergeant having his biweekly chuckle over whether copping a VW constituted grand or petit larcency), assault, aggravated battery with intent to kill, reckless endangerment, kidnap, rape, carrying a concealed weapon, reckless use of a deadly weapon, hitchhiking on a public highway, and several lesser crimes. "You forgot selling secrets to the Russians," the lawyer carped at the omnibus booking.

A full make-sheet was in on him that evening; it described Richie as a forty-five-year-old "regular on the merry-go-round"—police argot for the revolving door which opened by turns into penal institutions, work farms, training schools, homes for the wayward, homes for the criminally insane. He had last done hard time at the correctional facility in Florence for "menacing," earned a sabbatical for observation and psychiatric care in Flagstaff, then shuttled back to Florence where, having already served the minimum term peacefully enough, his motion for a new trial won his release.

The very first thing that Gary Stanton did was offer the prosecution a deal: drop the kidnap-rape and they'd plead on the remainder. But the County Attorney's office wasn't so sure. They had a "People's Case" so tight there was no need to bargain. "What do you think you can tell a jury?" the County Attorney laughed. "That she seduced this poor bastard?"

Now the legal-aid man, Stanton, was angry. He didn't like being treated so cavalierly. He was a better lawyer than James Hood, the County Attorney, and ten times the legal scholar. Except every time they came up against each other it was because some poor joker had been nabbed with his pecker hanging out halfway to China, with a return address and a stamp. He lost too many cases simply because his clients were guilty. "I'll tell you exactly what happened," he said. "Where's that inventory? Packed bags, wearing a skirt an inch below her snatch—off to turn tricks in Mexico or—"

"Rape bait?" the prosecutor screeched. "Those fucking skirts are the style! My wife wears one. My daughter wears one."

"Keep them indoors, then. I say this chiquita pushed my client past the point of reason."

"Wouldn't take much of a shove," Hood said scornfully. "Damn lot of conductors've punched that boy's ticket."

But the defendant's man only smiled. He was having his intended effect, pushing the prosecutor into a defense of the girl rather than enforcement of the state's laws. He continued baiting the prosecutor: "—so scared that he takes the car and lams it. But he makes no attempt to deny it when asked—because he's a decent fellow at bottom, who just fell into the wrong company."

Hood sneered, then shook his head and laughed, "You think you can get him made a Cardinal?"

"I think I can beat the rap with a jury or get him on a one-way bus to Flagstaff."

"Now look!" the County Attorney boomed, finally losing his temper. "This man is a public nuisance. You know that and I know it. There is no way you are getting him off. And if he goes back to Flagstaff? In a year they tell him: 'Nice maniac, you're no longer criminally insane. Just insane.' And out he pops. This time to kill somebody. Give us all a break, Gary."

"When *you* won't? How? Throw the case? I don't get paid enough to do you favors. Drop the big two and we can talk."

"Christ!" the County Attorney barked, angry to be still chasing around the same tree. "If I could, I would. You're gonna lose. Your boy's going up and you're just going to wipe the floor with some poor girl trying."

"I'm going to try, though."

"That's it. End of discussion. Your boy can enjoy a free turkey dinner on the state. I wouldn't want to break his string—unless he can pull bail out of his ass. We'll do pretrial after Christmas. Bob Marks will run you right out of court."

As soon as Gary Stanton reached the door, the County Attorney chuckled strangely. "Listen," he called. "Way off the record, I can see a whole defense for you. According to the detectives, she's some little honey. He may be a rapist—but she's a *carrier*."

Saturday noon, a day after Johanna came home, her family attorney came by to talk with her and Warren. He told them she'd have to see Deputy County Attorney Robert Marks during Christmas for depositions, the sooner the better, and have to make positive identification as soon as she felt strong enough. "It'll probably go to the grand jury right after New Year's," he told them. "It won't be too difficult. But you'll have to tell it all over again."

"Who's the judge?" Warren asked.

"Ronald Hall. He's good." Their lawyer, Edward Denning, spoke for a moment about proper posture for complainants "in matters of this sort," and they understood what he was saying. If they wanted a divorce, they'd better wait until this was done.

Warren waited until Denning was gone and said, "After this is over, I don't care what the hell you do."

Her head was still throbbing, and she closed her eyes for some gentle darkness. "Damn you, Warren. You—" She couldn't muster the strength to fight, and sank back, limp. "Oh, what-the-hell yourself." Then she looked up at him with the most frail and empty expression, peeping, "I'm sorry. Warren? It's very nice of you to do this."

Tyler Bowen's hours were filled with the Compound-bound wanderings of a nonperson, and each night was sleepless. By day, he and Zermatt tried to figure out how best to defend against the whim and caprice of Martin B. Gracie's merciless office. In the evening, Tyler forswore Zermatt's company and the hale drunkenness of the Crypto Club to write letters to Johanna he couldn't mail, and hair-shirted notes to Saint Paul, wondering in each how much he was responsible for all the terrible things happening around him to those he loved.

Saturday evening, near midnight, he wandered over to the commissary. Three Mexican cooks were making baked goods for the next day's breakfast. They fed him some cakes and spoke in the half-whispers people used in their awakening hours. He took a cup of coffee and walked outside, moving with aimless steps to the softball field.

He sat on the bench for a while and recalled baseball teams and legends, his frame of reference frozen at the point of his greatest youthful reverence for the game, when its myths and heroes were largest for him. He remembered Pee Wee Reese, shortstop for the accursed, luckless Brooklyn Dodgers, who were always losing the Big One to the Yanks. He remembered the last pitch of the '55 Series: It was hit right to Pee Wee. It seemed as if Pee Wee's life summated at that moment; all his hopes and fears and doubts, and everything which played on them, formed a giant pyramid behind the point of action. All things that went into the making of Pee Wee Reese were distilled in a moment's trial. All of Civilization resolved itself in Harold Reese's body, for in that instant he became the leading edge of history, determining whether half the world would be tied to heroes or to bums. "All I was doing," Pee Wee said after the game, "was praying, 'Dear God, don't let him hit it to me!'" Pee Wee handled the chance flawlessly. He was a pro. The Dodgers won; their fans were blessed at last—until next year.

Tyler Bowen took his place in the batter's box: the Skipper again, Big Red's Big Red, Rusty at the Bat. The *Daily Sun* had a dozen sobriquets to pick from. He eyed the imaginary pitcher sternly as moonlight played on the top of Gila's ridge. His conjured bat met the pitcher's challenge belt-high and he stood like his namesake, the Babe, observing the towering arc of the ball's outward flight until it disappeared over the mountain wall. Then he trotted triumphantly around the dusty, weed-choked basepath, landing with a two-footed jump on home plate.

He wandered around seeking satisfaction in different places, like the restless franchises of the Major Leagues. A gypsy, he played the infield, the outfield, and the mound, and pitched a pantomime inning. But true release would only come in the batter's box, where power, retribution, and revenge found violent voice against the cunning of the pitchers.

So he came to bat again, at last, a pinch hitter with two out, one on, and his team on the short end of a 2–1 score in the bottom of the ninth. There was no one left but the Skipper who could deliver the Big Hit. His best days may have been behind him in this boy's game, but the old warhorse was the man for the clutch or no one was. And if it could be known, such ego as a pinch-hit hero must own in order to act, to believe in himself, compels him likewise in his heart of dreams to wish his own team ill-starred fortunes—that he may be called upon to reverse them.

And here he was, in the wished and dreaded moment: all or nothing on a three-and-two pitch. The stretch. Check the runner. The pitch: Tyler strode easily in the batter's box, leaning into it. But he didn't swing. The payoff pitch and he stood idle, Casey in stone, the fans shocked as the unmolested ball nipped the outside corner of the plate, when, like no thing men or fans had ever seen, his quick wrists flashed, less the Babe than Henry Aaron, in the final instant of his graceful stride. He split the home-plate air with concealed fury and stole the strike away. His whole body poured into that dreamily effortless stroke. What seemed a sudden burst was the fulfillment of a long chain of mounting, combining pressures of hope and chance. There was no doubt. The swing was no less than the synthesis of a lifetime's moments. And the ball rocketed out with redoubled speed, in a long, low trajectory, flat as an old coach's arches, way into the left-center power alley, toward the mountain. Tyler stood halfway to first, in no hurry. He knew what the center fielder and fans did not. They could only guess. He knew that ball was gone from the moment he was born or nothing was certain. It would not land. It would just disappear, back into Heaven. And all fans everywhere released their breath in a roar.

Tyler Bowen circled the bases, wallowing in his predestined triumph, luxuriating in sweet revenge. He'd known it was a homer, for his whole life pointed to it. Nonetheless, a tight-lipped humility ruled his face: thankful for the gifts of talent, respectful of the fans' adoration, protective of their fragile hopes. When he stepped on the plate into the mob of grateful mates, he looked up and tossed back his head to accept one last coronation of cheers: the Skipper had delivered. A man could become their King or President on the crest of such love. He made them feel redeemed. He was what they'd been waiting for.

Late Saturday night, Baron Zermatt returned to his room and found a letter from Tyler Bowen on his bed. He read half of it and then raced over to Bowen's room. Tyler was not there, and Zermatt sat down outside to wait, glumly finishing the letter. The first part was formal, absolving Zermatt from any responsibility for what Tyler did. Then it said:

. . . when I was a kid, about ten, I had this paralysis for a few months. Nothing I ever told you about, and not really serious, it turns out. Just enough to keep 'em all on their toes. Now, it was Father-Son day at the club, with races and such. And the damnedest thing about this paralysis was some days it paraled and some days it didn't. I could tell when I got out of bed each day. I'd either fall on my face or I wouldn't. That day, I just tipped over on my ear. No races for little Tyler.

So they parked me with the invalids. And there was this real fat kid, who I was supposed to play checkers with for a little invalid kid tin trophy. He wouldn't shut up about how he was going to beat me and I'd have to crawl up for second prize. I mean, there I was, a crip, and he's not running because he's too fucking fat and likes to eat too much. Probably had a gland problem: each and every gland must have weighed ten pounds! His father came over and I figured, well, at least he's got to

315

behave now. And his father, who's twice as fat and bald besides, joins in! "Come on Johnny! You can take him. Beat him every game. He's just a cripple. Watch out, sonny. My Johnny's gonna wipe you off the board!"

Now, I have always thought it's not nice to brag. And of course you don't pick on crips. So I didn't say anything, because naturally it would just detract from the righteousness of my cause. Right?

He beat me every game. Him and his father went up to get the trophy together, and I just finessed my consolation prize. That was the last time I ever lost something I wanted, Bar. Now I have a room at home just filled with that kind of scrap iron. And I guess that piece of tin foil's still waiting for me somewhere, too. I figure it'll all work out: I'll be in the Checkers Hall of Fame and he'll get hit by a Pontiac. He'll be a grille ornament. Him and his fat and bald father.

That's a parable, Bar. Except it's true.

And maybe Crazy'll get Tobias's balls between the eyes as he's about to strike another cripple, and he'll fall in a heap. Say good night, Gracie. But you can get old waiting for the sons-of-bitches to go under from nonbuoyant belligerency. And I'm not a kid paralytic anymore. So what I do's my own lookout. Adios.

Skippy-as-in-the-spread.

Zermatt finished reading it and muttered to himself, *"Vaya con Dios."* He weighed the letter in his hand and put a match to it, letting it burn until it nipped his fingers. It fluttered to the ground, and though he had a quick urge to stamp it out, he watched it burn in hypnotic fascination. His whole mind danced inside the fire, and he pushed the ashes into the Gila sand until they were vanished. It was a humane thing to do, a risk. Bowen had offered him a free pass and he refused it. Zermatt felt slightly exhilarated, high, flattered to discern the instincts of friendship in his breast after so many years of dormancy. Bowen was just a good boy in bad company; a good man, really. And now he,

316

the Baron, could risk something in return. Right now, all he could do was go to sleep.

It was hot in the desert. Unnaturally hot for a desert night, unseasonably hot for even Tucson at Christmastide; Indian summer's dregs stayed through Advent and kept the night boiling as Tyler Bowen marched on the untended road from Gila to Tombstone. His spine itched in fear of wild animals and worse: loneliness. But his loneliness was for humans, and they were also his chief fear. The desert was alive at night with sounds and sudden noises: piggy javelinas, and far-off coyotes howling; kangaroo rats and even owls; woodpeckers named for Gila and insects no one wanted to meet by day or night. Not to mention snakes. But all of them kept clear of Tyler Bowen, for the animals—bats and nighthawks and poorwills, mule deer and spotted skunks—however desperate they were in search of the rare water holes or prickly pear cacti or the giant saguaro's milk, predator or prey, all knew enough of man to stay the hell away. It was an instinct with them.

More than the animals' noises frightened him, Tyler Bowen's presence, his scent, terrified them; their noise was of a flight for safety. "Nature," Baron Zermatt had observed on Tyler's first day-trip away from Gila, "sure knows her stuff."

The truth of that was plain and Tyler Bowen often thought that same hope-filled notion stood behind the continual inversion of the best, most awful work done at Gila Compound, as though Nature were bucking Man off her. Despite the evidence of the stars, Nature worked hard to keep things going. As a result of her complex systems, so arduously designed, and her fragile structures, so painfully evolved, her center of gravity was low. She was the fundamental engineer: her assemblies resist easy tumbling. Her own chief instinct was survival, and it would have taken every mean genius of man to undo that. So the black-tailed jackrabbits fled Tyler Bowen, knowing him as an ambassador from a deadly tribe.

Zermatt woke as if from asthma. His sheets were stained with sweat. It was still dark out, but more

317

sleep was impossible. He knew what he had to do. It wouldn't come without risk. It might not cost a penny up front. And really, all the money in the world couldn't buy the boy out of this one; only a man with brains and an understanding of what obtained, and extra balls, could pull it off in a Sunday blitz. What was money if you didn't spend it, influence if you sat on it? And Zermatt had at least one slim arrow in his quiver yet. He liked his face as he shaved, dark light of night still at the window. He nicked himself, thinking that friends, if they were worth anything, had to act unilaterally at times, like hospitals, deans, parents, and war heroes.

And the night boiled like summer. The promise on the far edge of the short desert was unclear, but it drew Tyler Bowen. All night he marched, twenty miles perhaps, between the yuccas and Gila monsters, the diamondbacks and the cholla cactus, from heat, through heat, to heat, toward a highway in the north.

Early Sunday morning Neal and Denise Poulson, Johanna's brother and sister-in-law, came by, in Denise's words, "to take Johanna for the day," as a favor to Warren. It was a favor to him because he had to go to Benson to claim his car and because Johanna was still, as he put it, "out of control." She objected furiously when she found he'd moved back into the house while she was in the hospital, complaining even more loudly that she did not need "to be babysat. It's not a continuing condition, Warren, despite what you think." But she acceded to these arrangements when her mother suggested that Johanna "come up to Scotts-dale for a while."

Warren said he'd be back after dinner, and would stop at Tombstone Center on the way back to catch up on paper work. As soon as they heard Neal pull away outside to drive Warren to the bus depot, Denise broke her silence. "Warren's absolutely heartsick, he's so worried. He called Neal three times yesterday, and your mother calls us every four hours. If there's no answer she goes crazy. How do you feel?"

"Stupid."

"You know, a little make-up and no one would ever know." When Neal returned he found the two women silently stirring coffee and he surveyed the soundless kitchen as though it were an after-battle scene, picking up pot-holders, dirty dishes, greasy frying pans. "What'd I miss?" he asked. "Mom call yet? Any score in the football games? Lemme guess: Johanna's lonely for Warren and you're jealous 'cause she's got a husband on a bus headed south. Am I the only person here who knows how to talk?"

"Did you know, Nealie," Johanna asked him, dredging up an old family name he hated, "that when Warren was a child, if you can imagine *that,* his mother used to walk him in one of those harness things? On a leash! Weren't they outlawed by the Geneva Convention?" She was moving toward the ringing kitchen phone. "Probably Warren, can't find the bus." Neal's eyes washed over his sister in pained love and he turned to Denise with a thoughtful expression that Johanna took, out of the corner of her eye, to be a thankful one. He was listening to the echo in his memory of "Nealie," and thinking of his brother Brian and Johanna when they were kids.

Denise's eyes were slits of scold. "You think she'd be a little less casual with the cheap psychology, just now." Neal's fond smile had dissolved to a curious stare, a sympathetic wincing with each slow movement Johanna made, his concentration straining further as he tried to eavesdrop on the phone call.

Johanna said to the phone, "No, no, not you. Yes," and her face lit suddenly with delight, then grew decorous for her family's gaze.

"Neal? What did Warren say to you?" Denise asked.

"Oh," he answered, "I heard a short talk on the dangers of ceding social authority to children, I swear it, letting them vote in family matters. Somehow that's supposed to lead to terrible television programming or something, I forget. I don't know. Who listens?" Johanna was off the phone then, asking him a favor. She said she wanted a lift somewhere, to be dropped off and left. Denise called it "outrageous," and Neal added that he'd promised Warren they'd keep her "out of trouble." When Johanna made a face, Denise reminded her "it wasn't Warren who nearly got killed, Johanna."

319

"And it wasn't me," Johanna snapped, "who dropped Michael from a Ferris wheel."

"You're goddamn out of control!" Neal hollered, rising. Then he threw his hands up, disgusted, sighing "Ah, I don't know what to do with you. When you were a kid you'd blame some imaginary playmate. Now you'll blame Warren, or us, or Mom."

"It's catching," Johanna sputtered. "You're all turning into Warrens!"

"You could do worse," Neal said.

"I could do better. Never mind. I'll walk. I'm only going to meet a friend for lunch, that's all."

Denise said, "Then have your friend come by."

"I'm going to meet a friend for lunch," Johanna repeated.

And Denise said, "You want us to lie for you." She waited for Johanna's reaction, but Johanna turned from her to Neal and then looked all around the kitchen, then back to Neal, saying softly then, "Yes, I do."

As far as Neal would go was to offer that if Warren called he'd say she was napping, and she could tell him she'd read a novel all day. "But you'd damn-well better be back at our house before Warren is, Jo."

Both Neal and Denise relieved themselves of obligatory statements about marital trust and Johanna insisted, "It's just a friend, but Warren wouldn't understand. Honest. And I'm going up to Scottsdale Tuesday! I just need some time with some of my friends. That's all." She was already braiding her hair and scooting them out the door.

When she met Tyler at the Royal Inn motel, she said, "You do cheer me up!"

"Because I look worse?"

"You make me feel all better."

"Then it was worth every step." She didn't ask why he had to go to such dramatic lengths; neither did he ask the details of her travail. They did not say much at all, just hugged lightly for a time, Johanna whispering "My bonny macaroon," and swallowing hard.

She told him how she'd gotten out, as though he'd known the details leading up to it, as though her life was now discussed on some wide-area party line. She said she had told Warren she didn't want him back at the house, she'd stay there by herself. "But it's not safe," Tyler said.

The sauna and therapy pool which so delighted the arthritic and the stoned were gratifying to them now. "We're both," she said, "retired microbussers, after a fashion." He held her loosely around the waist as she floated and said, with a vague look of wonder, "Shy, maybe, but hardly retiring. Hardly shy." But they were that, too, and sought out a small restaurant for lunch. Tyler gazed at her thoughtfully across the spaghettini, trying to discern what she needed from him, signaling his support when she caught his eye, as though to say, "I'm your biggest fan." At one point he said, "I bet you were glad to hit clean sheets."

She kissed his hand as it held hers, and felt a little better realizing that her task was to comfort him as much as he was thrashing about for some way to comfort her.

He reached out with his hand to touch her face at that white dot, and she rolled her head into his palm. She was afraid things stronger than their fitness would sweep him off and leave her prey to bogeymen. She wanted to look unafraid, wanting him on their original terms.

"Johanna. I don't know what's going to happen. But, when we get through this, we'll be together all the time. We'll go to New York, that's what. And we'll laugh at how terribly serious we were just now."

"I'd like that," she said.

"You'll like everybody. And they'll love you. My family's a little strange, but—" They both said together, "Whose isn't?" and she started to laugh painfully. "You'll love my friend Saint Paul and my Looney-Toon sister Mack and my bro—"

"I love you, Tyler Bowen."

In spite of her lawyer's warnings, they went back to his room to take a nap in the late afternoon. It seemed important precisely because of those warnings.

She was in pain, and when he kissed her, however softly, all he could see was her eyes, wide with anticipation. So they ate their way through boxes of pretzels and corn chips, talked, and slugged down soda, until Johanna felt calmer. But holding her only prevented her sleep. More than ever, for the first time, Tyler wished he was Warren, to have been there holding her the first time she needed it. Now when she needed him most, he could only reach out a hand of promises. So he petted her shoulders until she dozed off, and stayed in bed with her so she could feel the safety of his presence. He wished he could guard her from her dreams somehow, censor them for her.

All the next few hours she tossed. Once she awoke, breathless, and took a moment to recognize him, then fell asleep again, with her head in his lap like a child. Somewhere in the neighborhood, he thought, between the missiles and the telescopes, was a ghost-play being enacted in some phantom dimension of evil. As was done to her would be done forever, in her memory and in light rays speeding from the galaxy, a monument of vaporous energy, growing older and dimmer, one to die with her, one with a half-life of forever. It would happen eternally without pause or tears. His nostrils, in this hermetically sealed, air-conditioned room, filled with the smell of waxes and fuels, as though the echoes of smells that bounced off non-porous walls. It was the way an airport smelled, the way the one in Dallas smelled: the one that had no note or plaque or hint of awareness that it was the ledge of a special place, where eras parted.

Just before she stirred for the last time, a sleepless Tyler Bowen moved to a chair by the door, guarding Johanna from the evening hours, his eyes wide open, vengeance ready for any harmful spirits.

At this moment, he thought, he would die for her, certainly kill for her. There was little else he could do. There were no Christmas gifts to stand for what he'd like to give. So he'd sat awake instead, through the afternoon, into evening and the dawn of night, his finest soldiering of the war, battle-ready and fierce in defense of her against lurking demons from without, through the long and peaceful day around them.

He walked her to her brother's house, then stood halfway down the block, watching, while she went in.

He stayed another half-hour in that spot until he saw Warren drive up, and turned on his heel away from the light, to go back to his rented room.

In the morning, she called at the motel. "Warren's gone down to the Center. How did you get the day off?"

"I know the right people," he said. "Can you come by?"

"My mother's coming 'round this afternoon. She's going to drive me down to Benson to make an identification."

"I'd like to meet her sometime."

"How about today? She knows, kind of, and you're allowed to make courtesy calls. I need a little help today."

A nervous Baron Zermatt had been driving an inter-agency motor pool sedan around the neighborhood all morning. Warren had seen him, some blocks from the house, and beeped at him, tossing a friendly wave. Zermatt's circuits were large and long to prevent suspicion, and he added side excursions to each, once to the University, once to call likely motels, looking for Tyler. He knew Tyler would not be at Johanna's if Warren was, but he didn't want to call there, lest she call Tyler and scare him off. As Tyler rang her bell, Zermatt pulled slowly into the driveway and Tyler began to back off. "Stay put, dammit!" Zermatt yelled, stepping out of the car. "I only want to talk to you." Johanna came out and walked over to Tyler, as if to protect him.

"I'm not interested in what you're selling," Tyler said to Baron, holding him off with an arm and a backward step.

"You'd better be. You've made one hell of a mess for yourself." Johanna looked at Tyler, confused.

"By doing nothing!"

"Skip the ironies, Babe. I'm trying to help you. Now get in the car."

"No way," Tyler said.

"Tyler?" Johanna asked.

"Look, if they have to come get you, it'll go very

hard. You come back with me and I know a way we can work it out."

"What's he talking about?" Johanna asked.

"Tell her, Babe. Go on. Tell her."

"Nothing. It's just a bureaucratic nothing."

Zermatt came between them like a pastor. "Our boy here has it in mind to become a dead hero."

"I'm a hog for glory. Why don't you just head back and say you couldn't find me."

"Nobody's looking for you. Yet. But I wouldn't hang here all day counting on it. I can help you. Now trust me."

"Why?" Tyler asked.

"Oh, Jesus Potato! Have I ever lied to you before?"

"So many times I can't even count them. You and them—"

"Look. You're lucky. You're dumber than shit, but lucky. You've got a lot of good instincts. Now do this thing and we'll both walk out of here with the shit on them!"

"What's he talking about?" Johanna fairly demanded.

Zermatt offered a short course: "Your friend and mine is believed to have collaborated with the enemy— you. A fact he is not exactly being discreet about."

"This is crazy," Tyler said. "I don't give a good goddam what they think. You know and Johanna knows and I know that I haven't broken any—"

"Stop right there," Zermatt snapped. He went back to the car and fetched a sheaf of papers. "As a lawyer I advise you to keep your stupid mouth shut and stop protesting your innocence. You're only gonna make it worse."

"I'm not guilty of anything!"

"But you can't plea-bargain innocence. Your only way out is suicide."

"This isn't half as amusing as you think it is, Bar."

"I'm not making jokes. You've got to admit everything." Johanna sighed and sat down on the grass, watching the two men-boys argue with each other, interested, but tired, detached.

"I've got nothing to admit!" Tyler shrieked.

"Use your imagination. Make it up. Say you told her the World's Biggest Secret and everything else you know!" Johanna nodded amiably. "Perjure yourself. They gave you the tool. Use it!"

"No! The burden's on them."

"You are naive. And in bad shape," Zermatt replied. "I told you—you've got to take it to 'em. You wait to see what they're throwing, you're never gonna see it. Now I've spent all day yesterday and this morning getting all the little duckies in a row. Please don't screw it up. You don't stand a chance on your own. Believe me."

Tyler reached down and extended a hand to Johanna, to pull her up. "I'll risk it," he said, starting for the house.

"You're a fool, Tyler. Not only will they burn your ass whether you think you're innocent or not—but they'll goddam have every federal agency they can find grill your friend just for sport. You think they're children? You think they're playing? *You* are! I'm offering you a bye and you won't take it. You're a *fool*."

"What are you selling?" Tyler asked.

"I'll give you a choice. You come back, with Johanna agreed to be, shall we say, a stringer—for them. It's a very popular—"

"Fuck off!" Tyler snapped, flushed, clenching his fists.

Zermatt grinned and made a sucking noise. "OK. OK. The other is—if they believe you, if they believe you've been doing more than just messing around, then you've got something to bargain with. You've got to understand the way these things work, that's all."

"What would I have to do?" He was looking more at Johanna as he asked, but all he saw on her face was a look of saturated weariness.

"Just tell 'em everything you know and say you've communicated it all. That's the difference between you and Len Tobias—he didn't know what to communicate to whom."

"And they'll do to me what they did to him!"

"All you've got to do," Zermatt said, "is sign a new oath that goes right on top of your statement. You've got something they want."

"Which is?" Johanna asked. Zermatt turned to her, bowed and pointed at her.

"Your silence," he said. "And a button on the Boy Wonder."

"I don't want her mixed up with those creeps!" Tyler exploded.

"Why don't you let her decide that, huh? Trust me, Tyler, just once. All she's got to do is sign a sweet little security oath, just like yours. Yes, it puts her under penalty of law just like you if she divulges any of the things you never told her—but it's nothing over nothing, for Chrissakes! And it's the only thing that's got them worried."

"Gracie'll find another angle," Tyler said, still dubious.

"Gracie is the happiest man in Arizona right now. He got his Christmas present early. Two resignations with prejudice. Yours and mine. He's—"

"What the hell did you do that for? You're short."

"I had to sweeten it a little for the bastard. Besides, no sweat. There's more than one way to skin a son-of-a-bitch. He can't lay a glove on me."

"You know what he's like," Tyler said.

"There's a faster track called politics. Ever hear of it? Wherever he goes, I'll be there first with twenty friends." Zermatt grinned. "It's not how much you know, Babe, it's who."

Johanna took the papers Zermatt had been waving. They were various forms of security oaths, prewitnessed by friends of Zermatt, and a document which resembled a negligence release or a contract, ringing with phrases like "forswears all use of aforesaid information acquired through whatever means including and especially above-indicated associations from the Creation to the End of Time . . . contracting to embargo same in all manner and means . . ."

"Where do I sign this silly thing?" Johanna asked.

"You don't," Tyler insisted.

"You two can play Gift of the Magi some other time," Zermatt said, "but I'm either taking that batch of papers down with me signed or I'm going back alone. That's my final offer. 'Cause unless I've got them in my pocket, I've got a shit hand to play and they're not buying bluffs." Zermatt handed her a clipboard and Johanna signed her name with weak strokes while

326

Tyler looked away, deflated. She gave them both a kiss on the cheek and said, "It hardly hurt at all. Take care of him will you, Baron?"

"Like he was my own brother. We'll call when there's news."

On the way back to Gila, Tyler gazed out the window. "The revolution's over. And we lost."

"On the contrary," Baron Zermatt answered, looking jollier than he had ever seemed. "It's just begun."

It was late afternoon as they waited in the outer office of Central Security. The room was air-conditioned to the point of chill. Tyler examined the Yggdrasil tree on the Gila emblem while they waited, and said to Zermatt, "You didn't really think I'd let her take that other option, did you?"

"I didn't know you were running her life," Zermatt answered. "But no. It wasn't mine to offer. I just needed something you could refuse, a little working room."

"Scribes and hypocrites," Tyler said to himself.

"What?"

"That fucking tree. It's a whited sepulchre. Beautiful and sweet outwardly—but full of dead men's bones and all uncleanness. It's from the Bible. It's a message to the scribes and hypocrites."

"You'd think," Martin B. Gracie said, shaking his head pityingly as he came out, "a fellow with your smarts would know better."

Zermatt said nothing and Tyler Bowen felt sinkingly frail. When Gracie left to get some coffee, Zermatt burst into a happy smile. "He thinks you're sailing up Shit Creek—"

"He seems rather sure of it."

"He doesn't know what kind of rudder I've got."

"Paddle," Tyler said. "I hope you mean."

"Sue me," Zermatt laughed. "I'll tell you, Tyler. He's right. I'm one smart guy. You ought to be grateful you know me."

"Talk to me in about an hour, genius."

The legal staff man, an off-duty friend of Zermatt's, looked over the paperwork and grumbled, "This is a real mess!" He muttered about "straining the quality

327

of mercy till it's a bloody puree," then looked up. "First of all, Bowen, I should tell you that anything you say here—"

"Is confidential." Zermatt nodded.

"Can and will be used against you."

"What the hell are you raving about?" Baron demanded. "If you take the trouble to look under your nose, you will see we have been resigned—it's signed, sealed, and ready for your stamp, Fred. By-the-regs."

"Yes. Yes. Quite so. But Mr. Gracie wants a more complete statement for the files."

"All I know is on the statement," Bowen said.

"You expect us to believe that?"

"Yes."

"You realize that making an incomplete statement is perjury?"

"It's more than complete," Tyler said.

The man sucked his cheeks and fussed with the papers some more. "Concerning disposition," he said, "Mr. Gracie points out, correctly, that you should not be the beneficiary of your own avowed misdeeds. You still have an unfulfilled obligation to your Selective Service board—" Bowen rose half out of his seat, but Zermatt helped haul him down. The man held a staying hand up, half-cautionary, half in fear. "Toward which end we have communicated with your board concerning processing and, I don't know how to put this but—apparently your file contains a Red Cross Advisory about a family member. Consequently, Mr. Gracie has withdrawn his suggestion, let us say out of compassion."

Zermatt squinted skeptically. "Is that how you read it?"

The man shook his head quickly no. "Here's your disposition, Bowen. You will return on the next available flight to New York City, where you will report forthwith to the NSA Office at the Foley Square Federal Building. They will figure out what the devil to do with you. You will serve at their convenience in whatever fashion they deem appropriate, so that your training not go entirely to waste, but, that you not be in a position to imperil the security of—"

"Cut the shit," Zermatt snapped. "What's his liability?"

The legal staff man rustled through his papers, saying, "I must say, you're getting a rather special and rare—two-and-a-half years." He straightened up the files and smiled. "Gila Compound National Laboratories—on behalf of the staff and management thereof, it is my pleasure to bid you both a fond: Good Riddance."

On the wall as they walked out was a sign, and Tyler nodded to it: "Watch Your Hat and Coat."

The public road from Gila to Tucson winds over the dead San Pedro River bed all the way to Tombstone where it enters the World. Then the Interstate at Benson, then Mescal, Pantano and Vail. It was dark, late evening. It had taken them a few hours to pack and finish their out-processing. Zermatt had reassured Tyler before they left, "I've got a man who's going to bring us a very happy New Year's present—the originals of those statements, singing and dancing their way from the files, right into the old Yule fire."

"How?" Bowen asked, still dazzled by the day's movement.

"Cash. How else?"

Now, staring out into the purple desert as they were driven north in an otherwise empty jitney, Tyler asked, "You think your friend can get the whole deal wiped? Can he get me out of the two-and-a-half-year item?"

"Miracles—I told you—for miracles you gotta look elsewhere. Be grateful for the little stuff. You did all right. I told you once about putting out perfect games when they don't count for the scorebooks. You just don't listen."

"Why'd you do it, Bar? You could've just hung in and jogged out of here clean in two weeks."

"I've got my reasons," Zermatt said.

"Come on. You never bought someone lunch unless there was a fee in it—"

"You're not only stupid, Tyler, but you're a little bit of an ass. You know that? And cruel sometimes."

"I'm sorry. You're the one who's always saying there's no such thing as a free lunch—so why the free ride?"

"Because you're an endangered species—all right? It's my small contribution to the world. And one good satisfying chance to spit in that fucker's eye and walk. Is that what you want to hear? Look, Babe. We beat it. We beat it bad."

"Maybe."

"No maybe, Baby. How'd you like to have been in Nam? Or wiped out by Crazy-man? You had a damned good time. You're no one to complain."

"I'd almost rather have been in Nam."

"Are you nuts?"

"If I had gone—" He exhaled deeply and looked past Zermatt into the desert as they drove, experiencing a new taste in his throat, regret.

"I know how it is."

"We held off the whole enemy army—we thought—but every time, the attack came from behind. They won." Zermatt let him talk himself out, for he knew when every layer of current pain was stripped away, Tyler Bowen's heart beat out of optimism, else he would not be such a reckless protohero. Sweat stood out on Tyler's upper lip and he wiped it off. "She really made it for me, Bar—I mean, she saved my life. Pulled me through when things were bad—and some madman goes and—"

"Take it easy, Babe. Things work out. Hell, you're the one who says that all the time. Things work out. You'll see."

And another mission beckoned him, to seek revenge for Willie. That's what his experience at Gila had done for him. The Golden Boy who had so readily joined the starched Great White Fleet and so effortlessly accepted all moral compromise had been transformed by that. The All-American Boy was shy, but prone to action. And if this was the only way, in a pattern as old as the Eumenides, that too was part of his character, for the American morality, from Davy Crockett down, was personal and pragmatic.

They'd called her before leaving Gila and Johanna was waiting at the airport. Several times Tyler explained why he had to leave and though she said she understood, he didn't think she really did. He couldn't see any reason why she should have to understand. It wasn't her war. With each phrase he was asking her for reassurances. He said he'd come back as soon as he'd straightened things out in New York. "Maybe before New Year's."

"It wouldn't be good," she answered. "Not until after I'm finished with the court things."

"OK. As soon as you finish. We'll go somewhere for a few weeks. Or you can come to New York. I'll send a ticket." She had saved him, he was convinced, many ways, and he would not permit the madmen and the bureaucracy, or even the wheels of justice, to abort this romance, though all seemed part of the same malign cabal.

Her emerald eyes picked up gray from the walls and their blue turned violet with the neon lights. They swam with a cloudiness he had never seen there before. "Can you keep a secret?" he asked her. She nodded, timidly. "I love you. I promise, you, Joha—" She put a hand to his lips to permit him no more promises. But he took it away and said, "We're going to be great. We're going to be terrific."

In all her look, only her mouth smiled. But even that trembled under an awful weight. They hugged for a moment, Tyler afraid her strength was such that she would recuperate first: that the gambling instincts he so admired in her, her poise and daring, would enable her to pick up fresh without him. She was too much for him, and he was afraid she would spin off to new adventures when her powers returned, afraid he would recede in her life until he disappeared. He was afraid that the very things he loved in her would prove lethal genes for a love affair.

He looked at her and winked confidently. "Supergirl." Hugging her lightly he said, "We'll be together soon."

A stewardess tapped him on the shoulder like a death-row chaplain and he gave Johanna a last kiss on the cheek.

Johanna clutched him with a sudden spasm, and whispered hurriedly, "I love you," in his ear. Her look was terrified and he rocked her in his arms a moment longer, soothing, echoing her, promising a quick reunion. When he tried to let go she held tighter and

331

bit her lip. Zermatt was already on board, holding seats, and the plane was powering up. Tyler cupped her head in his hands and kissed her forehead. He turned to give his ticket to the stewardess, and then turned back to say a final word of reassurance. Johanna was hugging herself with her arms, and before he could speak, she blurted out, "Tyler? You won't forget me, will you?" And she whirled, tears streaming freely down her cheeks, and ran down the corridor from where he stood shaking his head, "no no no no no no no no no."

Then he boarded the plane, the only Bowen boy going home for Christmas 1967.

Part III

Bright
Children:
1968

MAUREEN POULSON'S WORK WAS AN ODD echo of her late ex-husband's, assonant with his interests. He mined the electromagnetic spectrum, concerned with questions of time and space and rate; she merchandised it. She was Vice-President for T&R—sales of Time and setting the varied Rates for advertisers—at her Phoenix television station. She could buy and sell "Sermonette," quote a price on "The Star-Spangled Banner." From this she knew, better than her children, something she would never say: that Christmas was a ruse.

Statistics proved it.

Holiday seasons were defined by irrefutable indices: ratings, and rates, went up, even though more reruns were slotted between the specials. Parallel to that were the Himalayan peaks of the national suicide rate at Christmas and Thanksgiving.

It was generally assumed that the striking correlation between those modes—recycled programs and vented wrists—was a statistical curiosity, not a matter of causality, the product of emotional variables best explained by O. Henry.

Maureen viewed these relations without illusion. Supply remained constant, but Demand at such times turned into pathologic need, and increased heroically. More people were at home, denied the alternative of going out. Families proceeded with the strict forms and rituals of dining together, as though Constitutionally commanded to. When done they would bolt toward every television available—football games, rewarmed drivel, heart-tugging lies about other people's Christmases, variety shows and cartoons—thankful most of all that such ordained celebrations were mercifully sparse, if crowded into one quadrant of the calendar. By unseen hands of market laws and enterprise, the Price to advertisers and to viewers streaked skyward.

Her personal understanding of these holiday functions was just so: they were functional. For some years she had tossed a monster Christmas gathering, considered by many to be a high social event. Maureen's dispersed brood was gathered in at her glass-walled house in Scottsdale for what Johanna called "the yearly weighing of the crown jewels." On closer inspection Johanna decided it more truly resembled the First Christmas: an imperial census from which Maureen Poulson could gauge her worth and how much her subjects were to be taxed. Her children were trotted out before Maureen's professional associates, each to admire the other and therefore her the more. Brian, Neal, and Warren insisted loudly they were dandy affairs, while Johanna steadfastly termed them "vulgar . . . chiefly of benefit to the figgy-pudding wholesalers." When one year's cancellation did not stimulate the redundant expressions of sorrow Maureen would have liked, the parties were dropped altogether.

Nonetheless, her maternal Yule duty was clear. Whether her family's current attenuated cohesion could be traced to the times, her own failings, or children's congenital ingratitude was no longer at issue: by presence and command she would remind them they were a family still. So attendance, attention, and good manners were required, if not good cheer, as a form of universal service. Maureen reigned at these shrunken occasions with benign regency, tolerating the delinquencies of her grandchildren as an indulgence befitting the season, flattering herself in this small way. And one and all gritted their teeth, resolving to be merry within the bounds of plausibility.

At this year's grim supper Johanna's full citizenship was imperiled by the majority: her brothers, their wives, the children, and her husband, who was still part of this holiday clan.

Warren was at this Christmas dinner because, for Johanna, it seemed easier than offering elaborate explanations of why he wasn't there, and might afford her some slim protection. But it did not. She was child-less and halfway out of marriage; her incompetence was proved to them by her inability to act her age, and by getting herself, as her sisters-in-law put it, "mixed up in the worst sorts of things."

On the way up to Scottsdale, Warren had tried hard to make married conversation, suggesting that "this could be an opportunity in disguise, you know. A fresh start with your family and everything else." Johanna said nothing. "Are you listening? When this thing is over you should think about getting your teeth into something serious."

"Like you."

"Like me, yeah. There are worse things than finishing your graduate work."

Expressionlessly, Johanna said, "I can't imagine them."

"I can. Why don't you ever think of other people for once?"

"What other people?" she asked.

"For instance your family."

"Exactly how did this get so crowded?"

"I can't believe you. Everybody gives to you—and as much as they give, you take. I try to meet you halfway, but that's not enough for you." Johanna was silent again. Warren continued, "I'm busting my ass to do my part in this business—"

"Which is what?"

"Which is pretending we're still married until your trial is—"

"It's not *my* trial. It's *his.*"

"God, you're a child!"

"Get it! I'm not stopping you. Get a divorce. But don't tell me you're acting out of gallantry. You just don't want to be embarrassed."

Warren veered the car onto the gravel shoulder and stopped it hard, a sound and sensation that reminded Johanna of stopping to pick up Richie Ellis. "You're wrong," Warren said evenly. "You're dead wrong. I don't care what you think. I'm doing what I know is right. Because—regardless, in spite of everything— I care about you. I do. And I don't want to see you hurt—anymore. I don't want to see you hurt by your

336

own—" He waved his hand around looking for a word between *childishness* and *stupidity*. "I still care that much. You don't have to believe it, it doesn't matter. It's still true."

Johanna said softly, "You just don't understand."

"That's it. That's exactly where it is. You've got a moral bludgeon. It's a new toy! This privileged status that mere men can never—oh, no!—we just can't *understand*. You can have a divorce, but I pity the next guy because this thing has made you a bloody virgin princess. You're holy as hell. You're practically untouchable! I strongly suggest you see a shrink if—"

"Let me out of here!" she demanded, shoving the car door open. He grabbed at her arm but she pulled away. "Let me go!"

"What are you going to do? Hitchhike? Keep running away, Johanna." She stormed out of the car and stood with her arms folded, in the headlights, facing the desert. Warren followed. "You know exactly what I'm talking about. You'll go from this thing to the next—and you won't be satisfied there either. You think this is the best damned thing that ever happened to you. Write a book about it! Show slides!" She swung at him awkwardly; he slipped it and pulled her close to him, but she struggled free and bolted a few yards into the desert. Warren, seething, got back in the car and raced the engine while Johanna cooled down in the empty blackness. He started to roll, then stopped, and backed up. Johanna got in and pulled the door shut sullenly behind her.

At dinner, Maureen watched helplessly as Johanna's attempts at casual humor drew strange looks from the others, who regarded her as if she were in the terminal stages of some ghastly disease or breakdown. Maureen recalled enduring similar patronization each time she'd been pregnant, as though fertilization had turned her into a moron. In a sense, Maureen understood, Johanna was pregnant, with experience. It was the others who, though smug, were barren. For the price of the comfortable immunities, the snug tidiness in being middle-class was ignorance by isolation from chance. Real pain and real passion's memories could not be summoned. Now, Johanna had known a brief, yet thorough, terror.

337

She was a pioneer with news of sensation's shores, though none of the others recognized that. Maureen knew that none of them except her daughter, and she herself when alone at night, had ever screamed in fear for their lives—in fear of their lives—aloud or in silence, or knew their measure from surface to depth. Only she and Johanna had priced their lives.

Early in the dinner, that very question of experience and commonality was approached, tangentially, by Warren. He ventured that "marijuana is the whole key to the generation gap. Forget all that stuff about war babies and the TV generation and nuclear threats. It's given a whole horizontal level of society a common—illusory—experience. Might as well be a religion. They wind up with a similar perceptual system, a shared cognitive style—"

"A *what?*" Brian asked, regretting it.

"They think alike," Warren said. "The same rhythms and patterns—with agreed-upon meanings; values the rest of us don't share. That—and their music—becomes a secret language."

"Their?" Johanna asked.

"Their," Warren affirmed. "When someone goes so far as to describe himself as 'countercultural' I think the larger culture can properly recognize his alienation—and protect itself by raising the tariff on the means—"

"Does that mean you're against legalizing grass?" Neal asked.

"It does."

"Why can't you just say that?" Neal wondered.

"Because things have to be justified."

After a long series of family reports and gossip, Warren tried again. Noting the Handel on the hi-fi, he became eloquent on the subject of "classical values and true culture," invoking a pastoral idiom he had never before used, to describe the pleasures of Salt Lake City's traditional Christmas: the snow and lights in Temple Square, the Mormon Tabernacle Choir's angelic concerts. Finally, Maureen said the Handel they were listening to was "hardly Christmassy. It's *Xerxes.* I like the Largo." The silence was unnerving. Warren looked at his plate. Johanna looked at Warren's plate, too. Everyone else squirmed uncomfortably except for Michael Poulson, who was eating up a storm. "He seems rather fully recovered," Maureen smiled.

The day before she and Warren left for Scottsdale, Johanna had stopped in at the *Intelligencer* office to see her editor, Arnie Logan. She needed someone in town to trust, now that Tyler was in New York, and he seemed the likeliest candidate, though trusting him was always risky. He waved giddily when he saw her come into the office, and excused himself from a coven of subalterns in a Page One conference to greet her. "You look super," he cooed.

"You'd never know, would you?" she laughed skeptically, pirouetting like a fashion model. "I'll just tell people I've been on an ocean cruise." He looked a little hangdog at this rough teasing. After all, he'd been trying to be kind, so she felt bad for her sarcasm, though it was the truest proof of her rehabilitation. She softened, saying that she felt reasonably well, "all things considered."

"Do you want to work?" She nodded vigorously. "I have a wonderful idea for you," he said, draping an arm over her shoulder. This was a ritual reporters knew well. He would enfold one under his massive, pterodactylian wing and parade around the newsroom with his gull, as though in a three-legged race. Such special attention was flattering. The victim felt like a friend and coconspirator on a special project. But con-manship being a large aspect of the editorial art, often enough it resulted in the assignment of a fruitless story, a snark hunt or a fool's errand, or some annual hobbyhorse of the publisher's sister in Tempe. Johanna knew the game, but was revitalized by it. "A wonderful assignment," he rhapsodized.

She laughed merrily. "You all think you can get whatever you want with a little sex appeal—get us to pick up after you—" Dealing with him was like playing with a muzzled bear. You had to let him roll all over you. You had to flirt well. But you had to set limits. "The *last* time you said that," Johanna told him, "was the Columbus Day pageant of some demented cousin of Jerry Morrissey—which you shirttailed onto some wire service feature—and the time before that, it was 'Cream, light sugar, and a prune Danish.' "

"Women!" he scoffed in turn, eyes heavenward. "Just to get 'em to do a little laundry we've got to treat 'em like the little tsarinas they never were. So: now that we understand each other—" he said, hugging her shoulders fondly, "how about helping on a new series?"

Johanna's eyes brightened. "I'm listening."

"How about all those crazy psychology groups popping up?"

"Have you been talking to my mother again?" she asked, quickly distant. He ignored it.

"I think you're just the person for this."

"Why?"

"You've got some idea about those things. You're a girl—"

"What does that have to do with anything?"

"Who do you think the market for those things is?" he asked incredulously.

"Frankly?"

"I'm sure there's need on all sides—but who do you think the readers for that kind of story are? And if you say men, you've only got one guess left."

"I'd rather go back on general assignment."

"Later."

"Later when?"

"When you're finished in court. I can't put you on breaking stories if you won't be available from day to day. Besides," he said, with mock hauteur, "I'm your editor. I don't need reasons."

As they marched past the door to the ladies' room, she loosed herself from his grip, saying, "I don't know, Arnie," and slipped into that sanctuary.

"Think about it," he said, holding the door to continue his pitch. "It's new terrain—no one's done it—"

"Arnie—please. There are things I don't want to—" she stopped and came back at him impulsively, without finishing her thought. He was trying to be sweet. He deserved her effort. She brushed him on the cheek with her hand and backed quickly into the washroom. The door closed slowly on him and she stood in front of the mirror, watching her face grow drawn until she

340

started inexplicably to leak tears. She washed her face and caught her breath.

When she reemerged, Arnie Logan was still at his post, looking at her now with a mixture of warmth and sternness, as though he'd caught her in some childish lies, impossible contradictions: she was saying that she was strong enough and reliable enough to work again, that she was neither different, nor sensitized—yet wanted considerations for precisely those reasons. And perhaps he also knew about Tyler Bowen. She'd been compromising the integrity of the paper. Logan enjoyed pronouncing that "anyone who makes it with a news source is screwing the readers." But he never said anything. She bit her lip and blushed.

"Stick with me, kiddo," Arnie beamed, taking her under his arm again. "I'll make you a star."

"Can we have a private talk, Arnie?"

He guided her to his favorite nook, a corner alcove where the wire service photo and dupe machines hummed relentlessly.

"Isn't there something else besides a lot of people screaming and feeling each other up I can do?"

"You want to pursue some of those Gila stories you were so keen on?"

"No," she said efficiently. "What if I—I know this sounds strange but—what if I did a story on what it's like to—"

"Absolutely not!" he cut her off.

"Why?"

"We're a family paper."

She arched an eyebrow. "I'm a family member. So is—"

Holding a hand up to stop her, he sighed, "Not only would it be exploiting yourself in the worst way—it wouldn't be a cathartic—it'd be demeaning."

"Why?"

"This isn't the only thing that distinguishes you. Look, if I thought we should do a piece like that, I'd go to the experts—psychologists, doctors—"

"I'm something of an expert, Arnie. My credentials are—intact. Is my objectivity in question? Are there two sides to it?"

"No," he exhaled patiently. "But there are to a

341

legal case. And I think this would be—I'm sorry—at this time, an unfair use of the paper. Frankly, I'm not even sure your by-line isn't."

"Do you want me to quit?"

He shook his head quickly no, then said, "I'll come up with something, OK? Give me a few days. You'll look better for the rest—"

"Hey, Arnie!" called one of the nearby reporters who was killing time with another of the endless diversions bored rewrite men dreamed up—plots for gothic novels, improbable movie scenarios, parlor games, lists of arcane trivia, newsroom contests. He sailed a paper plane made from a ten-dollar bill over to them. It was a payoff on an office pool called the "Must-Go List," a continuing series of bets on which newsmakers would drop dead first. Parlays were available on across-the-board bets: Palpably Evil, Unnecessarily Famous, Monumentally Boring, Stories that Won't Quit, Good-Bland-Ugly, and Putative Frauds. Logan picked up the crashed plane with a smile. He'd collected on his choice, "Top Twenty Rock 'n' Roller," while the smart money was hovering vulturelike over aged dictators and former Presidents. Otis Redding had taken the plunge that month.

"That's what you get for betting your hopes instead of your good judgment," Logan laughed. "Who'd you blow it on, the Rostow boys?"

The reporter grinned. "Wanna sail it back and let it ride on the Beatles?"

Johanna called, "Rock 'n' Roll will never die."

"That's what they said about vaudeville. Two to one they break up before the election—"

Logan answered, "How about three to one on you're being here to collect? What's the line on Ali being allowed to fight?"

"None. All he's gotta do is take the oath—or change his name back to Clay. Anyway, he's still a bum."

"Will you tell him that yourself?" Johanna laughed.

Logan patted her on the backside and considered the bookmaker. "Donald," Logan said, "do I have a *wonderful* assignment for you!" Johanna sparkled, knowing. "Whaddya know about these idiotic encounter groups?"

"Five to one they don't make it out the year," Johanna said. The reporter pointed a finger at her and began to write it down.

"No bet," Logan told him. "Wouldn't want you accused of conflict of interests—" then he turned back to Johanna and looked at her fondly. "Friends?"

"Absolutely," she winked, and stood tippy-toe to kiss his bowed forehead. "I anoint you Editor of the Garter," she said.

Feeling the moist crown of his bald dome, he raised his eyebrows and outlined a halo with a finger. "I'll never shampoo again," Logan said, shaking his head in wonder.

"Christ," the other reporter grumbled. "I gotta kiss him on the lips to get half a day off Sundays."

Logan walked her to the door and said, "If I'd known how much I'd be snookered by Poulson women in my life, I'd have stayed in the Merchant Marine."

The presents were opened, and second helpings of dessert fended off, at the Poulson family Christmas. As quickly as was seemly, the various branches made their exit speeches, kissing good-bye by rubbing cheeks. Johanna went upstairs for a moment's calm before the ride back to Tucson with Warren. She wondered, as she looked at her mother's bedroom mirror, if she had been streaked with tears all night and not told. One night earlier in the week she had walked around her empty house, short of breath, looking in each mirrored surface only to find an unfamiliar face, teary and sagging, staring back. She raced from reflection to reflection as if changing doctors, seeking a happier diagnosis, searching for a glass with a smiling face. The tears had no weight and she couldn't feel them come. They were just there, arrived like Topsy, the product of some invisible act behind her eyes. So caution became her preoccupation and she checked her features often, having lost confidence in her control of them.

Maureen came up to say, "Warren's watching television."

"I'll be right down."

"I want to talk to you, Johanna."

"Why?"

"Because I'm your mother. I worry about you—"

"You don't have to."

"It would be a novelty for once if we could talk without all the snappish hostility—"

"What is it?"

"What are you going to do?"

"I don't know."

"What?" Maureen asked.

"I don't know anything anymore," Johanna mumbled.

"What about Warren?"

"What *about* Warren?" Johanna echoed. "As soon as—" She breathed deeply. "He can divorce me if he wants—or I'll do it, whichever is easier. He can have the charge cards and all our friends. And my car."

"Are you sure that's what you want?"

"Were you?"

"We're not talking about me. I made a mistake and—"

"So did I," Johanna said.

"I'd like to help any way I can. You have some rough times ahead."

"I can handle it."

"Oh, you think you're so young and tough. These things take their toll, darling. There are only so many pieces of yourself to trade away—"

"It's less complicated than you think, really. I'm just tired of putting up with Warren. He's narrow-minded and an intellectual bully and—he's tired of me, too."

"He doesn't act it."

"If it rained, Warren wouldn't look wet. Maybe he's—" She had no end to the sentence. But she didn't want the conversation to end. Could it be, she wondered, that in ten years she'd never had an honest talk with her mother, and that for two years she'd stayed with Warren just to prove her mother wrong? Now that game was over, but they had to make it short. Warren was waiting to go.

"I'm also worried," Maureen said, "about the very lack of emotion you display—"

"For whose benefit?" Johanna asked, pulling back warily.

344

"Your own."

"What should I do? Rant? Scream? It's not emotional. It's cold-blooded rational. I learned it from Warren."

"I don't care about Warren. I care about you," Maureen said. "You've dealt with the whole thing this way—from the desert incident to this. It's a defense, Johanna. And sooner or later you've got to let go."

"You sound like you can't wait." Her mother's whole manner disturbed her, from the way she phrased things—"the desert incident"—to the way she smoked a cigarette: her conversation was a dilettante's, her attention partly given to her own needs and pleasures, concerned but wearing rubber gloves.

As though reading Johanna's thoughts, Maureen said, "You forget I changed your diapers once or twice," exhaling a breath of smoke in staccato wisps as she said it. Johanna didn't answer, fingering a loose thread on her mother's silk bedspread. It had the feel of a tufted peignoir she once owned. When she was very small, she used to rummage through her mother's wardrobe when Maureen was out of the house, to find her mother's silken nightgown, sniffing it for its scent of safety and its comforting texture against her face. So they bought her one of her own. Now she wondered what had become of it.

She looked up at her mother slowly. "I'll work it out," she said.

"Alone? No one can." Maureen reached over and put her hands on Johanna's forearm. The gesture seemed mechanical, programmed, even to Maureen. Her hands were too much the instrument of her will and not enough of instinct to be a new umbilicus. They had abandoned this power for years. Maureen shut her eyes for a moment and drifted. "You know, dear—" She stopped again. Her voice was breaking and Johanna looked at her with detached curiosity, finding her urge to pull away from her mother's grasp too cruel just then to act upon. Maureen's eyes stayed closed and her mouth moved silently, closing in on unfamiliar phrases. "You know, your father and I—" Maureen looked around and suddenly stood up, crushing out her cigarette and lighting another. She took a few

345

quick puffs and the contrived theatrics bored hollow
her words. "Whatever happened later, puss—it was an
act of love that made you."

Johanna wished she had stayed where she was a
moment before, as did Maureen. Both would have
leaned against each other and let go a long-held breath.
But it was past.

On the way downstairs, Maureen stopped Johanna
and asked again, "What are you going to do?"

Johanna drew a thoughtful breath and leaked it out
through her teeth, then made a noise of sucking an
orange rind and pushed her lower lip out, all of which
was to serve for a shrug. Finally, she replied, "What
I should have done is left on a plane last week." She
paused and looked at her mother intently. She'd told
her about Tyler, though not by name and with a
modest economy of detail, just "There's this man . . ."
as a way to tell her she was not, with Warren's absence,
lonely and unloved. Mostly she'd told her because she
had to tell someone, and Maureen seemed shock-proof.
Nor had she told her about the nature of his departure,
just that he was unavoidably away and that she was
satisfied with the reasons.

Maureen said now, "To follow some man again?"

"Uh-huh. If there's a happy ending out there as long
as I stay in Tucson, I'll just get older—no closer."

"Isn't that the same mistake all over again?"

Johanna brightened into a laugh. "As Warren says,
'The uses of historical analogy are limited and special.'
That's not what it's about, anyway."

Maureen still looked dubious. "How well do you
know this—person?"

Johanna chucked her cheeks around considering it.
"Not . . . enough—" Indeed, their brief time of intimacy was a very short flowering, whose compulsions
of continuance were based on its seeming fitness. "But
very." Her sole fear was that the air they'd thrived on
was poison; but so was New York's, Tyler assured her.

"Any way I can help," said Maureen. "You're not
letting that newspaper hold you. Surely that's not your
career interest."

"You know what I'm trained for. You said it—"

Maureen shook her head and embraced Johanna.

346

"Baby," she whispered. "It's been a long time since I've called you that. You could be good at anything you wanted. You don't have to be a stenographer for the world. You're too good for that. Let them write about you."

"They'll get their chance," Johanna said.

Maureen gazed at her daughter with a fragile eye Johanna had never seen before. "If you wanted to, you could stand the world on its ear. You know that." Johanna said nothing. She wanted to ask, "Are you happy, mother?" But if Maureen were honest, she might have to answer, "No," and so Johanna thought to leave it where it was. Had she asked, Maureen would have told her it was a child's question, and one that did not admit such simple responses.

At the Bowen family Christmas, in Pelham, New York, Vlad Bowen's dyspepsia slowed, but did not stop, the headlong dash of the dinner into shambles. His son-in-law, Alan, whom Tyler called Animal, pigged his way through the meal, offering opinions which, when they could be understood, caused fights with Tyler. Leaking sweet potatoes from his jowls, he said at one point, "You see the news? LBJ's flying around the world."

Tyler winked to the children. "So are Santa's reindeer."

"It's no use," Mack said, warning him off. "They think they're too old to believe."

"Don't believe in Santa Claus?" Tyler recoiled in mock horror as the children giggled. "Too old? When their daddy believes in Lyndon Johnson?"

Laura Bowen tried to mediate by ignoring the tension. "He's going to see the Pope," she said.

"Where's he gonna park the reindeer?" Tyler said.

"The President is," Animal explained with a patronizing grin. "Not Santa Claus. It's a peace mission."

"The President is not Santa Claus," Tyler repeated, nodding agreement. "Some peace mission. If Cardinal Spellman arranged it, he'll probably napalm Saint Peter's. Too little, too late." There was no response, until Animal cleared enough food off his tongue to say, "Maybe they'll arrange to get that knucklehead Mc-

347

Carthy excommunicated. You'd think in time of war there's such a thing as aid-and-comfort. It's damned close to treason."

"Since when did the Pope become a registered Democrat?" Tyler asked.

"Some of us here are rooting for Willie's team—" Animal stopped. By unspoken agreement they did not speak of Willie in the presence of the children, except to say he was still overseas and wished he could be home for Christmas.

With measured anger Tyler said, "You can root for the war, the Pope, and fucking LBJ for all I care—"

"Tyler!" his mother half-snapped, half-pleaded, looking at the children. And Vlad groaned then, announcing that to his mind the turkey was "chewy, and kind of gray."

For long periods no one spoke, and when they did, all scrambled to get their words in. There were trappings of the holiday but Christmas itself had been exiled. Toys were religiously laid at the children's altar, after much clamoring insistence that included the brand names. The children, without prompting, announced they had pooled their allowances to purchase a hockey stick for their Uncle Willie.

That was the bond that united the Bowen generations as their family table strained under its sore burden. Beyond all else they were huddled together in meek expectancy, hoping to change the past as they bribed the future. If they were a television soap opera, they might have sketched in scenes for Willie in the next week's episodes, obliging his continuity by mailing the schedule to *TV Guide*. Instead, they bought a hockey stick and other things, all potential, demanding a user to be made actual, laying fruits of the season at the catafalque.

They were waiting, merely waiting. Mack remembered the time little Willie sat with his head wrapped in bandages, mump-swollen, waiting for his sister and brother to come home from school to play with him. She couldn't get the picture from her mind. She always remembered him as that age, no matter how old and large he grew, no matter that her children were now older. It led to another image of Willie sitting with his

348

last baby tooth tied to a string whose other end was on a doorknob. Willie had sulked that he'd rather sit there forever and starve to death than have anyone come through the door. He was right, she now thought, to be in no hurry to grow up. She remembered that Vlad had burst through the door then, but dopey Willie had tied the string to a door opening inward. He was reprieved, until he absentmindedly trotted to the bathroom and stepped on the string himself. Now, the Bowens wanted the door to open less and less. Hope was all they had, and the illusions it permitted them. It seemed at first like torture, but as the days passed ignorance became a welcome shelter against the inevitable, obvious reality.

At Christmas dinner, only Vlad Bowen knew what sad presents had already come, special delivery, from the Department of the Army. It was a packet of official forms and letters. He told no one, not even his wife, for it added no news, just a spadeful of authorized language:

On behalf of the Secretary of the Army, I am required to advise you pursuant to Title II of the Revised Military Organization Act of Congress and Department of Defense/Army Regulations that the official 30-day waiting period for personnel designated "Missing in Action during foreign hostilities" has expired.

Accordingly, pertinent sections of the aforementioned Act and the Military Affairs Acts subsequent to it are excerpted and summarized below:

¶Legally valid assertions of entitlement for purposes of military and civilian insurance claims may be made as of this date. A presumption of death-incombat is authorized by statute.

¶Survivor benefits under current amendments to Social Security System and Veterans' Affairs Acts provisions where applicable are accruable as of the date of reported separation. Enclosed find disbursal information forms to be forwarded to the appropriate offices.

¶Military burial policy regarding National Cemeteries, should you request accommodation, is explained in a booklet, enclosed.

The booklet stated in blandly cheery tones—for it served double duty as a recruiting brochure—that increased demand for space in the National Cemetery at Arlington had required the establishment of a priority point system based on length of service, type of discharge, manner of demise (combat-related or natural causes), and civilian criminal record. Such was the crush that "you may be advised to seek admission elsewhere."

The advisory letter ended:

Specific exemptions from the above-cited sections may be made in (a) cases where remains are not recovered, (b) where casualty is by presumption, and (c) when no reliable eyewitness confirmation exists. Benefits will be held in escrow in interest-bearing accounts at the discretion of the Department of Defense until (a) a declaration of Cessation of Hostilities and (b) a full and complete enumeration of casualties or (c) one calendar year from the expiration date of above-named EP's enlistment (EDCSA).

Waiver of this regulation where applied may be had in cases of extraordinary hardship. Requests for relief must be made in writing through application to the Secretary of the appropriate branch of service.

Enclosed please find a citation and a letter from *The President of the United States, Hon. Lyndon B. Johnson.*

This was a certificate, resembling a diploma or commission, beginning:

To all whom these presents may come, on behalf of the Congress and the People of the United States of America, I, Lyndon B. Johnson, President of the United States, and Commander-in-Chief of the Armed Forces, do hereby declare that *William Charles Bowen* died bravely in the service of his country, in action against its enemies, defending the Republic of Vietnam. . . .

The letter itself, on White House stationery, also suitable for framing, said the Bowens' grief was shared "by Mrs. Johnson and myself," and that "the memory of your son's sacrifice will keep him alive in the hearts and minds of those who knew him and all who cherish liberty in America and around the world. You should take great pride in him." The whole package was sealed with greetings of the season and signed with a mechanical pen.

Vlad had slipped it all into a drawer and told no one. When the Army burial people and Survivor Assistance Officers called, he told them not to call again, he'd contact them when he wanted them.

Small joy for Vlad Bowen did come this Christmas from the way Tyler and Mack, after years of bickering, had mellowed into good friends. She helped Tyler pick out Christmas presents and listened to him talk of Johanna endlessly. She helped him construct small, personal gifts to send her "to show her how creative you are when you have your sister's help," Mack teased.

But Vlad himself, presiding over news he did not share, and a family which cracked and groaned even without that weight, found sleep difficult and laughter impossible. Perhaps he should tell them, he thought, and let them have release.

No, he decided, they needed time. They weren't prepared. Not yet. They'd been conditioned into insolence, and he had to ease their-transition. He knew, despite their childish japes, that death had always sat next to him at the head of the table. For his children this was always a source of mirth, as Laura Bowen gave solemn dinnertime reports on the daily tragedies of neighborhood children blindsided by illness and conked by carelessly thrown rocks; one who lost an eye horsing around, another who choked by swallowing too fast; for a few years, polio had been a good lesson in washing before eating, until they cured it behind her back without asking. The world was lethal. Once, having listened to one-too-many gruesome tales, Mack said, "That's what you get for going out of the house," and she and Tyler had laughed until they choked. Willie was too little then to understand her crack, but he giggled just to keep up with his sister and brother. Vlad knew the

351

truth though: parents were on the eternal deathwatch, while their frivolous children considered life a matter of administrating over pleasures, all gaiety and good luck. Perhaps he had shielded them too long from suffering, kept them innocent of reality. They would learn the art in their time.

They would tire, as he did, of petty battles and endless frustrations, the tiny cycles, retreats, and holding actions. Perhaps the only real measure of success at this game was outliving the actuarial charts. "If you don't get your three score and ten," Tyler marveled when Vlad took out life insurance in his name at age eighteen, "all you get is more money back?"

Such inspiration as Vlad drew came from Laura. With unflickering faith his wife wrote daily letters to her absent son, with no doubt in her tone they would be read; it seemed less ritual than sheer instinct, stubborn refusal.

Yet at some point, Vlad thought, one grew tired of holding out. It did not permit sleep, but there must be a letting go. Even Laura showed signs of that, systematically divesting herself of her holdings. She'd given half her best jewelry to her daughter already, as though having turned a final corner, seeing the light at the end of her own tunnel, turning off the lights behind her. "What are you doing?" Tyler had asked. "Going out of business?" She did, indeed, represent a shriveling empire, bowing to heredity. Her faith was strong because her ambitions were now modest.

Cousins and aunts and uncles came through the Bowen household that week, and such was the ease of those relations that it seemed as if none took off their coats. Still, a genealogical imperative commanded reunion, despite its morbid pains. No individual stylization could overcome the plasticity of the chromosomal skeleton, drawing them, regardless of the allied threat, toward an ongoing family plot.

The day before New Year's Vlad asked Tyler to come with him to get new tires for the car. It was a long-standing code of sorts. When Vlad wanted to talk to one of his boys privately, in an atmosphere conducive to male heart-to-hearts, he used the car as catalyst. "If Detroit ever built one that knew how to last," Tyler remarked once to Mack, "I think he'd have to write letters like Lord Chesterton."

"Chesterfield," she said.

On the way over, Vlad asked him what he hoped to do.

"Well, I've still got this crazy obligation. It's no big deal—but it's still there. I gotta go down and see them again this week."

"Will it be a full-time job?"

"I doubt it. All I know is they decided they didn't need me out West, which is fine by me. My guess is it'll be a consultancy thing."

"What about the draft board?"

"They're cool. I'm on waivers or something." He shrugged a small laugh for his father's benefit. "Even for a hundred bucks they don't want me. I'll tell you the truth, Pop. I got fired."

Vlad kept watching the road. He asked whether Tyler had given any thought to trying out as a free agent at baseball's spring training, and Tyler looked over at him as though he were kidding, but Vlad turned to him slightly and it was clear he wasn't. "None whatsoever," Tyler said. "I wouldn't have a prayer. Those are pros, Pop."

"If you applied yourself, Babe, you could do anything."

"Hey—there's limits."

"What are you going to do?"

"I don't know. I want to go out and see this girl I told you about or—I don't know. Mosey around, look for a job, I guess."

"You could do worse than to come and work for me—"

"I don't know, Dad—"

"Someone's got to take it over from me someday."

"That's a long way off."

"Not so long now. It's given us a lot of fine things. It sent you to Cornell and—the money's good." Vlad smiled at him proudly.

"Yeah, I know. I don't know. If I wanted to get rich, I'd become Jack Nicklaus's caddy."

"Let someone carry your sticks." Tyler said nothing. Vlad sighed and then grinned as they pulled into the service station. "OK, be a bum for a while." It was a favorite incantation of Vlad's. It always concluded: "I only wish I had a rich father to support me, I'd be one too."

As they walked among the racks of radials and snow tires, Tyler looked at him remembering that there was a time when he might have done it all for his father: tried to make the Big Leagues, taken up the scrap iron line, all out of unalloyed adoration. It was a point of equilibrium and good feeling when each of them fit their roles and the future looked sensible. It was gone now, all those elements. But there was, for a fleeting adolescent instant, that moment, when Tyler stood on the sill of manhood at sixteen. One morning back then, Tyler awoke to soft footsteps in the early morning household—his mother's as she stole downstairs to make breakfast. The sun was not yet coming through the windows, but he couldn't sleep any more. He tiptoed past his parents' bedroom to the bathroom. The door to their room was open. Inside he saw his father sleeping, and stopped for a moment to watch. His father slept like he lived, with no letdown in style. If you woke him, Tyler thought, he'd be himself right away. A deep-chested breath rumbled out, his whole body relaxed but strong: a ship's master off his watch but ready for any sudden crisis. Tyler thought then, "He really is the way he is. He lives it. He believes it." Now, in the midst of tire racks, recalling this, he thought maybe his father just believed his subjects needed to see a sturdy, strong, and worthy king. Vlad handed him a cup of vending machine coffee, and Tyler gazed at him with open love.

The night before she left, Mack and Tyler stayed up late talking in the living room. Each knew the other better than anyone in the world, better than any friend or lover might, and they savored the joyful privilege of knowing what annoyed the other most. "You let them worry you too much," Mack pronounced.

"Who?"

"You. Your parents. When are you going to move out?"

"I just got here!"

"Two weeks ago. Nobody else lets them get to them like you do."

"That's the difference between you and me. You just up and spat in their face—tossed away a good education to hole up with Ani-mule. Me? I'm thoughtful. Willie—he must've been raised by wolves. No one can lay a glove on Willie. I'm—thoughtful."

"Have you thought about doing something with your life, dummy?"

"Yeah. I'm gonna grow a beard."

"I bet you can get a federal grant for anything that will cover your face."

He made a face at her, but she just snickered. She had Laura Bowen's face, mostly, agreeable and, indeed, pretty. Tyler and Willie had versions of Vlad's, though Willie's was rounder, more open. When pressed to describe him, Tyler always thought his old man looked like a melding of every world leader he'd ever seen: Johnson and Kennedy and Mao and the Russians. "You're nuts," Willie swore. "He looks like Y. A. Tittle with hair." Still, in Tyler's mind Vlad's weathered face, his lined and leathery skin, and the sense of power in his gut and sinewy forearms, evoked world leaders.

"You know what your trouble is?" Tyler told Mack. "When you come home—on your old man's money —it's like some goddam high school reunion. Your chance to show everyone you were too good to stay here. You grab everybody and hoot in their faces— 'Nooooo, I'm not you. I'm fucking self-created. I've overcome you and all the discarded destinies.'"

"I'll tell you a secret, baby brother. Stay home for a while. Watch them work: they'll barrel in and keep on coming."

He hung his head and acknowledged it was true. "It's started already. Working those real good levers like crazy Casey Joneses. Two minutes after I got in the door I was encouraged to take off my coat, take a bath, and take a job with Dad—they're a series of tapes. 'Save.' 'Have a pension plan.' Your parents have been recorded live before an earlier child."

She was falling asleep and Tyler nudged her to stay awake. "You were asleep," she mumbled, "until you were nineteen—then you woke up and started causing trouble."

"Willie used to say babies should be given a shot when they're still in the oven so they could be born without the trauma—"

"I've got news for you boys. The trauma's mostly on mommy."

"He says we should keep the little jivers asleep about five years—"

"Amen!" she whispered.

"And wake 'em up slowly with shoes and socks on and schoolbooks under their arms. They'd be puzzled, but they'd figure all that junk must be what their business is, that they just forgot. They'd be too embarrassed to ask or put up a fuss—"

"Willie says a lot of dumb things and most of them he learned from you."

"Except we really do it! We keep 'em asleep till about twenty and then: boom! Wake 'em up with a smack!" Mack was asleep on the couch. Tyler spread a blanket over her and went into the den to call Johanna.

"I wrote you a letter," he said. "You want me to read it to you?"

"Silly! Mail it."

"OK. But I'm afraid it's hardly poetry."

"Maybe I should come and be your muse," Johanna said.

"Any time, way, or place. I'll put you over my door like the bust of whatsisname—"

"Pallas," she said. "I think you need me for a muse."

"Can you kiss a muse?"

"This one."

"The pay isn't that good."

"We'll see. Tyler? Why are you up so late?"

"I don't know—hey, I've got one mother and one pain-in-the-ass big sister already, thank you. That isn't the job I had in mind for you." She giggled, telephonically tickled. "Come see about me sometime, kiddo," he said.

The letter he wrote her had described his landing. Supersonic lack of sleep and too much bad coffee had sensitized his skin to the rude shocks of disembarkation at Kennedy Airport. "The lounge," he wrote, was full of people with dogs and small children, and someone's friend playing Sousa on a tuba until the authorities shut him up. Zermatt kept saying about every ten feet, "call me, let's have lunch." Typically, he hadn't missed the opportunity to advance his own arrival. Half his people were at the baggage claim. Not the first and not the last bureaucrat to treat a whimpering rout as a famous victory. One of the federal German shepherds sniffed Baron's bag for dope and lifted his leg. The embarrassed Marshall dragged the disappointed poochie away. (It was the smell of Zermatt's laundry. We didn't have time to do it—so it was unleavened, sort of.) Bar was engulfed by his mother and his not-so-bad-looking wife who, all sense to the wind, were glad to see him.

When I got home my room—which had mysteriously metamorphosed into guest chambers about an hour after I left for college—was still a guest room. My brother's was also "just the way he left it" —according to my mother. A little cleaner, maybe. Has aspects of a shrine, actually. Everybody wants to meet you. My sister especially, who figures I'm a retard and therefore you must be a woman of infinite patience. I believe she may be right. Her kids all squealed about my coming back being "the best Christmas present of all"—as coached. I didn't tell them all the unnecessary facts and didn't even tell them I was on my way till I hit the Pelham station.

Just as reasons of style and character had made Zermatt trot out his booster club, Tyler's dictated that no one greet him. He felt it would be obscene to be piped ashore like Nelson returned from the Nile, when the real hero in his clan had no flags or strutting majorettes, nor even the prospect of a decent burial. If he had an extra brass band, Tyler thought, better to spend it on Johanna who could at least enjoy the cheering.

I guess I like surprises. You surprise me. I never know where your mind has spun during the night (that's good). Sometimes I think I should sleep with one eye open, but then I realize my real job is to dream with equal fever. Got to be very good and invent furiously to match your moves, kid.

But I chickened out on this one. I think it has to do with Pig Juice Hackett. Pig Juice was this big log-like back-up catcher for the Yankees. ("They aren't anti-Semites," Mel Allen always had to explain, "they're just yelling *Jooooose!*") Anyway, during one of his last years on the team he left the late season pennant drive—isn't this fascinating?—with a groin injury. (It may have been, but from time to time there are epidemics of them in Major League cities.) So he went home to Georgia to surprise his wife. Did he ever!

I suppose it's better left to moral philosophers to figure the P's-and-Q's of dropping in unexpected with a cranky groin, though I suspect having a sweaty jock in the house with his crotch in a sling is no great delight in Georgia or anywhere. Whatever—it was his home and he was home. Only, some other guy, whose groin apparently worked well enough, had got there first. So there was Pig Juice, standing there in his invincible Yankee pinstripes, hard-hitting varsity backstop for the World's Hardy Perennial Champ Vanilla Yankee Bankers—and what the hell's he to do? Cream the guy? Compete—with a thing on the blink for reasons unknown? Cry? Retreat? Close the door lightly and go back to the vagabond Club-house for its bachelor comforts? He wasn't trained for this kind of work. On the field, you know, balls come from the plate or the fielders, who are your friends. They hardly ever come from behind and bite you on the ass. But once in a while, they do (especially if you're a Met). What is the moral of this seemingly pointless story? Call before coming.

But you, tootsie-wootsie, can come anytime, call or not. I'm a-waitin'

                                    Yer faithful etc.—

Mack left in the first days of January, 1968, bestowing on her brother Tyler a blessing kiss as only an older sister can, just as only she could dissect his personality with impunity. It said that to her discriminating eye he was turning out less dreadful than she had figured. Then she whispered in his ear, "Move, dummy."

By mid-January, Tyler and Johanna had increased their letters and calls to three a week, though Johanna insisted that count resembled "an old married couple's mating habits." But the press of her work and preparations for trial became greater, so her pace tapered off a bit.

"I've been to see the grand jury twice," she wrote, "and seen the County Attorney five times at least. Also I've started—would you believe it?—doing book reviews. I'll send you a sample if you ask me nicely. Loved your presents. The V-mail may trickle, but it won't stop. Try to understand and write in spite of my failings, please? I'll love you for it all the more."

Another said,

Warren has fallen back into his old ways after almost three weeks of being a sweetie pie. I knew it couldn't last. Form tells. (This time it may have been my fault.) My relationship with Mr. R. is generally brisk and businesslike and I only want to see him when there's a lawyer around. Tra-la. But I shall speak no more of the boring, only you and me until we get bored with each other. I miss you. Don't get jealous, but other than you my editor is the biggest pussycat I know. I almost understand why my mother—the Dragon Lady of KPTV—and he—Oh, I suppose I'm terrible for mentioning it. But what did he see in *her*?

You are absolutely right about lawyers. You wouldn't believe the *dramatis personae* in this play. First of all there's the County Prosecutor, whose name is Jim Hood, a fine handle for a man who specializes in getting maximum sentences for things like flag desecration. He resembles an intolerant evangelist, with an impeccable marcel, $100 cowboy boots, $300 worsteds, and $25 dollar silk hand-weave shitkicker shirts. If it sounds like I've been shopping with him, it's only because last year SDS voted him "Best Dressed Redneck," and quoted figures. The Law, as Warren is fond of saying, is only fortunate he is on our side. Who are "we"?

He's always wrangling with his poor assistant or Deputy or whatever they call such people. The one who is going to handle this case is named Robert Marks, and Hood doesn't like his suits at all. They're a little too trendy, and don't fit very well. How do I know this? Because Hood brought it up in the middle of an interview. He said we'd like young Marks, even though he "buys his suits in a Mexican supermarket." Hood says, "I told him, get yerself some clothes, boy, so you can represent the People." He also, apparently, doesn't like Marks's hair, which I judge to be artfully unbrushed to conceal advancing baldness, poor boy. Hood thinks—he keeps repeating it—it looks like a bird's nest. "You gonna hatch eggs in there?" he asked him at our first meeting. Marks said nothing. Makes me feel all secure inside.

Then there's the defense lawyer. In Pima and Maricopa counties they have a Public Defender's office, but in Cochise the court appoints one, which tends to be better for the accused, I guess. He isn't as cornpone as Hood, and from what I gather doesn't like him, personally or professionally. I keep forgetting I'm supposed to root for the government. He's not too thrilled about Marks either, and likes to make quiet cracks about Bright Young Men who don't know the game's rules. Hood says much the same sometimes: "You've got a great future behind you, Marks." Comforting things like that. Since we're doing a wardrobe analysis, Stanton—he's the defense man—seems partial to blue pinstripes and a dab of pomade in his hair. When it gets hot it greases up his forehead so it shines. I think he'd like to think he's defending some aging don or bold rogue—he wears a red carnation in his lapel even—but I'm afraid he's got a rather unromantic banana for a client. Do I sound blissfully detached? I am.

I haven't seen the judge yet, but I've seen his picture. He's got thin black hair and a broken nose, and he's short and a bit squat. Between Prosecutor Hood and Justice Hall, this has to win some name contest or other.

Speaking of winning contests, the sartorial prize goes to my mother's lawyer, Mr. Edward C. Denning.

Everything he does is tasteful. Tasteful divorces, tasteful commitments, tasteful will challenges. He is slumming in the criminal precincts, though I hear he was once thought to be the prime mover in a big stock swindle where widows and cripples took a bath, but nothing was ever proved—tastefully. He looks like—well, he looks like a portrait of himself. He's got silver-white hair, favors muted gray suits of some Venetian tailor, and a perfectly doctored tan—what God won't give him, Q-T does. He wears silver ties, silver or platinum cufflinks. I think he's a relative of the Lone Ranger. And, on the rare occasion that his jacket is ever open, there is a silver-white monogram on his breast pocket: ECD. His shoes! My God, his shoes. If there are any unsolved Negro child murders in Hood's file, I think my lawer may be in trouble. So soft! Oh, and he's got the most elegant and tasteful silver moustache which, with speech lessons, conceals a tasteful harelip scar. I am just terrible, I know. Warren says that if the jury has any sense, they'll lock me up on general principles. That was the nicest thing he said.

Help.

Love,
Johanna.

Through all this time, Tyler moped indolently around the house, like a probated prisoner, or a bomber waiting for a break in the weather. He divided his time between correspondence and waiting for the mailman—with brief side trips to have lunch with Baron Zermatt. Had he known it would take the NSA at Foley Square so long to figure out what to do with him, he'd have stayed in Tucson. Finally, they called. He went down to see what Zermatt called "Our Men in Suits," who confirmed his status:

He would be required to give training at NSA seminars in his specialties—Information and Biochemical Applications—at the pleasure of NSA. They would give him at least a week's notice and he would be liable for up to twelve weeks a year if they deemed it convenient. Particularly distasteful was the risk of being pressed into such silly service at NSA's whim during

361

"emergency situations" for, as they put it, "the duration." In any event, he'd be confined to reading from technical manuals and otherwise restricted to dealing with nothing the government would not readily concede to foreign operatives or the People. It did, however, indicate that Zermatt, true to his word, had pulled one more magic rabbit from his raggedy topper: there was nothing in Bowen's file to say he was untrustworthy, his low security status being simply the absence of higher clearances. "It was radical surgery," Zermatt acknowledged when Tyler informed him of his discovery. "What else did they hit you for?"

"Nothing. I have to drop in next week for more paper work. They'll have some idea of what's up then."

"You getting a *per diem?*"

"Plus expenses," Tyler said.

"Hit the bastards hard. Don't let 'em off for less than the Waldorf. Let 'em know you don't come cheap and they'll think twice before calling. Ha—I bet the last time they saw a Waldorf chit was General Dougie."

"Aren't you the man who said, 'Learn to steal by nickels and dimes'?"

"Believe me, to them the Waldorf is a ten-cent store. What are you doing in the meantime?"

"Gonna run up to Cornell to see some people. Hanging out, mostly."

"I wish I had your ambition. Listen, give me and the lovely and popular Mrs. Zermatt a call when you get back. We'll have dinner or something."

"Saint Paul's outside the walls," groaned Saint Paul Hooper as he drove Tyler Bowen to campus in an old Hillman Minx from the Ithaca Airport.

"What now?"

"I got mugged by the Dean."

"Not to say you haven't been asking for it. Consular service material you are not." Saint Paul gave a dejected sigh as he acknowledged his own legend.

High above Cayuga's waters is how Saint Paul Hooper had spent most of his undergraduate career. He'd never really intended to go to Cornell; it was his "safe school" application. He hadn't even trifled with anything outside of the Ivies, so certain was he of admission to Harvard or Yale. But they excused themselves in the late running to fulfill an obligation to the civil rights movement, preferring other bright lads who came with the additional ability to dunk backward. Saint Paul took that in stride, declaring, "The Nazarene, if alive today, would not have made the varsity. For it is not known if He had an Outside Shot."

From his first day on the plain above the glacial lakes Paul knew the course requirements would be no challenge. And they never were. What would test his stamina and ingenuity was temptation: unless he yielded to it regularly, he knew those four years would be but an institutional menu of pallid experiences. In his first term he recognized this: "Jesus Christ! The same yesterday, today, and tomorrow!" Though but a vest-pocket freshman then, he quickly understood that survival's key was a gift for the perverse, and an unslakeable thirst for self-expression. He called it individuality. Others called him a maniac.

Only a few recognized that the apparent contradiction between his religious blathering and his relentless debauching was no contradiction at all. For he was in his way a genuine revolutionary, going about the business of that craft: nagging and prodding, holding up a fun-house mirror to the self-satisfied, turning every stable situation on its head, unsettling every stone of complacent authority. He resisted domestication by a passion for the erratic. As much as he aspired to become Cornell's first prophet with Honors, he also designed to be the most inventive, unmanageable, bizarre, and frantically alive pain in the ass to all the prevailing powers-that-smugly-be, more than anyone who ever laid leather on Ezra Cornell's indentured cow pasture. Three times the Dean offered to write personal recommendations if Saint Paul wanted to transfer, but each time Saint Paul said, "I'm happy here."

This time, Caesar's local governors were resolute in seeking his eviction. And this time, they had enough nails.

"What happened?" Tyler asked.

"You wouldn't believe it."

"I lived with you, remember? Try me."

363

"It was the woman. She caused me to get a bad grade."

"What woman?" Tyler asked.

"The woman who taught the course."

"Right. What did you do to earn it?"

"Nothing! I didn't do anything. That's the injustice of it!"

"So why did she give you a bad grade?"

"Because I didn't do anything. That's what I'm saying."

"Where was it that you didn't do whatever it is—?" Tyler asked and Saint Paul looked sheepish. Tyler understood: "On the final."

"I wrote a great final. That's the thing. She even said so herself. It was a marvelous essay! She admitted it."

"What was the course?" Tyler asked tentatively.

"Symbolic logic."

"An essay? On a symbolic logic final?"

"I just couldn't see taking sides in those equations. Killing off the ones that don't make sense in *our* rules—"

"You can't write an essay in math, dipshit!"

"Well, I did and it was a good one. I wrote about how logic was the function of neurological circuitry—it was all neurotic and circular—and that proximity was the fundament of all sequiturs, which gives rise to cortico-xenophobia and how the first metaphysician was an algebraic scholar stoned out of his calculus—"

"And you were likewise. What'd she give you for this blinding surge of insight?"

Saint Paul groaned, "An A."

"Well, that's terrific! Congrat—"

"You kidding?" Saint Paul shrieked. "I *tried* to bag that course. They tricked me! For three years, they tricked me into taking extra credits. That's the way to grad school, they said. I've got too many credits now and they're trying to graduate me early—straight to 1-A City. I figured it out. I can get Ds and Fs until June and—I'd stay an extra three years if I could. Let the traffic to Nam ease up a bit. No big rush. So I was thinking, maybe you'd like to talk to the Dean's Committee—"

"About what? How you're too dangerous to let loose into an unprepared reality?"

"Oh, you could sort of hint I get homesick easily. I do. And how I'm thinking of buying this terrific rifle with this high-powered scope and how much I like the view from the Libe Tower, maybe."

"It's been done. I've got a better idea. Why don't you not say anything for about a week—it'll help your case immeasurably. And I'll just quietly slip out of town the way I came."

"It's a death sentence, Skip! They won't listen to reason. Can't. Most of 'em move their lips when they read a bar of soap. They think the school's motto oughta be *Lucrum Gaudeum*—'It's fun to make money.' I'm a ritual sacrifice for them."

"Maybe you can convince them they need you around to justify themselves," Tyler said, "the way cops need robbers."

"Listen, if I gotta go, could you use your influence to convince your friends I'm a security risk?"

"It's an earned rank, Paulie. An honor, sort of. You don't apply for it—even though I'm sure you could get terrific recommendations for quarantine. It's kind of a talent search. They like to think they discovered you—*then* they shoot you. When's the vote on your degree?"

"Tomorrow. I figure it's a choice between principle and politics for them. Principle and I stay."

"You're fucked."

As they walked across the campus the next morning, Tyler waved to bundled-up friends trudging through the snow. "You know," he said, "a year ago, it seems like longer, I remember walking by here and people'd be tossing oh, balls, Frisbees, maybe sitting under a tree necking a few rounds. You could just skip by and raise your hand, someone'd toss a ball at you or a Fris—it'd just nestle up, float on up like it had all the time in the world and didn't know there was a war on, right up to your palm. You know what it was like?"

"Cold," Saint Paul shivered.

"I swear, it was like drifting under a high fly ball."

"I was never very good at that," Saint Paul muttered.

"It's true. You'd pound your mitt and—sometimes you'd look like DiMaggio, and sometimes the damned thing'd sail right over your head and you'd look like a jerk. So where is everybody?"

"The snow's a little deep for necking, Skip."

"I did it in a snowbank once. Hell, you picketed in a blizzard once."

Saint Paul warmed to the remembrance. "They're all indoors getting seriously wrecked. There's very little faith the snow'll ever melt."

When Tyler did get to see the Dean, it was a purely social call, and the Dean was all glad hands for the visit of one of Cornell's more honored recent sons. "We were all so proud to see you'd won that fellowship in the *Alumni Magazine*," the Dean said. "Very proud. It would have been a tragedy to waste your talents in the Navy. That's the shame of these things, of course, as Rupert Brooke—"

"Yeah," Tyler said. "They never listen. I was lucky. But you know how it is with funds and all." The Dean grumbled sympathetically. "So they closed my program down and I'm among the overeducated unemployed."

"Really? Have you spoken to the departments here? They may have leads." Tyler said he had, and had even asked them if they had any openings, but they too were budget-strapped. At this, the Dean visibly brightened, saying, "I'd have to talk to some people, but there might be a way to arrange matters between the various budgets. Those things aren't chiseled in stone. After all, what kind of advertisement for our degree would it be if our own golden boy couldn't find work?" Now it was Tyler's turn to roll his eyes. "How would you feel about a nominal affiliation with this office, say, with minimal duties and—you'd be associated with Advanced Studies, but paid out of here."

Flattered by the idea, Tyler replied too eagerly that he'd like nothing better than to be "back where I belong. It's cold out there," casting through the considerations aloud, including a vague reference to "this unsettled obligation" to the NSA. The Dean took it as premature office-decorating, but patted Tyler's neck amiably, urging him to "Stay in touch. We'll see what we can work out. I'd like to do it if I can."

Before he left, Tyler said, "You were talking about bad advertisements for a Cornell education—"

Smirking, the Dean nodded, "And that brought to mind your friend Hooper? The thing in its purest state. Wouldn't be in half so much trouble if you were still here to hold his reins."

"Well, I was thinking. I seem to recall your saying once, relative to some sophomore's notion that his psychosexual confessions constituted poetry, that 'sincerity is no substitute for competence.'"

Agreeing with his previous stance, the Dean said, "Neither is neither. And as for your friend Hooper, the unexamined life is not worth living, as he is so fond of pointing out; nor is the unexamined transcript worth having. I'm not about to debase this institution's diploma by a graduation of convenience. He'll have to stay until he earns his way out. That's our real battle. I've got Trustees who suggest that instead of loosening up social regulations, we let the students molest the curriculum. And faculty who agree! My own feeling is they all envy the sex lives of students. I'm curious though—you're suggesting his grade be lowered to match his performance? A bizarre act of friendship, I would think."

Tyler shrugged. "Two parts academic integrity, one part give-a-kid-a-break. There are a lot of things A's can't buy."

The Dean looked at him askance. "If I accept your analysis, it doesn't mean I believe your math. In any event, I wouldn't recognize spring without Hooper fornicating on some rooftop. Deny myself the pleasure of having him around? It's one of the few unrestricted forms of perversion allowed for Deans, such sadomasochism. Besides, I enjoy the boy. Reminds me of myself when I was, oh, about nine."

When Tyler gave Saint Paul the good news, Hooper was more bemused by the Dean's logic than anything, shaking his head and saying, "'What is truth?' asked Pilate, jesting, as he washed his hands. The decision to do nothing has great appeal for him, I guess."

Before Tyler left the next day, feeling like the hometown hero he'd once been, he took a jump shot and sank it from twenty feet into a campus trash barrel on the sidewalk outside the student union. As he had so often at Cornell, he felt he'd come off the bench in the

367

late going to win one for the Good Guys. Nor did he discourage that opinion in Saint Paul Hooper, who said he'd have to come off the bench for real, turn his energies to some larger mission. Ithaca looked different, smaller, to his sun-bleached retinas. "But was it Ithaca," Saint Paul asked, when Tyler mentioned it, "or Odysseus that changed with time and experience?"

"Your conception of me continues to be overblown."

Saint Paul would not have it, telling him he'd better be "about the business of being Tyler Bowen again. It's been an awful long time and there's a lot of fans counting on you, Skip. Go get the bastards."

But the only adventure he had in mind was one. All through this time he carried with him a letter from Johanna, fondling it for support, as though it were a magic amulet, reading it again and again:

I'm almost ashamed to say—embarrassed really, my missing you has not diminished as much as I actually expected (there, you've got me talking like you—*actually*, indeed!). I admit it. I assumed time and distance would work their bleak wonders. Maybe that would have been healthy, because I miss you too awfully much. Much too much. . . . I may have to run away from home to see you and I might just do it. Can you take in a refugee? I can cook (not well but well-intentioned) and clean (not well-intentioned but well) and I'm quiet (not too) and no bother really (unless you'd like . . .) and I'm told when I behave myself I can be lovable. Love you to pieces and miss you wretchedly. Love your city and yourself until I get there to do it in person and claim my reward for being

Your Very Ftfl Cspdt
Once and Future Scooter-Pie
All my strength in one Big Hug,
JPR(?)

The taxi driver at La Guardia called him Skipper, an accident the same as if his name were Bub or Pal or Buddy. With two hours to kill before he was due at Foley Square to finish his paper chores, Tyler asked the cabbie to wait while he dropped his suitcase at the Waldorf, then asked to be taken to the Battery, and paid the driver extra, figuring that the government should be a big tipper.

And there, at the foot of Manhattan Island, the landed sailor felt at home for the first time, returned at last from his secret desert seas. This was the promontory that had jutted into sailors' and settlers' imaginations for three-and-a-half centuries, the Circean island in the crotch of two great streams. All that was left now was a grass remnant, fenced in, a park encompassed by cementation, surrounded by highways and circumscribed by sewery waters; a pericardium-tough shield for the precious artifact. It was barely fertile, a heart sustained by intervention, preserved by ukase. All around, the settlers' effluent took root as concrete and macadam.

He crossed the street and pressed against the chainlink fence, Typhoon brand, near the Port of New York Authority office, to glimpse the statue in the harbor.

In grade school they taught him to call her Miss Liberty. It was a proper name, yet intimate; Americans, bowing neither to Popes nor Princes, call their household gods on the telephone.

She bore her constant torch still, for him as for early generations; Promiscuous Promethean, Lady Libertine, for anyone. Over the gray-brown turgid Upper Bay a mist swirled, flinging originless snow flurries about. The continent itself was still under bright skies, untouched by this weather, while Liberty's allure pulsed in and out of obscurity. First he saw her through a veil, then with sudden clarity. Then not at all. Bright, then gone. She reminded him of Johanna in that way, a green sister perhaps, and he wondered if ever another living woman looked so sexy and unattainable, promised so much release and kindled so much desire as did this far-off legend's beacon. Unwary sailors drawing too near the light might be dashed upon the rocks of Bedloe's reef.

He walked the short distance up to Foley Square with his hands in his pockets, thrust deep for stolen warmth. From one open island of sidewalk to another, coat collar turned against the chill, he sloshed through a shivering Financial District crowd. The traffic nearly swallowed him. The buses gave no quarter and the snarling traffic pressed homicidally into every vacuum. In spite of this, he burrowed up the ascending colon of Broadway to the Federal Plaza. National Security Agency Headquarters, Room 619 of the Federal Building, had an antiseptic air to it, rather like a surgeon's office, the gore at some remove. It was the bureaucratic way. If they wanted to be mean they'd do so with prophylactic locutions, ATRA for one: Administrative Termination of Respiratory Activities; or PCI for a shiv: Preemptory Cardiovascular Interdiction.

When he was through, he called Baron Zermatt to make dinner plans. "They've got more computer print-outs on me than you'd believe. Like an astronaut. You should've seen it."

"I have," Zermatt said. "I trust they don't know what they don't need to know."

"They still think I'm the big team player. Got my weight wrong, too. What time should I come over?"

"How about eight? I've got a doctor's appointment at six. I'll be out at seven but—"

"A shrink? Congratulations. It's about time—"

"Smart-ass. I'll see you at eight."

Then he was back on the streets, a free man, wandering with new strength and odd purpose up Broadway. Fifty years' propaganda had elevated homecoming parades to a mythic plateau, the boys come back from their various wars victorious, proud as hell, ready to claim their reward: the country they had served. And now nobody, no madman institutional or private, would deny him as he stole this march on them, the Skipper returned at last from a shipwreck, angry for its casualties, looking for a new commission. He decided to walk the three miles to the Waldorf.

His personal parade reached the hoar-frosted carny of Times Square in late afternoon. Then he turned east at Fiftieth Street to see the daylight trade: blue whores, ashen, shivering from the cold. They ruled the sidewalks as insurgent Viet Cong owned the jungles. Firepower was useless, police impotent. Imposed conventions could not stifle anthropological imperatives. Only the territorial urge is greater: new construction alone could muscle them into the gutter, but even that was temporary, no more successful than evicting roaches while a plumper high-rise is assembled for their pleasure. He smiled toothily at one whore in front of the Time-Life Building and headed for Fifth Avenue's more subtle and thorough seductions.

He reached Fifth, gazing up with the tourists, then down in the native habit, easing into the pedestrian currents in the backwash of traffic patterns.

Someday, perhaps, he thought, he might travel Fifth in giant strides, have an office up high where friends could visit; Saint Paul, a little nearer God, could sail Him paper planes, and Zermatt could eavesdrop or expectorate upon Saint Patrick's spires. But Con Edison would rip the street apart a thousand times before then, so he put himself on hold and headed east toward Madison, with a sudden laugh at his own movie-bred fantasies.

His chuckle caused one passer-by to do a startled double take. He thought it was a nervous flinch. But then he realized it was New York's special tribal dance, the signals from stranger to stranger in the crowd. For New York was first and last a town of insistent comics, pantomimists, take-artists no less than wise guys. Everyone had a reaction and the First Amendment had nowhere any wider reign. Every phrase and gesture was turned and played with, twisted, reinvented, and exploited like some bright object found by troglodytes. Every source of humor was examined for variety, a hybrid of commercial and talmudic scholars' arts. No wonder Johanna thought so highly of the place; for her, too, irony was not only a rhetorical device, but a way of life.

Madison, dark and narrow, was lined with luggage shops at this latitude, galleries to the north. Past the derelicts and the women with their lives in shopping bags and their swollen venous ankles loomed Park Avenue. It should have been a garden cul-de-sac in the granite canyon. But it was worse than Madison.

Park Avenue was cold. Manhattan was the brain of the animal and nerves do not themselves feel pain; they only tell the limbs to hurt. Park Avenue was the thalamus, protected from the cruder things that filtered through, a kind of Gila, where only sanitized word of the nation's fits and sores may come or go. Here was the center of immunity, the board room where orthodox Brahmins packed other people's children off to shoot, while they stayed cozy and married their cousins, Brooks Brothers and Sisters, inbred as the Mountain Clans. He wondered if he wasn't getting a little proletarian for one who, in spite of all, was manifestly blessed by fortune and his father's enterprise. But a deporting wind made him shiver and he realized it was twice as cold, that wind, as the weather. Tucson, using simple tools, could spit hot air onto sand by airconditioner ducts; garbage may be flushed beyond a household's borders using only minor genius. But Park Avenue, so hardy in its insulation, aged-wood rooms wrapped by a Rubicon of privilege, had a bolder franchise: tossing cold upon the public sidewalks, disdaining the thermodynamic laws as only fit for pedestrians.

Over coffee in a luncheonette on Lexington, he brooded about the city, unwilling to face the Waldorf just yet. No less than Paris or Hollywood, New York was once fixed in some imaginations as glamorous and enchanted; to many still it made the whole world one place called Out of Town. Now it glittered more in distant myth than close detail, a derelicted place.

As he scanned the worn faces in the coffee shop mirror, Tyler wondered if concerted energy could make time run the other way, and what could restore the city from its ruins. Was it always so quick before the poisons took their toll; did all things always regress toward an ethical, statistical mean; were great men's offspring always indolent?

If Gresham's law decreed the Bad drove out the Good, that would require the local future erupting as Los Angeles: a panting land of disconnected lives and hamburg joints, overcrowded with pathetic fugitives from broken promises, all desperate to lay nearer idols, bent on making sterile union with celebrity, reduced to fantasy and gambling, with the One True God, Bingo. There was a town come together solely by the gravitation of its greeds, and as the downhill drain of all the nation's lunacies.

Even Chicago, city of a million butchers, doomed always to be the Second City—if every other village, township, hamlet, and municipality in the world vanished overnight and New York fell into the sea, Chicago would not rise above its runner-upship—existed, plainly, in Tyler Bowen's mind, for no greater purpose than to hold the top and bottom half of the American League together and keep the Nationals perpetually supplied with patsies. New York was the mainsail and the rudder. Without her, America would drift. As he entered the Waldorf he worried over this: was there some irreversible design which must end all things in chaotic obsolescence? He was morosely glad no one had come to his homecoming parade, for he feared this was no home to come to.

"Am I keeping you from a breakdown?" he asked, when Baron Zermatt opened the door.

"Wise guy. It's a very complex process. There's Mondays and Fridays and on Wednesdays is group. It's got terrific benefits. For example, next week we're on a charter to Montego Bay."

"An affinity group of paranoid schizophrenics," Tyler said, punching him in the arm. "You going?"

"Can't," Zermatt said ruefully. "I don't use my right name. No use having all this come out at a later date—"

"Except your mental health dividends are accruing to Joe Blow."

"I make out all right. Monday and Friday's during lunch. Keeps the old waistline down. Wednesday's to work out the Monday discoveries, and Friday's to patch up the Wednesday problems."

"And Monday?"

"Things don't always go as well as you'd expect the previous week. It's a very subtle thing."

"What've you learned so far? I see you don't suck your thumb anymore."

"I'll tell you what I've learned. Once you leave the womb you gotta spend your whole life apologizing for the insult. 'Wasn't it good enough for you inside?' I've learned apology is also the fucking price for visitation rights." It was his wife's doing that he was going he explained, "not mine. I'm happy. She's not, so I have to go if I want to stay married. It's craziness. But—"

he shrugged. "Look, I may not be the most faithful guy in the world. But I love my—marriage. It's like finger-painting: it's a mess but it has its charms."

"And where is the lovely and popular Mrs. Z?"

"My mother?"

"Your wife. Being shrunk?"

"She's being stretched. She's dancing and I'm cooking," Zermatt said, mixing drinks.

"Like jitterbug?"

"You know, like modern stuff, sort of ballet. I tell you, I don't understand 'em, I really don't. How is my getting shrunk gonna help?"

"It can't hurt," Tyler grinned.

"Yeah, but I'm not the one who's flipped her lid. There we were in law school. Close? And in my first year of duty; what a peach. Then she decides wouldn't it be a grand idea to come back and crank up a practice, especially since Gila's got nada, squat. So when I get home after busting my ass over a hot desert for all this time, what do I find? She's practicing all right. To become a hippie." Zermatt sighed and sank into the couch. "I'm twenty-eight and I feel like a middle-aged man!"

"You *are* a middle-aged man."

"Ah, but with the body of a boy. 'The hell with work,' she says. 'You work. I just want to dance!' Is that responsible? Is that parity? What if I said that?"

"They'd laugh you off the stage."

"Let it be a warning to you. Marriage is a withered arm. You know it's rotting and it's gonna fall off but—damned if you don't feel a little sentimental, soft about it. So she dances and I see the docs. It's nuts."

After dinner, they walked through cold streets strewn with brittle garbage and freezing drunks to pick up Zermatt's wife, whom Tyler had not seen since they landed at Kennedy.

Lesley Zermatt was dancing alone, doing lifts and exercises in a practice studio at an old hotel. "There's gonna be a recital," Baron said. "And all the daddies are gonna come and watch all the mommies dance. Isn't that nice?" They watched her through a one-way mirror as she did her routines, dancing for the reflection, unaware of her observers. Baron wiggled his fingers at her from time to time and chain-smoked as he talked. "What do you know about McCarthy, up in New Hampshire?" Tyler asked.

"Running away to Never-Never Land?"

"Going skiing for a few days and I thought maybe I'd cruise over and take a look," Tyler said noncommittally. "What do you think?"

"The word that leaps to mind immediately is 'moronic.' "

"Why?"

"I'll tell you. It's not that he doesn't have a chance. He does—only he doesn't know it."

"Try that on me again, slowly," Tyler asked, averting his eyes from Lesley's stretchings.

"Look: Johnson's vulnerable. Don't let anyone tell you different. Maybe not on the war so much—and that's McCarthy's mistake. But on straight-up psychology and resentment, Lyndon's a sitting duck. He can be taken. I don't know if this guy can do it, though. He's more like shock troops. If he shows any strength, Bobby's in right behind. Count on it. That's the smart money."

"Johanna'd like that."

"All women do. He's so cute. They think he needs mothering or something, like Sinatra. And he'll fuck 'em eight different ways. But he's the guy you gotta watch."

"What's he doing now?"

Zermatt smiled smugly. "Nothing. All part of the plan."

"Well, at least McCarthy's up throwing snowballs at the son-of-a-bitch."

"Wait for Bobby. Listen, Gene's a fine guy. Started one heck of a zippy dialogue up there from what I read, yessir. Ought to make him Archbishop of Canterbury or something. Maybe he'll write an 'Oratorio on Gross Bombing Tonnages' or something. But he's never been famous for his follow-through. See, the first requisite of leadership is—"

"Power," Tyler agreed.

"*Love* of power. A lust for it. You gotta get it first. A psychotic need to rule. I mean, you tell me how else you can *dare* make decisions for two hundred million jerk-offs. And the only guy who can run Lyndon off the pot and make it stick is pretty Bobby. Whatever your taste for them, Kennedys get things done. They're get-elected machines."

Tyler nodded to the sage. "So—this being his state and all—you're waiting for Bobby?"

"Not"—Zermatt looked at the ceiling lights—"exactly."

"What's that supposed to mean?"

"Actually," Zermatt fluttered his eyelashes, vamping, an aging con proud of his acute angles, "my registration is a little, uh, hazy on this point. I'm with the other guys. I believe you've heard of us—and proud—"

"Republican?" Tyler squawked. *"Since when?"*

Baron twinkled merrily. "You kidding? A long time. December."

"Christ, if you were a puck they'd call you for icing. No wonder she thinks you're nuts."

"Sticks and stones and go blow yourself. Look, it's really very simple. Consider the dillies of the field: Lyndon's a fucking maniac—and anyway he's all boxed in. Gene's sweet. Real sweet, but the sap's running a little early this year. He's a daisy in a hurricane—and a one-time monk or something to boot. You want *that* deciding policy? Humpty's an imbecile. If he ever won, they'd have to put a timer on the hot-line and a Band-Aid on the button just to keep him from playing with it. He'd pick at it like a scab."

"Which leaves Bobby."

"Who's got problems," Baron said.

"Such as?"

"He's the only guy who can bump off Lyndon, that's true. But among other things, Lyndon'd be so pissed he and his friends'd stick their fingers up their asses and basically help the opposition. That's us. Politics is knowing how to stand on line, which is why upstarts aren't popular."

"But turncoats are."

"Uh-huh. If you bring the plans to the fort. Look, I like Bobby, really. He's the only one in the bunch who can tell all those toenail pickers to get their asses in line—but the rest'd say he's got no ruths. And that's why he's so good: because he's ruthless. Which tells

me it's a Republican Year no matter how you slice it—
a Zermatt year. It's an investment. Listen to the Baron:
Buy now."

"Regret it later."

"You get no points for losing. Being right is nice,
but winning's twice the fun—everywhere but in liberal
circle-jerks. It's really quite respectable. Rocky, Romney, Scranton, you know, they're pretty good boys."

"Reagan, Nixon, Goldwater, Himmler," Tyler added.

"Never come to it. Besides, I could live with 'em—
bore from within. There is no solace being out, fella.
If there's gonna be a revolution, it won't be from the
streets—it'll come in the back door and be hatched
in rooms you and I would never in our whole lives
be in."

"Why don't you take your talent to Bobby? Maybe
that extra little bit would do it."

"Because I'll tell you something else. That time I
did the thing with Jackie at Saint Tom More's? I walked
out behind her, and when she finally hit the street—
wham! A zillion flashbulbs and strobes went off, some
of them exploding from the cold. I hit the deck, Jack,
but she just kept on walking. You'd think she'd cringe
—just a little."

"So?"

"So I'm thinking, maybe it's bullshit. The rest of us
are wearing hair shirts and Secret Servicemen're talking
to themselves. But them? They're marketing it. You
gotta admire it. But you gotta wonder. And figure this
—if Our Men in Suits know what she was laying on the
line—and who—imagine what they've got on Bobby-
kins. And guess who gets it if Lyndon's feeling sulky?
So now, what profiteth a man to save his soul and
lose the White House? It's lousy shit, hollering in from
the cold."

"I don't know," Tyler said, shaking his head.
Solemnly, he lectured Baron, "A man has to stand
for something."

"Why?" Baron asked, the innocence in his tone asking who was really the naive one. "Listen," he said,
wrapping an avuncular arm around Tyler's shoulder,
as Lesley stopped her exercises. "You go up there and
take your lady friend. Have a real nice time, maybe

do a little skiing after the ship sinks. It'll be very romantic—a honeymoon on the *Hesperus*. If your luck holds, they'll shout, 'Women and sentimentalists first!' "

"All I said was I might go skiing."

"Good. It'll be better for your eternal soul."

"I'm touched you're so worried about my soul, Bar," Tyler said as Lesley emerged, toweling herself off.

Baron kissed her on the cheek without a pause in his patter. "Fuck your soul. It's ballast. Drop it and rise. I'm talking about marketability. It might be worth something on the open market. Get a good price on the thing—don't dump it at a White Sale. That's the spirit that made America great!"

"What are you talking about?" Lesley asked her husband.

"I was telling Baron about my plans," Tyler explained. "I said I was going skiing and he had some kind of seizure. I really think you should get him some professional help."

After a few drinks with the Zermatts, Tyler returned to the Waldorf and called Johanna. He did not know that on any given occasion Warren might answer his call, and Johanna did not choose to tell him. Had she, he would have merely said that he understood. She said there finally was a trial date, and that Warren's studied pleasantness made her feel "creepy," and he told her about his day and his intentions to go skiing. "I could use the rest," he said. "I haven't been doing a thing, but I got bags under my eyes that'd give a sleeping car porter a hernia."

"You worry too much."

"Yeah, maybe. Everyone tells me."

She asked how Baron was and wanted to know all about what kind of wife he had. When Tyler finished, Johanna said, "In his next existence I think your friend Baron is going to come back as a cavity." Before they hung up, he said that he'd tried to sniff out the ghost of General MacArthur, "but the cleaning fluid's too strong, so I'm gonna watch Johnny Carson, who'll have to do."

Had Tyler Bowen been a real hero on parade that day, with papers to prove it and medals to trade on, instead of immaterial wounds, there would have been this at the end of the evening still. In the lamplight outside a siren and some screams faded, vagrant comets of the chill. On the television, the coup de grace was stars and stripes and jets, extinguished by a wrist flick, with only an orthicon baby moon remaining. He was home, at the Waldorf, and he was alone. Now there was nothing left but to douse the lights and jerk softly off on the Waldorf's white sheets.

Saint Paul was wrong about him, he thought in his drowse, and wrong about the nature of the bastards. They were only to be toppled in fantasies.

The night before Tyler was to leave for Vermont, his father came into his room late, while Tyler was reading. "Your mother's asleep," Vlad said, closing the door behind him gently. "I wish you wouldn't smoke in bed, Babe," he said, removing an ashtray, sitting himself in its place on the bedspread. "You'll burn the whole house down." It was clear Vlad was in some pain, and Tyler put his book down, assuming his own lack of direction was its source.

"This thing up at the college may come through, Pop."

Vlad nodded his head. "That's fine, Babe." He still looked subdued and unhappy, playing with the sheet's hem idly. He called his son "Babe" when he wanted to stress pride, or concern, or filial obligation. In those contexts it was less for famous namesakes than short for "Baby of mine." When he called Connie "Mack" or "Mr. Mack," he was cheerfully joining his children's irreverence, yielding to disorder. When he called her "Constance" or "Connie," it was usually to speak of problems. From his tone and squint in the glareless guest room it was evident he was troubled. "I spoke to Connie tonight. Your mother doesn't know."

"She all right? What's the matter?"

"She's fine, Babe. The kids—" he smiled faintly at the thought of them. "We talked about Willie."

"Take it easy, Pop. I wish you'd talked to me first—"

He wiped a hand gently across Tyler's cheek, into his hair, and said, "I got a letter from the Army people."

"What'd it say?"

"It's no use, Babe. I had to tell her."

Tyler's response was as calm as his father's had been, having lived with the odds this long. He asked only, "Does Mom know?" Vlad shook his head, but Tyler suspected that if she didn't, it was only because she hadn't seen his face for a week, or didn't want to know. "Where is it?" Tyler asked, and Vlad told him it was downstairs in the desk drawer. "Can I see it?" They went down to get it. Vlad had it under lock with the previous ones and Tyler had to read it three times before it changed from mere official words to meaning. He shuffled through the other papers sightlessly.

"What'd Mack say?" he asked, a little numb.

"She says she'll fly in for a service."

"Is that what you want? I mean, forget about Connie."

"That's not right," Vlad said, scolding softly.

"Well, I think it's a lousy idea. Look—it's a strain. On everyone—you and Mom and all of us but—this letter," he said, waving it to show its flimsiness, its insubstantial word, "this doesn't tell us anything we didn't know. It's got the time. One says thirty days, so now it's what? Seventy-five? Sixty? You want to have some kind of memorial? Sure, why not? But it's for the neighbors—"

"Mother, and Connie—" Vlad said. "It might be of some help." Tyler shook his head mechanically. "Then what do you want to do?"

Tyler looked around his father's warm den and wondered how to say this. His role in the family had been altered. As oldest son he had made them proud. Now, however, Vlad was standing down to his counsel. Yet in spite of this, no ribbons or cups had prepared them to talk of what moved them, of the blood and marrow of their beliefs. "I don't know. I just don't need it. A service doesn't do anything for me. I mean, if I'm going to get down on my shins and do the whole act, Pop, I'm not going to hit up on Him for a squiggie like 'Give Willie a nice room, God.' If I'm going to go that route, hell, I'll ask for the whole thing. What's there to lose?"

Vlad played with his brow between his fingers. He was trembling. "What are you saying, Babe?"

"I don't need it. Not a wake and not a funeral. You

want one, fine. I'll stay. But I'm a holdout. One way or another, Pop, he'll keep." Vlad's breathing stuttered. He closed his eyes tightly, and wrapped his giant arms around his boy. Tyler said he'd call Mack himself and tell her it was off.

"Don't be rough on her," Vlad said. "She's not you." Then Vlad returned to bed, abdicating in the most quiet generational passing of the colors ever staged, leaving Tyler alone in the den.

It was a radical act, in a sense, that they had talked themselves into. For to take the declarations of their government—under powers delegated to the President and Congress by the Constitution, under statutes and provisions of the Armed Forces duly enacted, to sort the living from the dead—and reject that out of hand, deny it further sovereignty in their household, was a rebellion undermining all the contracts of society, as much as if they stuck flintlocks through the louvers at the tax man. By law, the truth was nailed to their door in these writs: their son was numbered dead, however incorporeal the carcass. To leave him above ground was barbarian. *Antigone*'s precedent was binding; it was the fundament of social order. To be so callous, even in blind optimism, as to leave the process flapping raggedly on the jamb in such weather, to leave Willie's life without ceremonial finish, was to threaten neighborhood custom and the shared reality of their world.

But, Tyler's argument ran, this was war, between such beleaguered citizens and the corpus without head or heart in Washington, which commanded them to bury vapors. If Nothing, last seen alive, could be rechristened Something, dead, the first act of moral mutiny would be to declare such fiat unacceptable, refuse its rule by loosing its grip on language. They would reframe the definitions of hope and despair, deny the government's right to order the faith of their home, enjoining it as a violation of their First Amendment Freedom of Belief; they would secede.

January limped to a close in that way, with no news from the pulsing wires and flashing networks, just suspension. There was no resolution in New York or Tucson or South Vietnam. All were locked in a doldrum of postponed activity.

381

In Asian jungles they were celebrating temporary peace, a tranquillity in the diastolic lull of a holiday called Tet. It was expected there would be a systole when it ended, a throb of resumed activity. But there was not. Instead, there was a furied seizure, a thrombic hemorrhage that sent aftershocks across the ocean floor. All around, from the quiet, came a surging embolism toward the heart, a paroxysm in the domestic Tet, erupting as catastrophe.

William Westmoreland said it was a great defeat for the enemy, and in some peculiar ways it was. For by the Queen of Hearts logic used to measure these things the enemy was soundly waxed. Not perhaps the local enemy, but such potential ones as doubted American will: the casualty statistics in the wake of Tet were staggering, yet America was undeterred; indeed, each battlefield rout was further proof that the economics of conflict were not enforceable on America. As much as high body counts told of enemy losses, so did high totals of American dead, even if both were achieved by the same American bombs. It was a potlatch.

So, Westmoreland and Walt Whitman Rostow and the others said again, they saw the light. It was at the end of the tunnel. They said, "We have turned the corner"; it was one funny tunnel. And the light at the end of the tunnel shone more brightly to them at the Tet Offensive's end than ever before. The war would soon be over, especially if America kept bombing its own troops. It was also said that the light, so clear, was a train coming the other way. It wasn't Bob Hope who said it.

Secretary of Defense Robert Strange McNamara, who had two years before declared, "We have stopped losing the war," called the Viet Cong's Tet drive a terrible drubbing—for them. It wasn't Bob Hope again, but some seer replied, "Another week like that and the Viet Cong will have the lobby concessions at the Pentagon." They already had the American Embassy in Saigon. It was lamented that no member of the Diplomatic Corps strode forth in white ducks and flannels to read the natives the Riot Act. Instead, cables home from Saigon describing victory piled on victory were dictated from under the ambassadorial desk.

Dean Rusk, Secretary of State, joined in the optimistic chorus, insisting that the enemy had been crushed. His vocal worries about the possibility of there soon being "a billion Chinese"—with the implicit suggestion that perhaps someone ought to *do* something about that—had sent Senator Eugene McCarthy's wheels of candidacy spinning toward New Hampshire. Now, with the enemy standing on the State Department's rug, if not its chest, he seemed almost sanguine.

Senator McCarthy had been inspired to move by Rusk, by Allard Lowenstein's whispered encouragements, and also by Nicholas DeB. Katzenbach, whose blithe assertion that the War Powers vested in Congress were "obsolete" implied they were supplanted by presidential discretion and the pragmatic realities of *faits accomplis;* that no tyrant's urge to spread his personality across history's landscape need be justified by any niceties of law or process beyond expandable, magic, concurrent resolutions, enacted without a thought.

It was becoming plain that the Constitution had been, for all intents, suspended. Also, Cause and Effect. As far removed as government was from its popular source, it was also abstracted from all sense.

THE PEOPLE AGAINST RICHARD ELLIS WAS a matter of long standing, according to the experts. More than once they had found him suffering from a species of "personality disorder," phylum *paranoia.*

On each occasion, a psychiatric panel studied him and debated the appropriate nomenclature for this highly mutable creature, his mind. Whether his actions were the product of "personality disorder" or "psychosis" was key to his criminal liability. A professional curtain guarded any interior doubts or dissents in those expert findings. And it was possible, as their consensus had the binding force of the Supreme Court's slimmest majority, that the critical distinction in language might have been different had one member of the panel been diarrhetic during the vote. By majority rule, they found him, linguistically at least, this time on the "personality disorder" side of the ledger, in the kingdom of the sane. Upon the hinge of that determination Richard Ellis swung into the dock in early February 1968, in *State of Arizona* v. *Richard Ellis*.

Pretrial rulings upheld the psychiatric finding: Ellis was "competent to stand trial and contribute meaningfully to his own defense," as well as "understand the nature of the proceedings." His lawyer, Gary Stanton, had argued contrariwise that Ellis was "no more than in the crepuscle of awareness."

Judge Hall also ruled that Ellis's blurted admission upon capture was worthy of exclusion. His confession was "tainted" because neither had he been apprised of his rights nor had he made a meaningful waiver. Also decided before the trial, upon defense motion, was that Johanna Reigeluth would be required to absent herself from the courtroom except for the purpose of testimony.

The Tuesday the trial began (Monday had been Lincoln's Birthday), last-minute haggling was confined to Judge Hall's chambers. Defense counsel Gary Stanton wanted to bring in the psychiatric testimony and Ellis's history to convince the jurors, where the experts were not, that Richard Ellis suffered from "a mental disease" at the most, "a defect of reason . . . a state of mind incapable of distinguishing between right and wrong," at the least. But the latter required a formal plea of insanity which Stanton did not believe could be successfully established and would mean abandoning concurrent lines of defense. And all that stood between him and using the former as a strategy was County Attorney James Hood, Deputy County Attorney Robert Marks, Judge Ronald Hall and, as Hood put it, "the codes, canons, procedures, practices and Arizona Revised Statutes"; a diminished capacity to discriminate or control oneself was not a legal defense in

Arizona, nor did it mitigate criminal liability. But Judge Hall, who had himself testified before the state commission that was drawing up a new penal code, and had been considering the very question of a defendant's right to be both insane and aggressively defended, suggested that "undirected observations by the jury of the defendant may accomplish the same purpose. Though I warn you: no outbursts or lunatic behavior."

"So," Hood asked, "you going to put him on the stand?" Stanton shook his head. The Constitution and common law did not require a man to weave his own noose or drag his own cross. "Then what's your line?" the County Attorney sneered, "Consent?"

"It's all you've got, her credibility," Stanton said.

"She seduced him, right?" Marks scoffed. "Quite a swordsman—with a sharp implement."

"Show me a knife," Stanton replied, "and I'll discuss the point. One with his prints. The way I hear it you had six troopers combing the desert and you got diddly. You've got her word and I can't let it go unchallenged, because it's exactly worthless."

"I want to tell you, Gary," Hood smiled as they left Hall's chambers, "that I thought your brief was the best novel I've read in years. I especially liked the part about the State being responsible because we set the monkey loose."

"You people said he's sane. He never did."

As they entered the courtroom, Hood asked, "Maybe you'd like to switch ends of the table—have us on defense. Hmmm?"

"Good idea," Stanton agreed, all smiles. He slapped Hood's back lightly as they parted, and lent a guiding hand to young Marks, who crossed in front of him, the way one might offer a gratuitous lift to a nimble woman's elbow as she climbed a curb. To the spectators and the thirty-six veniremen awaiting the arrival of the Judge, this small byplay went largely unnoticed. Only a few wondered about such chummy camaraderie in an adversary proceeding. To most, the abutting tables of Prosecution and Defense represented a continuous spectrum from innocence to guilt: at the far end, the defendant, then his lawyer, Gary Stanton; the near end, County Attorney James Hood and his deputy,

Robert Marks; closest of all, the complainant's attorney, Edward Denning, assisting the State.

Empaneling a jury took the rest of the day, as considerations of strategy took bewildering turns. The prosecution in such cases usually preferred juries of young women and middle-aged, working-class men, whose chief compassion would be saved for the sullied victim. The young women would feel vicarious, sympathetic ravaging as the case unfolded, and the men would be avenging angels, vigilantes cloaked in legal wrath. So Stanton used his challenges to exclude the men: he felt they were dangerous, in fear and awe of women, likely to regard any sexual encounter as a small ransacking of the temple. When Stanton also asked that young women be excluded for cause, Hood rose to inquire "having in this venue but men and women, the State wonders who, in defense counsel's mind, in the wide realm of God in Arizona, is fit to be on this jury?" Stanton's request was denied. For its part, the prosecution used its preemptory challenges to exclude young men. Earlier that morning Hood had explained his reasons to Marks: "Who knows what's a crime to them? I don't want to have to defend the whole legal system to them just to hang one damned donkey." Still, two leaked through the sieve and Stanton was pleased: they were both vulnerable to the draft, and might identify with his client as the hapless victim of institutions.

They were joined by three middle-aged men, one retired; two white-collar workers whose sympathies and prejudices were equally obscure to both sides; and five women. The women were a puzzlement. Experience suggested they might be hanging jurors, but strange things were done with power and the secret ballot. They might be just as vicious and unforgiving to a loose-moraled complainant. Religious ones were known to forgive the Devil before the errant lamb. To them, rape might be poetic justice, accounts closed. Three of them were in their middle forties, too young to be surrogate mothers to the State's chief witness; and two were by all assumptions well past menopause. These last two hovered over the courtroom like disembodied consciences for the community, Madame deFarges knitting Girondist revenge in their brows.

Wednesday morning, Judge Hall's clerk called the assembled to order—lawyers, jurors, spectators, defendant, and court officers—in Division Six, room 376, Superior Court of Arizona in and for the County of Cochise, at Bisbee, the seat of the county of the crime's venue.

The clerk read the indictment handed down by the grand jury, in the stumbling-brook Celtic tongue that was the law's and then County Attorney Hood approached the lectern. He outlined the charges in more simple language and said they would be proved "not only beyond a reasonable doubt, but any doubt," through evidence and testimony he and Marks would present.

Then, briefly, he explained his case, so that they could fit the information into prepared slots as it came before them.

"By far the most serious charges," he said, "are, of course, kidnap and rape and attempted murder." He looked over his half-frames at Richie Ellis with barely contained violence and ill-disguised contempt. "You will quickly see the matters of kidnap and attempted murder as self-evident, by the facts we present. But let us look at the law as it regards rape." He then fixed the jury with a flinty, chilling look, daring any one of them to betray unnatural enthusiasms on peril of a beating. "As you will be reminded in Judge Hall's charge before you retire to deliberate, the essentials to be proved are three: There must be lack of consent. There must be a threat or use of force. And there must be actual penetration, no matter how slight. We will prove all these things.

"I regret that you will have to sit through the painful recitation of clinical details. There must necessarily be a lot of medical testimony and—" He looked over at Ellis as if to place the blame for the jury's woes where it belonged. "When it is over, you will have no doubt there was a real penetration, with force accompanying, over the complainant's objections, of her vagina by the defendant's penis." He took a deep breath and pushed back from the lectern, stretching. Now was the time to spike the defense cannons, so he leaned toward the jury again, and said, "It is the custom in matters of this kind to permit defense to attack the credibility of the State's witnesses, including and especially the complainant. This is only fair. We are trying a man for a terrible crime, a savage assault. You must decide whom to believe and how much.

"But bear this in mind. What is in question is consent. We are not trying 'the new morality' here. There is no rule that says the Constitution and laws of Arizona only apply to virgins." Once, in a similar case, he had said, quoting an old legal precept, "even a prostitute has the right to pick her customers," and found it a mistake, so he revised his phrasing.

"I urge you all to listen carefully," Hood wound up, "and hold your minds open until all the facts are in, then decide the case upon those facts as you see them. We are interested in only one thing here: justice. All of us. And I am confident you will conclude that justice points to the guilt of the defendant. There were some awful crimes committed out there in the desert. Richard Ellis stands accused of them. In the name of the People's Peace of the State of Arizona, I urge you pay close attention, so you can give this man what— you will see—he so obviously denied his victim: justice."

Hood sat down and Stanton rose for the defense, a zero-sum relationship; when both were up or both down it was only because there were logical problems. Hood quietly shuffled through his briefcase as Stanton began to speak. "May it please the Court," Stanton said, nodding to the bench and his counterparts. Hood looked up and blinked in reply. The County Attorney would depart after the morning session, leaving the trial to young Marks, having set up the courtroom as he wanted to: imposing his strong character over it all. He'd leave the jury as children told to behave until their father returns. Stanton knew this, but knew that Marks would have to work hard to keep the jury's confidence. For, to many eyes, Marks appeared simply too young to be wielding such power over a man's life.

Stanton stood away from the jury, by his seat, disdaining the lectern, almost shyly fingering the table's polished edge. His manner was benign, at times sweet, perhaps lugubrious, all of it studied, in contrast to Hood's commanding sternness—which masked slick political boredom—and Marks' eager, conceivably ambitious style. Stanton looked like a solid citizen and good neighbor, while Hood, hill-country in all manners, still looked like he had coexisted with crooks too long. As prosperous as Gary Stanton appeared, his reticence scraped his feet on the jury's doorstep. He cast himself wholly with his client, two innocents caught up in the wrong web. "This case is not so simple as the State would have you believe," he said, preferring the Kafkaesque chill of "the State" to "the People."

"Virtually all of the facts are in dispute. The main charges rest on the testimony of one witness who . . . whose story you will have to weigh. Can you believe it? Beyond a reasonable doubt? Enough to send a man to prison on that uncorroborated—" He was interrupted by Marks who jumped up objecting that the question of punishment was irrelevant to the jury's function, which was solely a finding of fact and guilt. The objection was sustained, and Stanton continued. Hood knew the objection was just what Stanton wanted. Irrelevant as it might technically be, punishment was ever in the jury's mind, and Stanton had flushed the prosecution out as legalistic hardhearts, neatly zapping Hood's pious invocation of "justice."

Now Stanton underscored it. "Usually," he said, edging closer to the jury box, "in cases of this kind, where corroboration is absent, the State will ask for a lesser charge. That has not happened here. So it is left to you and to me to search for justice.

"You will see witnesses testifying to peripheral matters. But there is only one—one witness—to the main matter alleged. She has this terrible power of the State at her disposal. And you must judge her, her credibility, whether you believe her story or not—for yourselves. I too urge you to dispense justice as we know it in Arizona. Fair and compassionate *equal* justice."

He ranged quickly over some of his technical arguments, soliciting the Judge's imprimatur for his vernacular translations of the law's convoluted prose. Then, out of this woods, he tried to dress up his main argument with a little cheesecake.

"What it may all mean, when all the voices are heard, is that my client may have himself been a victim, ladies and gentlemen, ensnared by the games of a clever and cynical woman." The last word rolled off his tongue with archness and sarcasm buried in it like the charge of an artillery shell. While not offending the female jurors, it would penetrate and explode in connotations: "woman," not, as the female jurors were, "ladies"; not "girl," "young lady," or "Miss"—too frail were the images they evoked. Not "Mrs. Reigeluth" certainly. That would associate her with estates and institutions of franchise, communities who rightly feared the molestor and sociopath. Stanton would rather she was lumped with nonfreeholders, transients, kinky, rootless outsiders. "Woman": even the female jurors shivered at the term, with its scarlet undertones of "the woman," "that woman," "younger woman."

"Ultimately, what may shock you most of all is the absence of facts. The charges are unreliable. They are based on insinuations, deductions, suppositions. An alleged act of force took place, you have been told. Look for a weapon: you will find vapors. An alleged act of intercourse—uncorroborated—you are told took place. What stands behind that but one woman's word?

"It may be painful for you," he concluded, "but I remind you a man's liberty is at stake." This time, Marks only raised a pencil and Judge Hall sustained his objection. Stanton wheeled around, and asked with fine moral outrage, "Does the State want us to pretend that this is a debate and not a grave—"

"The State," Hood barked before Marks could reply, "says learned counsel should be admonished for deliberately disregarding the Court's instructions." Nonetheless, despite Judge Hall sustaining the State's objection, the weight of the action again was to generate sympathy for the defendant.

"Our job here," Stanton finished, wanting to end more neatly, and so drifting to a position behind his client, framing him with his arms, as though personally sponsoring the man's innocence, "is to distill fact from fiction," wondering as he did so if he could have those excluded psychiatrists speak as character witnesses. They were members of the defendant's only real "community," they knew his reputation, could speak knowledgeably and well in his behalf, and one of them had summarized his prior history as including "chronic impotence." Stanton asked the jury "to sort truth from allegation, thereby to do *justice*." And he sat down, more priest than lawyer, his soliciting but for trust and confidence, his petition one for mercy from great magisterial and primitive forces, his very collar turned in intercession.

State's witnesses took the stand all day: the Highway Patrol and Sheriff's Deputies who had located Johanna's car and apprehended Ellis, the Pima County detectives who interviewed Johanna, the Cochise County detective who found Ellis's fingerprint fragments on the car windows and steering wheel. Ellis's aunt said her nephew told her nothing except that "a nice girl gave him a lift to town." If that was a point for the prosecution, it also did not exclude a reasonable contention that Johanna had indeed dropped Richard Ellis off. Nevertheless, it was a perfect People's case being built, sweeping away any posture of total ignorance by Ellis.

The jury was excused while Marks reargued, without success, for the introduction of Ellis's blurted admissions.

Then came a Cochise County Sheriff's Deputy who explained lineup procedure and how Johanna Reigeluth had, without hesitation, picked Richard Ellis out from among nine men, several of whom bore a passing resemblance to him.

When Stanton bothered to cross-examine, it was perfunctory. The afternoon droned on with torpor settling in as a parade of witnesses built the chain of evidence: the admitting physician from the hospital, the couple from the service station. Under cross-examination, the couple said the girl had arrived with a truck driver who vanished quickly, and that she said nothing about being raped, that she had, in fact, denied it when asked. "But if you want my opinion . . ." the wife volunteered, cut off when Stanton shook his head. Nor would Judge Hall permit it on redirect by Marks. Outside, in the witness room, as she left, the woman put a hand on Johanna's shoulder, offering support. She said, "They're with you, honey."

Stanton's probing was without any ostensible plan of attack, idiosyncratic, and generally fruitless. There were few soft spots to find—not only because his client was palpably guilty, but because Stanton, at this point, was bored. He questioned witnesses without moving from the counsel table; and aside from the dubious nuggets offered by the service station couple, he seemed to expect none to be found.

All Stanton wanted to do on this first day of testimony was stay in sight, riding the State's slipstream, drawing what strength he could from the obverse of every prosecution coin: Ellis making no attempt to escape capture meant surrender, perhaps, but also, if flight would indicate a guilty frame of mind, an air of innocence. Ellis had been docile because he knew the jig was up, the prosecution implied, while the defense hinted back that Ellis had had nothing to hide. Stanton's fallback position was still reasonable in any event: if not innocent, Ellis displayed repeated stupidity to a degree which was clinically alarming.

But by day's end, Deputy County Attorney Robert Marks had constructed a pretty pattern with a solid beginning and a solid end. The next day he would offer the missing middle: Johanna Reigeluth's direct testimony. It would connect every strand of evidence: the police and medical reports, the location of her car, the service station couple's story.

Marks wanted the jury to sleep on what they had, knowing that his hints had created a receptive environment. In the night their imaginations would supply the explanation, as much as if he had denied them the last reel of a thriller.

They would be ready to believe Johanna Reigeluth on the second day.

Thursday opened with the jury excused while Gary Stanton made a curious gesture. He moved for a mistrial on the grounds that "the complainant's membership in the local press" jeopardized his client's right to a fair trial. Robert Marks countered that "the Sixth Amendment cuts both ways. He is entitled to a speedy and public trial." But Stanton urged: "and a fair one. He is entitled to press coverage—but also to protection from its bias."

Judge Hall asked Stanton, "You are not contending that he is being tried in the press, are you?"

"I'm suggesting that his accusers are being unfairly protected at his expense, and I am prepared to submit comparisons between the reporting of other, similar cases and this one—which is chiefly marked by its subdued tone."

Judge Hall rejected this. "It seems to me you are asking for the kind of coverage that might pollute the jury's mind. I'm inclined toward the position that I can enjoin coverage with a gag order, sequester the jury, or hold editors and reporters in contempt—but not direct what kinds of stories they may write. That is outside the competence of this Court. I think the motion is frivolous and capricious. Denied." Then the State called Johanna Reigeluth.

The jurors were pleasantly surprised at how pretty she was. She looked like a girl on her way to Easter morning church services. Some, in fact, wondered just how dim-witted Ellis was if he managed such fine discrimination in his choice of victims; others, though, speculated at what provocations he might have been subjected to. The emotional reactions to a witness's unfair share of the limited resource of beauty or privilege was a common point of after-trial debate. Some citizens, even judges, regarded grace, access, wealth, the inelastic rewards of work or luck, as natural wonders, freakish for their very loveliness, entitled to protection from the meaner grime of democratic daily life. Others saw them as elitist, socially out-of-balance, and thus deserving of defilement. There were many ways subtle bias could run, all unpredictable. So County Attorney Hood had advised Johanna on presentment: "Walk slowly and keep your eyes on the ground. Don't look anyone in the eye too long—especially the jury or the defendant, though with the judge it's all right. Act demure, wounded, scandalized when you talk about sex——"

"Sounds like I'm running for Miss America," she had said, grimacing.

"You are," Hood replied firmly. "But don't look like you're enjoying it—you won't. Don't smile and don't, uh"—he smiled at the gloominess of these commandments—"dress like a hippie. How do I put this? You, uh, have to seduce the jury."

On the stand, she gave her name and identifications, the make and registration of her car, the time of departure on the day in question, and the direction of her travel. Marks repeated each of her answers as he posed the following question, in a near-monotone, unsure of the appropriate solicitude, but clear in the matter of building a logical chain. She said, with but bare hesitation to skirt clear of her security oath, that she was headed to see friends. It hardly mattered: she never got there. "Now you were driving east on Interstate 10, toward the junction of U.S. 80 and Arizona 90, from Tucson. Now this was a common route for you?"

"My husband works in Tombstone—off U.S. 80."

"Would you continue please, and tell us what happened?"

"I saw a man hitchhiking," she said. "I stopped to pick him—I saw him on the side of the road and I stopped for him. He had his thumb out. You know, trying to flag a ride."

"Can you identify this man at this time for us? Is he in this courtroom? And if he is, would you point him out, please?"

"Yes—him. The defendant." Marks was pleased she had not used a dramatic gesture to finger Ellis but, rather, an efficient and timid one, as though unwilling to confront him directly. Judge Hall stipulated for the record that the witness had identified the accused in open court. As Hall spoke, Johanna turned halfway toward him, then fixed her sight on her own knees. Out of the corner of her eyes she had seen something behind the judge: the bas relief scales of justice on the wall. From this angle, they looked rather like a crucifix wilted into fallopian tubes. Marks established that she had not seen Ellis at any other time before the day in question or since, except at the police lineup where she identified him.

"Now, Mrs. Reigeluth," he said, "would you describe

for us, in your own words, everything that happened after the defendant entered your car?"

She began to recall the incident, reciting in a dry, almost indifferent voice, looking at her hands as she spoke, taking slow short breaths. She studied her fingertips and cuticles as she described how Ellis had pulled a knife, made her turn into the desert, and tied her up. At odd moments she looked up suddenly from her lap for reasons not obviously related to testimony, a snorkeler coming up for air. At those times, Marks and the jury would take an instant's measure of her expressions, to see if her composure was deteriorating, then avert their eyes.

"Now this is important," Marks said, facing the jury. He turned to Johanna. "I don't mean to make you relive this nightmare—this waking nightmare—any more than necessary. But you must be very specific about what happened from this point on—"

"I'll try," she responded. Her testimony plunged into the part the jury had been waiting for: how Ellis slapped her and made her take off her shirt, which was offered in evidence. She began to worry that she might be boring the jurors, that her struggling for words from time to time, necessary to keep her own interest alive by finding new ways to describe the same things, was begging their patience.

She told of the rape and the beating, and it took longer than the actual events. At each junction in the story, Robert Marks summarized her previous testimony and restated it as a question for her to reconfirm before moving on. Her recital started off strongly and she even thought she might seem too reconstituted, too reportorial to have been so threatened. But the tale was still a painful one and her attention wandered from it at times. She played with her hem unconsciously, or watched to see the minute hand of the wall clock jump with startling suddenness.

She had described it all maybe ten times before, to policemen, to Warren, to Denning, to the grand jury, to the prosecutors. Only Tyler Bowen, of everyone she knew, had not pressed for details, preferring to soothe her cuts rather than dissect them. But now, with all the strangers in the courtroom, with its hard wood and impenetrably institutional ambience, its unforgiving angles and unfamiliar faces, she felt weak and silly. She was exposed again before all those jurors and court officers, before Ellis again, who listened dumbly, as though happy to be the focus of so much interest. She felt naked, in this wide and cold room, in a desert again, watching herself being watched by everyone as she described the penetration. The right of gynecologic privacy fell before the community's right to safe streets. She squirmed a little in her chair, feeling some nervousness in such exhibitionism; it did not come naturally and her excited state made her flushed and sweaty. She even worried that she might find her own story subconsciously stimulating, or its telling so dizzying, that she might give off signs and scents of sexual excitement. She edited the story down, to gain control of it, and did not tell how, the last time, she was forced, just to save her life, to seduce her own rapist.

When she was through Johanna looked drained, and Robert Marks said, "Thank you, Mrs. Reigeluth. I know what you've been through. I'm sorry." He turned slowly on his heel, eyeing the defendant, Ellis, with sad anger, then said as he sat down, "Your witness." Stanton was already on his feet, shuffling through some papers, wanting to change the tone and pace. Johanna sat still, vulnerable on the stand, waiting. She looked up at Judge Hall for advice and he raised his eyebrows at Stanton.

"Defense cross?"

"Thank you, Your Honor," Stanton replied in animated friendliness. He approached the witness box and Johanna flinched slightly. He backed off, and gazed at her warmly to put her at ease. "Mrs. Reigeluth, I know you've been through a very difficult, uh, exercise. So . . . Your Honor? May I request an early break for lunch?" He dropped his pose of concern when he turned to the bench. "I'd like to let the jury calm down and stretch before I start cross-examination," he said in a confidential whisper, loud enough for the jury to pick up. "That was a very emotional song-and-dance she gave them and I'd like them to put some pasta on it—so they can listen better and so I don't seem like such an ogre." With no objection from the State, Judge Hall ordered a recess until one o'clock. Everyone left quickly, but Johanna didn't budge until the bailiff told her to come back at one.

"Don't be silly, Warren. Go, by all means," Maureen said at lunch. She had been late for court that morning and had not gotten a chance to talk to Johanna at all, so when lunch began, she began. Warren had been in court both days, and now both Maureen and Johanna were urging him not to skip yet another scheduled appointment, this one a seminar he was to teach in Tucson. Maureen herself had not been in court the previous day because of a network affiliate's meeting she had to prepare for. "Face it," she said to Warren, not unfondly, "if you *are* sitting out there, darling, and they ask Johanna how things are at home . . ." She rolled her head back as though considering nuclear warfare. "You just know her inappropriate sense of timing about these things. She'd probably tell the truth, God help us!"

Unconvinced, Warren bowed to the group pressure when even Edward Denning, their lawyer, said it was "a perfectly all right thing to do," and Johanna fixed it by telling him she thought he was being very kind to her when he had no reason to be.

Denning had been there every day and always swept up the lunch checks, his manners nothing but palmy, though it would all be in the later bill, Maureen knew. "You're a good witness, dear," he told Johanna at lunch. "You should be proud of her, Maureen." Catching Johanna's gape of disbelief, Maureen winked and kept chatting with Warren.

"I'm surprised how tedious it is. Well, not surprised," Johanna said. At this, Denning embarked upon a short rhapsody on the law's grandeur, but though he spoke ever louder, only Warren was riveted. Johanna grew smaller, offering, "I still say it's boring. Sorry." So Warren and Denning wrapped themselves around an intense discussion of the law, while Johanna mouthed, "bore, bore, bore," in pantomime. Leaning over to her daughter, Maureen whispered, "They're *made* for each other!" and the two women giggled like sisters, while Denning compared the law to a raveling tapestry, "an evolving language, a symphony whose aesthetic is its adherence to its own grammar." Warren, intense, wanted to know about equity and fairness; specifically, he wanted Denning's thoughts on the notion that "justice comes from nature. Law comes from the legislature as the interpreter of power." Denning listened further before Warren would allow a response, as Warren built an argument which obliged one conclusion: that social law, human justice, should serve majority interests. For Warren felt as though Richard Ellis had stuck the knife into something soft in his own flesh, and he wanted validation for the unclear retributive urge he felt. "Is that what you think?" Denning replied. "Very interesting."

Another cup of coffee and Johanna kissed Warren good-bye, excusing herself. The conversation was calming, but as the hour-and-a-half elapsed her anxiety mounted. It would not do to undergo cross-examination with a full bladder.

When court resumed, Gary Stanton began his cross-examination. "I don't mean to add to your discomfort," he said, "but I'd like to go over some of your testimony from this morning. All right?" She nodded and he began to ask her about each part of her story, looking for weaknesses in character and plot. She'd been expecting an orals examiner and found a familiar figure, a skeptical editor: "Is that what actually happened?" "Is that a quote?" "Did you observe that then or reconstruct it subsequently?" Neither Marks nor Denning thought this a particularly useful approach. "You say," Stanton asked in the same drone, "you are married?"

"Yes, I am."

"And your husband is in this courtroom?"

"No, he isn't." In the gallery, Maureen sat forward and tapped Edward Denning's shoulder, glaring down her nose at him when he swiveled around. He turned back and began to counsel Marks forcefully.

"Why is that?" Stanton asked.

"He's teaching this afternoon."

"But he was here this morning?"

"Yes—and the day before—and he'll be here tomorrow." Judge Hall interrupted to caution her about volunteering more than was asked, and Marks rose to object to the whole line of questioning as immaterial. Overruled.

"I'm sure he will be here tomorrow," Stanton said, earning for himself the Judge's rebuke about gratuitous remarks. Apologizing formalistically, still scratching, Stanton asked, "How would you describe your marriage?" His curiosity at the faint, amused smile on Johanna's lips was distracted by Judge Hall's headshake rejection of a protest by Marks which had not been more than a raised pencil of objection.

"Average," Johanna answered, and Maureen was sighing.

"Not—happy, or unhappy?"

"Average," she repeated. The jury tittered with recognition, but Stanton's curiosity was aroused. It was a funny question to hedge. Why not say "happy" and be done with it, unless there was some extrinsic evidence to the contrary? Still, witnesses were strange birds, prone to unnatural fits of honesty over the most irrelevant things.

"Average?" he asked. "I don't know what that means. Do you fight?"

"About average," Johanna said, quickly unhappy for it, embarrassed at her own coyness. Marks winced and Denning squinted, shaking his head imperceptibly, trying to signal her. "I'm sorry. Yes. We fight a little."

He asked whether they had perhaps fought the day she met Richard Ellis. "No," she said.

"You're sure?"

"Yes," she answered firmly.

"What did you talk about that day?"

"I, um, don't recall," Johanna said.

"When was the last time you saw your husband that day—before the incident?"

Johanna answered again, "I, uh, don't recall."

"Well, did you see him *at all?*"

"I don't think so."

"I don't understand. You don't think you *saw* your husband that day?" he asked.

"To the best of my recollection, no, sir."

"I must say, I'm confused. Does one of you leave for work before the other one's up? Was he out of town?"

Now it was he who regretted being coy, so he rephrased his question before she could respond. In doing so he inadvertently eased her dilemma. "Are you, at this time, living together?"

"Yes," she said evenly.

"And on good terms?"

Johanna blushed. "Average." Even Stanton laughed at the exitless cloverleaf they were in. "It's—" she began, but thought better of it.

"I'm sorry? I didn't hear."

"Nothing," she said, wagging her head like an eraser.

"And at the time of the event in question, you were —you did not see him. *Were* you living together?"

"No," she said, as efficiently and softly as possible.

"You were not?"

"That's correct," Johanna said, sucking in her lower lip.

"Well, let me see. Have you been reconciled since then? Is that why you're living together now?"

Johanna hesitated and said, "Ye—I guess, yes."

"You guess? You *guess?* I'll come to the point: are you living together for reasons relating to this trial?"

"Well, yes and no."

Stanton half-whispered, "Pick one," incurring a harsh grumble from Judge Hall. *"Why* are you presently living together and—let's jump ahead so you can be perfectly clear in your answers—are you planning a divorce after this trial?"

"I'm not—uh—" Johanna wondered what to say. "It's not sure."

"Well, let me ask you: Was your separation at the time of the incident preparatory to a divorce?"

Johanna decided to go straight at the truth. "Yes."

"And have you changed your mind about that?"

"No."

He sighed, "Then why are you living together now?"

Johanna reclaimed some of her losses with a concession of error: "It seemed like a way to avoid embarrassment." She blushed as though baring her neck. "That sounds a little silly now, doesn't it?" And Stanton fattened her with a reassurance that it was an inconsequential matter. To the jury, however, it seemed at least like a clumsy attempt to manipulate their opinions.

"Your Honor," Stanton snapped, "I would like to move at this time for a mistrial." Judge Hall denied it in the same instant. "Very well," said Stanton, returning to Johanna. "Who, if anyone, advised you to do this? To resume cohabitation?"

"My husband, and my moth—*our* attorney, Mr. Denning."

"The gentleman sitting at the prosecution table? Your Honor, will the Court reconsider my motion?"

"No," Hall said. "But let the record indicate it was made in a timely fashion—and that the indicated party, Mr. Edward Denning of Scottsdale, is assisting the County Attorney's Office for the purpose of trial."

Then Stanton elicited the information that Denning had first suggested the idea—postponement of the divorce and a temporary end to the separation—after a meeting at the County Attorney's Office. Marks pointedly objected that such testimony was "hearsay and speculation—the witness is incompetent on this." And Judge Hall told Johanna to report only what she had firsthand knowledge of.

Gary Stanton approached the matter with a shotgun. "Did you at any time receive any instructions from the County Attorney's Office or any member of his staff or anyone in the employ of the State, from the police or members of the judicial departments, suggesting to you in any manner other than that you should tell the whole and complete truth, regarding your comportment and testimony?"

Johanna took a deep breath and said, "Well, I suppose, in a—" Stanton wheeled around as if to nail Robert Marks in the act of signaling the witness. He shot the young prosecutor a disapproving look, but Marks was unfazed, scornful of the trivial issue Stanton was beating to death.

"What were you told?" Stanton demanded, still looking at Marks.

"I object!" Marks finally said impatiently. "This whole line is—"

"Your Honor, the State has been coaching the one material witness. Its whole case is—"

"I did no such thing, Your Honor," Marks said, matching Stanton stride for stride to the bench. "I was there at all the interviews and she was told simply to tell the truth as she told it to us. I'll take the stand and so will Mr. Hood if you want—"

Judge Hall interjected that he'd rather see a "quick end to this nonsense."

Marks picked up the cue: "We simply told her to be honest and watch out for cheap tricks like this because he'd try to make her look bad—"

"Your Honor! This is not some cheap trick—but an attempt to preserve my client's rights from the prosecution's stage-managed testimony!" But Hall had heard enough and ordered Stanton to end the line of testimony after another question.

So Stanton thought a moment and asked, "In the time that your husband has been living with you—for the convenience of your peace of mind during this trial —have you had any sexual relations?" Marks, outraged, was nearly on his feet when the matter was mooted.

"No," she said. She had, unknowingly, stepped nimbly out of a careful trap Stanton had set, which would be to admit she might have loveless sexual relations, even with her husband; while not exactly a criminal offense, jurors had been known to disapprove.

"I'd like to yield this witness," Stanton said, "subject to recall for further testimony during defense's case." Both Marks and Judge Hall insisted there was no reason why the examination could not be completed all at once. But Stanton argued that this was the one eyewitness to the charges, and it was necessary to bring her back when the defense was building its refutation. Judge Hall expressed his dissatisfaction, but acceded.

On redirect, Marks asked, "For the record, Mrs. Reigeluth, what did the People tell you regarding your testimony?"

"To tell the whole truth and—beware of traps that might trick me into looking bad."

"Objection," Stanton yawned.

"Sustained," Hall said, and excused the witness subject to recall. The jury, initially happy to have Johanna's

402

testimony, was glad to have this confusing blizzard of lawyerly backbiting ended.

For the rest of the day, the State brought forth redundant medical witnesses, including an attending doctor from the University Hospital who mentioned that he had seen the complainant before "when she and her husband brought in a child who had fallen out of a Ferris wheel." The people from the gas station were also back. The husband heard Johanna's testimony read back, saying she thought the woman was "a busybody—she kept emptying ashtrays even when there was nothing in them. I didn't say anything because—I didn't think they had a right to know."

The woman's husband listened and then added, "I'll tell you—Carol is the biggest snoop. She's always poking into other people's news." He confirmed that his wife had speculated about rape from the moment Johanna crossed their threshold, to which Stanton objected. But the man added, "I think the girl was uncomfortable."

The man's wife denied her husband's characterization, saying, "He spends all his time with his nose in the paper—how'd he ever know? That and looking at pretty girls and pulling up weeds is all he ever does. You come out to our place. Weeds is all we have growing about. But he—" Judge Hall, with the consent of both sides, excused them from further participation, and they drifted off into the hallway, still bickering.

By the close of business Thursday, the jury had heard more police reports read in the dry monotone of civil servants who could find no emotional distinction between shoplifting and battery. Everyone in the courtroom by then felt the tight kinship that developed in an extended trial. They now had a multileveled set of shared experiences, from light interludes to open hostilities, unbeheld by outsiders. They were family.

The next day, Friday, opened with the prosecution resting, its case wrapped up with a ribbon. Stanton offered the formality of a motion for summary dismissal, but it was denied. Now the jury was impatient. Stanton stood between them and what was clearly a simple vote

403

before the gallows could be erected. Ellis was guilty or no one was, the jury already believed with utter unanimity. All Stanton could do was fight the tide.

The jury was removed while Stanton made another motion, for the admission of psychiatric testimony, "by the state's own examiners," and Ellis's history of unsuccessful institutional care. But Judge Hall and Deputy County Attorney Marks would have none of it. Yielding, Stanton was cautioned that if he tried to cause a mistrial by insinuating Ellis's dementia before the jury he risked a contempt citation, and what chance he might have of winning an appeals reversal on errors would be greatly diminished.

In the teeth of this he began his short parade of psychiatric "character witnesses" over loud protests from Marks. They had little of value to say about Ellis's character, and were not permitted to speak professionally, though one did range across that barrier until alertly enjoined. Those remarks were stricken from the record and the jury instructed to disregard them, which of course they would not. Nor did the jurors need to stretch their minds to infer how Ellis came to be in such distinguished company. They knew he was not Viennese; now they suspected that he was crazy or no one was.

Through all of this, Johanna listened for stray phrases filtering into the witness room where she sat. She busied herself reading a new book; she made lists of things to do before she left town. And each night, in the privacy of her home, she wrote Tyler Bowen a letter. "I know it's classic," she wrote, "but here I am, the thirteenth juror. Right now I feel like a child who's been sent to bed while the grownups stay up at a party. I *miss* being in the courtroom, even though when I'm there it's a little confusing and sometimes hurts. I'd just like to *see* it. And I know you'll say this is perfectly typical, but I also feel bad for that poor man. (Warren says I wouldn't have pressed charges if he was a Negro. Isn't that charming? And he also says I wouldn't feel so sorry for him if he *was*. I say that's a contradiction, but Warren doesn't.) I hope he gets treatment —not Warren, although he could use it too—yet from what I hear the care so far is pitiful. He must feel really abandoned. I do, too: I miss you."

When Gary Stanton called Johanna Reigeluth back to the stand for more cross-examination on Friday afternoon, Judge Hall repeated his scolding for not concluding it the first time. "We apologize, Your Honor," Stanton said perfunctorily. "But we expected to develop new lines of inquiry which require this witness's recall. I believe we have, sufficiently to justify it." Equally perfunctory was Marks's accusation of "thinly veiled theatrics to gull the Court and the jury." Stanton all but conceded it with a wink over his spectacles.

This time, Warren was sitting next to Maureen, a family in a pew attending one child's First Communion. Prior to the session, Warren had asked Marks in the hallway, "just as a point of information," what his opinion was of the irony in Johanna's repeated testimony, "while that son-of-a-bitch sits there snug as a bunny—silent—with his P&I," which was to say, "privileges and immunities," against self-incrimination.

"As a point of information?" Marks answered, feeling crowded, "You're right. It's ironic. Is that all?"

"It's bullshit!"

Marks laughed, "That, too. Tell you what: come the revolution and you and me, we'll decide who's guilty by the set of their eyes or their *names*—to hell with their civil rights. Right?"

"Let us calmly, now," Stanton told Johanna on the stand, "reconstruct your testimony about that afternoon." He was friendlier than he had been the other day, almost courtly. Indeed, he seemed fatherly. "You were driving down the Interstate—by your testimony, toward Benson?" Marks squirmed exaggeratedly in studied fatigue at the repetitive questions. Johanna said it was correct. "Why?" Stanton asked.

"Why?"

"I'm sorry if my question is unclear. It's my fault. Why were—*where* were you going?"

"To see some people," she said, not wishing to take the easy choice of saying "Tombstone, to see my husband," lest she be tripped again by a fib. And Stanton went on, wasting time, reconfirming details so staggeringly irrelevant that Robert Marks was not moved to object, even though Denning kept suggesting it and Hall looked as though he expected it. These questions were the gaspings of a beached mackerel, a vague effort to convince a doomed client of lawyerly diligence—even though for Richie Ellis it would take a postcard to get the message through. This tangential excursion done, with the jury half-catatonic from their week-long bouts with inattention, Stanton floated back to the narrative line.

"Uh-huh," Stanton grunted, still floundering. "The—examination of your car's trunk when it was recovered describes several items: a tire iron, a spare tire, a green suitcase—people's exhibit number seven. Was that yours?"

"Yes," she said.

"Where were you going?"

She answered, "To the Grand Canyon for the weekend," and admitted through the courtroom titters that, yes, she knew it was "the other way."

"You were not going to go alone, were you?" Stanton asked and she said no. "Did you tell the defendant you were going to pick up your husband?"

"Yes," Johanna answered. "That should show I had no—" Stanton cut her off, asking, "But you were not?"

She admitted she was not.

"Now, were these people male or female?"

She replied, "Both," and admitted they did not include her husband. If forced to, she would name Susan Carver.

Stanton then asked for the names of "these persons —these *friends*—you were going to—"

Robert Marks bounced up with a procedural objection about limits of jurisdiction, explaining that the individuals were under federal color of law, employed at the National Laboratory installation at Gila Compound, and at the moment out-of-state; in either event not subject to the local court's compulsory process. All this was as infinitely boring to Judge Hall as it was to the jury, and Marks assured all that there was no pertinent information to be had from Gila Compound. Only Warren seemed affected by this. He squirmed uncomfortably in his seat. "In any case, she didn't get there," Marks said.

Stanton looked dubious and shrugged. "I only wanted their names." He wavered on the edge of requesting a recess to get depositions after all this fuss, but decided against it, largely because he thought it was pointless.

At the bench, Marks assured him none were minors, but testimonial availability was limited by national security considerations. Stanton rolled his eyes, and Marks said, "Well, she's a reporter."

"So," Stanton said, returning to Johanna, "you were on your way to pick up these unnamed persons at—"

Marks, who thought he'd had a truce, threw his hands up in despair. "Your Honor, hasn't this gone on long enough?"

"Is that an objection?"

Admitting it was not, Marks sat down.

"But I understand," said Stanton, "what the State is worried—"

This time Marks did object, sustained with a scolding from Hall that "defense counsel will confine himself to examination and cross-examination and presenting evidence—and leave the editorials to our friends in the press."

"I am sorry, Your Honor," Stanton admitted, all the more for having lost his edge of maturity over Marks in a poor gambit. "Let me approach this directly, Mrs. Reigeluth. In the suitcase, State's exhibit number seven, the following items were inventoried: toothbrush, paste, hairbrush, Johnson's baby shampoo, one new, unopened, man's chamois shirt, labeled L. L. Bean—"

"I told you, I was going away to the Grand Canyon," Johanna said.

"Yes. Lemon splash moisturizer . . . and item seven-K, State's exhibit seven-K, a diaphragm."

"Objection!" Marks called out with contrived annoyance, meant to show the jury he fully expected Stanton to move this way. "Counsel is needlessly degrading the witness, Your Honor."

Judge Hall, too, had expected this turn and said, "I want to instruct counsel to be careful here about the tone of his questions. I will not permit the abuse of witnesses in my courtroom. But counsel has made clear to me the purpose of this line of inquiry and I will permit it. I want to warn the members of the jury, however, to be very careful in their thinking: the facts of this case cannot be mitigated by the deportment of the complainant prior to the alleged incident. But you may draw upon this testimony when considering the question of credibility and consent. I also want to reassure the witness that the Court will insure that all due respect is accorded her in this examination. Proceed."

"Thank you, Your Honor," Stanton acknowledged. "Now this device, this diaphragm—also listed, um, I think it's seven-L, was a half-used tube of spermicidal jelly. These were yours?"

"Yes."

"Do you *always* travel with these, uh, things?"

Marks sucked his breath in slightly, seeing the trap, but Johanna looked at Stanton unruffled. "I did not own them until a few weeks before. I used to be on the pill."

"And at this time you were separated from your husband?"

"Yes." In the gallery, Warren was flushed.

"I assume they were to be used in the expected manner and function?" She felt embarrassed, nervous, and looked blankly at the gallery. Warren looked away. It was good of him to be there through this part, she thought. It must be worse on him. She had met Tyler shortly after having given up the pill. In fact, the transporting deliciousness of their first night was partly her sense of abandon and total vulnerability: she had been fertile as a frog that night and didn't give a damn. She just let go and fell and fell, carelessly, knowing her insides were throbbing with lively opportunity. Now, when she was playing it safe: "Mrs. Reigeluth? I ask you—"

"Yes—but I hadn't used them that day—"

"Please. Just answer the question. You were going away with some people. Were they married—*to each other?*"

The jury laughed while she exhaled, "No."

"One of them was a man?"

"Yes."

"But not your husband. Is that correct?"

"Yes."

"Was one of these people, so to speak, your *date?*"

"Yes," she said firmly.

"The man?" he asked.

She fixed him with a curious look, answering, "Yes, he was." The jury's thinking ranged from delight in the lurid possibilities Stanton's suggested couplings forced them to entertain—this was stuff they read about but never encountered, as good as a movie obscenity case —to mild disapproval of so casual a regard for marriage; yet she looked so . . . clean, and *normal.* "Mr. Stanton?" Johanna asked. "May I explain something?" He nodded warily. "You asked me if I was going to *see* more than one person, and I said yes. I didn't say I was going *away* with more than one. You just assumed that. I'm sorry if I caused confusion."

Stanton turned away from her and then asked, "Prior to the afternoon in question, had you engaged in acts of sexual relations with any or all of these people?"

Pupils in the jury dilated eagerly. Johanna looked uncomfortable. Warren pursed his lips, while Maureen patted him sympathetically on the wrist, and Deputy County Attorney Marks jumped up frenetically even as Edward Denning was about to prod him, requesting that Judge Hall "advise the witness of her rights to remain silent."

"What the . . . ?" Stanton screwed up his face as though smelling something awful.

Snapping out of his own reverie, Judge Hall explained, "You have the right, Mrs. Reigeluth, to refuse to answer questions which might tend to incriminate you. If you answer one question in this particular line you must continue to answer all related questions. Now I would remind you that the ground for refusal is that such testimony would 'tend to incriminate you.' If you believe it would—and for example, adultery and certain acts are, however technically, still a crime in this state —or if it were your intention to cross a state border with another person for immoral purposes—you may refuse."

Johanna's head swam. She felt strange and diminished, mumbling, "I guess, I—I guess I won't answer." There was something deliciously shady in that to her, no less than if she had been afforded an off-the-books opportunity to murder.

Stanton shook his head at the injustice. "Are you taking your Fifth Amendment rights against self-incrimination? Is that what you're doing?" She nodded, and Judge Hall instructed the disappointed jury that for the privilege to have meaning, they must not draw conclusions or adverse inference from its invocation, or be prejudiced by Stanton's expressions.

But Warren was under no such obligation. He turned to look at Maureen Poulson, wondering if she was part of the cuckolding conspiracy. She was sitting ramrod-stiff, eyes straight ahead. He'd assumed something like this all along, but it had never been confirmed. How many people had also known, he wondered, people who must have regarded him as some kind of fool to be trifled with?

Stanton gave a small shake of his head, as though amused by something he had thought of. "Well now," he asked, "as long as we're about it, why don't we put all the questions you don't want to answer in one—" Judge Hall cleared his throat in warning, so Stanton went right to it: "Are you a user of any narcotic substances prohibited by law?" Johanna peeped another refusal to answer. "Were you under the influence of any drugs, narcotic, hallucinatory—tranquilizers or diet pills, prescribed or prohibited—that afternoon?"

"No," she said firmly.

"For how long had you known your date?" Stanton asked, on another tack.

"About—two months." Now Warren began to boil, staring more at Maureen than Johanna.

"And during that time, was there any exchange of money or promise of—"

Marks's roaring objection startled the courtroom by its ferocity. But Johanna's "No! Never!" was already tripping out to moot it. She added sternly, while Marks sat down, "He was a friend of mine and my hus—"

"You don't have to give his name. We can call your husband to—" This was badgering, but no one objected.

Johanna offered "Tyler Bowen," finding the name had a strange new taste in this context, feeling bad for the sacrilege of injecting Tyler unawares into this condemnatory environment. Warren, damp, whispered in Maureen's ear that he was going to go out for some water, but she grasped him tightly by the wrist and froze him to the seat. She was sorry he had to sit through this, but leaving would wreck Johanna's tenuous composure—and esteem.

Johanna explained that he "had helped considerably when we had an accident," and that she began seeing him regularly subsequent to that, "Well, a little while after that."

"All right, let's move on now," Stanton said. "Is there anything you haven't told us—I know we've gone over it several times—about your discussion with the defendant when you picked him up?"

"No. I don't think so. I told you everything." Asked if she perhaps had a falling-out with her "friend" that day, she gave a firm "No." And likewise denied that she had seen him at all within the previous twenty-four hours.

"You did not see any man, your husband or—any other man—within the preceding twenty-four hours for any—social—reason?"

"No."

"Did you have sexual relations with—" Again Marks splenetically objected. But Judge Hall said she now had to answer, having already done so. Johanna shook it off crisply and said she had not. "And you were on good terms with your—date?" Stanton asked ingenuously. Johanna answered that she was going down to visit him, yes. Gary Stanton turned instantly hard: "So why and for what purpose did you pick up the defendant?"

"I told you: he looked tired. And it was hot out and I try to stop for people in the desert, if they need help."

"Do you suppose that's dangerous?"

"Lately, everyone tells me so," she admitted. "It's never been before."

"Did the defendant ask you that same question—whether you knew it was dangerous?"

"I think—yes, I remember he did."

"And your reply was?"

411

"Just an answer. I don't know. I—it was just an answer."

"Did you say, 'I do lots of things I shouldn't do' or 'I like to live dangerously'? Did you?"

He made them sound unfamiliarly lecherous, and Johanna gave a firm "No!"

"What did you say?" he demanded.

"I *may* have said, now that you remind me—I may have—you have to get the context right. I was talking to myself, nearly—"

"Loud enough to be heard?"

"Yes." He asked her to do as she had done then. "Well, he said, I think, 'Don't you know it's dangerous to stop for people on the road?' And I think I may have said, sort of half to myself, half to—you know, the wind—'I guess I do lots of things I shouldn't'—I don't remember exactly."

"Did you laugh when you said that?"

"I honestly don't remember, Mr. Stanton. It was— it's possible," she said, flicking her hands into the air to show she was speculating.

"Is it also possible the defendant might have interpreted those remarks to—" Stanton never got a chance to finish before Marks and Judge Hall shot him down for asking a conclusion from the witness. "Tell me," he tried. "Did you first meet your friend—your date— hitchhiking? Did you pick him up, too?"

"No." Johanna recited the circumstances of the Ferris wheel accident, which resolved one mystery for the jurors.

"Could you describe your clothing on the afternoon in question?" As she did, Stanton checked off the items against the State's exhibit list. "Now it's hard to offer an item in evidence by its absence," he said, "but were you wearing a brassiere?"

"I'm not sure. I don't think so."

"You don't remember?" Stanton asked incredulously.

"No, I don't think I was."

"Were you wearing—stockings?" he asked.

"No."

"Panties?"

"Yes, Mr. Stanton."

"Of that you're cert—of course: they're listed here."

"I'm certain."

"But no bra?"

"No."

Stanton turned his back on her and screwed up in overindicated thought. "You see, I don't mean to quibble, but at first you said you weren't sure. Now you are sure: you were not wearing a brassiere. This confuses me."

"I was not. And it's also true I didn't remember exactly until I thought about it." She was fencing rather well, even Stanton felt, and he nodded at the plausibility of her response.

"How often do you wear one, then? For the record."

"Sometimes. It depends on—it was hot that day and—well—" Stanton was holding up the leather skirt. Hardly tropical attire. She reddened, no less a good dramatist than Stanton. "I don't have all that much need for one. A bra." Stanton conceded another round with a smile, while the rest of the court murmured pleasantly at this minor intimacy.

Still smiling, but shifting the beat, Stanton asked, "And today?"

"Yes."

"You're wearing one today. A bra. After our discussion yesterday, I trust it's not a gift from the State—"

Marks bleated an exasperated objection, and Stanton bowed in apology. He rose from it and leaned across the witness bar to Johanna, smiling, then frowning, an avuncular impatience crossing his features. He backed off, but only an inch. "Tell me—do you know the definition of the word 'perjury'?"

"Your Honor!" Marks detonated apoplectically. "Counsel is harassing and attempting to intimidate the witness because of an insignificant and momentary hesitation in certitude which she admitted and which, in fact, was truthful under the terms of the question posed—notwithstanding the aimless and trivial nature of this truncated cross—"

"Not so, Your Honor," Stanton rebutted. "I can and will show several instances where this hostile witness has anticipated the thrust of a question and given a shaded or misleading response which has later been contradicted. The perjury statute specifically"—Marks waved an arm at him in disgust—"pertains to sworn statements, including affidavits in any State or judicial proceeding under explicit oath or implicit burden of verity, given falsely or in a manner intended to distort, omit, or disingenuously withhold material information. I move for a dismissal." Hall looked a little annoyed at having the statute recited to him. Rubbing his neck to wonder how any of that could be proved, he spoke a few words about the frail nature of human memory and the differing emphases placed on different things by people, and denied the motion. Still, he wagged a stubby finger at the witness and the whole courtroom, demanding truth, warning Johanna to be candid and eschew further coy responses. Then he once again instructed the jury to draw no inferences from the exchange, as they would have to judge the entire testimony.

Stanton completed his picture by eliciting from Johanna the various scents, shampoos, and talcs she was wearing that day. The jurors kinesthetically apprehended a pretty girl, braless, wearing a leather miniskirt and a cotton blouse, driving a Volkswagen, smelling of baby powder and Jean Naté Friction Pour le Bain.

"What was the subject of your conversation with the defendant?"

"The scenery. Thanksgiving." She quoted some of his remarks, and the jury realized it had no idea what the man sounded like. It only knew the crime through Johanna's words.

"Were you talking?"

"Some. I was being friendly, yes. But, then I got a little scared. He was distant—*spooky*."

"You picked up this man, a stranger, in the desert. But you were scared?"

She sighed. "He wasn't so scary before he got in."

After a short recess, Johanna began to recite the details of the assault again. This time Stanton was less argumentative, gently guiding her over the terrain, until he hit snags. Then he would toughen up.

"I want to be very precise here," he said. "You say

414

he held a knife and he forced you—tore your skirt off and forced you to lie down—"

"*Knocked* me down!"

"And then he raped you?"

"Yes," she answered unemotionally.

"This is the sixty-four-dollar question again: Did his penis actually enter your vagina?"

"Yes."

Stanton took a deep breath and looked to Judge Hall for a signal. The Judge blinked, and Stanton asked, "Now, as the only material witness to this event, I wonder if you could supply some corroboration for your story by—detail."

Johanna didn't understand. "The hospital people already told you—"

"No, no. You say you were raped. Could you describe the defendant—that part of him not readily observable?" The jury sat up straight.

Marks was on his feet again, protesting that this was outrageous cross-examination—but Judge Hall permitted it, for it bore on the matter of identification raised on direct examination. Marks then insisted that the accuracy of Johanna's description could only be tested by putting the defendant on the stand to display the evidentiary member. But Stanton waved a medical affidavit that, he said, contained all the relevant facts, and Marks sat down slowly, not believing this at all.

Johanna's memory was shaky, but she believed he was not circumcised. Then, still trying to think, she grimaced (no more than Warren in the gallery). She mumbled, "It's hard—to remember. I've been trying not to."

"No distinguishing marks at all?" Stanton asked, his voice full of misleading clues.

"It's—difficult. He was hitting me, and it was very scary, and—he wasn't *exposing* himself."

"All right. Was the penetration complete?"

"Yes."

"Deep?"

"Yes—*painful*—"

"Did he have an ejaculation?"

"Almost immediately."

"Inside you? He ejaculated inside you?"

"Yes—I think so. I don't—he came—he climaxed so quickly."

"Well, now this is important, you see, because the examining intern's report says seminal matter was removed from your vagina and uterine area. Someone's—live, not spermicidally destroyed—"

"His! That's all. His—the defendant's—"

"He was inside you when he climaxed."

"Yes!"

"Did you have a climax?"

"No!"

"Are you sure? I want a definite answer." She looked to Marks to wonder why they didn't intercede in this badgering, but Stanton said, "I'm sure *he* doesn't know. *Did* you?"

"I did not!" Johanna snapped impatiently.

"Do you have one frequently with your partners?"

Now: "Objection!" from the prosecution bench.

Judge Hall agreed: "I am going to sustain this objection. I have permitted the previous question as it may shed some light on the matter of consent. But this—no. This is an area we don't belong."

"Your Honor," Stanton pleaded, "I would like to establish whether the woman was sexually satisfied, or on the prowl. Whether she was, in fact, returning from or leaving one unsatisfactory sexual encounter still excited—possibly trapping an unwary victim."

"You will have to approach that with other questions, sir," Judge Hall replied stonily. "And you have the witness's testimony concerning the prior twenty-four hours—"

"Thank you. All right, again—during the twenty-four hours before—"

"No!" Johanna wearily insisted.

"Very well. Here's a point which bothers me: You said there was a knife. Have you any idea what might have become of it?"

"No idea."

"Could you describe it?"

"A hunting knife. A black—or brown—ridged handle. A kind of, I guess, Bowie blade. About four to six inches. No, six to eight."

"Thank you. An excellent description of a knife—"

Johanna slumped a little in her chair, grateful to have reached dry land. "But you can't describe the defendant beyond 'maybe uncircumcised'? This knife is unavailable to us for comparison, but—"

"I think it wasn't circumcised. It was red—very red —and brown on the underside and that's about—I guess about—" She paused, flushed and breathing quickly, looking for the right phrase—"about as long as the knife. It hurt very much. It must be—must have been—longer than average." She sank back a little, tired.

"You say ejaculation was immediate upon entrance. Yet—he did get all the way inside you? You say it was painful. Are you—were you—ah, how do I ask this— was entrance easy?"

"No. It was *very* painful."

"But he slipped right in. I don't understand the discrepancy. His penis went way up in your vaginal cavity—were you lubricated, excited, or what?"

"No."

"And you did not, you say, have an orgasm."

"No, I did not. I did not enjoy it. He was hitting me—he *raped* me, Mr. Stanton, and he was hitting me—"

"Were you struggling?"

"For a while. Sometimes he hit me when I was struggling, and sometimes when I wasn't."

"I won't beat around the—I will not pursue this any more. Before you took the stand, expert—we have testimony that—" Marks objected so violently Johanna flinched, and so emotionally that he lost his advantage in being correct. His was the legally valid point: such previous testimony was not "expert," nor were any medical or psychiatric expressions used in those vague statements to be deemed competent or admissible. The jury was instructed what to disregard, but Johanna was not. Mostly they tended to disregard such instructions: an expert was an expert. "Tell me," Stanton asked a tense Johanna, "did you notice at any time that the defendant was impotent?"

"All I know is he raped me, Mr. Stanton, and he wasn't impotent. Maybe—" she was afraid some medical point had been established that would undermine her word—"if your expert was a woman—"

"She was."

"—out there in the desert. I don't know. I, all I know, is what happened. He wasn't. Not then. But—later, yes, he was. Soon." Stanton had headed back toward his table to get something, to begin another line, and the slight pause, his turning on his heel, frightened her, so she sought to make noise, to make her story more plausible, by adding truth, cautiously. "That's why he was hitting me."

"What happened?" he asked.

Johanna hesitated and looked to the floor between the witness chair and the jury box, then quickly away, then out toward her mother and Warren, not seeing them at all. "I, uh, well, he tried to do it again, you know. But it was too—soon or—well, he was soft. I saw it. It was shriveled, and, uh—dripping—useless." She sniffled. "That's when he really started hitting me again—because he couldn't get it, uh, in me again—" This information, which she need not have volunteered except to help supply logic she was not responsible for, to reconcile two seemingly contradictory elements, now posed as the key to larger matters. Her reticence was undone by her sense of pressure from other, small dissimulations meant to save face and preserve her credibility. Now she was afraid of being disbelieved entirely. So, wearily, she let the whole story out, knowing that her further embarrassment was inevitable—and this new information only made the deed more repellent.

"So. Now we have your testimony that he tried a *second* time—and failed?" Stanton asked. At this, Ellis looked up for one of the rare times during the trial. The jury was confused about him. Stanton's questions had to come from somewhere: Ellis couldn't be a total wipeout. But for all the days of the trial, Richie Ellis had sat like a dog which loved its master's voice but didn't quite understand his words. Sensing the movement of his head, the jury stole glimpses of him. Few of them had a sure notion of how to make out this recluse in their midst. He was there and yet he wasn't. Was his hangdog look one of guilt—or even awareness? From Stanton's often aimless questioning, one would have to infer that Ellis was either so undeniably guilty that no shadow could slip between the prosecution scenario and a plausible defense, or that, guilty or innocent, Ellis was impotent in terms of helping his lawyer—cretinism meriting, if not total freedom from criminal sanctions, certain mercies.

"He did not actually penetrate this time?" Stanton asked Johanna. Clearly, this much was news to Stanton. Johanna didn't know if "this time" meant at that time in the event or this time round in her testimony. She shook her head, confused, babbling her answers.

"Well, uh—he was beating me, because he couldn't get it up. And he hit me with the knife—the handle. I thought, you know, he was going to kill me. His eyes, his face—was crazy—and his eyes were rolled back, kind of. He was very—very enraged. But impotent. I still had my hands tied, in front of me—and he was very violent."

Stanton sighed apologetically, and asked, "Why did he stop beating you? Why didn't—I'm sorry. Why did he stop?"

Johanna felt very weak and thirsty. The food she had eaten for lunch simply bypassed her system and gave her no energy. "He had that knife at my throat—and I was cut and—I thought I would faint or—I was trying to stay alive."

"What happened?"

Johanna's ability to answer questions in any but the most hypnotically free-associative way had been long ago overrun, and all her studied efforts at intimations of ladylike delicacy were similarly ground down. She was helplessly unaffected, using her residual strength to concentrate and keep from collapsing in tears; her testimony was glum and distracted, and her gestures were unconscious. She even wiped her nose with her hand. "He—uh, he dropped the knife. He regained his potency."

"How—how do I ask this—how did this *happen?* How did he regain his potency—what part did you play?"

"I uh—" Johanna looked around for a friend. But Marks looked at her with open hands, indicating she

419

should tell the truth, open up, and that he knew nothing about this aspect of the event, for she never mentioned it before. The courtroom seemed warped and chilly and she had a hard time focusing back to Stanton.

"Did you?" he asked. "I know it's difficult. But please tell this Court what you did to effect this—"

"I began to—I touched him—there." Stanton's posture of solicitude changed swiftly to disbelief.

"A man with—you say a violent man, hitting you—a man, you say, with a knife in his hands—you say at your throat—you say a man who is looking mad and beating you—who you say raped you and now you say is raging because he's impotent—lets you take hold of his genitals? Is that what you did? You stroked —your hands were—oh, yes, in front—is *that* your testimony? You caressed his genitals? You touched his penis and his potency was restored. He lets you do this and stops being violent? And drops his knife. Is *that* what your testimony is?"

"I guess—yes," Johanna said meekly, worrying most about its believability.

"That's your testimony—or you *guess* that's your testimony? Now please, be specific. I don't like having to drag this out of you. You should have been reporting this when the prosecution was examining you. Now, when asked several times under oath whether you had told the whole and complete story you said, 'Yes.' But you never mentioned any of this! Now your sworn statements and testimony mention just that one rape— I will remind you again about the perjury statute and ask you: *Exactly* what happened?"

"I stroked him—and he regained his erection."

"Just like that?"

"Yes."

"And the knife?"

"It was between my throat and my ear—here."

"Now, and I mean step by step—what happened?"

"It became hard and—I was kneeling and—I knew —I thought—if it went soft again, he'd be furious so, I—it was my last chance, I thought. I *kissed* it and— I was trying to save my *life!*"

"You kissed it—his penis. Once? Twice? Did you perhaps perform what could be called fellatio?"

Johanna took a deep breath and said, "I suppose."

"You kissed his penis. You took it in your mouth and licked it? Sucked on it? Did he suggest this or force you to?"

"Well, no he—"

"Did he ejaculate in your mouth?"

"No," Johanna answered. At the same stage as the event itself, Johanna had moved beyond shock. All further pain was redundant and unsensed.

"Do your lovers generally?"

"Objection!!!" Robert Marks and Edward Denning screamed, jolting the jurors to fidgety attention and great disappointment.

Judge Hall agreed. "Sustained. Counsel, this will *not* happen again! You have been asked repeatedly to regard your questions with care. I know there is a fine line—but this is well over it. I will halt this line of inquiry—and regard you, sir, in contempt, if you do not use more discretion."

"Your Honor," Stanton appealed, "the question of—"

"Enough!" commanded Judge Hall furiously, and Stanton apologized.

"Thank you, Your Honor," Stanton said. "Now, Mrs. Reigeluth. You were performing fellatio on this man and—he did not, you say, have a quick climax this time? He did not ejaculate in your mouth?"

"That's correct. He did not. He pushed me down and raped me again and he ejaculated inside me—"

"In your vagina?"

"Yes."

"And then?"

"He raped me again."

"Did he remove himself between those two latter events?"

"No," she sighed.

"His penis stayed inside your vagina. He was laying on top of you. Were you kissing or caressing him—or trying to force him out?"

"The first."

"You were encouraging him?" Stanton asked.

421

Johanna closed her eyes and said slowly, "He had let go of the knife and—I didn't want to anger him."

Stanton honestly saluted her, "I think you showed great presence of mind. Was that the end of it?"

"He didn't beat me any more. He raped me that time."

"Did you struggle?"

"No."

"Did you encourage it?"

"Well—to him I did."

"So now, we have by your own testimony just now: you say he raped you. Then he tried and couldn't because he was impotent. He—you performed fellatio on him until he could achieve an erection. You continued to perform fellatio, after he had let go of the alleged knife, and then you had an act of intercourse—"

"Rape," Johanna peeped ineffectively, twitching out tears.

"Following that fellatio, he entered your vagina and had a climax. Then he stayed inside you while you caressed him and then you aroused him again and engaged in another act of intercourse—is that it?"

She stiffened in resistance. "That's the number of events." Stanton admired her stamina.

"Did he have a climax—an ejaculation after each?"

"At the end of each—yes."

He smiled briefly. "My mistake. Did you finally have an orgasm?"

"Objection!" shot Marks.

"Sustained. Counsel—rephrase the question," Judge Hall said.

"Did you at any time have an orgasm during or at the end of these events?"

"No."

"Were you trying to?"

"No!"

"Did you feel yourself getting closer to having one?"

"No."

"In no way closer?" She shook her head wearily, afraid that some mystical, observable truth radiated off her for all to see, as though she came equipped with her own truth sensors that revealed every doubt and complex feeling as a lie. Her head was swinging like

422

a metronome in such ardent denial that Stanton asked again, "On the verge of one?"

"No!"

"Not at all?"

"No, I . . . it's hard to remember."

"You don't *remember?*"

"I've been trying to forget." Stanton was about to ask again, but she cut him off. "I remember."

"Yes?"

"I remember," she repeated, measuring each word. "I did not. No."

"What happened?" Stanton asked.

"He stopped. He was through."

"I'm sorry. Uh, how did you get out of this?"

"He made me go——" Johanna said.

"You didn't want to?"

"I thought he was going to run me down. But he went off with my car." She told again of waiting for the rain, and walking out of the desert, how she hitched a ride herself and called her brother from the farmhouse behind the gas station.

"Your brother—not your husband?"

"Yes."

"Now, your alleged assailant left you your clothes— and nothing else. Not the rope. Not the knife. Nothing else?"

Johanna searched for an appropriate response, but settled for "nothing." Then again about the hospital and police reports. She apologized about withholding the details from her earlier testimony, but "all those people—strangers, my family—it just didn't seem important. I'm sorry. I thought the first was enough."

Stanton was soothing now, smoothing over his tracks, saying, "That's all right. It must have been very painful and difficult, I'm sure." His last question was not meant to be tricky, but was nonetheless disarming. He asked her if there was any other person whom she knew of, besides herself and the defendant, who might have first-hand information about the events. It threw her, it seemed so dumb.

"Only us," she said, sinking, as if the bottom would drop out on that insufficiency.

"Just asking. No further questions." He sat down

423

with a look of calmness, innocence, as if he were a different person now. He turned away from the jury, which he had eyed confidently as he sat down, and placed one hand on his client's shoulder in professional and moral support. He shaded toward the prosecution then, exhaling a long forlorn sigh of apology, a shiver at his calling's duty. Marks closed his eyelids, nodding imperceptibly at the gesture; Johanna and the jury thought it had been a sigh of exasperation at the witness.

She felt torn. She was bleeding on the stand, but she was not the one in jeopardy. It was not her trial. What she could lose here had been lost before or could easily be regained. She was just a witness. What hurt beneath her bruises was that though this time her ordeal was only with words, and though she was hopeful of Ellis's treatment, this time just to survive, she felt herself knot inside and turn mean.

Robert Marks reexamined her briefly, and she fixed her attention on his cheeks. They were soft and pastel, and his sideburns were cut to a surveyor's evenness. It was a pity about his balding, and the vanity which made him self-conscious about it. He asked just a few questions, establishing in the jury's mind that the final assaults were unreported from the shocks she had suffered and the attendant embarrassment of such proceedings. He asked her to reidentify photographs of herself and she turned away twice this time before she could. Then he passed them under the jury's noses. They were of Johanna in the hospital, and no matter how distressed the girl on the stand looked, she was a fairy queen compared to the battered wretch in the photos. Marks pointed out that the omitted items of testimony were damning to the defendant—"forced sodomy and rape on pain of murder." At this, Stanton objected that those events were not in the indictment, but Judge Hall ruled they were the continuation of earlier acts in the commission of a felony and had, in any event, arisen during Stanton's own cross-examination.

"So what happened out there in the desert, Mrs. Reigeluth, was this man, Richard Ellis, raped you again and again—and tried to kill you. He raped you, forced you into sodomy and tried to kill you."

"Yes," she said and, finally she stepped down.

Court was recessed Friday evening after three days of testimony.

T HERE'S AN OLD JOKE FROM THESE PARTS (c. 1940)," Tyler wrote to Johanna that weekend while he was in Vermont to ski. "Seems Emmett says to Reuben, as Down-easters all get named, 'Well, now, if the United States goes to war, I'll just move to Vermont and buy me a farm.' And Reuben answers, 'Won't do ye no good nohow. If the United States goes to war, pretty soon Vermont'll go, too.' "

Yet Vermont, when he arrived, was still snuggled in its Alpine neutrality, safe from the various wars around it. Up near Camel's Hump, where the Green Mountain Boys first spat in the eye of authority, he'd sought refuge in play, a fallow period of thinking and organization, at the same time the Tucson trial was in recess.

It was an act of avoidance. He hardly knew his own motives. Johanna had accused him once of "words that come too easily and lie too well." She had a theory: "Listen to yourself sometime. Listen to the speeches you give in the shower, and when you're alone in a car." For someone who had spoken so sweetly of listening to his very thymus, she teased, he should already have known that when the senses are stripped, or flooded, one can hear the tingling of a tailbone. "Your subconscious knows the way home." So, aware of his motives or not, he was doing his best to serve his better purposes.

He had received a letter from Johanna, in which

425

she'd enclosed a speech of Robert Kennedy's clipped from the Phoenix paper. The speech said, in part: "Our enemy, savagely striking at will, . . . has finally shattered the mask of official illusion with which we have concealed our true circumstances even from ourselves. . . . The time has come for a new look . . . to seek out the austere and painful reality . . . freed from wishful thinking, false hopes, and sentimental dreams. . . ."

She had things to wrap up in Tucson yet, and the prospects for Tyler at home were still uncertain. She wanted to leave Tucson, she said, again and again, but what was there for them in New York? Yet here, in the high country, in the clean, brisk air, some things became more clear. Skiing is a quiet sport, or at least its noises are subtle. But through the dense, muffling forests and over the age-worn Green Mountains and the Long Trail spur of the Appalachian Trail, a wail could be discerned, still and small, like a child's in a darkened nursery. It whistled across the Connecticut River Valley, from the White Mountains and the Presidential Range.

All his life Tyler had been trained to perk to that sound in its many guises. But he had never heard it, not in the draft's sirocco, in the service of his country, or in the many oaths he swore. Not in Gila Compound's hard wind had it ever found his ears. In Willie's letters under foreign fire there was no indication but for mocking. Yet here in the calm snows was this inchoate, alluring cry, drawing him toward purpose. There was a need for love, and help, and heroes who could heal; optimists, faithful naifs, romantics, gathered in the People's name to battle against the bullies.

"Let's see Bobby back it up," Tyler wrote her in reply. "Does he think he's discovered something new? I knew it. You did. OK, RFK; we're equal—my brother's gone, too. That's reality for me. Now if cutesy Bobby wants to help, he can come out of the closet and run, for the love of Christ! Other than that, all I see are words. And words alone don't make us any wiser, more noble, more fit to survive. You've got to get in there and take your cuts. He wants to talk about reality? Fine. I'm listening. Because the harsh reality is my baby brother's disappeared from the face of the Earth. He isn't going to have any more lines in this play, but he may be carried on the roster for another hundred years because the government's reality machine has not decided to count him in or out. He's stuck, and I am, too, because they live with lies, by lies. All right, I did, too. You helped me see that. And now you are the only reality I can hold. You are my chief truth and I need you. Come join me and I'll tickle your toes."

That such benign rebellion should descend across the plains from the northeast corner's hills was only part of a timeless pattern, begun by Pilgrims who made first landfall nearby. They set their roots and nourished them on hope alone through the winters of infancy. Spring's floods bore their creation west. Great wrenchings carried it over the Continental Divide until every basin filled, to the far sea's coast where the best ideas came last and the worst ones grew between times. The country was an isthmus in time connecting the high Atlantic with the Pacific's stormy currents. This, Tyler Bowen decided, was a tide to be part of. He returned to New York to prepare for the voyage, to help evict the interlopers and false suitors and effect a restoration.

He arrived home in Pelham at 2:00 A.M. and stole upstairs to his room. His mother appeared shortly. "What's wrong?" she asked.

"Nothing. I'm just tired."

"It's three in the morning."

"That's why I'm tired. And it's two. It was a long drive. Do me a favor? Wake me when Dad gets up, OK?" He shooed her out affectionately, and repacked his bags, exchanging skiwear for suits and sports jackets. He felt he owed them this much, an account. All their years of pride in him were endangered by his recent drifting. So many things had changed, so many things inverted.

When he was young, Tyler's father would drag him out to play ball with "the men," a group of Vlad's cronies whom Mack called "hairy goons that Daddy likes." The men played all weekend and most evenings every spring and summer then. Tyler warmed the bench and eventually earned his place in the lineup. But those first years were most important, though all he did was watch adoringly.

Vlad Bowen wasn't the best on the field, but he tore around third base as though it was the only thing in life worth dying for. He'd stick his face into every grounder, follow every bad hop, dive in the dirt and emerge from a cloud like a treasure hunter, clutching the taped-up ball. When Tyler got to Cornell he found that many of his teammates learned to play on concrete, where caution and reliable bounces instilled bad habits.

After three games or so, the sun would be setting and the infield smelled of beer. All day long Tyler would keep his eyes glued to his father, afraid he'd keel over on third and every moment would count. But the man was made of pig iron. When the others packed to leave, he'd pound his glove and motion to his boy, "C'm'ere, Babe."

Then Tyler would spring up and fungo shots to third until his hands hurt. Vlad would grab them, or stop them with his chest, and whip letter-high strikes to the plate. Tyler would slash at these and sometimes tear them back down the line, where Vlad would gulp a mouthful of basepath lime but nab the ball. From his knees he'd peg it over. Tyler would swing again and hit some, and miss some. Then Tyler would take third. But it was no contest. He admittedly lacked that extra measure of desire. To his father's ill-hidden disappointment, he later turned to pitching. For three years, though, he tried at third, every now and then making a pretty pickup or a bare-handed snatch of a bunt. Vlad would have the bat down and his glove on, blocking the plate before the throw came. "Your catcher will want knee-high, chest-high, or down-in-the-dirt throws, depending," Vlad would say like a madam instructing a new girl.

As darkness came they'd play pepper until Vlad was wound down, and Tyler as black and sweaty. "Time for the varsity to pack it in, waddya say?" Vlad would declare. "Your mother probably thinks we're out drinking. She's gonna yell like the dickens, us spoiling another dinner out so late." Then he'd grin broadly, for that scolding they'd earned was one of life's better delights. He'd put his arm around his boy on the way to the car and tell him, "You'll be a damned good ballplayer if you'd just stick with it and look at the ball." Rubbing Tyler's matted hair, he'd laugh, "Get your face down in there, Babe. It won't hurt if it hits you. It feels kind of good—after. Besides, you've got my face: it's not so much to worry about." A big chesty laugh would crown that. "Just don't pull back. Hang in there, Babe." As Tyler rubbed his stinging hands, Vlad would break out the great secret balm which only he owned: he'd smile at his son and say, "You did good."

Wherever they went, whenever they had a few seconds, Vlad would drill him, and Willie, too—though Willie was for the most part too young and cross-eyed and in his own world at that age to pay much attention —on the lore and statistics and legends of the diamond: the Babe's exploits on and off the field; Ty Cobb's records and investments; DiMag, Christy Mathewson, Gehrig. On the street, in church, while driving. If Tyler showed anger, Vlad might remind him of what Big Bill Klem, the umpire, told a player who tossed his bat in the air: "Son, if that bat comes down, you're out of the game." When the boys did something scatterbrained, Vlad would call them "Bonehead Merkles" or tell them of the wartime Dodgers: when they got three men on base, people would ask, "Which base?" The boys would bust up laughing, forgetting whatever the immediate worry was. Each time's telling seemed new. And as he laughed, oxygen would roar in and out of Vlad's chest like a Bessemer furnace stoked to bursting, mighty lungs with a lust for air.

When the day finally came that Tyler could blow three by Vlad and run him a little ragged at third, he did. That was that. Beat him bad, his father had to admit. "You really gave your old man there a workout, Babe," Vlad said, winded but happy. "Now you teach Willie." The shortness of breath betrayed him. He was old. He had just walked out of his prime before Tyler ever got a title shot. It was a sucker play. Like Sonny Liston, lying down at Lewiston, winking of his ancientness, refusing to rise for Ali, Vlad stole the victory's sweet bloody triumph clean away by being, all of a second, old.

Still, Tyler was set on a path. He made every team from Little League to college. He played with such names as "Slayton's Pelham Lounge" and the "Madame Curie Madmen" on his back. And when he made the Little League All-Star roster, still no match for his father yet, Vlad crowed to see it posted on the bulletin board outside their church, properly father-high. "Look, there's your name, right on there!" Vlad beamed wildly. No greater heights of esteem than that could Tyler ever scale, though he'd sent home many clippings of his late-inning heroics for the Cornell varsity.

Through it all he felt an obligation to report on his progress periodically, though progress toward what was always left as undefined as the Pursuit of Happiness. Some day the news would be of new generations conceived. But now it was just another step, faltering, no more sure than last week, on an uncertain road; as he would put it, "It's a thing."

He cut himself shaving in the morning, just a nick, and thought of what his father told him the first time he'd shaved. "Well, you're not dead, so I guess you can do it all right." He said that over any daring thing the boys attempted, after they'd succeeded.

"You wanted to talk?" Vlad asked, waiting at the breakfast table.

"Can we go for a walk?"

"What's wrong? You want money?"

"No. No. I'm set. I got a rich father. Let's take a walk, huh?"

They made three circumnavigations of the extensive block on which sat what Mack called the "certifiably pleasant house and expansive lawn of Refuse Manor." Each time they came around, they saw Laura Bowen sitting on the front porch in her housecoat, looking nonchalant, turning gray-blue in the chill, waiting to see if white smoke or black came out of her husband's ear muffs. "She thinks you must've got a girl in trouble," Vlad said, his tone adoring. "Your mother loves her sons."

"I just wanted to talk to you about it first."

"You think this is what you want to do?"

"It's in the right direction at least. I called that guy at school back: nothing. He said maybe not till the new fiscal year. Who knows?"

Vlad found openings for homilies about Ty Cobb's grit and Bill Dickey playing with a busted hand. Then Johnson, Walter. "That fast ball, Babe. If that didn't do it, he'd throw it faster. If that didn't, he'd throw it faster still."

"And he'd throw his goddam arm out, Pop, unless he came up with a curve or slider."

"Spitter was pretty big in those days."

"Still is."

"Of course," Vlad said, "Walter Johnson wouldn't use one."

"That's where he and Lyndon part company," Tyler said, and threw a snowball at a traffic sign. One reason he felt he had to leave was his fear that his unresolved anger might be viral; not in its contagion, but that when crystallized it would stay dormant till revived by a drop of moisture, then to attack the host. He did not want to add more toxin to his home.

So many others were leaving home at this time, some snatched in the darkness from their helpless families, to disappear and never to return. And some, from spite, vowing the same. The latter group believed that by an act of will and invention they could change the courses charted for them long before. Their vehicles were music, drugs, and proofs of social madness. But Tyler appreciated that such changes were precisely owed to parental efforts. The oath so many took on leaving home was enabled by a leisure granted them by those they left behind.

"There's that girl I told you about. She'll be joining me, I hope."

"That's fine, Babe," Vlad beamed. "Just fine. Your mother will be happy."

"And you?"

"Me too," he said. "I'm in love with my boys, too." Most of all this walk was for his father's sake. His mother seemed to have instincts that guided her toward vegetative things; gloom was repulsed by making

431

things grow, even things that grew without her: grand-children, children, plants. But Vlad, with all these terrible things going on outside his control, Tyler thought, needed some support. So he thought to let his father do something fatherly. At one point, Vlad misted up, unaccountably. Such paternity could only help the living, he had realized. So he lavished all his hope on Tyler. And Tyler wished there was some way his father could let it all go at once, and still believe his dignity intact. But it was that—dignity—as much as heart and resolution which held Vlad together while his parts lost the epoxy of desire. That and the determined optimism Tyler reflected with support.

"I'll be thinking of you and Mom up there."

"A lot's changed, hasn't it?"

"Not so much, Dad." Every laurel of his youth had lost its meaning in a year. Every honor had become a disgrace, every opportunity perverted. Each gift he'd been offered proved base. So now, for his sake and his family's, he wished to go to war, to make things right. He had come home to acknowledge he was created by his past and still was someone's child. The forces which attacked him and reversed his victories attacked his home as well. This malevolence had turned him from a middle child to youngest, to sole surviving son. He came home to say he had a home to leave and one day to return to. So it was history's mistake to characterize the effort he was bent on as revisionist. It was corrective.

"You all packed?" Vlad asked.

"Just about. Except I didn't leave out underwear for today. I guess I'm still a bonehead."

"No you're not. You're going to be something wonderful, Babe. You could have taken some of Willie's—"

"Well, yeah. I didn't—one of your T-shirts fit well enough. A little loose in the gut, maybe," he said, patting his father's belly. "But your Jockey shorts, Pop, I don't know."

"What's the matter?"

"I put 'em on but they just fell to my ankles. I gotta hold 'em up with a safety pin, like a diaper."

"You've got time, son. You've got time." He hugged

his pride in front of the house and kissed him on the ear.

Then the Bowens waved another child off to futile combat.

O N MONDAY, FEBRUARY 19, 1968, COURT reconvened in *State of Arizona* v. *Richard Ellis*. The morning was filled with prosecution rebuttal witnesses; the afternoon was devoted to some unrelated loose ends from Judge Hall's calendar.

On Tuesday, Court assembled for summations and the Judge's charge to the jury.

Deputy County Attorney Robert Marks sat at the prosecution table, exiled to the same extent Johanna Reigeluth had been during other testimony, and Edward Denning throughout. County Attorney James Hood was back for the summation. Hood always complained about the paucity of good restaurants near the courthouse. "There's better food for lawyers in Phoenix," he liked to say. "Even better in Washington." Summation's attendant publicity was at least a dessert delight. He dismissed Marks's point that the jury might become "psychologically angry" at this seeming usurpation, glaring at his young assistant. "Don't you worry about it, boy. They'll thank me for giving you the help."

Hood began with the throat-clearing formal obsequies required in court address, fixing defense counsel Gary Stanton with a hard, unforgiving look. Then he launched into a careful reiteration of the supporting testimony and evidence for the indictment's proof, "a true bill proved in every particular," he said. He stepped back from the lectern and straightened up, looming larger than ever, as though the giant who ruled this cavern.

433

"We predicted at the outset—and you saw—counsel for the accused try to save the reputation of a repeatedly dangerous felon by smearing the good name of a decent young girl.

"Let me tell you something: the institution of marriage is not on trial. And neither are Mrs. Reigeluth's marital problems and attitudes, whether you condone them or not. They are none of our business. We're not here to defend the concept of holy matrimony—or hers—or her morals, but only the public safety. We are here to prosecute a crime. I'll tell you—I don't care if this woman," he made a sweeping gesture with his arm back toward Edward Denning, "was having an affair with all seven Flying Wallendas. It's not our concern. She is not on trial. Richard Ellis is.

"And what Richard Ellis did adds up, no matter how you slice it, to kidnap and rape under the law. It's not our business that his victim had a date that weekend. And the contents of her luggage are not on trial. He hasn't been accused of stealing a spare tire and a suitcase containing a diaphragm—but of the kidnap and rape of a citizen. If he'd set that damned diaphragm on fire, do you think I'd waste the People's time charging him with arson?

"You've seen the evidence. We've got the—we've got him cold. The man is a sex criminal and a potential murderer and Mr. Stanton can turn the whole case on its head—it still comes out the same. Up and down.

"This man deserves no pity. What was his instrument of seduction? A hunting knife! What was the subtle hint that suggested fellatio? A savaging beating and the point of that knife. Quite a Romeo.

"And what have we learned just lately?" he asked in theatrical amazement. "That his hideous crime exceeded our charges! He defies imagination!" Hood then went over the chain of evidence again, with careful logic, leaning less on the rules of evidence and criminal procedure than rough-edged common sense. By his construction, the facts denied doubt: only Richard Ellis could be the car thief—his prints were on the passenger side, incriminatingly on the wheel and the driver's door. All other events fell into place like the last pieces of a jigsaw puzzle. Only one solution

434

would do to fulfill the picture: Richard Ellis was in the middle. And though enjoined from remarking on Ellis's silence, Hood was confident the jury would consider it a guilty silence, as damning as the compelling material and medical evidence.

"They want you to believe that Richard Ellis was temporarily in a spell. But then they hedge it and suggest that spell may have lasted twenty years. A sandstorm of gibberish has almost completely obscured the truth: he's as sane as you or me. I take a look at a pretty girl and, by golly, my heart goes thump-thump, too. Any sane man's does. And taking what you want when there are not witnesses? Well, that's not insanity —it's *criminal*, though. His strategy is too artful for him to pretend he's nuts.

"By the inescapable facts it is clear that Richard Ellis did, with malice aforethought, willfully abduct, rape, unlawfully imprison, commit forceful sodomy upon, and beat Mrs. Reigeluth until her very life was in peril. Then he sodomized her, forced her to commit a terrible act in literal fear of having her throat slashed, and raped her again, two times. He did abandon her and steal her car—and belongings. He did leave her to die in the desert—from which she had earlier rescued him. He was sane enough to drive a standard-shift car. Sane enough to get rid of the knife and rope. Sane enough to find his way. The man is sane. And he is a criminal. No other judgment is possible."

When Gary Stanton rose for the defendant, he prefaced his *ex tempore* remarks with an idle thought:

"What can you say about a twenty-three-year-old girl who lied?" He shook his head as he began his valedictory. "You can say her word, alone and unsupported, should not be permitted to convict a man. So let us look at the facts before us and see what there is to go on.

"You have heard a woman, whose marriage was a fiction, who, by her own testimony, had taken up with a friend of her husband's she had recently met.

"You heard her describe her outfit that day: a miniskirt and hardly any underwear, scents designed to seduce. It's enough to make your head swim: leather and silk and sweet fragrances. Cynically ensnaring—well, she succeeded!

"This very pretty woman—who I'm afraid knows *just* how attractive she is, dressed to kill, all dolled up—and what does she do? She invites a weak, unwary traveler into her car. She begins to talk about her 'free spirit' and her adventurousness, her *misbehavior.*

"The State alleges force. The woman describes a knife. Was one ever produced? No. We have only her word—this woman's—that a weapon was used, let alone existed. The medical reports? They say she was bruised. They do not say who bruised her. Or how.

"What sticks out is that, when allegedly panicked, beaten, raped, having allegedly walked out of the desert—that *alone* beggars the imagination—what did she do then? Did she call her husband—the owner of the car? Or the police? No. She called her brother. That was the very first thing she did: conceal the truth. Or what she says now is the truth.

"She has been a most reluctant witness on her own behalf. She has misrepresented, shaded, lied, told us different stories, withheld information, changed details. Is there any liberty she has not taken with the facts? Her every word stands impeached by every other word.

"From the moment she invited this man for a ride, saying she was visiting her husband, from the moment he entered her rolling salon, she led him on with tempting phrases—and led us on, concealing the truth—or what she now says is the truth—until the last, or nearly last words she spoke under solemn oath, lying at every stage. The reasons we can only guess. Where caught in her web of lies, she recanted and admitted her falsehoods, cleverly retreating, retrenching in other lies. I have no idea what the uncaught lies are, but the possibilities are many.

"For example, we know from the medical report that seminal fluid was removed from her. We do not know whose. We do not know if this was not some vastly clever scheme to secure a free and legal abortion—to benefit herself and her lover. I would not put anything past her.

"Even if we were to assume this woman had sexual

union with this man, was it in fact rape? Who is to say? She told us that she, herself, removed her shirt. It is untorn, in evidence. She wore no bra.

"When does that conversation which is seduction and intercourse become a violent, one-sided shout by one person? When does it cease being a conversation? May it alternate? We have her own testimony that she encouraged and, indeed, *seduced* this man—to the point that her own sexual climax was moments away. Is it not possible she raised his interest and changed her mind? Caught him in her aura of promiscuous sexuality —then having played with this simple, direct, and forthright man enough, changed her mind again? She pushed him past the point of reason, by her cynical manipulations. This temptress—this love-girl in a Volkswagen— shall we take her word and call it kidnap and rape, capital felonies? Class A capital felonies? Kidnap and rape in the first degree?

"She has lied in this courtroom about main facts. The State's chief witness and we cannot believe her. Some things, she tells us, seemed unimportant to her. Obviously, one of them was the truth. Another was the right of an accused citizen to get a fair and honest trial. I can only speculate what else was unimportant to her. Marriage was one of them.

"Speaking of strange marriages—the prosecution joined her in her efforts to relegate the right of a fair trial to a low estate by coaching her on how to prevent the real, coarse side of her nature, her loose and vicious ways, from seeing light. Only through persistent inquiry have we been able to drag the whole story—perhaps the truth, who knows?—from her.

"She tells us, now, a tale of terror—in the midst of which she seized upon an idea: *fellatio!* Her life was in peril and she thought of fellatio! The threat ceased and turned into erotic joy. They made love, she tells us, not once, but twice more—and she held him in her arms and stroked him between times.

"You can all construct your own hypotheses, but let me offer a few to rest your reasonable—considerable—doubts on. One: She was seeking to abort an illicit pregnancy. This elaborate ploy may be genius or it may be that scheme backfiring on her. Two: She had relations with some man—perhaps her lover, perhaps the mysterious truckdriver who we have heard drove off into the night—and perhaps even suffered a beating at his hands, winding up dazed and bruised. This may have happened before, or after, she let Richard Ellis out of her car. I frankly do not know. Three: She was unhappy and unfulfilled by some liaison earlier, or some emotional crisis, and seduced this poor man. I do not know about that either. If she did, she may have grown so scared of her own game that she decided to bring the house down on someone else. Four: Perhaps out for some revenge or thrill or who-knows-what, she *sought* this contact. And, when she realized she had not used her birth control device, she cried 'Rape!' Many scenarios will work. Every aspect of the case is open to doubt. A car—not just a Volkswagen, but a *truck!*—could drive through the gaps in the State's logic.

"And what of Richard Ellis? The State has had him in its care off and on for fifteen years. They say he is impotent, as well. Does not the State of Arizona own some responsibility for someone they have so continually, miserably mistreated? If you agree with the indictment in any respect, isn't the State guilty as well, of neglect? Must Richard Ellis suffer forever for its incompetence? 'Even a whore has rights,' yes. And the feeble?

"There is a sad juxtaposition here: on the one hand we have this woman, a member of that articulate and privileged young promiscuous college-educated upper middle class, whose access to the press and the State's ear is easy—and who is so spoiled, whose word is so tainted, that if you accept it you make the courts into her private tool, you give license to every other lover's spat to end with the cry of 'Rape!' On the other hand, you have Richard Ellis, who all his life has been an impotent victim of the State—until they finally brought him to the dock on a capital charge.

"It is a strange thing about defendants. The privileges and immunities we afford them make them seem rather like foreigners, protected from the rude mechanisms of local law. In a sense they are foreigners. Certainly this man is. He can hardly understand us, and we cannot

438

understand him. In his conscience and middle ear rings an alien idiom which tempts him to run an erratic course. So he spins out of the field we define as 'normal' and deviates past imprecisely charted boundaries into territory the majority may vote to call 'criminal' or 'psychotic' as it wishes. Then he darts back into common mores. He needs help, not condemnation."

Stanton disputed the facts of the case point by point, showing where each was built upon a supposition and an inference of circumstance. "But we are not dealing with normal people here—so normal assumptions of behavior do not work." He drew on testimony, citing particularly the arresting officer's report that Ellis had been "cooperative and unresistant, more bewildered than anything." Stanton said, "And yet, when they were through interrogating him, he was ready to admit everything, about *anything*. Unsolved murders? Sure! Putting the overalls in Mrs. Murphy's chowder? Certainly!" He shook his head and sneered, "Bah!"

Like Hood, he too stiffened for his peroration. "Some things," Stanton said, "are strange and tragic. But when we do not know all the facts, when so much remains a mystery, enfolded in the dark coils of sexuality and the tangled relations between the sexes, so confused now with the loose morality of our times—when so much remains an enigma, unfathomable and unknowable, part of an act which itself is largely seeking to define itself at every stage—it would be the greatest tragedy, and the highest crime discussed in this courtroom, to convict a man on this untrustworthy, uncorroborated testimony.

"We would not dream of punishing this woman for being the prisoner of her passions, even though it led her to adultery and the felony of perjury. Nor must we punish this man for being her victim—for coming close enough to her fire to be ignited and consumed. That would be stranger and more tragic still—to ruin a man's life on so flimsy a story, so precariously assembled a case. Haven't we done enough to him already?

"Both these people probably need help. They need compassion and understanding—not conviction and censure. We must help them reach that help. I will not say my client is innocent. Does that startle you? He is not innocent—any more than she is. I will say what I would say of his chief accuser. They are neither of them *innocent*. No. They are certainly not *innocent*. Yet—equally, they are *both:* not guilty!"

Stanton sat down and folded papers while Judge Hall asked, "Prosecution rebuttal?" James Hood rose gravely. He stalked to the lectern as though to give a eulogy.

"Words," Hood said admiringly. "You have to find the truth among so many *words*. And they are such putty in the hands of a—smooth lawyer. But justice. That's another thing altogether. That comes from the hearts of citizens such as you.

"You know, listening to Mr. Stanton's very eloquent remarks, and going over the testimony he filled the record with, you'd think that this girl committed the crime. He has tried to stand it on its head. Instead of submitting to the torture of sodomy, Mrs. Reigeluth—this tiny, brave girl—could have won Mr. Stanton's respect if she'd only have let Richard Ellis cut her throat! I'm glad Ellis didn't have a lawyer out there.

"Clothing styles are supposed to be important. I guess I'm supposed to indict every European designer as accessory before the fact—party to conspiracy—to impairing the morals of this poor man. I'll tell you—my wife wears one of those miniskirts, and my daughter wears that kind of perfume. Am I supposed to keep them off the streets? Lock up the sales clerks? Is their hem length our license to injure, molest, and ravish them? Are they guilty of *incitement?*

"I'll tell you how we look at the law in Arizona: a woman is free to incite the senses. That is her right, and her role as a woman. A woman could walk naked down the Tucson Speedway and her right to the physical integrity of her body would be protected by law!" He leaned chummily across the bar and confided, "We might curtail her stroll, but no one except that lady can determine who may be intimate with her. No, sir! You take the woman walking naked down the Speedway: is that incitement?" He winked at them broadly. "To *riot,* maybe. But to *rape?* No. *Never.* Nor is paranoia a justification for violating the constitutional rights of citizens. *Never!*

440

"Now, Mr. Stanton has raised a very clever argument about the line between seduction and rape. But it is what high-priced attorneys and law students call sophistry. And it's irrelevant. Whether you think it's fair or not, the law reads that when a woman says no, she means it until she says otherwise. And when is a man released from the obligation to be reasonable and responsible? Because he doesn't *believe* her when she says no? That line falls far short of pulling knives on people who offer the simple compassion of a lift through the desert. Far short of attempting murder, attempting and completing several rapes and a brutal, monstrous act of forced sodomy. Blame it on the miniskirt! That's what Mr. Stanton's telling you. You see: Richard Ellis didn't do a thing. Some guy in Paris is walking around getting away with murder!

"Mr. Stanton tried to destroy this girl as much as Richard Ellis did that day. He's tried to paint her as a seething sexpot—a siren and a harpy. As if she lured every passing stranger into wild sexual affairs. Nonsense. You saw her. She is none of that. She is a hard-working woman—a wife, a housewife, a reporter—she's taken graduate school courses—a bright and pretty and talented—and thoughtful—and friendly young woman, who any of us should be proud to know, would be proud to have as a daughter. And like every other woman in this land, she enjoys the constitutional privilege of saying, 'No!' Otherwise, rape means nothing.

"A woman's body is her own property. It is premises, if you will, of which she is the sole owner. She is the only judge of who may take what liberties and have what favors—who may have access rights, and who may be her guests, who may share her pleasures. And the miniskirt is not on trial. Neither is the State of Arizona. They did not rape her.

"If Richard Ellis did not commit these crimes, if by your verdict you hold him blameless—understand this —you will be saying: there has been no crime.

"So, I want to ask you something. I want to give you something to think about. If this young woman, who had the decency to help a man and had the courage to go through all of this—this legal torture—now, for-

441

tunately she's held up pretty well, and I hope you don't hold that against her, though I'm surprised Mr. Stanton didn't point it out with sarcastic alarm—what she survived out there in the desert: you saw the pictures, the terrible beating and how she looked, and how she looked when she was through here—if this girl, who went through all that to protect other young girls, if she should enjoy nothing but pain and scorn and humiliation for her efforts, having already suffered once for being a good Samaritan out there in the desert—if you tell her that her courage and pain was pointless, and you condemn her—" He stopped and looked them each in the eye; his voiced lowered. "What will you have me tell the *next* girl?

"Ladies and gentlemen: for the sake of this girl, for the sake of those other girls, for our children, for our streets' peace and safety—for our whole concept of justice, law, and order, you must find this man guilty as he has been charged. He must not be left to think he can walk among us and spread his terror, to prey on those good people of this state whose only crime is that they would spread the spirit of justice and Christian kindness. That he is guilty is beyond dispute. It is written in the facts of record in this trial. Now it is left to you to ratify that fact: to convict Richard Ellis and pronounce his true guilt." He held their attention all the way back to his seat, where he turned back to face them and said grimly, "Thank you."

Stanton rose immediately to move for a directed verdict of not guilty which, along with several technical motions, was denied. It took Judge Hall half an hour to explain the law's intricate logic to the jury and lay out their options. He went over the evidence and how it must be weighed, how it might be applied, and led them carefully through the thicket the conflicting experts had planted, showing them how to regard such testimony, what the precedents and standards were, and how much light such matters shed on Ellis's criminality. He finished charging them just before lunchtime.

As soon as the jury retired, Judge Hall said, "The Court also wishes to thank the members of the press for their admirable restraint in this delicate matter," adding the Court's hope that "you can match this fine

442

standard in future cases—even if one of the parties is not a colleague in the journalistic confraternity." His face glowed puckishly. "Although, knowing some of you, next time it could be as a defendant."

Over lunch, Edward Denning and County Attorney Hood apologized to Johanna and her mother about the divorce advice. "We took a gamble and we lost," Hood shrugged.

"Small potatoes," Johanna said, happy it was over. "Next week it'll be history." Already Edward Denning had drawn up a settlement agreeable to Warren. Johanna had told Denning, "I'll agree to anything but reparations. Anything at all. He can even have my clothes. I just want it done quickly."

The jury stayed out all afternoon and the fragmentary reports on how things stood were all speculative and inconclusive. It was simply a complicated mess the jury was sorting through.

County Attorney Hood stayed close at hand, dominating the waiting scene by his bulk, wanting to be there when the flashbulbs popped.

Finally, at five o'clock, the jury sent a note to Judge Hall, and Court was assembled. Johanna lingered at the water fountain for a moment before going in. Her stomach was fluttery in anticipation of hearing what had, in effect, become her judgment. The empty building around her seemed forbidding; in her fatigue and hunger, the courtroom even more immense than before, disorienting. The spectators swiveled as she came in, as though she were the judge. Only her mother was a familiar softness.

There was some confusion down front that brought all the lawyers to the bench in animated pantomime. Edward Denning came back to explain that the jury had reached a verdict on four counts but were still out on the rest. Judge Hall quieted everyone and lectured the jurors like a group of first offenders: "It is your *duty* to reach a verdict. No one said it would be easy or brief. Now you go back there and keep trying until you come out with a unanimous verdict—and a correct one—on all counts."

The foreman said they considered themselves hung

443

on several charges and the others nodded in agreement, until, with barely contained rage, Hall polled them, asking each in turn, "Is it your personal opinion that further deliberations will not be fruitful at all?" When a few wavered, intimidated by this scolding, he ordered them back, requesting they first render the verdicts they had reached. It was passed from the foreman, to the bailiff, to the judge, who asked, "Is this your true verdict? So say you all?" The foreman and other jury members nodded solemnly.

"Clerk will read the verdict," Judge Hall ordered. "The defendant will rise." Ellis stood up, and as the clerk began to recite the charges in the indictment, he thought he was hearing his conviction. The reporters in the back eased up a few rows, silently, as though at a theatrical rehearsal, afraid to disrupt the fragile illusion by breaking into the corona of light.

Then the clerk read, "We the jury, in *State of Arizona* v. *Richard Ellis* find the defendant, of count number one, simple assault: *guilty;* of count number two, assault with a deadly weapon: *not guilty;* of count number three, kidnap: *not yet concluded;* of count number four, aggravated battery: *guilty;* of count number five, rape: *not yet concluded;* of count number six, attempted murder: *not yet concluded;* of count number seven, theft (felony): *guilty.*"

Stanton looked over at the prosecution and sighed, "What a mess!" The obvious reason for the single surprise, all assumed, was the lack of an evidentiary weapon to support the charge. This did not imply loss of confidence in Johanna's testimony, for they had convicted on the rest; just a little legal rigor in their thought, or logic, or an urge to fix their doubts and mercies on at least one item. Nor did the other counts, the ones still out, the Big Three—kidnap 1, rape 1, and attempted murder—depend on a weapon, or fall by this logic.

Yet they were stuck at nine to three for conviction on kidnapping, the holdouts arguing that it was overkill prosecution for something that was an inherent part of a rape event. On rape itself they were ten to two for conviction, the two leaning toward their doubts. On the attempted murder they were seven to five for dismissal, feeling that here the suggestion of psychiatric problems was availing: Ellis's actions went out of his control more quickly than most men's. The genius of the jury system is not reason, for it has a committee's logic, but ordered compassion.

As the jury filed out to try again, Hood went into the lobby to answer questions. Stanton had moved for a mistrial again, but it was denied.

Judge Hall called both Gary Stanton and Robert Marks into his chambers. "Will the People offer a solution?" he asked Marks.

Young Marks looked at Stanton, who said, "Talk to me, Robbie."

"The State feels it can get a conviction on all counts," Marks answered. "But in the interest of justice and saving the Court's time, we will settle for having the indictment covered." That is, they wanted a conviction's equivalent on each of the main elements, but would accept a plea of guilty to lesser charges.

"Is that what your boss says?" Stanton asked. "Or does he just give speeches?"

"This is my trial," snapped Marks.

"You'd better check," Stanton repeated, fatherly. "Go on, I'll wait. Tell Hood."

When Marks did, the angry County Attorney growled, "Ya put twelve meatheads together and I guess you gotta take the hamburger they dish up. All right, Roberto, do the deed." Two reporters nearby pressed in to ask whether Hood's comment meant he had lost faith in the jury system, but he raised his hands plaintively, as if to say, "Boys, boys. Please. Just a figure of speech. Off the record, huh?" grinning.

"I will only accept this on one condition," Judge Hall told Stanton while they waited for Marks to return. "That he be given a full psychiatric. I want him kept indoors. And if this monkey isn't buggy—it's the slammer. Understand this: I want him off the streets." Then Marks returned.

After a one-way conference with his client, Stanton told the reassembled courtroom, "In accordance with the State's generous offer, the defense would like to change its plea to no contest to false imprisonment, rape in the second degree, and battery. We appeal to the mercy of the Court."

Accepting this, Judge Hall recalled the jury, explained that they were no longer needed, thanked them, dismissed them, and remanded Richie Ellis to the holding pens to await disposition. Before Judge Hall's words had evaporated he disappeared back into his chambers, taking with him the Court's center of belief, leaving the stragglers as strangers in a vacant lot, unsatisfied.

"What, pray, is second-degree rape?" Warren asked Robert Marks as the County Attorney finished his paper work at the prosecution table. "An accident?"

Marks shook his head and looked up, tired and annoyed. "No," he said. "The law."

Johanna, Maureen, and Edward Denning had dinner that night in Tucson, talking mostly of divorce, a happier subject. County Attorney James Hood ate with a young widow he frequently saw before going home, and Stanton had a late supper with his family. On the phone that night, Robert Marks told his girlfriend, "It's the code of the West. You can do anything you want to a person, but don't fuck with a car. I think Judge Hall is probably going over the transcript right now, thinking about how he can ask his wife to—might put a little magic back in his life."

Warren Reigeluth had tacos and an Orange Julius for dinner, and fell asleep in front of the television.

For a few days after the trial ended, Johanna worked and slept. The more she slept the more nervous she became about losing time. But she didn't have the energy, nor could she regain it in sleep, for it was a shuttling between two poles of restlessness.

Her mind, at night, in the blackness, would not shut down or dream in full dimensions. Only in the morning, between snooze-alarms, did her mind let go. And then, they were not dreams of release nor symbolic dreams of Richie Ellis, but small, mechanical, problem-ridden dreams. She was too aware of being asleep, and the images seemed contrived, a shuffling deck of picture cards, too finite a process and too conscious. Her

446

friends, when they appeared on this stage, came in disappointing roles.

In one dream there was a face. It was hard to say whose. It seemed from a time long ago and gone, but that could have been three months before. The face had holes in it. She would dream of falling into that face, but it would be a shadow, and she would fall and fall past it into some interior night, and spin all night until she awoke. She described this to Tyler on the phone, calling him in New Hampshire at the number he'd given her, in the middle of the night. "Jump," he said. "I'll be there."

Then Warren informed her she was a single woman again. "Just like that," he said. He'd gone to Nogales and done it in an afternoon. She felt then more tender toward him than she had in a year. "Do you want to have supper?" she asked.

"No."

He was a good person, really, she thought, in spite of everything. And he had a right to feel hurt. Yet she would have to let him go and consign him, with all these recent years, to some well-merited vault of memory. She wondered if she should note the date and celebrate it as a perverse anniversary, a birthday. That would crowd February even more with holiday remembrances, she decided, too much sail for such a small craft. She'd save the celebration for March, when she and Tyler Bowen were back together. March was too long anyway, unrelieved by Red Letter Days. And this long March might be the longest ever.

She did not know that hate mail from far-off towns was coming in to the *Intelligencer* addressed to her. One letter had come to Arnie Logan, and his eyes bulged at the venom scrawled in a feminine hand, at the gentle deities invoked to serve the correspondent's pathological wishes. Logan made sure all Johanna's mail was opened and read before he would give it to her. And when she finally returned to the office to collect it, she came to quit. He went through a repertoire of crushed expressions, chiding her for "arguing me all over the map and then—poof—skedaddling."

Maureen accused her of having fallen on her head. She said, "Johanna—dear. You have just shed one husband. Why don't you take a time-out before you go running after another? Ask yourself, really. Is it sensible?"

"Do I have to be?" Johanna laughed, and even Maureen was swept along by Johanna's renascent cheer. It was good to hear her daughter excited again.

Tyler was already in New Hampshire and Johanna was agreeably attracted to the fragile, ironic McCarthy. It was an obvious adventure to embark on, though in her linings she believed her own heart's choice was Robert Kennedy; by no political index or social style, but by the red-rimmed look of his eye, and the personal signs of wound he wore.

It took nearly a week to pack her things, to take them up to her mother's in the Scottsdale shadow of the Superstition Mountains. It took nearly all the strength she had, walking around the house in Tucson, flinging her past the more determinedly behind her with each layer stripped away. Alone in the bare house each afternoon she walked around pacing off the size of rooms, touching walls, finding places she'd never stood in, angles she'd failed to consider. She wanted to leave it so urgently, but she wanted to know this side, the inside, and other side of it before quitting it entirely. And her last day, all packed, ready to go up to Scottsdale, she sat in the empty living room of her empty house and had a warm Coca-Cola. There were mouse traps set in various places but she decided not to look for them. As she got up to go she turned around to take in what she was leaving, then turned around the other way, as though her life was a string that might get knotted.

The winter sun in February's wane was large and moonlike, hanging in the low shoulder of the sky. Its light was refracted through a lacy veil of ice, and it made illusions, casting elongated shadows, splashing muted colors in its path, bleaching what it did not spackle. Alongside this warmless sun was a doppelgänger, resembling the cold fire of an arctic morning, bright as a white dwarf but vacant, infinitely cold and quiet. Over the desert this sight was so clear, so crystalline, that it seemed purposeful, as though some inference should be drawn, beyond the lesson of illusion's craftiness and the subtle, fickle ways of change. But few could say just what the lesson was.

For an event so full of consequence and catastrophic change—as René Thom would have it—as his divorce, Warren Reigeluth was barely conscious of its date. He had to check his calendar to be certain. Somewhere in the annals of Nogales law its time was noted with astrological precision, he was sure: a moment before he was married, a moment after he was not. But for him, except that he knew the day of the week—Wednesday—it was an event as elusively marked as other monuments and points of moment in the pragmatic nation. If it was the fount of future change, his discipline told him, only the modalities of change would be retained. The Civil War's synthesis was shopping centers, sprouted from the carcass-fertile fields of past contentions. It was that way all over: great highways spanned the continent, the seams of time-space, hewing varied cultures to each other. They began with on-ramps, fed by tributaries of other, drying branches, ending with "All Exit." They demonstrated no fatigue for all that weight and travel, arriving with no pageantry. For every one of them, despite the narcissism of the country's pride, some place of history was moved for mere convenience, the true site razed and sown under, sealed in concrete. It was that way with Warren, too. Now "catastrophically" free of his wife's willynilly distractions, his personal energy enjoyed a phase change and he leaped into his future.

He sparkled with ideas and quickly shone as the keenest light at Tombstone in his study group's meetings. In their work they were at the stage of considering revolutions, precisely the point of historical development for which the theories of René Thom, which Warren now championed, had most dramatic application.

They considered first the phenomenon of associative pressure. Great strides had been made in studying the movement of schoolfish, and the patterns of firefly flashes. Seeming simultaneity of action compared well to magnetism's effects. A sufficiency of uniformity was all that was required, a bare majority of polarities

449

aligned, and soon constituents would further organize, atoms in collective bargaining with their ferrite neighbor. Or, by such community they might demonstrate their discontent, and move, however slightly at first, in a common way against inertia's policy. The Tombstone panelists sucked their pipes as one in approval. For thus could be explained the migration of the largest and most intractable mass to a distant point, somnambulant and complacent, seeking only safe conformity, as unaware of its own journey as a leaf on a gentle current.

This was rich with possibilities. Examples tumbled over one another. Electromagnetic forces with a fairy's weight, by measurement less massive than ideas, could displace entities totalitarian, beyond imagination's scope, in time. It happened daily: a solar wind consisting of the most intangible particles and ephemeral pressures disturbed the most immense things known. Objections were quickly made: gravitons, quarks, neutrinos, psions, cosmic rays, all did galley-slave work in the scheme of things. "But for or against the scheme of things as they will. It is random and self-canceling. It is no match for the mammoth tendencies of the status quo, the stubborn proclivities of dreadnought momentum": so read a critical rebuttal. "The probabilities are forbidding, unless there is manipulation, intervention, mediation, and communication. The sun is not, that is to say, a laser."

Soon an in-house revolution moved adherents to this view. "I'm afraid we're in a version of Zeno's paradox," the chairman admitted. "We've got the tail wagging the dog, forgetting that the tail is wagged by common consent to established systems of the puppy's parts. Control is surrendered to the central authority —nervous and endocrine. Now let's consider in this light the question of a hound's-tail revolt. What if the hind end wants to wag the mutt?"

Warren removed the pipe bit from his teeth, and said, "It's mediation most of all, and propaganda. Consider both words: The thing about all revolutionists is their idiosyncratic sense of time. They never know the odds."

To converse like this required half a life spent under fluorescent lights with tenure, or at least the hope of it.

"By sheer probability," Warren pressed, "so much random stumbling, by passionate romantics given access to roam at will, admits the case where a fulcrum's advantage is gained—perhaps the discovery of an imperfection in the confining vessel, perhaps the conversion of the great mass of the unattended, unbaptised, unpropagandized new generation. That's the question. And I assert it is straight out of Catastrophe Theory once again."

"Say I agree with you," the chairman asked, tamping his meerschaum. "What's your point of attack?"

"Exactly what our major question is: What are the 'other means,' the subtle interventions in reliable process—ours and theirs—that may change flow? Violence? I say all our work has told us something important: momentum is squared with each success; the differential of change is a logarithmic function. The airiest first push may signal the old order's demise, whether you use the old calculus or the new. Our task is how to stop it. How to forestall, reversing Zeno's paradox, catastrophe."

On the way out of the room at the end of that session, the chairman stopped to talk with Warren. "The more I see of your work, Reigeluth, the more I'm convinced you're a boon to the Center."

"Thank you."

"Bad business with your wife. I'm sorry."

"Over and done."

"I like that phrase of yours about revolutionists. You suppose it's true in all cases?"

"In the main."

"A fine and foolish ignorance to start with. Would you say then the amateur or the professional has the odds?"

"The house has the odds," Warren said. "The amateur has his ignorance. The professional may have technique—but he has caution. And that may cost him."

"Interesting. Fool's luck. Some say George Washington had it. Maybe so. Fools whose work survives are rechristened wise men, aren't they?"

"Unless they gain no better sense in victory—and will it all to first-born sons of fools."

The chairman liked that and took Warren's arm.

"Quite so," he said, "quite so," and waltzed Warren off to talk him into a more extensive White Paper on it all.

Robert Francis Kennedy, the junior Senator from the State of New York, was no revolutionist. Neither was he a fool. He knew the odds.

For all his emboldened talk in the early months of 1968, the distance he put between himself and his party's President, the man who survived to succeed his dead brother in office, who was in that place to do that thing because Robert Kennedy and his brother had been too tired to think straight when they offered the vice-presidential nomination to Lyndon Johnson, was a semantic crawl space. He used the cryptic formula that he "expected to support the Democratic nominee" in the 1968 election. Lyndon Johnson used the very same words. One thing that Robert Kennedy held to in the early months of 1968 defined him as a prisoner of the odds: his own noncandidacy.

He believed, perhaps correctly, that such value as he had must not be squandered in a losing effort; his magic derived from a kind of virginity, an innocence of failure.

He had been the first man approached by those who sought to topple Lyndon Johnson, as the strongest man in the party, the likely champion of a restoration.

But he was, most of all, clear-sighted, and told them the apparent truth: his very candidacy would detract from the main issue, which was the policy of war that Lyndon Johnson stuck by. From that policy all things went awry, more so than they did for having Johnson succeed John Kennedy by assassination. They argued back: that policy would not change so long as Lyndon Johnson held his office; and, the proliferation of quirky polls notwithstanding, a presidential campaign was the only way to take an issue "to the country" and get the people's answer. The fallacies in that were two: campaigns were rarely turned on issues but on personalities —they were the marketing of competing television shows, one of which, situation comedy or adventure, the public would be obliged to watch; and most of all, to Robert Kennedy, campaigns were mounted with the purpose of victory or not at all. They were not edu-

452

cational events but gang wars, struggles to the death for power. And he was in a bind that way: his power was his personality wrapped around the issues; but the debate over his ambition would make him a liability and obscure the issues. There must be, he urged them, another way.

Disappointed by Robert Kennedy's refusal, the war foes turned to targets of opportunity. They approached the Senate Foreign Relations Committee, which had stood as the only government body consistently questioning the war. That committee's power had been usurped by the White House, though fair to say its chairman, J. William Fulbright of Arkansas, helped in that by shepherding the Gulf of Tonkin Resolution through the Senate, brooking no debate.

Fulbright, too, declined to make a run. He faced a tough fight at home, and lacked a man who could secure a local ruling permitting both a national race and a Senate race as a Texan named Leon Jaworski had done for Lyndon Johnson in 1960. Other likely candidates demurred, and so the mantle fell on Senator Eugene J. McCarthy of Minnesota. He accepted the challenge and its risks with a mixture of eagerness and reluctance, a radical juxtaposition of styles that would prove his hallmark. When asked if this was "political suicide" he said he doubted it, that it would more likely be an "execution." He would run in the first primaries to expose the issues, and let citizens register their complaint with a vote for him without actually affecting the true course of electoral politics.

As for running to win, that was another matter. Eugene McCarthy would run to teach. Winning was only the dimmest possibility. That it was possible at all could only be guessed from the sight of Robert Kennedy fumbling with his toga, fingering his dagger in the wings, dreaming of the ides of March. Shakespearean images abounded. At first the press rushed to pin the tag of Hamlet on Robert Kennedy, then McCarthy; then they switched to Brutus and Cassius, tossing in a ghost or two as in Claudius and Banquo. It was a field day for the scribes.

For the moment, though, Robert Kennedy was stuck. He alone could make the contest credible, and he alone could flush out Johnson's trump: the argument that support of the war was a patriotic obligation, about which all debate became dissent, and thus was impermissible. For it was in no small way Robert Kennedy's war as well, carried on by invocations of his brother's name, perpetrated by the Special Forces and Counterinsurgency experts his brother had been so keen for, executing policies John Kennedy had begun. It did little good for war foes to contend that Jack Kennedy intended to pull out before the end of 1963; he did not live to do it, and no one but Robert Kennedy knew his mind. So Robert Kennedy, perhaps alone, could be the wedge. His renunciation of that policy as a great national—and personal, and family—mistake had opened windows into which considerations of humaneness blew. In any role, he was the war foes' best asset. And just as clearly, their worst, for his first move would make the whole matter one of clashing personalities and resentments.

But what a clash: the dirt farmer's giant son, who'd scratched and clawed and seduced and suffered judicious humiliations on his way to the master bedroom where he now indulged every venal and sadistic instinct, refusing to leave but on a slab, whose chief public zealotry was institutional benevolence, a Santa Claus in cowboy boots who'd provide the globe with American salvation, inoculate it forcefully against disease and local custom, give the world a New Deal, power mowers, Marshall Plan, and pony rides; this man, against the delicately featured squirearch who'd come into the house through the roof, the once merciless crusader now crusading *sotto voce* for what mercy he could inspire, who had been spiritually closer than any man to the greatest trauma of the age, enduring a rebaptism in its violence, who wandered now through the servants' quarters and the pantry in search of the education privilege denied him. Each would raise so many conflicting sentiments, resentments, loyalties, and anger, so many would identify with so many different parts of them, that Baron Zermatt's prediction looked certain: like antiparticles, protean Johnson and antiprotean Bobby would annihilate each other, leaving nothing behind except energy.

But for now it was McCarthy who ran, almost apologetically, into the ten-second attention span of the nightly news watchers. He looked like Ray Milland, the actor, reporters said, and he acted more like George Plimpton, the Mandarin amateur, though his speaking manner more resembled Jimmy Stewart reading from André Malraux. He did not seem serious, though he was very serious. He did not seem energetic, though his record and very daring spoke against that. For a radical, if radical he was, he seemed too politic yet to call for more than "halt the bombing" of North Vietnam, shying from the radical proposals that said the best way to halt the war was to halt the war, the best way to get the boys home, "boats."

That reluctance was a clue to his serious intent. A politician's vanity cannot countenance embarking on a losing effort, even for so high a national purpose, even with the emolument of hearing his own voice. No politician would sail westward toward the Indies over untracked seas unless he thought he had a secret passage to those riches. It's not a gambling man's calling, but an insider's art, not an explorer's life but an investor's. McCarthy had a map. In his heart, he was confident he could win precisely by pretending he didn't care.

So he pledged himself to public discussion, adopting the diction and the logical rigor of the latent theologian. Were it not for the snow in the streets as he strolled the New Hampshire towns, preaching about the uses and the limits of power, his effort might be seen as of the Peripatetic School, entirely Socratic: his questions obliged ordained answers and led, he hoped, to larger understandings. He sipped from endless teacups along the way. And he grew thirstier to win.

Though no revolutionist himself, McCarthy also knew that philosophy is hardly pressure on those who choose not to listen. One man, however attractive, is only vaporous force. A movement requires an army, marching into the teeth of the prevailing stasis. An amalgam of vapors can then be mighty as a rocket exhaust, with limitless potential.

There was an army, preexistent to the march. They'd expected to serve under Kennedy pennants, and shivered through the winters of the past three years without a leader. They were young and, as most were initially inspired by John Kennedy, their allegiance belonged first to his legates. Many came from the Peace Corps; some, angry at the turn that noble idea had taken since John Kennedy's death, directed their community-organization talents to problems at home. Others came from the civil rights movement, with baggage tags from every scene of domestic blood, where they were schooled early, harshly, in the brutal politics of die-hard resistance. Most, though, enlisted during the serial madnesses that followed the phantom Battle of Tonkin Gulf. Many came from the campuses, where administrators and trustees had found them thankless.

That was at the bottom. The victors of World War II had supposed that victory and abundance entitled them to unquestioned loyalty. The giant engine of progress was complete, they had thought; America could meet all problems. It was not thought that victory, abundance, and benevolence could become a generation's poison, infecting it with a sense of arrogant mission and moral dominion. But now, in the most wonderful prosperity, the most dizzying boom, the most widely shared plenty the world had ever known, something was sickeningly wrong. The children of the victors had been given everything and had been asked for precious little, only to serve graciously. Now they refused to serve at all: they wanted to overthrow it all.

So there was an army, ready to be mobilized, waiting for a general. The cause was attractive; it appealed to all ideals; its failure would likely consume them, every one. McCarthy stepped into this leadership lacuna, commanding a vast, unheralded network of partisans.

From that beginning, the first battalion of fools could be raised, in McCarthy's idiom, to a crusade, to sweep into Jerusalem and boot the Saracens from the sacred places. For it was, as Warren Reigeluth had it, fools who were "the stuff of revolutions." Only fools could believe, before the evidence, that mere hope and high purpose might have purchase on so unwilling an unmoved entity as an Empire's politics. And in the early weeks, surging by jalopy, bus, and Volkswagen, dragging textbooks, leisure time, and parental funds, these fools entered the fruitless fields of New Hampshire, where any farmer knows the year's best harvest is the rocks. Among them had come Tyler Bowen. In the second wave would come Johanna Poulson, with new-old scars and an old-new name.

When he first arrived in New Hampshire, Tyler listed his useful skills as Biochemistry and short relief. Under previous occupation he put, in deference to his security oath, "Information Officer/Civil Affairs Associate." That was good enough for them. He was immediately press-ganged into service. On reflection, it was funny and reasonable. Johanna thought he sounded like he was leering when he said he was working in "Press Relations." He was. His job was to seduce the press, bend it to his will. They'd taught him a few things about it at Gila Compound.

These early fools believed, in the advanced rapture of innocent faith, that a successful campaign could begin with half a candidate, in a barren state, whose only statewide press called them worse than fools. This paper, the *Manchester Union Leader,* did its inane best to ignore the doings in its back yard, and the entire twentieth century, on the theory that if not encouraged such things might go away. Its publisher was, it was said, starboard of Caligula: if Caligula would have his horse named a Consul, William Loeb would go one better and have his counsel named a horse. When this paper stooped to coverage it treated the campaigners as "outside agitators," and developed a lexicon of sobriquets to identify them. "Quislings" being a favorite.

Oddly, the paper's publisher was no fan of Lyndon Johnson's. This supported the assumption, Tyler Bowen urged the inquiring press, that the man simply fancied war, though certainly, he pointed out, not at the peril of personal service. The paper answered with a peculiar sensitivity to the young campaigners' morals, accusing the McCarthy volunteers of all manner of license. This, too, Tyler Bowen noted with delight, was a curious accusation, considering the source. In Loeb's overpublicized life he'd singlehandedly given adultery a bad name.

It was all funny to Tyler Bowen, and even the other fools. It was hilarious, as they sucked a heady weed of impact. And within a few days, a strategy emerged.

At Tombstone Center, the lessons would have been clear. They trucked in alien newspapers from the metropolitan centers, papers that referred to them as "Pilgrims"; an honored name in that region, it had been suggested by a McCarthy press staffer to the newsman who first wrote it. That lent the weight of history and institutions, and softened initial attitudes for the waves that followed.

And the waves followed: thousands, pooling talent, time, and witness, gathering like the D-Day Armada, ready for the suicidal Great Assault. Each came with insufficient force, but in sum it was enough to initiate the energy required for consequence.

After arriving in New Hampshire, Tyler's first impression had been that Baron Zermatt was right: Robert Kennedy would not tolerate such an amorphous state of organization. Yet somehow, slowly, over the weeks, order began to impose itself; form could be discerned as even the land showed its shape in the melting of the snow. "It took some time to get the Fleet looking sharp after Pearl Harbor," one staffer explained. "Only for us Pearl Harbor was the day the candidate announced."

Tyler Bowen's rank within the organization remained as vague as the organization itself. With each successive pulse of eager workers from nearby campuses, he rose by sheer seniority.

"Looks like I bought IBM at three-and-a-half," he announced smugly to Zermatt on the phone. "Whaddya say to *that,* sucker?"

"Sounds to me like you bought Edsel at fifty. A lot of hamsters running around in their cage. Lotsa luck, fella."

Still, Tyler was convinced this was a suitable outlet for his urges: a legal crack at regicide, an honorable way to purge his anger, a mutual enterprise with Johanna—and a way to show his real decency to her. He could wear himself out at this, and prove his better angels in the process. He did not believe that the candidate, such as he was, really had a chance, or that the movement, such as it was, did either. Rather, he had a chance. So that at the end he might say with Johanna, in moral and political consolation, "We tried."

By THE WEEK JOHANNA LEFT TUCSON, Tyler had risen through the ranks, or on the shoulders of them, to traveling coordinator of press and public relations, ambassador without portfolio. Great attention had to be paid to the manner of campaign worker discourse. It was one thing for the candidate to use an urbane tone of learning, quite another, as a memo put it, "for us whippersnappers."

The enlistees alternated between displays of surprisingly shrewd political calculation—not everyone was a battle virgin—wishful nods to philosophy, and high-school civics class notions. Nor were they far from the heart of the local myth: New Hampshire license plates read "Live Free or Die." This was at once a stirring command, and a strange thing for convicted felons in the state penitentiary to be stamping out. But most of all it was a reminder of that first assault on Kings which ended with a world turned upside down; one mounted no less than the present one for reasons of ardent philosophy and local economy.

In Concord one morning and in Manchester that afternoon, Tyler briefed a group of canvassers, and told them how to deal with voters who were veterans of Word War II. "Ask them," Bowen said, "if they fought so their sons and neighbors could die for Ky and Thieu —working in that Mr. Ky's favorite historical figure is Hitler. Politely. Don't spell it for them. Then start talking about inflation in the supermarket. Make friends."

Some of the volunteers had to be cautioned that referring to "The Good People of the Granite State" or

"TGPOTGS" as "Geeps" or "Woodchucks" sounded snide and smacked of attitudes detested overseas. These problems, though, were easily corrected, and the Geeps were analyzed, cajoled, implored, and flattered by wave after wave of the overbright and the overeager. All references to Sartre and Camus were strictly and specifically enjoined, though like planaria, the severed bodies grew new heads: Bernard Fall, John Kenneth Galbraith, and Hans Morgenthau cropped up instead.

"I know your educations were very expensive," he told one group. "But as you go through life you'll have to learn to forget it all anyway. I know it's hard in the face of some grizzled geezer who's gonna vote Republican or write in Johnson and who's hitting you with quotes from John Wayne. But try. Turn the other cheek. Ask them what army John Wayne ever served in."

For a while, his assignment changed every two days. Some nights he slept in borrowed beds, a quartered soldier in peacetime. From one he wrote Saint Paul, "There's this picture of everybody's favorite Blessed Virgin and in her belly's the thermostat. She's either been doing it with the man from Mobiloil or God's truly the Light and the Power." He found the town of Berlin, near the Maine border, "closer to the Canada of 1938 than D.C. now."

In every town, and every storefront, campaigners and sympathizers reported one thread uniting their garnered support: "Anyone But Johnson," people said, just as Baron Zermatt had predicted. "ABJ" buttons did a brisk business, though the candidate was not flattered. "Whoever's responsible for putting New Hampshire first on the list," Zermatt said on the phone, "should have his head examined. Oh, it's great for the Geeps! You're their biggest industry. But the same guy who put this primary first is the guy who put Fort Kearny in the middle of the Sioux Nation. With all those colleges around there! If you guys can't do decently . . ."

"Wanna take points on 20 percent?" Tyler asked.

"With fifteen registered Democrats in the state? You need six friends to be geniuses!"

"What's your guess?"

"Anything over 25 percent is a new ballgame. Lyndon's got a built-in 75 percent approval if he takes a shit on the lawn. That's a fact. I'm just going to count the number of stitches that open on his gallbladder scar, for clues. Fifty percent and his intestines drop out."

"Hey, Bar, we're gonna do it! You should see it. On weekends you can walk to Boston on the car tops and never touch the pavement. It's like foliage season," Tyler said.

"Frankly, I don't know why it's written in such big letters in D.C. Any fool can do it if he doesn't fall down. But boy, if you win outright will Bobby be sore. And if you lose—well, I'm sure Lyndon'll let you plead to lesser charges. When's your honey coming in?"

"Day after tomorrow. Start the month off right. Bright and clear."

"Maybe it's an omen. It's a white shit-storm down here. I hear it starts off clean, but it touches down brown. Close your windows, pal, the shit's on the way north."

"You changing registrations again?"

When Baron hung up he told his wife he hadn't heard his friend sound so chipper in months. "He's jumping right up the organizational ladder. What a kid! I told you he was something. They take one look at him and say we want you on our side."

The storm that had strangled New York extended to New Haven and Philadelphia, and so a plane headed for Kennedy Airport was diverted that afternoon to Bradley Field, Connecticut, north of the weather's fringe. The passengers were loaded onto buses there for the city. By the time they would reach New York it would be late evening. It was some mess to arrive in, after the sunshine of northern California they had left that morning.

One of the passengers, Staff Sergeant Sam Kinney, lived in Dedham, Massachusetts, and the Hartford landing didn't bother him at all. He could cab it from Bradley Field to the nearby Springfield, Mass., bus terminal, catch an express bus home, and arrive ahead of his previous best estimate. The weather in Boston and environs was good. In fact, this diversion was further boon to him, for if he had gone to New York City he would have been obliged to run a time-consuming errand, which he could now duck out of. He had been in Willie Bowen's sector and Corps in Vietnam, and he carried in his black PX bag a thick mustard-green envelope, such as might protect books in the mail, or might keep ice cream from melting. The bag was hermetically sealed against spillage or spoilage. On the outside were several official stamps: "Special Handling," "Department of the Army/Official Business," some serial numbers and code numbers meaningful to its special handlers, and a seal affixed in the Republic of Vietnam, with an official regimental cachet. This would indicate to the Oakland Army Terminal Receiving Station inspectors that the contents were "Official" and "Sensitive" and discretion was advised during arrival shakedown inspections. The in-country seal of Regimental HHC said that the contents were licit, and the package merited care and immunity from inspection: it bore no dope. It was addressed to Mr. and Mrs. V. Bowen, at their home in Pelham, New York. Staff Sergeant Sam Kinney was to hand-carry it.

At Bradley Field, Kinney tapped an officer headed to New York on the courtesy bus and implored him, "I'd really appreciate it, sir, if you'd see that this here's delivered when you get down there, post haste. I know that's asking a lot but—"

"Yes, it is," the officer responded, trying to refuse efficiently. "I'd like to get home, too."

"Yes, sir. But, see, I'm going the other way and—this is a personal thing, you understand."

"Not official?"

"Oh, official as hell—but personal, if you know what I mean. It's got to be hand-carried—ASAFP."

"F?" the officer asked.

"As soon as fuckin' possible," Kinney replied grimly. "If you could see to it—"

By then the officer had been snared in the exchange too long. He had spent three years in a stateside pleasure trip at Fort Ord on the Monterey Peninsula, and at Oakland, preparing and shipping fresh meat to the Far East and receiving the ground-chuck results. His compliance was already impelled by the guilt feelings

Staff Sergeant Sam Kinney's extensive battle ribbons spawned. "What's the blue bar?" he asked Kinney, thinking he had changed the subject, his finger enviously brushing Kinney's fruit salad.

Kinney scratched his cheek modestly as if he wasn't quite certain. "It's a Presidential Unit Citation. Not exactly sure what for. I was R&Ring at Long Binh hospital when we got it. Tet stuff. Graves detail, that's what we were. Most of the guys who picked it up, I expect, would rather be alive."

The officer looked at the floor and Kinney knew he had him.

"Haven't taken a poll about it," Kinney continued, laying it on, "but I'd guess they'd just as soon live without it, what do ya say?" He laughed at his own joke but the officer grunted nervously. "Tell ya what, sir—I've got a Bronze Star in my ditty bag here. Snaps broken and all—keeps falling off. But if you'd like it—I got no more use for it. I'd sell it to ya." The officer shook his head frantically as if to convince himself he wouldn't make the deal. "Well, I'd *give* it to ya, sir, if—see, you'd be doing a real good turn to get this thing here delivered. Not for me, man. For a guy who really put it on the line for you." He tossed his head sideways and back as if to indicate some remote place and time he was referring to. "You know what I mean?"

So the officer carried the packet on his lap, gingerly, as though it contained nitroglycerine, all the way down to New York. He off-loaded his hot potato on the Arrivals Clerk at the terminal, pointing out that it was a top-priority hand-carry item. The Spec-4 at arrivals said he understood and tossed it in a hopper, where it was picked up by the next troop headed for Fort Hamilton, directed to the Provost Marshal's Traffic Controller there, who would know what to do. The Provost Marshal's Traffic Controller dispatched a courier with the parcel to the S-6 officer.

At the S-6 shed, the MP courier asked if the S-6 router had "someone doing Westchester tonight."

"Whatcha got?"

The MP handed him the six-by-nine-inch packet and recited its various priority designations, but the router cut him off, saying, "I can read, punko. Don't give me

463

that priority shit. Everything's priority. End of the line like everyone else." The MP repeated what he'd been told, and the router peered up in annoyance. "You can repeat yourself all night. I got a fucking snowstorm outside and I can't slot this shit."

"All I know is what they asked me to do," the MP retreated.

"Well, *fuck* 'em if they can't take a joke," the router laughed until he coughed. "Look, punk—I did you guys a favor last week. Busted my hump putting out a DGR-283 and it crapped up my whole sked. This dude's iced, he can stay in the cooler overnight, right? Whatcha got in there, anyway?" He shook the package jerkily. "Teeth or something? Ashes? Dog tags keep. Just make like you couldn't find me, huh?" Then, with a disgusted wave as though to chase away an offending smell, he acquiesced, "Ah, the hell with it."

"That's very nice of you."

"Yeah, I'm a peach. Christ, what a day! Lucky bastard. The next stiff takes standing room or walks his own fucking ass home."

A half-hour later, an aggravated Lieutenant, drummed into sled-dog duty by the S-6 router, telephoned the addressee, Mr. V. Bowen, in Pelham. "Mr. Bowen? This is First Lieutenant Anthony Higbee at the S-6 Section at Fort Hamilton. Army, yessir. I have a parcel here for you. Will you or Mrs. Bowen be in this evening? No, sir, my instructions are to deliver it personally. It cannot be mailed. Yessir, that's correct, sir. It's marked 'Special Handling/By Courier Only.'"

Vlad trembled, dangling at the mercy of a reedy voice on the telephone. This personless voice could not "divulge the contents or discuss the nature of this matter over the telephone," except to say that it was "under Official Seal, Department of the Army. I am not authorized to open it except in the presence of the addressee. This is an official parcel—a DA communication. My inst—I hope you understand, sir. Here is a number you can use to verify the authenticity of this call." Higbee read an official directive providing suitable phrases for every conceivable response, however shaken or hostile, thereby to prevent the compounding of injury by insult. He knew his part by rote, but the regulations required he actually read the lines, nothing more, and that he read them in a manner indicating they were being read.

There was silence on the line, then Vlad Bowen asked if he knew the way. "Yessir," Higbee answered. "I've been in the neighborhood before. Around ten, sir? Will that be too late? No, sir. I'll be accompanied by WAC Lieutenant Tipton. We will both have identification. Yessir, ten then. Thank you, sir, and have a pleasant evening."

Vlad Bowen sat at the kitchen table thinking how to tell Laura. He passed an hour in a near-trance, broken only by the phone's ring. Amid much static, no doubt due to the weather, a distant operator asked if he would accept "a collect call for anyone," and then drifted away, saying as she faded that she would call back. Laura called down to him asking who it was, but he yelled back, "Nothing. No one—" and nervously roused the local operator, whose advice was that he hang up and wait. When no call came back, he concluded the storm had foiled Tyler's attempts to call. Or maybe he'd gone off to do something else.

His belly felt weak, its muscles slackened by an over-long match with an unrelenting foe. His insides, blood, and heart felt heavy, on fire. He buried his head in his arms and closed his eyes, to let the feeling take him. It was an awful, disorienting sense, and he wept. Children were such slender filaments, vulnerable to so many winds, pregnant from birth with morbid consequence.

He sat there, motionless, thinking of how fathers sired sons who would then father other fathers, and he felt amputated. He thought of those special days set aside to honor that, of Father's Day, when his children would take him out to dinner, though of course he'd pay the check and thus feel even more a father; or they'd busy themselves all day in making a meal for him and he'd have to dine on a child's idea of supper, loving it nonetheless as much as he loved their presents of terrariums and artless drawings, snakeskin belts and basketball hoops.

Later, quivering but dry, Vlad left the table, looking for something soft to touch. There was nothing for the living to hold on to, no bones to bury, no memento to hug. What would they dare deliver? There would likely be papers to sign. The last act of paternity, begun by loving made actual, would be concluded with a pen's flourish, a contract sealed. His own signature and paraph would be the only shroud. He grimaced: would they ask a neighbor in to be a witness?

It had been a long time since he'd cried this way: the night World War II ended. He and Laura and their little girl Connie were in Washington that week, splurging their gasoline ration stamps on a summer's trip. It was then that Tyler was conceived. To celebrate the Victory they'd visited the Lincoln Memorial, and there met several thousand others with the same idea; something about the faith and purpose of that struggle to Victory brought them. Vlad broke down, as did many others there, and took some time to compose himself. And again, that night, after Laura was asleep, filled with the stuff that would be a son, Vlad Bowen sobbed to heaven in prayers and dreams, wept in prostrate silence for the country that had blessed him so continuously with wealth and happiness and safety, and he prayed that such children as he might breed would give back to their land as much in blessings as it had given them. Now, for that good fortune, in some awful form of taxes he had never been told about, they came to take his boys away. One was gone, one was in confusion's grasp, raging futilely to unwind the sheet. Only Connie was untaxed, and she too brought forth boys to lose. What a rare day that had been, V-J Day; and this one, too, the Leap Year Day, even robbing him of an annual remembrance.

At 10:15 the doorbell rang. Vlad was at the sink splashing water on his face; at the sound of the bell he gagged, then spat in the sink. He rushed to head off Laura but she was already at the door. Knowing he would not even be allowed the comfort of rudeness to the heralds, he came up behind his wife and gently guided her aside. "Mrs.—Mr. Bowen? I'm Lieutenant Higbee. I spoke to you earlier? This is Lieutenant Tipton—" he offered tentatively, half in question. "Yes, come in," Vlad said.

"I'm sorry to be disturbing you so late, Mrs. Bowen," Tipton said. Her job was to tend the mothers and the wives, part of the Survivors' Assistance Program of her Community Liaison Unit. Laura turned suddenly to her husband with a gasp of comprehension. She blocked the entrance, as though making a last stand on her doorstep. Vlad eased her aside to let them enter, looking only at his wife with a gaze of wild love and admiration for her iron.

Making small talk about the weather's driving problems, the four went into the living room, seated in the arrayment regulations required, Lieutenant Tipton near at hand to Mrs. Bowen, Lieutenant Higbee close enough to Vlad Bowen to look him in the eye while speaking. Vlad held both his wife's hands tightly in his lap, as Higbee opened a briefcase. "Sir?" Higbee said, as he handed over the small polyurethane-sealed packet. It was a strange fillip, that covering; Willie Bowen had once said of his mother's prideful mounting of the various certificates of her children's merit, "I think she'd like it best if she could just wrap us each in Saran Wrap and hang us on the wall." She begged Vlad's attention from the young officer, to ask, "Are these people here about Willie?"

"Mrs. Bowen?" Lieutenant Tipton said, with schooled concern, "We've been requested to deliver this." She leaned toward Laura, who only cringed toward her husband, demanding of the officer, "By whom?"

"Ma'am," Higbee said, Vlad nodding him on, "we are a Support Community Liaison team, from Special Services Section, Records Branch." Vlad took firm hold of the plastic package and softly lowered it to the tea table in front of him. He stood up and extended a hand to Laura and she rose to him, moving alongside him as he thanked the two officers for coming out in such dismal driving conditions. But he wanted no more apothegms. "We appreciate your effort," he said coldly.

"That's quite all right, sir," Higbee said, folding up his briefcase, pushing a receipt form toward Vlad. "I'm just sorry about—" Vlad cut him off and scribbled his signature. The form resembled nothing more than the invoices he used for consignments of scrap. "Sir, Ma'am? If there's any further assistance we—"

"You can leave right now," Vlad instructed. Laura made a gesture to ameliorate his harshness.

"Well, we do have to push on," Lieutenant Tipton said. "I hope everything will be all right. If you need any assistance——" She surprised Laura by pressing her cheek against hers. "I am—terribly sorry." She stepped out the door, followed by Higbee, turning to bid goodnight efficiently, "Mr. Bowen, Mrs. Bowen."

Higbee echoed her: "Sir, ma'am."

The packet sat in their gaze like a bomb. There was no reason to open it, so they let it sit, dormant monstrousness, still wrapped in the cloak of hope's illusions. Vlad seethed at the bland way they dropped it in his lap.

Finally, slowly untangling his arm from behind Laura, he walked to the phone to call his daughter. Connie's husband answered. "May I speak to her, Alan?" Vlad asked mechanically. "Yes. *Well,* thank you. We're all—no, not so well, Alan. Let me speak to Constance, please. Would you stay by the phone? She may need—yes. We just did. No. Not good at all."

Connie came on, half-distracted by one of her children, who had been socked by the other and required her leg for a hugging post. "What is it, Daddy?" she asked, while her husband pried the child from her; it only promoted real screaming and tears.

Vlad told her. "We haven't opened it—I'm not sure there's any—I suppose. Your mother has it." He gestured to Laura to bring it over and she ripped the plastic off. Vlad took the packet and found there were two envelopes inside officially stamped. He wasn't sure he had the strength to endure them.

He ripped open one quickly, knowing care would not avail. The notice would be economical and immutable, though the envelope was fat. "It's two——" The phone slipped. "It's two more—one's addressed to Tyler and oh, dear God, it's in Willie's handwriting——" Just another of the ironic indignities the Army subjected them to, having the men address these letters when they were shipped overseas, as they did when they arrived at boot camp. "This other's addressed to us. It's typed—some kind of official—just a moment." He ripped it while Laura held the receiver to his ear, leaning her own against it. It was a several-page document and it had been awkwardly, not at all properly, folded. "Connie?"

"Yes, Daddy. What does it say?"

"I don't know what the hell this—it's some kind of *inventory,* mimeographed. I don't unders—" He turned it over and saw crowded typing on the reverse side. "It's—" He went violently weak and this time broke down bawling, "Oh, Jesus!" hugging his wife and the telephone as he slumped against the wall.

"Connie!" he sobbed hoarsely into the phone, "Oh dear, dear merciful God, dear merciful—Connie!! It's from Willie. I think he's *alive.* I think—" Laura was rifling through the pages wildly, bobbing her head and weeping. "He's alive, sweetheart. Our baby is alive!!"

With Laura nestled crutchlike under his arm, shuddering, Vlad tried to read to Connie. It took some faltering starts before he could see clearly. Focusing was difficult and the letter was typed on the cheapest inventory paper, marginless and single-spaced with blinding compactness: It read:

Dear Mom and Dad and Ty and Connie and Animal and all the little Macks and all the people Mom's going to call when she gets this letter:

Hi. I suppose it might seem like a shock to hear from me after so long without even a postcard, but I wasn't near a phone for a while, and if I haven't spoken to you by the time you get this it's just as well as I don't trust Army Operators or the civilians working here (with good reason—and you shouldn't either) so if I have already spoken to you by now I probably didn't get to tell you the truth. There is a complicated business as to why. But first of all, if you are reading this, as you can tell, I am alive and sound. I only mention that because I understand that I'm supposed to be lost, stolen, or strayed. Not so. I hope this letter finds the rest of you in good health, too.

His letter went on to refer to a call he was going to try to make, but apparently never did, explaining that "it would cost a tooth and a foot anyway." Then, "if I didn't, here's what happened, or something.

First of all, as everybody knows now and I knew all along, I'm alive and as well as can be expected

469

in this part of the world. I'm just repeating that for emphasis. All parts of me are working—especially, at last, my head—and at this very moment I'm even better looking then when you last saw me, though I know that's hard to believe.

I guess you already met Sam Kinney. He's in my unit—I don't really know him all that well—and he just got out-processed—and since even the mails are slow and nosy (because if they knew in Westchester what we are doing in I-Corps it might somehow hurt the War Effort, I don't know) I had it specially wrapped and asked him to hand-carry it, sort of smuggling. He seemed like a nice guy and I told him to expect to be force-fed and adopted for bringing home good tidings. Hope you weren't too rough on him. He's from Boston and he's only got seven sibs —better move your ass or *whatever*, Mack! I guess he can take it.

The reason for all this and why you haven't heard from me in so long is supposed to be secret (except every Oriental in the world already knows)—that's why the Official packet. They'd never open one. Ha-ha. I should've sent some dope, I guess, too.

Uncle was no doubt diligent in getting you the details of my disengagement. Even I didn't know the whole story until my paper work caught up, and I found out what a scare story they had out on me. I wasn't missing—although I was scared for a while. Most of the time I knew just where I was—and just where I didn't want to be. . . .

There was this napalm attack on a village we were looking at. Our napalm. Except I was in the bushes taking a dump. Most of everyone else got a one-way ticket to Kingdom Come, except me. But the Army didn't know that. All they knew was there was my rifle and shirt (and dog tags)—which was more than was left by most. I got knocked half-silly into a drainage ditch or sewer. I didn't really check which. It must have been built by your tax dollars and some very earnest Peace Corps types a few years ago. Thanks, y'all. Anyway, between the War Corps and King Cong, most of what was left was me on my butt in that ditch—trying to tell my . . . from a hole in the ground—and a lot of well-done everyone else, like I said. My shirt caught fire, which woke me up smartly, as you can imagine. I only remember rolling around a little and passing out a lot. When I came around I was hurting and I stuck my nose out and saw the mess. It stank worse than the sewer or whatever I was in and looked like Mars. My rifle was melted better than a candle, and I'm only lucky my burns weren't worse. (They've mostly healed now and you can hardly tell I had any.)

There was exactly no sense hanging around waiting to see who got there first, so off I went like Tarzan into the boonies. That wasn't maybe so smart as it seemed, but I'd never been in such a fix before, and evacuation had a large appeal just then. Except I went in the wrong direction. (Well, right for *someone,* I guess.) I'm also sorry I left my rifle as I remembered later there was a letter to Tyler in the stock, which I suppose got burned up. (But at least *I* wrote, Babe.) . . .

Every step I got loster, until I snuck up on this village and staged a one-man raid on their vegetable patch, like Pvt. P. Rabbit. (Mack's kids would've starved to death—nothing but veggies to eat for a week!) I made it through all right without any flak from Farmer MacGregor-san.

One time I got a good angle on some shelling. I stayed with it a while to check it out. We were losing. I didn't think getting dead with a lot of guys who used to speak the same language as me was really much better than being lost and talking to myself. So I stayed neutral on it. We lost, and I had to move out by night the day after, scared silly, and with a cold.

After a few more days—I was having a pretty good time, seeing the countryside by myself, a lot like going to Europe, I guess—I began to run out of gas. Sometime during that week I forgot there was a war on—except that I was cold and had no shirt and was pretty bruised. At night I made out with leaves, like Adam before he lost his rib. But pretty soon I decided that being a POW had its advantages: they give you shirts, I hear. It seemed like the second worst thing that could happen. The first was starving to

471

death. So, at the next village, I just forked myself over. Well, the people were real great. You'd really like them. They reminded me of those people who used to live in the Kinsolving's house but they all had better skin, except yellowish, and the usual Namese features (which are quite lovely, you know). And they were all real old. They treated my scrapes and burns with some plants, and it really worked well. I had lost some weight, tho I weighed more than any two of them—and I had lost my zest for The War, which I had decided pretty early on was not such a hot item. They gave me a nice shirt.

They were a pacified village and every so often a VC unit would come by and they'd hide me. Once in grain bin—which upset me because this whole thing started when a guy in my unit found a suspected VC kid hiding in a grain bin. They adopted me as their American Foster Child. Someday I'd like to go back and thank them all—if they still speak to Americans then. I swear, there was no one younger than forty and they all looked ninety. I was getting into being their community project, for about a month. I'd gotten a real good tan, and learned a little Namese and some agriculture stuff, put on some weight, and got real healthy again. Somewhere in there I had a nice Christmas, I think, though my dates were a little slippery.

Now, we were up near the Cambo border and I decided one day to hit the trail and head for Sweden. I'd had it. I figured I couldn't hang out there for the duration. So I resigned. But there was some shelling again, and I spent a lovely day on the hillside watching us lose again. Also there were American planes pounding the hell out of the other side of the border —unless they moved the border. That had me confused. Maybe the old folks had given me a bum steer, because our guys were creaming something deep in Camboland. Maybe I was headed for the DMZ? No—it was Cambo! So I jollied back to my village—it was really *my* village—whose name I would spell if I could but it's all dirty in English. You may not believe this, but after about three days, all the trees on the perimeter suddenly bloomed into a whole Armored Division or something! I felt like France being freed—except I was still undecided.

I was surprised to find out they were not, in fact, looking for me at all. But, they were so genuinely glad to see me that they did something very official right there: they put me under arrest for desertion. I told them, "You're making a mistake," and this Major came up with his side arm out and said, "In a war we could have you shot!" and cracked me across the face. I figured, what-the-hell, if I'm going to get shot, what do I have to lose: so I bounced one off his pubes and another off his nose and dropped him for the count.

Apparently, my lack of regulation fatigues and my glorious tan did not testify well to my keen desire to rejoin the crusade for dead hearts and minds.

There was a radio silence, but they broke it in my honor, just to get permission to shoot me. Boy, were they upset when they couldn't find my records! Some Colonel decided I was a home-grown pinko who had come over to help the Cong. (I told them this was a peaceful village, but they showed me on their maps that it wasn't at all. It was a war zone all right. Sure fooled me until they got there.) How I ever convinced them to recheck my records I will save for future use on girls—and sure enough, the clerk in charge of them had been out to lunch the first time, and they were in the MIA drawer. When they found out I was truthful they were sore indeed. I had two technicals and should have been in the showers.

Intermission: I have lately learned that after I got back, they rechecked with the guy who filed the first after-action report the day I got lost. He was at Guam being fitted for a new body and had been set to go home. But they held him up, and for all I know threatened to turn off his IV glucose and saline—but he stuck to his guns, and if he's anything like the other guys in the burn wards, the sheets, too. Burns are bad news, and this guy deserves a decoration for after-action courage, I believe.

Back to the story: The Major's not speaking to me, but the Colonel said he knew, just *knew,* deep down, that I was pulling a fast one. I looked in his eyes—

and I saw murder. *I* began to believe him. My tan was too good and all. I was getting away with something, he said, and owed Sam my life—the implications of which I was not anxious to discover. (They don't mind if you miss a little duty and come back mangled or missing pieces. But six weeks and a tan? Oh, no, you don't!) But still, I was supposed to be dead, I guess, which saved me. So they dusted me off, gave me new socks and a shirt with no name and a recently inherited rifle. In its stock was some other guy's last letter, which reminded me of the one I wrote. I sent it on. Disregard mine—false alarm. Hope his was, too, but I doubt it.

Now, this Colonel tells me that with any luck I'll get offed with no ID and save everyone a lot of paper work. I could get lucky and make Unknown Soldier of the Month and go to the finals. Well, excuse my language, but I told him, as we say out here, "Fuck that shit, man!" I put most of my all into surviving after that.

The only problem was that we were on a four-week highly hush-hush Op—which is to say we weren't where we were welcome or supposed to be. Nobody stamped my passport, but we went well past the clump which separates Nam from the World, and Not-Cambo from Cambo. Anyone who could have been was shot when he stood up. I asked where the hell we were and I got told, "Nowhere," which I knew all along. The whole thing was "Embargoed," stamped SuperTopSecret, and all pens, paper, and carrier pigeons were confiscated. You probably know more than me. I don't know nuttin about nuttin. Mum's the word, chief.

Anyway, they had me stamped Secret for a while, which must have added to your distress. I'm sorry. They're a rotten bunch of bastards, as you probably know. I'm lucky I got found now—otherwise I might have to pay late penalties on my taxes.

So I'm back in-country now, and I'm working at a desk job starting yesterday, where, unless I get swapped North for some officer POWs I will be able to say that, as you read this, I am alive and well, and about to go on R&R in Thighland in a week.

I'll write (and call) often to keep you posted.

I think this only proves that only a silver bullet can kill people with real Vampire Blood in their veins (and a little Scotch to keep you warm). No VC can get a Bowen! But if Tyler doesn't watch out, VD will, ha-ha.

> Love to all and I'm sorry I let 'em scare you like that.
> Your son (and whatever to whoever),
> Willie/Me/X

P.S. Along with this one there is a letter for Tyler. Please send it or give it to him unopened, as I don't have his address. Tell him to give somebody—any-body—a big kiss and cop a cheap feel for me—and tell her I did *too* respect her in the morning. Ha-ha. Don't read Tyler's mail. It's bad form and besides it's just dirty about whores and drugs and you don't want to know about that shit.

P.P.S. Please give Sam Kinney maybe twenty-five dollars and carfare because he was a nice guy to do this and because I promised you would. Thanks. See you all soon. Love. Good to be sort of halfway back. Call the colleges I applied to and tell them I'm ready if they are. Love—Willie/The Kid

All through Vlad's reading of the letter, Vlad, Laura, and Connie communicated by shout and sniffle, pausing to let each other catch up like three hikers on a weary-ing trek, finishing with individual exclamations of joy. Every few lines, Connie would shriek out loud, "That's Willie, all right! Oh, it's wonderful! Oh, that little dope!" hugging one of her own children desperately.

The light was at the end of the tunnel for real. The corner was turned and the mask of jesting brought down from the attic. The world was made anew; the Bowen family was graced.

It was not until the next morning that they finally reached Tyler with the happy news. He deliriously ac-costed strangers with the information all day. They seemed genuinely pleased for him, and took it as a good augury for the campaign. He didn't mention the Cam-bodia aspect, and suggested his parents keep that out of circulation, for he didn't want to add any danger to

Willie's life, knowing how jealously the government husbanded its information.

Vlad and Laura sent the second letter up to McCarthy Headquarters at 3 Pleasant Street Extension in Concord, as Tyler instructed them, without reading it to him on the phone. "I'll either be staying at the Wayfarer in Manchester or a Hojo's in Concord after tomorrow, so send it to the State Headquarters. I'll let you know where I am as soon as I find out." He didn't want to subject them to "stuff about whores and drugs and all" either. They did this without protest, having already read the letter, of course.

"It's a good thing February 29 comes only once every four years," Tyler said before hanging up. "I don't know if I could take this every year. But I'm sure glad it's *this* year!"

Most of all, Tyler and his parents and sister felt, with Willie, it was suddenly good to be a Bowen once again, and sweet beyond words to be alive.

It had taken Johanna a week longer than she planned to leave Arizona. As anxious as she was to evacuate, there were still good friends to see and small errands to attend to. Indeed, in Scottsdale she felt a recuperative calm, with no pressures or obligations, on a furlough from those inside her. Then, good-byes exhausted, what she called "the longest dying scene since *Camille*," and not without a little trepidation, she got on that plane she wished she'd taken two-and-one-half months before.

She took off for Boston the morning Tyler received Willie's letter. Some measure of the excitement he was feeling in the campaign was that the second letter hardly dented his good spirits. Willie was alive, that's all he read. The rest, however disturbing, was small stuff compared to that.

The second letter read:

Hey, Babe!
How's it hanging? Suppose you've heard the good news by now: The Kid's back! Bigger and stronger and prettier—and I want my football on my bed when I get home or I'm gonna kick ass, older brother

476

or not. (We have supermanners over here. How do you like 'em?) How's your ass otherwise?

I told the rest of them I got a desk job, which isn't exactly true. But they've had enough, I figure. You know what I mean? And I had a desk job for a week, so it's true. *Was.* I'm back in the saddle again, out where a friend is expected to live thirty seconds shorter than you do if he's any kind of friend at all. And I don't know if I'll ever get back to Recon and Graves. Right now I'm at the mercy of a Replacement Center and I go where I'm told and the only thing that connects my assignments is that in all of them you're A-lone. . . .

I swear, they ought to let wives and girlfriends come along. Someone you could count on. Forget the lunch wagon in the sky—three out of five times they can't figure where to bring the rations. The evac ships never quite make their skeds. Forget buddies. Forget the Army—I can't believe any Army in the world could lose to us unless they really tried. All the time you are A-number-one-lone. Zee-row.

Dig: I know who I am—better than I know any of them except that I know most of them are Turkeys. I know how much I can be counted on: zip. Anybody waiting for me to come crawling under machine-gun fire with the ammo strapped to my back, leaking from seventeen holes a bloody fucking noble mess had better not hold dinner. I wouldn't get out of my 80% duck-down Posturepedic sleep-sack if it meant doing beaucoup bleeding, that's for sure. And that's the thing. You're supposed to be able to count on it. But till the crunch comes all you know is promises. It's like sex—isn't everything? So, you think you're a great lay, maybe even a sweet guy—kind and tender and all that shit—but when the blood's pounding in your ears and all those good juices are juicing that's when you're who the hell you should've been saying you are. They're all the same, all your standard lusts are: fear, fighting, sex, revenge.

Anyway, you're out here and it's all by your lonesome—don't count on the cavalry or AirCav, or America, or some Kennedy or Jesus Hisself or the

477

White Buffalo to stand between you and the news when it's coming. They got better things to do.

I finally understood what you used to mean when you talked about how at finals you always hoped to get some epilepsy or maybe an insignificant aunt'd crap out so you could do a makeup. One morning we had an early A.M. road patrol—go step on the dirt to see if it blows up—and I didn't care who I had to trade: you, Mom and Vamps, Mack, Animal (bonus!), the kids, all my buddies. Let somebody else die instead of me today, just so long as they come get me the hell out on a whirlybirdie. Turning into a junkie for living. Getting over it—it's the only way to survive.

A buddy of mine said he was pinned down next to this wounded guy, and he prayed all that time, all night, that the fucker'd die so he could use his extra clips and wouldn't have to tote his bod out of there. That's pretty common, really. He died. My buddy, too, last week, alone. One round clean, in his eye. Took the back of his head clean off. Painless.

The only way to explain things is, back in the world maybe you're driving along and some guy's changing a tire and you just imagine what it's like to blast thru him like he isn't really there, or right up some lawn through a picture window and into some living room (like that friend of yours who got drunk, whatsisname?) or maybe just between two headlights. But you don't because you figure it's awful or painful and hurts and so you stay straight. Like there's an invisible bottle of imagination and fears—a Buck Rogers force-field. What I'm saying is there's so much fear inside and out all over that it's like air.

Sometimes I think about these heroes, the guys who go out there in cold blood and get shot up just to do a bene. I don't know. They got to be surely stupid or something. Anything I do that smells good is probably just perfume on the fishy selfish reasons underneath it. I even think that guy you and I helped haul off the ice up in Maine—the one who we almost fell in trying to help—were we just do-gooders, or afraid he'd go down on our watch and someone'd see

478

us cooling our heels? I don't think any of us are cut out for this kind of work.

Listen, I'm really sorry about that scare letter back when I got separated, if it came. Forget it, I didn't mean any of it. But if I ever get a Post-Human ribbon or anything, don't believe it. I was probably running away or stoned or smacked out daydreaming about getting laid or trying to kill a friend to make a hit with the VC.

If you're wondering how I managed to type that other letter but couldn't call, it's easy. This guy in the field hospital let me do a little every night on his machine, but I haven't seen a phone in maybe three months. Now I'm back to where we don't even have field hospitals, so you get the scribbles. Sorry. It's a way to stay up on guard at night. Also, sleeping is a way to stay up. I woke up with this real horror show playing, among others. Pretty weird stuff: a tank burning ever so pretty in the night and I'm on skis. Beautiful. You can be sure I will not get within a hundred yards of one. They're fucking dangerous. . . .

If you have any kids and I'm a DOW (the last two words are "o' wounds"), don't name any for old Willie, OK? And don't let 'em think I was some kind of hero in some kind of war or anything, no matter what. I wasn't any hero. I was me. And I wasn't at any war. I was at Nam. Do you know what Mox Nix means? Is it back in the States yet? It's a phrase everybody uses here. I think it's already back in the world, along with our undetectable and incurable siff and clap. They got it (the phrase) from Deutschland or someplace like that, because I think it's German: Mox Nix, like macht's nichts or something: Makes Nothing. Mox Nix. Makes No Diff. Mox Nix. Makes Nada Lada Fucking Difference. If I get to the Big A put it on my rock, eh, Babe? OK?

But don't you worry, because I got no plans of going that way or any way but HOME. Come out and see about me if you got a steel hat. Better yet, tough guy, help get me the hell out of here before they take me home in a Shake 'n' Bake Bag. I ain't heavy, Babe. I'm your only lonely brother. Help.

Only joshing. Wait'll you see my VC ear collection. You'll be pea green with envy. You still selling secrets to the Russians or have they got you teaching basketball to the Canadians now? If you see Mr. LBJ —stick a rocket up his ass for me.

Love to all who buy bonds,
but wash afterwards,
William the Conqueror

Johanna arrived, as promised, that evening. She stepped from the ramp at Logan Airport in Boston and Tyler was stunned. It was not the radiant and bouncy girl he remembered, but a pastel imitation of a sophisticate, all made up, wearing a dress and high heels and holding a hat box she carried as though she were walking a Pekinese. She looked like someone who'd won the trip on a quiz show. Still, she looked wonderful to him, and he supposed he looked different, too. So he buried his head in her neck to find the secret spot he knew and felt a familiar squirm of delight. "Same girl," he whispered, having checked her credentials. He hugged her happily, then drew back to see the eyes which were the homunculi of her nature, and fell in love all over at the sight of her. "I'd forgotten how—Let's get you up to New Hampshire and out of those clothes."

"You don't waste time, do you, stranger?"

"Oh, uh, no—I mean, I—Are you—?"

"Aren't you going to say hello?" she asked, teasing, though scanning his face, uncharacteristically, for signs of approval. He melted entirely, and laughed at himself for his fumblings. He held her at arm's length, saying, "Hello yourself—gee, it's good to see you. The whole world is—"

"Now!" she smiled, folding her arms around his waist. "Where can I get out of these clothes?"

"You know you're the only person in the world who can confuse me?"

"I don't believe that—but I like it." She pulled his ear and whispered that all her plans for being a blushing maiden for a while, now that she was single again, "to see if it's any fun"—had suddenly gone all to hell. She managed to blush, and said, "You're such a bad influence on me, Tyler Bowen!"

As soon as they arrived at Concord Headquarters, he

introduced her to everyone. She ultimately dragged him by the necktie to a corner while he dumbly asked, "What? What?" She pressed herself against him and planted a moist kiss. He fidgeted in uneasy rectitude. "Jo—*What?* What?"

"What? What?" she mimicked as if he were a doltish ape. "I missed you. That's what."

"Is that all?" Then he squeezed her until she thought he'd break her ribs.

"What happened to your big talk about taking me back to your room and having your will?"

"Momentarily, toots—"

"Hey, Bowen," one of the staff coordinators called out as he passed by. "Take it easy—it's only supposed to be a slogan, 'Make Love, Not War.'"

Johanna asked him if he was aware of introducing her, "like a firstgrader at a new school?"

"I'm trying to make sure you don't get put in the slow reading group," Tyler answered.

"I *am* slow, here," she protested. Then they found the other staff coordinator Tyler had been hunting for.

"Mark, this is a friend of mine: Johanna Reig—*Poulson.* Can't be too good a friend if I don't remember her name. Johanna Poulson. Just joined us and I'm trying to get her a good spot. Anything?"

The coordinator asked him how come he hadn't fixed it up before.

"I did. Had it all set up in Scheduling and Advance —but they filled it—somebody else's friend."

"What does she want to do?"

Tyler laughed. "Work for Bobby Kennedy." The co-ordinator whistled sardonically, conceding it was not such an uncommon desire.

"How about speech research? What are you good at —uh, let me rephrase that: You in school, or what?" She said she had some experience as a reporter, and Tyler added, "a good one." "Perfect," the coordinator said. "Speech research needs a liaison to the press. It's a good place to start—and you could see each other at least ten minutes a day." He flipped Bowen's tie out from his jacket with a conspiratorial smile. "And she can work on touch football plays with Goodwin."

Johanna thought it a marvelous offer, and even felt

moderately qualified, albeit nervous. The job was tailored for her. And Richard Goodwin was the best-known, most professional campaigner on the lot. For a time, he alone gave it credibility. The story went that when he first arrived in New Hampshire a skeptic asked him where the campaign was. "Here," he said, tapping his typewriter case.

Johanna was further softened to her task when she learned that the Robert Kennedy speech she admired so much was run through that very typewriter in an early draft. In fact, so was the inspiration for the dump-Johnson movement itself. While Tyler didn't fully understand the attraction she felt toward Robert Kennedy, he was happy with her accommodation. Perhaps, she decided, the candidates were really only symbols, and the vital center of the matter truly resided between the margins of Dick Goodwin's typewriter and the space between his unelectable ears.

In the first few hours after her arrival, there was so much noise and distracting activity that she and Tyler were never quite alone with each other. But in the late evening they found a trough of silence. They were a little frightened at first. It had been a full winter season since they had been similarly alone. Again it was a cold hotel room.

And, like anxious artists, paralytic in the face of a major, long-postponed work, they were somewhat afraid to test the reality against so much invested hope. They sat, half-dressed, feigning casualness, talking, smiling, telling each other how good it was to see each other, over and over until the words were stale. They had never before been without the limits of time, circumstance, and pressing obligations. Now they were free and frightened.

False drama became apprehension. Kisses so readily tender seemed untrue. She had flown so far, done so much at his behest, gone through so much alone when he could not help, that he felt impelled to court her. But his own nervous fear translated as impotence. Her features returned greater nervousness, and a quizzical impassivity. He fell back laughing at himself.

"What's so funny?" her voice, a little girl's, asked, worried he might now be able to laugh at her.

"Me. I'm so damned dumb. I missed you so God-damned much—" Then he kissed her like he meant it: because it was good and his emotions directed him to.

"I missed you. Oh, I wished—" He put a finger to her lips and kissed her again, then kissed her smooth shoulder. There was no sexual urgency in it, only an admiring caress. He touched her face with his fingers, guilelessly. "That's how much I missed you. Just to touch you. Memories wouldn't do it. I need the straight stuff."

"And now?"

"So much it hurts." Her eyes were open as she kissed him, and stayed open, even as he kissed her neck and shoulders and belly and breasts and lap. He had promiscuous affairs with each inch of her world; heartbreaking ends for each, farewell kisses lingering at departure, false good-byes, with a new courtship already begun in a neighboring firmament.

She sensed only his lips, softly brushing her skin. It tickled. He scaled her sides like a funny centipede, dragging a man behind. There was sense, but not sensation. Her skin had somehow toughened. How absolutely odd, she thought: my lover seems to be no more than a giant pair of lips trailing a useless carcass. He was a ferret scurrying along for hints of food.

She felt tense and shuddered, but when he looked up she faked a contented smile. Her brow furrowed at her own strange impotence, this objective remove. She was immune to the larger flow. She squeezed herself to shake out the tension's anesthesia, resolving, "Try. Relax. Easy. He cares." She thought of how she used to regard Warren: a skeptic at a land rush. And so she closed her eyes to allow the impulses to build. The small feelings became sensations. Sensations combined orchestrally. Her mind slid sideways, in and out of sexual thoughts, wishing she could overwhelm herself with erotic images.

Their distance was slowly narrowed by an awareness of mutuality, swelling. He entered her and her mind went awash with new feelings: What did he sense? What did he feel? He was trying so hard—to be gentle —but what did this mean to him? Was this gift of entrance some achievement? Did it rule men from their cribs to deathbeds? Was it some instinct for affection, unconcerned about its source? Was it an unfilled urge toward some primal womb, a male prerogative alone? Was it an unfulfillable desire to go deeper than a womb could be? Was murder just beyond it? How accessible men's urges were, how easy their articulation! When done, they were done, sated, off again. Was it ignorant and greedy, a masturbation at its heart; was it ego alone in that gluttonous root?

He was in her, wearing her. What did it mean to him, that she could never do the same? A voice, clear as tape, was saying, "Penetration . . . no matter how slight." That was the controlling relation, penetration. He was at-large inside her and she only knew his surface. Her head hurt. She was leaking tears. He didn't notice.

He was saying something. "I love you, Johanna." She embraced him tightly, urged him deeper still, wondering was she inside herself where he went searching? Doctors found no magic there, just a tropic membrane. Yet some new thing, some event of mind, was made at the kiss of tissues until, residents of different worlds, in different times, they met, and held each other in that coincidence with all their might and all the urgency of their momentary lives' worth.

He lay beside her, stroking her, and asked, "Where do you go when you go? And what do you do while you're there?" She shook her head with no good answer, and rolled against him, elbows in, shaking.

From Nashua, where the charter buses dumped the Boston students, and Keene, where the New Yorkers and Bennington girls came, and Concord, where the planes landed; at Manchester's factory gates, in the streets of Newport and the town meetings of Salem, and Littleton, from the front porch of Myer Goldman's Rexall Pharmacy in Peterborough to the boarded-up summer towns along the midland lakes, to the ski towns along Route 93, from the bohemia of Franconia's mountainside to the ghostly clinks and echoes of Bretton Woods and Bethlehem, a loden-coated cascade of Minuteboys and girls, already calling themselves the

Children's Crusade, had waged a six-week war to revive a faltering myth they learned in grade school: that the wishes of citizens might turn governments around.

They dared The Good People of the Granite State to help them. Their ante was a ritual sacrifice: more than one haircut and shave was commenced on a voter's doorstep for two bits of time; hence the label "Clean for Gene." If hair obscured—or was—the issue to unsophisticated minds, cut the problem short. The emotional issues were translated into common coin: the war's most personal wages, its cost at home. A Salem school board budget meeting was turned into a debate on the war: Resolved, American treasure was being drained by a mortgage on Asian swamp lots. In every town they prodded, coaxed, exhorted, pamphleted, argued, and asked nicely. They courted the stiff-spined conservatives they would otherwise spurn on campuses. They wheedled, nagged, flattered, played the innocent, and showed flashes of silken strategy, until a nominal democracy was forced to face its own most cherished vanities, to comprehend its theory, philosophy, and moral roots, at precisely the most vulnerable level. The invasion resembled an attack of ants at a church picnic: person to person until the congregation was overwhelmed.

If they were watching at Tombstone, they might have seen validation for their primary model's postulates: how a flimsy, indeed weightless force can have outsize impact when multiplied by media, genius or timing, thereby to move a people. They could have explained it all to the campaigners. But it would be as necessary as coaching a shortstop in the ballistics of a baseball. Some, like Johanna Poulson and Tyler Bowen, picked the skills up quickly. Others, like Richard Goodwin, knew it all by reflex.

At Tombstone they would have proceeded from the "factual": the psychological evidence that retention and understanding are functions of the simplicity of information which the brain must process. They would cite the "Verbal-loop Hypothesis" as confirmation. They'd validate it further, adding the "Seven Plus-or-Minus Two Principle." They'd thus arrive at the well known: slogans are the grease in campaign gears.

485

Goodwin knew this. Elsewhere in the state, Richard Nixon's campaign knew it.

No better proof could have been provided than the rising of Eugene McCarthy's star in pace with the regular broadcasting of a simple radio message. It ran every half-hour in the week before the voting. Goodwin wrote it. Johanna Poulson helped refine it. Tyler Bowen added his initials to a circulating memo on it. It translated the motives of all those thousands of volunteers into terms acceptable to The Good People of the Granite State:

"Think now how you would feel to wake up Wednesday morning, March 12, to find that Gene McCarthy had won the New Hampshire primary—to find that New Hampshire had changed the course of American politics." Thirty-six words. All gaps were bridged, as the negative ions of discontent were fused with the positive ions of promise to make a compound, the whole point altogether.

They would have said as well at Tombstone that the men of politics learn their art on green baize tables, where the rules of poker are informing. If the dealer tries too artlessly to stack the deck, the odds can suddenly invert.

Johnson helped. He stumbled gracelessly. He knew he could steal the headlines with one bold stroke. Any President could. But the public had seem him do it one too many times. He tried another gambit: patronization. He praised McCarthy for "bringing our young people back into the system"—out of which LBJ had driven them—gagging as he uttered it. He'd once said of J. Edgar Hoover, "I'd rather have him in the tent pissing out than outside pissing in." Those young people were under the canvas again, many of them, but Johnson felt a dampness rising to his ankles anyway.

And others under the Big Top became incontinent, too. Ministerial utterances, once deemed The Truth by editors and publishers, who also enjoyed the perquisites of indecent recumbency with the powerful, were beginning to be disbelieved: "How long is the damned tunnel, anyway?"

"If you only knew what I know," Johnson scolded, and to make the point he gathered in his best advisers.

Some in the press already rose to say perhaps they knew *more* than he knew; perhaps he was misinformed; or, maybe, lying with his whole heart and mind.

Johnson's Generals publicly promised a faster end to the war. But then, a Defense Department aide named Daniel Ellsberg leaked the truth to Robert Kennedy; others, to newsmen. Neal Sheehan and Hedrick Smith shared the credit on the *New York Time*'s front page the Sunday before the New Hampshire balloting. The headline shed this light on what was down the tunnel: "Westmoreland Requests/206,000 More Men. . . . Enemy Hammers 7 Sites/On the Outskirts of Saigon."

A howl, like a wounded animal's moan, shuddered coast to coast all Monday. Goodwin's radio tag had its purchasing power trebled as the bond of Government word was devalued. In New Hampshire, Monday was frenetic, the last seconds of lustful rushing toward a culmination, before the dawning silence of the polling day.

The weather Tuesday remained easy. Omen watchers and journalists took note, the last believers in the pathetic fallacy.

The predictions in the press gave McCarthy a 15 percent share of the voting, as much as 20 percent in some polls. That would be grand, and would encourage the Crusaders to carry on. Twenty-five would be grander, but unlikely. "And if it tops 25 percent?" a reporter asked at the Press Office.

"Then something's happening," Johanna Poulson answered.

"Something?"

"Something that's not being understood in Washington."

When Tyler Bowen heard what she said, he grinned. "Perfect!" He had seen the confidential poll circulating among higher aides. It estimated 33 percent for McCarthy. Attached was a note urging them to "poormouth it. Anything over 12 percent is a famous victory." Thirty-three percent, he knew, and all hell would surely break loose.

The afternoon of the voting, there was little left to be done but start packing up. They had nothing left but busy-work. Reporters wanted colorful tidbits for late files. A few meetings were held. But most of all there was the waiting. The momentarily slackened pace—a Christmas truce of sorts—permitted staff and press to unwind a little, to have a moment's chat. So slight were McCarthy's chances that he was covered by lower-ranked, younger reporters, hungrier than usual. The heavies, the majors, the in-and-out glamour boys who needed to be dipped in the Potomac once a day, or at least have it splashed in their bourbon, concentrated on the aborted efforts of George Romney, and the re-treaded tire that seemed to run on and on and on, Richard Nixon. "Poor Nixon," the consensus seemed to laugh when Romney dropped out. "He's gotta prove he can *beat* somebody—and they won't let him." Running unopposed would not prove he was a winner. You didn't get to the White House unopposed.

Before dinner Tuesday, the courtesy suite provided by a major network was a boozy wash from the stock laid in for just that purpose. Though not given a chance of victory, the McCarthy campaigners were favored by the working press for conviviality.

The millisecond after detonation of the first nuclear device, despite all surety, the best minds assembled wondered if they might have missed some vital thing: might it be a dud or set the atmosphere in flames? No one could be quite certain, but behind their eyes was something flashing before the event: tachyons, particles that grew younger, moving faster than light, arriving from the future with the news, swiftly racing into the past. So it was Tuesday evening.

And all were assembled.

The best minds.

Self-congratulations preceded the results. The campaigners felt they were a new elite, humanists who found injustice offensive. Rebellion was not naturally in their blood any more than was bombery in the blood of wartime men at Alamogordo. A sizable number came from the aristocracy. Names of the famous abounded; children of historians, musicians, legislators, scions of the favored classes, soon-to-be professionals. In Washington, D.C., this was a much-noticed phenomenon. The wives and children of top policymakers worked against the war while the worry-lined husbands and fathers persisted in Asian error; having read reports late at the office, they'd missed the evening news.

Brief flashes. Some towns reported early, fragmentary results. It was boosterism, nothing more, the best way to secure a brief monopoly on Walter Cronkite's attention.

Doubt.

Then all hell broke loose.

The bomb worked. The partying began as soon as the outcome was clear. McCarthy was there all the way. He even had a majority for a while. It was a roisterous, emotional, crazy, believing-but-disbelieving celebration. The story goes that when the first atom bomb was tested, J. Robert Oppenheimer did two things: he spoke lyrics about the awesome power; and he tore up strips of paper, dropped them, then paced off how far they were carried by the shock wave, saying simply, "Twenty thousand tons of dynamite." It was the same with canvassing and straw polls.

When the write-ins were tabulated (and McCarthy's PR troops managed to obscure the fact that all of Johnson's votes came by write-in), Eugene McCarthy, or opposition to the war, or animosity toward Lyndon Johnson, or love of beagles, or fans of proud man's contumely and foes of the insolence of office pulled a fat 42 percent of the vote. More significantly, Johnson was held to 48 percent. The President could claim a plurality if he wanted to, but he didn't dare. It was, for all intents, a tie. Twenty kilotons of dynamite: the world forever changed.

In the halls and offices and ballrooms of Concord Headquarters they were screaming and sobbing and running around in mad circles. They had done everything they knew how, and now the victory almost dazed them. Then suddenly they knew what had happened: they'd seized the long arm of the lever in New Hampshire and the world was budging from its ordained path.

Older partisans said they had not seen this kind of reckless elation since V-J Day. There was nothing else to compare it to. The noise alone was overwhelming. Otherwise poised and sober campaign staff members ran amok and yipped their triumph, socking the air with fists as they danced manic jigs. No gesture was strong enough to convey their joy. They grabbed previous doubters, shaking them, demanding, "Do you *feel* it? Do you *feel* it?!"

It was there to be felt. It was tangible. It was unbelievable, but there it was. That staggering 42 percent told a story well known in the Northeast: the ragged Minutemen and farmers had made it safe across the river and busted up a fine, but premature, Tory bash.

The war might soon be turned.

"I would hesitate," Baron Zermatt said, awakened in the middle of the night by Tyler's drunken telephone demand for a concession, "in the words of Winnie the Pooh, to endow this deliverance with the attributes of victory. A few more forty-two–forty-eight triumphs and they'll have to send small boats for you. So the guy stumbles on his way downhill—"

"Vinegar in the honey, pal," Tyler said. "That's your style. We knocked the old buzzard on his can!"

"Yay for us, hooray!" Johanna shouted tipsily in the phone.

"Have fun, kids. You're gonna hate yourself in the morning."

"Sourpuss!"

In the morning, the battle was reduced to litter and hangover. The victory was chiefly over the odds, but it was satisfyingly solid. Its sublime momentum was crated up and, along with several thousand individual enthusiasms, shipped Wisconsinways, while a sleepless and giddy collection of newly minted geniuses divvied up the world and Cabinet posts. The day was filled with postgame analyses and revised strategy planning, and the evening saw a hastily assembled banquet at the Concord Headquarters. The reporters offered songs they'd written in derision, now as crow, and put on quickie skits. Johanna had spent the day helping rewrite the songs, because she sheepishly admitted to Tyler, "it was my idea." She had told a reporter looking for a Sunday feature story that McCarthy reminded her of "something out of Simon and Garfunkel. And Bobby? He's all four Beatles. Sergeant Pepper's Lonely Hearts Club Band. Kennedys are a whole production."

"And Johnson?" Tyler asked.

"Why, Lyndon Johnson is Bob Dylan or no one is."

In tribute to McCarthy's penchant for obscure and highfalutin references, the reporters waddled out as a Greekish chorus, chanting, "Of charms and the Man I sing—"

Their leader, tagged "the Muse of News," stepped forward, screeching in falsetto: "I sing of Johnson's Pride—" The crowd moaned, delighted. "His fatal flaw —wax lyric and—" Hisses and groans, all in approval. "Glow, coat his gall with stoned rockers' verse—of Genie's Teenie Big Bright Green Election Machine!" Cheers and whistles. The chorus showed a lot of hairy, pudgy leg, and the soft, mostly white underbelly of American politics: the bleak wit of its reporters. So they parodied Simon and Garfunkel's "Big Bright Green Pleasure Machine," and the equally upbeat "Feeling Groovy," in self-celebration. But no McCarthy rendering would have been on the mark without a wry poke at their introspective champion. Thus, with a cowbell's gift of tune, they essayed a version of "The Dangling Conversation," this way:

> It's a still-life watercolor
> Of a presidential race,
> With an existential candidate
> Who runs—but stays in place . . .

> • • •

> And he spoke to them of Guernica
> And quoted Robert Lowell,
> While Bob Dylan played harmonica
> And Lyndon read the polls.

> He's a poem not a novel,
> He's character and contrast,
> Meter, wit, and rhyme—
> No plot or grand design.

> He's the dangling politician
> Of the Jean-Paul Sartre line:
> —a hero out of time—

491

And they all wound up singing to a Beatle tune, together:

> Now that we're older, losing a war,
> Changing points of view,
> Must we still be *unter* Lyndon—till he's through
> With a term—in Seventy-two?
>
> After he told us he was for peace,
> Then he bombed some more,
> Let us relieve him,
> Who can believe him—after Sixty-four?

Bleary music of an ebbing winter drifted down from the hills Thursday, as Tyler Bowen and Johanna Poulson drove through the gap in the Appalachians between the Berkshires and the Green Mountains, toward the West. Spring was moving in on the northern towns, under soft white-blue skies, over the lower peaks and glens, through the snowy woods to start a thawing in the valleys. At noon they were between the Champlain and Hudson catchments. Northwest were the Adirondacks, southwest the Catskills. Ahead, the farmlands, plains, and lakes.

All day they drove, alternating at the wheel, taking turns picking out songs to sing. Across the flat New York State afternoon, their shadows long behind them, they lost ground to the sun. They booed lustily when they passed an exit sign near Utica that read "Westmoreland," and they met Saint Paul Hooper in Skaneateles for dinner. Then they split the highest knuckle of the Finger Lakes, picked up two hitching volunteers and headed toward Milwaukee. Through the Pennsylvania and Ohio midnight, cruising recklessly at eighty on Interstate 80, eager and impatient, they drove and sang and yawned, in manifold love and on a joyride.

They were one more in an old, unbroken chain of pioneering Conestogas gone west. As in each age, they were running from something, seeking something, offering sweet optimism in their sweaty, salty, and sturdy faith, toward that original promise made once to the future.

At the same time, Robert Kennedy was seriously

reevaluating his position. Which is to say, he had already decided to run, troubled only by the infelicitous appearance of muscling in on Gene's fiesta. In another dimension of the same space, Richard Nixon's advisors were already auctioning ambassadorships.

In yet another place, in dimensions even more removed, the pragmatists at the Tombstone Center for the Applied Social Sciences were filing into a conference room to scrutinize a political biopsy.

"Warren, you'll like this," the chairman of the study group said as they took their seats. "You know what my son told me yesterday? He's almost your age—and he makes more money racing motorcycles than I do teaching. He said, 'The only people who really believe in authority are the Authorities.' "

"Sounds like my ex-wife talking. What'd you say?"

"What could I? I had to borow his car this morning while he fixes mine. I've been thinking about some of the things we talked about yesterday. You may have a point. We need a fresh approach to some of this. Windows."

Warren raised his eyebrows and said, "It wouldn't hurt to look outside for real. It's happening, Sid. And they're winning."

The chairman sighed and raised his pencil to tap the panel to order, but turned to Warren again. "Perhaps. What it tells me, though, is your point about political process being a paradigm of morphology has a lot to it. Dynamic topology or whatever you call it."

"I've changed my mind," Warren replied. "We're missing something we could pick up from Gila. It's a question of scale but it's a strict parallel to cellular activity. We're looking at the growth of a neoplastic entity. A tumor. The question is will it set up a vascular system to sustain itself. From there—metastasis and it's all over. Oncology redelineates political economy."

"Let's talk about it later," the chairman laughed, and called the group to order.

STATELY, PLUMP, BUXOM MOTHERS AS-
signed the sleeping quarters to the volunteers in Milwaukee. Such benign concern filled these matrons'
cheeks that they reminded Johanna of teachers signing
up children for Salk vaccinations. Some volunteers were
housed in borrowed beds of sympathizers, some on
cots in church basements. Johanna and Tyler had priority space. "You're on staff, aren't you?" the woman
said to them. The words "on staff". meant everything
they did at newspapers and other large organizations:
rank, privilege, commission. Wings. A hotel room. As
in New Hampshire, seniority placed Tyler Bowen near
the pyramid's tip as it erupted from the grass roots.
Johanna was on a lower peak, but each jerky spurt of
growth reduced the significance of that difference.

What they lacked in credentials and purity of ideolog-
ical commitment, they acquired by timeliness alone. "I
could be completely exposed," Johanna said, "if some
kid asks me the difference between the Bolsheviks and
the Mensheviks." No one did. The latest volunteers
knew Tyler and Johanna's names before they met them.

"You were there when it all began," one said to
Tyler in a corridor. "What was it like—back then?"
Tyler struck a veteran's pose, while Johanna grimaced.

"When you're through telling about the hardy pioneering," she said, "would you explain to me again the
difference between Stalin and Trotsky?"

The dark, cold days of February had turned into
legend, but Tyler Bowen had no heroic tales of battling
for a cause to tell. Nor did he have the articulated
philosophy of the antiwar movement cadres or the civil
rights regiments. Those were the holy of holies, *plus
Catholique que le Pape*. His motivations then, and

now, were vague, conflicting, and considerably personal. In a sense he had drifted into this effort, as he had drifted into naval service, and rank at Gila. And here again, by luck and grace, he was a presence. He was a staff coordinator. Just what that meant was indeterminate, but God must have loved them, Johanna said, for He made so many of them. Basically, Tyler had responsibility now for coordinating the burgeoning, volunteer office with the Operations Office at State Campaign Headquarters, and coordinating that with Johanna's liaison at Speech and Research. It was bizarrely military for an organization so resolutely anti-bureaucratic. The reason was that the cause itself was larger than personal tastes.

"Warren says," Johanna recalled, "revolutions are programs, not people. The first to go are the drunks in the streets."

"He's said stupider things."

"I've heard them," they both blurted.

Indeed, just three days after McCarthy's stunning New Hampshire showing, Milwaukee looked like an occupied city.

Drab green was the predominant color of volunteer clothing, except for the suit-and-tie-clad staff. The rest, the ones not dealing with the public, nor requiring dress to show position, the boiler-room crews and back-office workers, wore pacified Army surplus. They took its ferocious mien and banalized it beyond all recognition. Democracy, it has been said, is death to style. "You know, we really ought to reconsider the impact of ending the war quite so suddenly," someone in the Research Office told Johanna.

"It looks like we'll have plenty of time yet."

"I mean, the cruddy refuse of our Army is the greatest agent of world culture since Mohammed—the flotsam of our wars makes half the world's civilization." The person who said it wrote it down when he was through, a member of another army: the sociological scavengers who, having sensed the blood of a phenomenon, came to pick its bones with participant observation, in full defiance of Heisenberg's principles. Saving the world was a side interest.

Also passing through the campaign on their way to

other rendezvous were radicals with abrasions from every protest of the last decade. Hovering above it all were a few professional politicians, confused and elated at the handiwork of so many amateurs. Half the pros were maddeningly calm, riling their co-workers by that arrogant ease. The other half were so intense they ran up the mountain and down twice in the time it took the amateurs to run up; as a consequence, one nervous man quit daily.

And came more volunteers, then still more, beyond the campaign's capacity to use them all. But it was as though some kind of pledge had been made to all these young people, and employment was found for them, lest they drift off discouraged to some new love.

Most of all, the campaign was marked by ambivalence, despite the energy, starting at the top. At first, McCarthy himself had urged Robert Kennedy to run. Now, as that seemed imminent, McCarthy affected wound. Johanna's nominal boss, the superspeechwriter Goodwin, worked in his pajamas to squeeze more hours out of the day because, as word had it, "We won't be seeing much more of Dick. He's pledged to Bobby, you know—the only man left in America who thinks McCarthy's a stalking horse for Kennedy." But there were others in the campaign who hoped it were so, and still others who wished secretly for New York's dashing—although Republican—mayor, John Lindsay. The call of celebrity and beauty, it was assumed, was mighty. Chiefly it indicated how fragile was McCarthy's hold.

Then Robert Kennedy called a press conference.

Even to his well-wishers, Kennedy's timing was painful. It was still McCarthy's hour. Moreover, Kennedy chose the same room his elder brother had used to announce his campaign eight years before. Not only did his timbre and diction build a momentary illusion of something lost, but he used the same opening words as had his brother Jack: "I am announcing today my candidacy for the office of President of the United States."

His obstacles were partly of his own devising: the brusque nature of his entry into Eugene McCarthy's miracle play, and his public rivalry with Johnson. Hoping to dismiss the latter with one rhetorical sweep, he said, "I do not run merely to oppose any man, but to propose new policies." Oddly, McCarthy having legitimized the enterprise, the issue of a personal Kennedy power-grab mounted against Johnson was never to be compelling. It was the McCarthy-bustling that was the sorest point. So Bobby saluted Gene's "valiant campaign" and, echoing Johnson, praised the "remarkable" way McCarthy had brought back "our children," who had—it was unsaid, but left to be assumed—wandered astray, leaderless, waiting for Robert Kennedy to fulfill his and their destinies. One could almost hear Kennedy's teeth grinding with the congratulations; McCarthy's, too.

McCarthy's reaction to the Kennedy announcement was sarcastic lack of surprise. He had never suffered well at the hands of Kennedys, nor they at his. Years before he had joked, "I'm twice as liberal as Hubert Humphrey, twice as smart as Stuart Symington, and twice as Catholic as Jack Kennedy." And he liked to say, as Lyndon Johnson did, "Bobby is not Jack." McCarthy would smile and add, "He's not even Teddy."

"It's a pretty straightforward thing," Baron Zermatt said when Tyler called him to salute his prescience. "Kennedys understand power. They're sons-of-bitches. I mean, Catholic or not, they understand that there's no immortality. This is the whole show. You don't get points for sitting down, and monuments count for shit. Get it while you can. They're having fun."

The press immediately and unanimously decided that, while McCarthy was a novelty, Kennedy was The Story. McCarthy observed, "They're like blackbirds on a telephone line. One flies off, they all fly off. One flies back, they all do." And, paraphrasing journalist Murray Kempton, "the function of liberals is to observe the battle and then when it's over, go down and shoot the wounded."

Overlooked at first, in the rancor, was that Kennedy had been out front on the war, against it in 1963, by the records, and had a broad program of social concerns he wished to champion every bit as hard as he opposed the war. In fact, while his personality was his single most powerful weapon, Kennedy would try harder than McCarthy to articulate policies to match his personality. As much as McCarthy offered himself as a low-key, intellectual, anticharisma, issue-oriented would-be President, he was nonetheless resting most of *his* case on one issue and his own offbeat, appealing personality.

Kennedy insisted he'd made up his mind before New Hampshire, for the same reasons that voters were moved to vote against the Administration in that primary. But he had wanted not to confuse the matter, he said. And, not wishing to crowd McCarthy too suddenly he would stay out of Wisconsin, too, urging his supporters to help McCarthy there. The key issue was still, he said, delivering a resounding message to Lyndon Johnson.

Yet the issue was also, to McCarthy and his legions, that their man had been subjected to an undeserved brutalization. A staff conference among high McCarthy aides decided to exploit any resentment of "Kennedy's unfair treatment of us."

"Where was Bobby in New Hampshire?" went the refrain, and McCarthy made wry references to "bonfires in the hills" and "dancing by the valley moonlight." Few people understood him entirely, but most assumed it was a criticism of Kennedy. It became the first political movement in the history of the world that determined to run on a pout.

Halfway round the globe, they were still sleeping, tired from an all-day mission the day before, waiting for new orders, dreaming of the previous day's Search-and-Destroy results. Before eight in the morning local time, the choppers had put them down in a village designated on their maps as "pink."

They had suffered severe losses for some time, and were frustrated by the decimating effects of booby traps, ambushes, and an elusive enemy. Those who had seen the huge military hospitals told of horrifying sights: men without faces or limbs, made that way by teenage sappers. Those who had seen the civilian hospitals said the enemy had no mercy on noncombatants.

Babies lay five and six to a bed, hopeless cases, reduced to a barely vegetative state, gnarled, mangled, half-burned alive, missing limbs and eyes. They looked like sausage links. The hospitals were giant open graves where only the frantic activity of the doctors smelled of life. The enemy was inhuman.

This village was a center of enemy activity, they were told. The threat was always in disguise. It could be anything that moved.

They had entered in strength, scared, nervous, undertrained in this kind of warfare, well fed, overarmed, and largely ignorant of the subtleties and rules of land engagement.

They separated everyone they found in this Pinkville into three groups and carried out their orders as they understood them.

A few heroes were present. One shot himself in the foot, and played very little role in the mission. One other, a helicopter pilot, risked court-martial by interfering with a mission-in-progress, taking the enemy's part. No clearer instance of single-handed aid-and-comfort could be imagined than using a U.S. Army helicopter to ferry personnel designated "enemy" away from the scene of an authorized patrol's interdiction. One hero was not there. He was back at Headquarters wondering how he could advance his career. He was already a Major General at Division Headquarters. When the first reports came to him that morning, he embarked on a course of action which could end his career if not carried out correctly. Acting on the example of company and field-grade officers below him, he courageously ordered the most massive, individual, inconspicuous mendacity in the history of American military activities, a cynicism not to be equaled until another officer ordered himself decorated, and another, his two pet dogs. His success led to his appointment as Commandant of West Point and a third star.

At the village, two groups of Vietnamese were taken to dispersed locations. Seventy or more of them were led to a sort of ditch on the eastern perimeter of the hamlet. As many as fifty were taken to a trail on the southern edge. The remainder of the inhabitants numbered as high, perhaps, as two hundred and eighty, though a more likely figure is in the low hundreds.

The platoon's nervousness was, happily, not justified. All these people were civilians: those civilians that these troops and the whole Military Assistance Command/Vietnam were there to help. These were the hearts and minds they hoped to win. Some reports had it that the U.S. forces regularly committed acts of personal violence—rape, assault, looting—against civilians or suspected enemy. It is even alleged some did this day, though none of the villagers ever testified to that effect. The villagers were no threat, already pacified, and acquiescent to the orders they received from their American guests. They went where they were told, stayed where they were put, and gave no resistance to the search and the operation's further fulfillment. It was a complete success from that standpoint, and all the reports reflected it. Big numbers pacified.

Then the mission was accomplished. While Robert Kennedy was taking his first steps as a presidential candidate, the men of the First Platoon, B Company, of the Americal Division, murdered every man, woman, and child in the hamlet of My Lai.

Tie askew, sleeves rolled past his elbows, Tyler Bowen slumped against a wall at Milwaukee McCarthy Headquarters outside an empty ballroom, flipping through a stack of papers dense with scribbled notes. His eyes were glassy and he puffed his cheeks up as he read, grunting or nodding wearily as people brushed by, never lifting up his head. Coming around the corner behind him, Johanna saw him and stopped to watch his exhausted concentration. She knew he'd had only two hours sleep each night for a week. She walked by him humming a familiar melody, la-la-ing its beats. As she passed she said, out of the side of her mouth, "Ain't all fun and games, is it, pal?"

He shook his head and snapped up in recognition, "Wha—?" She was waving cheerily over her shoulder as she went. The melody pleased him and he whistled a few bars to himself: "She Loves You." A happy Beatles tune. Then he remembered it was one of the songs she'd monkeyed with for the reporters:

You think I run today
Just to be a ruthless spoiler,
To take on LBJ,
And to be Clean Eugene's soiler,
But I'm a Dove, too!!!

. . . .

And with my past ignored,
You know I'm not half-bad,
Yeah, Yeah, Yeah—Yeeeeeeaaaaaah

"I've created a monster!" he yelled after her.

There was much to do by Primary Day still. Canvassers to be assigned, throughout the state, as volunteers came and went by the quirky calendars of college recesses. What Fort Lauderdale had been in other years, Milwaukee was now. Coverage was required for everything. More coverage. Staged haircuts were arranged for the cliché-junkies in the press. Every network wanted a shot of shearing. Envelopes were licked by volunteers who insisted on keeping their hair. Phones were set up and, quickly, triple their number were required. Office supplies were piling up and some were running out. Highly skilled professionals in advertising, press, and campaign techniques were landing every day to lend their talents to an already successful enterprise; big contributors arrived to lend their presence. The staff grew faster at the top, and that was where it was least organized. Advance men advanced for advance men. Specialists in coordination coordinated other specialized coordinators. The National Staff arrived from Washington. So did consultants. So did celebrities and rich liberals. Money was coming in. Money was going out even faster, much of it in pursuit of other money. Deals were made with local office-machine, car-rental, and communication companies, all of whom doubted they'd ever see more than three cents on the dollar when the bills were paid.

Half the staff was engaged in a UN peace-keeping effort to prevent open war among the factions, state and national, professional and volunteer, high-strung and low-key. Multiple structures bloomed. Some things were covered in manifold layers and some missed altogether. Of the latter, the most frequently missed were the candidate's scheduled appointments.

The smoke-filled rooms smelled of rotting cigars and adolescent lubricants, panatelas and peanut butter. The staff no longer called it a Crusade. The Flying Circus was their name, and so it was. They lurched into the final week of March on the back of the oddest menagerie of partisans as ever saw combat. There were political savants who had to fly off to take exams and write home for money. "It's just like Stevenson, Dad!" one was heard exclaiming on the phone. The receiver rattled with the bellowed reply, "Stevenson wasn't worth a damn, either!! Not another penny!!!"

There were campaign workers who had means and were not paid, and others in lesser jobs who had none and so received a stipend: "Isn't that socialism?" a reporter asked. "We call it scholarships," Johanna answered.

There were those who had to streak home from their antiwar labors to attend Reserve and National Guard drills. "If they declare us seditious," Tyler said to one, "half your office is going to change clothes and beat up the other half."

The missions vital to seizing political power and countering the glamorous competition included finding a beer plant open at night to guide a blue-eyed movie star through and recruiting bodyguards for him when he visited a local convent school. One day a driver was needed to go to Oshkosh. He drove off frenetically with six people who wanted to see the town. Only he forgot his cargo, the candidate's daughter.

Somehow, as it always does in varying degrees, it all worked. The polls held. The troops stayed energized. Defections to the Kennedy staff were negligible. Conscientious resignations were glossed over. Sixteen hours a day. Eighteen. Then split shifts of ten on, four off, ten on. It was wartime footing.

With four days to the voting, the polls had McCarthy with a solid, fat 68 percent. The Kennedy people in the electorate were sophisticated enough to know it was the anti-Johnson tally that mattered if Robert Kennedy's candidacy was to remain credible. So they threw in with McCarthy even as the Kennedy campaign apparatus in Indiana and Nebraska was being readied for the first Kennedy-McCarthy head-to-heads. The main question in both camps was how well the dam would hold after Tuesday. Johnson was the chief target, and the twin candidacies would have to be subtly carried on. Richard Goodwin was taxiing at the end of his runway, ready for the shuttle back to Kennedy-land.

Saturday night, Johanna Poulson first mentioned to Tyler Bowen that she might switch, too. He insisted it was unfair to McCarthy. "I know you'll say this sounds silly," she told him, "but Gene reminds me of—well, Warren, in a way."

"Warren! *Your* Warren—your *ex*-Warren? That's the most ridic—"

"He's so—so cold. Bobby touches people—"

"Shoves."

"Now *you* sound like Warren," she replied.

"Where was Bobby when the chips were down?"

"Where was anyone? Where were we?"

"So much for loyalty."

Johanna smirked. " 'Loyalty' he says, after making off with another fellow's wife."

"That was war . . ."

"I thought it was love."

"You're impossible. *This* is politics—and I didn't do anything you didn't."

"I flew three thousand miles to see you, hotshot," she said. "That's being pretty—*possible,* in my book. What're you going to do for me?"

"Show a little principle for once."

"Do you expect any less from me?" she asked.

He grumbled, "I think I liked you better when you didn't take yourself so seriously. Me too." And she smiled contentedly, impish enough to infuriate him again. He was mulish. But it was only a matter of time.

Sunday night, Eugene McCarthy was in Waukesha, Wisconsin, giving a speech, hardly heeding his prepared text. It was the sort of thing that drove reporters batty, as they'd actually have to listen and take notes or scramble for a transcription later. This time they weren't taking notes. They were outside, listening to radios. David Schoumacher, the CBS correspondent, whose transparent elation when reporting the New Hampshire results had made him a McCarthy staff favorite, rushed inside to get the Senator's reaction.

At the Hotel Wisconsin in Milwaukee, the ballroom was filled with a hundred campaign workers. Johanna was scribbling notes. Lyndon Johnson was on the tube and she would have to oversee the manufacture of some kind of release within the hour. McCarthy would say whatever popped into his head, ad lib, and probably say it best, if he didn't offend half the electorate with an offhanded observation dripping irony or sarcasm. But a position paper on everything Johnson said would also be required.

What bombshell was the old buzzard going to drop?

What could he have up his sleeve this time? Would he declare a real war and drag 75 percent of the country to his side? A Texas stampede was possible. The polls could be tumbled in a trice. An eleventh-hour trick was just his speed. The hundred in the room waited for the sky to fall.

Instead, he was cutting back the bombing of North Vietnam, one of McCarthy's main issues. It was a concession. Enough to undercut them? Would they be left carping at his peace move, secretly wistful for the bombing issue? What a flanking job! A McCarthy reaction claiming credit would hardly do: it would still leave the focus of praise on the Oval Office. Johnson was still talking, and a hundred hearts were sinking in anticipation.

The man on the screen raised his right hand and appeared to be wiping some sweat from his temple. "Flies!" someone yelled. "Bullshit attracts flies!" Johnson spoke sorrowfully of "America's sons in fields far away." What could he do? He'd already fired Westmoreland earlier in the week. He drawled of "challenges right here at home . . . with the world's hope for peace in the balance." It was plainly a play for sympathy. The hundred moaned mockingly when he spoke of "demands on my time."

"*Quit,* you shit!" someone shouted, others shushing him as Johnson continued, speaking about "my party," and "your country." He was near tears. As always, his contradictory expressions—tearful elation, disjunctive grins—confused the viewers. Then, with a "God bless you and good night" it was over and just as suddenly his words reached home: He would not run again. The realization erupted in pandemonium.

"He quit! He quit! We did it! He's *out!*" they screamed, while the still image of the blood-drained fighter on the screen lingered haplessly. One partisan rushed up to plant a kiss as the face dissolved to Eric Sevareid's. Others danced wildly about, remembering that wan smile of abdication. He'd tossed in the towel.

The first doubts came: "It's a trick—an April Fool—"

"We did it! He's out! He's not coming back!"

One of the dozens of Bright Young Men mounted a table and waved for attention. "If we fumble it Tuesday, he'll say it's a mandate—" He thrust his hands in his pockets in the self-consciously unselfconscious manner favored by student politicos, cautioning them to be careful and restrained. It was a one-upman's gambit to explain why joy was premature, and all else inappropriate. But they'd have none of it, reveling in anarchic, classless delight, screaming, "Hell no! We won! We won! We *won!*"

On the television, learned faces admitted their own loss for words, at length, and could only evoke the resilient genius of "the system," as they did for everything this side of subway fires.

Monday was quiet. People reminded each other that they were still "only in the suburbs of Jerusalem." Others spoke of "premature ejaculation," and a lot of people looked at their laps. Talk began about what Hubert Humphrey might be planning. "Do you suppose Johnson bothered to tell him?"

For Johanna it was a time of floating, in the balance of delicate forces. Here was proof she could do something real. Her weight on the lever had added something. Tomorrow they would win. The day after, she would be, by invitation, on Robert Kennedy's campaign; Tyler could work out the details of getting himself assigned to the same places as she. Tucson seemed so long ago, though its memory remained. Tyler and this work were so restorative. The fears and ill-ease she'd brought from home were banished now. Tyler had been patient. He understood enough to let her find her own way. And through that, new potentials grew. Still, she wondered what would happen to them if this glue were gone. Dizzying thoughts filled her mind, exciting but frightening, full of promise and dread.

At night now she would lay with him, and they would find new paths and patterns to touch. They'd joke, and speak and tease and wrestle. After making love she would feel warm and glad as Tyler stroked her, a friend, a lover, a secret sharer. The filling sense of herself would lead to grand and rapturous imaginings: of the space between content's own constituents, as barren as the space beyond—yet: pollution, remnants in those vacuums despising emptiness, or craving being, became as obdurate as masses of grave density. They talked of these things, understanding that they stood, or lay, on the doorstep of all possibility.

And for a moment, for a month—for a while at least, they and their world could be well. It was despite the rush and panic, the time of their lives. Her time, his time, all times, real time—all were relative, imaginary. The infinite was made intimate by thought and sense. All distances were warped by imagination. Connections were made by will and action. In her self-weaved womb of timelessness, she wondered: was a first creation so astounding, second and third ones so unlikely? There were all these small creations: the ability to make fingers move for the desire of it, unconsciously, life begin for the love of it, passion rise for the very need of it. Impossibilities were only doomed by man-made logic. Self-willed existence was possible in other faiths, realities only functional myths. She could reach out and touch these things, behind her eyes, as she fell asleep.

Anticlimactic Tuesday brought the expected McCarthy victory in Wisconsin. It was smaller than hoped, but a clear, clean win: 57 percent. Headquarters wallowed in its spoils: they'd turned the war around, pried Johnson from his seat, won the primary outright. Now on to Indiana, Nebraska, Pennsylvania, Oregon, California, New York, and all the way to Chicago. Then, the "Victory Special" to Washington.

"There was another winner here in Wisconsin," a network newsman said to the camera while McCarthy's celebrants cavorted behind him. He grabbed one and said, "In Nixon's Headquarters they're just as happy—but more subdued. What do you think of a McCarthy-Nixon race?"

"I try not to think about Richard Nixon," Johanna replied. "But—we'd win. Anyway, all he beat was a pigeon of a dove in a hairpiece."

"Well, what about Senator Kennedy, now that this is over?" he asked. He meant: How would they counter him?

She shrugged nonchalantly. "That's something people will have to work out for themselves. It depends on what's important to them." Tyler stood off camera going over some moving plans with another staff worker, but caught the answer and turned around to see her smiling at him deliciously.

"And that may be the difference," the reporter told the camera. "McCarthy's young legions are all around here whooping it up—and all over the country. His staff is dedicated, thoughtful"—he turned to acknowledge Johanna—"and very, very smart. Robert Kennedy's machine is made of guts and fighters and pros from the wards. Across town, Richard Nixon is celebrating his easy victory over Harold Stassen. What will happen when, and if, he—Richard Nixon—comes up against this, this amazing force, this machine that runs on hope and milkshakes, that uses more acne cream than chaw tobacco—will be something for the books— From an"—he gestured behind him, directing the camera's eye to the crowd—"ecstatic McCarthy Headquarters in Milwaukee this is—"

"Some joke," Tyler called when the camera went off. She dared him to find fault with anything she'd said. He just threw up his hands in surrender. On ethical grounds she did not attend the postelection strategy meeting at the Sheraton-Schroeder and packed their suitcases for the Indiana trip, seeding Tyler's with mischievous messages.

The meeting was a rehash of a fiery one the week

before. After that first one, the campaign Press Officer and his chief assistant quit, because the candidate was not making a significant effort in the nonwhite ghettoes. Success had bred caution and Milwaukee's white ethnics were the key to victory. But that same posture continued would, while winning a few votes in Nebraska, concede great chunks of Indiana, California, and other urban states to Robert Kennedy. The McCarthy campaign was being personified as a white middle-class suburban conceit, a Volkswagen caravan with flower decals—an unappealing concept in Gary, Indiana. A tentative pitch had been made to Milwaukee's embattled civil rights activist, Father James Groppi, but nothing came of it besides McCarthy dubbing the American system of black exploitation "domestic colonialism." That was only words. Symbols were important, and Robert Kennedy had the two best: Cesar Chavez and Martin Luther King, even though King was off supporting a garbage strike in Memphis, the kind of thing middle-class white ethnics were terrified about: being held hostage by their service classes. "All I know," the meeting's conductor kept repeating, "is we better do something. Before it's too damned *late*."

It was.

The nation lived on two timeclocks, in two realities, and while the white liberals were celebrating their impending release from the bondage of their own acquired power, the black clock spun erratically and ran down.

The crest of young, white, nascent hopes occurred contemporaneously with the trough of black despair. A white man blew up the Reverend Dr. Martin Luther King, Jr., in Memphis.

"One more cretin heard from," Tyler said, when they heard the news, checking into the Antlers Hotel in Indianapolis. "Always some guy with a thing for humping celebrities. Just once, why don't they take aim at a pansy movie star for a change?"

"Tyler!" Johanna scolded.

"You can't even say it. That's it. Some clown'll go out and do it! What a time!"

Also landing in Indianapolis that night was Robert Kennedy, who learned of the shooting then. Perhaps feeling the burning of a dormant lesion on his own brain, a scar that refused to heal, he reached back to Aeschylus for a moral: "In our sleep, pain which cannot forget falls drop by drop upon the heart until, in our own despair, against our will, comes wisdom through the awful grace of God."

Johanna watched Tyler as they watched that statement on the television. She was even more confirmed in her own decision, and Tyler said he was moved by Kennedy's feeling. Kennedy had reflexively called for compassion and a turn away from polarization. "My own brother," Robert Kennedy said, "was killed by a white man."

The next few days attention shifted to the funeral in Atlanta. Campaign headquarters in both camps were quiet. Tyler again admitted to Johanna that he was impressed with Kennedy's manner in a way he had not been before. "He's a very nice man," he said. "Very decent."

"Kind," she said. "Feeling."

"I had him wrong."

"Will you come over?"

"I didn't say that. I said he's a nice man. He's not nice to fight against."

"There's a remedy for that," she smiled.

"Johanna, you have no scruples whatsoever! Anyway—if Kennedy wins, they'll make you a judge and you can support me in the style I'd like. If McCarthy wins, I'll see you get paroled to a warm climate. We've got the field covered."

But his softening toward—or growing affection toward—Bobby Kennedy was a manifold thing: part honest reappraisal, part romance, part unconscious identification, and part, no small part, the desire to be with a winner.

For Robert Kennedy was looking like a winner, and Tyler Bowen regarded himself, no less than Kennedy, one also. His nature sought its own level. He was just as glad for Kennedy's success, though he continued to labor diligently and honestly for McCarthy. Gene was too much a poet; in the week following the King assassination, McCarthy had sulked in his hotel room, pondering existential things, communing solely with his muse.

From a standing start, Robert Kennedy was gaining steady ground, and had Indiana locked up in the polls. McCarthy was lagging in third place, behind Lyndon Johnson's stand-in, Governor Edgar Branigan—who attempted single-handedly to breathe life into the honored soul of Know-Nothingism. Kennedy's victory was so certain that Tyler began to call Johanna "Your Honor," amending it to "Your sort-of Honor. I know better."

Certainly, another force in his attraction to Kennedy came from sleeping with "Bobby's best and prettiest staff aide," he admitted one morning to Johanna.

"Irrelevant," she said, brushing her teeth, her mouth foamy with paste.

"So are you. So am I. So why not?"

"Uh-uh—do it for the right reasons."

"Which are?"

She grinned—"He's cute"—and winked.

He'd stay with McCarthy as long as he was wanted, though the entreaties grew more plentiful, from Johanna and others he was meeting from Kennedy Headquarters. She was growing in importance, doing for Kennedy what she had done for McCarthy, with even greater expertise. If Tyler shipped over, she teased, "I might be under pressure not to fraternize with enlisted personnel."

It was a foregone conclusion in McCarthy Headquarters that Kennedy would not only take Indiana on May 7, but that same night would lap the field in the District of Columbia. And a week later, they were privately conceding, on May 14 he would take Nebraska. Eugene McCarthy was shaping up all of a sudden as everybody's second choice. If McCarthy didn't hold a grudge and threw in with Kennedy at the convention on Ballot One, they could lock it up. McCarthy might even get Secretary of State for his pains. The first votes had not yet been cast in an election with Robert Kennedy's name in the lists, and already people were conceding him the nomination. You don't bet against a Kennedy in any brawl when there are real marbles in the pot.

By mid-April McCarthy strategists were thinking about how to hold their own troops in line and how to offset the Kennedy psychology. During this time, Tyler Bowen was admitting to Johanna the shaping of an admiration for Robert Kennedy, despite the mauling Gene was getting in the polls, or maybe a little because of it. For as Baron Zermatt had said, "Winning's nice, too," and it was not obvious McCarthy had heard about that, the way he ran. The more Tyler learned of Kennedy the softer he became to Johanna's beckonings, though she did not make things any easier by constantly telling him "You'll come over. I know that. I just want to know when—so I can get you a good job."

As Indiana slipped, a new mood came over the McCarthy staff. Their antipathy to Kennedy increased in the conviction he would so divide the Democrats and unite his opponents that his candidacy would permit the Republican nominee to slide home unmolested. And the Republicans, they shuddered, were demonstrating their pathology: a love of Richard Nixon, whom no one ever accused of being a charmer and who, decked out once again in a self-proclaimed "New" self, resembled, behind his excess of toothiness, beneath the Grandma's bonnet of his latest style, nothing more than a shark in wolf's clothing. And that Robert Kennedy was exciting strong passions and emotions in the streets of every town he came to convinced the McCarthy loyalists all the more of their own man's superior merit: he appealed to reason.

More than could be said for McCarthy's turbulent staff. The national office sent out new plans daily, then changed them overnight. The staff itself was having civil wars, and each faction took on new generals every few days, each made overtures to the other's loyalists, each suspected their own. A former CIA man joined the staff and no one was quite sure for whom he was working. Tyler Bowen was sent to Nebraska in advance of the Indiana voting, having begged off a Florida assignment. He maintained hotel rooms in two cities, so frantic was his shuttling around that state, and he never knew until his body gave him notice whether he would lay his head at Omaha's Chicago House or Lincoln's

Cornhusker, or with Johanna. Or at the Menninger Clinic.

Every step each one of them had taken for the last six months, every misstep and bad fall, had been in some way for the other. He had joined McCarthy as much to show Johanna he wasn't all Gila Monster as out of genuine commitment. She was the one who cared about politics. And now his rationalizations began to arrange themselves. McCarthy had taken the solitary lonely step—but even Goodwin and Allard Lowenstein had shipped over to Bobby. McCarthy might just not be the man to run the engine of rebellion or build the hope-founded empire anew. It was no longer a battle to change one policy, but to rearrange the nature of the world—a rejoinder to those others who abdicated to the hard-hearts by choosing disengagement or fruitless radical revolt.

Johanna wasn't helping things. She was just too smug, too sure of her hold on him for Tyler to switch with any pride.

He objected. "You expect me to just give up my convictions?"

"What convictions? And why not? Look what I gave up for *you!*"

It finally got to him, and he blistered. "The only thing you give up is men—one at a time. What the hell do you believe in besides yourself? Bobby's cute, you said it. So off you go!"

She was not immediately angry, but disgusted, wounded, though unwilling to show it fully, wondering how she could have been so wrong about a man again. Were they all the same or was she just prone to a type? "You know what, Tyler Bowen? Drop dead."

"Yeah, that's right, terrific. There's a rational approach. Appeal to the mind—"

"Go away from me!"

"Wait a minute—What am I?—What the hell are we doing? Fighting over two politicians? Look, I'm sorry. Really."

"If you were, you wouldn't have thought of those things."

"Come on, you know me. The words come out before I get to think about them. I don't hear 'em till you do—"

"Listen to yourself some time. I—I wouldn't kiss you again be—because you'd turn back into a frog—" He started to laugh and she took a sock at him furiously, hitting his back as he turned. "If you were an instrument, you'd be a bass drum in your own parade. You—kazoo!!"

"I haven't stuck with anything except you since I got out of college, for Christ's sake. And you ask me to just toss the whole thing over—"

"I just ask you to show a little kindness. That's all. Just a little."

Kindness was the clef of Bobby's romance, people said. "Decency," he said, "is at the heart of it." Bobby, the former strong-man whose wet footprints were on both sides of the civil rights and civil liberties streets, was standing for kindness. And Lyndon Johnson, who wrote the Great Society, no more humane a program than which ever sprang from office, saw his works crumble in mean, base statistical vanities before him. Kindness was the only thing missing in social equations. And it was romantic, because only in the most naive lobes and sentimental chambers did anyone dare hold that kindness could prevail in a noxious world. The lessons of so many years were plain: things fall apart. On Earth, brutes survive. The order of the heavens is disorder.

After some hours of mutual funk, Tyler courted Johanna and said, "I'll try, that's all I can promise."

Johanna said, "That's all I ever ask."

It was the most romantic and paradoxical of times, for kindness had a decent, fighting chance to survive the harsh, unfiltered, ultraviolet rays of politics.

In the last week of April McCarthy's national staff descended on Lincoln and determined that both states, Indiana and Nebraska, were in disarray. Kennedy's momentum was making the McCarthy campaign welter in confusion. "My God, *look* at this!" a National man bellowed when he surveyed the Lincoln operation. "It looks like the inside of a nose in full sneeze!" He started firing people who had been there twice as long as he had.

A plan emerged after all the fumbling, based on New Hampshire's strategy. It was to lose. They would take a standing count in the plains states, then back-pedal and slip west quietly to regroup in Oregon and California for an ambush. You could only lose your cherry once, they felt, and someone said, "Bobby's whole mystique is his inevitability. He can't afford *any* loss." Kennedy was expected to win every time, so one McCarthy victory, straight-up, would stall him. It would shatter the Kennedy veneer and be the start of Bobby's finish. Indeed, they'd hurt him in his home state, New York, where they were already better organized, and in Pennsylvania. By losing Nebraska and Indiana, they'd set him up to look silly later. "We'll just hang close until he stumbles. Then we shoot right past. That's the virtue in running second."

"We're third," someone pointed out.

They'd make Robert Kennedy the first of his clan to drop an election since Jack got set running for the Harvard Senior Class presidency. If they could take Oregon, they might just keep the tide going through California. Someone asked what good did winning Oregon do Rockefeller in 1964? "That was different. That was then. This is now."

So, McCarthy staff was sent to Oregon, California, and New York, ten days before the first midwest voting. People were being shipped around like office supplies. Tyler Bowen gave his car to one headed back east. "Just do me a favor," he said, "and carry identification. I don't want my parents getting called out to look at your body if you roll it." He'd asked Johanna whether she had any use for it, but she just said, "No, I get to ride with the motorcade." It was true: she was in the circle just past the bodyguards, both by virtue of campaign position and because Bobby liked to see her face nearby. He talked to her, seemed to seek her out to pass on quips, and the number of times Tyler saw her picture in the paper near Bobby set his teeth on edge.

"Don't be jealous," she chided. "He just likes my work. And I like you better."

"I'd think your reporter friends would catch on that his crowds are the same faces. He's got a portable riot."

Then, the day he was to leave California, Tyler was told he was being sent to Philadelphia instead. "Wait a minute," he objected. "This is already set up. I'm supposed to meet Mark Siegel and Marty Munn in San Francisco to—"

"It's changed, that's all," he was told by a new gun from Washington.

"Could you see if you could maybe change it back?" Tyler asked. "I already shipped a suitcase out—" The man asked what the big deal was and Tyler explained that his woman was flying out to San Francisco that afternoon.

Grumbling that "it's not a fucking pleasure cruise, Bowen," the man said, nonetheless, he'd see what he could do. Later, Tyler was summoned to the State Campaign Chairman's office where the man he had spoken to was fuming. "You told me your woman was going to California—"

"That's right," Tyler said.

"So I thought I'd do you a turn and get rid of this motherfucking hostility that's shot through this campaign. Be a nice guy and get her shifted to Oregon—" Tyler winced, knowing what was next. He also wondered how pure the man's motives were. Factions in the campaign were literally offering bribes to staffers for support in the internal struggles. Presidential campaigning was fading to a distant second place in their priorities; future political careers were being made and broken, and never did integrity figure in the process. Nor was doing a good turn in the repertoire of this man unless he had good reason. He squinted hard at Tyler Bowen, stalking closer, trying to read him. Then, "You didn't tell me, Bowen, she's working for Kennedy!"

"I didn't ask you to change her plans. I asked you to leave mine the way you found them."

"Are you kidding?" the man half shrieked. "Are you—"

"Hey! I don't know who-the-hell you think you are, but I won't be shouted at. Got it?"

"Are you putting me *on?*" None of the other staffers

515

in the office betrayed any allegiance, though most had known of Bowen's arrangement for weeks. No one went looking for a fight they could avoid. "What's the story here, Bowen? Are you two—shacking up? Are you?"

"I don't think that's any of your God-damned business!"

"Everything in this campaign is my business. Everything that affects the efficiency is—"

"You must have better things to do while we slip a point a day," Bowen marveled.

"Don't you tell me how to run things! What are you—a fifth column—?"

"Screw off!" Tyler snapped, starting to walk out. "I'm getting fed up with your whole act. Get it: I'm on the team—and until I hear different from the Senator, he's my boss, not you!"

The man blocked the door. *"Which* Senator?"

"If you're looking for a busted face, keep standing there."

"I want to know what you did before this campaign? Who'd you work for?"

"The government. The same as Senator McCarthy."

"I hear it different."

"You hear it wrong."

"I hear you're still working for them—and there's only one candidate in this race who knows people who tap phones—"

"You are over your head, buddy," Bowen said.

"And you are on your way out. God! To think we gave you a position of—"

"You didn't give me anything but a pain in the ass. I was here in February—when we were *winning*. Where were you? Don't think I haven't had offers from the Kennedy people—"

"I'm sure—every night." Tyler shoved him forcefully into the wall. They had been arguing chin to chin like an umpire and a disgruntled batter; now, Tyler had already thrown his bat in the air. He remembered his father, quoting Bill Klem: "If that bat comes down—" No one was really sure what the fight was about: power, alliances, resentment over the good press the young volunteers received, jockeying for influence

516

with the halfhearted candidate. The mixed marriage was a spurious issue. There were too many others, official marriages even, at the local level, where husband and wife worked for different slates.

"You've got it," Tyler said, backing off. "You haven't lost a program coordinator. You've gained a hotel room. Keep it up—you'll have a whole hotel. Just try and fill it." He stormed out disgusted with the whole episode.

When he called Johanna, from a pay phone, he was still heaving mad. She laughed salaciously, "I happen to know that you're a pushover—"

"Is that thing about open arms still good?"

"Some of us," she said.

"You're so smug I can't stand it."

"When I'm right, I'm right. You can't beat that logic. All you have to do is pass a test: explain the difference between the Bolsheviks and Mensheviks in twenty-five words."

"Christ, I can't even tell my own team without a compass."

Within fifteen minutes of arriving at Kennedy Headquarters, Tyler Bowen warmed to the virtues of his new candidate like an old hand. Johanna said his praise for Kennedy seemed "a mite too effusive," and his scorn of McCarthy was "delivered like a dowry."

"It's true," he insisted. "I just never got the sense McCarthy was there. He's like Mr. Phlogiston—there's burning all around, but is he real? Or just some gimmick to explain the fire so the engineers can thrive? He's a stalking horse for the Invisible Man."

She frowned. "Spoken with all the conviction of the recent convert. A week ago you swore McCarthy was the greatest thing since donut holes. Is that how you'll talk about me when you're through?"

"Are you kidding?" he said. "I'm Mr. Loyalty."

"Do I contradict myself? Tra-la! I contain—*platitudes!*"

"I'll tell you the truth," he smirked. "I liked Gene because he reminded me of you."

Unlike Eugene McCarthy, Robert Kennedy was accessible, all the more during the small crises of scheduling and personality that arose. Yet there were similarities: both men enjoyed the administrative prerogative of dispensing justice, and both pursued the despot's art of shaping it creatively, styling it poetically. In this instance, Kennedy suggested that the campaign's interests would best be served, embarrassment be avoided, if its newest young associate was kept on a lower rung, out of view for a while. He suggested that Tyler Bowen be made assistant to Johanna Poulson. Kennedy's adept anticipation of and intervention in staff conflicts, his ability to resolve them by wise counsel or fast lessons in power, only convinced his followers further of his suitability for high office. In the Kennedy campaign there were no illusions as to whether it was the candidate or his entourage that was the attraction. He was the product and he was, from his own early career, better at each campaign task than most of his aides. He could patch together his own speech on his feet, with more pungent references and more shocking citations than his writers. He could charm the press, even the cynics. He could get on a telephone, cold, and twist a never-met alderman's arm, knowing the right tone to use, whether flattery or spiritualism was demanded, and the favorite brand, confirmation name, voting record and list price of every ward heeler on the mainland. He could organize people more efficiently than seven layers of organization experts: he could inspire. Yet, he had time to rib the reporters, kid with his staff, mock himself, be private with his wife, grab a revitalizing nap or officiate when a prank was played and, with a word, recharge a tired friend.

On the plane to San Francisco, one of the reporters told Johanna he remembered John Kennedy as "a Fitzgerald guy in a Hemingway book and the other way around." He said it wistfully. "Bobby? Bobby was always something else. The runt of the litter; but Jesus, did he do a job for Jack. I remember when he worked for McCarthy—the other one. It was always funny how much Bobby despised Roy Cohn. We used to say, 'The difference between Bobby Kennedy and Roy Cohn is— I don't know. What's the difference?' Anyone who calls him ruthless now didn't know him then."

"He seems so sweet," Johanna said.

"Yeah. Timid, sort of. He's changed mostly that way." Seeing Robert Kennedy moving about in the aisle ahead, the reporter raised his voice to make his presence known and insinuate himself in any hatching action. "I wouldn't want to wrestle him for the last piece of— chicken," he said, his voice trailing off as Kennedy headed back the other way, "but yeah, I know. He's become less assertive than . . . than just about everybody. Except they're not running for president. If you told him he had the second worst stutter in the world? I wouldn't want to be the guy in first place!" Johanna had noticed odd signs of this: Robert Kennedy seemed to shade his eyes, not in embarrassment or modesty, but shyness, as though afraid of personal trespass. Yet he could look up and, one eyelid drooping, there would be a gaze that was so intimate it was disarming; it burned through one's eye into a place deeper than the optic nerve could go, and seemed both to understand something and be begging something. He competed terrifically, but never on the expected ground. He seemed at times so tough and, in the midst of the same moment, so soft, more vulnerable than she ever would dare be.

In power, confident, unbruised by pain, Robert Kennedy was unforgiving. Out of power, he was shambling, meek, contemplative. His reputation as a dextrous man with a hatchet preceded him, so even his closest associates were surprised by his true character: sensitive, self-deflating, amused at his own pretensions. As delighted as he was by the enthusiasms he provoked, he was a little frightened by it all.

Were it not for his unfathomable energy, the reporter told Johanna, "he might have made a great librarian."

She repeated the conversation to Tyler Bowen, who had just been with one of the Senator's speechwriters. Tyler said, "We were talking about it, too. He told me Bobby said, 'Irony did not begin with Oscar Wilde, or end with Gene McCarthy.' "

"Two, three, four . . . ," a glee club of reporters crooned tipsily as the plane descended into the San Francisco glide path, Johanna's hand evident again in their work:

We're Brother Bobby's Lovely Heart Throb Clan,
We hope you will support his race,
Brother Bobby's Lovely Heart Throb Clan,
Come forward and receive some Grace. . . .
From Palm Beach to Hyannisport,
We feel at home with your support,
You make us feel at home. . . .

The candidate and his staff were delighted, though the landing cut short the show. "I should like to hear the rest of your fine efforts," he deadpanned, as the motorcade prepared to zoom him away, "if we ever meet again."

Whatever the assigned causes, as they knew at Tombstone now, this was an extraordinary moment in the world's life, another in the periodic high tides in the culture and politics of men—a syzygy, where the sun and moon and earth align, making for the highest of tides—a year to have schoolchildren memorize with the multiplication tables; a year like 1848, 1917, 1932, when revolution was itself the natural order, at the peak or on the cusp of epochs, a time when politics and culture combined and altered each other. All across the planet, the music invented in the last decade reached its most elegant phase, made its most felt statements, took its most romantic form. The discontented sought focal points, clustering around their champions, turning romantic ideals into programs, programs into demands. They believed this was the last chance to believe. This was the first year of their collective majority, young adults forced to live in their parents' house overlong because there was no place to go; the world was too crowded and too poor, despite all affluence, for shared ground and power. So they made bold to say they wanted the master bedroom. Now.

Passion was shot through every craft and every stratum, spread to every open space on the planet, as though some new element was in the air. Pundits declared that a decade of nuclear testing had altered social weather patterns, made mutations in the young;

this was fallout from the fifties, the result of energies released at the end of the last World War; something in the milk fed to a generation who were never spanked.

It was a worldwide thing. In West Germany, on whose behalf the North Atlantic Alliance periodically risked war with the Soviet Bloc, the favorite posture of students was hip Marxism. They spread it, west, to France, as though a Continental fad, where it was dubbed "obsolete," and supplanted by a more chic form of radicalism. In both countries, leaders attacked such dangerous games by the young, while they made sweeping gestures of accommodation to the Warsaw Pact.

In Czechoslovakia, a fragile sprout of democratic experiment ascended to the daylight through a crack in the socialist pavement.

In Paris, cobblestones and paving blocks flew from the student quarters at the Sorbonne and Nanterre. With them, a solid cry, *"À bas l'état!"* Young French radicals taunted and tottered the last pillar of the Grand Alliance that had forged this world. He swung back at his tormentors, but they were too manic to be frightened. Left with but invective he called them bed-wetters: *"Non à la chienlit."* They yipped back a bitching pun: *"La chienlit c'est lui!"* That is, "dogshit." And to him, who had liberated them before their very conception, freed their parents from the burden of their own collaboration with the Fascists, they declared the estate of being young in his reign as one of German Jews: *"Nous sommes tous des juifs et des allemands!"* He sank in the agony of his heart, his world crumbling from an era's weight. Arteriosclerosis was in the veins of empires. And though they almost tumbled a government, those demonstrations were finally most noted for their artistic posters, *les affiches du Mai.*

American students would learn from this and henceforth delegate roles to the talented as well as the committed during campus clashes. Poets and artists would yet be in the highest revolutionary councils. And future demonstrations would be financed by the mass-marketed artifacts sold for wall hangings in a million homes: strike symbols silk-screened on T-

521

shirts, epic slogans lithographed for every den, commercial ripoffs before the fact.

The politics of the time became its art, because the art of the time was its politics.

WILLIE BOWEN COUNTED THE STARS. IN the sultry damp of midnight, he looked up at the hills around him and continued to wait. He rested his eyes and his concentration by trying to count the stars over the silent hills. Somewhere around three thousand he lost track. Wisps of haze kept interfering.

They were out there. This much he knew. Everyone knew it. They knew it in the fire base and this hole and they knew it all the way back to Washington. They were out there, all right. Behind rocks and bushes. In caves and makeshift bunkers. Who knew what kind of nests they lived in? Gopher holes and trenches—a tunnel system under the whole rotten country, maybe. Moles. Every time, they emerged from a different reality. Oh, they were out there, all right. And they would wait. They wouldn't breathe or move or exist at all. Just wait. Until Willie Bowen and the others in this tiny hole of a forward fire base were one step past being tired of waiting, and then . . . Somehow, they just knew.

So Willie's mission was, apart from the futile watching, to serve as sitting duck. That's what everyone said. There was no other reason for this outpost. There was nothing to do but sit here and be harassed. He'd come with a recon patrol of seventy-five troopers. Why, nobody quite knew. There was no resistance along the way. Only, when the Hueys came to withdraw the detachment they were relieving, fire from nowhere chased the gunships off. The hole in the middle of nowhere suddenly became important. But the enemy—wherever they were—played a strange game. They let troops in, but not out. It seemed they wanted them there. The hole couldn't be that important if they were letting American strength build up, could it? But, experience showed, they were damned clever. Willie didn't actually think they made strategy or tactical decisions—they just had a sense of how to bamboozle.

Willie respected them for it. He was afraid of them and would freely admit it. They knew his cracking point and just how long to wait. They had animal cunning, and he was just a skinny, broad-shouldered kid, nineteen years old with good lateral moves, and not much more than an M-16 to rely on. He waited. They would come. But not tonight. No, Willie knew it would not be tonight. Two more nights, maybe. Maybe three. They'd wait until the clouds blocked the moon, and a vague, gray glow made the mist shine with anarchic, dislocating fierceness. They'd wait until *Time* magazine arrived with its weekly morale-downers: its stories of campus riots, antiwar demos, the whole political structure turning against the war, sexual liberation, people groping each other coast to coast—all the evidence that a goddam party was going on back home, while they were stuck where they didn't want to be, fighting for people they didn't give two warm shits about, at the command of people they wanted to kill, against the wishes of friends who were fucking up a storm and rooting for the other team.

Then they would come. They'd lead with invisible sappers' satchel charges. Claymores would fail somehow or blow backward. Technology's wonders would come a cropper. Mortar would pour in at impossible angles ("Incoming!" someone would scream, always too late) —up the ass if that hadn't been tried yet. Who knew where the tunnels led? It would happen again, as it always did. You'd be on guard, projecting cues, trying a key in a thousand doors of night sounds. When your mind's ear corresponded with the world's voice it was coming and already half-over. Until then—nothing: just the expectancy mounting in your fearful head. Just the cadence building toward a final beat. The Army's rhythms were all 4/4 time. But theirs were different. There'd always be an extra beat or more. And infinite cadenzas and codas before the last measures. It would come soon, Willie knew. Maybe as soon as tomorrow or the next day. If he was lucky, he'd be sleeping. If it came bad, he didn't want to be on guard and have so long to think about it. On guard he'd certainly be overrun before the others woke to defend the hole. Asleep he'd have a chance. It would come. We'd bring in the choppers and gunships and bombers then, even with a mist. The Air Force would wait till dawn if they could, the lazy, comfortable cowboys. But at least they'd get there, if needed, by night and fog. You'd have to call them twice, though, and swear to the urgency.

That was Willie Bowen's one ultimate faith as his blurry eyes scoured the anonymous hills in the dark. If all else failed, and it surely would, despite all his cynicism about chickenshit comrades—we at least had the Big Stuff. If he was ever in Really Big Trouble, no matter his open unbelief, there was this secret creed: Sam would come rumbling down the pike with tanks, he'd split the waters with the roar of destroyer fire. Battleships would spit flame as accurate as Willie's own rifle from a hundred times as far with a million times the punch. The air would be betrayed by the sudden claps of a thousand bombs, from planes already past and turned for home. Sam had infinite resources and infinite potential when he cared. Sam would move the heavens and the earth, rechannel rivers overnight and rechart the seas to save his nephews. He'd drop the atom bomb if he had to. Sam would not let them down. Sam was God if there was one, and the grunts were His Chosen, elected by His draft, or enlisted in His priesthood, warring in His Hell. He wouldn't let some slant-eyed heathen slope-gook-dink-greasy-VC be the sword of his wrath. No one had the right to tax them but their Uncle. We're American citizens, that faith snarled. You got that, Charlie! No one's got the right to waste us. Not yet, anyhow.

Yet: they were good at waiting, Willie thought. Better than we were. We're so impatient. He almost wanted them to come. And they had an Uncle, too: Ho. And they'd waited very long. They'd outwaited Lyndon. What a victory that had been! Ho-Ho-Ho, LBJ.

But Sam wasn't Lyndon. Sam was larger than that. Sam was unaffected by all that, not yet moved. Soon. Sam would be sitting back, waiting. He'd outwait the waiters and then: Sam would roll up his sleeves and pave 'em over. He'd do it all just to bring his nephews, and Willie Bowen, less a few, home to all those nice aunties again.

So Willie waited. His ears perked to an occasional toad or cricket. His eyes burned from efforts to uncover treachery in the hills. Sometimes he'd hear the fluttering of helicopters passing nearby, or feel the rumble of vehicles through the earth. Mostly nothing. And he had hemorrhoids, with nothing to rub with but his loaded weapon's muzzle. DOD would have a hell of a time figuring that wound out.

After his guard was over Willie sat up half the night, with some others, scared and edgy. "One good rain," a guy said, "all the Chung King Charlies in the world'll wash right down in our laps."

"You like rain? Wait a few months."

The sky seemed already set to burst with thunder, hanging heavy; cloudless, but saturated with vibrations. The dull drone of nearby movements continued. Choppers maybe. Armored vehicles. "Good," one said. "I hope they see a lotta action. As long as it's outta here." Willie smiled at that. As long as the tanks and choppers stayed away, the hills remained quiet. So the less help they had now, the better. Just like his feelings about Johnson: hating him, but requiring him, for Big Bad Sam was still the meanest dude on the block, standing just behind them with planes and tanks and bombs and ships and helicopters, trucks and—"HELICOPTERS!!!!! WHERE THE HELL DID THEY—GET—" a voice screamed as a gunship opened up on the hole. "INCOMING!!!" it bellowed, Willie's own voice, muted by the blade's gurgling roar as the craft swept out of the mist. "IS HE CRAZY? IS IT OURS? ONE OF OURS!!!!" The men scrambled, grabbing what weapons they could, firing hysterically at the helicopter. "THEIRS??" "THEIRS!!!! OMYGODOGOD—"

"WHERE THE HELL—" Fire blasted from all over and the helicopter pulled higher, joined by another. The first wheeled around on its sky hook and swept

back to flank them, and both were joined by "TAAAANKS
—THE FUCK—WHERE THE—"

The rumble turned into a roar. Four tanks fell in
behind the choppers, through an opening between two
hills. The night turned into a quilt of flames and whines
and screaming noises of machinery. Explosions and
wild lurches were the rhythm. Dirt thickened the fog
in a choking stench that whipped about beneath the
helicopter blades.

The men in the hole ran around their position like
wild panicked rats, evading the choppers' crazy-angled
fire, dashing into the tanks' path. Men screamed orders
to each other in command and complaint, cried for
help as each one's world blew up. "Get up into that
hill! Go! Move the hell out!" one officer yelled. He
crashed ahead in the darkness, clutching a 7.62-mm
machine gun. Troops in underwear and unlaced boots
and others in shorts and socks or barefoot, carrying
what they could, burst into the hills for mere survival,
unconcerned about those left behind. "Over here!—
Somebody—Take that tank!" one man howled before
it ran him over.

Willie ran straight for the very hill he had been
watching before. He knew he would be greeted with
a sudden burst of final fire—just make it quick. Behind
him the world was coming unstuck. On his right, a
barefoot Sergeant caught his ankle on barbed wire and
ripped himself free, leaving a length of flesh, flapping in
ignorance of its birth agony, on the rusty barbs. His
tugging set off trip wires down the line. It killed two
men hurdling over. Caught them in mid-vault with the
blast. Blew their bottoms off completely. One crawled
a few yards still, intestines dragging.

Willie cut to his right toward some bushes for cover.
A helicopter blasted it away. "Why me?" he wheezed.
"Why me?" Dirt kicked in his eyes from the rounds.
He fell flat and rubbed them clear, and the ground was
torn apart by furious fire. There was no place to hide.
He ran back toward the hole and got tangled up in
barbed wire, tugging, snorting like a hog in the dust.
The gunship tore the ground where he had been seconds
before. The second ship burst into whiteness and Willie
had a moment's breath to think someone had blown

it up—but the whiteness stayed. Arc lights! They were going to hunt them down like animals. Screaming for help, he freed himself from the barbs. A few feet away someone else was screaming, too. Men were howling and smashing into each other, running over the wounded. Crying men were ignored. Dying men were trampled. The chopper with the arc light swung into a bad angle and Willie and some others ran underneath it, firing blindly to cover their movement. No one knew where he was going or what he was hitting. The tanks tore up the hills they fled to. The men were delirious, isolated, hoping for lucky hits. Some were groping in the darkness with their insides hanging out, some were lying face up waiting for the end. The lucky ones, already in the hills, were under constant tank fire.

A sudden blast brought a small burning cloud into Willie's nostrils, and his face was splashed with the blood of someone close by. A young Lieutenant had stepped on his own carefully laid mine. He'd reeled backward into the pulverizing blast. Willie was toppled by it and slithered around the site like a frightened weasel, clawing hysterically through the Lieutenant's entrails, over another corpse. A few feet away, someone was screaming, "Help me!—for God's sake—pleeease—God! God!" Willie crawled away, fearing him as much as the tanks.

Then the tanks lined up and pounded every place in front of them. The men staggered and cut, dashing out and into the path of fire. One chopper chased them, belching machine-gun rounds and rockets. The chopper skimmed over Willie's head and as it passed he thought to escape behind the tanks. There was nowhere to go. For a moment he just lay there, unable to breathe, reducing his life to the length of a minute, believing he was at peace. The chopper pivoted for another run and the other moved toward him. They pulled away fearing a collision: he alone was not worth that much. Pieces of rock zinged by rounds struck him in the face and he was knocked over and over, back toward the hole. He struggled to his knees and the arc light chased him. He gasped for breath. It still came after him relentlessly. All he could do was perform for it: dodge and roll and tumble. It had him by the tail.

He was exhausted and he put his hands behind his head, unable to move further. Why didn't it get bored and pick somebody else? The floodlight caught him full. He knew he was dead, shaking and whimpering and his nausea rose to greet it. He gagged as the fire struck all around. There was no place to hide or escape. He scratched his way to the left, without breathing, unable to take air as the fire sprayed around him. It would be like sleep, he was sure. He'd never feel it. Dizzy and disoriented, rolling, eating dust, whining. Gravity repealed, falling and tumbling. What was up? Sideways, spinning, running down, changing every axis, pitch and yaw and roll, swallowing dust, leaning on air—tears in his throat turning the dirt to mud—mad, still moving unconsciously, imagining it was personal, only him the gunners sought. Gasping, furious: he'd expected his Americanness to give him dignity in dying, make Death respect him and his nation. Now he was just some slave to the brutes in the sky, a puny thing for slaughter, leaping up into the light, screaming, "Fuuuuuuuuck!"—blinded by the glare, saved from another sweep of fire by falling over sideways on his head and tumbling ten yards toward the hole. He rolled and rolled—unwilling to die obediently. "Fuuuuck!" he bellowed with misty self-pity in his eyes and a frightened defiance in his voice, cut off from the rest again, off the team. The chopper's eye picked him out of the darkness and moved remorselessly past. He played dead, staring up into the star-spangled night, until he was in momentary eclipse. Some fire struck nearby and he hollered louder than he'd ever screamed before, "Fuuuuuuuck!" and poured the last of his clip into the crew's faces. Another survivor was doing the same on the other side and hit the pilot. The ship tilted over and spun around one-half revolution, bursting into a black-spotted ball between two tanks. Willie gagged and dry-heaved at the sight, then ran as fast as he could along the edges of that fire for cover, smashing into the broken bushes where the remainder of the decimated unit quivered. The latecomers were the luckiest. The first to safety had been torn apart by the repeated tank volleys. The remaining helicopter strafed all around and half the survivors were struck along the way. No one paid any attention to anyone else as they dug their way past each other to safety.

They were scattered all about the hill, living and dead, shattered and bleeding. Men with bellies gushing out and men with sucking chest wounds didn't cry or tell of pain. Others with mere abrasions moaned and sobbed. Some lost limbs entirely and some would bleed to death that night. There was no Med-Evac or rescue possible. The first things lost were the phones.

Scouts were sent to find the remnants and by late night all were together. They sutured what wounds they could, and watched helplessly as the tanks gave every place a pounding. Some shots hit and killed survivors. By the end, less than a quarter were still whole.

The NVA crews picked over the remains. They stripped the dead and moved through their waste like vermin. In the lulls the men in the hills could hear voices—calm North Vietnamese officers finishing up their detail. Patient voices in the still night air.

"Where'd they come *up* with that shit? Where'd they get it?" one survivor moaned while his buddy dressed his broken head.

"I heard they had some—but not this far south— Tanks! Choppers!"

"Too early," someone said to Willie. "Too fuckin' soon—too much!" Willie lay on his side, holding his shoulder. It throbbed painfully, as did the bruises on his face where ricocheting rocks had struck him. He was only thinking, "Jesus Lord, I'm a-fucking-*live!*"

They took turns sleeping, though it was hardly sleep. A man would let his eyes roll up and pass out for a few minutes, not so much trusting his buddies as simply accepting the inevitable. The rest they took was what many had promised their bodies, then had denied them in the wild flight. They took turns watching, for what it meant. Willie tried to fall asleep, but as he fell, he felt a surge and vomited for fifteen minutes. Every time he thought he'd fall off, he woke up startled and sweating, freezing with fear. When he took his turn on watch, he still smelled the blood of strangers and tasted his own vomit in his teeth. His ears rang and his head spun from motion sickness. He could still feel, across his arms and stomach, the bodies he had tripped and crawled over, the parts he had shoved furiously out of his way.

Before dawn the tanks finished up below and pounded the hills for cover as they pulled out. There was nothing left to do but go down in the hole and get the hell out. There was no point waiting; they weren't coming back. There was no one in the hills, after all, but them. Now there was no more hole to guard from phantoms. Just a lot of dead men who'd tried. "We fought nobody," someone said to Willie as they helped carry an unconscious man down toward the hole, "and got creamed." Behind them a troop limped along between two supporting men guilty from their lack of scars. His murdered leg hung onto him more by habit than tendon.

No one in the hills today. Nor last night. And though a few men held their weapons high, for the most part those who still had them slung them loosely, or dragged them. They were out of danger, no more threat to the enemy. The dead would stay until they were ferried out. The ragged remnant would go to a good new hole while men with modest wounds went to look for someone with communications gear.

Willie's wounds were deep gashes, caked with dirt. Some cuts and tears would mend by themselves. But his shoulder worried him most. His good right arm's good shoulder was torn and aching. He wondered if he'd have nothing more than eternal bursitis to remember the war by—or whether the sum of his wounds would be not so great as to entitle him to benefits: just enough to rob him of his shoulder fakes, pass-catching moves, and the strong right arm that could work an option play. He stumbled through the scattered wreckage in the hole and wondered if all promise of a football scholarship had vanished overnight. He laughed suddenly, thinking how much trouble he'd be in if he had to limp along on his brains. Just as well he didn't rely on his head, he thought, or that would have been the thing they'd have picked to wreck. He bumped into one of his buddies who was staggering aimlessly around with his weapon across his shoulder like a prisoner's yoke, aimed at Willie's head. Willie pushed the muzzle away gently, and the man lurched in a new direction.

The rest of them sat where they could or wandered where they wanted, sleepless, hungry, too beaten to retreat. They hoped some enemy would rematerialize, declare himself the master of all about, capture them and lead them to the peace of sheets and hot water.

Willie and two others with ambulatory wounds were sent to get help. He watched his feet as he walked. But he tripped over rocks anyway, watery-eyed with visions of the chopper's crew and the dead he'd slept with. He coaxed his feet to late fourth-quarter heroics. "Just one more great move. You gotta want it! You gotta want it! Just one more time!" he mumbled. It was a chant, for survival where rational thought had failed. All that came were the homilies and maxims drilled in him over the years by unscarred coaches. They were meant for now, when thought was slow or too irrational, when minds wandered to notions of surcease, when action stood between the players and destruction. "Meet it head on, boy. Go out there and meet it. See what the hell's out there, Willie. Stand up and do it, boy. Stand up and shoot." His greasy, dirt-smudged face ran free with tears. "Don't ever die easy, boy. Stand up and shoot." The purring chuffs of whirlybirds swept over the trees and they froze. The three men didn't care who it was, but they'd put up a perfunctory struggle just for form. The ships hove into view, festooned with U.S. Army decals like some child's model, and they sniffled and straightened up.

As expected, on May 7 Kennedy took Indiana, and then took Nebraska the week after. It added momentum and a sense of inevitability to the West Coast efforts and made their frantic flights around California and Oregon all the more roisterous, made the campaign itself, in victory, all the more manic.

They were only in San Francisco a few days, but it was long enough to squeeze in some fast visits to friends of Johanna's in Berkeley, enlisting them out of their torpor, and a dinner with Tyler's sister and brother-in-law.

The four of them dined on the wharf one muggy mid-May night. "This is a hell of a thing to say after six months," Tyler whispered as he and Johanna walked in to meet Mack and Animal. "But I've never seen you look this lovely."

"Gearing up for combat," she said, clutching his hand tighter. Revisiting old places of happiness had helped, too. It confirmed her high expectations for the future. Tyler introduced her as "the future Federal Judge—"

"Not quite," Johanna blushed. "But it's better than Postmistress."

During dinner, Tyler mentioned how he'd almost gotten a free trip to San Francisco once before, but if it had worked out he and Johanna might not have known each other. "And the way I figure it, the course of American history was changed right there."

"To think," Johanna marveled, "the whole campaign is just a vehicle for your megalomania."

"The way *I* figure it," declared Tyler's brother-in-law when the check arrived, "the outrageous prices my old man paid for Papa Kennedy's Depression booze just about covers dinner."

"Are you telling me," Tyler asked, "that somewhere back in your family tree was a man who paid for his own drinks?" At that, Tyler dug in his pockets and came up with air. Johanna offered her campaign American Express card but Tyler interceded. "Alan— this could be your first contribution to enlightened politics since the last time you didn't vote in the Nazi Primary. I'll even see to it Bobby sends you an auto-graphed picture—he loves children and animals, you know."

Before leaving, Mack drew Tyler indiscreetly aside and whispered in his ear. He pinched her on the cheek and said, "I'm not as dumb as I look."

She pulled his cheek out in turn, twisting it tortuous-ly. "Sure had me fooled."

All the way back to the Jack Tar Hotel, Johanna kept asking him what his sister said, but he clammed up. She tickled it loose later, under the covers, despite his protests of "unfair advantage! She said—Stop it! Stop it! I'll talk, G-Men—"

"I should have done this to you in Tucson!" she said, poking around for ticklish spots.

"I had a poison pill in case I—*stopit!*—Is this any way to run—"

"What did she say? Out with it!" she demanded, triumphantly astride him.

"She said—she said, 'If you let her get away, you're a bigger dope than I thought.' Satisfied?" Johanna hugged herself with ill-disguised glee. "Pretty proud of yourself, aren't you, lady? What if I want a trade-in?"

"You're stuck, Mr. B."

"The B. stands for Br'er Rabbit," he said, pulling her down to kiss her.

"That starts with an *R*—but you're cute anyway." She sighed melodramatically, "Take me!"

"I think I'll take an aspirin instead," he said, flipping her over. He pounced on her and they jounced through a happy, laughing, mutual ravishing she would never have been able to endure three months before. She was effectively whole again.

The Kennedy efforts in northern California helped unite scattered factions. San Francisco itself might be conceded, wharf and weavers, to McCarthy, but the countryside could be salvaged. A few noted the resemblance between this strategy and General Giap's, but did not speak of it.

In southern quarters, Kennedy's problem was reversed. His strength was in the bilingual cities and among the migrant farmers. McCarthy had the suburban upper middle class. In one place McCarthy was the moderate to Kennedy's radical, in another McCarthy was the radical of choice. Kennedy was making a lot of mistakes as well, and McCarthy enjoyed watching him squirm: at one point, Kennedy made a clumsy opening to the Orange County burghers, all the while frightening them with his support of lettuce pickers.

And the McCarthy strategy was working well in Oregon. Kennedy would take a drubbing. At the start of Bobby's campaign, some backroom noises had been made about a little deal: McCarthy would let Kennedy have Oregon in exchange for Kennedy staying out of Nebraska. But Kennedy had needed to get his vote tally started, get the string of successes he required begun, so it was rejected. It was not a decision he enjoyed being reminded of. Identification with blacks, an advantage in Indiana, was troublesome in Oregon. Neither would he flinch from alliance with Chicanos and a strong gun-control position. Headquarters appraised the Oregon resistance to Kennedy charm this way: "Oregon needs to have a ghetto airlifted in." McCarthy found it easy pickings, the white-middle-class suburban flavor of his campaign served him well in this state; demographically, it could be a sister to Minnesota.

Yet Oregon was just a sideshow. It might have some slight psychological impact, but it was to California, before the Oregon votes were even cast, that the Kennedy staff turned its greater attention, because that was where the delegates were. They were mindful of Oregon's potential for harm, but confident that it would be only a setback, and not the beginning of a panic or rout, just a small detour on the way to a big win. Indeed, there would be benefit for them in a McCarthy victory in Oregon. Gene would have had a fair run, bloodied them, and they could stop campaigning apologetically. They'd put him out of business. Already, wave after wave of Kennedy enthusiasts were hitting the beaches in California, more to follow. "OK, Gene's gonna have his little triumph," a close Kennedy aide said. "Give us a bloody nose. Swell. Now we can get him in a fight, at last, gloves off. They can't complain anymore. After Oregon—let's tear his throat out!"

But most of all, first and last, Kennedy's strategy and mounting success rested on an insubstantial thing, transcending temporal issues and momentary allegiances, something in the psyche and breast, a mania his presence inspired. For his genius was to leave no one cold about him, so that portion of the population that did not revile him was soon gripped by a powerful myth surrounding him. It was a light, radiating from his body, a gift which the ancient Greeks and modern hacks translated as a charismatic glow; one which, mistranslated, misapprehended, could also be seen as horns. For he stood as the personification of a bewitching promise. His voice was the subtle cues of morning sounds by which a nightmare might be exiled, a neurosis dispelled, history recalled.

It was this belief, that what was behind could be undone, that animated this idyll and the energy of so many strangers. His motorcades wound through more and more hysterical throngs. A fearsome crescendo was building. It dwarfed the fantasies of Hollywood by its participants' dynamism. And no mere star ever received such desperate embrace by screaming, sobbing crowds. He was seen offering something more than dreams, something close to deliverance.

To blunt the well-conceived McCarthy inroads in Robert Kennedy's home state, a reinforcement squad from that surging national team was detailed to New York in the weeks before the West Coast votings, among them Johanna Poulson and her "assistant." Just before she left San Francisco, she went up to the candidate's suite to give some material to one of his aides. Inside, an exhausted and barefoot Robert Kennedy was having an informal session with advisors and some favored reporters.

"I'm told your group is leaving for New York," Kennedy said as she entered.

"This afternoon, yes," she answered.

"I can't say it will be lonely here," he told her, turning his head to the crowded room. "But we'll miss you."

"Give his regards to Broadway," said one of the reporters, sprawled amid a pile of papers on a mussed-up bed. "Tell them how homesick he is for a place where people wear shoes."

"But tell them," Kennedy smiled, "after the polls close here."

Johanna said, "I only wish we had something to take back with us."

"Take Jeff Greenfield," Kennedy replied. "He's about to go into corned-beef arrest."

"I meant something personal to tell everyone."

"She's right, Bob," another reporter said. "Those crowds aren't coming out to grab cufflinks from the great issues. Why don't you cut up one of your bathrobes into small pieces—?"

"Does this imply," Kennedy asked, with a look of less amusement than those so familiar with his streak of self-mockery would have expected, "some judgment about my ego? Or does it simply speak to your own cynicism?" Then he relaxed and added, "If I thought I were God I wouldn't be running here. The competition's too organized."

Then Kennedy gave her that personal message. It was a stock charge that seemed nonetheless intense, for the effect of his self-consciousness was to make those trite things a candidate was called upon to say seem, if he was not embarrassed to say them, the more believable.

He walked Johanna back to the door, leading her by the hand, a slight man, almost feminine in his wiry grace, but with a suppressed torque inside him. Impulsively, Johanna leaned forward and kissed the surprised candidate, who brightened suddenly. "People," he called over his shoulder, "that was off the record." He grinned at Johanna, and caught her chin with a crooked finger. "And on the cheek." Then he repaid the kiss closer to her ear. Returning to the room he said to one of his aides, "You know, we should look into the English system. Lloyd George knew how to conduct a campaign," with a sly, self-satisfied smile.

When they landed in New York, Tyler called Baron Zermatt. "You can still save your soul and change your mind. You said it once: Bobby's the man."

"The Baron already has a candidate," Zermatt averred. "That other great sometimes-resident of New York, Mr. Nixon."

"My God, Bar! I've heard of self-interest, but—"

"There's more?" Zermatt asked incredulously.

In Tombstone, Warren Reigeluth was looking out his window. His employment was sufficiently covert to be free from Hatch Act restrictions, yet he felt bound by conscience to request temporary leave from his fellowship. He told the chairman of his study group that he found philosophical kinship with the Republicans probable.

"Philosophical?" the chairman asked skeptically, as though Baron Zermatt had it straighter.

Proof of Kennedy's assertion that the nation "could do better" was nowhere more explicit than in his adopted home state, New York. It shocked Johanna when she first saw it after all these years. The Enchanted City, if it ever was, was gone. Of course, it was gone in San Francisco, too, after less than one year. Already coming in were reports of young people dead of drugs and even starvation. These two coastal open cities, discrete circuses insulated from cruel reality, were now grim charnels while the hope they each had spawned swirled all around them.

Before they'd landed, Tyler tried to explain the street map, comparing it to "a great graph. The origin is—well, there are a couple of concentrations of greed: Rockefeller Center, Wall Street, Madison Avenue." On the way in from the airport, he elaborated, explaining how, slumped along the ordinate and abscissa were the great depressions of Harlem and the Lower East Side, while random, drunken prophets and castaways lay in heaps, or meandered in the Brownian staggers of survival. "Where's Bedford-Stuyvesant?" she asked.

"Off the graph until Bobby found it. That's the weird thing. It's not as if you needed a microscope." So abandoned was Bedford-Stuyvesant that its neglect extended to lack of notoriety. Harlem and Watts were the famous urban ghettos, and others came to renown only in the embers of riots. But Bedford-Stuyvesant, in Brooklyn, the largest, most impacted cavity of urban American misery, was unheralded until Robert Kennedy adopted it as a personal concern. All the emotional drive he could muster, all the arms he could twist—even as he had years before to raise a ransom from corporate heads for imprisoned veterans of the Bay of Pigs—were lavished on Kennedy's causes. He gave them publicity, attention, programs, and no little hope. The kindest way to explain their prior anonymity would be to say that perhaps it took a newcomer's fresh eye to see these things as aberrant, as wasteful, as intolerable.

Nor was Robert Kennedy's eye always so keen. It had required a freshening of torment before he could shed the glib tough-guy scales he'd worn. And if he was thus positioned by prior fortune and recent pain to be a symbol of stubborn faith in the efficacy of work and commitment, there were many still whose history was only one of desolation, who remained apart from the wave he rode, because nothing in their lives permitted them to believe. Still others shunned the traditional path he took because they believed that injustice was built into systems and institutions.

Uptown, at Columbia, the students challenged liberal universities' imperial rights to build upon the squalid parks of slum-bound neighbors, demanding theirs withdraw from contracts with the government, its assistance in great destructive enterprises. When the university refused, the students ran mad, seizing buildings, quoting Trotsky on social justice, Marx on paying one's overdue rent, smoking the university president's cigars. They might have been rehearsed by the Radical Saint, Paul Hooper, Tyler Bowen thought, for their sacking was a fornication in the eye of administrators. It was a clash of style and symbol and morals. They showed no respect in dress or manner, no sense of place or occasion. They turned the very school cheer into a nasty question: "Oh, who owns New York/Oh, who owns New York . . . ?" And though they were disparaged by the press and split themselves into racial camps, their self-righteousness stayed high, as though they'd tossed the bingo players from the temples and would yet be honored in the Latter Days.

"What are they putting in the Yoo-Hoo and tuna fish these days?" Tyler asked Saint Paul Hooper on the phone when they talked about Columbia.

"Tear gas," Hooper said.

The Columbia students were routed by the police in a bloody, indiscriminate assault.

It put the campaign and the forces feeding into it in bold perspective. There was a tension between two cultures: those who believed in possibility enough to risk a bloodying, whether by traditional political efforts or radical, against those who took arms to hold the day's distribution of influence, who felt threatened by changes in style and mores around them. It did not matter whether one joined campaigns or dropped out doping, or did nothing: a common fever was sweeping everyone susceptible, and it made them all extrapassionate, even in disassociation.

It was a time of paradox in art and politics and passion. By far the most bizarre of all was that though the anti-Administration forces of Robert Kennedy and Eugene McCarthy polled a steady two-thirds of the vote in every state, the stubborn mechanisms of a republic under siege responded to democratic impulse by yielding up more delegates to Lyndon Johnson's surrogate, Hubert Humphrey. And he was, artless as he was, the soul of paradox itself.

His claim to the Populist mantle stretched back to Robert Kennedy's school days. He'd inspired Eugene McCarthy to enter politics. He was the chief living architect of the national liberalism the other two struggled for leadership of. Nearly every liberal dream of his youth he had shepherded into law.

So good was his heart, so generous, so complete his faith in his fellow man, so strong his desire to create a decent, just society that he offered himself in sacrifice. He bartered his independence for a share of power, the vice-presidency, to achieve a little more. But the power he received was useless, and in the bargain he became an Establishment apologist. His personal act of coalition allied him to an enterprise whose consequences cost him moral leadership and self-respect. He'd lain with lies one year too long.

Once, twenty years before, he'd been a radical for a cause of liberal principle, and nearly turned the New Deal coalition from a perpetual majority to a collection of warring splinter groups. Now, he'd learned the dangers of that and campaigned as a party unifier. He ran for the presidential nomination in the most disruptive year in a quarter-century, promising "the Politics of Happiness, the Politics of Joy." It was a pitiable sight. Except he was winning.

The contest in California was winding up with hysteria its major key. In the last days of the race there, McCarthy and Kennedy had a "debate" on California television, broadcast nationally, whose sole enlightenment was to show the country what California called a news format, a sneak peak at the future. McCarthy, capable of being charming, was unlovably stiff. Nor did Kennedy appear at his best. And both were degradingly required to sell themselves as if they were competitive breakfast cereals. "Who produced this?" Kennedy grumbled when it was over. "Nixon?" McCarthy made a slight gain.

Kennedy supporters carped that Gene refused to address himself to the broad program Kennedy stood for, while drawing Jesuitical distinctions between their nearly identical positions on the Vietnam issue. "Gene hides in the war like a cave." But Kennedy's coming victory was in no peril.

People fresh from the Coast said the California madness was intoxicating, a surging, wild, continuous parade. Still, one or two observed, after Oregon they'd noticed something changed about the private Bobby. A kind of pallor could be seen beneath his sunburn. He'd sensed his own weak flesh for the first time then. His hair was sun-streaked and his tan turned sallow, as though from a failing liver. It was but a one-day thing. And the pressure continued to build.

In New York, an aide warned, "Anyone who doubts we're going all the way to Washington had better get off the train here. We are not about to preside over the first losing Kennedy campaign."

Johanna realized she and Tyler had been in New York nearly two weeks but hadn't seen a thing. There was no time. It was a high-wire act on bicycles, with no chance to fawn at the scenery, only a few late evening strolls. They hadn't seen much of California either. Warren was right, she reluctantly admitted. Though the adventure was heady, politics was programs, nothing more or less.

Such were the daily chores of campaigning that they were not in New York City for any three consecutive days, and it was not until the first day of June that they had time to visit Tyler's parents in Pelham. Johanna tried to be her flippant casual best beforehand, but inside she was in full panic.

When they arrived there, Laura Bowen bathed her in a most adoring gaze, and then, as Tyler made drinks, proudly announced, "We've been telling all our friends to register so they can vote"—Tyler's cocky smile at his mother's zest fell into a dumbstruck blankness, as she finished—"for Senator McCarthy." He looked at Johanna, who suppressed a titter.

"Uh, Mom? Remember all those wonderful things I

540

told you about McCarthy and what a stinker he was running against?"

"Your mother's been telling everyone she got it from the horse's mouth," Vlad said.

"Wrong part," Johanna muttered as Tyler walked by her with the drinks.

"Yeah, well, uh, Mom, Dad, could you go back and tell 'em I meant it the other way?"

"Kennedy?" Vlad asked. "What happened to the other fellow?"

"It's just a little mistake, really. I forgot to tell you. Gene's a nice guy, too. No doubt about it—"

"Tyler," Johanna said, in imitation of a proper young lady at a tea, "It's not nice to argue about politics. You wouldn't want somebody telling you what to think." He flipped an ice cube at her as his only weapon.

The elder Bowens took it all in stride. As Tyler told Johanna later, driving back to the city, "She probably didn't hear a word I said, too busy thinking, 'I hope the children have her looks and his—taste.' Listen, we didn't have to drive back tonight. What was the big-deal rush when they asked if we wanted to stay?"

"I had the feeling your parents would appreciate it if you confined your promiscuity to politics."

"They wouldn't care!"

"I might. Did you ever think of that, sir?"

"All right: you could've had Willie's room."

"I just didn't want to stay."

"I wouldn't blame you if they made you nervous, measuring you for a veil and all," he said, chucking a quarter into a toll machine.

"They're very nice and I liked them. I just didn't want to stay. Can't that be enough?"

"Sure. Why not? Accepting the award for strangest performance by a lady in a starring role for Miss Poulson will be—"

Johanna said nothing. What made her nervous was the sense of being instantly assumed into a family. It felt so good and warm, but it had been a long, long time since the last time. There was something less threatening in the randomness of the campaign life, hotel rooms, and restaurants and musical-cities.

"Strange bedfellows," he said, then turned to her and winked, squeezing her hand until she squeezed back.

Baron Zermatt was having dinner in Chicago with Warren Reigeluth, to talk about Warren's working in the Nixon southwestern states' campaign.

"It all depends on how much you want it," Zermatt said. Warren said he wasn't sure, he'd still have to give it thought. "Do the appropriate thing," Zermatt counseled. "I think you know what it is already—you flew here, didn't you? Face it: you've got talents, know-how —they're highly valued by the right people. Your choice."

"I know."

"You can work your ass off in a library all your life or take the fast track—and float up like a cork in the professional seas." Warren smiled, not only for the possibility but because his very presence and his doubts were both echoes of the study group's report and what he drew from it. One section, titled "Perspectives on Activity," defined his dilemma.

It said: "Within an inertial space is a shared illusion of stability, a commonality assumed from contemporaneity." Warren thought that best descibed Tombstone's own remove. His hesitation came from an inversion of that ideograph further on: "Furious motion within the inertial space may be inconsequential when viewed from outside it, if the inertial space is itself gripped by larger forces." Ecstatic atoms in a sublimating fit might be fast travel going nowhere, all in all. And the lurches that suggest eventful motion may be the quaking of the surrounding world, or the universe's shudder, or the pulses of the void.

"Look," Zermatt said, "you can slice it different ways. Either it's all illusory or it's all manipulative. You're a smart fellow. What do you know?"

"Less and less," Warren admitted for the first time in his life.

"I bet you know enough to know you've got to work with it. Be pragmatic. Don't tell the walls they don't exist. Respect 'em. *Deal* with them. They may be illusions. But they bite. So what do you say?"

"Yeah, sure."

"I like your enthusiasm."

When Tyler heard from Baron about the meeting, he said to Johanna, "They're made for each other. All three of them."

In his hotel room in Chicago, Warren had watched an illusion within an illusion on the television: a television studio in Los Angeles. In such, an actor employing earnest expressions under judicious closeup could recite the Nicene Creed wearing Bermuda shorts without seeming silly. And a presidential candidate could feign uncontradicted sincerity within its inertial womb.

Reception required illusion. As with movies, the flat and discontinuous picture was perceived as something more. The mind's calculus corrected the image, reconstructing to its tastes and needs: assuming movement, depth, and contour. It imagined real causes for afferent effects, supplied history and sequence for what scenes it apprehended. The mind could fool itself at every level as it desired, and editors and directors knew this, working well with this, juggling, distorting, creating out of fantasy, fabulous effect. They could make an object seem to reek, conjure apparent depth from perfect flatness. For every dimension collapsed in the art and economy of transmission there was an exponential level of resources available for interfering with the truth. And all of this was based on one primeval truth, an instinct known for ages: the audience's desire to be deceived.

The television studio in the picture had a cutaway backdrop to imitate a conference booth, contrived to soothe the viewer, not the interviewed. The subject knew the game: the public wants its leaders washed in glamour's hue and glow. The audience coaxes chromatics to frantic brilliance, compatible with this need, so that leaders, famous freaks, demigods of media stand above the common colorations by their intensity, pitch, and light. They are seen through a glass, prismatically, glory found in their coronas. They are calm when all are agitated, and they are energized in the calm. They have influence invisible but believed. In their spotlight they are beautiful: sweatless, bloodless, and divine, heroic by definition. They are royal, they are celebrated, they are holy, and short-lived. It remains for their wives, their children and valets to hide the doubt-filled truth.

In this studio, the questioner asked joshing, rude impertinences. He exposed the mortal strains of his guest, briefly debunking his myth. Some viewers were shocked. They thought more respect becoming. The candidate was being treated like a quarry. But, Warren thought, now that California was won, this candidate had to show his more pliant sides to the unsold.

"Are they squeezable? Are they solid?" the questioner asked the candidate. Robert Kennedy winced at this backroom jargon.

"I don't like either of those expressions." His face yielded up a plaintive "Why are you doing this to me coast-to-coast, Mudd? Those words! That odor of calculation!" Against the flow of his apparent victory in California's primary, Robert Kennedy's expression insisted, as Theodore White's joke had it, "I'm trying to be so *ruthful* today."

It was late in New York City and so Tyler Bowen and Johanna Poulson watched the returns from their hotel room, preparing to be off in the morning for Buffalo. There was a party at Headquarters but they had more work tomorrow. Their sleep would be that of victors, people who had changed their lives and the world's: their own colors intensified like the celebrities they might become, feeding on the television's glow, immortal.

Roger Mudd's lips moved, stopped, began again, "Bob—*Senator*—Do you have no way to . . . draw the Vice-President into a fight?"

Again the painful grimace of a broken pose. "No, I —do I have to put it that way?"

"You would not be willing to join with Mr. Humphrey?" Mudd asked.

The Senator drew breath and spoke with care. "No —well, no I wouldn't. I'll be glad to help the Democratic party . . . but I—particularly if Richard Nixon is the nominee of the Republican party, which I think is unacceptable to the country, and I have strong disagreements with Hubert Humphrey . . . particularly what he said this week—that he would step aside if

Lyndon Johnson wants to run . . . that I don't understand . . . it doesn't make sense to me."

In their hotel room in New York, Tyler Bowen and Johanna Poulson turned away from the screen's image, giddy from prior celebration of the far-off victory. They'd come a long way from Tucson, from the hopelessness of having to lie without recourse. He kissed her gratefully for her part in this, and she laughed softly at the candidate's television complaint, "It doesn't make sense to me." As if things were ever under such compulsions as minds desired. As if shocks to conscience never exploded from unreason into waking life. There was the fallacy in Warren's study: Catastrophe Theory was the bedding on which things lay, there were no strange bedfellows, only lack of surprise was surprising.

In Los Angeles, the red light beneath the camera eye blinked off as the candidate said, "Let's see how things turn out," leaving viewers with that odd ambivalence, a hesitancy at the core of confidence. "Let's see how things turn out . . . I've said all along that—it's a long road to Chicago." The red light out, the hollow eye insensate now, Kennedy shook his head at Roger Mudd and laughed as he left the room.

In New York, Johanna turned the sound down and got into bed. The air conditioner hummed remorselessly and made it cool enough to snuggle comfortably. They both smirked at their sacrilege: did it dishonor love-making to leave the TV on, or dishonor the candidate to sport like this while watching? They decided it was honor to the candidate, his message in extremis. "We can do better," Tyler whispered. There was love in their lovemaking. But there was interest in the California numbers, too. This was an honest compromise, and so they shuttled back and forth in their attention. There were worse ways to celebrate the totals.

The only falsity was the style of their ardor. They were tired. Every day was a new crisis. They were on the master circuit, so each surge of tension jolted them both. Johanna had spent more time traveling in the last two days—on a series of short plane hops to upstate areas—than she had in any one place. She wanted this lovemaking to unknot her fatigue and tensions. But he was simply sleepy. Attempts to choreograph lust into

545

artful movement were beyond him just then. The random movements of inventive balletic play required too much thought at this hour and made him more tired. So he played a somnambulant game: using his hips as a fist, he pretended he was a pen, writing his name on Johanna's inner walls.

To Johanna it felt convincingly subtle, mysterious, full of urgent messages encoded but not quite revealed. It was political.

He finished his signature with a grand flourish. It was not known to her that he was literally writing his name on her insides. But she wouldn't have minded, believing it true of lovemaking in general.

On the silent screen, Robert Kennedy was tracked by fisheye lenses, moving from the interview with Mudd to his suite. He was chuckling still. Soon to the main ballroom. The latent images, to the keen, caught him with the masks of candidacy askew. Exposed now was the face of a younger brother, ever to be a younger brother, despite his recent role as eldest surviving son.

Then on to see the well-wishers. To a favorite he confided what he had denied Mudd: "I'm going to chase Hubert Humphrey's ass all over the country. Wherever he goes, I'll go." Then, smiles for the strangers.

At the crest of his wave, he was the tough Irish kid. At the trough, the overscrubbed altar boy in sissified, embarrassing skirts, with his Oregon shiner as the badge of honor's successful defense: "You shoulda seen the other guy." Along the axis, joining crest and trough, was a scrapper who would not rest until the pudgy loudmouth took home a bloody nose.

Awash in a sea of love, Robert Kennedy was unable to contain his pride at the hopes and good energies he animated. Yet inside that smile, deep in his marrow, was a fear like he feared no natural thing: crowds were animals, jungles full of unknown terrors. To losers, who only saw the smile and glinting eyes, he seemed an awful winner.

Eccentric thoughts flashed through Johanna's head, while Tyler moved lethargically to grander prose in imitation of Eros. No more would the mere signature of Tyler Bowen alone move her. So he wrote in flesh, "We, the People of the United States"—an echo of each word carved in the soft insides of her thighs; the main manuscript was within her—"in order to form a more perfect Union. . . ."

Johanna only sensed the nuance of this body English, not the body's politics or syntax. Her head throbbed with inner sights that were wide ranging and impressionistic, organizing themselves in patterns back of her eyes, designed by the dynamics of awareness and imagination.

Tyler continued to write like a caveman Federalist: "And to secure the blessings of liberty to ourselves and our posterity. . . ." Her breathing was short and rapid and her limbs drawn in by her own gravity. She had acquired a new reflex: an urge to hold onto herself when she seemed ready to fly apart centrifugally. She was tentative and nervous before her final nakedness, as Tyler etched, "do ordain and establish. . . ."

"Thank you all very much," the clean white lips on the silent television said. Candidate Kennedy spoke from the ballroom podium, his voice coming from somewhere above and behind his larynx. Through the microphone it sounded tinny, and more like Bugs Bunny than fair jokes (and Ethel's continual family condition) would allow. "And so it's on to Chicago," he charged the throng. Wild applause to his stabbing left fist—the pugnacity of the gesture artfully muted by the use of his weaker arm—"and let's win there!" Cheers of delight and love tore the ballroom. Hope and redemption, release and compassion, all around the corner. Santa Claus was on the rooftops in sun-bleached locks and Cloroxed jeans. Kennedy waved to them and made them winners with him, on his wave. "On to Chicago and let's win there!" he repeated, surfing on the chanting beats of "Kennedy! Kennedy! Kennedy!"

The candidate shook his head and grinned as he dismounted the small stage. Erotic screams of love trailed him, bodies pressing, coming after him like an unsatisfied beast.

In the screen's glow, Tyler Bowen wrote on and Johanna's cheeks flushed crimson. The picture over Tyler's shoulder flipped in reply. She quivered and she

547

gasped, cascading all about him, drawing him deeper, while wrestling to break free.

And then it was soft, quiet, timeless: the mournful, moody Fifth of July with its litter and soggy cigarette butts in half-filled Coke bottles, and its fizzled roman candles.

Slowing pinwheels of blue spun at the outer edges of Johanna's sea-green irises. And there was red in the corner muscles, twitching with each heartbeat as she nuzzled his soggy, groggy face; and white, vacant, trusting, pure, pure white between the colors, while he lazily rocked in her embrace.

The candidate stepped from the prying cameras' range for an instant and asked aides if he could skip out of further interviews in preference to a nap before the big victory party. They told him the press was waiting, and he had to give them a chance because it was already late in New York. "Why aren't they in bed asleep?" he laughed.

"I'll tell them you're coming," one said, ducking back through the mob to bring this news. Kennedy wished there was just fifteen minutes for a nap. There were never enough naps. It was campaign time around the clock on two coasts. A two-ocean war. The screaming never stopped. Only an occasional wall muted it. But why should it stop for him? Why should it permit him to stop? No naps.

No time to catch his breath or have a dream. What-the-hell: this was a dream, he thought, pumping hands as he moved down the parting aisle like a bride, to the doorway. This was it: the breathless caravan, the Bouncing Ball campaign with movie stars and folk-songed minstrel shows, the Cannonball Express of happy faces, reaching hands and laughing, tinkling voices. Shouts: "We're on our way!" Echoes: "Ken-ne-dy! Ken-ne-dy!" Choruses: "Bob-by! Bob-by! Bob-by." The noise swirled about him as he ducked out of the ballroom. Poor Nixon, he thought, wryly: he'll never know how nice it is to ride a wave of good intentions, to feel the pure erotic thrill of union with so many joyful noises. It was like the most thorough nighttime dream. And this was a waking dream, better than the night ones, better than the bad ones: blink and the dark visions are chased. "We're on our way!" He was. Sneaking off through the kitchen, conspiring with his other self to steal a nap. One of them would get some sleep.

Congratulations from surprised chefs. Talking to a boy named Jesus. Kid wants an autograph. Really insistent. Won't they leave a body alone? All right, an autograph to get some peace and then a nap. The greasy-faced salad boy wants an autograph and won't take no and wants a shake and oh, what the hell. Here, take the pen but it's a gun.

The candidate's eyes stared wide at the ceiling as he rested, lying down at last, a breather from the business of saving others. They could hold his tired head now. Bless the People and the Angels, he thought. It all made sense behind his eyes; he knew his part.

He mumbled things, "How's Paul? Is everybody all right?" A name, "Ethel. . . ." No tears. Tears are for surprises. White lips, sunburnt clean, whispering, "Ethel." Then, barely, "I love—" while a rosary dangled in his spastic hand. He lay in her lap serenely. From the front there was no damage, the image intact, undisturbed. He had angelic features resting, peaceful; the choir boy again: impish, gay, and pure. The decorous small-bore hole behind his ear betrayed the only clue to his recumbency, and the blood sluicing down his neck from that aperture, onto his collar, coat, and floor. "Plug it up! Plug it up! Plug it up!" cried a voice, in weepy, broken innocence of the complexity of breathing's miracle.

Plugged-in televisions crackled with sudden life from their listless fade-outs, the picture resurrected. Great changes in potential stirred transistors and tubes. The image came alive. To Tyler and Johanna, who sat naked on their bed's edge. To others, frozen-footed on their ottomans in the act of switching off. They were all coaxing details from the box, all limp. The magic of TV is universal impotence: events hurled across the miles, coaxial rapists in the living room, in color and alive without a vital third dimension. All substance gone in those reductions, the holographic truth catabolized for commerce, all potential for effect is denied the lonely

549

viewer, as the box commands: "Watch! Accept! This is the Age, unalterable: your heroes lie bleeding in their good wives' laps, again. You cannot even change the channel!"

The candidate lay still. In her arms. On a stretcher bed. On a table under lights. On a plane. At home across the continent. In the nave of St. Patrick's, on Saturday, before the noble amassed, as his last brother, Edward, called a eulogy:

"My brother need not be idealized, nor enlarged in death, beyond what he was in life"—he swallowed slowly, to master his voice—"to be remembered simply as a good and decent man . . . a husband and father, brother and son . . ." For the barest half-second he could not go on, but the Gaelic way with heartbreak is to sip bravely, if not gladly, from the cup of its occasion.

The statesmen were up front, again. Tyler Bowen and Johanna Poulson were further back. Behind them were those thousands in the streets who'd stood on line two days and nights to file by, and others by their televisions, those thousands of the millions the press called "Bobby's people"; which was to say they had to belong to someone to count, and that is why they'd come. ". . . who saw wrong and tried to right it, saw suffering and tried to heal it, saw war and tried to stop it." Tears flowed freely down Edward's puffy cheeks, but his voice held firm, and held too many memories for the other mourners' restraint. They were less Irish, and the reedy sounds of their soft weepings reverberated in the vaulted caverns of the cathedral. Johanna shut her eyes and rested her head against Tyler's shoulder in their back pew. He stroked her hair, his chin trembling against the top of her head as his own tears slid down onto her hair and his fingers. "Those of us who loved him, and who take him to his rest today"—Edward's voice wobbled—"pray that what he was to us, and what he wished for others—will someday come to pass for all the world. As my brother said, many times, in many parts of the world, to those whose lives he sought to touch"—the voice quivered—"and who sought to touch him"—it faintly cracked, breaking but in silence—" 'Some men see things as they

550

are and ask, Why?' " The pale echoes in that Brahmin *ahsk,* of the others, now vanished for all time, gently stoked the sad hearth of so many different griefs, and they expired a sighing shade of resignation. " 'I dream dreams that never were and ask, *Why not?'* "

Then down the old Pennsylvania run to Washington, through trackside crowds so thick the trip took twice as long as planned, pacing the Post Road, the guitars picked out farewell songs.

And just outside the gates of the District of Columbia, by Bobby's brother and his brother's babies and half a million strangers, in Arlington, they laid down the body, in the damp, hot, false-spring night. They sang, as if it were a dirge, "His truth goes marching on—" without believing it at all, having moved past such fragile faith.

RAIN-STREAKED, WILLIE BOWEN COUNTED the hours. Sweat-stroked as well from the intermittent tropical sun, he was damp and uncomfortable, clammy as he sat cross-legged under a tree on the longest day of the year.

His buddy Timothy Franks mentioned it to him on the chow line that morning and the possibilities amused Willie. "Longest day, huh? You sure?" Franks said it was so. Their boredom in between events, even events comprised of terror, was so acute that anything distinguishing one day from another was seized upon and celebrated: "Wanna toke, man? It's Arbor Day!" "Hey! Back off, Jack—it's the goddam summer solstice— don't you know any better?"

"Maybe there'll be a solstice truce," Franks suggested. They were in the paralimnion of the rainy season, and when the first rains in several months fell,

Franks was stoned. He looked outside his hootch, a corrugated tin ammunition bunker, and said, "This is where I came in." He walked out as though heading home.

The drizzle stopped. The sun broke through. The drizzle started again. Willie held out his hand to catch a few drops. "What do you think?" he asked, as Franks left him under his tree. "Ours or theirs?" It was never certain who Uncle Sam's rain makers hurt most.

Frank yelled back at him, " 'sgotta be ours. It's all wet and don't work." Overhead they heard the drone of far-off jets, assuredly "ours." The rain didn't ground them. Repairs did. Losses multiplied with frequency of maintenance, because the ground crews, no less than the grunts, hated their jobs. The command experimented with reducing maintenance by half, and malfunction losses dropped dramatically. So startling and dismaying was this finding that the maintenance schedule was redoubled again, lest the unsettling news reach the pilots, who liked their jobs. But even they were overcome by doldrums when the rains kept the enemy indoors. So they amused themselves by doing tricks above the clouds, barrel rolls and flips, wing stands and stallouts. When the clouds broke they peppered targets of opportunity. They played Blue Angel over North Vietnam and zoomed under the few remaining bridges; then they blew them up. Some flew stoned. They laughed. They took exotic risks to pass the time; their real missions were boringly programmatic. In playing, many were shot down, and many just blew up, unaccountably.

Willie Bowen had the worst of both worlds, boredom and explosions. When he had one he wished for the other.

He sat under his tree, Buddhalike with the only thing, save dope, that made the hours bearable: a letter from the World.

"Now I understand what you meant," Tyler had written,

> when you said about that wounded guy—how you hoped he'd just fade out. I've been feeling guilty about this since Bobby died—while he was in the

hospital I felt the same way. It sounds shitty, I know. We were on the death watch so far away and I thought, "Oh, Christ—why don't they just let him slip off. Face it: it's over." It wasn't going to get any better and I thought it should just end there. How can you say you sort of loved somebody but hoped he would die? It was like a broken love affair, and just as well buried. I'm sorry for his family, too.

The strange thing is, all the time you were lounging in the MIA file I never felt that. I kept insisting it could be pulled out in the bottom of the ninth.

The news Willie really wanted to read about was of love affairs that were still working. Anyone's. And Tyler had obliged, writing about Johanna and their plans. There were hints of problems, but nothing major. Tyler mentioned

a funny thing—not so funny, really—about how we both felt. Like I said, I sort of gave up early. Johanna took it a bit harder, I think, and didn't understand my reasons. That's the thing I can't figure, and she hasn't been too good at explaining: my defense mechanism is to move on to other things with a more likely payoff. She thought I was being too pessimistic. Then when it was final, I kind of spat on the ground and said, "Oh, hell, let's do something else and see if that works," and she's just lost all her fight. I suppose a few weeks and we'll be humans again.

He wrote that he had driven to Ithaca for something to do,

to see St. P. get commissioned as a taxpayer. Seemed like a good place to hide for a while. He kicked and screamed but they excreted him anyway. Between that and the fact that Doc Spock took the count in his trial—I always said if you were caned more you'd never have turned out the way you did—it was a banner week for the Meanies. Speaking of which, I put in a good word for you at Admissions and told them how well you were doing keeping the world safe from democracy. Told 'em to ignore your CEEBs and recommendations—to use their imaginations, which is always something of a challenge for them, you know. It may help, though, my good man, as I have acquired something of a good Rep in those parts. You remember I told you about how the Dean—the one who tried to stomp St. P.—approached me, while I was trying to put the touch on him, about a job? Apparently he's under some kind of pressure to make nice with the students—almost unheard of in my day. And there's old me, broken-down jocko, unskilled and unwanted—makes me a perfect administrator-type according to the by-laws. It's practically a prerequisite. As I told you, my main interest was getting a fellowship at the Advanced Studies Labs, and after a few quick phone calls, he says, Swell, there's a spot for a Junior Fellow in Biochemistry that'd be perfect. I said, Gimme. He said, Can't have it. I said, Why'd you mention it, then, you son-of-a-bitch? He said, They've got the spot but not the scratch. I said, I've been mooching off the fat of my dad for a year already. He said, Oh, ho-ho. He sort of laughed and said I could take the spot and also be Assistant to the Dean, see, and we can fiddle with the funding through the Administrative Budget, maybe even get a foundation grant to sport us to it as an experiment in student-administration communications. Why won't the world ever let me be a Biochemistry student, you may well ask. Well, it was a good offer and I told him I'd think it over. Johanna thought it was good. Your parents thought it was one step to the Nobel Prize. I thought it was a job. A little investigation and some subtle arm twisting and we found a very nice job Johanna could have in the publications office. She wouldn't be assistant to anybody and the pay'd be better than —starving. She's less than wild about it, but game. If I took this deal the letterhead alone'd lock you up with the college of your third choice. So don't you do anything dumb like try for a medal.

We spent ten days putting mileage on my car, at the Cape and just around. I don't mean to spoil your vacation, but (a) your parents could stand to hear from you, (b) they have very loyally kept a certified check they made out when they didn't think you were alive—in spite of your return they still mean to lay it on you—for a car or some such. It is presently mildewing. So are they. So are you I gather, and (c) did you know New England is the size of Nam—roughly? We took the place in less than a month, buddy. What's taking you so long?

He didn't write about why Johanna was reluctant and he hardly knew himself. She just was. Too many shocks, he thought, had changed her sight. That was very close to true: she was seeing the world through cleansed eyes, and her very revival in the spring seemed premature and maladaptive.

Under his tree, Willie was shielded from both sun and rain. He slouched against a huge crate of explosives he'd helped unload from a cargo hauler. A tarpaulin covered some of it. All around him were the perquisites of his throne room: spools of det-cord, a ropelike explosive of great practicality, and other percussives: two cases of dynamite, thermite bombs, and foo-gas—a gelatinous first cousin of napalm, made of similar basic ingredients: petroleum base and soapflake M4 thickener, mixed to taste. There were boxes of blasting caps, C-4 plastique, and some canisters of code-marked substances which were sinister blends of phosphorus and potassium compounds. None of it would suffer from a little dampness—they were too well packed, sealed in cotton, flannel, Cosmoline, and chamois. If they didn't work, it was because they were fucked up at the factory. The percentage was nearly half.

For reasons best known to the anonymous authors of the "Incendiary Drill and Explosives Regulations," most of the merchandise so casually littered around Willie Bowen was classified "Non-Accountable" or "Expendable"—just like him. This effectively meant that odd lots could disappear without anyone's approval or awareness in case of attack, say. Or, say, theft. So they did, quite frequently. And there hadn't been an attack in weeks, though the books spoke of "returned harassment fire" to justify reorders. On the other hand, those items already rushed to the secure munitions bunkers were "Strictly Accountable." They had priority for storage, since their control was a matter of bookkeeping urgency, according to the regulations. They were sped to shelter while the nonaccountable languished in the short light.

It briefly struck Willie Bowen as queer that such fuss should be made over items benefiting no one who did not possess American heavy pieces. Neither, unlike the mess around him, could any of that stuff detonate spontaneously. Nevertheless, he had come to accept the fiat of regulations to this extent: he was moved by neither their anomalies, nor the dangers around him. When his tour was over he'd go home, and if his number was up before his tour, all the careful treading in the world was not likely to prevent it. This laissez-faire approach to logic and safety was a sustaining philosophy, and in consequence, he wondered over Tyler's letters, "What kind of war's going on back there?"

Another letter Tyler wrote was shown to the few people Willie called friends. It was a funny letter, and as such, a rare and wonderful thing to have. People admired you if you received one, wondering aloud what you were doing there if you were the kind of person who knew folks who wrote funny letters. You obviously deserved better duty.

"You know how roaringly popular your war is?" Tyler's letter asked.

St. Paul, who you'd expect could get as many people to testify for his sanity as R. Nixon can get as character witnesses, could not convince anyone that his every effort to avoid getting blown to smithereens—drafted—is anything less than laudable shirking. His latest effort was to convince them he's dangerous to have on our team. Maybe if you wrote a letter saying you don't want him, they'd believe it. His commitment (always a good word to use with St. P.) is so strong to staying stateside that he stared down a big semi on the clean Norwegian streets of Minneapolis. Grinned it down in actual fact, according to reports, Davy Crockettish. The truck jackknifed and pacified a Flower Shoppe and a Fannie Farmer. The papers said it was "a miracle" no one was hurt. So did St. P. Says he flushed the Holy Spirit out of the woodwork. It only speeded up the induction process. The mills of God may grind slowly, but the draft board's another thing altogether. So St. P. took to the air. Except he doesn't own a TV station (hardly stopped Ruby, Sirhan, or any of America's more beloved maniacs ever). He burst into KSTP (says he liked the initials) and damned if he didn't *hijack* the Nightly News. That made 'em sit up and listen! He had the whole crew intimidated while he rattled off a series of (not entirely untrue) reports, like: "The President says we will continue to bomb them until we—*understand* them!" Apparently, there's no law against that sort of thing, but it did convince his local board to award him their One Allotted Conscience of the Month with an Almond Cluster. . . .

The poor boy had, believe it or not, been planning a wedding, and his girlfriend Cathy called it off. I guess Conscience fucks up blood tests or something. St. Paul says it was all a mistake anyway: She had a yeast infection and thought it was love. Cured of both, I take it. Now she's Closed for Repairs, according to St. Palsy. . . .

Ultimately, this letter, like the other, gravitated back to one thing:

We keep trying to make sense out of the RFK thing. I always figure, cockeyed optimist I am, that things have to make sense. Fates are earned, not sealed, right? But who deserved this? Bobby? The K's? Us? It's just too much to chalk it up to chance and accident *again*. And who's the chief beneficiary from *this* one: Johanna's ex! (The X stands for x-treme asshole.) He had half a leg in Hell—about to work for Nixon—when the eagle swooped down and plucked him up. I read it in the papers and Johanna almost went bananas: he got named to the staff of President's Commission on the Causes and Prevention of Violence! Seems he's something of an expert. It's true: I always wanted to punch him out, myself.

557

I can hardly believe that the net effect of Robert Kennedy's life was to give Warren Reigeluth a job, but that's the way it seems. It's all a Big Raffle. You might win a yacht and you might win pancreatitis. There's cosmic rays and there's the chance you might honk at a mobster with a temper.

"Some months," Tyler wrote,

are just bad for the living. Leap Day was extra good to us this year—we heard you were back. Maybe we should make it a yearly thing and drop Junes and Novs altogether. You'd have a Memorial Day Weekend that ended July Fourth. It'd be hell on traffic, but it's worth a look. And a Halloween that ran to Advent. Not so bad.

If there's sense about this it's like a foreign movie. You have to look very close and follow the line under the action, because everything going on is in a language we don't think in. Johanna said the other day, on this, "The universe isn't responsible for our problems"—which works both ways you can read it.

Who gives a shit? Willie wondered. If Tyler could find no sense in the Kennedy shooting, what was so strange? Willie had given up demanding sense from things. The most intelligent comment he heard about that came from Timmy Franks, who said he'd given up smoking in November '63 and again at the start of this June. "I'm gonna have to wreck my lungs, it looks," Franks said, "just to keep that son-of-a-bitch Teddy alive."

"Psst. Bowen," a voice urged from behind Willie's tree. "How long they gone?"

"Half-hour," Willie answered. "You better move your fat black ass, Collins. There's two crates over there open and all jumbled. Under the tarp. Grab what you can and blow. I never saw you."

"Right. Right. Diggit. Goin' Double Eagle this time. Interested?"

"Catch me later," Willie answered. "Just hurry it up, huh?"

Two edgy troopers helped themselves to what they wanted, while Willie reclined in the shade and pulled his helmet liner down to avoid seeing them conduct their business.

"OK, Bowen," the two men said. "Check you later," and disappeared into the brush before the munitions loaders returned.

As far as Willie Bowen could tell, the world's biggest problem was seeing that his brother didn't go down the tubes over things he couldn't control. Was that what they were doing back in the States? At least he was having a laugh now and then where he was. Maybe going home wasn't such a hot idea after all. Between people getting their brains blown out and Tyler's rotting, it didn't seem much different from right where he was, except less safe. Either place could blow at a moment's notice.

Willie missed the Double Eagle that night, and everyone said it was something special. But on the night of Bastille Day, which has never been much of a holiday among the indigenous peoples of Indochina, some of the blasting caps and det-cord that Collins and the other troopers had liberated were connected to two cans of foo-gas and strategically placed for the Turkey Shoot. It was the fourth one this month.

Six stoned troops, Willie, Franks, Collins, two noncoms and a guilty-conscienced Second Lieutenant sneaked up on their target and wired the explosives. The foo-gas had been preplanted that afternoon. When all was set, and a hundred other enlisted personnel were in a position to watch without seeming obvious, Collins fired a short volley high overhead into the roof of the wooden outhouse they were attacking. This was an accepted signal by now. Its occupant fled frantically.

Collins then touched two wires together to complete the circuit. The explosion consumed the entire wickiup in one gasp, and two distinct fountains of orange shot fifty feet in the air. No one bothered to take cover, for this was routine, no enemy attack. The charred remains fell backward, while raucous laughter and applause crowned it. Into the burning pit fell a fatigue cap with twin silver bars. Then the whole hut caved into the yawning hole of eddying fecal muck. It sloshed along with a singed and splintered two-by-four that once had been lovingly etched "Officers Only."

Willie could never understand why they bothered with the warning shots.

I T WAS A NICE CONVENTION," BARON ZER-matt said. He was treating Tyler to lunch, and was overweeningly confident and indigestibly smug, having returned from Richard Nixon's Miami coronation. "Going to Chicago?"

"I think we'll sit it out," Tyler said. "Catch it on the tube. Right after Labor Day's the big move to Ithaca."

"You should have been there, Tyler . . ."

"I thought the best part was when Harold Stassen's nephew nominated Don Quixote."

Zermatt said, "I read it in the papers—didn't see it. Personally, I think he should take the same speech and give it for McCarthy."

"How you can find Nixon adorable after this," Tyler sighed, shaking his head.

"Never said he was pretty. Only that he was gonna win. He's the man who's gonna get your brother home—"

"He's short now."

"Well, sure as hell McCarthy's out of the picture and Humpty's sucking Lyndon's teat. So what are you doing?"

"Nothing."

"I keep forgetting to remember," Zermatt said, "it takes you longer to bury dead issues than most people."

"Most of whom wanted to bury my brother—"

"This other guy's dead, Babe. I never cease to be amazed at how sentimental you are. Look, I'm sorry he's dead but dead he is. So's his whole game. Wise up to the news. Stone, cold, rotten-in-the-ground dead. It's a goddam pity and a shame. But it's a goddam fact. It's tissues now, for the ragpickers and the vendors."

"Terrific."

"The Revolution is over, pal. And we lost."

"We? When did you get religion?"

"Look, waste away in melancholy for all I care. But understand something. We all hated Lyndon from Dallas to yesterday, because why? Because he had the bad manners to survive——"

"Want about thirty more reasons?"

"Yeah, well he survived to make them—made the world you're bitching about. So you can indulge the luxury of sulking—go kick the dog of the world for its nasty assassinating ways. But it was on the program from Day One. Me? I'll plant some lilies and keep on working. You get no points for sentiment—even if you got fouled. Bobby was a sometimes nice son-of-a-bitch who's dead. Martyrs are losers. I'm sorry. They don't count for shit. I see what I want and I'm going after it. And Nixon's gonna do it for me."

"He's a thug. He's a goddam mobster on the verge of the grandest heist of his career! And you're holding his coat."

"I got news for you," Zermatt said. "You win and you get the *keys* to Fort Knox."

"Don't leave fingerprints, Bar, that's all."

Shortly before the Democratic jamboree in Chicago, Tyler and Johanna attended a party thrown by some people from the Kennedy press contingent. Some spoke of how they envied their colleagues headed for the convention, "But Jesus, you should see the stuff the desk issued them—gas masks and crash helmets. They look like the California cops." Others said they'd like to have gone if the reasons for their not going could somehow be revoked.

In the background, a grotesque tape was playing: the recorded songs they wrote for Robert Kennedy. It sounded harrowed. "I thought you threw it away," Johanna said to the owner.

"Couple of people wanted to hear it again," he shrugged. She shut her ears to it with a shudder, then wandered around the airy apartment while Tyler went off to fetch them drinks. But the familiar music chased her:

> What would you say if I entered the race,
> Would you say that I'm ruthless or bad?
> What would you make of my building a base
> On the best pal a pol's got . . . my dad?

> Oh, I can buy better help than you friends . . .

In a corner were some reporters, one just back from Vietnam. He was talking about how everyone he knew was "compulsively writing books no one wants to read. I know five guys doing it right now, books about the war. The thing no one understands is—I mean, forget the names are hard to pronounce and the place is overrun with political roaches—there's still some honor and heroism going on."

Another said, "To my mind the biggest victims of the war—among the survivors—are the guys, the first reporters to call it for what it was. Look at 'em. One by one they got the axe. But dammit, they made the rest of us possible. Shock troops—they changed the voice of the world as they fell."

Johanna went looking for Tyler, hiding from the music.

> Picture yourself in a house with Rose Gardens,
> With Red Carpets, Blue Rooms, and white lies
>   all day;
> Somebody hauls through, his accent is Texan,
> A man with a brand: LBJ.
> Oval Room odors of barnyards. . . .
>   (Two, three, four—)
> Lyndon in the White House with gallstones.

She went through the kitchen where two men were talking. One was saying how every Sunday morning he and his wife "do it all over the *Times.*"

"The whole paper?"

562

"We save the *Entertainment* section for the TV listings, sure. But I mean, we really get down in it like hog slop. *Classified, News of the Week, Book Review*. Get that *Magazine* under her ass and it's dynamite—you need an acupuncture chart to list her erogenous zones. I dunno—it's magic."

The tape spun on:

For the benefit of LBJ
There will be a war today—on foreign ground . . .

Tyler was not in the living room where two women were trading mugging stories. One told how her blind neighbor had been assaulted in the hallway as the other residents pounded on their doors and cursed the hoodlums.

Tyler was in the bedroom in a tight circle of men when Johanna found him. She came up behind him and hooked her fingers onto his belt, then pressed against his back, trying to signal her restlessness. "Can we go?" she whispered. But he merely slipped his hand behind and patted her hip. "Please?"

"Mmmm—just a few minutes." He was intent on hearing the end of what an advertising copywriter was telling the rapt group about how his company had tested a vaginal spray. "We wanted to call it Pubi-Care, but we got shot down," the adman said. "So anyway, we round up the usual gang of volunteers: anyone in front of the Standard Brands Building at a quarter to ten who wanted to make a quick fifty. Randomized. Told 'em it'd be a little, uh, un-u-sual. . . ." Johanna beckoned him again. "Couldn't we go—*please?*"

"In a minute, sweetheart. I just want to hear—"

She eased her grasp of him as the adman was interrupted by someone who had to tell a quick story about how he thought he had VD one day and "spent an afternoon sitting in a pail of pHisohex, trying to convince myself it was only a pimple. It was—but now they tell me the stuff causes cancer."

"In rats. Don't screw any rodents—"

Johanna let herself out onto the terrace, while the party burbled on inside. There was talking and sar-

563

donic laughter, marijuana and hashish, wine and hard liquor, sexual advances and ego wrestling going on back there. She could hear it tinkling through the terrace door, feel it in her chest.

> He goes downstairs to a TV speech he has just
> prepared,
> Quietly adding a personal word,
> Says he is quitting for Lady Bird . . .

Someone turned the television on inside to see the evening's convention session and it drowned out the song. She was glad for that, though she could remember the music despite the din:

> He . . . (we gave him all the war Congress
> could buy)
> Is leaving . . .

But it was not the music on the tape deck that caused her upset, nor the tone or substance of the conversations she overheard, but something more basic, and it was enough to make her bones cry. It was the very idiom of the city. There was enclosure all around, an insistent verbality in its citizens that made her jumpy. They all scurried around an interior landscape looking for a roost in the concrete. It made her feel claustrophobic, temporary, transient, all the more estranged and homeless. Once she had sought surcease in the desert, in its lazy unbounded dimensions, and the free expression it enabled. But the desert had been closed off by pain and by what others made of that very liberating atmosphere. So she had a desire for faster movement then, and a vision of what the city promised held close in her mind. Now its hurricane of words and images seemed oppressive. Idiom was the difference of worlds, and there was none she now felt comfortable in. She felt distant from Tyler, too. He fit in, glibly, anywhere; she had no home at all.

There was noise on the television, noise from the party, noise from the music, and noise inside her head to make her hurt.

(Two, three, four—)
We're Brother Bobby's Lovely Heart Throb Clan,
We hope you will support our kin,
Brother Bobby's Lovely Heart Throb Clan,
It's time for us to rebegin;
Brother Bobby's Lovely,
Brother Bobby's Lovely,
Brother Bobby's Lovely,
Brother Bobby's Lovely,
Brother Bobby's Lovely Heart Throb Clan,
The future's just around the bend,
Brother Bobby's Lovey-Dovey Lovely Heart
     Throb Clan,
It's getting very near the end—
Brother Bobby's Lovely,
Brother Bobby's Lovely,
Brother Bobby's Lovely Heart Throb Clan . . .
I read the news today oh boy. . . .

Tyler found Johanna sitting outside on the terrace by herself. "Kind of muggy out here, isn't it?" He sensed something was disturbing her, but not what, or how early it had started. Her skin was flushed and he picked some stray hairs from her cheek.

"It was smoky." She looked at him as though he were a stranger.

"Remember me? I'm the guy who's sometimes dumber than he looks, your old pal. Why didn't you tell me you were having a bad time?"

"I didn't say that."

"You didn't have to. What's the matter, honey?"

"I don't know."

"You want to watch the convention?"

"I think I want to go home."

"OK. Let's walk."

"I mean home. To Phoenix—just for a while."

"Yeah, sure. We're both tired. Let's talk about it later. OK?"

"Never mind," she said.

All he could gauge from this frightened him a little. But then, maybe a short vacation would be a good idea. "A little breathing space to get refreshed," he said, as they walked home to their borrowed apartment.

"You do that. Go do a week or two, however long, and I'll set things up in Ithaca. Maybe I can get them to let me do my NSA thing while you're gone. Just make sure you come back—"

She said she'd fly back in two weeks. "Remember," he told her the next day when he put her on the plane, "you're the best thing that ever happened to me."

Driving back from the airport he came across a toll booth stuck open. By all evidence it looked to be another lucky day.

In August 1968, things, people said, were in the saddle. Again.

Great events and natural disasters arranged themselves around the convenience of impacted politicians.

The highways were filled with travelers. In Europe, Charles de Gaulle was packing for Colombey-Les-Deux-Eglises for the last time. And the Russians, having heard so much about the delights of Prague, embarked on a journey by tank.

In America, regular and insurgent Democrats descended on Chicago, with journalists and protesters. Five summers of ghetto riots had ceased. A season of campus rumpuses had ended for vacation. Instead, a savaging of children would be staged in the Chicago streets. The enemies of the state called themselves the People, and were identified by their lengthy hair and stubborn faith. Most people observed this from in front of televisions.

Halfway round the world, at the beginning of the Chicago convention week, the benign face of Czechoslovakia's tentative democratizations was stamped on by the Russian-booted boys. The news of this was handed to Dean Rusk, Secretary of State, as he talked to the Democratic Convention's foreign-policy-plank platform committee. He excused himself to see what he could do.

Eugene McCarthy said it was the sort of thing a President should not be woken up about, because there was nothing one could, or should, do.

Loving neither the messiness of Vietnam, nor Hubert Humphrey overmuch, the Mayor of Chicago was in bad temper. He had been identified by Lyndon

Johnson as a "royal pain in the ass" for his continued kvetching about the cost of the war in terms of urban disintegration. He had been Robert Kennedy's ace in the hole against Hubert Humphrey and McCarthy. He, Richard J. Daley, along with a couple of other well-placed pols, had oiled John Kennedy's path to nomination in 1960; and, it was alleged, swiped for him the margin of victory in the general election, voting some friends whose last forwarding address was "Deceased."

But Robert Kennedy was dead, and Eugene McCarthy was a threat to Daley's regular organization power. So Richard Daley sighed, and hied to Hubert Humphrey, hating most of all, above war and power threats, messiness, disorder.

Nor did Hubert Humphrey love the war. But he was stuck with it, the albatross of his loyalties. Neither even had the Secretary of Defense loved his war. Robert McNamara's friends insisted he detested it, found it wanting, statistically. But Humphrey's friends, like McNamara's, said he had no way to separate himself from the policies he so vigorously supported, but disliked, without offending Lyndon Johnson. Others asked, what then was to say that he did not love the war? If not lacking spine, they asked, did he not suggest that all statements by men in office be assumed untrue?

Yes. The delusions and lies of Lyndon Johnson's winding sheet became a straitjacket for all his associates. They lived in a land of mirrors where all things were inverted: the best intentions in the world murdered and maimed and ruined. Thus Hubert Humphrey offered something refreshingly, breathtakingly new into the language of political campaign: he asked the public to accept that what he said he did not believe.

And so, the more brutal beast hatched weeks before at the Miami Republican Convention could promise what the Democrats had always offered: peace and hope and unity. That he intended to deliver crueler things, extract a greater toll, was almost unbelievable. So it was not believed.

And the Democrats, like laboratory rats forced to choose between two pains, shriveled in the symptoms of nervous collapse. Another choice came in that bind:

to die or to turn violently against one's own, competing for survival space. So the Democrats were left with madness, and commenced to send policemen against their offspring, friends and delegates.

It was seen on every television set at home and around the world. Yet the authorities borowed a leaf from Tombstone Center's book of public information techniques and called it a UFO, an "Unfortunate Overreaction," not specifying whose.

No lever was left at hand to move the world. The box was slammed shut, with only the hope that hope remained inside.

In the teary poison swirling into every nostril was the barest trace of wishfulness that from the many shattered energies of spring across the planet, someone, some way, somehow might survive, to one day repair so many fractured dreams.

The desert in September was dappled tan. Johanna spent a week with Maureen in Scottsdale and even had dinner with Warren before he flew off to Washington again. Without saying as much, both reminded her that she had run away from many things for reasons she could not articulate.

In mid-September, after a ten-day stay, she flew east to Ithaca and Tyler Bowen.

SEPTEMBER WAS GONE, AND THE VIETnamese days Willie Bowen counted were getting even shorter. The last equinox he would see in Vietnam was behind him. The nights were very long and, because of the monsoons, less filled with threat. And the days belonged to him.

When last measured, Willie Bowen was six feet, two

inches, lanky and big-boned. Too big, in fact, for standard-issue body bags. Now they called him "short." In Army argot it meant his time in-country was almost up. He lay on his cot in his fetid shelter, in his boredom and his safety, through early October. The roof leaked and the mud grew slimier and he resolved to strike, and to war no more.

The raindrops trickled onto his face to wake him. And when there was no rain there were insects. There was never a solid eight hours of sleep for his dollar. Sometimes none at all. Just the intermittent annoyances of drops on a tin roof and canvas lining, the weird counterpoint of water splashing off sheet metal and the flying pests all buzzing—and the thud of mortar.

Though enemy action had slackened from the rain, every night brought enough mortar to keep Willie sleepless. It was unpredictable, mixed with thunder, maddeningly unresponsive to anything. Neither weather nor countermeasures abated it. The enemy had his own schedule and his own reality. The break in harassment that came with the rains wasn't enough to matter. And it wasn't the first prediction that didn't pan out. What the rains had brought was a flood of Montagnard refugees who wanted food and shelter from the Army that had chased them from their homes. Their children and animals were all over the place. More annoyances.

Most of all, the mud was a reminder of the viscous and intractable nature of Willie's situation: the Army had tacked his too-brief sojourn from the war to the end of his tour. They deemed it Solomon's justice, their means of settling accounts with him.

They hadn't been so brazen as to say that, for that would leave him some appeal. They'd taken a simpler course with the same effect: declared his paper work "missing in action." There was no chaplain or Inspector General riding circuit out there to complain to. Even the Pizza Trolley shied from the rains. Just when it seemed he'd waded to a safe shore, they'd contrived to nail his young ass to the barn door. Hence his strike. He knew when they'd relocate his files: when he'd given them every one of the three hundred sixty-five— this was leap year, make it three hundred sixty-six— days they demanded. That or four red quarts. Every day now he should by all rights have been out-processed, out-country—T-*FOOH,* as they called it: "The Fuck Out Of Here."

He was stuck in the mud, still. It was all slime and insects and nothing worth getting out of bed for. So he stayed on strike and listened to eight-track tapes until he thought he'd turn black from the incessant soul music.

Some distance from Willie Bowen's static nest, the whole planet Earth was spinning crazily, thrusting itself closer to a failed machine.

The tops of triple-canopied trees, fierce and shiny in the wet, rushed up to enfold a flightless craft. Inside it, a crippled Recon helicopter, the pilot's face became a child's, distraught at the breaking of his toy. The instruments were frozen by the sudden impact from a rocket of unknown origin. All systems, primary and backup, failed in that concussion, a blow to the ship's occipital region. Compared to the glistening mosaic spinning outside, the dials were hypnotically serene. Twilight images flashed in the windows. There was silence from all hands. The pilot was enthralled by his glowing dials. Crew members braced themselves.

A sudden jolt catapulted the grinning pilot from his seat. His lap belt tore loose and he tumbled from the fuselage into the trees, screaming softly as he crashed down through the branches. Two others by the rear door shook out like piggy-bank coins. All others on the manifest, four crew and two passengers, were incinerated by the rupture of the gas tanks and the explosions of spare armaments aboard. The three survivors smashed their way through branches and bushes, splatting into the mud outside the explosion's perimeter.

It took an hour for the three to find each other. They were a bad-looking group. The pilot's multiple broken bones were all above the waist—one arm, several ribs, and his collarbone—and he had apparently suffered a shock in his brain. Soundless tears rolled down his face, scooped up by his moronic smile. He wondered why the rain tasted salty, and dizzily believed it had to do with being near the ocean.

More conscious and in more torment was the door

gunner, a saucer-eyed boy who wore a string of foil-wrapped prophylactics like a lollypop chain around his neck. His leg was mangled and the white, virgin bone was showing through, splattered with mud.

They were joined by Brigadier General Kermit A. Loudermilk, fair-haired boy of a dozen superiors, an odds-on favorite to be Chief of Staff in God's Good Time. He was Adjutant of G-2, Intelligence, in this combat zone. His only serious injuries were a broken cheekbone and a chipped tooth, both suffered when the empty upside-down pipe he suckled was jammed backward in the impact.

Loudermilk took stock of the situation and removed his poncho from his web belt, then took off his jump suit and helped the pilot into it for what protection it might offer. The door gunner, who needed it more, would be too difficult to get into it. The pilot's own suit was torn in a dozen places and sticky with mud and blood and soaking wet from rain. General Loudermilk donned his poncho and stifled a laugh at having come through this murderous crash with hardly any mud on his trousers or a crease in his Dacron summer tropicals. It was like his whole career. Then he turned his attention to the door gunner's wounds and applied first-aid measures.

"Why're we out here, sir?" the boy asked.

"Our craft was hit," said Loudermilk.

"But why're we out here?"

Loudermilk wished he could say, if that would help the boy, just as he wished he could find a mother's kiss in his first-aid pack. But to say anything would place the boy in a more vulnerable spot if they were taken. The boy was easy prey for interrogators as it was. Loudermilk answered, "I can't tell you. I'm sorry." Then the boy said he was scared and cold. "You hang in there, trooper," the General told him. "Help's coming. Just hang on." He assumed the chill presaged the boy's dying. What he couldn't tell the boy was that the craft had gone on a run of compounded mistakes and now six men were its price. Maybe seven soon.

Clay Merz looked over Willie Bowen's sloppy quarters and spat on the ground. His muscles stretched his

T-shirt tight, and he looked more like a streetcorner hood than a Captain. "Bowen," he barked. "Up ya go. Lessgo. Up, I said." Willie Bowen groaned, pretending he was still asleep. "Up 'n' at 'em. GET YOUR ASS UP AND OUT OF THIS FUCKING PIT, BOWEN!"

Willie opened one eye and moved his hand to the stock of his M-16, saying "Fuck—*off*."

"Come on. Move! Up. Let's go. I haven't got all night, Bowen. I don't care for this shit any more than you do."

"Blow, Captain."

"You gotta problem?"

"You," Willie said.

"This time, Bowen, you're the solution. We got a ball-buster and you're on the rotation. You are *It!*"

"Do it yourself," Willie grumbled, rolling to his fore-arms. "I'm on strike."

"Tell it to the I.G. I've had all I'm gonna take from you in the way of shit."

"I'm short. Get yourself another sucker."

"I don't care if you're *overdue*—"

"I am."

"You'll go where you're told till I get orders pulling you out. The game's over. Now you get the hell out of that rack and get it on. You've just gotten an order!"

"Get stuffed," Willie said.

Willie rolled onto his back and yawned. He tilted his M-16 into the air so it pointed from his hip to Merz's nose. "Get yourself another boy, *sir*. I don't like your batting average—*sir*." He clicked the safety off and stared at Merz's unyielding blue eyes. "You're dripping on my mud."

Merz made no sign of being intimidated. He calmly told Willie to be in his command hooch, dressed and ready in five minutes "or I'll have you down on so many charges you'll wish you'd had the guts to shoot that thing!"

"You know? These mothers got an awful problem. Keep jamming and—" He fingered the M-16's trigger housing. "Sometimes the bastards fire off by accident at the damnedest—I wouldn't stand there all that long if I were you . . . *sir*."

"You'd better pull that trigger if you're not coming, Bowen—while you can."

"Don't tempt me."

"Try me," Merz snarled. Willie slowly squeezed the trigger to see how far he could push himself in cold blood, hoping to bypass his irresolution by easing through the point where the mechanism tripped itself into action. He lowered the barrel to the Captain's chest, then slid it down his gig line to let the weapon rest in the trough between his crossed feet, pointing straight at Merz's crotch, still off safety. He stretched out full to warn the Captain not to hold his breath waiting. Merz turned smartly on his heel in the slop and left. Each member of the Recon and Rescue patrol he was forming had put on a similar show. Someday they'd all just refuse and that would be that.

When Willie Bowen crowded in with the others in the cramped headquarters hut, a full ten minutes late in reporting, Merz seemed to have forgotten his earlier threat.

"OK," Merz addressed the sleepy quintet, "here's the scoop. There's a chopper down six to ten clicks out, azimuth deuce-trey-niner. Last signal we got was well before radar contact was lost—putting it *here*—" He indicated the spot on a field map. "It continued along and should have lost altitude until it was below radar—and it may have been hit or crashed in this general area." He swept his finger around to a small arc to indicate the possible impact zone. "Now there's a lot of fancy-assed tech shit on board, of an electronic nature. Been no signal in two hours, no Hicom or Loran contact. Some ground fire was reported in the area. Brigade and Division are, needless to say, curious."

One of them asked if he expected them to drag the stuff back. Merz said, "Just destroy it."

"We're good at that," Willie grumbled.

Merz snapped back, "Yeah, make like it's a latrine. You check this out, Bowen: you're short but you're not through. So wise your ass up, buster—your shit's flaky." Then Merz explained about the brass abroad, joining in the troops' derision. "Just bring the fuckers back."

"And yerselfs if at all—" one mumbled.

Merz growled. "Just neutralize that shit and get them back. Take det-cord and thermite and C-4 and any nonaccountable destruct materials your friends haven't already ripped off."

"Nonaccountable?" Timothy Franks asked warily.

"Damn straight. This whole show's off the books," Merz said. "Extra cookies and milk when you get back. Now check out."

Willie knew it was less simple. Being "off the books" meant it was a complicated mess, more likely than not the result of incompetence, malfeasance, or just plain traditional criminal negligence among field grade officers. People who died in off-the-books operations were routinely figured into whatever vague mass action's statistics could accommodate them, then bumped up one grade and decorated for their service.

Merz had one last item of business and he groaned at the idea. "God, I hate to do this. Lemme guess: who's senior? Ah, Bowen, how did I *know* it was you? Christ! OK, you're my main man: number one. Franks —you're in charge of seeing your patrol leader doesn't drive your guests nuts. If he pops off to anyone over Major—shoot him."

When they left, Merz took out his after-action report forms and squared them neatly on the top of a pile made of each man's DA 201 individual records jacket abstract. If they made it back, *bueno,* he'd put them in for a little something. If not—his ass was covered with Battalion at any rate.

It took Willie and the four others nearly three hours to make their way through the thick wet bushes to the site of the crash. Six to ten clicks my ass, Willie thought. Ten, easy. In actual fact, it was seven.

A small fire had burned off the tops of some trees and a dwindling one still licked at the mostly burned chopper's hull. But besides the continuing rain, everything else was very still. One of the five spat disgustedly that it was a false alarm. "Work's done—so's they. You think? Or captured."

"We gonna look for 'em?" another asked. They were all itchy with fright, Little Lost Boys, looking to their leader.

"I guess," Willie shrugged. "For a sec—then head the hell out."

Franks suggested that any survivors might think they were VC, though any VC in the area probably had them in their sights. "We might have the guys we're looking for scared."

"Their prob—not mine," Willie said. "But you wanna go sing 'The Star-Spangled Banner,' be my guest—" Diego Lupe, an eighteen-year-old Chicano, launched into it. He didn't get through two bars before Willie and Timmy Franks smothered him. "Another peep outa you and I'll cut your throat, I swear it!" Willie rasped. He and Franks looked at each other, as if to ask who was the crazy one.

Then a low rustling sound came from the bushes and they all reeled, dropping to their knees in the mud, scared witless, clicking their weapons off safety. Two of them rotated nervously to cover the flanks and rear.

The bushes began to shake, and leaves glistened with rolling water. The green was black, deep, and shiny in the wetness. The undersides of fronds were lighter, matte green, and each bush seemed an array of faceted jewels, emeralds sparkling with a million eyes, all stunning and threatening at once. From between two bushes stepped Brig. Gen. Kermit A. Loudermilk in his poncho. His hands were raised in surrender. When he recognized them he recovered by pretending to adjust his cap, and then motioned imperiously. "Good to see you, men. Come with me." He led them to the pilot, who was bundled in Loudermilk's orange dayglo flight suit, and the door gunner. "We're all there are. The rest didn't make it."

"You sure?" Franks asked. "You checked?"

"Quite sure!"

Willie knelt by the pilot and said only, "Jesus!"

Loudermilk moved over to them and pulled two of the patrol with him, ordering, "Take care of this man. He's hurt." But Willie wasn't listening. He smelled something awful: shit-and-spinach. In sweaty fear he swung his head around, blinking the rain out of his eyes. He spun on his knee, whirling his rifle around, aiming at the peripheral vegetation. "What the devil is the matter with you, troop?" the General demanded.

Willie poked around, ignoring him. "I said take care of this man," Loudermilk repeated to the two who had abandoned their charge to join Willie on his snark hunt. "He's hurt." Willie's heart pounded and he bumped with his patrol sideways around the clearing, his weapon for a beech rod, divining the source. The smell was worse. He snapped his head toward the jump-suited figure who looked blank and whimpered at him. It was the pilot who stank, not some portent of disaster. When the chopper had tossed him out, the pilot's entire system of security, his steady dials and fixed trusts, were taken away, and his head was rattled. The hard, wet earth was painful and confusing. He had instantly given way to his fears: he peed and cried and lost bowel control. There he was on the ground, stewing in his mess, smelling like a toilet, babbling about a new Caprice he'd ordered.

They made a sling for him and dressed his wounds, as best they could. Then Willie and Franks went to look at the door gunner. General Loudermilk, having determined who was in charge by the way the others responded to Willie's cues, pulled Bowen away. "What's your plan, troop?" he asked.

"Plan, sir?"

"Your plan."

Willie gestured openly and said, "Check out the craft, destroy what's left—then get you back to our cozy little camp, sir. Mostly get out of the fuckin' rain —in one piece."

"Good," Loudermilk said.

"Glad you approve." The two were locked in stares until Franks called out, "Hey, Will—c'mere. Take a lookit this, huh?"

Willie pulled Lupe and another off the perimeter guard and said, "We'll keep an eye out—you go ask General Custer there for the layout. Then do a little Search and Destroy on what's left of that bird so's we can pull out quick." Lupe started off and Willie called him back. "If there's any way you can delay the fuse, lemme know—so we can get a little distance. But make sure you got the fucker rigged right—I don't wanna come back here." He pressed his eyelids. He had a headache. He was surprised at his own capacity for leadership, and stuck a finger into Lupe's shoulder, saying, "Look for code plates and—ah, shit—when you got it all wired I'll look it over. Just set it up and I'll tell you when to burn." He knew they'd get most of it fouled up.

The door gunner's face told the story silently. His mouth and eyes were wide open. His head lolled and blew out sweat. His left leg was badly fractured near the hip, twisted and black. Blood from all around the main wound soaked through his fatigue pants. An early attempt to stanch the blood flow left a cake of poulticelike mud at the site of the break, inside his thigh.

"We can't do anything for him here," Willie sighed. "Oh, Christ, it's gonna be murder dragging him—"

The door gunner looked up at their urgent conference, begging for a merciful, efficient deliverance from pain.

"I'm sorry, fella," Willie said, fingering the gunner's unbroken bandolier of condoms. He winked to comfort the boy, "You'll be reamin' your way through these in no time. You'll see."

"I'm sorry," the door gunner repeated, breathing out his pain in staccato gasps. "Drafted—*sorry*—Nam— *sorry*—gonna take my leg—say *sorry*—"

Willie looked away toward Franks and bit his lip, then said, "I'm sorr—yeah, I know. What can you do?" He lit a joint and stuck it in the boy's mouth, while they fashioned a splint for the festering leg. During that time Lupe came back to report on the progress of the destruct mission, and Willie told him to "go back and get the other guys. I want to hear it from them, too."

For the wounded boy's benefit, Franks began to tell Willie a tale showing how the wheels of injustice rolled over everyone. "I tell you I was home last month? Seems like longer. My mom—she died."

"I'm sorry," said the door gunner.

"That's OK. She was sick, you know? But they wouldn't let me go till she was just about—they said 'she might get well'—ah, the bastards. Then they whisked me right-the-fuck back, 'cause I was short on R&R bank. I didn't half-get time to get laid."

"They don't sell Fourex at the PX," the boy winced, one hand on his contraceptive string.

Willie pulled the splint stays tight, using the remaining det-cord Lupe had brought back to lash it in place. He patted the gunner on the shoulder. "Don't fart if you care about your ass."

"The thing of it is," Franks continued, "is my girl was off fucking her brains out with my best friend—doing more dope than anyone here, while I get shot up. How you figure?"

"Typical," Willie said.

"Sure is," Franks agreed. "Guy's 4-F. Combat fatigue, he says he's got—from too many protests. Combat fatigue in California!"

"Sounds like my brother," Willie laughed. "How'd you like The World? Our man here's going that way soon, I expect."

"It's not here, is it?" and they both turned to smile at the wounded boy, whose pain eased under the salve of having new friends.

"You're on your way. Almost a hero," Willie said. "Pretty soon you'll have the medals—bet you get a DSM at least. Yup, almost a hero now." He patted him on the head, and stood up as the other men returned to report. "In an almost-war."

Franks soothed the gunner and whispered, "You'll make it. It's tough, I know. Just take it easy."

Willie and Franks inspected the wrecked chopper and Willie was satisfied that it was set up well. But General Loudermilk was hungry and cranky and wanted to know, "What's holding us up? Let's get out of here already, troop!"

"You're absolutely right, sir. But—" Willie cocked his head in the direction of some soft thunder. "You hear that?" A cushioned, rhythmic booming had increased by degrees in the half-hour they were there, from the faintly audible to the distinct-though-distant. "Sounds like someone's going to war out there."

"It's mortar," Loudermilk answered. "So what?"

"Just—we leave here and everybody and his aunt's gonna be trying to kill us. Both sides, 'cause we're moving and it's cheaper than asking. And when we light the scraps they're gonna know where we've been, and where we're going, and which way we came. So we even have to get a new route."

"What do you suggest?" the General demanded.

"Not a damned thing, sir. Problem's the same if we sit put. I'm just readin' you the score. We can touch off the rest of that wreck any time you want to travel." Willie's unspoken idea was to shoot the General and go home, but he quelled it.

They waited another hour until it seemed that the rains might have parted for the night. There would be light in an hour or two, and so they began to thread their way back to the base camp, the wounded being supported by the patrol members, half-carried, half-dragged, on a path wide of the one they had had come by.

Around the first bend the mortar sounds grew louder and explosions blocked them.

"Should we wait?" one of the patrol asked, hoping majority vote would prevail.

Willie thought a minute. "That shit'll just walk right in on us. We gotta get out of here. Get near it and duck around. They're just playing hunches."

General Loudermilk said, "Let's go that way," pointing to a different path. Willie wondered whether that was a strategic decision or just one supported by the belt of authority. He'd been there a year now and he still had no idea about such things. He wondered if the General knew his ass from his helmet about the bush.

"Why?"

"Because I said so," General Loudermilk replied.

"I'm not sure."

"I am. Let's move." And the new path seemed good. The mortar sounds were loud, unmuffled by trees, but they judged them farther off. Willie walked point in front, and Franks took the rear.

Willie looked up and down and sideways with every few steps, his nervous sweat mixing with the hot raindrops. Every now and then he took a look back at the General, marching smartly, weaponless, behind him.

The mortar sounds continued to grow louder, and they knew they were getting closer to home. No safer, Willie knew, just closer. He didn't like the idea of coming out from the mist into a target area for random death-kits. His left foot stepped on something soft and without thought he jumped backward and to the left, pulling Loudermilk with him off the road. His foot had hit a spring-loaded pop-up mine and despite the mortar noise and his nervously shifting attention, he somehow had heard the tiny "click" of the spring and catapult as it engaged. Such mines were designed to leap straight up, four to six feet, and blow off a head. But the mud had slowed it, and it flew backward, past the spot Willie and Loudermilk vacated. The others dove also, but the two men carrying the door gunner froze in panic and dropped him. He screamed. Both reached instinctively to pull him up and they were killed. The enemy never intended such efficiency. The door gunner lay on the ground moaning from the weight of his heavy busted armor: the remains of his escorts.

Willie wondered if he hadn't risked his own life and killed two men in trade for Loudermilk's. But such calculations could be traced back further, to Merz, and Operations, and Washington. So he turned to practical considerations. What to do with the dead pair? Leave them? If they weren't picked up by VC, more men would have to come get them—maybe himself as a pathfinder. Bury them? They were surely and uncomplicatedly dead, gristle beyond repair. Yet, being stuffed under this stinking country's shitty soil was no one's wish. He'd want to be sent home, even if dead, himself. He couldn't bury them. And he couldn't carry them back, either. So they dragged the bodies off the path and covered them with branches to hide them as best they could. When he was through, Willie shook his head and wondered how long they'd remain like roadside garbage, and who'd get to them first? Then he wondered what made him jump. In the midst of all the noise in the world, he'd heard the click, as clearly as a chime in an empty ballroom, felt it, as a chill. But worrying about the price those reflexes had exacted on his two dead companions wasn't in the rule book. It wasn't his fault.

The now-reduced party paused at the crest of a rise to check their path. Willie scouted up ahead and reported the worst news: a mortar emplacement commanded the road on the next hill with, from what he could count, three machine guns guarding it. Franks began to look for a way to circle around and avoid it, but Loudermilk curtly said, "We will take it out. It's what we came for—they're the ones."

"Look, General—" Willie said.

"Look, Specialist!" Loudermilk nearly bellowed, modulating when Willie shoved his muzzle into his belly. "We will not avoid it—we will take it out!"

"Goddam it!" Willie snapped in a hoarse whisper. "Two of my men are dead. We got one idiot and one crip and one fat-ass *you* to carry back." He fought for control and rasped, "I'd rather be carrying those two dead suckers—now who in hell's gonna take you in if me and Franks and Lupe buy it playing—"

"You will do what you are told, troop—and I will personally have you on report for every minute you fail to do so!"

Willie roared back, "I'm not getting my ass blown off for you, fuckhead!" and Loudermilk's eyes popped. "So stick it up—" Loudermilk slapped him ferociously and Willie spat in his face, snapping his weapon up to butt the General's skull, but Franks dragged him away. "Lemme go! I'm gonna climb all over that bastard, I'm gonna kill him!"

"Willie," Franks warned him, wrestling him until he was subdued, "we're giving away our position."

Loudermilk addressed Franks while Willie seethed. "You've got your orders. Follow them," at which Willie drove his weapon's stock into the general's solar plexus and the man groaned miserably, collapsing in a heap, the wind knocked from him. Mutiny seemed appropriate, abandoning the General a good second choice. Third came looking for another route, and because Willie's generalized sense of rebellion was mitigated by uncertainty and fear, the fourth was worked out in the slop off the road like a razzle-dazzle play in touch football. They pulled Diego Lupe over, and Franks said, "You go long." Diego hardly understood a mess menu. Then they went back to gather up what they needed from where their three charges sat.

"In case I don't get back," Willie said, and Franks tried to stop him, but he wouldn't be denied: he kicked the General in the kidneys. The door gunner's pain fled momentarily, and he smiled with delight.

Franks took the det-cord from the door gunner's splint and replaced it with the pistol belts he'd taken from the two dead patrol members. He wrapped it around some leftover incendiary material, thermite, and C-4, and attached it to two hand grenades until it resembled a massive pair of bolos.

A curious morality made Willie designate himself as the one to perform the most dangerous task in this maneuver. He had no more notion of what to do than either of the others. He had never done this kind of thing before. He had used his weapon, and had gotten bailed out by support many times. But never this junior commando junk. He'd only seen it in the movies. None of them had any idea if it would work. Willie wasn't even sure he was capable of thinking straight at this point, let alone accomplishing the task. He had no surety the emplacement was arrayed as he had indicated. He might just get killed going up the hill. Or wind up killing some ten-year-old Vietnamese kid.

He slithered up the hill as best he could, slipping all the way, until he could survey his target. Franks was in sight at the bottom and he nodded to him as Franks crawled under—he hoped—the machine-gun sights. From Willie's vantage point there seemed to be a good angle for cover on the far side of the hill. Since they didn't trust Diego Lupe's command of the language, they spared him any elaborate assignment or difficult instructions. They had dragged the door gunner to the cover point nearest their original position. There they propped him up, and stuck an M-16 in his hand. The pilot, incompetent, they let guard Loudermilk. Then they continued on: Franks to the closest approach up the hill, where he waited, and Diego Lupe in the far bushes, slithering in the mud and slime to a cover point diagonally opposite Willie, working his way slowly, it was hoped, under the sights of the mortar guards.

Willie moved in closer and Franks eased in from the front. Lupe arrived at his post without incident. Willie carefully pulled the pins out of the grenades and held the whole package against his chest, the det-cord, thermite, and C-4 holding the levers down. A loop of det-cord hung loosely between the two mounds. He could just about manage the whole rig in both hands, and throwing it would require exactly one, sure heave. Even with the wrapping, the levers strained against his slippery, trembling fingers. He crept closer still, keying on the slightest sounds above, pushing forward on side and elbow, using a scissor kick to advance up the slimy hill.

Franks wondered what was taking so long. He hefted a grenade in his right hand, enfolding it in casual sureness. His M-16 was on full automatic in his left hand, as he crept, grenade up in periscope fashion, for easy tossing in the first moment's need. Where was Bowen? he wondered, hoping he wouldn't have to blow up Willie to save himself.

Willie paused for breath, and realized that this was where their amateur plan broke down. His part was to heave with his good right arm the device they had made. But it wasn't until he got this close that he fully appreciated the bomb's cumbersome weight, and began to doubt his poorly healed shoulder's ability to meet the task. He thought a moment and crept closer still, his nerves and impoverished strategy getting the better of his sense. Overriding his fear was the sense that the others were counting on him and were in impossible positions awaiting his key, not realizing that his position was equally impossible, and that they were key. The whole movement had been well devised in three dimensions. But the fourth—timing—was forgotten. Nor was he at all clear what events should come first.

He entered the VC's periphery of awareness at the same time Franks did, and hackles rose in warning among the VC. Then, what no one had supposed: a fourth machine gun, set wide to guard the position, spotted Willie and opened up. Lupe saw the frenzied jerk of two gunners wheeling around to aim at Willie, and opened fire in a flurry. The door gunner and Franks crossed fire at that fourth machine gun. Friendly and hostile fire ripped past Willie Bowen and he rolled violently to his right and tried to get up without traction or the use of his arms, nestling his violent cargo. Fire was all around, and he slipped and slid hysterically halfway back down the hill to cover, tumbling head-over-heels, hugging the explosive mass to his chest. Frank's grenade was spastically launched when a burst of fire from the mortar nest took out Lupe. The grenade killed one of the machine gunners, but the other opened fire on Franks, who tumbled down the sloppy hill to safety, as it chased him. He lay hugging the ground, breathing frantically, while the fire skipped over the small gully he lay in, pinning him to the ground, moving on in search of the door gunner, who had no good angle after all. In the short breathing space, Franks scampered to a safer spot. From there he could see Willie on his knees, trying to crawl back up the hill. Franks reached for his other hand grenade, but the machine-gun fire raked near him and he had to lie flat. Franks was pinned down completely, and Willie dug furiously to the top of the hill, without the use of his arms, tripping, panting. Franks had to take a chance. Willie was desperately naked as he crested the hill. Franks slithered to a spot the gun had been hitting and then scratched and clawed as fast as he could another few yards. He pulled the pin as the gun stopped and wheeled toward Willie, who was crashing up the side of the hill. Franks raised his M-16 and squeezed off a volley closer to Willie than to the gunner. His unpinned grenade was clutched to his chest. Willie fell flat over his weird bomb, in complete panic, wondering if the thing would work. The door gunner gave him jerky cover fire, and Franks's fire goaded the VC machine gunner into return fire. It was the opening Willie needed, all he knew he'd get. He drew close enough to heave his package and drew a breath for courage. Franks figured Willie needed another lull to work in and so began to throw his grenade as Willie stood up to get better leverage. "No! Don't!" Franks screamed, unable to stop, *"Will—"* as he and Bowen let go of their parcels in the same instant. "No!!" And Willie tried to fly, hurling himself back down the hill as it ripped open in a series of blasts. The fourth gunner, bleeding to death but not stilled, trained his weapon on Willie's body as it skidded, slid and tumbled down the hill until it slammed limply into a tree. The door gunner blasted away at that remaining position while Timmy Franks raced toward Willie, tripping and stumbling into the ravine. Rounds tore through Franks in the arm and upper thigh, and he cartwheeled helplessly through the glop down close to where Willie lay tangled and moaning. Willie's legs were in the air and he was pitched helplessly up against a tree. The haze was choking, and it was soundless but for their wheezing.

Willie's breath came short and with difficulty in the acrid mist. He sniffled about his own pain as Franks lay ten yards away. The two of them coughed and dragged their way to each other, and then fell exhausted in each other's arms, crying.

Willie's back and chest and gut were achingly ripped, and he groaned a soft "Fuuuuuck," thinking of his nineteen years and the slime he was condemned to lie in. Franks could hardly move, and lay back weeping, as Willie tried to pull himself into a sitting position. He did the best he could with both first-aid kits to bind Franks's wounds, and Franks kept reaching up with his good arm to stroke Willie's face clean of mud. Then Willie collapsed backward. He pulled his own shirt and trousers open. Blood trickled out of a wound at his belt line, where a metal shard was stuck next to his navel. His chest had a funny aspect to it, and he coughed up blood. Franks could hear a horrible gurgling sound from Willie's lungs, and saw blood come out with each of Willie's coughs. From the blood and spongy sound he guessed Willie had something sticking through a lung.

They lay there for a half-hour, and the door gunner grew frightened by their absence. He finally yelled for General Loudermilk to go investigate, and the General found Willie and Franks half-conscious lying in each other's arms in the soaking leaves.

It was daylight by the time Loudermilk got them both back to their original position. Franks couldn't walk, but Willie could manage, so they left Franks and the door gunner, while Willie, General Loudermilk, and the still-crazed pilot walked the remaining few kilometers back to get help. Willie paused to kiss Diego Lupe's half-blown-away skull for that brief measure of protection he had given them at the full cost of his life. Bending down to do so only drove a rib deeper into one of his lungs.

Willie's belly was tearing and his chest was aching, filling with blood with every step. It made him light-headed and nauseated, but he kept going. Every few yards he spat up blood, and every hundred yards he doubled over to cough out what he could. But that only made it worse. His anger yielded to his pain, but he still managed to be resentful: Loudermilk was unhurt, his own wounds weren't million-dollar tickets home, and Franks was surely going to lose a limb if he didn't bleed to death before help got to him. His own external wounds were slight, but he thought, "Who'll fuck a guy with two belly buttons." Loudermilk walked stiffly, maintaining his valorous pose. He hadn't thanked them for getting shot up. Willie's whole body, inside and out, wanted to go away and hide, and he once again thought of shooting Loudermilk, when the General made his misstep. Loudermilk's boot hit another pop-up mine, and all Willie could do was stagger into the dim-witted pilot and fall on top of him, further aggravating both their wounds. Loudermilk stayed erect for the mine's act.

Brigadier General Kermit A. Loudermilk faced the menace as sternly as a Christian Scientist would a microbe, not believing it at all. The tiny device reached its zenith between the General's cold hazel eyes. They considered each other for an instant: steely man and mangling steel. Loudermilk's determination was fierce, his glint-eyed stare and self-possession commanding. He regarded the infidel gismo with scorn. Its mechanism went "whrrrrrrrrrrr," and it fell to the soggy ground between his feet, a dud whose bluff he had successfully called.

Willie spat blood at the prick's good luck, then he raised himself and the pilot up. "Nice going, boss" he told the General, shaking his head in disgust. "Sure showed it." General Loudermilk said nothing. He stood where he had stopped, staring blankly, with a sweet, tired smile. His eyes drooped in the wide corners of their sockets and his head hung languidly, listing to one side. He looked like an expressionist statue of Brig. Gen. Kermit A. Loudermilk. "Hoooooly shit," Willie moaned. He shivered and then eased in front of Louder-milk, whistling of terror. He spat a bloody geyser at the

586

General, who did not blink. "He's jumped the tracks," Willie muttered, and laughed in spite of his pain until he hacked relentlessly. Doubled up coughing, he said to the equally insensate pilot, "Damned thing shoulda went off." He wished there was some useful way to strip the General for parts to restock the more deserving.

He pushed Loudermilk, and the General stumbled forward, falling every few yards. But they went on, like ragged Rockettes, Willie Bowen, General Loudermilk, and the pilot, staggering their way home to Oz from the Munchkin Forest. It was a strange conga line and the last two kilometers took an hour. Willie had to rest more and more, and he was losing a lot of blood. When they reached the perimeter, Willie shooed the pilot ahead, in case the guards opened fire. The pilot tore for the camp like a horse smelling the barn. Help was within sight, and Willie Bowen had no further need to march, so he gave way to his wounds. Dragging Loudermilk down with him, he collapsed by the roadside, unwilling to let his booty go that easily.

A detail scurried out to portage them back to a field hospital which was staffed by three paramedics and four assistants. While they tried to silence him to take his blood pressure, Willie rallied to tell them that Franks and the door gunner were still waiting for help, and where they could find the dead.

Merz came by when the next patrol brought Franks and the gunner in. "Go 'way from me!" Willie gagged. "You got three of my—friends—out there—" He spit the blood onto his pillowcase, and most of it ran down his jaw. "—waiting for the garbage truck—"

"We're bringing them in now," Merz said calmly.

"—stuff 'em in a Dempster—Dumpster . . ."

"Take it easy—"

"Why'd you send—*Lupe,* for Christ—"

"You saved three lives, Bowen," Merz snapped. "Maybe more."

Willie looked at the door gunner and Franks when they were carted in, wondering if they'd spend their days sitting around VA hospitals trying to get laid on Veterans Day, with wooden legs and wilting pansies. And the pilot and Loudermilk, who couldn't feed themselves. "Fuck you. Some—favor," he winced. "Fuck me."

The door gunner said, "They don't sell Fourex at the PX."

Merz went over to him to put an understanding hand on his shoulder, looking back at Willie. "You did good, Bowen. Real good."

They stretchered Willie out when a top-priority Med-Evac chopper arrived with real medics. But Willie was no help in the diagnosis. He'd gone into shock from the loss of blood, and took three units on the way to Long Binh. The fresh blood almost killed him, as it added to the pools in his lungs, so a makeshift siphon was inserted down his esophagus, to bring out the blood as fast as it dripped into him. Franks was watching all this from his rack, heavily doped with morphine, but conscious all the time. He smiled and kept muttering, "Come on, Willie. Come on. Just hang in there another few miles. Come on, man."

Already shot full of pain killers while they had waited for evacuation, Franks had answered Merz's questions for the after-action report. The door gunner gave corroboration. "Listen, Cap'n," Franks had said. "I saw it all out there. The whole thing. I mean Willie showed me guts you wouldn't believe." Merz nodded. "You oughta make him a Sergeant, truly. He's a real leader like that."

Merz sighed heavily and said, "I want everything you can tell me. You, too," he said to the door gunner. "Everything. And I mean each time one of you guys *pissed* heroically."

"Yessir," Franks said. "Don't forget the General. He held up like a real Trojan—or what's under one."

"I won't," Merz replied.

F̲OUR YEARS' ACCUMULATED VICTORY AND honor in the old school's name," nagged a familiar voice outside Tyler Bowen's office door and Tyler rose toward it. "Unmarketable in any way except this!" A grinning Saint Paul Hooper shot his head into the office, past the lettering on the door that said "Assistant to the Dean."

"Get in here, dink," Tyler laughed, embracing him. "Let me tell you how much I hate this job."

"You're doing it, aren't you?"

"Until I can figure out what I want to be when I grow up, it's doing me."

Saint Paul stood distant to him, as though under a white flag on hostile territory. "You were better at it when you didn't care."

This was the place of Tyler's many heroics, his timely savings. Politics was well behind him, a bitter lesson in futility; yet not until now, Home-coming Weekend in October, did he feel fully arrived in Ithaca, his odyssey ended. And even then it was only to wonder whether they had moved the world out from underneath him in his absence. So many things had changed since he was an undergraduate. "All except the Coke machines," Saint Paul said. "And they'll outlive us all. But the Coke machines don't know shit."

Saint Paul was back for the weekend with safe passage as an alumnus. The only conscience he had purchase on after four years of turmoil was again Tyler Bowen's, and he spared no time saying how disappointed he was that Tyler should be so cozy with administrators. "It doesn't matter, Paulie," Tyler reassured him as they went over to the Faculty Club to meet Johanna for lunch. "They've had their wings clipped.

And it's only part-time so I can work at Advanced Studies."

"It's still collaboration," Saint Paul insisted.

When they sat down in the well-appointed dining room of the Faculty Club, Saint Paul was too busy greeting Johanna to look around. "You know," he said at the first silence, "they never let me in here before." He examined its ambient comforts with a class-conscious eye, looking, to Johanna, like a sparrow, new-hatched, peering over the edge of his nest, as he ran his fingers over the damask and admired the clear crystal of the water glasses. "Now I know why they fight so hard for tenure."

"We're supposed to be the government in exile," Johanna said, sardonically. That's what McCarthy had called them in Chicago, all those weary-faced youngsters whose torn efforts came to naught but funerals and busted brows. Most were now in domestic exile or disarray. "Some exiles," she shrugged, "are cushier than others."

"What'd you think of Johanna's story in the alumni mag?" Tyler asked.

"What? The piece on your Advanced Studies project?"

"Not exactly mine," Tyler said. "All I do is hold the great men's coats and every now and then they give me a tip."

"Is that why you didn't mention his name?" Saint Paul asked her.

Johanna pursed her lips and said, "On past experience, I wouldn't say our boy here is the most trustworthy source."

Saint Paul looked surprised. "Why don't you ask him why it's not a good idea to pick crops bare-assed naked, and how, if that's true, people can eat them?"

"I'm sworn to secrecy," Tyler said, trying to make light of it.

"But a 'No Comment, National Security' would sure get people wondering."

Tyler lolled his head, saying, "I think I'll just have to stay out of that kind of action for a while."

"Still hold the record for the one-man standing straddle," Saint Paul teased.

"The project director really liked Johanna's piece," Tyler said. "Suggested she help write the popular press version when they get down to journal articles."

Johanna added, "I suggested Tyler do it." She was not engaged by this kind of work, and did it only to pass the days, a kind of housewifery until Tyler was through at Advanced Studies, a thing she hoped would only take a year. What pleased her most of all was that some poems she had written were accepted by the campus literary magazine, and one received the politest rejection from *The New Yorker,* encouraging her to try again. These were something all her own and true.

It was not obvious that Tyler would be through at Advanced Studies in a year. If they could clear it, he wanted to have a full-time legitimate affiliation, and drop his administrative chores, which he found loathsome. He told Johanna that if they couldn't find funding for him for the next year, he would chuck it all and go somewhere else. Already he was dusting off graduate school applications. But it wasn't much of a promise to Johanna.

As minor as his role in this project was, it filled him with excitement, just to be a witness and protégé. For, according to Johanna's story, it was a great step in understanding the special energy relations of the biochemical process, how that determined the unique capacity of some molecules to act biotically. Physicists and geneticists, computer mathematicians and chemists lent their time and resources to the biologists running the project. Tyler's subgroup on cellular identity looked to be an action corner, perhaps the fulcrum on which it all hinged. She had written, "At the basic level it is the ability of organic molecules to replicate themselves exactly that is the first step in the ladder of life. At the higher level, it is the ability of cells to distinguish their own stuff from counterfeit—their idiosyncratic organization from an invader's—that makes life tenable from generation to generation. And, of course, the ability to synthesize an identical twin of a gene from the random nutrients ingested depends on the information those giant molecules have about their own arrangements, information that is based on energy relations between atoms. . . ." The possibilities down these roads were wildly promising, and they were very close to important understandings. Though but a junior member of this team, Tyler would not give it up for anything.

Most of their lunch was given over to Tyler and Saint Paul recounting campus adventures for Johanna, like old war veterans swapping brags. It was a shorthand, coded recitation, with salacious laughs at the raunchier stunts they'd pulled. Johanna listened politely, and was about to ask a question when Tyler interrupted to give Saint Paul an update on Willie. "He was all busted up for a while, but he's OK now. My parents wanted to fly out and see him, but first my mom got sick and then the Defense Department, or State, or somebody withdrew their permission, a big mess. But from what I hear, he's getting along."

Saint Paul replied, "When this is all over, when I'm finished holding the hands of probated laddies in Pittsburgh, you know what? I'm just gonna take my marbles and move to Canada. The more I think about it, love it or leave it makes great sense. Not before, but after, so no one'll have any doubt."

"I take it," Tyler said, "this decision results from an audit of your marbles."

"Mostly, there are days I get the feeling my telephone calls and letters from the Big Guy are being screened in Washington."

"I wouldn't be surprised," Johanna said, "if they were written in Washington. He may be just a pawn in some plan."

Saint Paul was toying with his napkin, as though loath to leave such finery behind, then said with an unaccustomed clarity, "It occurred to me, just before I got my deferment, when I was considering that truck, that the whole course of American politics depends on the latent stupidity of a lot of rednecks. Specifically, how badly the South feels when it gets out of bed with whichever party it's getting laid by. It was Democrat because the Republicans freed the slaves, until the Democrats proposed to make them a little freer, so it conjured up a liking for the Republicans again. That Richard Nixon should be the ultimate beneficiary of the Civil War is just too much for me. However long it takes 'em to wise up again, I think I'd rather be a dog catcher in Toronto than King of Ithaca."

"Dog catcher," Tyler repeated slowly, considering it. "There's only one thing wrong with it. It's one of those things that's great to have been, but lousy to have gone broke in. Like politics."

"So much for the great struggle?" Johanna asked.

"Look around you," Saint Paul said, with a sweeping gesture meant to take in the whole Faculty Club. "It's been won. I spent four years beating my brains out over the social regulations and what happens? My best friend becomes one of *them*. But it doesn't matter, because the fight wasn't won by them, it was won when no one was watching, by the faculty. And what's the first thing they did? Go to war with themselves." Saint Paul began to speak derisively in loud tones about the "professional survivors" in the faculty, "many from the Pleistocene epoch, some of whom knew Andrew White as a boy," and their struggle with the insurgent wing unfondly known as "the Young Turks." He said, "It's a case of the new braves trying to push the old bulls into the sea, off Seal Rock where the grants are."

Trying to quiet him a little, Tyler said softly, "They used to grumble all the time about the revolting younger faculty. Little did we know."

"But see, now here's the thing," Saint Paul said, more loudly. "Who's their big ally? The administration and trustees! Why? Because *they* don't want little boys and girls to get laid in the dorms and they can make a deal for support from these bucks, a little log-rolling. So the faculty gets the power, and all they had to give up was any measure of competence in favor of relevancy. And that is guess who in the faculty. There's nothing so irrelevant as relevance. But it bought off the students. What a mess they've made! No wonder the old guys abdicated in favor of stupefaction."

Johanna was charmed, even if dazed, wishing she had, years before, had a friend like Saint Paul was to Tyler. But then, why had Tyler never been swept up in Saint Paul's exotic current? So as Paul spoke it was with a keener interest that she looked at Tyler. "Look," Saint Paul insisted, "it's one thing to savage traditional class values: tradition itself, antique departmental divisions, the Byzantine protocols of the faculty meeting, archaic tenure procedure. But that's not what the upshot is. I bet you, the Assistant Professors' Putsch will go down in pedagogic history—a more arcane field, I might add, than which none exists, and a more useless one—"

"Political science," Johanna corrected automatically.

"Anyway, it's the biggest thing to hit the knowledge biz since the introduction of edible paste in the lower grades."

"Paulie, you sly bastard," said Tyler, smirking, "I do believe you've become a cranky conservative in your old age."

"Not a bit. Not a smidgen. Look, what was surrendered to the three-credits-for-jerking-off guys? Right, the core. Since World War II what have we been reading? The collated, translated, received wisdom of the ages. Great thinkers, revolutionaries every one, never satisfied. It was highlighted in yellow streaks in ten million texts that whole systems, orders, philosophies and worlds will go down. No more! Now we're back to hobby-shop and memorize these dates, except now it's fashionably left hobbies and dates. But you can't beat down walls with bullshit. You need the hard stuff. So maybe," Saint Paul said, a little sadly, "you just never understood what I was saying."

From the table next to them, a young history teacher in a corduroy suit said in a voice to match Saint Paul's, "Not that you ever did, Hooper."

The three of them spent that weekend larking all over the Finger Lakes, attending a football game and concerts, dashing to distant restaurants for dinner, then back for a student theater presentation, then home to get stoned, then up early to go exploring, seeing new things or experiencing old ones with wondering eyes. It was a giddy, happy time-out, as though a step back into the past. But for the most part, the Cornell Johanna had heard so much about was not in evidence. There were new campus leaders now, none in student government; new sports heroics, with apathetic following. Glories had come and gone and been forgotten. What united students and faculty and administration was not frolicsome bearding, but shared drug connections.

In the pile of memos and mail on Tyler Bowen's desk when he returned to it Monday morning were faculty committee meeting notes, course cancellation notices, requests for room changes, requests for use of campus facilities by special groups, schedule changes for lecture sections falling on holiday dates—all the junk mail of the administrative life. "Look at this," he said to Saint Paul, who was about to leave for home. "My mother didn't raise me to do this."

Saint Paul sifted through the pile and came across a list of dusty demands from a student group. "Do something about it," he said to Tyler. The date on them was early September, and they'd squatted on a dozen desks already, collecting initials, mastodon bones unaware of their vestigiality in the Ice Age coming.

"The best I can do is put my initials on it and send it back the way it came," Tyler admitted. "It's not much." Then he scribbled a note across the top of the sheet: "It's nearly Pumpkin Time. Has anyone done anything about this? Does anyone care?"

That was the last he would hear of it. It disappeared without a trace. And he, too, lacked the energy to pursue it further.

Lyndon Johnson, having eased the bombing of North Vietnam when he withdrew on the eve of April Fool's Day, halted it completely on Halloween. This he did for All Saints and for Hubert Humphrey in particular, a last-minute electoral boost for the Democratic candidate. So appalling was the threat of Richard Nixon's election that Johnson even made a spectacular pitch to disgruntled Democrats on Humphrey's behalf, as desperate as it was stunning, praising him as the peer of Robert Kennedy and Eugene McCarthy. Neither that equation nor his embrace hurt any of the three, really. All were either beyond pain or redemption. And it could not have helped Humphrey, to protest his independence by his master's proclamation. But it must have cost Lyndon Johnson half his heart.

Even Eugene McCarthy broke out of his brood long enough to offer Humphrey an endorsement of sorts, or rather, as Robert Kennedy once described a Papal offer to pray over reporters, one that would not compromise nor hurt, "just a small blessing." McCarthy had observed most of the campaign from the Riviera, interpreting it with bright but cryptic metaphors which passed for wisdom, as balm to those he left behind. To them, though, it seemed as if McCarthy had led the stampede to the edge of the mesa and then stood back, just as Baron Zermatt had suggested, while the herd thundered into empty space to be dashed upon the rocks below. They imagined him sighing contemplatively at the wreckage from his safe roost, "You didn't believe all that stuff, did you? You mean you took it seriously? Come on, you're kidding, right? It was just to raise a dialogue. Didn't you understand that? And didn't we do that?" The residue was bitter. Some said McCarthy would be a paragraph in future textbooks, or a footnote to an otherwise inexplicable succession. In that way, perhaps he was a catalyst, unchanged. Others said he'd join past and future candidates in the place where go the men who break a civic trust.

Election Day itself was a hung-over affair. Tyler and Johanna had gone out to dinner the night before to celebrate the publication of her poems and continued drinking through the night at an election-eve party. Statutory sobriety by a closing of the bars on voting days was fashioned in the finite wisdom and infinite vanity of legislators, in no way anticipating that the choice might one day be between repugnancies. In the morning, they gritted their teeth with other tired revelers, held their noses, and pulled the lever for Hubert Humphrey, hair of the dog, withal to avoid a greater hangover.

When it was done, Hubert Humphrey had, of course, accomplished two political miracles. "It used to be impossible in this country," Allard Lowenstein said, "for Richard Nixon to be elected President. It was up to now inconceivable that he could beat Moshe Dayan for Mayor of Cairo." And—perhaps it was Humphrey's purpose all along—in defeat, Humphrey, the loyalist, made people instantly nostalgic for Lyndon Johnson, just as Stokely Carmichael had once warned of his successor, H. Rap Brown, at the Student Non-Violent Coordinating Committee: "You're gonna miss me 'cause the next guy coming, he's a *Bad* Man."

596

An emotional grimness followed, ineluctably. At dinner that weekend, Tyler broke the prevailing silence by demanding of Johanna, "All right, I give up. What's wrong?"

"Nothing. And I wish you wouldn't do that."

"Do what? What'd I do? You're the one who's acting like we're inside a fallout shelter waiting to crawl out and look at the debris!" Johanna just shook her head in disagreement.

"If I don't chirp like a bird, you take my temperature every two minutes."

"Do I do that?"

"Yes," she said, turning to her salad.

"Well, I do it because I want you to be happy. I care. You know?"

"I wish you wouldn't," she said.

"Care?"

"Tyler. Don't you think I'd tell you if I wasn't happy?"

"Loudly—except when you do it quietly."

"If I wanted to tell you something, I'd tell you."

"Like taking dancing classes."

"I do it for the exercise, the same way you play ball. And because it's fun."

"That's what Lesley Zermatt said. Only in her case it was because it was cheaper than divorce."

"I'm not Lesley Zermatt," Johanna said, getting exasperated. "And I *am* divorced. Believe me, everything's cheaper."

"What's that supposed to mean?"

"Tyler, don't *do* this!" She shook her head, frustrated, with lowered eyes. "Exactly how long do you think I'd stay in a place like this if I wasn't happy—in some important way?"

He reached across the table to tilt her chin up, asking, "But?" She just shook her head again. "No, come on," he insisted. "Talk to me."

She seemed almost ashamed, embarrassed as she spoke. "Just understand that—understand that it's not so easy for me. You have your—you have all the things you want around you, in easy reach."

"And you?" he asked gingerly, watching her watch her silverware.

597

"You're lucky. Things come to you."

"Great things! The war. Gila. A job I hate, to do one I want. It's easy to make a choice when you've got none. You're the lucky one, Johanna. You've got the whole world open to you—take a bite. Nobody's forcing you to make choices and compromises."

"You don't make choices, really," she replied, looking up at him, her eyes like two telescopes peering beyond his head. "You avoid them."

"Hey, you can cut the moral high horse, too. You weren't there and you didn't see. You didn't have to choose. Yeah, you've had a lot of rough stuff happen to you, but it's not like it's off the charts. We've all been through some bad shit. And it's not as if you went looking for it—it found you, just like it found the rest of us. And if I'm not enough of a moral hero for you, fuck you, run off with Ralph Nader or something, because all I know is every time I did have a choice I took you, at whatever cost, and I'm still paying for it."

He stopped for a moment, almost panting. "So don't go push that crap with me. What'd you ever do? All right, you got beat up and raped. And you got your feelings hurt like everyone else with Bobby. Well, I got fucked over, too, royal, and mine wasn't any fun either. And half the time it was because I felt something about you. As far as I'm concerned, I don't give a shit about the rest of it anymore, not politics, not my job, not the whole fucking world—just you—when you let me."

"I'm sorry," she whispered. "Really."

"You know what it is? Time perspective. Everything's the end of the world to you. OK, maybe you feel like you're living a postponed life. So do I. We are. I've lost two years—but it's going to take some more time, so let's have a little fun while we're about it." He slumped grumpily, then looked up at her, mugging a funny face to chase their seriousness. As she began to reply, he picked up his water glass and slowly turned it upside down in his lap, without changing his expression. Nor did she crack a smile.

Too many things had happened in too short a time for her to integrate, so despite her initial flush of enthusiasm in Ithaca, she had become subdued except for outbursts of diversionary play. She considered it a time of dry dock to scrape her barnacles, for she was still working things out in her mind, things more than a year old.

Still, she was willing to give this every effort because she felt something undefinable about him, something about the very fitness of their being together, and because the economics of her life had been refined to an equation where the risk of laying down roots was a better gamble than the caution of surrendering to her doubts. It was an inverted notion, a paradox that made her fitful, for as Tyler understood, her life was becoming one of infinite postponements, with each new day a further postponement. She was not yet the self she wanted to be. But each possible decision meant a backward step, if she even knew what she wanted to step toward. Only aging was getting closer. Her life thus far seemed a function of the men she was with.

And so she lost herself in details. As much as she was scared of putting down roots, she became intimately absorbed in the process of doing so, embracing their apartment as though it were a lover, decorating it with an erotic involvement with its walls and space, caressing each corner with concern, exploring its forgotten and neglected crannies, seams, joints, as though they were the toes and elbows and eyelids of a paramour, adopting the strategies of a rapist to overcome her reluctance. For it was day-to-day living, as she fell deeper into that pattern, that made her itch. She would wake up some days and wonder why she was next to this person in this place, look across a table and wonder who he was and how she'd gotten there. It seemed to her at those times that she'd fallen asleep not hours before the night before, but years before in some other place.

As for Tyler's feelings toward her, they were unchanged. Ignorant of time and season, he could find a bright October in her November, see hazy aureoles where she saw cold pale light. And one Sunday morning, she heard him stir next to her in their bed. The sun rays coming through the windows carried bursts of autumn from the trees outside, tossing rainbows lapped by shadows on the wall. He sat up marveling at the lacy gold that fell upon them, hoping that his voice would wake her in pitch with the day. "My God," he said. "My sweet God."

She lay there, halfway in and out of sleep, lost among a jumble of quilts and sheets and comforters, down-stuffed pillows and ruffly things. And he turned, delighted, to watch her sleep, as though finding himself in her bed for the first time.

He pulled back the bedding a little to admire her before smoothing it out over her again, and she shifted, but did not waken. Indeed, as he watched her face, a dreamy untroubled air came across her, as if she knew he was watching. She made a purring noise of contentment at some inner thoughts, and her light, fine eyebrows raised in appreciation of her visions; then she purred again as Tyler stroked her hair. "A cat," he said. "I live with a cat."

Her hair seemed innocent of gravity, whose laws, like other worldly constraints, were not made for cats or her. It spun out of her scalp like the unbridled product of dreams within, taking a willfully unique course to her shoulders, moving here and there by urges of its own heart's pleasure, downy and self-possessed, in this light dappled with the color of peaches and apricots, lighter than her normal shade. Her shoulders had something of peach in them, too, more so than her face, where old suntan, new sunburn, and yesterday's smudged makeup created a funny archipelago of reds and tans and saffrons on her cheeks and nose. Her shoulders had a uniform tone, and his hand slipped from her hair with trembling fingers, afraid now to disturb her, but unable to hold back from petting her, for her skin was so custard-smooth as she slept, and soft, though firmed with tapered swimmer's muscles beneath. She seemed liquidy, a warm glass mobile to him, in bed beside him. Nor did she wake as he ran his hand lightly over her shoulders and traced the route down her side to her back. He did so with the simple wonder of a child running its fingers across a cello. The angles were so gentle, but the changes brought by each so fundamental, a G clef's outline, or a pear's. And there were so many surprises, from the rillet between her neck and shoulders, to the rivulet of her spine, the freckles he had never noticed and the twin dimples, like buttons on a mattress, just beside her tailbone. His hand waved on her form and except that she was visible it might have been floating in a breeze, and he on some raft. "You're not a cat," he said. "You're music." She shifted then, rolling her shoulders, twisting herself around herself, her trace smile broadening into a grin as she stretched languorously to find him on one elbow raptly gazing at her.

Scrunching her face up further as she opened her eyes, she turned on her side and arched her back, her breasts pointing toward Tyler and the sunlight. "Don't aim 'em unless you mean to use 'em," he cautioned. And she squinted her eyes shut with a little-girl giggle, only to open one eye and in a sleepy way ask, "What're you doing?"

"Watching you," he murmured.

"What're you thinking?" in a whispery singsong.

His easy smile fell away, replaced by a self-consciousness, as he replied, "I was thinking what a privilege it is to be here."

"Silly," she said, laying her arms over his shoulders to squeeze his neck with her elbows. "Silly, you live here."

In the middle of November, as though Nature were regarding the grim trends outside and conserving good cheer, came news of Willie. Not bad news at all. Rather astounding.

Willie wrote that he had been "R&Ring at Uncle Sam's expense" for a few weeks, "watching my extra belly button take root. The docs at Long Binh also found a hernia which they patched up free. I'd never have known." He said he'd demanded a local anesthetic, as "nobody fools with my best parts without me keeping one eye open." They had him in a constricting set of harnesses while he was hospitalized " 'cause they said fixing the ribs was like trying to glue moving parts together in a hurricane." His extra belly button "would make a nice flower vase." His only complaint was: "As soon as I got well enough to trot around they put me to mopping floors." Otherwise he was gaining strength.

His lung had been punctured, and the internal bleeding was serious, but his ribs hurt more and "only when I tried to grab a nurse."

Timmy Franks, whom Tyler had never heard of until this last series of letters, would keep his leg "after coming within an inch of not." Willie also said Timmy

should be writing novels. I had to read over this after-action report he wrote for concurrence and such, and our CO Merz polished it up about 15 percent into Army talk. I thought there may be more to it than that when I got visited by a stream of higher types and really grilled about the whole op. Now I hear there's going to be a hearing board, which means some people are gonna wear tin badges. (Or go to jail.)

It turns out that while we were out looking for those jerks the base camp took one class-A pounding from everythefuckbody who wasn't on our side, it's supposed. If we stayed home maybe we wouldn't have made it to laugh about it all now. Who knows?

Now, this General is of exactly no use to anyone, least of all himself. They'll pension him off and add expenses. His wife'll love it and maybe visit him at the Green Dragon Nursing Home on alternate Flag Days if she's not too busy taking yoga lessons and driving her Mercedes. The pilot might get a job as a traffic sign, I don't know. Otherwise he just smells and that's all. The guy with the leg lost it. He had pneumonia and bad rot, too, I hear. They're spending a lotta bucks on rehab types to tell him how fortunate he is to be alive. I haven't been asked my opinion on that. I slipped a nurse a couple of million piasters to blow him, but she took a gander and a rain check. She makes a cozy living that way when she's up to it. Got my investment back with interest: thought I was such a swell fellow for doing that for a buddy she did me gratis. Two other guys tried it and got sent back to the field. Now she doesn't talk to me anymore, because she thinks I told. It's just that if you do that kind of thing in the ward pretending you're changing bandages, somebody's gonna suspect—they keep a careful inventory on bandages. (Show the clean parts of this to Mom and Dad.)

Between Timmy Franks's pathological imagination, the simple gratitude of the door gunner, and the fact that General Loudermilk had had more information in his head than was on the craft, with great friends in Washington—and the fact that Willie, Franks, and the others were said to have volunteered for Merz's mission —"everyone gets to take home a little piece of silver or bronze." Everyone on the helicopter won the Bronze Star and everyone in Willie's patrol won Purple Hearts and Silver Stars. "They're pretty lax about these things," Willie admitted. "And I don't think they should be encouraging people to save Generals if they ever want to end this thing. Of course, this guy's no longer any help to anybody, so maybe that's why we got it." Both units received Presidential Unit Citations for the action, and Loudermilk himself was awarded the Distinguished Service Medal.

The initial lie was that they volunteered. Merz had not wanted to be caught having sent so few people out on the mission. Any time less than a hundred people went anywhere, whether to search, destroy, or buy dope, if anyone got wounded, the reports read, "Action embarked upon by individual initiative."

Only General Loudermilk had actually volunteered, and that was only to save his ass. He was on his way to check out a monumental fuck-up, for which he was responsible and for which he needed to assemble a full and complete cover story. A Special Forces and Marine position under harassment had called for help. Loudermilk's command relayed incorrect coordinates to Naval Artillery and the shells erupted through the low-hanging clouds onto the beleaguered outpost. The doubly besieged troops radioed frantically for more support. So B-52s picked up the faulty coordinates and flew above the weather in a risky operation. Help came when it was called. It came and came from every branch of service, an all-service show, until it killed them all. The totals weren't tabulated, but over two hundred troops —a hundred American, the others ARVN, half of whom, it was estimated, were loyal—were annihilated.

A friendly village was erased. General Loudermilk's condition closed the accounts, made it a self-suturing wound, and gave the command a better story to put out.

Her eyes told things about her she would not herself reveal. "There's nothing to tell," Johanna answered every time Tyler asked. "Please stop. It makes me feel creepy."

"You're a funny lady," he would sigh. "Strange."

"You're a nice man."

In New York City at Thanksgiving, despite the Bowen family's and Tyler's friends' raucous celebrations, when he and Johanna were alone together they were halting, quiet.

One evening they went to the theater and, while walking from their parking spot they passed a doorway where an old black was being tormented by a young Puerto Rican. In the violet night the old man's face was a canyon of lines and scars, gold teeth and warts; each point and stratum the sum of a moment's or a lifetime's agony. They watched the scene and hurried past, ready to jump back if it spread beyond its borders to engulf them. Others paid no heed, airline passengers feigning confidence despite the turbulence of their vessel. Johanna grabbed Tyler's arm when the young man burst past them clutching the bottle that had belonged to the old man, who lay fetal in the doorway holding an empty paper bag.

All night, she kept bringing up the sight, as though, Tyler thought, it was one of those things she feared might be her own fate. "Why did he have to steal a bottle from a drunk?" she kept asking.

"Maybe he was thirsty. It's a lot easier than knocking over a liquor store. You know, you've got to be careful about drawing conclusions. Last year there was this guy who found two teeth and thought he had the Missing Link. Till he dug a little deeper and came up with a Good Humor wrapper." That wouldn't do for her, so he tried another. "Maybe the kid was trapped. I mean it. At least the blacks can move white guilt, ooze it out like pus. The Puerto Ricans don't even have that. They weren't dragged over in irons. They came over for the scraps, everyone thinks—and they resent it. They get it coming and going. They're not black or white. They're just a Latin Polish joke: sixteen to a car in undershirts on Bruckner Boulevard on the Fourth of July or something."

"That's terrible," she scolded.

"It's also true. While you're at it, I'll show you some good old WASPS to pity: all those snowy-white nymphettes paying fifty bucks for fifty minutes' company. If they had a little color, they could splurge it on some Red Lightnin' and keep the change." She looked at him hard, not knowing what to think.

When they returned to the car, she remembered the last time she'd been on that street. It was when they were in New York campaigning for Robert Kennedy. They'd taken a rare lunch break, "for medical reasons," they'd both insisted. "If I don't get out of here for a couple of hours I'm going to use the window," he had said, and so they had a parkside lunch and just forgot the campaign and the world for a few hours. They walked down this street singing rock songs and songs from Broadway musicals, believing them, standing on a streetcorner crooning to each other, waiting for the light to change. When their song ended, a woman asked them, "Are you two actors?"

In early December, a representative of the National Security Agency came to Tyler Bowen's office to tell him his schedule for the coming year. They wanted him to spend a few evenings tutoring a group of semiliterate National Guardsmen in Binghamton bound for Fort McClellan's Military Chemistry School. The man also told him that he would be required in Washington, D.C., for the summer at the NSA seminars there. "All summer?" Tyler asked. The man nodded. Then the man shuffled his feet and wondered if Bowen wouldn't like to get a better deal by compiling information about campus radical groups and potential troublemakers.

"You got a title number for the U.S. Code section I'm violating when I throw your ass the hell out of here?"

The NSA man left with unruffled aplomb.

Later that week, another letter came from Willie, this time slightly crazed: ". . . Gonna be home soon now, so watch your ass. I'm all patched up and pretty again and I even spooked them into an early out by threatening to extend. I'm gonna take the long way home so I can see the place before we do to it what we've done here.

"And why have they stopped trying to kill me? Politics.

"See, it's that and promotion and a lot of other things—and I'm yet to win lasting friendships among the command over here—but!!!!—Franks and I are getting set up, sent up, put up and over—for the Whole Thing, Babe. The Whole Thing. They want heroes bad enough to invent them."

Brigade sent back the citation forms with several corrections and reconvened the review board, who added to their previous findings that Willie's band had "braved intense fire and shelling," "continued in the face of sure and certain sacrifice," and "repeatedly spurned opportunities to cut their losses." They "engaged enemy positions on their own recognizance," according to Brigade's corrections, "destroyed a critical mortar and machine gun emplacement, suffering severe wounds and several fatalities during said assault." And so on. Brigade moved the site of the first two deaths—the patrol members carrying the wounded door gunner —to the hill assault, and depreciated Loudermilk's estate in a manner that would do a tax accountant proud. Only, they had the mine working and Willie Bowen recklessly interposing himself between the General and its rough manner.

The mortar emplacement, which had been the annoyance to the Special Forces outpost, was dubbed "the key impediment to the success of Operation Grand Old Opry," which operation had never been heard of before, and hasn't since.

All this was originally contrived to churn out a little publicity on the fortitude and dedication of the fighting man, but red tape got stuck in the machine's offswitch. So Brigade got the message and continued to append phrases like "enterprise and intrepidity" where "they had no choice" would have served. An unrecognizable tale emerged when all the review boards and revised reports were finished: one report told of how the embattled men struggled to "save a pilot, his crew, and a general staff officer being sought with supreme vigor for capture and interrogation by a cruel and vicious enemy."

Again it came back, this time from Da Nang, tagged "NMI"—"Needs More Information." Division and Brigade had run out of ways to juice up the story, but Da Nang's Eat-Me-After-Reading note explained how very much someone in Very High Authority cared to have as many high decorations handed out by year's end as possible. Back to work.

By this point, all hands agreed that the level of horseshit on the reports had reached Augean Stables depth. But still they strove. A further delay arose because several files were absent without leave from Personnel. Further inquiry demanded to know why the devil W. C. Bowen was still in-country at that late date, his tour having expired some time earlier. Battalion coolly responded that he'd extended, and sent two envoys to chat with Willie about it.

"In it goes and now its up to the gods," he wrote just before he was released from the hospital in Guam. "They've added the Whole Act. Cross my heart and hope to lie: 'Conspicuous Gallantry.' I *like* the sound of that. 'At certain risk of life in action with the enemy' and—you realize this is all just different ways of saying what they've said before, and no more true— tell you something about inflation?—oh, here's a familiar phrase—you'd better sit if you're not already—it's on account of that 'volunteering' we didn't do: 'By personal actions . . . above and beyond the call of duty.' At least they spelled our names right.

"I suspect you're 70% happy and 30% hope I get hit by a truck. Well—just do me a favor and wait till I get home before you start telling the world what a crock it is. Besides, it's still up to some people back in the Good Old U.S. of A. I told you war was a good investment. Ha, ha, only fooling. It stinks like always.

"My friend Timmy says there's an old Russian proverb—how the hell he knows, he won't say—that goes, 'Truth can be seen even when she is lying down in the kasha fields.' I sure hope she hangs low in the rice for a while till I get home.

"Best laugh: it happened on one of *Their* days. I should have been rotated *out* by all rights. Mox Nix—just like the election, eh? Any way you slice it. That's all there is, there ain't no more."

At Christmas, Tyler flew down to New York early and left Johanna the car in Ithaca. The plan was that she would leave the car at the airport in Syracuse and fly home to Phoenix, where Tyler would join her at New Year's for a week of skiing in Utah before they returned to Ithaca, via the Syracuse airport. Tyler was especially proud of the logistics. "Why don't I just meet you in Salt Lake," she said.

"Who are you ashamed of, me or your family?"

"It's just going to be so rushed, and it's so—unnecessary."

"You've met my friends. I'd like to meet the storied Mrs. P. and your brothers. I've already met your California friends. And Warren."

When she got out to Phoenix, she called Tyler and suggested they skip the skiing trip, that she'd meet him back in Ithaca after New Year's.

On Christmas Day 1968, the World's Biggest Secret went up in smoke, and the security of Gila Compound, the National Labs, and all it housed was in jeopardy. It was an accident. The first thing anyone noticed of it was that the entire side of Gila Mountain was in flames. A ball of fire rolled off the mountainside, but didn't penetrate the surface. The Secret burned, but it was not consumed. The fire hovered as a gloss, carefully etching the shape of the sign on the side of Gila Mountain. Nothing else besides that configuration was combustible, and the logo rolled on the thermal currents off the edifice, into the sky, a gargantuan smoke ring in black and orange flame, drifting north on the airstream, toward Tucson and divulgence. Against a stunning cerulean sky it spelled out in brilliant relief, "GEMS—TOP SECRET."

On the other side of the mountain, the order of the day was extreme panic. Labs were evacuated, experiments dismantled, sera, animals, vials secured as per the "Fire Scuttle Posture" bill posted at each station, part of what was called the AESOP Table—the regulations for Accidental Emergency Situation Operating Procedure. Heavy labor crews donned fire-control garb and manned their stations, while the important personnel huddled in shelters with goats and pigs and other clean control animals. The SOP was clear for emergencies: "The substitutes will go down with the ship."

The fire swept into Gila Historical Forest, while fire-fighting crews raced around helplessly. Over the main section of the holocaust, two helicopters burst out of the haze like ghost riders. A mighty cheer went up from the smoke-blackened men below, expecting a gutsy display of fire-jumping Rangers. The first of the two turned out to be a rented chopper packed with newsmen from Tucson and Phoenix papers. The second carried electronic media. The two whirlybirds swung around in daredevil positions, jockeying for camera angles like dancers on "Dick Clark's American Bandstand," until jet fighters without markings arrived. A hair-raising, ersatz dog fight concluded with the helicopters limping off sullenly, while the forest burned to the ground. Luckily, the fire stopped short of the Compound's labs.

The next day's papers screamed:

FREAK FIRE RAGES AT GILA;
ANCIENT STAND OF TREES SAVED

This headline almost ran, but was killed by consent of editors and publishers:

FLAMES SWEEP HISTORICAL TREES;
LOSS 'PRICELESS, TOTAL'
IN ALL-DAY BLAZE

This was also killed:

SAY FIREFIGHTERS HELPLESS AS FOREST BURNS
(pix, bckgd inside)

This ran in all editions:

THOUSANDS REPORT SIGHTING
STRANGE DISC IN SKY,
FLOOD POLICE WITH CALLS;
'NONSENSE': KITT PEAK

Susan Carver, Director of Gila Compound's Office of Public Information, handled the dissemination of authorized accounts from her command post behind her desk, which, with her sofa, did double duty that week, serving also to barricade her door; she wore her rug like a shawl. She pulled in every favor due her from news executives around the state, but most would only promise her that they'd sit on what they had as long as they could: until the competition went with it —"Then it's anybody's, Susie." But when she called Maureen Poulson in Phoenix, to further ice the compliant KPTV cake, Maureen would only say, "I'll see what I can do. Remember, I'm only one vote, and I'm on the T and R side, not news or programming." What Maureen could and did do was: march into her station president's office and say, "Jesse, I've just screened the half-hour we're holding, and it's time to cut these people loose. Hal tells me the news department can pull together another seventeen minutes by tonight. I can sell what you can't fill, Jesse, and I can sell it at premium rates over the phone in an hour. The market is ready for it. The wires'll pick it up, network will—and there hasn't been an affiliate that's had something like this in a year!"

Susan Carver hissed and sputtered, but to no use. And though Maureen would never admit it, a small part of her fervor on the question, besides its commercial potential, was that she considered it a sort of Christmas gift for her daughter.

On the KPTV broadcast, an aide to the Arizona Governor said, "When they're through fricasseeing our precious Arizona heritage they will probably declare themselves no longer interested in the area and return it to the Indians. It's their favorite sport in Washington—the ever-popular sacking of other people's wilderness." Another aide, however, denied those were the Governor's own thoughts. Susan Carver's sole video appearance was a brief but Churchillian recitation of a statement by one of Arizona's U.S. Senators, dictated to her aide over the phone, which she read before she had a chance to review it: "Well of course now," the Senator had declared, "we regret and mourn the loss of those trees. Yessir. No one is a greater champion of Arizona's wilderness than I. I'm on the subcommittee, it might not be known, which had the original jurisdiction over that hunk of woods. Yes, that's right; you didn't know that, did you? And I don't mind telling you we were convinced, and I'm sure the good people of Arizona who don't have cynical hearts would be too if all the facts could be made available to them, of the compelling reasons for off-laying that responsibility to another agency. No, I'm sorry, I don't think I want to get into that just now; I'm doing you people enough of a favor. But I can say I'm also on the subcommittee which, as it happens, oversees that very agency, and while I really don't want this to get so involved, there's no question but it's a tough and thankless job that Gila Compound does down there, no doubt about it; and those trees, for my money, if you want to look at it practically, are but a small price to pay for our freedom. . . . Yes, thank you. You too, Merry Christmas yourself." She was pleased to have the statement, in the main, but ultimately felt required to call it, despite a throat-clearing attempt to swallow the word, somewhat "schizzy." She didn't like having to sandbag a congressional friend, yet there was no other way to hold on to her ebbing credibility and the "brush fire" story. She was convinced, and historically correct, that if denied often enough the thing would still resolve itself into a dew: truth crushed to earth will slink out of sight.

The Churchillian manner of her reading was in the way her gullet jiggled, and her eyes betrayed a softness for brandy.

Security had its hands full fighting tourists who thought they'd seen an apparition promising GEMS there. It made sense: as schoolchildren they'd learned the state motto, *Ditat Deus,* God Enriches. They came with picks and shovels and cameras and left without them, while Susan Carver, in a grim prospect, mined deeper and deeper to find out what had happened, the better to say "Nothing happened."

But she would never say it to Maureen Poulson. Not that she wouldn't lie to her. Only that she resolved to speak no further to her, nor anyone at KPTV. They were flush from the success of their embargo-busting. They were breaking down doors to get it all, though they never would. They were one step behind, and sometimes ahead of Susan Carver's own investigations. Their leaks were coming from somewhere in Central Security's own office, but they were attributed to an unknown source "close to the Gila Administration," thought to be someone's unhappy wife or dependant. Central Security was happy with that assumption and did not attempt to set anyone straight. And once the real story was pieced together, they did manage to keep the lid on fairly tight.

It was all very simple. Someone had gotten the bright idea to strip the paint off the mountain with a laser weapon under development, to win favor by saving Gila all that expensive painting. What the laser operator didn't know was that the area was thick with underground electronic sensors, waiting ostensibly to detect information poachers, but instead usually registering the tread of trespassing teenagers who liked to fornicate upon the mountainside. The sensors picked up impedance from the laser pulse and sent a charge surging through the old arc-light circuits. The carbon arc lamps blew sky high and one flipped over the mountainside to set the forest burning, all of which escaped the notice of the dreadnought laser operator who sharpened his aim and bore down on the sign's first letters.

At Gila, as elsewhere, the men of pure research and the engineers enjoyed a cordial chilliness between them; similarly, the physicists, biologists, and chemists spoke through seconds. So which of them knew that the Biology people had been experimenting with a polymer-digesting pest on the paint, and the Chemistry people with a rain-resistant overcoat of olive green? The bugs and paint enjoyed each other's company immensely; the bugs spent two weeks excreting a long-chain polysaccharide that had exciting possibilities as an incendiary weapon. This would have gone entirely unnoticed, save for the serendipity of research, when a man ventured out one bright afternoon with a laser. A few high-level nucleic acids were also found in the debris.

Johanna watched the unfurling of this story in disbelief and regret: that she could not have broken it herself a year before, that she could not contribute to it now, and that there was doubtless more behind this security hysteria than a stupid decalcomania on a mountainside, which no one seemed to think about.

She didn't call Tyler Bowen all that week, and finally he called her the day before he was to fly out. She again told him not to come. He said he'd talk to her about it when he got there.

They exchanged Christmas presents New Year's Eve. He'd brought her a silver-plated cactus burr, which he swore was the one he sat on the first night they met. "Well, it's like it, anyway," he admitted. "The other one died."

She gave him a lovingly calligraphed version of a poem she'd written, dedicated to him; and a little circus of odds and ends she had assembled in a shoebox: feathers, shells, and rocks, some glitter and a piece of bark, angel hair and agate. "Aren't you going to say it looks like the inside of my head?" she asked.

"No," he answered with studied surprise.

"Why did you come out?"

"To see you."

"Why?"

"To keep you."

"Why?"

"Because I love you."

"Why?" she asked again.

He stood up and walked with that Christmas box to the corner of the room. "If I could give you reasons, Johanna, it would be an investment. It's not—it's pathological."

"But you ought to have *some*."

"If I had some, I'd lack some. What are you trying to do? If there were reasons, you could take them away —by acting like you're acting and like you've been acting. You're right: after a while I suppose I'd say,

613

'Hey! This isn't worth it, pal.' And you know what? I can't think of a single reason why I should—but I do. So what can I tell you?"

"I don't understand that," Johanna said.

"All I know is what I feel. That's all anybody knows. You figure out why from that. Don't ask me to explain why."

All through the conversation, he played with her present, peering in it as though for clues, finding none.

The next day, they drove out into the desert, aimlessly rambling around. He felt as though she was a hair-triggered bomb, and every time he tried to touch the workings, she hissed dangerously. He was beginning to resent the very circumspection required. But as long as he did not express direct concern, she was happy and open. Just, there had come up this distance, closer than which he was not permitted.

Finally, she said, "I don't want to go back."

"I don't suppose this is a sudden decision. I've been asking you for weeks what's wrong."

"It's not—oh, I don't know, maybe we started out wrong, out of, y'know, need, rather than—"

"Bullshit! Who cares how it started, for Christ's sake? It started. Jesus! Every foundation in the world is sunk in glop—so *what?*"

"Tyler, don't."

"Don't what? Don't tell you the truth? I want you with—"

"Things have changed," she said.

"*Johanna,* we are people. You and me."

"We're not immune to the world."

"Oh, for Christ's—what are you? Warren?"

She took a deep breath, and exhaled slowly. "Things don't happen to you."

"What the hell are you raving about?"

"It's true, Tyler. You get by, you survive."

"So do you! This is really useless, you know?"

"You're not listening," she said.

"I'm listening. I just don't believe it." He trailed off, understanding too well. The discussion was being held on her turf, not just the desert, but the emotional geography only her mind knew. He was a stranger in both places, a guest. In frustration he scooped up some pebbles to play with, letting them slide off as he flipped them from palm to the back of his hand. "I don't know why, but I love you. I do. Doesn't that count for anything?"

"Please. That's not it."

"I can't read your mind, dammit. I can't do magic tricks—you've got to let me try."

"No."

"Why?"

Her face was blank of all expression. "It's been fine and wonderful—when we were on . . . holiday from reality."

"That's all? Haven't we had times?"

She smiled softly. "We've had times." But she was saying that she felt removed, that companionship, sex, even love was not strong enough for some burdens.

Again, the next day, he tried. "You saved my life, you know—You made me be who I want to be—you make me glad to find you in the morning. Won't you let me try, at least?"

She smiled. "And I like waking up with you."

"But? All the times I couldn't be there when you needed me—*now*—"

"That's not it, Tyler. You belong there. I belong here."

"Ah, this is crazy! What are we, salmon? You sound like a teenager."

"We're different."

"You're damn right! If I wanted another me, I'd buy a fucking mirror! And for all the scrambled eggs and applesauce under your hair—try to find somebody else who can figure out what you're up to. I'd say I'm pretty close."

"We take different cuts in the world. Maybe we should just leave good memories—"

"Johanna! This isn't a picture album! You're what's important to me—Look, I'll quit. I'll come out here. OK? Over. Settled."

"No. We'd be spending time trying to live up to one good moment once."

"Once!" He spluttered. "Absolutely wacky! No sense—"

"Just try to understand," she said. "Please?"

"Not when you're talking crazy—"

"Sometimes you just don't listen."

"I'll listen. You: make sense."

The words came before she knew their meaning. "We've come as close as we can, I—I just don't think we can come any closer. It would be nice—but it won't happen."

"I wish I had a tape recorder so you could hear yourself. Or so you could play it for a shrink, Johanna."

They went on like that for an hour, in substanceless code, shadow boxing, knowing that they were on opposite sides of something, but not what that something was, where it came from, or why it had been on the program, only that they were there to disagree about why they were there to disagree. And it had been on the program from the start.

Finally, he threw his hands up in surrender. "I'd like to take whoever sold you all this garbage and—" The fight had left his stomach. It was over. "And—ah, *shit*," he mumbled, "kick the dog of the world." Logic's pull was strong, a comfort in confusion, drawing him back to formal patterns, a useless language in this terrain. He could no longer follow her down the convoluted paths inside her. His maps were no use. None were, not his or any man's, anyone's. She drifted freely among her hunches and feelings. There was a place for these things inside her, which he could visit, but never really share. He admired those traits in her, the willingness to gamble a good stake for something better. It made her different from every other girl he'd known. To an extent, he had the trait himself in some situations; for a while with Johanna he'd had it enough to change his life. The cost to her he couldn't calculate.

She was an artist in his eyes, whose talent was her sensitivity to her insides, her ability to find a voice for her urges, or the daring to seek one. Her dues for that grand gift was a sense of incompletion. And the last thing he wanted was to make her shed it, even for himself. Even if that was what he thought the world required.

So they were two cowpokes on panting ponies, anxious to be off on new, diverse adventures, having last words while their mounts pawed the ground. He would not force her to mortgage the future to enshrine the past. "I goddam fell in love with you and stayed in love with you," he said. "And—that's all I have. Everything I have. But it doesn't dent it at all, does it? It doesn't slow the world a bit. Like everything we did last year. I'm getting my head bashed in for glory."

She said something then, so practiced and tuned that he took it for a quote from some book. "All that would be fine and just and elegant—despite the encouragement of romantics and poets—is under no ordination to be."

"Who said that, your father?"

"No."

"It sounds like you're giving dictation to a stone-cutter."

"It's true. It might not be what history had in mind."

"Oh, how the hell do you know?"

"I don't, that's half the problem. You didn't listen. It doesn't matter what we want to believe."

She drove him to the airport that night, to catch a flight to Salt Lake City. He'd go skiing alone, and then go back to Ithaca to send her those things she'd left, and make her excuses. She leaned against him, calm, relaxed, and whispered at the gate, "I love you, Tyler Bowen."

"But?"

"But—we'll get older." She looked up at him, nearly serene, so untroubled, and asked, "Would you still be my friend?"

Unwilling to lie, he shook his head. "Not just now. It's too much for me. No."

On the short flight to Salt Lake, he thought of childish things, as his mind scrambled around dry recesses for a sense-making metaphor. He thought of the Man of Steel, called Superman; how when he was just a Superboy he wandered through a solar system with a red sun at its core. He fell weak under its rays, for he was super only under the yellow sun of his adopted Earth. Poisoned, he crashed upon a strange planet of that sun and might have died there in its russet glow, senselessly and unmourned. But a youngster who was gifted with great powers on that world found the crippled champion, was drawn to him by a compulsion of consanguinity, and nursed him back to health.

Together, they frolicked like young gods among the stars, cavorting between the heavenly hazards until it was time for them to return to their native worlds and fulfill their appointed careers of good works. Their destinies beckoned.

The following spring, on Earth, Superboy's new friend paid him a visit in Smallville, U.S.A. But the atmosphere and yellow sun of Earth were likewise peril to Superboy's pal. Each one's home was lethal to the other. Where each might thrive the other would perish. Only in the great voids could their love, and it was love as only the super and the crippled know love, be realized.

In sadness, they flew apart. And over time, their friendship withered to mere memory; dead, according to the comic book writers, "by a jest of circumstance, cruel fate, and the curse of a foreign sun."

He thought about the last time he had left Arizona, scared and rowdy and full of passion, ready to tackle the world come spring. Romantics, they found the leaving good, knowing what was on the far side. But if he'd known how much those battles would take from them . . . well, he thought, it's not the kind of thing you can predict.

Now she'd slipped past him, in search of something he was sightless for, past his power to do anything, untouched by his suit. He needed her, but she needed herself more. Would she defy tracking down in some months' time? Would she be changed, or work things out in ways that must exclude him? Would she need him, want him, or permit herself to? Would she tend the memories? Would he have the energy for the pursuit, the heart?

Before Tyler had met her, Baron Zermatt had joked that they of the "Gila Monsters" carried "Pox Americana." And when he'd first encountered Gila's true nature, Tyler had foul dreams of being kidnapped by the law's own trusted servants; of deadly "beauty marks"; of a wife dying in childbirth, killed by his love. Was he now passing poison seeds, killing with his kisses? His class had been raised to believe that their birthright was effectiveness and access to power. And then they'd learned of violent impotence. Yet, so many were still convinced of Tyler Bowen's good purpose that he wondered: did not those programs that selected him, found him from among all others, know the stuff of greatness when they saw it? Or would his ego, weaned on corrupt nonsense, move, as every recent monster had, to lock the whole world from its dreams?

And then he had another drink and thought about the goats and losers and devils and suckers: Tracy Stallard, serving number sixty-one to Roger Maris; Dale Mitchell, striking out to end Don Larsen's perfect Series game; Ellie Howard, grounding out to Reese in '55 to hand the Bums their first World Flag—the chumps who made the bums look good by inadvertence. There was Tony Kubek, fielding a hot grounder with his throat; Joe Pepitone, choking away at first; Branca, forking over a pennant; Floyd Patterson, outpsyching himself with Ingo and Sonny. Something of the world was handed over every time when heroes missed the bus. The hard-luck guys, the big losers, boneheads and the turkeys. The ones the leaky, rotting ship went down beneath, whom fate made fools of: Marv Throneberry, Francis Gary Powers, Charles Van Doren. The kind of guy you shook your head about and said, "Poor bastard."

At Christmas 1968, Lyndon B. Johnson, thirty-sixth President of the United States, pardoned several federal convicts of compelling feloniousness. By these greetings he conferred on them a gross immunity from judicial process for past crimes against the United States and its people. This was an honored tradition, culled from Kings and Pontiffs. Feasts were always celebrated by imperial gestures. The year past he'd cut back bombing on one and halted it completely for another. It would prove to be a holiday tradition soon, to bomb or not to.

Shortly after Christmas, Lyndon Johnson also laid a blessing upon, among others, Timothy Franks and William C. Bowen, United States Army. He completed the actions necessary to bestow on them, "in the name of the Congress of the United States," the Medal of

Honor. No higher award exists for valorous service to country.

He decided to leave the privilege of actual decoration, however, to his successor, just as he had, involuntarily, bequeathed him the naming of a new Chief Justice: as a courtesy *du régime*.

An Assistant-to-the-President explained, off the record, to an inquiring newsman, that "it's only fair" to leave this small ceremony, "in its utter meaninglessness," to the new man. "After all," the aid said, "he's left the son-of-a-bitch the war."

Part IV

The
New
Calculus:
1969—1970

THE MAN OUTSIDE THE WHITE HOUSE LED a chilly line of picketers in the shadow of gigantic implements of process, the stands and loudspeakers still up from the Inaugural Parade. They marched in a constricted loop. "There is no justice in the world," he declared of some peculiar and neglected cause.

"Damn little, anyway," Willie Bowen admitted, passing by, somewhat giddy, heading for the East Wing entrance with his family. The evidence of this was strong. Willie had thrived at war: gained two inches and twenty pounds—mostly in his shoulders—and all of this, despite ages of dire counsel, on tacos and watery Cokes. "Too bad you didn't gain a little weight up here," his proud sister said, tapping his skull.

The only price Willie had paid was in injuries that would prevent his becoming an object of fevered bidding among football powers. Instead, he would humor the course attendance requirements of Stanford University, promising only to demonstrate his academic maturity at a summer session, to forgive them their trespasses, and not to blow up anyone above the rank of Associate Professor.

After some unfortunate stories in *Time* magazine the previous year, the Army had wised slightly up and, as SOP, flagged the files of anyone considered for a high decoration. Such daring as won citations for wanton courage was likely chronically self-destructive, and they needed live PR men more than tragic ironies. So the monster coughed twice, grumbled gassily, and passed Willie Bowen from the Army altogether. He rolled home after the New Year the wrong way 'round the world, arriving in a T-shirt and a World War II bombardier's jacket he'd swapped for in Amsterdam, with no more self-conscious ceremony than if he'd been in Bermuda for a week. "Hiya everybody!" he greeted his personal airport throng. Vlad Bowen rushed his son and kissed him on the lips, clutching him fiercely. Dumbstruck, Willie reached through his father's bearish embrace to pump his mother's hand like a Rotarian. "It's a good thing," his sister observed, uncontrollably glad, "they don't require mental tests to get out."

Though aware of the imperfections in his storied repute, even embarrassed by them, once Stateside he cooperated with the process of exploitation. His parents and the local press ate it up, in his estimation, "with a spoon." He did not go so far as to say anything good about the Asian conflict, only that "there's a lot of brave people over there. Some of them died. I was just lucky. Yes, I'm proud. No, I went because they sent me, because it was my fair share—of a bad deal that everybody got. No, I don't think I'd like to do it again, it wasn't fun the first time. Yes, I was in the Boy Scouts, well, the Cub Scouts, really. When I was little." In the pictures he was an orthodontist's pride. And with his family he journeyed to Washington, D.C., in the last week of January 1969, to smile for *The Big Picture* cameras, to show "the boys in the boonies," as Timmy Franks put it, "what happens if you eat all your rations, including the licorice Chuckles and the dried prunes, and shoot straight, if you know what I mean."

Both families were treated to VIP tours of Washington and were honored by all who received them, then given a private White House tour the morning of the decoration ceremony. Timmy and Willie laid out their clothes carefully the night before. "Where do you think you're going?" Tyler marveled. "The moon?" Both were given "Gratuitous Issue" new shoes, spit-shined to a high gloss by some anonymous supply clerk in the Pentagon Protocol Office. Willie cooperated further by shaving off a fungal growth of beard he'd begun. "Don't have to, you know," his brother chided him. "It's your party. It's appropriated."

"Their war," Willie said. He was standing in brand-new underwear, which he said was a gift from the

Secret Service. Tyler asked if he expected to be checked for wrinkles. "I dunno," Willie shrugged. "I mean, look, suppose they rode up and, you know, pinched. I could bolt into the guy and *Je-sus, kill* the fucker. I'm, y'know, dangerous that way."

"Promises, promises," Tyler laughed, messing up Willie's carefully parted hair. "For you, Slick, brushing your teeth is a tuxedo. You're so worried about killing people, how about starting off with a shower?" Willie turned on him with an aerosol bomb of shaving cream while Tyler wielded a tube of toothpaste like a dagger. They wrestled playfully and half-destroyed the hotel room. Though physically larger now, Willie said uncle. He could still not best his brother in a head-to-head on a good day, and this was his best day.

As they were shown around the Mansion, it was Vlad and Laura Bowen and their grandchildren who were most absorbed by the guide's narration. Mack and Tyler were more involved with teasing Willie, their glee incandescent. Mack's husband lagged behind, measuring the house for refurbishing to his tastes.

Willie, for his part, was intoxicated, partly from all this attention, a little from the Laotian Purple he and Timmy and Tyler had blown the night before, both honorees having solemnly vowed then to "whip it out on the guy"; but mostly from the imposing sense of place. This was special space, and he gazed around numbly, overwhelmed by sensations, caressing the walls with his eyes. It was not just the belly of the whale. It was so filled with sensuality, pulsing out in waves, so disorienting, stuffed with unimaginable potentials. It seemed like an immense vagina overladen, in its emptiness, with myth. He felt indecent, a trespasser of sorts, whose discomfort was far more than political. It was emotional, sexual, personal, total. He was of different tissue, unalterably apart.

They were led to the vast, gilded East Room where, twenty minutes before the ceremonies were to start, the seats were half-taken. Cockeyed rows slowly filled with reporters, come less to record the honor devolving on two families than to stand by in case the President did anything improbably bizarre: to report what he did if he didn't and assure people he didn't if he did. The seats, despite the absent President, were arranged as though iron filings in a lodestone's field of influence.

A lectern in front commanded this respect, the King's surrogate, flanked by the blue presidential flag and the American flag drooping from tawny staffs like two bored princelings.

Willie had no illusions of having fought for the cloth. Still, the flags' arrogant slouch was bothersome. These were damn privileged flags, he thought, as he and Tyler sat down some distance from their family. These flags never hung out at ballparks or hustled through a sales career alongside pennants and bunting. They weren't trampled underfoot, abused, ignored, and rained on at picnics and grand openings. They suffered no war, nor gale, nor dirty paws of children at summer camps: stains of blood and jelly didn't sully them. All they knew was royalty and honor. They were born to rank and station, well removed from democratic strife. They'd never be sewn on a hippie's pants seat or be washed in guerrilla theater, or fly from a Deputy's lawn. Until ceremonial cremation they'd be coddled, kissed when they scraped the floor, and spend their days as the podium's lapel pins.

"Hey, boy!" a voice from behind said, startling him. "How's it going?" Willie turned around to see his brother shaking hands with a toad-shaped man. "Some friend! Not even a phone call," Zermatt sighed. "Ah, you must be the boy of the hour, the justly famed Willie Bowen!"

"I must be."

"Still selling infected blankets to the Indians, Bar?" Tyler asked.

Zermatt beamed egregiously. "If you'd taken the trouble, you'd know. Internal Security. Justice."

"Why did I think Criminal?" Tyler laughed. "I suppose that means you can make certain crazy people sit up and bark."

"I told you," Zermatt said. "Good out of bad. Weren't for you-know-where it might've been Lands and Deeds."

Zermatt's job was a reward for efforts in the campaign. Specifically, that included hitting disgruntled

Democrats for over two hundred thousand dollars in contributions; Baron was discreetly glad for Tyler's political efforts, for it was in such that the disgruntlement was born. Baron had wanted to siphon this money to Las Vegas to be wagered on a Nixon victory. His plan was hatched when Nixon's lead in the polls was slipping in October. The Republicans' early cushion from Humphrey's Chicago curse began to erode as Nixon's personality metastasized in public. Zermatt's idea, deemed genius, was to use the money to push the betting odds back toward Nixon. This would tell bandwagon watchers where the "smart money" was going. Lonely voters, craving majority's comforts, would conclude Nixon was still The One. For the energy, if not the idea, Zermatt had won his post at Justice.

Zermatt poked Tyler's rib cage. "Go ahead, ignore the received political wisdom of the ages. See where it gets you. How do you like the suit?" he preened. "Matching cravat, custom-tailored."

Nodding, Tyler smirked. "Like your principles. Very handsome."

"The cream," Zermatt said, sitting back proudly, legs crossed, his arm around Tyler's chair, "rises. And truth will out."

"For all our sakes," Willie mumbled. "I hope it's slow."

"That was quite something you did out there," Zermatt said to Willie. "Quite."

"What?"

"You know: the whole thing."

"Not really," Willie demurred.

"Let's call it modesty, shall we?" he winked knowingly. "Remember, that piece of tin's better than bail money when you need it. 'Cause when the shooting stops they only know you from the medals."

Just as he was about to tell them of the benefits accruable, a white-gloved Marine usher came to escort Willie to the podium, where Timmy Franks already waited nervously. "If I'm not back in three days," Willie said, "send out the dogs—but not the Marines!" Zermatt grimaced and turned sideways, saying hushedly to Tyler, "It's not right to joke about the war. Not here. But believe me—we're going to stop it."

"Which? The jokes or the war?"

Zermatt's mask fell slightly and he nudged Tyler. "Can't have one without the other."

"Uh, speaking of absurd stories," Tyler said nonchalantly. "You still in the sack with Reigeluth—politically?"

"Jealousy is not your best mode, son. At least he stays in touch. He's a very bright guy. You ever read his thesis?"

"I heard about it for a week one night. All that shit about power relations. It's full of holes and the holes are full of jargon. Pragmatism gone amok."

"Ain't nothing succeeds like success, m'boy. I thought he laid it out pretty well, frankly. All that stuff about executive power being democracy's only effective weapon. Strafed it with Kennedy quotes even."

"Swell. Except he's wrong," Tyler said, scanning the press office hand-out on Willie.

"Yeah? Well, he's got a job here whenever he wants. You know what he did? He had that thing bound in leather and slipped it to Dick. I hear The Man nearly creamed. Read it, too. He loved it! I'll tell you, Warren knows something about self-promotion you don't, that's for sure. Wonderful stuff, really: 'A world in the balance every day—the last best—' "

"Laugh's best? If that shit's coming out of your ears next year, we'll know who to blame."

Baron smiled a Baron smile. "Come on, let's go fill in next to your folks."

"Listen . . ." Tyler stopped him, then shook his head. He wanted to ask if Warren had said anything about Johanna. Zermatt waited, but Tyler only clapped his shoulder, saying, "You're OK, Bar."

As they slid in next to Mack's children, Zermatt looked down the line and grinned greetings to all. Then Tyler squeezed his arm. "Where is she, Bar?"

"I don't know. Warren said she took off from Scottsdale and her mother called him."

"Didn't call me."

"What do I know?" Zermatt said. "Anyway, he says she was gone about two weeks, maybe. They even put

627

it through Missing Persons. And uh, well, she turned up."

"Where?"

Zermatt looked at him kindly. "Seattle."

"She all right?"

"I thought you knew."

Tyler shook his head. "No. No one told me. She OK?"

"I guess. She was hitched up with some guy in a rock band or something."

"Still?"

Zermatt said, "Split back down to Berkeley, by herself, I think."

"Getting quicker," Tyler snorted, heaving his shoulders as though from a chill. "Missing Persons, huh?" He put his arm around his nephew's chair back and tousled the little boy's hair, whispering, "Can you see all right? Want to sit on my lap?" The children were all straight upright, bouncing on their hands as the adults chattered in anticipation. Only their little wagging legs and craning necks, their constantly crossing and uncrossing feet showed any impatience. They wiggled some to keep their backsides from getting sore, but they did not whisper or giggle. Everything these children knew came from television, and so they instinctively suspected the entire affair was "a program." Their modified behavior was in the nature of a studio audience.

Back at the hotel, though, over breakfast, when their mother had explained the day's schedule of events to them, the youngest blandly asked, "When do they shoot him?"

Johanna had only been an official Missing Person for a week. When she finally called her home and Maureen Poulson told her how "absolutely frantic we've been," how she had even gone to the Police, Johanna's apology contained the slightest hint of amusement. She muttered something about enjoying the designation "Missing Person."

"You are less than funny, Johanna," Maureen rasped. "Totally irresponsible, and you don't give a damn about anyone but yourself. I'm coming up there."

"Don't," Johanna said. "Please."

"What are you going to do? How are you going to live?"

"That's what I'm trying to figure out."

"Do let the rest of us in on it—in your own sweet time."

"In my own sweet time," she repeated in a near-whisper. "Please. Don't be angry."

"How can I help it when you act so thoughtlessly?"

"I need you not to be. I'll make out."

"Johanna, darling. I love you. Let me take you home."

Johanna for a moment said nothing. Then: "I'll be all right. I think I know what I'm doing, now. I hope so." Then she rang off.

Into the East Room marched a VIP contingent from Congress. They entered through the Green Room along the south wall, having come from the State Dining Room where the reception buffet was being set up, through the Blue Room and Red Room, behind the velvet ropes that separated the accessed from the public. Earlier, some had been at a coffee-and-crullers briefing on domestic policy at the Executive Office Building, in the Indian Treaty Room on the fourth floor.

A Marine in dress blues called out their names. To Willie, on the podium, the Majority Leader, Mike Mansfield, looked like a scholarly Roman Senator, or just the man to play Sherlock Holmes in the *Congressional Follies;* Minority boss Hugh Scott's titular eminence was undermined by his beclouded Gildersleevian aspect. Carl Albert, Speaker, seemed chipmunkishly happy to be inside his tiny suit, and House Minority Leader Gerald Ford resembled a cuddly Newfoundland puppy, except his tongue wasn't hanging out. Then came a series of lesser legislative lights, the Senators and Congressmen who represented the Bowens and the Frankses, followed by some people from the Executive Branch and military who were unfamiliar to Willie, uniformly badger-faced but tanned and hale. Next came a crew-cut angular figure, whose entrance made Tyler's head snap, and sent Zermatt's elbow into Tyler's side:

General Armistead ("Buzz") Sheaffer, whose insulation from the news of half a decade had worked to his career advantage. It had enabled him to reach the seventh circle.

Zermatt hissed out of the side of his mouth, "Lucky bastard jumped ship before the fire. Straight to NSC."

"If he's here," Tyler whispered back, "your pal Captain Crazy can't be far behind." Zermatt sneered confidently. "Why not?" Tyler asked.

"He blew it on the fire. And, big news: we're shutting down Gila."

"Ladies and gentlemen," the head usher called, "the Vice-President of the United States." A loud shuffling of chairs and all rose. Spiro Agnew strode in, a double for Johnny Carson's shill Ed McMahon, waving cheerfully. Before they could sit, the band struck up "Hail to the Chief." And nothing happened.

"Where is he?" Tyler asked.

"He's still out there, maybe he'll get a station chief spot in a soft—"

"No, Nixon." Two Secret Service men, tasters of presidential porridge for treacherous lumps, entered to see if hostile fire came from the gallery. "You'd think he'd leave 'em at the gate. He's safe here." Zermatt held a finger up to his lips. Then, safety assured, quite as suddenly as he had not been there, he was: the Super Chief, arms waving, all smiles, Richard Nixon, President of the United States, and his wife.

Willie sat facing the audience, expressionless as a graduation speaker, while Tyler's thoughts erupted in a broad grin. He poked over the children's heads to jab his sister, then lifted his nearest nephew onto a seat. Tyler thought of how he used to dream, even as Nixon did, of someday being President, mostly when John Kennedy was. He'd hold press conferences and toss back sweet, clever answers to the tough ones, set the moral tone, reassure people, "We're not so scary, really." Outside the White House as a boy, a photographer had snapped the family picture and said to little Tyler, "Someday you could live in there." Now, he thought it was only likely if the woman he married was a politician. When Nixon shuffled in, Tyler imagined himself on the inside of Nixon's suit, and felt the dream

630

fit rather better than the garment. The President asked everyone to please sit.

He bobbed his head to the dignitaries in a stiff, halting way as he welcomed each. "Mr. Secretary . . . Mr. Senator." Willie was surprised by his ill-ease, but thought, well, he hasn't been doing this long.

The President spoke of his "personal and intense pride" in the heroism of those he had been called upon to commend, and the "new but age-old courage of the men who have fought in Vietnam." He quoted two lines from a formerly popular song called "The Ballad of the Green Berets," which bore not the least relation to Willie Bowen and Timmy Franks.

The President shuttled phrases around like heavy equipment, ramming them this way, jolting them about, joining end to front by sheer force. He snapped words together with a utilitarian disregard of harmony, making bad ideas from good sounds, erecting a vast housing project of the mind. Then he began to construct an elaborate caste system, selling leases on those modular condominiums of citizenship: those who had served their country when it called were of one class, those who had not, of another; among those who had served were those who'd been under arms, and among those, the few who'd seen hostile fire. At the apex were those who had acquitted themselves with great distinction, a tiny group of Brahmins. Not accommodated were those who declined, those who never had the chance, and, inexplicably unmentioned, those who did not survive.

Nixon smiled broadly, enjoying this function, dashing with relish into lines about heroism, honor, and courage, taking a perverse delight in quoting from "young John Kennedy," stretching the adjective unnaturally to full condescension. Newsmen sat with their jaws unhinged as he cited his own dubious war experiences which, in truth, amounted to hauling toilet paper around the South Seas. One reporter scribbled a speedwriting note to himself; when fleshed out it would read: "RMN settles definitional distinction between 'guts' and 'balls.' "

The President continued, invoking his own civilian travails, seldom connecting a thought with its neighbor, as though impoverished of conjunctions.

631

Willie, watching his gestures from behind, was swept up in wonder. The man acted so like a spastic mario-nette, so nervously. At one moment he huffed into the embodiment of his office, verbally, and within a second shriveled in an exhibition of fearful self-pity. Queer mannerisms, Willie thought, for one so thoroughly honored just to be standing where he was. Schizzy. But maybe, Willie thought, he too felt that disorienting apartness, that vaginal vertigo of personal remove from place, and was concerned he might be hounded from the hall as a poseur. So perhaps he was discovering there existed no final cure in this life along the upward axis for the great ailments he suffered. But who was he afraid would notice? Surely the glaucomic reporters would be the last to indicate a psychic shortfall in their accountings.

The President had difficulty remembering details out-side himself, such as the names and deeds he was called upon to celebrate. Nonetheless, he was certain of one thing. Tilting his head back, eyes closed in apparent sensual delight from the pronouncement, he said, "This is, this conferral of this great, great decora-tion, this medal, the Congressional—the Medal of Honor is the very first time this award has ever been given in the first two weeks of a President's administra-tion to two men in the East Room—"

Tyler leaned into Zermatt, whispering, "To a left-handed tight end of Scottish-Rumanian—" Zermatt shushed him.

Timmy Franks and Willie Bowen maintained grim faces of tight lipped gratitude throughout, holding them-selves in check like true champions: men who'd been on the rubber-chicken circuit long enough to accept celebrity's incumbent indignities. There was some possi-bility Franks might fall off his chair, so hard was he squeezing his sphincter.

Willie could only see the back of the presidential head from where he sat. He targeted his vision on the bulge of the man's skull, puzzling over what subcranial pressures and edemas made him act so. The few brief times the President turned to gesture at him, Willie gave a winsome smile, and was left thinking about Richard Nixon's face. Willie wondered if, more than the

632

flag, that face was worth dying for, and how long men and boys would do so. For it was in his face that the man's personality came through loudest: his jowly, floury, loveless mug was the man's epitome.

As Nixon read of the heroic assault, dealing with Timmy first, Willie became obsessed with faces, visions of heads exploding by his own hand, Diego Lupe's shattered skull. His dispassionate sanity enabled him to live with this as best he could. Dreams at night were something else, but with these at least, he could switch the images by a mental dial flick. Abruptly, the proceedings were halted, and Willie's attention snapped back, afraid his daydreaming had embarrassed him. The fuss, however, was over the President's daughters, who entered, starched as crinolined birthday cake figurines, to a standing ovation. They smiled at Willie, Timmy, and the others, faintly curtsied, and took seats.

The previous evening, when Franks had vowed, had *sworn* to whip it out on Nixon, had absolutely pledged himself in the name of dead ex-comrades, Tyler, equally stoned, remarked, "He'd only turn it to advantage. They have special reflexes, same as shortstops. Move right or left, make the backhand stab. Like priests, too: smack a Padre and he'll pop around like his head's on a spring, turning that cheek, right back for more—make you feel like shit. Spit in a politician's face and he'll start selling tickets on an Ark. Try it! Hock one at 'em."

Special reflexes, Willie thought, were the price of admission to this room: from his own reckless insensitivity to danger, to the journalists with their glaze, to Tyler trying to find sense in things nonsensical.

Suddenly, Willie heard his own name, and forced himself to recall what had just been said in his lapsed attention.

"—Bowen—Sergeant Bowen, as I was remarking the other day when we had the—signing the documents honoring Specialist, uh, uh, Frank, Franks and him—is another fine example"—Willie realized he'd missed nothing—"of why I say the young people of America is, our youth who will one day run this country are, our last, best—" Tyler was too keenly involved with his brother's name to note the usage. Then

633

Willie was jowl-to-jowl with the President, and even Baron was grinning as proudly as any of them.

To Willie Bowen, this man appeared, hands down, the worst looking he'd ever met. No Lincolnesque radiance turned his homeliness beatific. He was pasty-faced, fleshy, nasty to behold. Reluctantly, Willie conceded Nixon's command of all present, despite his surface tension. Yet he wondered if the man wasn't rotting from within. In the cathode rays and klieg lights, the man quickened, all doubts and tics were banished to his shoes. Timmy Franks was staring at the President's shoes.

Willie towered over the man who placed the silk ribbon around his neck. In manner, the President acted like a State Senate candidate certifying a livestock show winner. He grinned broadly at the cameras, for the honor he shared with Bowen and Franks, assaying a lovable coziness with the two boys.

"Uh, uh, Sergeant Bowen now—I understand that promotion is very recent," the President said, twisting Willie and Timmy around to different camera angles. They went where they were shoved. "I know something about that—you might say I was just promoted myself!"

Willie said, "Yessir," and the President continued.

"Well, congratulations, Sergeant—what? Oh, yes— you're civilians now. Then, congratulations, *Mister* Bowen. You know—but, ha-ha, that sounds like your father's name, 'Mr. Bowen.'" The President's eyes widened. "Are they here? Of course they are. Let's bring them down front for the picture boys." He waved them energetically to the podium and Willie marveled dumbly. Now he knew who the president most reminded him of: Ed Sullivan! He could probably introduce a jockey, a safecracker, and a Bishop all at once. He knew no shame.

While those families trooped forward, the President's attention was distracted by an aide whose forehead shone like Plexiglas. He was whispering something apparently delicious in the presidential ear, his hand lightly touching the man's sleeve. The President smiled, bobbed his head vigorously, and scooted him off. "Get it, get it," the President beamed. "And hurry."

The Frankses entered from the wrong side, surprising

him. Then he maneuvered both families around mechanically, pretending, old hand that he was, that he knew what kind of setups the photographers wanted, conversing uninterruptedly with the videotape machines about the exemplary American families before them, his arms around the mothers, while the cameramen groused.

When he'd shipped her things out to her mother's house in Scottsdale, Johanna sent Tyler back only the briefest note. "Have a nice life," it read. That was all: "Have a nice life, Tyler Bowen."

"What the hell's *that* supposed to mean?" he demanded in a return message. "Morbid melancholy is hardly becoming." And though she did not respond, nor her mother tell him where she'd gone when he called, it was not so much a valedictory, though it would serve, as it was a wish: for those she loved, and for herself.

She had gone back to Berkeley seeking what had eluded her, nearly desperate. She'd taken a hunch, played it, changed her mind, and now resolved to honor her instincts with redoubled investments. She laughed to think that in her way she resembled the war she'd been so bruised trying to stop: pursuing a chimera she could not identify, struggling more determinedly with every painful misstep.

She had been struck more harshly by the Robert Kennedy rupturing than had Tyler. After a period of trying to find sense in it, his innate optimism took over and led him to more fruitful paths. But it was also true that she, too, was an optimist. That was what informed their whole campaign, and made its collapse the more devastating. It was an American serum, a humor in their blood. And she too was a believer in sense. She was trying to find a sense for Johanna.

"The world," Tyler had quoted to her from a book, "is a comedy to those that think, a tragedy to those that feel." She could do both with blazing intensity, but a critical lack of stamina. So she burrowed inward, withdrawing to a self-made shelter, and wandered egotropically toward the places of her past, looking for the self she once loved being.

She was caught, balanced between the poles of emotion and reason. She wanted a man, if any man, who could do a simple thing, really: assume the weight of her beliefs to be the equal of his, even when her logic was not as accessible, and to honor her that way. Tyler had tried, but still she had to leave, because she felt she'd lived too long as an appendage in other people's worlds; too long on the short arm of the lever, being tossed when institutions ordered others' fates and when the world's events happened to her.

Yet her own life instincts were strong. She was stubborn and proud. She believed at the bottom of things there must be some way to feel her own self in her own place, perhaps then to be confident enough to live with someone else.

The very fact that she was trying, however close to the ragged edge, was proof of her still-quick spirit. Warren had said to her in one of their arguments, "The test of character, in a person or society, is the ability to hold a difficult ethic when it pinches." The pinch was squeezing the breath from her, bleeding her by drops. But she would not let it dominate her yet.

The President's aide returned to the podium with a sheet of paper while Timmy Franks and his family were posing for the cameras. The President read it, smiled, and pocketed it. He turned to the Bowens, toothy. "I have something of a surprise," he said to Mrs. Bowen, whose husband was telling some reporters to ignore the name on the releases and write him up as "Victor." "You have another boy, don't you? Taylor?" Vlad nodded.

"Tyler," Laura said.

"Yes," the President replied. "Well, this is something of a double pleasure. This is the very first time that—"

In the far back, Tyler gaped at Zermatt while he listened. Baron grinned beneficently and punched his shoulder, as the President called him down front. He went, stunned, his head swimming with too many things, the manic cycle of varied news he'd heard in one short hour. The President was saying that Tyler Bowen was part of a research group "at prestigious

Cornell University" that had been awarded National Institutes of Health fellowships for the coming year to enlarge their project at Case Western Reserve University in Cleveland. "I don't think anyone will mind my breaking the release date," the President chuckled. Murmurs of echoing chuckles and a smattering of applause approved his noblesse.

Tyler arrived dazed and dry of throat. His eyes felt receded into his skull as though they were rattling around inside a statue of himself. He accepted the President's handshake—a firm one—and stepped backward into the bosom of his parents, clutching the paper announcement, while the President offered an estimation that "this is a wonderful, remarkable family we have here, an American family—"

The press release rattled in Tyler's hand and he stole glances down at it while the President continued. His father reached over his shoulder to point to Tyler's name. It said he'd been a "1967 recipient of the coveted Vera and Benjamin Trovato Fellowship at the Gila Compound National Laboratories, serving in an administrative capacity," explained what he'd been doing at Cornell, and that he was to be an NIH Fellow with the rest of the Cornell team. Tyler's puzzlement over why they picked Case, other than its well-reputed cancer research, was resolved when he saw that the head of the Cornell unit had been made a chaired Professor there, a chair worth far more than the fellowship grant. It was still Willie's show, so Tyler folded the release neatly and gave the President his full attention.

"And you, William—or is it Bill?" the President concluded. "You know, you and Specialist Franks here, and your two fine families are proof of what a wonderful year this has been for America—for our brave men in uniform and for the special brand, breed of, uh, we, uh, we who come from this country, America, the United States of America." Each time he said the name "America" his eyes closed in extreme unction, and a devout, purgative shudder passed through his body. His nostrils flared and his whole frame swelled with a fearsome passion. It seemed an invasion of privacy to stand so close.

"I spoke to—last week—our three astronauts who

flew to—around the moon. And you know, later this year we're going to land men there. I called them from Air Force One, and we had a conference call to Houston, down there in Houston in Texas—and I told them I'd be giving out these medals to you men this week, you know. Well they said, and I pass this along to you, Bill and Specialist, uh, uh, Franks—they said, 'Mr. President, you be sure to add our congratulations and our thanks, sir, for a job well done!' I said to them, 'Roger,' I would. You see, we are all, all of us as Americans, and I know I speak for all real Americans, and I know your families are especially, all very proud and grateful for the courage of young men like yourselves, who help support America as you help save the brave people—the Republic of Vietnam."

"Thank you, sir," said Timmy Franks and Willie Bowen, tripping over each other.

"I was wondering, Tim, Bill, if you remember, and might share with our friends here from the news media"—he made a sweeping gesture to include them all in his show, granting clemency, sarcastic amnesty by that pass—"just what were, just what your thoughts were and feelings as you braved that—the Communist fire."

Timmy Franks shivered, blinking rapidly, swallowed, staring ahead, then fixing his eyes on Nixon's shoes again, his jaw grinding in panic, while without hesitation, Willie said, "Yess—" He cleared his throat. "Yessir, I—"

"That is, Bill," the President cut him off, "if, heh-heh-heh, they're printable!"

"Yessir," Willie answered, his gaze unwavering from the President's eyes. "I was thinking that flowers grow best under the breath of dragons." Nixon looked at him for what seemed a whole minute, his grin undisturbed.

Among the benefits of Warren's participation on the Commission on the Causes and Prevention of Violence was a shuttling between Washington and Tombstone on the wings of an Air Travel card and full expenses. At Maureen Poulson's request, he flew out to Berkeley in late February, at her expense.

It wasn't hard to locate Johanna. She was staying in the guest room of a young faculty couple they had known, though looking for her own rooms. He told her he had to spend a day in Palo Alto at the Hoover Institute of War, Revolution, and Peace—"Which one is your favorite?" she had asked—and one at Berkeley's Center for Law and Society. He suggested they have dinner and she accepted. She even thought it would be interesting to sleep with Warren for old time's sake. In her present thinking it was a trivial event; she'd put a half-dozen men behind her in the two months since she left Ithaca. As it turned out, the question never arose.

From what Warren said about himself it was obvious his work had been noticed by the right people. Warren had a gift for that. She permitted herself the honesty of admitting she admired his sure purpose and adroit pursuit of goals. He made progress. None of the horrors of the year past slowed him a whit. A chill ran down her spine, realizing that he had, indeed, profited by them.

Before she could offer him the hospitality of sharing her bed Warren mentioned a woman he'd been seeing. "One of the better perks of this Commission experience," he said. "She lives in Virginia."

"Are you going to marry her?"

"Oh, I think it's a little, uh, premature to—" She smirked at that, but he ignored her. "Well, we'll see. Perhaps."

"You never can tell," she said.

"No, you never can. At all events, I'll be making permanent headquarters in Washington when the new fiscal year begins."

"I love your sense of time. Did I ever tell you why my mother never married Arnie Logan?" Warren shook his head as though to say he'd never asked nor been interested. "Because between her television station and his newspaper, their wedding night would've been an antitrust violation!"

"We don't have such problems," Warren said icily. "I can't tell you what, but I've had a very solid offer—"

"Do I detect the slithering hand of—da-dum!—the Baron?"

639

"Oh, he's dropped that crap now that he's where the real action is. Quite a guy, though."

"Warren, you can tell me. Who would I tell? Who'd care?"

"Partly it has to do with your old friend Gila Compound. I thought you'd like that."

"The fire?"

"Not exactly. There's going to be a special commission to determine how best to dismantle the place, where to reassign its functions, the ones we're going to keep. And—"

"I take it your affiliation with Tombstone was instrumental."

"Somewhat."

"As you say," she smiled warmly, "you can storm the castle or build a scaffolding outside."

"Uhm. Supposedly, when that's wrapped, I've got a spot of some permanency waiting. National Security Priorities Staff."

"That's very nice for you," she said, and she knew she meant it.

He gave a quizzical laugh, and she cocked her head, inquiring.

"Oh, just, Zermatt's running the talent-search committee—he's counsel, and—" Warren shook his head in wonder. "He just about insists on having your friend—Bowen—on board to consult in some fashion. Asked me if I minded."

"That should be nice for everybody."

"Knowing how these things operate I doubt we'll ever be sitting at the same table, not that I give a damn. Still, it's funny, don't you think?"

She puckered her cheeks, admitting, "More droll than a laugh riot, but funny, yes. You can hold veterans' reunions. I can be guest speaker."

"So what *are* you doing, Johanna?"

"I thought you'd never ask."

"I'm asking."

"Taking one day at a time."

"Dandy. What does *that* mean?"

"Reading. Doing a lot of that. Talking to people. Thinking."

"Are you thinking about *doing* anything?"

"Sometimes I think about reading or talking to people," she said with a mischievous twinkle.

Warren was disgusted. "You're still a baby, that's all."

She agreed vigorously. "Uh-huh. A creature of impulse." She was delighted with herself. "Some are better than others." Now she wore a great grin and reached across the table despite his scowl, to pull his head close for a kiss. But he stiffened, so she settled for twisting his cheek. "You're such a cutie," she squealed.

"I don't suppose there's any threat of your finishing your Master's."

"In fact," she brightened, "I may even talk to the department. If I get around to it."

"To what may we attribute this revolution—besides impulse?"

"You were always such an inspiration to me. I want to be you when I grow up."

"English? Philosophy? Or childishness."

"Oh, maybe a little of each."

Warren just sighed and rolled his eyes in despair of her. His stomach fluttered uncomfortably. "You're in your own world, Johanna. I hope you're happy there."

A sentiment she had not expected came over her when he left. Her confidence trembled as though succumbing to age. All the frontal shocks she'd suffered left her nonetheless undimmed, still willing to take her own steps. But this shook her: Warren was jetting to and from Washington with all the shiny opportunity that implied and she felt a little wrinkled, left behind in Warren's past as he entered a new age. A year ago she had left him, a year before that compared faculty marriages to government ones: they were fatal to the wives. The men were rejuvenated by power, by the act of emigration to position. The women tended old skills learned in a receding past; often cut loose, set adrift, too unhardy and unyoung to make it in the new world.

She who had found her own vitality and racing wit demanding more than Warren had now outlived her time. She'd adapted herself to an era already gone. Warren survived, hedgehog to her fox. She cut him loose and saw him speed off without her ballast. It rattled her.

WILLIE BOWEN KNEW BETTER THAN MOST that his medal and its alleged honor counted "zipworth, squat, *por nada*," a form of understanding he shared with other celebrities. Even so, he suffered a minor decompression on the city streets when his renown went singularly unnoticed.

Save for his conditional acceptance at Stanford, the main benefits of his return were a lingering cold and the new car his parents had whistled him to. Amherst College had resurrected his old application and informed him they felt he was "satisfactorily matured to be reconsidered for admissions," but he wrote them a nasty rejoinder complaining that "you didn't love me before I was a star."

When his cold cleared up he developed an allergy to the inside of his skin and shuttled between various friends' campuses. "Doing a little outside agitation of the local females—with my ribbon around my neck, pretending they're Tricia Nixon—mostly trying to convince them I'm not some crazed killer, in preference to working for dad's company," he wrote his sister. She replied that she devoutly hoped Stanford would drill him in the rudiments of grammar and syntax, for the sake of posterity.

In March, Willie let himself be dragged by friends in Boston to a manifestation there. It was to be a day of protest and resistance organized among the academic institutions which fed the nation's technical appetites. It was another day of teach-ins, preaching to the already-converted, a moratorium on all study that contributed to the detested foreign war. At this one, an American Nobel laureate, whose prize work explored the chemical mysteries of vision, the role of carotin in sight, spoke of the lack of luster he saw in his students' eyes. He ventured his opinion of the reason, calling them "a generation in search of a future." And he described the nation's political impulses that had occasioned this as "criminally insane," to great cheers from his youthful audience. His remarks were reprinted around the world, to nearly no effect.

Such future as there was, common lore suggested, was invented in a cauldron of cheap sensations along the Sunset Coast. It drew the rootless, and Willie Bowen. "Don't believe any messages you get there," Tyler cautioned him before he left for California. "There's a national case of the runs that gets flushed that way. Don't expect to find any frontier or Indians, Willie—or is it Bill?"

"I've had enough of that, thanks."

"Good, because all they've got is about a thousand miles of McDonald's stands. How long you think you can mooch off Mack and Animal?"

"Long enough to get a job before the bread runs out. I'm pretty good at demolition, you know. Want me to look up that girl?"

"Yeah, sure, see how she is. Look, but no touch. She's heard a lot about you. She'd be thrilled."

"And maybe nudge her a little?" Willie asked. "To drop a line?"

"If you remember," he said casually. Before Willie left, Tyler brought it up again. "You'll recognize her. She'll be the anarchist with the blue-green eyes."

Johanna had pioneered the same path as Willie, and found the veins were mined out. Only fool's gold was left, glistering at a distance. She'd hoped to find the future, by locating the past, the shadow she had lost. But she had changed with the world. The cheering culture of two years before was gone. Cold and broken-spirited young were in the streets. Hard drugs replaced the soft, a narcotic Gresham's law.

Good ideas went sour in their westward travel, it was said, and bad ones sprouted first in that sunshine. Nihilism was California's crabgrass, a new cash crop. And if tidal waves were on the national docket, California would feel them first, for it lay philosophically, as well as topographically, closer to the sea. And once again in California, spreading east, as for the previous five years, in rites begun at Berkeley, campuses were swallowed up in waves of bloody uprisings.

San Francisco State College was on strike over demands for a Black Studies Department, a grammar of thought incomprehensible to the Japanese-American linguist who was the school's acting president. He wore a tam o'shanter while officiating at the busts. San Fernando Valley College saw a black sit-in result in mass arrests. A grand jury convened by the Governor—who had gained office railing against student excesses, while he popped jelly beans—charged those aggrieved students with "kidnap, burglary, larceny," etc.

A backlash of freeholders was forming. In San Diego, a self-created bubble of boosterism, a bond issue to fireproof the elementary schools went down, two to one. This, despite an imaginative media blitz showing newsreels of screaming tots fleeing an inferno. A shrill disclaimer followed, to no avail: "NOT ONE"—(goddam)—"PENNY OF THIS MONEY WILL GO TO THE COLLEGES AND UNIVERSITIES OF CALIFORNIA." It was unconvincing to those two-thirds who thought it wiser to catch the baby rattlers in their nest.

In California as a whole, faith in the future was at an ebb.

The lower Gold Coast was clearly insane. New religions sprang up promising varieties of psychosexual experience and job success, as all other payoffs proved unfulfilling.

To the north, the idea of "Dancing in the Streets," emblematic of the Bay Area two years before, was a grotesque irony now: such dancing came from overdoses, barbiturate tremens and a Saint Vitus reaction to shotgun attacks. Over the Washington's Birthday weekend, an attempt to protest a University of California Regents meeting at Berkeley was routed by troopers firing birdshot from helicopters. The diehards were warned by a casual terrorization.

Johanna Poulson had withdrawn from such political battles, as much as she could. Still, she was caught innocently by the tear gas while browsing in a bookstore. There was no place to hide. Others became even more abstracted from political and social reality, delving into dark things: magic, Satanism, mystical idolatries, and faddish mentalisms. Many studied morosely, moles whose eyes were seared by vicious light. A few unregenerates rallied for another stand, but the rest found the whiff of grape and lachrymetics sufficient. Even the Minutemen at Concord might have given up in the face of that. The flowers were long dead, poisoned, and unable to serve as humus for new ones.

Rampant rumor in early April insisted that the San Andreas Fault would twitch to quarantine the continent from California, submerging an entire state of mind. There was no panic, only partying. Liquor stores, limping along between cataclysms by selling groceries with the booze to justify cashing welfare checks, promoted the rumor with glee.

The catastrophe never came, a considerable disappointment. Its arrival would have been a welcome break in the routine, a season in a certifiable Hell, agreeable to all sacerdotal groups, potentially satisfying to the parched imaginations of bored natives. So California remained attached to the mainland, and the tremors rippled east.

At Harvard, in time for a holiday called Evacuation Day, a week before the anniversary of Paul Revere's ride, the students went on strike, setting new standards of style in propaganda, going so far as to parody the form, their wit exceeding their anger: they lifted their elongated "Strike because . . ." manifesto, a blank-verse chanted slogan, from a Douglas MacArthur speech to the natives on the eve of the invasion of Manila.

At Cornell, what the war had been three years before, and was still, what the privileges of co-ed room arrangements would ever be for many, the long-standing frustrations of the black students were this spring. "Jesus H.—" an experienced hand in administration moaned to Tyler Bowen as they staggered from a stormy late-night meeting. "They've already got their own *department!* Isn't that enough for one year?" Apparently it was not. The black students wanted a say in faculty hiring. But faculties, while always willing to mediate in other people's business, show surprising signs of fiber when the medieval sanctities of their own prerogatives are threatened.

Tyler Bowen had thought he might fly out to join his brother at Mack's for Easter, but the campus situation prevented it. He volunteered to help negotiate the issue. "Since I'm not going to be here next year, maybe I can be impartial." But a new element, or an old one, entered the question, to cast a shadow on anyone's impartiality.

White fraternity boys in Ithaca, their wit unimproved since Ezra Cornell granted his farm to higher learning, placed a burning cross in front of an all-black sorority. Anonymous death threats and obscene phone calls followed. The humor of it escaped the black students, who prepared for a defensive struggle. Over Parents' Weekend, not without an eye to publicity, the black students seized the administrative offices, including Bowen's, at Willard Straight Hall. And they took the Afro-American Society Center at the too-aptly named Wait Hall. The fraternities let be known their intention to "liberate" the captured territory, and so the blacks' friends brought in armaments. The national press worked into its stories the intelligence that Cornell was founded in the last year of the Civil War, and played with the images of its cloudy altitude, its soft shale, and its surrounding gorges. They wrote that Cornell was on the verge of full-scale racial war.

Days and nights of negotiations brought no relief. The moment was supersaturated. The slightest agitation would precipitate the whole. So the Administration offered a late compromise, and a settlement was reached. For its apparent capitulation, the Administration would be sacked by the school's Trustees, a lesson noted for the future by others across the country.

From her vantage point, when she read the news of Cornell's turmoil, Johanna thought it funny that Berkeley should be enjoying an uneasy peace of nerves and apathy while Cornell went wild.

Indeed, the police deterrent had worked at Berkeley. Despite the traditionally emotion-fraught political atmosphere, Berkeley's students had retreated to their long-neglected textbooks, licking wounds, frightened.

It would be hard to incite them again. They were nearly back at the stage where their former University President, Clark Kerr, the reigning genius of higher education in the 1950s (and fired by the Governor in the first antistudent moves), had listed the three things necessary for administering a great university as "sex for students, sports for alumni, and parking for faculty." The politically acute Berkeleyites had conceded the Maoist point that political power began at the end of a gun barrel, and the State had a near-monopoly.

The threats had been so weighted that only one kind of issue could revive their flagging energy: one whose dialectic defined every difference between students and their institutions, the purest kind of existential question; for they were absorbed now in considerations beyond politics, in pursuits informed by understandings of what in life was worthwhile. They'd turned to simple, nurturative things, away from policy battles to small community projects of indisputable merit.

One was a small, fallow, rubble-strewn lot which the resourceful neighborhood people converted into a children's park. The local residents covered the ground with sawdust and grass, set up swings and slides, hung ropes from an old tree, placed barrels and tires around for kids to play with, built little dirt hills and handmade picnic tables.

Mothers sunned babies there. People gathered for a cool drink or smoke. It was peaceful, rustic, calm—the kind of thing educators were always urging students to direct their energies toward instead of politics; at some colleges they were now giving credits for just that sort of bucolic hobby.

It was the scruffiest little island, but it was covered with a naive, preurban glow, as though some proletarian conception of a small-town green. Or Walt Disney's. For at Berkeley, where lived youths who never knew innocent times, who came mainly from large cities, Walt's myth found most lively animation. His heirs and defenders-in-spirit were the long-haired, leftist, pacifist, dirty-talking, obnoxious, blues-rock-playing, cynical, dope-smoking, Mao-quoting, authority-baiting, sassy radicals of Berkeley, U.S.A. Some thought themselves modern Jesuses, but they were really updated Toms and Beckys. The only difference was something subtle and something obvious: Disney's world was static, made of humanoids and petrochemicals, while theirs was a jolly mess, mutable and breathing. Anyone could come to their People's Park and take enjoyment; Disney's legates barred such youngsters from his amusement park: their freaky looks and antics frightened paying customers. They loved their grubby spit of handmade Main Street, it was their Adventureland and Fantasyland.

The State wanted to destroy it.

Disney had also given them the myth of Davy Crockett, a drunkard whose motto was "Make up yer mind what's right then go ahead and do it." They believed that, called it "Do It!" and heard it translated by the Moses of their Free Speech Movement, Mario Savio: "There comes a time," he had said five years before, "when you have to bend, fold, spindle, and mutilate, . . . you've got to put your bodies upon the gears and upon the wheels, upon the levers, upon all the apparatus." Now it was: AND SHUT THE MOTHERFUCKER DOWN!

The University Regents were headed by the Governor, an ex-actor whom the Berkeleyites called Ronnie Ray-Gun. The student-hating he had based his campaign on kept the San Diego lower grades, and the University, flammable. His line of argument was simple: the University owned this lot, and pioneers' squatter's rights were no longer honored at law in California. Property values were too high to permit "adverse possession" by the community. The world was too competitive and crowded for the easy ways of the Founders. The State and its many bulldozers had eminent claims. The University wanted its land, they were not embarrassed to admit, to pave it over—to turn it into a parking lot.

Seeds versus concrete. The issue seemed to the students a pure dichotomy between all things organic—people, flowers, children, grass, community, creative, throbbing life, flesh—and all things toxic: property rights, bulldozers, cement, the internal combustion engine, Ronnie Ray-Gun, and monoxide.

An eleventh-hour compromise offer by the University refined the issue even further into its nonnegotiable polarities. Submitting to faculty pressure, the Administration proposed a deal: they would turn the park into an athletic field.

But the street people refused. They loved their homely child for its ungainly beauty and the spirit of its conception.

A brass chuck wagon gong hung from the park's apple tree, over it a sign: "Bulldozer Alarm / People's Park / Power / Fresh Air / To the People!" They would not be budged. The students—and some were students only as Cubans are Soviets, satellites of the campus, nonmatriculants sharing only a frame of mind—laid claim to the land, casting themselves exuberantly as the "People." This drove the Regents into apoplexy. For the Regents were the only duly appointed representatives of the People, selected by the Governor, under authority of the Law. The Regents were nothing if not the People. The students said very well, they're nothing. For the students truly believed themselves the People. People versus People: it would be a Civil War, a battle, really, between democracy and republicanism.

The Governor, an experienced Indian fighter in a score of movies, said the State could not sanction mob confiscations, Robin Hood extortion, and moralized theft. The issue, he said, playing to the fearful ranchers in the valleys, was "who owned the land."

So here the battle-weary students of Berkeley would make another stand. It would look like one of the enactments of battles at Disneyland. Only at Disneyland, they didn't use real blood. There were days of stomach-churning waiting. Some preliminary clashes, then disengagement. The street people knew what would come next. The Army was over the horizon, waiting for its orders to destroy the park in order to save it. The rumors came from a reliable source: the government's own leak. Eying the Russian takeover in Czechoslovakia enviously, the State wanted a nice, quiet, efficient operation, resistance softened by scare reports preceding it.

But the only warlike creature about was Willie Bowen, up from Mack's place in Carmel, visiting friends. He warned them, "I've seen this shit. You don't want it, believe me."

One of his friends said, "I thought you said the Army couldn't beat its own meat."

"Who says you're any better?"

"Don't you believe in anything?" another demanded scornfully.

"Nah."

"Isn't there anything you'd go down the line for?"

"Nope. You know why? Because you're stupid, and I'm tired of officiating at bloodbaths."

"Apathy begins at home."

"Yup," Willie said. "And that's where I'll be hiding when the shooting starts."

In the predawn hours that night, the girl friends and roommates of National Guardsmen who were detained at armories spread the alarm. Those who had not attended drills joined the shorts-and-sandals-clad hundreds on the wrong side of the barricade. Before dawn, before the evidence, the crowd swelled, an impassioned mob bent on preventing the Sheriff from committing a lynching.

Out of the dawn came the troops, the wrong way down the streets, in olive drab, on jeeps and trucks, in dark green sleepy grimness, in the bulldozers and half-tracks of the Combat Engineers Willie Bowen knew too well. He'd hitched enough rides on their stiff iron backs. They came in cargo haulers and deuce-and-a-halfs, with Cyclone fencing to secure the land when they took it. They even came with an American flag to hoist in victory.

The first truck stopped at the head of the column. Two troops looked out at the growing mob and smiled. The driver turned back to his impatiently honking Commander and yelled, "What am I supposed to do?"

"Pull that damn thing to the side," came the reply. The commander waved an MP jeep around the column and ordered the other trucks to reverse and form their secondary advance lines on the other access streets.

The MP jeep pushed slowly toward the students, a

bedspring-frame cowcatcher wrapped loosely in barbed wire fixed in front of it. Alongside, gas-masked troops proceeded with fixed bayonets.

Someone in the crowd was yelling that they might shoot, and the crowd gave ground reluctantly, like a lion before a tamer's whip and chair. By this they dared the driver to be aggressive, backing up so slowly that he stalled out twice. The third time he stalled, they surged around the jeep and immobilized the guards by sheer pressure. They shook the jeep until its two dizzy occupants bailed out. The crowd tore their helmets from them and seized their empty weapons, dragging both men to the ground and sending them off pantsless. To the rear, the Bulldozer Alarm rang wildly.

The troops pulled back for a moment and someone in the crowd asked whether they shouldn't all consolidate and fight at the park. The answer was that the troops didn't care: if the park was destroyed, it would take the fight out of the defenders faster. Still, someone argued that morale would best be served by fighting on their native soil. Most agreed, wandering off the street into the park area. Then the troops came back, from all directions, boxing the defenders in.

The Commander rode up like a Cavalry officer, roaring his orders from a bullhorn. A student answered with his own bullhorn and they moved at each other in a joust, knights and seconds in long trains from their wings. Two elongated semicircular lines faced each other as the two leaders jawed through electronic amplifiers. It seemed a reactor pile simmering near criticality, an inevitable dance of war, with one admissible conclusion. Few had seen this kind of thing before.

Willie Bowen was in bed, dreaming, as the troop Commander yelled "Mask!" He dreamed with frightening vividness that he was standing between great cogs of a machine, his puny arms breaking as the gears turned. They spun him round and the gears became cars and exploding faces in a wildly spinning landscape, a glare of faces with the entrails he had crawled through hanging off like leeches, dogs flying apart, a woman whispering something indistinct as he seeped erotic joy.

651

"Dispense gas canisters!" the Commander bellowed. Canister after canister was fired. Mighty-Mite blowers churned out more. That illusion of limitless wealth which saw frightened infantrymen empty clips into every breeze-rattled bush in Southeast Asia, leaving the floor of that country a thick carpet of shells—the greatest single copper deposit in the world!—had panicky Guardsmen firing ten, twenty, fifty canisters of CN and CS tear gas into the crowd.

Inexperienced warriors fell flat on the street to suck clean air from the ground. Others smeared Vaseline around their eyes, stuffed cigarette filters up their nostrils, and masked themselves with wet hankies. But all were poisoned. The gas drifted on the morning air into every neighborhood window. Willie woke up choking. There was no place to hide.

A helicopter buzzed overhead with helmeted State Troopers manning shotguns. Its rotors dispersed some of the gas, but in those clearings the Troopers fired random blasts of buckshot. Having done so at the last riot, not to fire again would suggest remorse. Some of the defenders broke and ran at the sudden noises in the disorienting haze. Some waded rashly into the Guard ranks seeking cover from the Troopers' fire. They tore into the National Guardsmen, their faces twisted by torment and rage, swinging sticks, wrestling for rifles, murderous at the betrayal by their generational comrades.

The bulk of the crowd sought escape down avenues blocked by trucks and bulldozers. A girl fell and broke her nose on the street in front of a steaming earthmover. The troop chasing her pulled her to safety. Three troops saw their girl friends and ran off into buildings with them. Other troops gave discreet aid to the hopeless students.

Chased every which way, the bulk of the students were trapped in a pentagonal pincer, their lungs seared with the gas's indelible pain. They watched helplessly while the big-tire wreckers ripped their park apart and scarred their lawn. In one desperate outburst of gagging frustration, they surged into the main body of troops and clawed at the National Guardsmen's masks. Students and troops stood in the nauseating cloud, slugging it out in a bloody street brawl under the lovely western dawn.

The noise and burning vapors shook the whole neighborhood. Inhalation injuries were suffered by combatants and neutrals alike; Willie Bowen, roused from sleep, was choking. The foolhardy defenders suffered lacerations and broken bones as well, some beaten severely enough to require hospitalization. A few were stung by birdshot. One succumbed to complications and later died. Three dozen Guardsmen needed treatment for wounds inflicted by their own weapons, the gas and the rifles torn away by maddened students. Two were bayoneted, others butted and clubbed. One Guardsman was hit by 00-gauge shotgun pellets and another had his foot run over by an MP jeep.

But the engineers kept coming and coming and coming and they had the fencing up and guarded before the last fighting was finished, in time for breakfast, as the sullen stragglers limped off coughing, crying, chanting exhaustedly, "Pow-er to the Pee-pul! Pow-er to the Pee-pul!"

Scores of the losers were arrested, transported to a hospital where, under guard, they were treated for their wounds and then, prisoners of war, removed to pens.

"Have you ever had tuberculosis?" an Emergency Room doctor asked Willie Bowen when he was admitted suffering inhalation burns. Willie shook his head weakly. The chest X ray had shown scars.

"Had a puncture once," Willie rasped. "Nothing serious."

"Were you in it?" the doctor asked cursorily.

Willie wheezed, "Not when it started. Sleeping."

"It just found you."

He shrugged painfully. "I was trying to get out of the way."

"Picked a funny place for it. How'd you come by this?" he asked, holding up the gas mask Willie had arrived with.

"Found it."

"Where?"

"On a Major." The doctor's eyes opened incredulously. "Look for the guy with the broken head—that's

653

him." The doctor nodded, said nothing, and left to attend others.

The papers were full of the People's Park story, but it had to share space with a Pentagon leak William Beecher of the *New York Times* had received: that for two months, on orders of the President, a secret war was being waged from the air against the neutral country of Cambodia. The results of that disclosure were not immediately clear. The bombing would continue unabated for a full year in violation of the U.S. Constitution. And so maddened was the President at this leak that he asked his Secretary of State for a list of likely perpetrators, their telephones to tap. He set up a secret group of investigators, intramurally dubbed the "Plumbers," to stop these leaks. For continued leaking was at once a threat to his ability to govern and, if anyone cared, a public reminder that his whims exceeded his constituted authority.

Once again the stores along the Telegraph Avenue strip put up their mocking "Riot Sale" signs. "Tear-Gas Damaged Merchandise, Half-Off."

A few days after the riot, Willie walked into a record store on Telegraph Avenue and idly thumbed through a stack of pirated recordings. The girl behind the register had blue-green eyes. "Don't tell her this," Tyler had instructed Willie, "but they're very close to the shade of penicillium mold."

"Only you would think of that," Willie had replied, amazed.

She approached Willie in the store, asking whether she could help him. He nodded his head rhythmically, and smiled, looking not at her eyes but the tiny scar by the corner of one.

"Hello," he said softly. "Can I show you something?" She backed up half a step, warily, as he undid his bottom shirt button. "See?" he grinned. "I got one just like yours."

"Congratulations," she said impatiently, and turned her back. She knew these customers pretty well. For most, conversation began and ended with "What's your favorite drug?" He reached out for her elbow but she jerked quickly away, snapping, "I think you'd better get out of here!" She retreated behind the register, heaving angrily. Willie just folded his arms and pouted. He followed her to the register, and leaned on it.

He cocked his head cheerfully. "I don't know, I was told you'd be friendlier. Maybe I got the wrong girl. The clues were pretty vague, but this——" He reached forward gently as she recoiled, reaching farther than her recoil to graze the small depression by her eye with the barest touch. "He couldn't've got it wrong."

Her mouth hung slightly agape, tentatively, and she turned her head slightly to squint at this rough-cut, rude boy. She could feel anticipation's heat and moisture fill every facial cavity. Her features lit up electrically. "Who——?"

"What makes this such a trip is you're exactly like I had you pictured."

"How did you——?"

"I got a friend who's got a friend and all that—somebody knew you. I ain't as dumb as—my brother."

She came out from behind the register, bouncing ecstatically, to give him a bear hug. "You had us all so worried!" she squealed.

"I'm supposed to tell you the same thing."

"How *is* he?"

Willie shrugged, "Busy. Seeing a lot of action."

"I read it," she said.

"Not so much gas, though. You get hit?" She put both hands on her head, and said she too had gone to the Emergency Room. "Now *that* would've been a place to meet up."

Taking his measure, she squeezed herself gladly. "I heard endlessly about you. We were so—you're exactly as advertised."

"Better looking," Willie said. "Gotta be."

"Exactly as advertised."

She was off work in a few hours and insisted Willie tell her "all about everything" for the rest of the afternoon. "It's so good to *see* you." So they bought a bottle of the cheapest wine available—"Are you old enough to drink?" she asked; "I'm not old enough to be sober," he answered—and headed into the Berkeley Hills, which bloomed lavishly in the salty May air. They found a bosky cemetery for a picnic site, incongruously gay for its fertilizer.

Her skin was radiant and stunning as ever, her eyes gleaming with apparent fire. She was glad old friends, even those she'd never met, had a secret lease on her.

"Boy," Willie said, wine slobbering down his chin, "I know at least one guy who wishes he was here—" Then he looked around at the gravestones. "And a whole bunch who wish they weren't." He burst out laughing, a crude, howling laugh. Johanna supposed it was a triumphant cackle at having beaten the odds. But Willie said, "It's an old superstition from the boonies. Supposed to wake the fuckin' dead—I guess it doesn't work too well. Nothin' ever did—"

"Like your 'Famous Wolf Call'? I heard about that one—" Willie flushed in embarrassment. "Look at that—isn't that marvelous?" she said, pointing to a headstone. "Goodenow, 1866–1957! Imagine! Covered wagons to rocketships. Good enough."

"I'd like maybe about a hundred more years. Then I'd like 'em to put something up that made no sense. Give people something to think about, something to do. Maybe just hang my little badge on it—that makes no sense—remind me to show it to you. It's a beaut. Mox nix. Zippers. Nada. Nulleroonie. Hot damn Veet-Nam—*nuthin!* Just a big hole in the ground."

They chattered away the rest of the afternoon, Johanna delicately keeping the wine out of Willie's reach. At one point she said, "What I'd like on mine is, I think, Fermat's Last Theorem." She explained that Pierre de Fermat, a seventeenth-century French mathematician, had left behind a theorem "like the Pythagorean one—you know, a-squared plus b-squared equals c-squared."

"Yeah, sure," Willie mumbled.

"Except he said it couldn't be done with cubes and any higher powers."

"I don't get it," Willie admitted.

"He *said* he had a proof. He wrote down that he had it—but he died in his sleep."

"Oh, I know that guy! Tyler told me about him. It's been giving computers a hernia ever since, right? Boy, you and Babe, really—uh, I'm not supposed to be that direct, I think," he said sheepishly. "Listen, is that what you're into? Math? Like that?"

She shook her head. "Fabulism," she said in a confidential whisper. "Mythopoesis. If they let me."

"What's that?"

"*You* know," she coaxed him. "Legends, tales with a moral."

"Bedtime stories?"

"Adult versions. Modern ones."

"You know what Tyler said? He goes 'The smartest girl I ever met. The prettiest, and the best.' He said I was too young to understand the subtleties. But I've met some of the others. Boy, you wanna see white bread some time—aw, *shit*. Give him a call. You know? A letter. Drop in."

"Maybe I will," she winked.

For a moment, their eyes aligned and held for one bare beat, tugging back as they darted off. The conversation rattled on in ignorance of this. There was something they shared, but wouldn't speak of: a common love for Willie's brother.

Willie idolized him. No honor he could own blessed him more than his brother's pride. He was content to be a younger brother, helplessly weak at the thought of his big brother, devotedly chasing his footsteps. He might talk wise or tough, or wrestle Tyler, but he knew he could never hurt him in a precious spot, nor would he dream of it. Willie loved his brother in the inchoate way he first fell in love with a ten-year-old girl. Unable to understand the rushing blood, he bopped her on the head, socked her, and ran away.

And if Johanna's eyes were any clue, she loved Tyler also when she spoke of him. It made her apposite with Willie, sharing an equivalent feeling, an orbital plane that could be reached only by a similar love. He felt an urgent, fluttering passion for his brother's woman, as the closest he could ever come to his own brother. But he forced it from his mind.

Unlike Willie, Johanna was old enough and sophisticated enough not to be undone by strange sensations. She had learned to discriminate among them. Eros had lied to her too often. Part of her, a corner, a layer, would always hold a memory of Tyler. It could never rinse out, with a half-life of forever, that's how brightly they had burned, fierce and hot, cauterizing the wound, leaving no ash, just the memory that something once was there. It was a wordless, awful feeling. She looked fondly at Willie while he picked at weeds, wondering what would happen if she were still with Tyler. Would they be two mighty lovers, or disappointed souls? Could their complement last or would they have grown apart, destroying each other, vulnerable to worldly ills? Being old friends and former lovers was a warm port of remembrance, and just now she would prefer to stay there.

"My dear miss p," Tyler wrote in early June, breaking their six-months' silence,

I am informed—by auspices I cannot reveal, but bearing a remarkable resemblance to a talking panda —that you are thriving by the seaside, but that a nasty gang of thugs broke the fingers on your writing hand, thus explaining why you haven't dropped your old buddy a line. It gets expensive sending family ambassadors west, so maybe I should change the economics here. The next one out will break both your legs if you don't pick up a pencil. Write—or limp!

The kid said he'd look you up, but of course I didn't believe him, not so much because I doubt his retentive ability or good sense (which I do), but because of his history. In D.C. he swore he was going to expose himself to the Maximum Trickster. Eleventh-hour pledges of candidates (and lovers probably) and the midnight conspiracies of war heroes are not supposed to be taken seriously, I know. But we were all disappointed nonetheless. Still, I'm glad he didn't get the two promises backward. (I hope.)

The kid tells me also that you are a Mything Person, after a fashion. From his garbled transmission of detail I gather you are on to something terrific.

Having given some (amateur) thought to this myself I have wondered "where did we go wrong"— not you and me so much: all of us, that everything got inverted. Lots of people suggest the First Assassination, and while it's a compelling notion, I personally think it goes back a little further.

Parenthetically, knowing your interest in four-part harmony, it has always been my contention that Masters and Johnson had less to do with the Sexual Revolution than did the Beach Boys getting "Wouldn't It Be Nice" on the radio. That tore it, as it were. (Tellingly, the flip side, a romantic love song, lost air play because its title was "God Only Knows." He may indeed, but it's a phrase not fit for the public waves or something. Hoist by their own petard were they.)

Willie tells me part of your thing—I should have guessed—is the dissemination of myth and meaning and values through pop culture. How the media makes proto—Bridey Murpheys of us with understandings that exceed our histories. It's a peachy excuse for the right to listen to a lot of records for credit— and a dandy idea. He also said you're using Tales from the Labs and some of the ones I have bored you with about baseball players and other Jockularities. I will dutifully scratch out as many as I can think of and send them Bayways if you like. Which, circumnavigatorially, brings me back to the Big Derailing. Viz:

Things were going nicely once. Mickey Mantle wore the Triple Crown. Yankee Stadium was not yet obscured by slums. Elvis wriggled out Golden Records (not *everything* changes). Hungarians were revolting, but came up short, while Pat Boone wore white bucks to his Columbia graduation. On the Big Stage were Sputnik and Castro and Danny and the Juniors singing "Rock 'n' Roll Will Never Die"— and Big Chuck de G. who looked good for the duration, too. (Adolescence Will Never Die, it seemed.) Then, of course the Twist, and Dion and the Belmonts, and John Glenn and Whammo (Double Whammo: Hula Hoops and Frisbees)—this is not just a laundry list but a *thesis,* sweets—the One Event, miss: One fine afternoon in 1961, at Yankee Stadium, Roger Maris jumped on a Tracy Stallard Special (a Beantown Meatball). He parked the Big

Asterisk (Number Sixty-One) in the right-field box occupied by Sal Durante's girlfriend. Broke the Big One, the Bambino's Best, and no matter what was ever broken afterward, records, vows, or hearts, the world would never be the same. A common delusion of meaning had been swept out, logic too, on the fractured carcass of a Great Man. When cretins kill heroes, right away things go out of whack.

And they did: Dylan ambled in and sang "The Times is a-Changin', Jack," until Pope Jack dropped dead. And while the Singing Frigging Nun was boop-boop-de-dooping between Twist lessons on Ed Sullivan, the Supercretin of the Century had a bad night with his wife and took it out on Jack Kennedy. The funeral meats were hardly cold, as they say, when the Beatles broke in, tearing up the place and all remaining old assumptions. Harlem flew apart, something happened off the South China Sea, maybe, and Dylan went electric (eclectric, actually) and got his ass booed off, as you may recall. But a lot of folks must have gone that way because one night all over the East Coast the lights dimmed once, then surged, like Ossining at Frying Time, and went out like— well, a light. When they came back on, Lyndon had the Marines frugging in Santo Domingo.

They must've changed more than the fuse, I think, because a lot of people never turned the lights back on. Just sat around with incense and candles and stuff. Anyone who could poke his nose over the counter was going "Keep the Bull Durham, man, just gimme the papers." Magic in chemistry, just like they always said on "College Bowl" or somewhere. So it was "Good-bye, all, we're goin' to Ape-shit City!" Fare-thee-well, parents, pasts, and preordained futures—this while the Red Guards raged in the night. And butterfingered Lyndon dropped an H-bomb off Palomares, Spain. What a time!

And of course, the Big News now is that the Beatles, the Thousand-year Rock is breaking up (are?). That leaves you and me, toots, unless the rumors are true and they let Ali fight again.

Where, you may well ask, are Frankie Lyman and the Teenagers, now that we need them? Probably casualties of war, shed like so many veils of innocence after Roger Maris squared off against Tracy Stallard. The bum could never even hit a good change-up. But, I suppose they gave him enough of those. Except that it was a day game (I was there, though, typically, in the wrong section), Saint Paul's phrase commends itself: Ages End at Night. It seems they're generally changed by the morning, moonbeam victims. From something you once said I would infer that we are now in the Age of Aging, Danny and the Juniors notwithstanding.

Not quite apropos of all this, our mutual friend B. Zermatt has connived me into being attached to a study commission set up to close down you-know-where that we're not supposed to talk about (you and me). While I can hardly imagine a more worthwhile activity (Zermatt, being Zermatt, stressed the point that 'it won't hurt your résumé and think of the leverage in reassigning projects to other places whose love you'd like'), it's giving me kind of a full summer-fall sked. One of its lesser pleasures is the increased odds of bumping into the esteemed Mr. R. as well. So the question arises: how come the only non-compulsively reuning alums is thee and me, eh? I'd sure like to swap old war stories with you.

I asked Zerm-the-Worm whether there wasn't maybe something relative to this that didn't have to be done in S.F.? He said no, but if I'd like, any time there's a demo in D.C., he thinks he can clear it with the Bad Guys to have W. C. Bowen flown in, gratis, for propaganda purposes against the thing. Which missed the point, I think, two different ways.

Among the many quotable things you've written/ said at me, sometimes when angry, sometimes when blue, I think, was "Have a nice life," which you may have meant to be an exit line, I don't know. I am here to tell you that it's that much more difficult for your having exited. If your memory is as good as mine, you may recall once I told you how absolutely terrific waking up with you was—and what preceded it—at which you suggested we share the credit. But ah, the point was, I've been here all along, that's the difference. And as much as I like/love being me, I like it that much better when you're there.

Zermatt, referring to the giant cookie cutter looming out of D.C., likes to say, "Adjust. Make do. Cop a Galileo and brush up on recanting techniques." He also likes to say, "Go ahead, ignore the received, collated, and stapled political wisdom of the ages. See where it's gotten you."

In your absence—which I continue to construe as something between an extended holiday and a period of infirmity, thinking to the time when you "get better"—but not even a *card?*—I can adjust, sort of (to Cleveland???). But I don't see how I can Make Do. And you? Next year I'm applying for a Fulbright and every graduate fellowship on Earth, other parts of the Earth especially. Keep those cards and letters coming and sing a happy song for me . . . call if you find a few nickels . . . I'll send you a souvenir from D.C., Cleve, maybe the moon.

F LOATING TO THE TILE FLOOR, HIS JUMP shot splashing in the last can of the row, Tyler Bowen was laughing and proud. He was charmed, enchanted, immune, riding the tiger's back.

The Goat's Song, a swan song, was sung over and over that summer in this place in Maryland, as Tyler Bowen watched. When the Heart-Line rang, it was to say the goats would be replaced by beagle puppies.

Men walked ghostlike on the lunar plain and the selene umbra covered many things whose toll would not be tallied for a while. As boys played in the lunar dust, expelling Earthly wastes in that pure soil, a kind of madness settled in at home. Demons were believed to be about.

The last living Kennedy brother pushed his Chrysler off a wooden bridge into a murky tidal inlet. He ran screaming into the Martha's Vineyard night, afraid, he said, of curses and hobgoblins, folding behind him the last tent in the public Camelot. Opportunity sutured closed above the car. So shattered was his future, or so meaningless his life without a higher office, that his best friends and cousin let him swim, bad back, shock, and all, across a mile of open sea at midnight. Then they and he, they said, went calmly, all, to bed.

But from Tyler Bowen's employers' viewpoint, the summer was a grand success. The students learned. Other instructors liked to grumble, "I taught it, they just didn't learn it." Not him. His efficiency reports glowed with "natural leader," "an asset," "fine teacher." One had him "a real politician," meaning it as praise. His manner was low-key, agreeable. He wove anecdotes and put-ons into his lectures, though it was hard to tell what was real in such matters except by his wicked smile.

If their concentration wandered, Tyler would talk about "olfactory parameters of pheromones"—sex-attractant chemicals, and the wonders of methane and ammonia: "Guy ran a spark through a mixture—it's what the primitive atmosphere was like eons ago. Name was Miller. Forget it, you don't need it for the final. OK: all that gas and lightning and he winds up with a first-class amino acid. Now, unless you're a biochemist I suppose that's kind of boring. So let me tell you about another guy, a friend of mine who repeated the process on a bigger scale. He assembled *all* your basic life chemicals. Seasoned it with a little potassium, calcium, iodine, iron—all the right weights and measures. Then he ran a spark through it twenty, thirty, six hundred times! And by golly, he's got himself some protein. Which is also kind of boring, you say. So he got really ambitious and hooked the whole thing up on a time-sharing link to a string of computers with some very fancy gadgets and some highly sensitive data he filched from Rockefeller University—that's in New York. Programmed in every conceivable type of parameter—spectrographic, structural, all that, all the proper readouts—for a perfect simulation of the components, surface dynamics, etc., of Miss Tuesday Weld." They roared and drooled approval. "The theory was if you could grow your own, you'd save a lot of energy—you know, like no dinner and four hours of talk afterward—" The whistling and hooting was deafening, and the rhythmic pounding on desks. He'd borrowed the kicker from Baron Zermatt. But his friend wouldn't mind. He'd be proud as hell. And it wasn't the first thing he'd picked up from the Baron.

Later that day one of the students asked Bowen, "What happened to that guy's paper?" Bowen wasn't paying attention. He was more absorbed in a letter he'd gotten from Saint Paul Hooper.

"Huh? Oh—he sold the screen rights to Paramount for a million bucks." The man looked satisfied. "Watch for it."

Before the Moonmen would leave quarantine, Tyler would be through with his. In the meantime he doodled aimlessly, filled out fellowship applications, and chewed Turkish Taffy bars each time the mottled goat was laid low.

The light was at the end of the tunnel. His "consultation" still remained, both with the newly formed Commission on the Allocation of Life Science Research Facilities and with those "interested parties" the NSA required him to brief in the subtleties of biochemical mischief. But of the latter, he was satisfied that whatever their "need to know," so poorly had he taught the "practical applications and tactical operations" sections, knowing little about those himself, that if they wanted to use such knowledge, they'd have to send down for a high-priced specialist. He'd bragged to Willie that "if I'd taught those troopers at People's Park how to use gas, there'd be grass growing in the streets right now. Maybe a hundred Guardsmen taken hostage, too." He felt clean.

Saint Paul had written:

Good show on the box the other week, eh? Do they let you Mad Scientists watch? Old Wally Crankcase reeeely pulled out all the stops, dintee?

"Virility Base is Down! They're on the Moon!

Man is on the Fuckin' Moon!" I thought he was gonna pee in his videotrou, I did, and short the whole show out. Fuckin'-A! He sounded like Mel Allen.

It occurs to me in this strange land we serve, you in your *haut monde* lab coat (learning, I gather, to murder nuns and orphans and other good works), I by advising, through a well-tongued chic (Miss Cathy's fine, thanks, if a pain at times), probated Pittsburgh (City of the Big Steal and Flammable River), laddies to hew close to the straighten-arrow, forswear the evil Weed (Makum Takum Hypocritic Oath) and to Play Fuckin' Ball with us White Middle-class Coddled Conscientiously Objecting Authorities (this is just a Family spat, all you Lazy Black Underlings—never you mind gettin' any shuckin' and jive-ass ideas about nuttin' 'cause you cain't C-O the armed robbery laws and if you don't got no diploma, you can't get no diplo-matic immunity from packin' off to shoot the yellow folks—'cause they don't give out no consciences til the 14th Grade), whether the Winning of the Moon is what the Public Really Wants? Would any of the humanesque rubble on "Queen for a Day" ask for it? I mean, it's their niggle out there in Videoville, right, Skip?

A small test: Put Bonnanzai on NBC. Put any old Kennedy Funeral on CBS. Put the Moon Epic on ABC and throw in "Wide World of Sports" coverage, with Cosell and McKay on the spot ("You've heard the stories. You've read the re-ports. They say you're lackluster in the third stage. That you fold in re-entry. That you can't go the distance. They say that when you splash down it'll be the biggest dive since Jacques Coos-toe last went down in the Marianas Trench . . .") What are they gonna watch in Tee-veetown? The Funerals, that's fuckin' what!

The way I see it, since they were only sending them up there to dance a jig, they missed the point. They should've sent Walter Hisself! "And *that's* the way it is . . . This is Walter Kangaroo, CBS News, on the Fucking Moon! How's *them* apples, you guys?" Everybody knows he wanted to go. They really ought to have done it. (Hi, Walter, missed you at Martha's Vineyard this summer. Where were you?

The Hamptons? Fire Island? Maine?: No, I wasn't anywhere. I went to the Moon . . .).

I'll tell you, Mein Herr Daktari—without background music le mondeal was, how you say in Inglis —oh, yeah: Shit. "Bleep . . . Bleeep . . . Bleeep . . . 'We're . . . bleep . . here' . . ." Big Bleep Bore is what! No guts on the table. No grinding of dreams and machines. No agony. No screaming bodies. No d-e-a-t-h! Izzat what we pay you guys for? No death? Bring 'em back alive? Are you naive, son, or what? Is that why we lavish all those stripes and pretty ribbons and medals and good lodging and fellowship and tons upon tons of chipped beef and creamed chicken on you? To survive? Holy suffering—would Jesus be worth a prayer if He hadn't crapped out?

Martyrs, m'man, martyrs. Once you're in it you've got to go all the way. No halvesies. Bring 'em back in a body bag or a paper bag, an ox cart, a goat cart, or a pushcart. *Then* we'll talk turkey and Thanksgiving. How the hell can we thank the Good Lord if nobody's dead?

Like you say, America needs heroes to eat for breakfast, slipped soft between the cornflakes. Lindbergh and the Baby were delicious; Jack's been good for snacks.

Keep your ass down and your chin up and don't accept rides from Teddy the K (you go to limbo). He should have gone to the Moon, poor bugger. What do you figure?

So don't put your faith in heroes, they might just miss their bus or drive off a bridge with a broad who can't swim. And don't be anyone's whole prayer if you can help it: you don't want to disappoint. I hear Armstrong pulled rank to be No. 1.

And speaking of which, enclosed please find a word from the Big Guy, Who, after all, is everywhere (even in dirty books) and especially likes to hang around with me (and by the way, I am fine— no thanks to you—how are you?).

He speaks: "So long, sucker. I'm sorry I ever knew your aunt when I see how you turned out. By-the-by boy, I'm doing Final Galley Edits on the Book of Life for 1970–71. Do you happen to have a large animal around the house? I'm not sure We're gonna extend your option. We'll see. Shape up. It's one, two, three strikes you're out in this league. The Earth, Bowen, was not invented when you were born, nor are yesterday's promises binding. You dig?—Me-Three."

Listen, Ty, He may not mean it. I had no idea He was so pissed. He's been a little grumpy lately because whatsisname, the guy who thinks he runs the place, said the Moonshow was "the Greatest Week Since Creation." It turns out that He's kind of partial to the Flood and Easter One. I heard Him grumble, in fact, that He saw *Gone With the Wind* and the New York World's Fair in one week back in '39. . . . But, *chac-Un à son goût,* I say. 'Snow reason to take it out on us.

Here's the big pitch though: some accident's got three stars coming together and He's got diddly on the back burner to show for it. He may get unpissed and tap you for a Bene. (Says He's sure as heck not going to fool around with a Jewish girl again after what happened last time!) I reminded him there's a big rockfest coming up at Bethel (of all the hubris) but He says He's gonna make it rain like hell. He really doesn't stay mad long, and kind of nods off now and then. Once He didn't talk to me for a couple of months because I dropped His name to nail that chick from Campus Crusade for Christ, then wouldn't tell him the details. So be cool. He just wants you to believe, that's all. He's, well, lonely. He's American on His Mother's side, you know. Keeps the radio on for company.

If you doubt any of this, Cathy was on the extension, the little princess (the phone, not Cathy—but she's pink and cute, too, and falls off the table when you . . .). She can vouch. Vouch. There, she vouches. I vouch, we vouchons, they vouchent—how'm I doing so far? I must say, though, He and we take a dim view of modern goat-hunting. Pure tragedy. He *knows.* And He *tells.* Can I believe what I hear about *beagles?*

Wait for a Call, but if you need Him in a flash

He can be a Prince. He's in the Book, you know.
Listed under "One True Big Guy"—first name, *"The."*
Paulus

Johanna paid close attention to the summertime
events at her remove. She noted how children like herself had discarded street battles for songs and mass
pleasure. They showed their potency by chanting mightily for sunshine. And the heavens opened, pouring
buckets. In her notebook she wrote, "We are stardust,
we are golden, we are full of shit."

And while the aging sixties' youth chose drugs and
music in a farmer's field one muddy weekend, massaging their waning zeitgeist, the far side of stoned reverie's moon waxed on the western coast. It shone in
foggy Angeleno night, traces in the clouds observed
as antiparticles. A coven of children crazed by drugs
and dark charisma sloshed through blood like surfers.
It was later thought they'd killed the Lennon Sisters'
father. They'd left their desert hideout where a score
of movies had been shot and searched for a rock 'n'
roll producer who thought little of their master's voice.
They came upon the home where Doris Day's son had
lived the year before with Edgar Bergen's daughter.
Inside was a starlet and her party guests, a hairdresser,
a coffee heiress, and others, all linked by dope and
curious couplings. The starlet was the new wife of a
director who turned horror into art. She was the midnight fantasy of Playmate idolators. The synthesis was
deadly energy, spreading fear down the canyon roads
to the suburban streets. It was visible, palpable, red
in the moonlight, as the mist that Hollywood, the womb
that spawned them all, once used to signify the last
plague on the Pharaohs.

Future plagues would come in more benign disguises,
from more banal beginnings, by familiar urges and
simple means. There would be poisoned wells and
choking air, killer love, and Great Engines run dry of
gas, irresistible cans of hairspray.

All of these, Johanna noted, were clues in search of
meaning, rootless images. But she remembered something about the cusp of times: these things came in on
moonbeams, in the night.

In late October she finally wrote to Tyler, having spotted his picture in a magazine story about the research at Case. "I see where they say, 'Not since Pythagoras played with triangles in the sand . . . has there been a closer approach to the secret of nature's mystic beauty as this biological hegira. . . .' *Whoo!!* Dear, dear Tyler, is it true? Or are you all like Fermat: almost touching something in a dreamy state?" Her letter hinted not at all of her long silence. Tyler picked up her clue, and did not mention it either.

"You know what they say about Monsieur F.," he wrote. "Tetched in the head. Deranged. Intuitive, but, er, ah . . . wrong, except that he's right.

"My own honest opinion is we're on the verge of positing an elaborate new conceptual system of fictive constructs. Pragmatism dominates. (A reality based on error is as good as any if it works, better than some.) Personally, I think our greatest result will be defining the limits of understanding. Try selling *that* to the public. That's not exactly a better toaster-oven or a brighter picture on the tube, but. . . ."

She answered in early November with a photocopy of her father's memorial for Einstein, and a pleasant surprise.

"I'm working on your almost-annual Christmas present. If I can't finish it in time to deliver by Yuletide, I'll have to hand-carry it." She said she was proud of him whatever shape the project took, as he was part of a great promise "to release so much benign energy." Still, he wished she'd share it with him.

Carl Poulson had written of Einstein:

"In my heart I hope a Unified Field Theory might be true, and provable, just as I hope, in faith, that an extant Deity will reveal Himself to skeptical eyes. As Einstein held, 'The Creator is subtle, but He is not malicious.'

"Yet, sometimes there comes a despair that says any effort to distill the universe into symbol must fail. Nature may be, at long last, a series of statements about what is, fiats of existence, with provability—even plausibility to us—an incidental trait. Our tools, our logic, have limits. There may be stations of the cosmos, islands of reality unreachable from where we stand, except by giant leaps: imagination, intuition, intellectual arrogance—or faith. All of these were abundant in Einstein's work. Especially faith.

". . . The leap from nothing to something, from inert to organic, from chance to purpose to consciousness—from ignorant and certain atoms to creatures capable of . . . doubt, is more than Math and Chemistry can account for, and minds explain. . . .

"His was a bold journey, then, but it was doomed to incompletion. . . . No man may ever see to that road's end. But should we disbelieve the road itself, we would be left with the promise of today's bleak philosophy, whose moral Einstein so strongly rejected: anxiety would be loose in the universe. There would be a need for faith without a reason. God, even if living, would yet be playing dice. Beauty would not be truth and whim would have the upper hand. So we are left, in the middle of the journey, simply with a choice of faiths. . . ."

Tyler was wildly flattered by the comparison her note implied, however modest. He wrote back, "To think that if all our work goes well, if we find the means to understand so many enormous things in our piecemeal way, and so many greater, smaller things, that our reward might be such lovely words! (Not to mention serenades by Princeton boys in yachting pants!!) . . ."

She did not respond to his letter. In late November, Tyler wrote her again, this time from Washington, D.C., on stationery of "The President's Commission on the Allocation of Life Science Research Facilities." He'd gone down there at Commission expense that week, and he and Saint Paul Hooper had spent the fifteenth marching against a war, again.

"While Bar was riding shotgun in a whirlybird," the letter read,

St. P. and I trudged like troopers. I understand Willie was going to do the same out your way, maybe even make a public gesture. (He turned down a plane ride here on some kind of principle. Both sides wanted to exploit him. Could be an auction next

670

time.) Did you? We were not what you would call alone.

I was wondering as I walked, how many kids knew about the goat business I wrote you about. How many really *knew?* How many still believed in heroes and the Cavalry, the U.S. Army'll Save the Day and Send the Marines? Get Congress to Pass a Law and the Supreme Court to Strike It Down, because Good Guys Win in the End? How many of them knew the actual truth—that while the poor damned goat lay dying the Cavalry took its union break and had a smoke? Maybe they learned it in other ways. You know, there's that optimism that molecules believe in, that binds them from the first step above the inert all the way to life, the thing that informs them, tells them to try, to keep on keeping on, hang in there, strive, live, exist, be unentropic. But things can filter down, too. And if the lesson is the good and fine must perish, the base and mean have achieved dominance, it won't take long before it drifts down to the molecules themselves, and tells them not to bother.

But there must have been a half a million of us, anyway, shouting against the infamy of it. We carried names of dead in Dixie Cups, Ours and Theirs, from Arlington to the Capitol, a candle in the cup for every soul, and laid them in wooden coffins. At Willie's request I carried a boy named Diego Lupe's name. I also marched for Baron Zermatt's elusive soul. (Mine can take care of itself.)

The route took us across a bridge and around the Lincoln Memorial. It was brown and frigid. Then we marched past the Presidential Palace. We were supposed to shout the name we carried. I thought of what Willie had told me about a Good Laugh, but chickened out. I doubt it would have woken the spirits or the sleeping Commander in Chief. My breath was frosty and I could see it drift past the iron gates into the morning.

After lunch, with the great gray government build- ing hiding the afternoon sun, adding to the chill, we marched—flowed, really, a river—toward the Wash-

671

ington Monument, into an ocean of others. You should have seen the faces. At least they were alive.

The speakers spoke. Everyone from the past year was there, even Gene. But not Bobby. The musicians played. The freaks grabbed the mike for a turn or two. And all of us called "Freedom," and "Peace"— and "Sunshine" while the freeze settled in waves. Then one more time, half a million of us (and no fewer brands of ideology!) calling to the White House a hundred yards away, just to Stop the War. Maybe it was too much of a miracle we were asking.

Around the castle were a ring of buses. Then the gates. And the gardens. The lawn. The white walls and catacombs. And we screamed a prayer to the Commander in Chief of all dead goats and children. But voices can't raise the dead, and no surge of rectified emotion and music and prayer could budge him from his easy chair to turn off the bloody football game.

I forgot to tell you something Saint Paul said Friday. The boy said, "He isn't really dead, you know, He's just a hostage." Then he mumbled something morose, so I had to spend an hour telling him it really didn't matter, anyway. He couldn't prove it.

The Commission finished its work in the first months of 1970. Weighing on their deliberations were priorities imposed by the year-old Administration. It was getting expensive to conduct both an undeclared and a covert war while the people craved domestic extravagances, too. Surtaxes were not enough, though they imposed a harsh economic reality on such demands. Some things had to go.

Unexpected cooperation came from the military itself. Those malign things under study at Gila were an embarrassment now, the United States having committed itself to accepting the 1925 Geneva Protocol against chemical and biological warfare, "with certain exceptions such as tear gas and other agents of control." A representative from the Army War College at Carlisle, Pennsylvania, told the Commission, "The accidental deaths over the years make it difficult to say this, as it's never easy to admit men may have died in vain, but these things are frankly more of a nuisance. And most of the stuff is obsolete now anyway. Further development is not cost-effective."

He explained to them that lasers and masers were where the action was. Using the same principles of microwave technology that promised crispier fried chicken in home ovens and made long-distance broadcasting cheap, antipersonnel weapons made practical by miniaturization brought this technology into the field. The maser, he explained, "can take an individual enemy miles away and fry him alive from the inside out." It could turn a heart to stony ash, turn blood to steam, and render irises sclerotic—"the translucent jell of the vitreous humor would become a hard, callous scar," the man said.

And the laser, so useful in fine surgery and industry, able to fuse or vaporize anything, already could be found ringing missile and antimissile sites, irresistible, the perfect light, blindly waiting. Above them, perched in the nostrils of Minutemen and Titans and in Poseidons under the sea, were the elements sufficient for catastrophe. A would-be enemy would become "a festival of minerals," the man assured them, his land resemble Uranus.

"So you have no problems with the closing of Gila?" he was asked.

"With its closing? No. Our problem right now is learning peaceful coexistence, to coin a—" Amused Commission members lurched forward and asked him to clarify. He smiled easily. "Just a phrase to get your attention. We have to learn to cohabit with these poisons. Right now the warehouses are stuffed to the gills. We don't know where to put it all."

"You could destroy it, you know," a Commission member from the National Science Foundation said.

"Maybe you'll tell us how. At present there is no safe way. The surplus is stacked in every shed and bin from Fort Detrick to the Rocky Mountain Arsenal." He said it was "in dumps, on the ends of runways, at the outskirts of twenty cities," in so many secret stashes "the bookkeepers can't give me a hard count."

What pleasure Tyler derived at the dismantling of the monster was mitigated by his memory of lying in behalf of it, of burying Len Tobias in cant and continuing, by his subsequent silence, to laugh about it. Inside Tyler Bowen, the price of his wartime compromises signaled him in a small voice. "Are you even *aware*," an angry black student at Cornell had demanded, "that your contemporaries have been busting their chops against Mr. LBJ's and Mr. Trickster's war?"

"I did my share," Tyler had replied. "Don't let it worry you." It only worried him and made him another of its casualties.

The man from the National Science Foundation was appalled at the locations of these stored venoms. "Are the engineering tolerances fine enough to forbid some kind of catastrophe?"

"Gentlemen," Armistead Sheaffer assured them when asked, "I have made the relevant material available to the President. And his answer is that he, at least, has faith in the capacity of our engineers to solve these little problems."

"No big deal, really," Zermatt said to Tyler at the buffet dinner when the Commission wrapped up. "Piece of cake. Easy aces."

"You ever read the charter of Gila Compound, Bar?" Tyler asked, filling his plate. "Study it?"

"Many a night when I couldn't sleep. I've even read the supporting documents. Better than hot milk. It's all inoperative now."

"Including all that jive about the slim, poor, dim chance that in the heart of here alone on the globe— what's the rest? 'The resource, the potential, and the willingness to heal the infirmities of the globe—' "

"That's not even the best stuff," Zermatt laughed. "There are drafts they threw out that're *really* purple— about 'rendering mercy, bounty, and kind succor'— stuff like that to—this is my favorite—'the parched lips and twisted bones of the suffering half of humankind.' Ya gotta love it!"

"Who?"

"You. Me."

"No. I mean, if not us, *who*. Who'll do it?"

"Skippy, I never thought I'd say this, but you are a closet imperialist! After all this time! You want to be Lyndon Johnson and give 'em all their measles shots.

674

Ya gotta understand the imposed economics of the situation and—maybe they don't want it. Don't forget individual choice. You can't forget that."

"Where'd you get that phrase—'imposed economics'?"

"Reigeluth. Oh, hey, there's an item of minor amusement. Last week Warren drank himself silly and—"

"It's not a far fall."

"Well, he was moaning how nobody here *reads* anything. No Montesquieu, no Locke, no Mill—not even Mao. No Hobbes—"

"I'd add the Constitution to that list," Tyler said.

"What a crybaby he turned out to be. Said he doesn't want to stay in town, so he's going back to Tombstone in a top spot—coming in, so to speak, through the roof."

"His new wife should love it as much as the last one. He didn't happen to say if he'd heard anything, did he?"

"Your department entirely, lost-cause lover that you are."

"Some are more lost than others. We write. Sometimes talk." He lifted his wine glass in mock salute. "She should be preserved like a National Monument."

Zermatt took a long draught and swallowed dramatically. "When you're through erecting statues to all the ladies in your life, Skippy, there won't be a dog in this country with a bladder problem or a pigeon without a place to park."

Tyler shook his head lugubriously. "Only one, Bar, only one." Those other women were different. He'd grown tired of their twists and gyres quickly; theirs were a finite repertoire. Whenever he wanted to explain himself to anyone, even another woman, he had to tell of Johanna, and they grew tired of that.

He did not talk to her, as he had claimed to Baron. Her failure to answer his latest letters kept him from calling. All that remained now was remembrance, stubborn belief. That, too, was withered, dwindled with time. She didn't send her promised Christmas present, and Tyler allowed himself to forget her half-promise that she would be hand-delivering it. Willie said he ran into her from time to time, that she looked well, seemed well, asked about him "politely." It should have been enough to convince Tyler there was not a chance. But still, he returned to her in his thoughts, as though a shrine, to get his bearings in the world.

At times Tyler found himself cheating off those memories, exposing her to unclean strangers, telling about her as a fable of calculated impact, useful in the coping or mating games like a novel read in college. Too late he recognized it as another form of rape. But equally often, even in the flush of making love to someone else, he'd think silently "one more time, Johanna," and see her eyes in a rear-view mirror.

"Stick with me," he'd told her. But, as with Willie, he had to admit "you could never lay a glove on her." That's why he loved her, he recalled, trapped in the paradox of things. Her memory had left only the small scar, a lesion on his brain, and the feeling, like the unquiet traces of a former life, that something, once, was there.

CONSIDER HER EYES: SO PRECARIOUS THEIR balance between visions past and possible, things seen and wished. They were too kinetic and informed to be called beautiful. Their extraordinary color was added grace, unnecessary for the many miracles besides. They were, in any shade, delicate, and passionate, alive. They held seas of luster and dread, and the brew that only came from living, dreams and tears.

Johanna's limbs could open up to let her out, then close to wall the world off. By will she could bring things in or withstand oppressive gravity.

She was a creature of imaginings, all personal, unique; so fragilely special.

Now her mind simply hurt. She'd come to distrust

her hunches and her words. She analyzed the intuitions of others for course credit, but couldn't find her own. The music she loved seemed different on hearing now, transposed to a minor key. The poems she wrote resembled her true nature as the product of seven mighty streams run through a single duct would their sources. A membrane stood between herself and her expression, like a sheet between two lovers; flimsy everything.

Her time at Berkeley was not without men, but each of them came with insufficiencies. "What do they want from me?" she asked an analyst she'd started seeing.

"To be yourself. If you knew your own needs, perhaps—"

"They change daily," Johanna said. "My needs."

The woman said, "Not the real ones."

"What are they?"

"What do you think they are?"

With one or two of these men, Johanna was briefly touched, taken by surprise, moved slightly. Barely budged. Most of the time she remained clothed in her apartness, unwilling to believe any of these men were intimate with her fate, seeing each as, somehow, kindly, not enough.

She always had a bad taste afterward, feeling prodigal in squandering her days tending boys' unworthy vanities. One was an undergraduate of affected gentility. Another was rougher than the common run of graduate students; he said he could see inside her brain, match her stride for stride. He frightened her, made her feel "trapped," she said, and "owned." One day he struck her, and even as she ran away, he shouted after her the reasons why she did so.

Once, years before, Carl Poulson had spied his daughter looking broodish. He asked her what the matter was, since her gaiety was key to his. She answered that it was something he'd said. "To you? Did I scold you?" She said that wasn't it. "Well, I can't imagine anything I would say that I might believe if it made you unhappy. That would conflict with what I love most." She said it was something he'd told her about never knowing everything, not anything finally, because the heavens were still exploring their own possibilities.

Surprised to find she'd understood that, he sat her

down and soothed her. "Sweetheart," he said, "that's the beauty of it. I wouldn't want to know all there was because every day it becomes even more beautiful. Like little girls. They just become more wonderful. It'd spoil the fun of tomorrow." He called her a "happy Archimedes, who could move the world with laughter." Now she wondered where she'd misplaced that simple tool.

Her mother was exhausted by it all. Over an Easter visit, Maureen said, "Darling, look at me: I've made my life happy. I've made my mistakes, too, but I live with them."

"You mean me?"

"My God, the self-pity! You have had everything. More than that. Let me tell you something. I knew a girl, when I was a child, whose father rowed her into the middle of a lake and said, 'I don't like you, Sally, or your mother. You were an accident.' And he dove in, just like that. He was mad. That woman has a career, she's raised good babies, and she leads what I think you'd agree is an exemplary life. She's tired at night from good efforts, she's a woman of quiet decency. And you, you've had it so easy—walking around as if you're a zombie. I just don't know what to do. What does that doctor tell you?"

"Results, she says, take time. And even then, they're very hard to gauge. It's not medicine, it's a life-style."

"Does it do anything for you?"

"I'm fine, really. I'm quite happy. I don't know why everyone assumes I'm not. I'll even have a doctorate to prove it—I can tell other people they're not happy."

There was a nightmare Johanna had often, she'd told the analyst. The woman nodded understandingly. "The rape?" Laughing faintly, Johanna said, "No. It's an impotence dream. I thought only men had those."

"Not always. It depends on what you're missing."

At a farm one weekend in Monterey, Johanna made the uncharacteristically public effort of attending an encounter group. She thought the others showed a morbid, sadistic interest in each others' pain, and hers. It felt rapine, sarcophagous. She did not like her whole measure being taken and she fled before the weekend was over.

A friend of hers brought her into a women's group in Berkeley, and Johanna mentioned letters she had received from "this man, a friend of mine—"

"A lover?" one of them asked.

"Former," Johanna said. She told them about one letter and at their request read parts of it to them at the next meeting.

"I should tell you," Tyler had written,

that I still perk up to noises that have overtones of your voice. I jerk around at familiar backs of heads —almost dropped a coffee maker the other day (important work going on here, yes)—and when I see similar walks. But no one has your face or voice. They are not you.

The other day I was out walking on Euclid Avenue and I heard a telephone ringing. It was snowing and there was no traffic. I thought it might be you. There was a man walking, that's all, and he didn't hear the phone. (I even had a notion for a moment that somehow the Baron knew where I was strolling, or maybe even St. Paul's buddy was back in town and found a dime.) But I was hoping it'd be you. The man didn't hear the phone because it wasn't ringing. Nothing. Pure thought, an understanding of ringing, but no Call. I phoned a lot of friends that night because I was, well, lonely, and there was a cold wind coming off of the lake. No one was home. I called you and your line was busy. Then there was no answer, so I watched TV and fell asleep, deciding somehow you didn't want me to call. . . .

My name is attached to the work here (and that Commission Report) rather like a loose tooth. But we seem to enjoy the unnatural affection of the Prexy of the U.S.A. (I think he's a fan of Chemistry to the extent that his daily reality may be a function of Ups and Downs he's popping, pity for us all) and that doesn't hurt. From which I judge there to be a Good-to-Poor chance (just about covers the field) that I'll nail that Fulbright and be Yanked to Oxbridge next year. It's neutral territory, Pilgrim. Interested in seeing Jolly Olde (me?), what ho?

She said she didn't answer the letter, and he'd stopped writing weeks ago.

"I forgot why you brought it up," one of the women said.

"I forget, too," Johanna said.

"He sounds like he's in love with you." Johanna nodded, but another woman offered, "Only men have faith in those Calls. Fate opens for them; look at his luck! Joan of Arc is a myth. All burning, no glory."

They all agreed: she and many of them had had experiences of a level and intensity that would cast a man for greatness, certainly happiness. If one could believe in such Calls, power and prominence could be theirs, insights convertible as leverage. But the world conspired to confine heroic women to lives of heroic frustration, heroic sadness.

One said hypnotically, "I watch my face in the mirror. It's starting to slide and sag. I don't think there's any courage or stamina that will prevent it becoming my mother's face. It's just a short drop. She gave me cadaverish bone-structure."

They agreed: each of them had victories and routs the envy of any ribboned General. But Generals didn't have the fear of winding up like the thousand sad-eyed secretaries, divorcees, ex-lovers, and disappointees who haunted chic bars: women who must barter for affection's salve, mistresses to the snap-tied businessmen. Women, each and all with stories that could shake your spine, women whom the world wore down.

They would disbelieve those nightmares if they could, because accepting them would be to despair of the world, and that was contrary to their deeper needs. But faith just now would be more naive than public tolerance would permit. The lesson of their reinforcement group was to reinforce a melancholy and pernicious notion: that the rule of getting older was to accept the bowing of one's head.

But as much as she won their esteem, they became to her people whose esteem she did not want, defeatists, a group who watched themselves watch themselves. This, too, made her uncomfortable, a binding paradox, and she felt as though her friends now fell into three categories, all insufficient: those who loved her unconditionally, as though she were a star immune to social obligations; those who made her feel as though she had to earn their love, prove herself, a thing that made her withdraw and become perverse; and those who she felt closest to, uniformly the farthest ones away. She told her analyst about her feelings and the woman asked, "What makes you feel that way?"

"I feel that way," Johanna answered. It was another double-bind of self-consideration, an endless loop.

"You don't have to feel that way," the analyst said. "How?"

"Don't feel that way." Johanna burst out laughing, wildly, uncontrollably, until tears freckled her cheeks. When she caught her breath she said, "You know what? I've really discovered something. I'm always happier when I leave here, but not right away. I'm always miserable when I first leave, then I get happier, until I come back. I don't think I've ever left here feeling better than when I came. Maybe it's because I feel stupid being here. Or maybe it's because I feel so stupid being here when I know it's so stupid."

"Which do you think?" the woman asked, unruffled.

"I think you're crazy. I really do!" Johanna said evenly, and she left.

But such moments of determination were short-lived; they depleted her shallow store of energy.

When she'd sent Tyler Bowen her father's essay, Johanna had thought about the Unified Field Theory in Physics and the biological analogues in Tyler's project. Why wasn't there one for people? The lessons of the years said the whims of nature took no heed of poets. At best, a sweet—bittersweet—paradox of eternal imbalance ruled, made motion. Feelings were not to be fixed in time-space any more than particles were. Vague outlines. Nothing at the core. Even poetry did not exist, really. But one had to believe in something.

She wanted to believe she could rip free from the gravitation of chemistry or curses. "If anyone can beat the rap," Tyler insisted, "it's you." But it was so hard when the pain was immaterial, and analysis could not unwind it.

Even as she worked toward a future she dragged

this sledge. Every step made her less sure of the last one and the next ones.

There were unguarded moments when this fell away from her, moments when she laughed herself dizzy or played like a pup. The few times she ran into Willie Bowen, she felt on her mettle to be sunny and terribly good. And it always made her feel good afterward.

There was another paradox: Tyler's letters had made her happy every time they came, and now she'd forced him to let them lapse.

The central paradox she lived was she was frantic for liberty, a junkie for it, yet she yearned with equal fever for connection's order. Tyler's very patience made her feel diminished, even as it made her feel well-loved. She wished she could go back in time, or leap over all the impossible-making things she'd said, or failed to say. She felt like Fermat, dying in the face of the unsolvable, in the ambiguous battleground of the heart.

It had been a month since his last letter and that one had been tart with annoyance. "Has anyone told you it's bad manners not to answer your mail? The next unanswered note will be the last, for my own peace of mind." Still, he held out the offer: "Come to Cleveland and see the Indians. Be a cowgirl if you like. Come to Akron, enjoy the aroma on Tuesdays when they burn the rubber—smells just like Speedway at noon. Come to England and translate for me. I still have your toothbrush but it's getting kind of limp. In spite of yourself you are missed. What can I say? I can't lie."

She could not bear to write him a reply. Now, in April, it had been three months since she'd shown the simple courtesy of responding to the person she held as her best secret friend.

So she sent him a "delayed Christmas present," scribbling across the top of it "Sorry so late, my calendar broke."

It was a long scroll of rice paper, elegantly hand-printed, dedicated to "the fellow who understands— yet likes me anyway."

Her letter arrived in Cleveland the day Willie Bowen called Johanna for the first time in six months. He'd seen her here and there, talked to her a few times and always greeted her warmly, like a favorite sister. But to Tyler he reported the stray rumors and observations he'd picked up from common acquaintances, that she seemed "subdued" and sometimes "kind of glum." With the Fulbright locked up, Tyler enlisted Willie's help in a small subterfuge. "Listen," he told his kid brother, "why don't you tell her I'm blasting off for the dark side of the moon and she's invited to the launch at least."

"What if she says take a hike?" Willie asked.

"Then tell her I've got leukemia. It's worked before. Use your imagination."

So Willie called her and asked if she'd heard about Tyler winning the Fulbright. She said that he'd mentioned it in a note, and that she was thrilled for him. "Yeah, well, see, we're having this send-off bash for him in two weeks. He thinks he's gotta be in New York by then for my mom's birthday. Gonna be a terrific surprise."

"That's lovely," she said.

"So I was thinking, how'd you like to be the surprise of all time, the mystery guest?"

Johanna looked at the receiver and wished she could see Willie's face, to squint out the truth. "Did he put you up to this?" Nonetheless, she allowed herself to enjoy the idea, despite the clumsiness of it.

"Honest. He doesn't know a thing about it. Whaddya say?"

"I can't afford it," she said.

"If you wanted to, you could——"

"I'd like to," she repeated patiently. "And I can't."

"You gonna let me finish? Me and Mack were thinking and really there's only one present he'd like, y'know, and Mack says Animal's figured out a way to deduct his part off his taxes anyway, see. And me, well, it all comes out of the Mom and Pop Foundation 'cause Uncle's got the tab for school."

"It's not right, Willie."

"Tell you what. You want to make a small contribution? You can pick up my share—or Mack's. The rest is Robin Hood. Boy, I just wish we could get his

683

face on film when you hit the ramp instead of me. I mean, I'll be right there behind you, but boy, what a sight that'll be! Huh?"

"Are you sure this is all right? You've asked your parents?"

"Are you kidding? Sure I'm sure. They ate it up. Our gene pool's getting kind of weak, y'know."

"Willie, let's not get carried away. This is just a party."

"Yeah, sure, I forgot. See, it's no big deal for me, I'm gonna see him in Europe anyway this summer. You're the big deal."

"OK, John Alden, I give up. You've called my bluff." Her whole face felt warm and tickly. "Both of you."

"Far out. I'll get your ticket to you as soon as I get my check from them—you don't mind going student fare, do you? I know this girl whose ID you can——"

"I'd even go by bus." She felt shot through with a queasy energy that day, laughing giddily for no apparent reason. The next morning she still felt nervous, and called Willie to say she was having second thoughts, embarrassing herself by doing so. She wavered and left it that she was tilted in favor of going, but didn't want anyone's plans contingent on it. That made her feel better. She would go, but didn't want to lose her freedom until the last moment. Still, she felt deliciously full of silliness and beans at the prospect. Wild, unprepared-for imaginings made her weak, delirious, and very much younger, all of a late April day.

In Cleveland, Tyler mounted Johanna's present on the wall where all his colleagues could see it. One laboriously copied it to show his children and another urged it be sent in to some kind of journal. "Somebody's got to be right for it. Surely you can find someone who'd publish it."

Tyler shook his head more in admiration than doubt. "The lady herself is a shape for which there is no description. If there was a category she fit into, she'd fight her way the hell out of it. Ya just gotta love her."

The scroll read:

The Sweet Paradox by Johanna Poulson
(after C. Poulson)

The last thing Monsieur Fermat wrote
Was just a cryptic little note:
"A most *enchantant* thing occurs
    When adding squares of integers:
    They often yield another squared!
    Can we infer this trait is shared
    By cubes and other powers higher?
    Can other figures so conspire
    To make (of that pow'r) something new
    At superscripts above but two?

"We know that squares of *A* and *B*
    Can summate in the square of *C,*
    But can *D* cubed plus cube of *E*
    Make some *F* at the pow'r of three?
    Mais non! Toutes seules Pythagorean
    Groupings (squares) are not plebeian:
    Squares *uniquely* can be summed!
    At no pow'r greater can it be done.

"Now I've a *charmant* proof, *petit,*
    C'est *simplement* and *tout* sweet.
    Oui, it's so basic, plain, and wise,
    'Tis odd it's yet escaped all eyes.
    I'll jot it down before I sleep.
    Merde! Tiny margins! Well, 'twill keep.
    I'll write it down tomorrow morn.
    It's waited this long to be born—
    Such beauty will not fade away,
    With dawn it shall see light of day . . ."

And that is all he wrote, that night.
He never did see morning's light.
He died, *en pax,* while in his bed,
His proof tucked silent in his head.

Now there's the thorn in math-men's side:
The pain which goes before their pride;
This thing they feel—and *know*—as true,
Its proof eludes them, though they do

Devote their years and sweat and hopes
To reconstructing Fermat's notes.
Computers now have joined the quest,
Submitting new proofs to the test.
But nothing seems to show just why
He wrote that on the night he died.
Oh, they've tried algebra and graphs,
Tried calculus and higher maths,
Tried every trick in every text,
But come up empty and perplexed.
The theorem's *true:* no series show
A contradiction. Did he *know?*
Or did he make some minor flaw
And pass with error in his craw?

Another view, less current than
The facile words "mistaken man,"
Might say that Fermat knew his time
Was running out and that the prime
Problem for his friends on Earth
Was finding proofs of living's worth.
For when all things are plainly known,
All proved and catalogued and shown,
The role of minded man is moot,
When laws are stagnant, absolute.
Perhaps his mind, as sound as clay,
Devised a clever game to play
Eternally: the proof's absurd!
For possibly, that night he heard
A Voice. That is to say: a Word
Bespeaking powers of the third.

Consider: all our formulae
Are also just another way
Of stating properties observed
In forms straight, angular, or curved.
The exponentials of one tangle
Chart for us a right triangle;
Graphs of other shapes revealing
Grand equations they're concealing.
But yet: no process known on Earth
Nor shape the human mind can berth
Has yielded cubes of *A* and *B*
Which added make the cube of C.

The closest few approximations,
Oddly, are the field equations
Locked within another soul's
Death-sealed hunch, his lifelong goal.
'Tis thought perhaps that Einstein found
The root of form and Being's ground,
Uniting diverse paths, in sooth,
Revealing Fermat's basic truth:
   Perhaps in some vast reach of space
   Quite different from our time and place,
   At fringes of the universe,
   The first is last and last is first.
   That is to say, as matter dies,
   It's re-created in some eyes.
   In some dimensions passing five,
   The past has yet to come alive.
   A cosmic topographic riddle:
   Outsides find themselves the middle;
   Farthest out, the closest in;
   What's finished, ready to begin.
   Thus is the cosmos made anew
   By powers greater than but two.
   Of course, no graph could chart this truth;
   This paradox eludes all proof.
   The riddle's root was thus begun
   When Nought contrived to equal One . . .

So possibly in Fermat's ear
That voice made these conundrums clear.
The voice would speak but one more time
In whispers full in Einstein's mind.
To Fermat, saying, "When men know
All riddles' answers—all must go.
So quickly now, one moment's jot,
That's all the patience I have got.
Your time, *Monsieur,* is closing now,
You'll have this last breath to endow
The world with some bequest to stall
That time when I must end it all."

Thus at his end the dying man
Took up his quill and book in hand.
He penned those words. His gift to be:

A tail to chase, eternally.
His final theorem has *no proof;*
It's paradoxic'ly aloof
From solving. Fermat's testament:
A last will. An encouragement
To mathematicians 'round the Earth
A present of galactic worth:
The heavens' chart, in earthly signs
Sweet Paradox!—creating time.
Unknowable; unmissable:
It makes all things permissible.
This simple theorem, ever turned,
Will stave off that day all is learned;
Forbidding last things, fatal, dire,
Making entropy a liar,
Preventing consummation's fire,
By flawless truth: unquenched desire.
The heart of conscious history,
Existence's whole mystery,
The roots of all Eternity,
Are found in that Affinity,
For Being of One Trinity.

And thus, within the theorem's core
Is held the promise: something more.
Infinite preface to "Amen"—
The deathless words, "World without end."

Attached to the bottom was Maureen Poulson's duplicate of a police report dated January 1969:
"White woman, 24, 65 inches, 112 lbs, Hair: Lt Brn., Eyes: Bl-Grn. Not considered dangerous. Detain and contact this office, Attn: Missing Persons."

THERE WERE QUAKES ON THE MOON, according to the Smithsonian Institution's Center for the Study of Short-lived Phenomena and Arizona's Deep Space Communication Center; and blood on the Earth. According to Kitt Peak's astronomical observatory, there was such severe sunspot activity in late April that normal radio communications and weather patterns were disrupted.

Of man-made things, late April was a time of quiet catastrophes: an oil spill in Alaska, mercury contamination in Lake Erie. Of unaccountable things, reindeer were dropping dead in Sweden. Saint Paul Hooper was writing deranged letters to Neil Armstrong and John Glenn. Both had relocated themselves, inexplicably, to Cincinnati, and Saint Paul peppered them with requests for information about what they'd seen from their stellar vantages "and Who." Also unaccountably, Willie Bowen was defying all natural law by getting straight honor grades at Stanford. In Phoenix, Maureen Poulson was informed by Edward Denning that "a hustling young ACLU lawyer" had secured a writ of error for Richard Ellis, setting his conviction aside. They agreed there was no point pursuing the matter further.

It had been four years—an internalized measure to a college generation—since Johanna Poulson had left San Francisco for the desert. Not quite three years since she met Tyler Bowen and found him complementary; a little more than two since the world consented to be their epoxy; over a year since they had last seen each other. She was back in Berkeley, but planning to surprise him by flying to New York to celebrate his good fortune; she was willing to risk reunion's allied threat.

It was spring in California, a time of sumptuous bloom. Thoughts turned to regenerations as the world greened. It was known that moods depended greatly on environment and so the seasons were always news. The environment itself was now news as well, and in late April a day was set aside, made official by presidential proclamation: "Earth Day." As the weather was news, so had the news become a mere weather report: delivered authoritatively, people were its hostages, lives were affected by the storms and torment, but they could not alter it. Yet how they did talk about it!

To the keen-eyed, late April's skies were scuddy, green with static overload, the anxiety of undischarged electricity and unrevealed events. The source was known abroad, all over the world, but not in the United States. Alone on the globe, America was ignorant because of a theory of governance devised at Tombstone Center, refined at Gila Compound, and adopted throughout the government: that ideas and information were parcels, quanta, particles not waves, and were amenable to regulation, control, and interdiction. It was a long way from Boston Harbor. The information was denied the right of transit into the United States, prohibited, quarantined offshore, embargoed. American journalists were uneasy over this, but an Assistant Press Secretary said, when they pressed for release from their vows, "If the people had to choose between no news and no dinner—no dinner is bad news."

Then the blister was lanced and what had been known to be occurring nine thousand miles away was revealed through its very mutation: the secret bombing of Cambodia had finally ceased, and American troops in Vietnam had now invaded that nation. Stocks on the Big Board plunged to new lows and all across the country American campuses erupted one more time in the fatalistic rituals of anguish. All around Tyler Bowen colleges exploded. Miami of Ohio, Kent State University, Ohio State University, and Ohio U.—all went wild. His own reaction was sympathetic to the protesters' when he heard the invasion news on television. His eyes

690

bugged wide in disbelief and he screeched, "Is he mad? Is he out of his fucking *skull?*"

But he confined his own protest to that expression. Case Western stayed calm, except that a symposium scheduled to discuss "The Legacy of Earth Day: Quo Vadis?" turned into a free-for-all merely for the presence of a participating Department of Commerce ecologist. A woman in the audience had stood up when the government man began to speak and shouted, "Eat shit!"

He'd tried to gloss it over saying, "Well, as a recycling suggestion, its merits are—"

She screamed back, "Recycle Nixon! Recycle Nixon!" He looked ill at ease, as though the walls had ears. She was asked to leave and a small scuffle broke out with catcalls and obscenities pouring from the audience.

"Please! Please," the man from Commerce implored. "Let the lady stay. She's told us what's on her mind—" They booed him lustily and he wagged an elegant finger at them, "I should think those of us opposed to violence must be consistent in opposing its subtler forms—"

The moderator tried to calm everyone down, his voice crackling through the microphone: "A university must keep a neutral stance—to preserve academic freedom—"

"It's academic," a heckler yelled, "but is it freedom?"

The moderator closed his eyes in a sign of exceeding patience. "Violence and mob action have no place at a seat of learning except on the football field. You know that."

"Where would you have been at Lexington and Concord?" a voice from the far back demanded. The panelists looked at each other, confused, so the man from Commerce tried again, "If you had a gun as loaded as that question," he shot back, "we'd both be in danger." They rejected his wit by voice vote and howled angrily.

In the din, a chant began, "Up against the wall, motherfucker! Up against the wall!"

The beleaguered man from Commerce's smile faded and his face turned white. He screeched back, "I've seen walls! Have you? I've seen them in Cuba and when our Army liberated Europe!" His hands were squeezing sawdust from the tabletop. "Even those of us who believe in nonviolence"—the laughing rejection of this did not slow him—"know it can be social suicide. This government will not price itself out of the ballgame—and become the prey of anyone with sticks and clubs." People were standing up, hollering epithets. "And let me tell you something—if a man leaves his door open wide because he's got some ideal against property and territory—he'd better not complain when madmen and wild animals invade his home!" Their silence was largely because they had no idea what he was talking about. "You want violence? You'll see it. There's a limit to our patience. Dialogue, yes. But walls —to keep the wild things out. Force to meet force—"

"I think it was Lincoln," the moderator interrupted, hoping to calm them all, "who asked: 'Must every government suffer from this fatal problem? Must it be too weak to preserve itself and too strong for the liberties of its people?' "

"Don't make us choose!" the man from Commerce warned. No wonder the President called students "bums," he thought.

"If you're not part of the solution," another heckler screamed, "you're part of the problem. Out of the road!"

"What a slogan!" the Commerce man fired back. "I work on the solution. What's *your* problem? What's your *solution?* To let a handful of kids at Harvard and Columbia turn a great nation? Guns? Bombing? To clean up the environment? To save the peace?"

"Castrate the bastard!" a woman's voice burst through, delicate as crystal.

In the middle of this pandemonium, the last panelist in the row pushed back his seat and bumped his way off the platform. By the time he reached the rear of the auditorium, Tyler Bowen was being cheered. "I'd invite you all to follow," he said to no one in particular. "But I'm just going to take a pee." For the audience he pumped a good-natured clenched fist in the air.

In the bathroom was a graffito in the style of a historic marker. Through the walls he could still hear the arguing in the auditorium: "Work within the system!" "That's not democracy!" "Up against—" The wall writing said: "In this place in October 1964 Lyndon Johnson composed a speech for delivery in Akron—'We are not about to send American boys nine thousand miles away from home to do what Asian boys ought to be doing for themselves!' Flush before leaving. The life you save may be your own."

Below it, someone wrote in a different hand, "Flush twice if you love Jesus." Bowen took a felt-tipped pen and added his own comment: "God lives! He lives! But He's an awful liar. We are truly, finally, existentially, alone—St. Paul." And: "God doesn't play dice. He throws darts.—Anon."

Nine thousand miles away the blood was unabated by expressions of outrage. The Great Good Nation lashed out heedlessly.

Friday was Mayday. The newspapers and airwaves were filled with stories of domestic campus violence. The first reports were calmer this time, more measured, even if the reality was not. In translation to cold type and electronic signals the news became as stripped of passion as commercial items, though commerce itself still dictated front-page play. In the slick pages of the offset news magazines, felicity of expression led observation around by a nose-ring. Radicalism, rebellion, and violence had become domestic pets.

In a way, this was accountable to styles of mind engendered by the economics of two different media. Those who reported and edited the news were raised in the dynamics of films. They assumed those who made the day, and watched, took their sense of scenario and history from television. And movies were a sensational form, necessarily bold. To lure the patrons' interest at a price required greater changes with each attempt. Movies were exciting when they were unsettling. Film credited customers, who might otherwise stay home and suck at tubes, with a sense of the past and a discontent that demanded fantastic twists of plot and new invention, small revolutions that subvert predictability.

Television, as a great pacifier, was an evolutionary art: succeeding generations of its product bred from the hardiest strains, hybridized and unsurprising. And, often, as a consequence of that inbreeding, demented. Television was without boldness because it was, like a charming cat burglar, a guest whose fortune required remaining welcome. So it avoided insult and indulged contempt. Television was wives; movies, whores. Audiences would watch their televisions and read their papers with regularity but detachment. To be shaken, or thrilled, or engaged, they went to movies.

The protests were seen on TV as a minuet of roles and expectancies, entirely deterministic. They had become a rite of spring, whose symbolism was its whole substance, and a tired one at that. If, as the demonstrators repeatedly urged, such actions were protected as a form of free speech and petition for redress of grievances, then they were not spontaneous outbursts of rage, but stylized debate about a political issue deemed settled, or at any rate boring. Demonstrations had run the course of audience tolerance. It would take greater circuses to move the populace.

But what was missing from the news reports that week, making the events seem so tediously repetitious, was precisely that sense of saturated patience that even the demonstrators felt. That was the character and heart of those protests; they would be as wars to end all wars. For there had been a sea change in their manner over the years, from the intensely philosophic appeal and formal logic, the schooled decorum, of the first Free Speech Movement rallies at Berkeley a half-decade before, to the anger-informed rhetoric and slogans of the latest ones. They had evolved to suit a hostile environment, because, while they attracted attention, their cause was not surviving. So, long gone were polite dialectics beneath arrogant moral postures. The footnotes and historical citations were dropped. Once, over issues of principle not prone to parsing, the aggrieved were willing to talk compromise. Now positions were deemed nonnegotiable. This was so because the lesson passed down to each new class in the colostrum of Orientation Week was that the sources of their dismay had shown little willingness to negotiate and none to be swayed by argument. They would not even listen. This was the only lesson of history accepted as unconditionally true. History was otherwise abandoned; reason, exhausted: power ruled.

So the unseen content of the May Day protests was appropriate to the day. Their mood was anguish and frustration with no available vocabulary to articulate it. This was something more than ritual. It was a wild, final howl of pain by those refusing to let go of faith and no other language to convey their level of desperation.

In Ohio, in Cleveland and Columbus and Athens and Kent, in Yellow Springs and Oberlin and Gambier, students ran rampant, setting fires, breaking windows, reverting to primitive expressions. All over the state it was the same and, north and south, all over the country.

"We just thank God our children are no longer in harm's way," Vlad Bowen told his eldest son on the phone Friday evening.

"If you speak to Him again, thank Him for me, too," Tyler said. What did panic his parents was when he reported, "The only agitation around here's an anniversary orgy tonight. Big bash." It was thirty-two years since LSD was discovered at Sandoz Labs in Switzerland. "And ten," he told them, "since its discovery at Case, give or take a few months."

"You're not taking any drugs, are you?" Laura Bowen asked timorously.

"Just a beer bust," he reassured her. "Purely symbolic. You gotta seize any chance you can to celebrate in Oh-ho-ho, so you don't atrophy."

"Have a nice time, then," she said.

"I plan to. It's my last chance to outrage the senior fellows, throw a show."

The next day, Saturday, he spoke to Willie: "You'll love this, meatball," he said, "it's just your speed: the big rumor is an angry horde of kids from Oberlin and Kenyon are going to sweep down on Canton for a little sacking and pillaging of the Football Hall of Fame. Supposedly they're going to defoliate Memorial Field there as a gesture. And I thought *I* was hallucinating last night!"

"I thought they had astroturf," Willie said.

"Probably. Squat's come of it. Maybe Monday night."

Tyler had heard that peculiar rumor from a straight source, in the early hours of Saturday morning. A representative of the Governor's Office of Public Safety had called him and said, "You have been detailed to us in this matter by the National Security Agency."

Groggily, he complained, "In the middle of the night? It's 5:00 A.M.! I'm a chemist—not some kind of pediatrician."

"You are a qualified chemical expert—"

"Instructor."

"—and you will report at 0730 hours to OArNG HQ, High Street, Akron, by order of the Governor."

"I don't understand a word you're saying. How do I know you're not some crank? You better put it in writing." He yawned. "Don't hurry."

No one at the Ohio Army National Guard Headquarters in Akron was the wiser for Tyler Bowen's absence, nor for any of his previous trips there, when he had taught them the rudiments of chemical and biological "defense." Nor did the Governor's aide call back.

But by Saturday night, a message carrying Tyler Bowen's name clattered onto a teletype link in Chicago's National Security Agency Field Office. The man who read it blinked twice and then grinned manically as he tore the printout off, tugging delightedly at his crotch with his free hand. He gleefully rerouted the message on a Telex circuit to Washington, with a notation: "Dupe/Attn: B. Zermatt/JustInSec." He signed off "MBG/GS-18/NSAChi." It rang a few bells at the Justice Department and the FBI man on duty gave it to the night courier who called Baron Zermatt at home to read him the wire. "Is that all it says?" Zermatt asked mechanically.

"Affirmative."

"Nothing more?"

"Negative. That's all she wrote."

"He. Yeah, thanks. I'll handle it from here."

There was no answer when Zermatt called Cleveland, not until Sunday afternoon. "Where the hell have you been?" Zermatt demanded.

"Out."

"I hope she was worth it!"

"She was. Actually I did more scoring in a softball game we had this afternoon. Christ, Bar, I was in the middle of this great nap just now. How you guys know just which dreams to bust into I'll—"

"Are you through? Listen to me, you dumb shit. You want to see England? Go ahead, take that nap!"

"Hey! If you're calling to hassle me about that bull-roar in Canton, eat it."

"Fuck you!"

"Fuck me? Fuck you! I'm not getting out of bed to stand between the National Football League and brown grass! I'm packin' to get *out* of here Tuesday!"

"Fine. Good. Just stay there. In two hours, maybe less, a man will knock on your stupid God-damned door. He will be just as stupid and evil and mean as the law allows, maybe more—"

"You're coming to visit?"

"Hey, smart guy. He will cause your arrest for being a God-damned jerk."

"When did that become a felony?"

"I'm looking at the sheet right now, Skipper. You are under contract to these guys, remember? And you have refused a lawful—"

"You're all off your rockers. This whole—"

"Tyler! Your personal opinion of it has no legitimate standing. A contract is a contract."

"You're my lawyer, Bar. Let's litigate it."

Zermatt blew an exasperated sigh into the phone. "Hey, Skippy? Grow up! You've got yourself an obligation. My own suggestion is you get your golden bod over to Akron and look like you're enjoying yourself and your shit's straight. Because in about two hours you won't have any choice: it'll be permanently flaky."

"Bar, you've got hemorrhoids on the outside, pal."

"Listen to me, Babe. We're talking about your fucking freedom now. And if you want to know why they didn't just haul you away yesterday it's 'cause the Chicago Chief of Station wants the pleasure all to himself. He should be arriving shortly. His name is Martin B.-

for-Bozo Gracie and he might just beat on you for the heck of it. Are you beginning to understand me?"

"Perfectly. Now why don't you maniacs fold it—"

"Tyler," Zermatt said, with grit in his voice and a tremble of concern, "the law will be obeyed!"

"Tell me about it, Bar!" he shouted, slamming down the phone. Tyler exhaled, and he got up to dress. "Aw, shit," he said.

In this surly mood Tyler Bowen drove to Akron, arriving at the National Guard Armory just before sundown. He stalked in still wearing the jeans and frayed-collar oxford-cloth shirt he'd played softball in, a sweater tied around his neck. He was one of the few civilian-clad people in evidence, and the only one with a football. Milling in the halls were tired, bored, edgy citizen-soldiers in fatigues and dress greens, unwilling to die in the war, preferring to kill in the peace. Some were wearing ridiculous short-hair wigs, the military being more fond of humiliation than good sense. Others were jousting with their weapons, drilling in large assembly rooms, relentlessly preparing for the Armed Forces Day parade; still others were reading, studying, sleeping.

Outside the Commander's office, two dour-faced young officers were talking. "I knew that NFL thing was a decoy. Even the ROTC building at Kent is a feint. You watch: it'll be Antioch students at the Wright Air Force Museum. You've got to think like them—"

Tyler looked at his football sheepishly. "Is Colonel Woodin around?" he asked.

"Inside," one said. They both examined his casual outfit and turned to each other blankly as Bowen went in.

"What the hell is *that?*" Colonel Woodin snapped, staring at the football.

Tyler extended it across the desk at him. "My weapon. I figure we can co-opt—" Woodin slapped it away furiously, demanding, "Where were you yesterday?"

"Home."

"You were notified yesterday. I could have you court-martialed for dereliction! We're mobilized!"

Still feisty, Bowen gazed at him with undiminished

scorn, shaking his head. "Look, I'm a civilian, a grad student, not one of your toys. I was told to report here and that's all. You want to hard-ass me by the book? I didn't get a reliable notification till today. So here I am. Now, you still think you can court-martial me?"

"Yes," Woodin nodded.

"You're nuts."

"Or arrest you. We are under martial law. You are in the area and under my jurisdiction. So you are either with us or against us, but as far as you're concerned we are the legal authorities in this region." In but a mere century the word of *ex parte Milligan* had not penetrated that deep in the Ohio command structure. "We are for all intents the military, civil, and criminal authorities." He sat back pleased with himself. "Now then, I am advised by the Governor's office that you are a highly trained specialist in civil disturbance procedures."

"No, that's wrong."

"What's *that* supposed to mean?"

Testily, Bowen replied, "Your information is in error. Check your source."

"My intelligence is that you are highly trained. You will be highly trained."

"But not qualified! I don't know tactical shit. I just lectured and showed films."

"Good!" Woodin barked. "You can show them again. We're understrength in that element. Sergeant, get this man a projector and all the films on CBR. Bowen, you will take the officers and NCOs from each unit and drill them on procedures, then you will take the available units and show your films and give your lectures on gas deployment if it takes all night!"

"Where they going? Korea?"

Woodin squinted at him hard. "Training reports are going to Washington, with after-action reports, to the NG Bureau."

"Why?"

"So that everytime there's a little flare-up we don't get the 101st Airborne jumping down our necks. We're going to show them we can take care of things just fine. And, by God, if you didn't come to me from

Washington, I'd send you right back the way you came. You don't fit in with this team picture."

"OK. Dandy. I'll tell 'em everything I know," Tyler relented. "And then I go home."

"Officers and liaisons will be billeted at the Ramada Inn until we stand down," Woodin said. He was a Good Humor plant manager between weekend wars. "There'll be a consolidated mess in the dining room there."

"Hey, look. Fun's fun. But I've got a conference in Cleveland tomorrow morning and things I just—"

"Can't be helped. Now get started. And find something that looks like a uniform." Tyler slowly shook his head, with a sneer of contempt, and Woodin conceded the point with a wave of dismissal.

Until midnight, Tyler Bowen showed movies and lectured to the various units. Several platoons had already been dispatched to do precisely what he was teaching. "All right," he wearily addressed the last group, speeding a little as he neared the end. "You guys all know this junk, right?" They nodded somnambulantly. "But I'm supposed to tell you anyway."

In a singsong recital he detailed the steps in checking out protective masks, setting up dispensers, treating burns and inhalation casualties, firing canisters, and, should they happen to be at foreign war, identifying exotic pathogens.

"Now, how can you tell if there's a chemical agent in the air? Well, most likely you guys are the ones putting it up, so you can figure it that way: ask. Otherwise, take your masks off. Let one guy do it first: draw straws or something. If he doesn't fall down, it's safe. This is called the Noah's Ark Test in the manuals, if we had any. OK, now I'm going to show you some of the worst movies ever made about the use of the M-17 and M-9-A-1 protective masks. I understand officers and NCOs have M-17s with special adapters to enable them to speak through them for orders and such. I'm sure you're all very happy for that. And we'll also see a short on the M-79 canister launcher, and the Mighty-Mite pump and other terrific handy items. Try to say awake and don't reveal the surprise ending."

When the last class had seen the goat films, about

nerve agents they would never in their lives encounter, he said, "Now what are the lessons in this? Very important. First of all, don't let anyone tie your ass to a stake. Second, never listen to a slick-talking salesman, especially if he's wearing rubber gloves. And third, have faith in your Uncle Samuel. He may fuck you over, but if he does, he's the only one's gonna pull your ass out of the fire. Remember that."

Of tear gas, he said, "OK, with this stuff we're not interested in LD-50s; that's your Mean Lethal Dosage. All we want to know is the ID-50, the Mean Incapacitating Dosage. But compare those two figures and what do you see? Right. This tells us two things about incapacitating agents, and where not to use them: indoors, where we don't have a fine enough control of the tolerance to prevent fatalities—better to use a stink bomb—and *outdoors,* where the stuff is dispersed easily and doesn't do much good. About all it's good for is, oh, blocking an alley, scattering a street mob. But for open areas, like campuses, best to use Bran. That'll knock the shit out of anybody. Or yell out, *'Quiz!'* What else? If you're thinking of bayoneting any girl students, tell 'em you promise to only stick it in a little way. It usually works."

"Bowen?" Colonel Woodin's ragged Sergeant asked when Tyler wrapped up. "I've got a change of situation for you."

"What's that mean?"

"There's no room at the Inn." He said it with a straight face and Bowen started to laugh uncontrollably. The Sergeant looked at him with curiosity.

Wiping a tear from his eye, Tyler said, "Tell me I get the manger, with the cattle and the goats."

"You're in the Best Western Motor Court across the street." The command post, the Sergeant told him, would contact him in the morning if they received any "new intelligence. Keep yourself available." He handed Bowen a wash-and-shave kit for use in the morning.

Monday morning, all over America, the invasion was protested anew. The pressure on Washington was enormous, the frenzy of the protests unparalleled. But for every previous cry, the government had responded with

701

stiffer beatings and sharper reasons to scream; this time, after pledging itself to ending the war and the protests, it was an invasion of neutral Cambodia. Yet this time, so widespread was the protest, so bloodcurdling the choking, inchoate seizure of despair, it seemed possible that the protest might avail. In the U.S. Senate itself, members rose to denounce the invasion. Ohio's own Republican Senator questioned the President's sanity. But that question, or the temperament that gave rise to it, was precisely why no manifestation, petition, or imploration stood a prayer.

That weekend, in one of the grotesque ironies that appeals to a nation of *Time* readers, though it went largely unnoted, three diverse communities in the Southwest reported incidents of accidental deaths associated with the consumption of romaine lettuce. Health officials were at first strangely silent, then put the blame on the Botulinum family, the mafia of toxins: it was always convenient for unsolved murders. In the morning papers that day, May 4, in the back pages, new cancer statistics released by the federal government revealed a pandemic increase in the occurrence of tumorous growths, despite years of massive endowment to government-sponsored research facilities.

There was something malignant in the air. And in the water.

The day's local papers dealt most prominently with the events at the Kent State campus, under banner headlines. Stunning pictures showed the ROTC building crackling in its juices against a night sky. It had been set blazing, perhaps fire-bombed, by students Saturday night, and as it burned the glow it cast on the National Guard troops called in to protect it was macabre. When he saw the pictures, Tyler muttered to himself, "If only they'd let them have girls in the dorms, we wouldn't have this problem. They never listen."

Sunday night, at the government's expense, Tyler had called everyone he knew who lived in more westerly time zones or who wouldn't be disturbed by a late call. "You gonna see any action, troop?" Willie asked.

"If I do, which I doubt, I'll use the patented Willie Bowen gotta-take-a-pee strategy to skip the heavy stuff."

"You got a uniform and everything?"

"And be an easy target? Are you kidding?"

"Yeah, but if the students capture you without a uniform you can be hanged as a spy," Willie teased.

"The way I figure, it's a toss-up. The cowboys've got the guns and the Indians are right. Either one's the wrong team, so I'll just watch soap operas or something."

"Who are you rooting for?"

Enervated, Tyler snorted, "Me. These guys couldn't round up sheep from what I taught them. Just to even the score I snuck in about a half-hour on amino acids. One of my boys might be the guy who cures cancer, you can't tell."

"Are you paying for this call?"

"If you wonder why your GI Bill benefits are so low, you know who to blame. On my money, I have better people to call. What's the word from the lady?"

"Why don't you call her yourself and ask?"

"Maybe I will, punk."

"At your own expense?"

"Maybe."

"Well, if you lose your nerve, I'll say hi for you tomorrow."

"Maybe I'll break your leg, punk. Or is it Bill?"

Twice he started to dial Johanna but didn't finish, afraid it might be awkward, that neither would know what to say. Rather than upset her precarious willingness to "surprise" him in New York, he decided against calling.

Saint Paul Hooper said, "I knew that guy Zermatt was no good. Just be glad he didn't kiss you on both cheeks and feed you spaghetti."

"He's not that bad," Tyler replied. "Just misguided."

"I've got a riddle for you."

"Riddle away," Tyler said, lying back on the bed with the television going in the far corner of the room, picking idly at the tassels on the bedspread.

"OK. Dig. What would happen if you told the people that the health of some poor mutt was tied to the Gross National Avocado Consumption level?"

"Tell me."

"You'd see a guacamole festival that'd turn your hair

green. People would stuff avocados down the throats of the senile and the paralyzed. And what would happen if you told them that the health of a lot of mutts, and people too, were tied to the number of *bombs*—"

"You're losing your sense of subtlety, Paulus, if you ever had one. Stick to avocados."

Then he thought again of calling Johanna, but fell asleep.

At ten o'clock Monday morning, Tyler Bowen was contacted in the Ramada Inn dining room and sent to "observe and reinforce with a chemical-instructional capability" the units bivouacked at the Kent State campus. Already there were over one hundred enlisted men and nearly a dozen officers: Alpha and Charlie Companies, First Battalion, 145th Infantry; and G Troop, Second Squadron, 107th Armed Cavalry Regiment, Ohio National Guard.

"All I know," Colonel Woodin's Sergeant told Tyler, "is my ass is getting reamed out with a corncob for more gas and qualified personnel. They're depleted from injuries." Tyler told him they were all zippy as loons.

The specific task Monday was to prevent a scheduled noontime student rally, because martial law required the dispersal of crowds. But the students had not been told their rally was forbidden. As for crowds, classes were still in session and would be changing at the time of the scheduled rally. And as for martial law, the commanding General who invoked it was mistaken. Martial law had not been declared in any legal sense. The informaton he'd relied upon was false in every particular. It was prepared by the General's own aide.

A TV editorial that morning praising the National Guard's policing efforts reminded viewers when, "over a hundred years ago, America was being torn asunder, Ohio men met their duty, and President Lincoln exclaimed, 'Praise God! Ohio has saved the Union!' " It went on to say, "The men who make this day and come safe home from keeping the peace will stand tall when this day is named and rouse themselves at the name of Kent. Their names will be a brand on our age."

Tyler Bowen arrived at the Kent State campus at

eleven and was put to work checking out masks and equipment. The masks and dispensers all seemed adequate, though the weapon these overweight, sloppy troops carried was the pitifully outmoded M-1.

He distributed the resupply of tear-gas canisters among specialists in each unit and quizzed them on the operation of the launchers and dispensers, about which he knew nothing but what he'd seen in films. When he protested that fact, he was curtly told, "Do it!"

Finished, he reported: "They all knew more than me except the guy I came with. Now he knows more than me. When can I get a drink?" The officer handed him a hip flask from his web belt. "Actually, I was thinking of a Coke."

"You'll stay here with us," the officer said.

"N-A-F-C."

"What?"

"Not A Fucking Chance. I look like I'm with the home team. And you know what? I'm not saying who I'm rooting for. But I see too many bananas with loaded weapons for my taste. Now where's that pop stand?"

Reluctantly, the officer said, "There's a machine in the basement of the journalism building."

"Which is that?"

"Taylor Hall, over there." He pointed to a building that must have been designed to house the world's largest pair of Thom McAn's. "And I want you back here in five minutes. You're an official observer."

Tyler took the man's elbow and pretended conspiracy. "Look, I'm wrapped here, see. This op's a lock, right? Now, you can write any damned report you want and sign my name to it, it's fine with me. But I've got better things to do. I'm going home to apologize for blowing a meeting this morning, and then I'm going sailing."

"Nice day," the officer averred. "Not too gusty."

Tyler nodded. "And then I'm going to pack my bags and tomorrow fly the hell out of here. So why don't you just admit you can jolly well live without me, right?" The man shrugged. Tyler winked at him and said, "Adios."

It was eleven forty-five.

At noon, Tyler Bowen was among a crowd of students and faculty onlookers outside Taylor Hall, on its porch. The Guardsmen had already begun their maneuvers. There was no point leaving the safety of the bleachers for the playing field, so he maneuvered himself next to a pretty girl in a polka-dot bandana and started a conversation. She was taking notes, and said she was a journalism student. He chuckled to himself and shook his head. "Gives you kind of mixed loyalties, doesn't it?" he asked. She frowned at him for clarification. "I mean, wouldn't it be nice if the Martians just went home and nothing exciting happened? But where's the story in that?"

"The story," she said, peering over sunglasses at him, "is the story."

"Is it a class assignment?" he asked. She said it was. "Everybody gonna have the same story or a different one? Or different versions of the same one?" Probably, she admitted. She caught his eye with a smile and, some effects of spring being ineradicable, added that the assignment wasn't due until Thursday. He offered her some soda, and said, "I'll keep watch for you." With great fumbling she rearranged her pen and notebook to take a swig. "Listen," he ventured, when she gave him the bottle back, "if you don't have to have this in tomorrow, I could tell you things about this—these guys and all—you'd never get standing here. Now, I've got this friend who's got this little Sunfish on the lake he lets me borrow. It's a lovely afternoon, no clouds, just perfect for picking up some rays."

Not believing the first part at all, she nonetheless looked up at him flirtatiously, and said, "Sounds too good to pass up."

"Beats sitting in a hot room," he winked. "And this. Life's too short to waste being serious. You've got to screw around and play on pretty days."

"Amen," she said, taking the Coke bottle again to toast the notion.

For the next fifteen minutes they watched from this perch as the National Guard troops showed a strong flair for low comedy: marching in the wrong direction, dropping weapons, stumbling into each other. "Those masks," Tyler explained to her, "constrict your view. They also make you nearsighted, they've got such

706

scratched-up lenses. Astigmatic tunnel vision, quite a combo. Write it down." She looked at him oddly and he gestured vaguely. "I told you. I'm an expert. Certified." The troops boxed themselves in along a baseball diamond backstop and the growing crowd on the porch whistled and applauded at their antics. The troops spun around and bumped like mechanical toys in spastic confusion. They fired canisters of CNS tear gas in every direction, but these fell uniformly short, affecting no one. Bowen loved that. The instruction he'd given was completely useless. "I taught them that," he nudged the girl, who was shaking her head in laughter at the display. Merry tears were rolling down her cheeks and she wiped them away, asking, "What?"

"I told you. How to screw up. It's not easy. Takes training." He cocked his head to admire the way the sunlight glinted off her hair and face, making a glory behind her. He brushed some moisture from her cheek with his fingertips. "Next, they surrender. Watch." She began to blink as some tear gas wafted by. "Don't rub your eyes," he told her. "Just let the air clear it out. Here—" He handed her the Coke, "take another sip and spit it out. Best mouthwash going."

In their uniforms and smothering masks, the troops were sweltering and growing disoriented. The crowd had swelled with the changing classes to outnumber them by ten or twenty to one, though scattered in different places. The various unit commanders shouted out indistinct orders through bullhorns, but it was only so much noise. Reckless students rushed toward this hapless patrol and picked up the tear-gas canisters, hurling them back farther than they'd been fired, bouncing them into the Guard ranks. Others threw rocks and waved taunting flags. Some cursed and hollered epithets.

On the porch, Tyler Bowen was one of the few people not taking notes. Many were laughing and jeering, some, still affected by the drifting gas, were coughing. But for most it was negligible, nothing serious. Mostly funny.

Tyler enjoyed it immensely as the troops, having been encircled by phantoms, huddled and then broke out of their stymie to retreat past him. It was like being at the races. Their frantic officer was screaming for

"more tear gas, dammit! Gimme more, godammit!!!"
He was begging, backtracking as he was pleading into
his radiophone. On the far side of the building, a more
successful phalanx was pushing students around this
way, but this unit was in full rout. Whistling and laughing chased the Guard troops as they fled. It looked
like the streets of a Central European town with the
partisans resurgent. It was theater, with waving flags
and flying bottles and rocks and defiant oaths.

A student with tumescent bravado ran down toward
the Guardsmen and hurled some hard object at them,
then ducked into the crowd. His fans on the porch
offered cheers.

At the same rate as the Guardsmen were retreating,
Tyler had moved the girl down the porch by crab steps,
loosing her grip on duty with each pace. "Believe me,"
he said. "I've got the whole story and it's gonna be
great. Gonna be terrific." He felt boundaryless, intensely
free, delighted with himself and full of good air; despite
the drifting CNS gas, he was kissed by sunshine. He
threw a big wet one to the bright blue sky. It was in-
fectious and the girl moved another half-step away
from the action, smiling in the self-seduction of a glorious May afternoon.

He was sucking on the soda bottle, sticking it into
his lower lip, then popping it free, whistling and making
foghorn noises, when a student who had run down the
little slope from the main section of the throng, to imitate the last crowd hero, suddenly darted onto the porch,
lurching into Bowen. The bottle banged into Tyler's
mouth: "Hey! Watch—" He shoved the stumbler away
with annoyance. Coke spilled on his shirtfront and he
looked at the girl and they both laughed. Some had
spilled on her, and he said, "I'm sorry" and brushed
gently at her shirtfront where her breasts pulled the
blouse out. She pointed to his lip. "You're bleeding,"
she said.

He reached his hand up to his mouth to check this
fact. "Maybe there's a medal in it," and took a swig
to rinse the cut. There was a coughing sound and they
twisted around toward it. The retreating troops had
stopped retreating. They were kneeling, aiming down
the porch, up the grassy knoll, firing. Tyler jerked

backward, grabbing at the girl, and blew the syrupy pop out.

"Hey!" She wheeled around to look at him, a confused smile on her face. *"Hey!"* The cough became a sharp barking noise and the Coke bottle exploded in a brown, iridescent sunspot. Sticky glass shards sliced into his face and hand, scrambled and overlaid with matter from the girl's throat. She piled into him from the force of the hit, her face frozen in that quizzical expression, and they crumbled to the ground. He was cringing beneath her convulsing body as the troops continued firing. The officer was smashing his men on their helmets with his baton, screaming, begging them to stop. Up the hill, the laughing kids were falling, flying apart.

In less than twenty seconds fifty-five rounds were fired. And then it was quiet. A few wailing voices, but they were piercing a vast, open quiet, a forbidding silence slashed by screams.

Tyler's face burned, and he could hardly breathe. His face stung, bleeding from the glass and caustic cola. It had barely missed his left eye. But the girl's blood was cascading into both eyes, over his face, into his mouth, down his shirt, soaking him. He slid out from under her and saw the massive exit wound torn from her cheek. Blood poured out from it, and her mouth, and the back of her neck, and pink-gray brain tissue flopped out, flotsam on this tide. He draped himself over her, crying, frightened, and then pushed up to his hands and knees, retching hysterically, until he fell over backward. He pulled himself up to sit between her blood and his vomit, dripping with both, sniffling and heaving as the troops rushed up. One helped him to his feet, and Tyler tugged himself free, furiously. His face and left hand hurt terribly, his own blood slipping down through the mess all over him, as he spun away from there.

Dazzled, he stumbled up the hill. There were other bodies on the sidewalk and in the parking lot, wounded, dying, dead. Troops rushed up to surround the ones that did not move, and Tyler Bowen saw them, small reefs of green enclosing red lagoons. He stumbled past without stopping, sightlessly wild, fighting a faint. A few people tried to take hold of him, "You're hurt," but he fended them off. Some others, running neither to anything nor from anything, bumped into him and crashed on, staggering about.

It took a minute for him to remember what he was looking for when he reached the parking lot. His car window had been blown in and he eased himself into a front seat covered in broken glass. Trembling and nauseous he started the car, then stuck his head out of the opened door to vomit again, losing consciousness for a moment as he hung limply against the cool metal doorpost, halfway to the ground.

His thoughts came crazily: if only he could get to New York and keep Walter Cronkite from telling everyone, it wouldn't really have happened. He could get in front of the light rays and rearrange them. Or get help. Or disappear. Or never have been. His head was buzzing with the ringing of the Heart-Line, blood running into his mouth. He swallowed some and spat the rest out in a pink explosion, like a fireworks chrysanthemum. He stalled out at the parking lot's exit, and restarted the engine frantically, afraid of the noises and frenzy behind him as though it was personal, chasing him, and he bolted ahead, lurching into the street traffic.

There were signs he passed on the highway that other days would have delighted him: an ad for a restaurant gave its location as the town of River Styx, O.; nearby, a Bible group's billboard asked "Who Made This Day?" But he did not see them for his squinted eyes, pinpointed and recoiling from the unshielded wind as he sped west into painful light. Nor did he see the huge one for his exit, "Cleveland/North/Shoreland," though it was the biggest thing around. His mind was too soaked with clutter and noises, stray phrases from songs, mumbled half-words and wild images, reeling from the smells of blood and vomit and gasoline and soda. He gagged from the sensations of the mucus and puke half in his throat and the gore all over him, spat it out and felt it dribble down his chin, while his throat filled up again. And the noise was deafening between his ears, and he was feverish, sweating and shivering. It was hard to breathe in all the confusion, hard to remember how. There was no way to destroy the noise,

710